Praise for Michal Ajvaz

"Ajvaz's [*The Other City*] is a gorgeous *matryoshka* doll of unreason, enigma and nonsense—truly weird and compelling."

—Publishers Weekly

"Michal Ajvaz is a literary magician creating worlds of worlds, worlds of words, worlds of objects. He is the fantastical baby of Borges and Timothy Leary. He is a cartographer on mescaline. He is Czech."

—Salonica

"Through the sheer force of imagination Ajvaz manages to achieve that particular velocity required to slip the pull of the familiar and effect that marvelous feat of literary transportation to a world of uncompromising strangeness."

—Full Stop

T0006981

Other Books by Michal Ajvaz

The Other City
The Golden Age
Empty Streets

Michal Ajvaz

JOURNEY
TO THE SOUTH

Translated by Andrew Oakland

DALKEY ARCHIVE PRESS

Dallas / Dublin

Originally published in Czech as *Cesta na jih* by Druhé město

Copyright © 2004 by Michal Ajvaz

Translation © 2023 by Andrew Oakland

First edition

Paperback: 978-1-62897-444-7
Ebook: 978-1-62897-471-3

Library of Congress Cataloging-in-Publication Data: Available.

Cover design by Nuno Moreira
Interior design by Anuj Mathur

Dalkey Archive Press
www.dalkeyarchive.com
Dallas/Dublin

Printed on permanent/durable acid-free paper.

Table of Contents

Part One
Two Brothers

The Story of the Wire Book I

Part Two
Cities and Trains

The Story of the Demons of the Night Train and the Corso Café

The Story of Meditating Ants, Gunfire on Gogolevsky Boulevard, and the Sociologist Who Tries to Hang Herself

The Story of the Underwater Lettering, the Keter Sapphire and the Beautiful CIA Agent

The Story of the Colored Threads, the Harmony of the Universe, and the Fruit-gum Candies

PART ONE
TWO BROTHERS

Libyan Sea I

1. Loutro

I sipped strong Greek coffee from a small cup and watched the surface of the Libyan Sea. A moment earlier the sun had disappeared behind a rock that cut into the water at the western end of a small bay and now looked like a heap of black stones someone had dumped in the sea. For the moment, the outline of the heap was eaten into by a dim red light, as though there were a quiet blaze just beyond it. The Albanian youth who brought my coffee had not yet rolled away the blue-and-white-striped awning that from early morning shielded the customers of the taverna from the blazing sun; I heard the slap of the fabric's edge in the breeze that was now rising from the sea and carefully modeling low waves with serrated crests on the shiny, metallic surface. The invisible sun still hung around on the eastern side of the bay, where the top of the cliff was brushed by the last of its orange light, casting shadows in its winding clefts. On the other side of the bay, the white tavernas and boarding houses were bathed in bluish shade, although their walls would continue to exhale the heat of the day long into the night.

Every day at this hour a stillness settled over the bay that was very different from the languid stillness of midday, when the sun was high in the sky, burning all the thoughts in one's head; it was different, too, from the stillness that fell on the bay soon after midnight, when the last customers left the tavernas for their beds, the stillness that flooded my room through the open door to the balcony and whose lovely sounds—the creaking of boat chains, the rustle of branches groping walls—transformed the nightly magic into the voices of characters from an impending dream. Although in the past three years two new bars had opened in Loutro, it seemed unlikely that this village, which comprised only an arc of little white houses squeezed between the bay and the cliff, would ever abandon itself to a nightlife.

The stillness that reigned in the moments between late afternoon and the onset of evening was woven from the splashing of low waves, the flapping of awnings, the rustling of soft paper tablecloths as their tips were lifted in the gentle breeze, the distant tinkling of bells as sheep converged on the trough into which at this hour a magnificently tan old man poured a grayish mash. Sometimes the distant whir of a boat came from the sea, this sound growing ever louder until the boat touched the low stone wall, gave a roar and fell silent; but not even this disturbed the fabric of the stillness, as it was woven into it like a distinctive pattern on a faded carpet. Often these sounds of stillness caused thoughts to begin their smooth slide down the slope to sleep and dreams; marked by this descent, they came apart lightly, so summoning images distant or held deep within. The mind also had a tendency to hear in these sounds of stillness the whispering of many stories—here on the shore of the Libyan Sea, it occurred to me that the tales of *One Thousand and One Nights* and all their wonders and marvelous encounters originated in the murmur, buzz, rattle, and rustle of the stillness of the south.

I heard a regular creaking sound: The Albanian was turning the winch that drew in the awning, opening up a purplish sky above my head. It contained a single motionless cloud that still shone pink, although the sun had by now disappeared beyond many horizons—the many strips of mountain that descended to the sea and were piled one behind another like sets on a giant stage. Tanya, a girl from Ukraine who worked at the taverna as a waitress, chambermaid and kitchen help, had also succumbed to the spell, although it dominated the bay every day at this time, and this was her fifth year here; I saw her stop with a tray in her hands on the white steps that led to the kitchen and stand there motionless, staring at the shining water of the bay.

This moment of the late afternoon was my favorite in the whole day. Although it was the end of September, the high peaks of the Lefta Ori mountains prevented wind and cloud from the north from reaching the coast, so that here on Crete's southern shores the daytime was as hot as in August. In recent years I'd gotten used to coming here when the rocky landscape above the sea was lit by the year's last hot days—I'd learned that by cleansing my life in bright light and planting it on a distant horizon for a few days, the restlessness, insomnia, and despair I experienced in winter arrived later and in milder form. On the small beach in the middle of the bay, several guests from the Porto Loutro hotel still lay on blue sun loungers, exposing their heat-damaged bodies to the cooling breeze. Others were getting up, shrouding themselves in bathrobes and going off to change for dinner; I heard the squeak of wet pebbles under sandals. The rocks to the west lost their aura of burning as the dim orange light left the cliff. Soon the first of the tavernas on the other side of the bay was switching on its lights, and the others quickly followed suit; on the steel-gray surface of the water, the tremulous columns of light grew in number. I saw a waiter at the Blue House taverna remove the cover from the brightly lit glass box in which the evening's meals were displayed, producing a new strip of light on the water; I watched Vangelis and

Jorgos, brothers and proprietors, weave their way through tables at which the first customers were seating themselves.

2. Martin

Then, practically in an instant, all distant outlines dissolved as night fell over the bay and the rocks. All that remained of the deluge of light—from which my eyes were still aching—were shimmering dots in the sky, the flashing red of a low lighthouse on a rocky islet, a string of lamps along the bay, the quivering columns on the water and, to the east, an unmoving luminous horde that glittered like gold dust on black velvet; this latter, I knew, was the distant lights of Hóra Sfakíon. I saw that there were guests at most of the taverna's tables. I realized that for some time now I'd heard a hum of voices mixed in with the lapping of the waves; out of this hum, I caught snatches of English, French, German, and Greek. I could smell meat, which was suspended on a spit slowly turned by an electrical device over a deep metal tray in which charcoal was burning.

An acquaintance I'd made the day before yesterday was weaving his way through the tables, a thick book under his arm. As he passed, he greeted me with an almost imperceptible nod of the head. I saw him hesitate as he wondered whether to join me, but in the end he sat down at the next table. He smiled at me a second time before turning to his book and leafing through it; then he set the open book down on the blue-and-white tablecloth and, like me, turned his gaze to the lights on the water. His name was Martin, and I already knew he was an avid reader with remarkable taste in literature. I'd fallen into conversation with him owing to a longstanding, incurable, compulsive, bad habit of mine that expresses itself in the need to discover what strangers are reading. I practice this everywhere and by all possible means, some of which exceed the bounds of decent behavior.

I'd first noticed Martin two days earlier at the pebble beach known as Sweetwater or Glyka Nera, in a small taverna that was little more than a crooked metal shack with a few plastic chairs and tables squeezed into it, which sat under a holey reed roof on a block of concrete in the sea, and was crossed from end to end in four paces. As I was approaching the taverna across a narrow bridge composed of a single swaying plank, I spotted the slim figure of a man of about twenty-seven. In near darkness because he was set against the bright marine skyline, he was wearing bathing trunks and a T-shirt, and he was bent over a book. My mania was aroused immediately; I sat down at the next table and squinted at pages awash with the striped shadow of the reeds, but the print was too small for me to read a word. After a while, the stranger laid the open book on the Formica table-top, sipped slowly at his milk-colored ouzo, and looked toward the island of Gavdos, which appeared as a glowing cloud on the marine horizon. Then, having taken a final long sip of his drink, he called the waiter and closed his book. To my surprise, I saw that this was the third part of the Czech translation of *One Thousand and One Nights*—the one that contains "The Adventures of Sinbad the Sailor."

I was delighted to come across this book this far south: It had once meant so much to me that I'd often read myself to sleep with it. But whenever I encountered a Czech on my travels, I was overcome by a sense of unease. Over many encounters I'd convinced myself that a tourist who happens upon a countryman abroad considers it his right, maybe even his duty, to engage him in conversation and make a nuisance of himself by talking of boring matters at inordinate length. For this reason, whenever I hear Czech spoken abroad, I take measures to prevent recognition of where I'm from. This time, too, I quickly finished my coffee before returning to my towel on the beach and hurriedly slipping into my bag two items that would give away my origin—a Czech magazine and a carrier bag from a Prague supermarket.

The reading stranger was also alone on the beach, lying not far away from me. The fact that I was concealing my nationality to avoid conversation with him didn't prevent me from taking an interest in the several books scattered about his mat; when he went for a swim, I stood up and walked toward it inconspicuously. I was greatly surprised by what I saw. In addition to *One Thousand and One Nights*, there were six books on the mat. Resting against a tube of sun cream was a disintegrating, pre-war copy of *The Adventures of Sherlock Holmes*, and next to this was a tattered paperback in English with the title *Live and Let Die* and a smiling, tuxedoed, white-shirted James Bond holding a pistol cozily against his cheek. From underneath the Bond a book poked out whose author was Giovanni Pico della Mirandola; I couldn't see anything more of it. Farther along the mat lay a book whose cover declared: Novalis, *The Disciples at Sais*. Beneath this were two books, one very thick, the other very thin; of these, I was able to read neither title nor author.

The next day, I saw the stranger at the taverna on Glyka Nera again. And again he was sitting with a glass of ouzo in his hand, looking across the sea toward the horizon. The wind was slowly turning the pages of the slim volume that lay open on the table in front of him. From the illustration, I saw straight away that it was a collection of Lewis Carroll's mathematical brainteasers. What did folk tales from the Orient, detective stories, a spy thriller, a philosophical work by a Neoplatonist of the Renaissance, the prose of a Romantic poet, and mathematical puzzles of an Oxford logician-cum-author have in common? Suddenly my desire to know what kind of person takes such a mix of books on holiday was stronger than my aversion to

Czech conversation, and so I did something I'd never done on my travels before: I addressed a fellow countryman. In so doing, I felt extremely embarrassed to be placing myself in the role of nuisance-maker; and from the expression on the stranger's face, it was obvious that he had as much enthusiasm about the chance to converse in his native tongue as I tend to in such situations. We soon established, however, that a distaste for speaking Czech in a foreign land wasn't the only thing we had in common, and that a conversation with someone from the same country didn't have to be a horrible experience. Although we didn't speak together for long—we exchanged a few sentences only—we discovered that we read the same books and both liked the sun and the Mediterranean Sea. Martin also managed to tell me that he had recently finished his studies and was now working as an assistant lecturer at the Department of Philosophy of the Faculty of Arts in Prague. In answer to my question about when he had landed in Crete, he told me that he hadn't flown, instead coming by train and boat. I had the feeling that he was about to say more about this unusual way of traveling from Prague to a faraway island, but then he changed his mind. Instead, he told me that he had stopped in sleepy Loutro because he was quite tired after his journey and needed to rest in a quiet place; he was waiting here for his girlfriend, who was in Crete already and would come to him in a few days. He didn't tell me why they weren't together.

3. All Because of Kant

The thick volume that now lay on the table was probably the only one from the pile on the mat that I hadn't been able to recognize. I heard Martin order baked eggplant with feta. As he waited for his meal, he leafed through the book absent-mindedly. I realized that I'd never seen him read for more than a minute or two; he'd brought so many books on holiday, yet plainly he was unable to concentrate on reading. As Tanya set down in front of him the plate bearing the egg-plant and white goat's cheese dressed in hot olive oil, together with a brass jug of the local wine, he snapped the book shut, and I stole a look at the dark spine; at its center, I saw an oval that contained a silver outline of the head of a man wearing a wig with its pigtail raised, and, above this, faded silver letter-ing that declared: "Immanuel Kant, KRITIK DER REINEN VERNUNFT." We each raised a glass to the other, performance of a remote toast. I wasn't surprised to see Kant on the table—indeed, in the company of Martin's other books, it wasn't out of place—but I couldn't stop myself from pointing at it and remarking: "Rather unusual holiday reading."

"My thesis is on *The Critique of Pure Reason*," said Martin, as though in apology. "And I've got some catching up to do. I've not been doing much writing recently: I've been traveling since mid-September." He paused before adding: "Yet if it hadn't been for *The Critique of Pure Reason*, I wouldn't have taken any trip, and I wouldn't be sitting here . . ."

Obviously, Martin was telling me this so that I would ask him how his trip had come about. Yesterday, too, I'd had the feeling that he wanted to tell me about it, yet for some reason he'd been afraid to. Most likely, he needed to deal with certain things that had happened to him, but at the same time was apprehensive about returning to them. Also strange was the way he pronounced the word "journey." There are many ways of doing this; although Martin's suggested a long, adventurous pilgrimage across several continents: By his own admission he'd left Prague only two weeks earlier, and I doubted that he'd reached Crete from the Czech Republic by taking a detour through other continents.

Martin plainly felt the need to tell a story and had the impression I would make quite a good listener. But I wasn't sure I was ready for a long narrative that would drown out the beautiful sounds of the Cretan stillness, of which I couldn't get enough, even though I'd been listening to them for a week— even if this story was more fascinating and thrilling than that of Sinbad the Sailor. Yet my curiosity was piqued; as well as being perturbed by the tone in which he'd spoken of his journey, I was keen to know why a journey he'd taken because of his thesis on Kant had brought him all the way to a beach in Crete rather than to Heidelberg or Freiburg. What did Loutro between the rocks and sea have in common with Kant, of whom it was well known that he never left Königsberg? Then it occurred to me that this village wasn't far from the university city of Rethymno, and I asked Martin if he'd come to Crete to meet a local expert on Kant.

"I'd no idea that this was where I'd end up," he said. "The night I left Prague Central Station, I thought I was on a one-day trip to Bratislava . . . Actually, what I said may have confused you. I said that I set off on a journey because of *The Critique of Pure Reason*, but I should have said that it wasn't because of the book."

"You mean to say it's the title of something other than a book? Is there now a film based on Kant's work?"

To my surprise, Martin didn't take my question as a joke. He paused as if considering whether he'd ever seen anything based on Kant at the cinema. "I don't think *The Critique of Pure Reason* has ever been filmed," he said, "but someone has composed a ballet around it."

"You set off on a journey because of a ballet? Did you fall in love with a ballerina and then chase her around Europe?" I said with delight.

Martin didn't even crack a smile at this; he just shook his

head, as though he thought that something of the sort might easily happen to him. He took a sip of wine and then said: "I left Prague because of a crime committed during a performance of the ballet *The Critique of Pure Reason*."

"A crime committed during a ballet? A fur coat stolen from the cloakroom?"

"Oh no, it was a murder," he said calmly. "At the end of the second act, someone shot Petr Quas, who was on the board of the Phoenix Finance Group."

I was astonished. "Do they know who did it? Don't tell me it's you! You killed someone, so you've put half of Europe between yourself and the police?" That would be the best explanation by far. But Martin didn't look like a murderer to me.

"I didn't kill him, no," said Martin. "The murderer was The Thing In Itself."

"I don't get the joke."

"It's not a joke. The murderer was the person playing The Thing In Itself in the ballet. *Das Ding an sich*."

"Then all the police had to do was reach for a program and read the names of performers."

"It wasn't so easy, unfortunately. It turned out that The Thing In Itself was being played by an intruder, whom nobody knew."

I was still in the dark. "But when he was dancing, he was on the stage, surely—so everyone in the audience must have seen him."

"The trouble is, as no doubt you know, Kant's 'thing in itself' is inaccessible to the human senses and human knowledge."

"So?"

"The dancer playing this role wore a costume that expressed this. He was covered from head to foot, and so impossible to recognize."

"Okay, that I can understand. But what I don't get is the

connection between your journey and what happened at the theater?"

"I went away in order find out who the murderer was." Again Martin paused for a moment. Then he corrected himself. "Actually, I went away with the intention of finding out who had committed a different murder, but it's rather complicated, you see . . ."

By now my curiosity was stronger than my longing for the sounds of Cretan stillness. "How about you tell me the story of your journey from the beginning?" I said.

Martin had been waiting for this. He picked up his jug of wine, carried it over to my table and sat down next to me. He fixed his gaze on the dark sea and began.

Murder at the Theater I

1. The Tortoise

"As I said, I'm writing a thesis about Kant; it's on differences between the first and second editions of *The Critique of Pure Reason*. I began working on it in the fall, and continued all through the winter. Every day I sat in the large reading room of the university library, arriving so early in the morning that it was still dark. When dusk fell across the great windows, and I switched off my lamp, there would be several handwritten pages before me on the desk. By the time I left the building, it was dark again. I live in Libeň, and in the evening I tended to go home on foot. On the way I would think over what I'd written that day, and often the solution to a problem that had been bothering me would occur at the corner of some street or in front of some store.

"Just before the Libeň Bridge, I would pass a wall plastered with torn posters. I never looked at these; apart from the little red and green men on the traffic lights and puddles on the sidewalk, I took in nothing of the streets, always the same ones, that I walked. I always registered the wall of posters as a great, multi-colored carpet that moved past me in the pale glow of the streetlamps. Then spring came, and I walked home from the library in daylight. I never missed my ritual walk, even in rain or stormy weather. One day in May, I was walking past the posters and their inundation of letters, when out of the corner of my eye I spotted the title of the work by Kant I'd spent the whole day thinking about. I was convinced that these words had been conjured up by the mosaic of my subconscious—such things happen to me quite often. Wondering which words had been transformed into the name of Kant's book, I took a few steps back and began to study the posters, which were still damp and wrinkled from the afternoon's rain. To my astonishment, I saw a poster of a greenish color on which was printed in black lettering:

Tomáš Kantor
&
Immanuel Kant

The Critique of Pure Reason

a ballet
based on the book by Immanuel Kant
music and libretto by Tomáš Kantor

performed by the Flamingo ballet company

Performances will be held from 8 P.M. every Wednesday in
May and June
at the Tortoise Theater.

"And that day happened to be a Wednesday. I knew that the Tortoise Theater was nearby. A low building next to the railroad track, it used to be a cinema. In my childhood, I'd attended this cinema nearly every week. Owing to the shape of its metal roof, it really did look like a giant tortoise that had stopped at the track in confusion, wondering what to do next. I looked at my watch: It was seven. For a moment I stood undecided in front of the posters. I was tired, and my eyes were aching; since I'd set off on my walk, I'd been looking forward to stretching out on my bed and listening to music. Yet I was curious about a ballet with such a strange theme, and to this curiosity was added the desire to sit again in the auditorium where as a child I'd seen the most amazing movies of my life.

"So, a few minutes later I found myself in a little square, looking across at the Tortoise, which I was seeing for the first time in years. I was standing next to a restaurant, against whose front wall four tables were set up on the sidewalk. As I still had some time, I sat down at a table and ordered a pickled sausage and a small beer. The setting sun was weaving its way through the branches of the dark trees, the overhead power lines for the trains above them. At first, the little square was quiet and empty, but then the first knots of theatergoers appeared. Young people in sweaters and jeans stood in front of the Tortoise and called to others who were approaching; apparently, everyone knew everyone. Just before eight, I picked up my check and walked across the square. The box office where I bought my ticket hadn't changed at all since my childhood; nor had the dark swinging doors with the little round windows in them. The new owner of the place hadn't even changed the fittings in the hall. As I stood in the aisle, I reveled in the musty smell that recalled all kinds of images; my gaze wandered over the indented rows of folded-back wooden seats, which so far contained only seven or eight people. Even the gray-haired usherette in her blue nylon coat was like a ghost from the past. I bought a program from this lady and took a seat in the middle of an empty row.

"For a while, I listened dreamily to the creaking of seats being folded forward, as though to enchanting music. Then

I looked at the program. Most of its content was a long description of the experimental, amateur Flamingo company—I scanned this but briefly. As for the ballet, I learned that its three acts followed the three parts of Kant's work in being called 'Transcendental Aesthetic,' 'Transcendental Analytic,' and 'Transcendental Dialectic'; only on the final page did I find mention of the composer and librettist. *Tomáš Kantor, it stated, was born in 1968 in Prague, where he lived all his life. Although his primary activity was as a writer, his work remains in manuscript, with the exception of two extracts published in periodicals.* The Critique of Pure Reason, *to which he wrote the music and the libretto, is his only ballet. Tomáš Kantor died tragically in Turkey in July or August 2006.* I wondered what could have happened last year in Turkey that the exact month of Tomáš Kantor's death remained unknown. Then the third bell rang out, and the lights in the auditorium slowly dimmed to nothing."

2. First Act

"A moment of silence was broken by the commencement of the overture, played through speakers. This was a composition for two pianos. I had the impression that the melody described a struggle between dogmatists and skeptics, which Kant writes about in the preface to his book. But I realized that this idea was inspired by the name of the production; if the ballet had been called *Twenty Thousand Leagues under the Sea*, probably I would have imagined that the melody was telling of a submarine voyage through the reef.

"The overture played out, and a heavy crimson curtain was raised. Beyond this, all was dark at first, but then two cones of light appeared, illuminating two groups of figures that stood stock-still on the stage. On the right were eight men in costumes stitched together out of numerous brown, orange, and green rags. The second of these groups was composed of eight girl dancers standing motionless center stage, their bodies twisted in unusual attitudes; it occurred to me that they looked like letters of an unknown alphabet. Their costumes were white, apart from their pale-blue pointed caps. Soon, another cone of light appeared, illuminating a figure in a violet costume that was standing alone on the left, at the edge of the stage.

"The two pianos started up again. I had the feeling I was hearing two compositions played simultaneously—two compositions with nothing in common. The swirling notes of the first piece reminded me of rain falling on a tin roof; the second piece was a simple melody. Soon, the men set up a chaotic, undulating swirling; as they performed this, the soles of their feet remained rooted to the spot, so that their bodies resembled aquatic plants caught up in the current. Then, as though with great force, the men tore their feet from the floor and began to dance about the stage. The white girl dancers stood where they were, like the letters of an inscription. The violet figure, too, was motionless, apparently taking in nothing of what was going on around it. Then, one after another, the girl dancers awoke from their torpor; their gestures slowly developed into movements; the letters burst out of their confinement and spilled across the stage, erasing the inscription. The girls came together in two groups of four. The dancers of the first group held hands and formed closed figures—circles, squares, stars—by constantly changing places; the girls of the second group formed a line that rippled first this way, then that, never forming a closed figure, and with the sequence of the dancers unchanged.

"As the dance of the two white groups progressed, the whirling of the men became calmer; their movements lost their chaos and gradually began to imitate the figures being performed by the two groups of girls. At this point, the two lines of music were reconciled: The chaotic swirling attained structure and took on melody as its notes grouped themselves around the motifs of the second line and developed these; and the melodies, which were played by a second piano, took on the randomnesses and variations originating in the chaotic current, and reinforced *these*, although at the same time it was as though they were fraying and losing their original simplicity. Now the violet figure on the edge of the stage was in motion too; its dance comprised no more than slight, seemingly hesitant movements of the hands, but still there was something authoritative about it. It took me a while to realize the connection between this dance and the movements of the white girl dancers. After each gesture made by the violet figure, the patterns drawn by the bodies of the two groups of girls changed: The violet figure was covertly directing the girls' dance . . ."

I heard a boat engine: The ferry *Daskalogiannis* was approaching the shore. Having spent the night in Loutro, it would leave for Hóra Sfakíon at nine in the morning before pursuing its regular course along the south coast, to Palaichora and back again. Martin paused for a moment as we watched the approach of the large, illuminated boat glued to its reflection on the dark surface. Soon, the ferry struck the landing stage on the opposite side of the bay. There was a thud as the open front of the boat hit concrete, then the rattle of the anchor chain. A few passengers, who had taken the late bus to Hóra Sfakíon, disembarked; they would be looking for a bed for the night in Loutro. The boat closed itself up again with a screech, and all its lights went out.

Martin picked up the story. "It was some time before I noticed another spotlight, which must have come on slowly, as I was watching the dance of the men and the girls. It was directed at a back corner of the stage. In its pale green glow, I saw a lone, indistinct dancer shrouded in a pleated robe. The broad hood of the garment cast the wearer's face entirely in shadow, so that it was impossible to tell if it was a man or a woman. The dance of this figure didn't correspond at all with the movements of the men or the dance of the girls. To top it all, the green light would fade and sometimes die altogether, casting the mysterious figure in total darkness.

"Suddenly it dawned on me what I'd actually been watching all this time. The program wasn't lying: The dancers of the Flamingo company really were presenting the first part of *The Critique of Pure Reason*, which Kant gave the name 'The Transcendental Aesthetic,' and which deals with sensory perception. I was sure now that the white girls represented Conviction, i.e., forms by which material is ordered that brings us the senses; forms of Conviction allow us to perceive floods of colored spots and clouds of sounds and touches as beings spread out in space and time; the group of young women that formed a closed figure represented the conviction of space, the other group the conviction of time.

"The men represented sensory matter as a disordered whirl of color, sound, smell, taste, and touch. To be perceived as reality in space and time, the men were arranged in forms supplied by Conviction, which the work expressed by having them copy the figures made by the women. I liked the fact that the pure forms were danced by women, even though symbolism tended to associate femininity with matter and masculinity with form. The violet figure probably represented Transcendental Apperception, the source of all arrangement, which we refer to as 'I.' The mysterious veiled figure at the back was probably 'The Thing in Itself,' which hides behind our forms and is unknowable to us. Judging by the reaction of the audience, few of its members knew Kant well enough to understand what the dancers were conveying. Even so, no one looked particularly surprised or bored; apparently the ballet aspect of the performance was enough in itself. There was a short intermission. According to the program, the second act would be a representation of the Transcendental Analytic."

3. Second Act

I found Martin's description of a work of philosophy retold in bodily movement in what once was a cinema in the Prague quarter of Holešovice quite entertaining, but as I knew that *The Critique of Pure Reason* is long, I was beginning to fear that his story would end as the sun was coming up over Hóra Sfakíon. Maybe Martin noticed that I was getting restless, as he said: "Don't worry, I'm not going to describe the whole ballet to you. Besides, I didn't even see the performance to the end . . . But I must tell you something about the second act, because at the end of it a murder was committed, and that's the reason why I'm sitting here with you now.

"When the curtain came back up, in addition to the men and women from the previous act, a new group of girl dancers was standing on the stage. Although also dressed in white, these girls were wearing white caps. Seemingly, there was some similarity between the girls in blue and those in the pink caps. At first it was as though these two groups were kept apart by an invisible line that none of the girls dared cross; indeed, whenever one of them approached the imaginary boundary, the others quickly pulled her back to the territory designated for their group. Also, a third piano was added to the two pianos already. Now that I had the key to the production, it was immediately clear to me that the women in the pink caps represented 'pure understanding' and the patterns of their dance were categories in which sensory material was arranged, bound so far only in forms of time and space that presented to us a meaningful world of objects, activities, attributes, and relations.

"The violet figure stepped out of the shadows. The quiet movements of its body opened into a dance, which the girl dancers of both groups followed and imitated. At the same time their movements were guided by the movements of the male dancers, so that there was perfect harmony on stage; the dissonance had vanished from the accompanying music, too. I had little doubt that I was watching the Transcendental Deduction, its aim to show that the category of understanding can be used as a sensory opinion, even though the concept and sensory experience are apparently heterogeneous. The members of the company performed this unusual harmony in that the group of girls in blue caps (forms of inner sense), and the girls in the pink caps (categories) were directed by the movements of the violet figure (Transcendental Apperception, or 'I').

"As the second act was drawing to a close, I was expecting an enactment of joyous harmony in a dance performed by all groups of dancers. But then, in among the white female dancers and the many-colored male dancers, a figure stepped forward: A representation of The Thing in Itself. As I'd been watching the progress of Transcendental Deduction, I'd completely forgotten about this figure; I wasn't even sure whether it had been standing at the back of the stage the whole time or had vanished into the darkness for a while. Having hitherto rippled in the half-shadows at the back, now this hooded figure was engaged in a strange dance that had about it something of a shamanic ritual but also of the frolicking of savages around manacled prisoners, the motions of a Catholic priest at mass and the gait of a sleepwalker along the ridge of a roof. This dance seemed to demolish the idyll of the harmony of all the other dancers—of all powers of the mind attained by Transcendental Deduction. By movements now aggressive, now eerily languorous, The Thing in Itself worked its way right to the front of the stage, to where the violet figure of Transcendental Apperception was standing. I was nonplussed by this part of the ballet. What on earth could it mean? According to Kant, The Thing in Itself cannot enter the realm of understanding, let alone the region of forms of opinion, but here at the Tortoise it was behaving as though it owned the whole stage. What did the author of the ballet intend to express by this passage? Might he be polemicizing with Kant? The girls in white toward the front retreated from The Thing in Itself in confusion. Suddenly, I lost my certainty that what was being enacted on stage was part of the performance.

"The Thing in Itself was standing in front of Transcendental Apperception, which had stopped moving and was now staring at the other figure in amazement . . . Some of the others had stopped dancing too, although some were still trying to keep the ballet going. I wondered what was about to happen between The Thing in Itself and Transcendental Apperception. But then the shrouded figure turned its back on the girl dancer in violet and took several steps to reach centerstage, where it stood on the very edge with a hand plunged into the folds of its costume. From these folds The Thing in Itself then pulled something that flashed in the glare of the spotlights. Then it stretched out an arm in the direction of the auditorium—and a gunshot rang out."

4. After the Crime

"For several seconds all was still on the stage. The shrouded figure representing The Thing in Itself stood at the front of the stage encircled by petrified male and female dancers. Music was still playing from the speakers, expressing the harmonious union of forms of perception and categories of understanding. Then The Thing in Itself, pistol in hand, walked slowly to the back of the stage, the other figures stepping out of its way. I was still clinging to the idea that what was going on onstage was part of the performance, telling myself that someone who made a ballet out of *The Critique of Pure Reason* was probably eccentric enough to insert a scene in which the *Ding an sich* fires blanks from a pistol at the audience. I tried to imagine the philosophical meaning of the gunshot, but I didn't come up with anything.

"Once The Thing in Itself had disappeared backstage, shrieking broke out of the kind that usually accompanies the discovery of a body in a thriller. In this case, however, there were several dozen witnesses to the murder, onstage and in the audience, so before the first screams had died away other screams had started up, of many different types, from a simple squeal, through howls of hysteria, to sounds in which words were articulated as yells. Mixed in with all this was the playing of three pianos issuing from the speakers. There were moments when I imagined all these sounds as a wild avant-garde composition. Had the ballet truly ended? I still don't know the answer to this question. I'm still assailed by a sense of uncertainty as to whether the performance that began when the lights went out in the Tortoise theater isn't still going on . . ."

Martin paused for a moment and looked about. I saw his gaze slowly take in the arc of lamps that lined the bay before coming to rest on the large white spot that was the ferry at anchor, in which now only one cabin was lit, by the changing light of a television set.

"The dancers flocked to the front of the stage, then jumped down and bent low over something. If this part wasn't in the script, it was pretty clear that the object of their interest could only be an injured person or a corpse. Members of the audience got out of their seats, forced their way chaotically into the aisle, tried to push through to the place where the probable victim lay. I was as curious as the rest of them, but the space between the front row and the stage was clogged with a jumble of bodies, some wearing street clothes, some in dancer's costumes. It occurred to me that I might climb onto the stage, by now abandoned; I reached it in the glare of the spotlight.

"And from the front of the stage I saw below me, half sitting, half lying in a seat in the exact middle of the front row, a slightly rotund, clean-shaven, crop-haired man in an elegant, obviously expensive suit. He looked to be about my age. His arms were thrown to the sides across the armrests, his palms turned upward. His head was lolling backward, and the eyes in his pale face were wide open, shining, and looking toward the ceiling. His mouth was half open. Right in the middle of his forehead was a hole; from this hole, a thin red trickle ran toward his hair, dividing his forehead into two halves. It was as though the hall, too, were divided into equal halves by the bloody line on the forehead of the victim. The precise symmetry in the killer's work produced a dreamlike impression; I was confronted with a phenomenon apparently so contrived that again I had the feeling that the performance was still in progress.

"Maybe the others, too, were struck by unreality of the scene: Movement in the hall became less chaotic, and all the excited, worried, hysterical, and compassionate voices died away until a last, whispered word was heard. Meanwhile, the soundman had switched off the music, so there was complete silence. No one moved. It was as if the ballet had ended with this motionless, incomprehensible image. I was almost expecting applause; for everyone, the corpse included, to take a bow . . . Then the silence was broken by the siren of an ambulance, joined soon thereafter by the siren of a police car. As figures in green suits and black uniforms burst into the hall, the magic dissolved. Several police officers, pursued by members of the company, ran to the backstage area, into which the nefarious

Thing in Itself had vanished. As there was nothing else for it, I followed.

"In one of the dressing rooms, they found the girl dancer cast in the role of The Thing in Itself. She was lying on the floor in her underwear; there was a smell of ether in the room. Once she had been revived, this ballerina testified that as soon as the green spotlight had gone out a hand had pressed an ether-soaked handkerchief over her face; this was the last thing she remembered. Obviously, the intruder had dragged her unconscious body to the dressing room, stripped off her costume, and put it on. By the time the spotlight with the green filter came back on, the killer was standing on stage in the ballerina's place.

"The door at the end of the corridor was open, suggesting that the killer had fled through it. Just beyond the door was a steep railroad embankment overgrown with bushes. Although by now it was dark, the moon was shining brightly amid the high metal constructions along the track and above the black silhouettes of the bushes. The police officers clambered up through the prickles, followed eagerly by the dancers in their Kant costumes, with five or six of the most inquisitive audience members, including me, bringing up the rear. On reaching the tracks, the police officers stopped for a moment, wondering what to do next. The members of the company jumped from tie to tie, the white costumes aglow in the moonlight. Transcendental Apperception tripped over a large nut that was sticking out of the rail and moaned that she had sprained her ankle; the forms of Conviction attempted to examine this while Sensory Matter exasperated the police by offering advice. A girl from the category of Pure Understanding group ran to something light among the dark bushes and returned with The Thing in Itself's costume, which plainly the killer had discarded.

"Beyond the tracks, a wire fence stretched into the distance. On the other side of this was a large, untidy area containing workshops, storehouses, and a parking lot for trucks, with scattered islands of earth overgrown with dry grass and dusty bushes. One of the dancers discovered a hole in the fence. Having gathered in front of this, the dancers pushed one another impatiently as they climbed through one by one; meanwhile, the police officers called to them in an attempt to stop them from what they were doing. Infected by the restlessness and curiosity of the dancers, I joined the queue and then slipped through the hole after them. The space beyond the fence was divided by more wire and wooden fences into small squares, giving the impression of an enormous chessboard. It turned out that there were holes in all the fences, so we were able to go over the whole board, square by square, like movable figures in some crazy game. I wandered about with the others for about an hour, tripping on rusty machinery hidden in the grass, marking an area between two towers made up of stacked wooden pallets. Girls in white habits and men in suits made of colored rags emerged in the moonlight from behind enormous spools, immobile machines, and tall piles of breeze blocks and wooden boards. Several times I ran across the lame figure in violet, and occasionally I encountered a worried-looking police officer in uniform. We didn't find the killer, of course; apart from the costume in the bushes, he or she left no trace."

5. Investigation

"By morning, the first reports of the shooting at the theater had appeared on the internet. The following day the story was picked by the newspapers, as you probably remember."

I no longer read news in paper form or on the internet, I told him. Martin took note of this before continuing.

"It turned out that the body in the auditorium was that of

Petr Quas, quite a well-known figure in the world of business and a member of several supervisory boards as well as being the presidium of the Phoenix Finance Group. I was surprised by this: I wouldn't have expected such a person to attend a performance by an avant-garde ballet company. He had been thirty-eight years old; in death, he looked considerably younger. A letter was found in his jacket pocket—an unsigned letter that was composed of upper-case letters cut out of magazines. It invited him to attend a performance of *The Critique of Pure Reason*, and to this end, apparently, it contained a front-row ticket for the show . . . As I read on, I discovered that when he was twenty-two, Quas had published a collection of poems, after which he had quit poetry and turned to the writing of pop song lyrics. His career as an entrepreneur had begun twelve years ago, when he and some showbiz friends founded a music publishing company. Apparently, he hadn't given up writing altogether: One newspaper had found out that Quas had co-authored the screenplay of an American science-fiction thriller called *The Larva*, which would premier in the States the following summer. Word had gotten around that one of the characters in the movie was Jan Evangelista Purkyně. At the time, I thought that the journalist must have had this wrong, or that someone had been pulling his leg. What would a scientist who lived in nineteenth-century Bohemia be doing in an American science-fiction movie? Had I only known that I would get to see this odd movie while on vacation, in a cinema in Rome, and that I would give a lot more thought to it . . .

"The next day, the newspapers came up with something else that surprised me: The murdered man had been the step-brother of Tomáš Kantor, who had written the ballet. Now they took the opportunity to go over the details of Kantor's death. I learned that his body had been found last September in the net of a Turkish fisherman, in coastal waters near Bodrum (the

Turkish name for the ancient city of Halicarnassus). Someone had taken a dagger to Tomáš Kantor, stabbing him thirteen times in the chest and abdomen. Around his legs were remnants of a rope, to which, it was presumed, a weight of some sort had been attached.

"Apparently, the police weren't connecting the murder in Turkey with what had happened at the theater. A month before Quas's murder, a sniper's bullet had smashed through the skull of another rich man; and a week before the killing at the theater, a car had been blown to smithereens after the owner of a soccer club got into it and turned the key in the ignition. The investigators seemed to consider Quas's death a fitting sequel to these two crimes, not least after the business relations between the two murdered men and the Phoenix Group became known. This hypothesis was reinforced by Quas's willing acceptance of the anonymous challenge to attend the performance at the Tortoise. Had he believed that someone wished to talk with him, someone who knew too much about his business? As the case may be, no one succeeded in finding evidence of anything illegal or even suspicious passing between the Phoenix Group and the murdered businessmen. Nor did they find evidence of any dubious business in which Quas had been implicated.

"The journalists occupied themselves with the story for several days—at first with enthusiasm, I think. It is rare for criminals to demonstrate a sense of originality; most of them pay little attention to formal aspects of their deeds. What the journalists had here was an original work unlike any other. After a while, however, I noticed in their writing a certain irritation, probably resulting from the fact that they didn't know what to make of such an unusual crime. The detectives, too, were at a loss about how to interpret the deed: Its strange language was too much for them. Soon the journalists began to look askance at what had happened at the Tortoise, much as a lover of landscapes looks at a work of modern art. They had five or six templates for murders, which up till now had always sufficed, and they tried to apply these even now, although it was obvious that none fitted the Tortoise case. So five days after Quas's death, on the discovery of the body of a businessman implicated in a number of fraud and corruption scandals who happened to be friendly with cousins of certain well-known politicians, the journalists breathed a sigh of relief: This was the crime they'd secretly been longing for; the killer had done a sound job, and in the central idea and manner of performance all the proper motifs associated with the 'murder of a rich financier' were present. So the journalists abandoned the murder in the theater and launched themselves into the new case. Now they could make up for the time lost on a crime that was too avant-garde and obscure. No sooner had the newspapers forgotten about the murder of Petr Quas than so, too, did the public.

"The criminal investigation went on for a while, of course. At the Tortoise, the police had written down the names and addresses of everyone present. I was summoned to the police station several days after the murder. I waited almost two hours in a long, light hallway with an unpleasant smell and high windows that overlooked a yard. About ten of us sat in silence on wooden benches. I recognized two or three faces from the theater. A couple of us flipped through magazines with lots of pictures in them, but most of us just stared into space. From time to time, the silence was broken by a cellphone ringing, followed by a muted conversation; sometimes, someone stood up and paced the hallway from end to end before sitting down again. Periodically, the door of one of the offices would open and a man's voice would call out the next name. Opposite me sat a girl with wavy red hair who spent the whole time with her eyes fixed on a duplicated university textbook. When she looked up, I saw an unusually pale face and a freckled nose, and I recognized her as a student I'd seen in the corridors of the Faculty of Arts, and at the Tortoise, too. She was studying art history, I'd heard.

"At last, my name was called and I stepped into the small office. Most of the room was occupied by a large, scratched desk with an ancient computer on it. One look at the face of the policeman behind the desk told me that the police were as fed up with this case as Prague's journalists were. And the way in which he put his questions confirmed my impression that he resented the killer for the unconventional style he or she had introduced to the realm of crime. It seemed this officer took it for granted that crime and its investigation were parts of a game whose rules should be respected by prosecutor and prosecutee alike; the arbitrary violation of these rules was an unforgivable dereliction. The questioning was a formality, more or less, as the officer had little expectation that I or anyone else from that audience would tell him anything of substance. As far as I could tell, he didn't even know what he was supposed to be asking about.

"I was preparing to leave when he asked me a final question, apparently out of personal interest: 'As you work in the Philosophy department, maybe you could tell me what *The Thing In Itself* is.' I explained that according to Kant, this is something independent of all the ways we have grasping reality, meaning that it is altogether unknowable for us. The officer sighed as he turned to his computer keyboard and began to type slowly with two fingers."

6. Kristýna

"I was at the police station on Friday. I spent all of Saturday and Sunday working on my thesis; now members of the Flamingo company were dancing through every sentence of Kant that I read. I continued my notetaking on Monday morning. In the afternoon, I went to the Faculty of Arts to listen to a guest professor of aesthetics from Vienna speak on American abstract expressionism. This lecture was held in a large, light hall on the second floor whose windows looked out on the river and Prague Castle. I sat at the end of a long row next to the door, so that as I listened, I could look at the castle and the streetcars crossing the Mánes Bridge. Among one of a series of profiles bent over their notepads, I spotted the girl I'd seen at the Tortoise and again in the hall of the police station. A moment later, her profile moved back, like a fold in a closing fan.

"When the lecture was over, a group of students remained in the corridor outside the lecture hall, discussing the opinions of the professor from Vienna. The girl from the theater was among them; those who knew her called her Kristýna. For the first time, as the cold light streamed in from the courtyard through large windows, I was able to get a good look at her face. I was struck by the seriousness I read in her features, setting her apart from the other students. Kristýna's fragile frame was awash with this seriousness. She stood straighter than the others, as though setting herself against a great weight that was bearing down on her; I was reminded of the caryatids on the balconies of the Neo-Renaissance buildings in the street where I live. I had the impression that something bad had happened to her recently, and that this experience reverberated in her body, like an etude for piano through the rooms of an empty house. She spoke slowly and deliberately, choosing her words with care; maybe she was afraid that the utterance of something stupid or banal would contaminate the empty space left by the tragedy I knew nothing about. While the others gesticulated, her arms rested mostly at her sides, stirring and sweeping upward only when the cadence of her words demanded it, before returning into the pool of dejection, resignation, and waiting that her body apparently contained.

"I was attracted by her secret, which reached into the smallest movements of her fingers and the tilt of her head, like the last foam of the surf. It was the secret of some past sorrow, I suspected. But the girl scared me too: I knew that by getting close to her I would have to enter the strange space around her person, where I would struggle to hold on to the life I was used to; I would have to undergo a painful transformation.

"As I watched Kristýna and pondered, with limited success, the ciphers of her face and figure, I didn't pay much attention to what the group in the hallway was talking about. It was a while before I realized that the debate had gotten around to Jackson Pollock. An ardent admirer of abstractionism was complaining about how the human figure re-emerges in his later paintings; he took this as a betrayal of the magnificent world of splashes and smudges. Kristýna spoke up in Pollock's defense. 'What eventually appears on the canvas—be it a swirl of color or a human figure—isn't in the artist's power,' she said. Although I had no clear views on Pollock's late work, I joined the dispute on Kristýna's side, invoking Anaximander's statement that the formed and the formless are fated to pass one into the other without the one ever conquering or being of higher value than the other. As I was speaking, Kristýna looked at me for the first time; I tried to read in her expression whether she had noticed me at the theater or the police station, but I couldn't tell. The gathering in the hallway gradually dispersed; before long, Kristýna, too, walked away quietly, without having said goodbye. I hurried after her, catching up with her on the stairs. I'd be happy to talk to her some more about Pollock, I said, even though at that moment I had no thoughts of art. It was obvious that Kristýna had no desire for company, but she didn't brush me off. Maybe she felt a duty to explain in full the idea she had half-developed in the hallway before it had been lost in the confusion of the debate."

7. Plinth of the Stalin Monument

"When we reached the covered walkway at the front of the building, I asked Kristýna where she lived. She was going to Letná, she said. I decided I was going the same way. As we talked on about art, the impression I had that Kristýna inhabited some dark, possibly haunted house of the past became stronger still. Perhaps she was drawn beyond its threshold only because the outside world contained names that had once meant something to her. I could tell that she didn't feel good out in the open and was ready at any moment to bolt back inside and close the door behind her. I attended less to what she said than to the rhythm and melody of her utterances, seeking a clue about the unsettling house she inhabited—and about its secret. But these told me as little as had her earlier gestures in the school hallway. Besides, I had the feeling that her gestures and her words were products of a great variety of dissimilar spaces that had little relation to one another. As I wondered about the strangeness of her palace, my confusion grew. Only later did I learn how many worlds Kristýna lived in.

"I managed to keep the conversation going as we crossed the Mánes Bridge, passed the Straka Academy, and ascended the steps to Letná Plain. On reaching the top, we sat down on the granite plinth that once supported a great monument to Stalin. Kristýna said something more about Pollock, and then silence fell between us. We watched the white steamboats on the river, the streetcars, and the rest of the traffic on the bridge, and the flocks of tourists on the Pařížská boulevard. I could tell that Kristýna was about to return to her secret house. So I turned to her and told her that I'd seen her in the Tortoise on the evening of the murder, and then again at the police station; I added that I hoped the police hadn't kept her there too long. She didn't let on whether she remembered me or not, but she did say that she'd spent several hours in a police interview room. I was surprised by this: Could she have seen something at the theater that the investigators considered important?

"When I put this question, she shook her head. 'I don't think I told them anything of interest.' She hesitated, before adding: 'They kept me there for so long because a year ago they had me in for questions about the death of Quas's stepbrother. The investigating officers probably thought it strange that one of the witnesses had known the brother of the victim, when that brother, too, was murdered.'

"'You knew Tomáš Kantor?' I asked in amazement.

"'I lived with him for two years,' she replied. 'But we broke up a few months before he died . . .'

"I asked if Tomáš Kantor was as rich as Petr Quas.

"Kristýna laughed. All his working life, Tomáš was a dispatcher for public transportation, posted at a streetcar terminus. The stepbrothers didn't see much of each other. She never once saw Petr Quas. 'At least not when he was alive,' she corrected herself.

"I learned that the brothers had neither father nor mother in common: Tomáš's father had married Petr's mother when Tomáš was thirteen and Petr a year younger. I asked Kristýna if she had any idea who the murderer of Tomáš and Petr might be. It was as much a mystery to her as it was to everyone else, she said. Tomáš had no enemies—no friends either; when they were together, she was the only person he had anything to do with. As for Petr, Tomáš used to say he meticulously avoided all suspicious acquaintances, in his business and his private life alike.

"Naturally, I was far more interested in Tomáš Kantor than

his brother, particularly as I felt a pang of jealousy toward the dead man at the news that Kristýna had been his lover. I still can't shake off that jealousy . . . Anyway, at that point I knew one thing for sure: The misery Kristýna carried around with her was a strange fruit of her love for Tomáš Kantor. I asked her to tell me about him. What could a man be like who wrote a ballet that painstakingly transformed into dance the thoughts contained in *The Critique of Pure Reason*, and who ended up in a Turkish fishermen's net with thirteen wounds, although he was poor and had neither enemies nor friends? The first look Kristýna gave me was one of horror, as though I had made an indecent proposal. I had the impression that she was yet to speak with anyone about her relationship with Tomáš; I also felt that she longed for a visitor to her house of sorrow, so that she might show him around its rooms and tell him what had happened in them."

I told Martin that it seemed to me that he and Kristýna had a lot in common. Apparently, he, too, struggled to decide between the need to keep a secret and the need to confide in someone.

Martin smiled before going on with story. "Kristýna looked down on the roofs of the city and said without turning to face me: 'I got to know Tomáš three years ago at the streetcar terminus . . .' And in the melody of her words was an echo, albeit an indistinct one, of a long story as yet unknown to me; it came like the sudden view from a mountain-top of a landscape whose contours are glowing through the mist. There on the plinth of the Stalin monument, Kristýna began to tell me the story of Tomáš Kantor. That day, I learned about his childhood, which he had thought of often and spoken about with Kristýna many times. When I asked her if she would go on with the story the next day, she showed no reluctance.

After that, we met every afternoon for three weeks, mostly

in the outdoor seating of restaurants on the Letná Plain, and Kristýna spoke of nothing but the story. At the end of the first week, she brought me the novel *Damp Walls*, Tomáš Kantor's only finished book. It comprised seven hundred and eighteen computer-printed pages. Until then, I was still trying to spend my mornings working on my thesis, but I gave this up and read Kantor's book till lunchtime before rushing off to meet Kristýna and hear more about her lover. I had no thoughts of anything but the life of a man I'd never seen so much as a photograph of—a life most people wouldn't consider particularly interesting or colorful—and the lives of several of the characters he had invented for his book.

"I came to realize that the strange building Kristýna lived in was actually a huge museum to Tomáš Kantor, containing pictures from his life and works. I was proud to be the only visitor she let inside. In this labyrinthine house, she was at once the guide and a figure in many of the pictures. I wondered about the strangeness of a fate that made a quiet girl like Kristýna mistress of a monstrous memorial, whose corridors of pictures and phantoms she wandered alone for many months, until she herself became a picture and a ghost. I understood her fear of visitors but also her longing to show the corridors and halls devoted to the dead man, so that someone might share in their oppressive vastness and solitude. And the stories emerged from the tremulous, astonished, and sorrowful stream of her voice like crystals, and these crystals spread themselves before me before dissolving and soaking back into the stream, so that all stories brought me back to Kristýna and transformed in her aura . . ."

Tomáš and Petr I

1. Father

Martin paused and looked about. For a moment I sensed the picture in his mind of outdoor restaurants on the Letná Plain had blended with his view of the nighttime bay. Although most of the taverna's customers had paid up and gone to bed, there were still a few people there, sitting outside.

"When she first met Tomáš, Kristýna lived on the edge of the city. Every morning, she traveled from the streetcar terminus to the Faculty of Arts. There was a little house next to the track loop. Rising from the roof of this house was a pointed tower, three of whose sides were made of glass. Whenever she looked into the glass she saw, beyond the reflected sky, the face of a man of about thirty-five, who was sitting on a swivel chair in front of some kind of panel with levers and colored buttons. At first, Kristýna had the feeling she was looking at a homemade space rocket that was about to take off, although in the six months she'd been using that streetcar stop the tower had remained where it was. Before long, she noticed that the astronaut in the cockpit was playing some mysterious game; most of the time he was bent over a notebook that lay among the buttons, writing slowly and intently. Whenever a streetcar arrived or a colored light showed on the panel, he would zoom away on his caster-wheeled chair to the other end of the desk, where he pushed various buttons and wrote something in a large book; he would write with remarkable speed. A moment later, he was back in his original position, having resumed writing in his notebook.

"The terminus was beyond the last houses in the street and skirted by tall wooden fences. So few passengers got on there that Kristýna and the man in the tower were often the only people around. The man in the tower soon became aware of Kristýna, and for several months they would wave to each other whenever she appeared on the platform.

"When Kristýna ran into the astronaut from the terminus at an exhibition, she couldn't resist asking him about the rituals he performed in the tower. That day, however, she learned nothing because he glossed over the subject, joking that the glass tower was actually the top of a shaft two hundred meters deep, which ended underground at a diamond mine so secret that the miners were forbidden to speak of their occupation, even in front of their families; his job, he said, was to receive and write reports on finds in the mine. After the exhibition, he walked her home, and within three weeks Kristýna knew almost everything, not only about the two occupations he performed on his castered chair at either end of the dispatcher's desk in the glass tower, but also about the life of Tomáš Kantor. Kristýna fell in love with him straight away, and she's still in love with him, even though he left her, and even though he died over a year ago.

"Both of Tomáš Kantor's parents were lawyers. Tomáš didn't remember his mother: She had died in a train accident when he was one year old, after which he lived with his father and his mother's mother in an apartment block on a Prague housing estate. His grandmother had a key to the apartment so that she could take care of the housework, the child, and the father, who wouldn't have managed otherwise; she left the Kantors' apartment to return to her own home late every evening. When Tomáš was thirteen, his grandmother introduced his father to Mrs. Quasová, a divorced teacher of geography. Following the marriage of Mrs. Quasová and Mr. Kantor a few months later, Tomáš's grandmother left them to it, although she determined to keep an eye on Tomáš from a discreet distance. Not long afterward, however, she went into the hospital, where she died without fuss. From her previous marriage, Mrs. Quasová had a son called Petr, who was a year younger than Tomáš. When they first met in the Kantors' living room, Tomáš and Petr faced each other across a platter of open sandwiches in silence, and with probing, jealous eyes. After Mrs. Quasová and her son moved in with the Kantors, the boys had adjacent rooms. Once Tomáš realized that Petr, whom he saw at dinnertime only, would give him no trouble, he ceased to take any notice of him. For Tomáš, Petr became a colored smudge behind the frosted glass of a door.

"Tomáš was thought to be a daydreamer, and it was true to say that he was often unaware of what was going on around him. Although he imagined himself becoming a famous painter, writer, or composer of music, apparently there was nothing he was truly gifted at and no hobby he attended to with any consistency. Before he so much as picked up a pencil with the intention of drawing something, he would spend hours picturing himself being congratulated at the opening of an exhibition of his paintings. His father looked on anxiously, for in the son he recognized a sickness from which he himself had suffered as a child, and which had marked his whole life. The father, too, had lived his childhood in a continuous dream of glory, in which he appeared in dozens of different roles. At sixteen, he'd decided he would write, but the literature he finally opted for was in many ways undecided, as the decision to become a writer isn't exactly a choice; it doesn't have the firmness of true choice, in which we discard all options but one: Somehow words contain all rejected possibilities and return them to us in the ghostly form of reality formed by language.

"Although the father never spoke with the son about his literary attempts, Tomáš could imagine what he must have gone through. When Mr. Kantor died and his stepmother passed his father's papers on to him, Tomáš's suspicions were confirmed. On beginning to write, the father had had a strange, striking realization: The opinions, thoughts, likings, values, and feelings he had hitherto considered his own didn't in fact belong to him at all. Although he had had occasional suspicions about this, only when he saw his opinions, thoughts, likings, values, and feelings made into words on the page did he realize the full extent of this piteous, ridiculous truth. He stared in surprise, disappointment, and disgust at the wobbly, threadbare scratchings he had dragged out of himself; he told himself that amid the junk that filled his mind, he would surely find something that was truly his, if only the germ of an original feeling, or a hazy opinion—but there was nothing at all. Once he had brought out all the things that didn't belong to him, he was goggle-eyed at the vast emptiness of it all. He had collected these opinions, thoughts, likings, values, and feelings at random and God knows where, and he didn't even know if he held them near or far. They were detritus of other people's minds, which he appropriated only so as to cover the dreadful emptiness that was—he now realized with horror—at his own core. How was it possible, he asked himself, that the core of a person could comprise nothing but a gaping hole? Now he spent most of his time lurking at the very edge of that dark hole. Surely, he told himself, he would find something—some feeling, liking, object of admiration, aversion, penchant, something that truly belonged to him; but there was nothing. In the end, the father concluded that he was a monster, unhuman, and he thought how difficult life was likely to be with this knowledge.

"So it was that when Tomáš's father, aged sixteen, decided to become a writer, he met a Sphinx that set him a riddle: How can a player win a game when his only choice is between repellent masks and an eerie emptiness? He never found the answer to this riddle. In the few more years he continued in his attempts to write, the disgust he felt at the sight of the faces of others clinging to and growing into his own skin gave way to horror at the emptiness he looked on, and vice versa. Later he emptied the drawer filled with pages covered with his own script into the garbage. From what was to hand, he built himself a flimsy shelter, which he strengthened by force of habit; somehow his life went on."

2. Tomáš

"So from the moment the father first saw symptoms in the son of the sickness he saw in himself, he lived in fear that the son would be forced to repeat the father's experiences and likewise end up a ruin. The fear was counterbalanced by the hope that this couldn't happen twice—that Tomáš would succeed where he had failed and solve the Sphinx's riddle, which, it seemed to him, had caused him to waste his life. By such a success, he felt, Tomáš would write the last, hitherto missing act to the silly, failed drama of his father's life, thus making some kind of sense of it.

"As the father watched the growing son walk the well-known path of confusion, his feelings swung from agonized anxiety to hope, although he spoke to no one of either emotion. The torment gave way to despair: The idea that the son should have strayed into the same absurd maze as the father, making of Tomáš's life a desperate, ridiculous remake of his own, was intolerable to him. He was still unable to imagine the complete meaninglessness of his own ruin, and that the life of his son should be a mere echo of it. The hope—stronger at certain periods of his son's life than others—grew out of the feeling that traces of his own malady had entered Tomáš's bloodstream like a vaccine that would save him from the sickness.

"The manifestations of the son's sickness differed a little from those of the father, but the sickness was definitely the same. On several occasions, Tomáš's stepmother suggested to her husband that this child who lived in his own imagination and was mostly oblivious to the outside world might benefit from a visit to a child psychologist, but his father always rejected the idea: Psychology would only conceal the sickness under a false name. He knew that what Tomáš was going through was a response to the cold breath of the void inside him; he knew that Tomáš lived in his dreams because the void kept calling up new images, and that all images disappeared into it. He knew that also Tomáš's childish yearning for fame grew out of the emptiness inside him, and that perhaps the only means of filling and counteracting this bottomless, all-engulfing emptiness was the extreme brilliance of fame that touched the whole world.

"Tomáš was fourteen when his behavior changed suddenly. He decided to become a painter. For the first time in his life, he concentrated on one thing, determined to learn it properly and to work hard at it. He filled his sketchbook with fantastical cities, dreamlike landscapes, and contorted figures in dramatic poses, and with careful studies of objects and figures. He used handbooks to teach himself perspective and shading; he studied anatomy for artists, and art history. At this point, his father was confirmed in his hope that Tomáš would find a way out of the labyrinth of dreams, and that he would vanquish the dragon of the void and the monster of revulsion, the terrible pair to which he himself had succumbed.

"His anxiety returned about a year later, when from one day

to the next Tomáš dropped painting in favor of music. Now his room was littered with books on music theory and lives of composers. Tomáš and his father carried through to Tomáš's bedroom the upright piano Tomáš's mother used to play on, which had stood in the living room with its lid closed since her death. Over the next few months, the sound of the piano issued from Tomáš's room, in chords developed into fragments of melody that frayed into silence. In the evenings, Tomáš's father sat with his wife, nodding at what she was telling told him about that day at school; but he wasn't listening to her, he was listening to the notes coming from Tomáš's room, and searching them anxiously for signs of their shared sickness. Although he had no understanding of music, he heard in certain of his son's passages—in their rashness, lack of concentration, and booming pathos—a foolish attempt to drown out the loud, colorful silence of the void. In the way the melody rose and fell, he recognized the oh-so-familiar revulsion that arose from knowledge that one's own mind was a randomly gathered storehouse of others' feelings and that it could never be anything else, as nothing could grow in the barren void at its bottom. And he sensed that sometime soon, the revulsion in his son's melodies would eat into his music like gangrene."

3. Poems in Drawers

"The father wasn't mistaken: Tomáš's obsession with music, too, lasted only about eighteen months. One evening, it occurred to the father that for two weeks he hadn't heard a single note from behind Tomáš's door. Tomáš wasn't at home, so he peeked into the room. Although the biographies of composers and manuscript paper marked with clusters of notes were still there, there were books of poetry piled on top of them. The father opened the drawers of the desk and found exercise books whose lines were filled with Tomáš's still-childish handwriting. He took to paying regular visits to Tomáš's room, to raid the drawers for the poems his son had written. He tried to cover his tracks, but Tomáš could always tell when his father had been through his desk. In those days, Tomáš knew nothing of his father's anxiety, believing the expeditions to his room to be a demonstration of ordinary curiosity; he would leave poems he was especially proud of where his father was bound to see them.

"The poems were of little value; few sixteen-year-olds write good poems. But what concerned the father wasn't the naivety and lack of originality in the son's poems. As he scanned the pages filled with crossings-out and insertions for signs of the family sickness, to his sorrow he found them on every line; he would have known them even if knew no Czech, by the pen strokes that now rushed onward in pursuit of images with which to fill the void, now labored across the page as if plowing through a snow drift; above all, he would have known them by the furious intensity with which lines and sometimes whole stanzas were scored out, so that in several places the pen had torn through the paper. Only a writer whose work causes him such revulsion, who is so terribly ashamed to look at it that he can't bear that a fragment of even one letter should remain visible, can treat it in this manner. Notebooks filled with the father's writing had looked just like this.

"The drawers would later contain not poems but unfinished short stories, plays, essays, fragments of novels, even comic strips and film screenplays. The father would monitor these regularly for traces of disease, like a doctor checking the extent of a virus in the blood. Soon he saw that his son's writer phase was coming to an end—far sooner, in fact, than Tomáš himself saw it. And it was just as he had expected: One genre gave way to the next ever more rapidly, until eventually Tomáš lost interest in literature and turned to philosophy, mysticism, linguistics, and, for a while, higher mathematics . . . Tomáš didn't get around to any other arts and sciences: When he was eighteen, the toboggan ride came to an end, and he fell into a void indistinguishable from the one he had known at the start. The difference was, now he was so exhausted that he felt it would take his whole life to get over a series of excursions that had left behind not a single fruit or a single germ of meaning.

"On finishing high school, he lacked both the desire and the strength for a deeper involvement. All his feelings, thoughts, deeds, and plans had disappeared into the void. A week after graduation, he spotted a notice at the streetcar terminus: Public transportation was about to employ a dispatcher. Looking up at the glass tower, he told himself that this could be his room—and such a room was the only thing he wanted. His father knew the uselessness of trying to talk him out of it. Having settled in the glass tower, Tomáš stayed in it for the twenty years until his death. Although he had many years of emptiness, the sight of the track loop sparkling in the sun, wet with rain, or lined with a new fall of snow provided an incomprehensible solace."

4. Petr

"You're speaking of Tomáš and his father as if the two of them lived alone in that apartment," I said.

"The chapter I'm about to begin features two more characters," said Martin. "Even though her husband never shared his worries with her, Tomáš's stepmother soon became aware of the painful bond that existed between father and son. She didn't know the basis of the drama her husband and stepson were enacting, but she was moved by their mysterious torment, and at that time her emotion and the compassion she felt for the two of them was a source of her love for them. But this love was like what we feel when we look at a photograph of people on some distant continent who have suffered some catastrophe. The love she felt for her own son was of a completely different order. It was an emotion joining two people who would spend many years in a foreign land without hope of ever being granted citizenship there. She would have liked to help her husband and stepson, but she didn't know how; and she considered it an incomparably more important responsibility to protect her own son, as it was by her doing that he was forced to spend his childhood among peculiar strangers and was at risk of infection by some deadly disease.

"Tomáš's father wasn't the only one who explored his room; Petr, too, would sneak in. Only much later did Tomáš consider the feelings Petr must have had, and he often spoke about this with Kristýna. The incomprehensible figures of his stepfather and stepbrother were a cause of anxiety to Petr, but this was mingled with germs of admiration and hatred. Although he breathed a compound of fancy and sorrow, numb despair and maniacal, self-consuming endeavor for several years, the dose of Kantor poison that seeped into everything in the apartment came to him too late to destroy his health, or to redraw the contours of his world. Obviously, Kantor the father's hope that the poison he had passed on would act, by dilution in the blood, as a strength-giving vaccine, was a vain one; it was still strong enough to destroy his child. But it reached his stepson in a form too weak to harm, and which perhaps was even medically beneficial.

"Petr had the feeling that the room next to his was occupied by a fairy-tale creature. The moment he heard the click of the apartment door, marking his stepbrother's departure, he would hurry into that unknown land and go on with his research. He would examine the layers of paper that captured the sequence of Tomáš's transformations: publications and notebooks filled with poems and prose, followed by scores, with drawings at the very bottom. Usually, however, he stayed at the upper stratum of his brother's wanderings. What fascinated him most were the books of poetry. Often, he couldn't get the lines he read in them out of his mind. The fact that he couldn't make heads or tails of them caused him to suffer: Although every word had an obvious meaning, and the words were arranged in a clear structure and submitted humbly or guilefully to the rules of grammar, still he couldn't make sense of many of the lines. Sometimes, he felt hatred for the authors, whom he cursed silently and accused of posturing. But he returned to their books to pick over the nonsensical clusters of words again and again. He would sneak his brother's books into his own room, where he would lie on the bed and read the same page, sometimes the same line, over and over. While he was doing this, he always heeded the sounds of the building; the moment the elevator stopped at their floor, he would leap from the bed and put the book back.

"One day, after countless hours spent poring over books from Tomáš's room, the isolated words began to come together on the page. Suddenly, Petr knew that the words were groping in the fog for subtle vines that formed a network on the page; all at once, this network was so clear to Petr that he felt like taking a pencil and drawing it in. At last he saw meaning where there had been none; it was like a sap that coursed through the intertwined veins of a book's pages. The tips of the tangled vines at last shot forth from the book and touched the surfaces of objects and bodies, marking them with their image, so transforming Petr's view of objects and bodies.

"There was a further outcome of the time Petr spent with his brother's books—it inspired him to write. A few years passed before he wrote his first real poem, but by the time he was twenty, his work was appearing in magazines. He published a book of poetry, *Columns and Beams*, when he was twenty-two; the critics wrote about him as a promising talent. This was in 1991, by which time Petr and Tomáš each lived in shabby apartments of their own—Petr in an attic studio, Tomáš in a first-floor room with a view of a yard. Mr. and Mrs. Kantor were left alone in their large apartment on the housing estate. Where once they had discussed their sons' progress at school, now they were silent for want of something to talk about. For several months, Mr. Kantor was seriously ill, and he shuffled about the apartment in flannel pajamas; when he got hungry, he heated up food that his wife had prepared and left for him in the fridge.

"Petr's mother was surprised by her gleeful satisfaction when he brought her *Columns and Beams*. She was ashamed of this feeling and tried to dispel it, but finding that she couldn't, she yielded to it and came to revel in it. She realized that this new happiness was the joy of revenge. Although she didn't understand the sickness and proud despair Tomáš and his father shared, she sensed that Petr's book would be a humiliation for her husband. Perhaps she realized only now that at the very bottom of the love and compassion she had felt for her husband and stepson, remnants of which endured, there had always been hate—hate for these people who had held her captive in a strange land where she and her son were forced to live alone, without knowing its language. She could have forgiven them if this incomprehensible, unhappy foreignness had applied to her alone, but she couldn't reconcile herself to the fact that her son had been made to spend his childhood in deepest Kantorland.

"One day, as Mrs. Kantorová was passing the open door of her husband's room, she saw that he was standing at the window, which looked out on rows of windows of the apartment buildings opposite. His hands were resting on the sill, and he was laughing quietly to himself. She walked on without saying a word. She didn't realize that her husband was reading Petr's book and laughing at the practical joke fate had played on him: It had never crossed his mind that the long story of his anxiety and two wasted lives could end this way. In times when he and his wife tried conscientiously but clumsily to make a family out of the four of them, he made touching attempts to treat Petr as he treated his own son, and often this expression of his favor worked against Tomáš. Mr. Kantor was fond of Petr. He'd been neither unaware of nor unmoved by Petr's status of confused foreigner in the Kantor household, although he'd been unable to help him with it. Even now, he was glad that his stepson had succeeded in resisting the mixture of fever and lethargy that had hung about their apartment like stale air. Yet he was bitter, too, because Petr's victory reminded him of his own and Tomáš's defeat. It answered no questions about the peculiar drama of his own life, because Petr didn't figure in it: He and Tomáš had always been its only characters. In thinking with malice that Petr's book would bring her husband pain, Petr's mother hadn't been mistaken.

"When the book of poems was published, Petr and his step-brother hadn't seen each other in over a year. After a few days' hesitation, Petr mailed Tomáš a copy with a dedication. Tomáš read it and was enchanted by it. He called Petr up, and they met in a café, where for the first time they shared a real conversation. Petr confessed to his brother that he was first inspired to write by his secret visits to Tomáš's room, and Tomáš was glad that the childhood he had daydreamed his way through wasn't entirely without meaning. Nor was he sorry to be reminded by his brother's book of his own failure. The emptiness that had apparently taken full possession of his mind a few years earlier also acted as a palliative, a snow of conciliation that covered old wounds."

5. Visit from the Darkness

"In those days Petr was working on a long poem, and he thought of nothing but poetry. He was so possessed by the need to write that he had no thoughts of anything else. When he abandoned his studies, his mother, secure in the belief that her son would become a famous writer, raised no objection; from time to time, she gave him some money. One day, a friend who played in a little-known punk band asked Petr to write some words to a song he'd composed; Petr produced these overnight. After this, he sometimes earned a little extra money by writing lyrics for various rock bands. He also wrote—under a pseudonym—lyrics to two or three songs for a famous pop singer. Although he didn't like doing this, sometimes he struggled to feed himself, and he didn't want to keep asking his mother for money. Besides, it would be a pity if he starved before he could complete his long poem.

"Tomáš told Kristýna about an evening that changed Petr's life. He spoke of it in such vivid terms that at the time Kristýna was certain that it happened just as he said. Only after Tomáš's death, when she was going over all the moments they had spent together, did she reach the conclusion that Tomáš had dreamed up the whole episode. Indeed, she was amazed at her ability to believe a story that contained so many literary references and suspicious props and was obviously a parody. She couldn't even be sure of the accuracy of Tomáš's description of what happened that evening. His story sounded very much like literature, but fact often resembles fiction, doesn't it?"

Martin paused again. In the taverna, the few remaining customers were finishing their last glasses of ouzo, retsina, and beer. We called to Tanya, ordered another jug of wine, and paid up.

"So tell me what happened to Petr," I prompted Martin, who appeared to be lost in his thoughts.

"As the story goes, late one winter's evening, the doorbell

rang in Petr's attic studio. According to Kristýna, there was a blizzard outside, although she admitted that Tomáš had mentioned no such thing; the picture of a raging snowstorm was probably formed in her own mind. Petr opened the door to a burly man in a fur coat glittering with melting snowflakes. The man introduced himself as the general manager of a theater. Petr invited him in. The man unbuttoned his fur coat but refused to take it off. In her mind's eye, Kristýna still sees his round face and pointed black mustache, even though she suspects she added these details later. He sat down at the table and asked Petr to write lyrics for a musical his theater was planning to put on. The fee he was offering was higher than Petr would have thought possible for the committing of words to paper. Even so, he declined the offer out of hand.

"The general manager wasn't disturbed by this refusal; apparently he'd been expecting it. He stood up, shook Petr's hand solemnly, said that he understood his attitude and congratulated him on it; then sat down again. Petr found all this rather confusing. The general manager went on to say that he shared Petr's reservations about such writing. But there was one thing Petr should take into consideration: There was a huge difference between money in the hands of a poet and money in the hands of a banker or an official. Money was neither printed paper nor figures in a bank account; it was the seed that produced stories, experiences, adventures, artistic creation, and days of meaningful work. Money was the future in its freshest and purest form. Money was more than just the possibility of this, that, or the other, it was the *ultimate possibility*, the initial purity of an act imbued with a dream.

"He reached into the breast pocket of his fur coat, pulled out a thick wad of banknotes, and laid this on the table. 'In the hands of some,' he said, 'riches spawn a villa lacking in taste. In the hands of others, it can be a fountainhead of experience in search of the absolute, spreading itself out like a flying carpet that delivers thousands of adventures. It'll allow you to know the breath of hot walls in the alley of a medieval hilltop town in Italy, or the rank smell of water in a Portuguese fishing port, or to stroll about nighttime Manhattan looking at the hundreds of lighted windows in the silhouettes of skyscrapers, or to drive a jeep through an aboriginal village in the Australian bush, or to sip tequila in a bar on the square of a colonial town somewhere in Central America, or to read your favorite poet on the terrace of an Alpine chalet, overlooking snow-covered slopes glinting in the sun, or to drink a liqueur in the dining car of an express train passing a lake whose shores are lined with white villas set in gardens with tall, dark cypresses, or to stand on the balcony of a luxury hotel sipping chilled champagne as lights come on in the blue Parisian dusk.

"'And all experience, no matter how deep in the memory, will mature into words, and you will write wonderful poems. My favorite poet is Rainer Maria Rilke. I read him every evening. Rilke said that for a poet to be successful, he must gather a lot of experience; he must travel, and get to know lots of people, landscapes, and different seas in different seasons. And I ask you: How could he do this without money? Who should have money if not the poet, who transforms it into unique experience, images of light, encounters with unforgettable scents, and unrepeatable gestures, creating light and shade in the streets of strange towns, and flavors of dishes unknown to us, so revealing to us mysteries of distant lands? Who else shows us many women, and many loves, be they tragic or happy, heavy, or light as the breeze? His experience is transformed into poetry; indeed, experience itself becomes poetry. Poetry is a gift bestowed by the poet on others. In fact, it's the greatest gift he can bestow. So if a poet earns a lot, first and foremost he does it not for himself, but for others.'

"The general manager said a lot more in this vein. The way

Tomáš told it, the part of the speech about experiences that could bring Petr money was strikingly similar to what Sara de Maupers says to Axël d'Auersperg in the final act of Villiers de L'Isle Adam's play *Axël*. 'I myself earn money only so that I can cultivate such a poetry of experience,' said the general manager, 'as, regrettably, I've been denied the gift of creating poetry in words. But you could bring together the two streams of poetry. Does it not make you dizzy to imagine what could come of such a fusion of life and poetry? Although other people consider them mad, poets are wise. Your book was a source of great pleasure to me. I read it closely, several times, so I know that you're wise enough to laugh in the face of the silly, small-town lore that says a poet must not be rich.'"

"At this, the general manager laughed, as if it were impossible not to laugh at such a good joke. When the laughter had passed, he picked up the wad of banknotes and said: 'I can give this money to anyone; there are dozens of lyricists who are decent practitioners of their craft. Their lyrics wouldn't be as good as yours, of course, but that hardly matters to an audience that can't tell the difference. And between you and me—and I'm being straight with you—not even lyrics by Baudelaire would save a musical that was going down. I've offered the work to you because I know and admire your poems and I'd like to give something back to you for them. I can imagine how unpleasant it must be for you to write lyrics for pop songs. But consider this: It would be a one-time thing, and you'd earn enough to be able to devote your energies to writing true poetry without distraction.'

"The general manager fell silent and remained calmly seated at the table. While he spoke, Petr had been pacing the narrow room nervously. He sat back down at the table, the wad of bills between him and the visitor, the snowfall heavy beyond the window. We know that Petr's discovery in poetry of meaning that grows in the lines as wild as weeds had caused the way he perceived landscapes of the world to be purified and sharpened. Petr took more from a naïve mascaron on a wall, masonry reduced to rubble, or an old factory than others did from a trip along the Loire. He had often regretted how his poverty caused him to miss out on wondrous encounters; travel was out of the question. The general manager had chosen the very words Petr couldn't ignore . . ."

6. Sorcerer's Apprentice

"So did Petr accept the general manager's offer?" I asked.

"As I was saying, it's unlikely there ever was a general manager in a fur coat. I suspect Tomáš invented the whole episode. But it's true to say that Petr accepted somebody's offer to write lyrics for songs in a stupid musical, and it seems to me that in his story of a nighttime visitor, Tomáš managed to express what he thought about this pretty well."

"So what happened?"

"Petr never finished his long poem; indeed, he published no more poems. Perhaps he gave up on poetry altogether. He wrote lyrics for pop singers, and after a while began to attend their gatherings. He would appear in photos in tabloids taken at celebrities' parties; as a result, his earnings increased. In 1995, his showbiz friends established a music publishing company, in which they offered him a stake. Having become a co-owner of this company, Petr soon started doing business elsewhere, too. Eventually, his work was more about financial transactions than the writing of song lyrics."

A young Dutch couple, the only other remaining customers, waved and smiled at us as they passed our table and left the taverna. There was still a light on in the kitchen. Most of the other tavernas were empty; the only sound that carried to us across the water was quiet music from a bar at the other end of the bay. Loutro was either sleeping or lying down to sleep.

"Thanks to his decision to write lyrics for a few musical songs, his whole life was changed?" I asked Martin.

"That would be a bold claim to make. Such sudden changes probably happen only in novels, like the kind of mistake that destroys absolutely everything forevermore. I don't know what caused the poet to become a popular lyricist and the popular lyricist to become an entrepreneur, and neither did Tomáš. He often spoke of it with Kristýna, making whole stories out of it, but that was more of a game than a genuine attempt to find an answer. While reading *Columns and Beams*, he identified impure tones at the heart of Petr's poetry. In and of itself, however, this didn't have to mean anything. Indeed, Tomáš said that it was as it should be: Having been torn away from the complex system of veins from which a work draws nourishment, unblemished purity was sterile, and also weak. Is it truly possible to distinguish a fascination with radiant reality from complacent hedonism? In the act of writing, what is pure and what is impure are born out of each other, and vanity and self-indulgence lead to an encounter between the miraculous and stubborn righteousness on the one hand and rigidity and arrogance on the other; but that in the mix which is dark may also distance itself from the interplay in which strange alliances originate, and it may make itself independent and begin to govern on its own.

"It may have been a mere coincidence, a single moment of malevolence. Maybe among the components of the hot, stinking, bubbling mixture from which a book is born a bad relation was established, putting the whole slightly off kilter, and Petr paid no attention to this; there is something of the sorcerer's apprentice in every writer. Maybe for some reason he suffered writer's block, and while this was going on a demon seized the opportunity to obtain a position of advantage. To me, it seems entirely plausible that the incredible career that followed his fall was an expression of despair at the loss of the treasure he had found in childhood, as he sat over Tomáš's books and listened for the elevator . . . Maybe he knew in his subconscious that this loss could be compensated for only by something equally huge; maybe he acquired ever more money in the belief that his bank balance still didn't make up for what he had lost. Maybe he became a financier as a punishment to the poet inside him for his failure to write. Or perhaps he first approached his business as a kind of experiment performed out of curiosity and it simply got out of hand—experimenting in money-making as if it were poetry is like poking about with graphite rods in the core of a nuclear reactor. Maybe this was a test he had set for himself; he wanted to see if he could make his way in the unpolluted world of money, pop stars, and trivial versifying. If this were so, then it's likely that the idea of a test was whispered to him by his demon (demons tend to beget such good ideas). What if he had convinced himself that the distant world of business and finance was for him what Africa was for Rimbaud? Until he became accustomed to it, I can imagine him wearing his expensive manager's suit as Rimbaud wore the burnoose. But things may have been completely different, of course; we'll never know, as Petr Quas is dead. But we can be almost certain that he never wrote another poem, and as a result he was unhappy to the end of his days. This unhappiness manifested itself in boastfulness, the well-known temper tantrums he directed against his friends and closest colleagues, and a tendency to alcoholism, which he could never shake. On top of this, Petr Quas became an insuf-ferable snob who bragged of knowing worthless celebrities. But unlike other snobs, who envy others, Petr Quas knew the agony of jealousy directed at the self; he envied the person who had written *Columns and Beams*.

"Petr saw Tomáš rarely. He built himself a villa in a small town called Dobřichovice. He joined the boards of various companies; his mother didn't even bother to ask him about the abbreviations that appeared in their names. Eventually, he found himself on the board of the Phoenix Group, which bought and sold other companies. Petr discovered in himself a strange ability to solve mergers, purchases, and sales as though they were complex equations. Wasn't this unexpected gift another result of his skill in reading the complicated network of obscure relations—a skill he'd acquired by reading the books of poetry borrowed in secret from Tomáš's room? Who can say?"

7. Snow in the Yard

"Meanwhile, Tomáš was sitting in his glass pavilion on the roof, looking at the streetcar track loop. Or he was lying on the divan in his apartment, with its view of a yard in which there were several piles of junk covered with pieces of fiber cement. The void that ruled his world had various faces; there were times when it looked something like a mystical union with the cosmos, and others when it resembled imbecility; sometimes, it was a bringer of despair, but there were also times when it brought something akin to joy. Tomáš took these changes as they came, as different weathers over the land of emptiness in which he lived, neither thinking much about them nor trying to influence them. The rule of emptiness erased from his mind most of the aims people set themselves in life, while transforming the rest; what drives others on in the form of desire worked in Tomáš as a simple mechanism that kept his life in minimal running order from day to day and from hour to hour. But this muffling of life freed up space for an enormous quantity of things, shapes, hues, and lights that—as they were considered of insufficient interest or usefulness—rarely penetrated the conscious; if they did, they were immediately expelled by the memory as superfluous ballast, the waste of experience.

Tomáš's main activity was aimlessly wandering the city. Over the years, he came to carry the whole city about in his head, like some useless load. His memory retained details of even the most remote suburban backstreets; he believed himself capable of recalling the expression of every building, right down to details found on crooked wooden sheds in the allotment gardens. In those days, he seemed to be dragging around a great quantity of images to no purpose, as he had neither the strength to resist the flow of time that deposited all this useless junk in his memory nor the energy to tidy up his mind by disposing of the useless things it contained.

"He read all kinds of things, although all the words in the books faded and came to lie on the pages like dead insects; from time to time, with amazement and a feeling akin to sorrow, he recalled how the very same words had once glowed with an almost unbearable radiance. At times such as these, he felt as if he were recalling life in another body. A workmate gave him several dozen inherited issues of *National Geographic*; Tomáš got through them all in a few months. It would be untrue to say that he read them with interest—in those days he really wasn't interested in anything—but while he was reading them, he had the feeling that from deep within he heard an echo of muted desire for strange lands, especially cities—a desire that diluted the Kantor void to an almost imperceptible shiver of sorrow.

"He bought a television set. Although he struggled to pay attention to dramas and psychological thrillers, he sometimes watched adventure films. Often, however, he just listened to the trickling of rainwater from the gutter next to his window into the drain, experiencing no great difference between this water music and reading or watching TV. He had no dealings with his stepmother; indeed, he never gave her a thought, and rarely thought of Petr. But Petr often thought about his step-brother, and he sought him out every two or three years. Petr wondered if he should offer Tomáš some money, although he never brought himself to actually do so.

"Although he was almost never sick, in December, 2001, Tomáš came down with the flu. For the first time in his life, he was confined to his apartment for several days. On the third day, he awoke as the sun was coming up beyond his window. He brewed some coffee and turned on his bedside lamp, so he could read a few pages of the magazine lying on the nightstand. Moments later, he laid the magazine aside, lay down again, and looked, via the pattern on the curtain, through the window to the bluish gulf of the yard, specifically at a broken cupboard that someone had dumped there at least a year before, some kind of a machine with cogwheels, and a tin barrel; all these things were coated thickly with snow. The light came on in the narrow win-dow of the kitchen where people made breakfast and prepared to leave for work. He listened to the early-morning sounds of the building—the flushing of toilets on all floors, music from radios, the calls of children, the purr of the elevator as it rose and fell . . .

"He didn't know what to do. Having decided he would read, he couldn't find a book that held his attention. A pile of twelve volumes pulled from his bookcase at various intervals lay on the nightstand. He had read a few lines of each book and been dissatisfied with all of them. In the white quiet of the early morning—which turned the creaks and rattles of the building's bowels into a quiet music that reminded him vaguely of the forgotten joy of listening he had known in his composer period—he found the problems of love and marriage experi-enced by fictitious characters an irritation. For the first time in ages, he had the feeling that he knew what he wanted to read about. The book he wanted to immerse himself in would deal solely with the life of things and spaces. Only the words of such a book would leave the tranquility of early morning undisturbed; only such a book would be admitted by the white snow. He longed for long, calm descriptions of a people-less world, where humans were present only in creations they had left behind, impressions of gestures, and traces of past events. In all books, however, the life of things and spaces was intruded upon by the uninteresting stories of people, with their exaggerated gestures, boring words, and drab thoughts. It occurred to him that he might find descriptions of things in *National Geographic*; he pulled a few issues from his bookcase and started reading several articles, all of which he laid aside after a few minutes. At first, he was happy that the people in them appeared only as participants in travel, but before long he became annoyed by the authors' assumption of the right to decide on what was important about a city or region, and what wasn't worthy of description.

"He realized that he had no books that provided indiscriminate descriptions of everything the gaze fell on. Maybe no such book existed, he said to himself. Who would write a book that was nothing but endless descriptive details of city streets or country roads that ran between fields? And even if someone did feel the need to describe such things, no publisher would entertain the idea of taking on such a manuscript . . . Then he had an idea: If no such book existed, he could write at least a part of one, perhaps describing the empty streets of some strange city. Tomáš had no thoughts of starting on a work of literature; he didn't want to encourage the return of his old malaise, its feverishness, and the exhaustion that followed. But surely he wouldn't be producing literature by describing an imaginary city for his own amusement, so there was nothing for him to worry about. He remembered the loose-leaf streetcar schedules in his briefcase. He sat up in bed and wrapped himself up—it was cold in the apartment. Then, by the light of the bedside lamp, he began to write on the back of one of the schedules."

Escape to Parca I

1. A Strange City

"None of the world's cities were in his thoughts; he didn't even know if the city he was going to write about was ancient or modern, a great metropolis, or a small town. He wanted to think all this through, but as soon as his pen touched the paper, to his surprise he learned that there was no need to think about anything; indeed, there was no time for such thoughts. Immediately, his mind conjured up a picture of an empty street, and it was as though this street had long been waiting for the moment when Tomáš would turn on it the gaze of his other, inner eyes. The pen embarked on a journey of its own, the hand unable to keep up. Tomáš wrote of goods and tubs of flowers in store windows, streetlamps, Neo-baroque ornamentations on walls, and shapes made by patches of peeling stucco. Although he lay in bed, he was wandering along a street in a strange city. Reaching a corner, he turned into a side street, and this, too, opened itself to his view; he saw stains on walls, tufts of dry grass growing against buildings, cast-metal acanthus ornamentation on streetlamps.

"To his delight, Tomáš realized that there was no need for him to set about the laborious invention of the city, as it was emerging from the mist of its own accord. All its streets were there, as were its facades, with their scratches and scrawlings in chalk. He had no difficulty writing down everything he saw, and the writing in no way disturbed his view or interfered with his pedestrian progress through the strange town. Indeed, as the sentences rolled out onto the paper, as well as driving his imaginary legs, they sharpened his inner gaze by asking questions and setting tasks. Although the street would sometimes fade and disappear, it was enough for him to look up from the page at the snow-covered yard and the incipient daylight for the strange city to emerge from the bluish, grayish areas of the window. Before long, the yellow glare of the lamp was lost in the light that came from the yard; Tomáš switched off the lamp before going on with his writing. He once told Kristýna that sometimes he had the feeling that the dim light of a December morning in the narrow yard between the apartment buildings contained all the images and stories yet to arise in his life, and that this light should take most credit or blame for what happened later. I asked Kristýna if he saw the light in the snow-covered yard as a disguised image of his death, but Kristýna couldn't answer.

"The city announced itself through the other senses, too. It was pleasantly quiet in the streets. All Tomáš heard was the sound of a distant car or a snippet of radio music from a window he was passing. After a while, his mind grew imaginary arms to go with his imaginary legs; he used his hands to touch a wall and feel its rough surface. He inhaled the pleasant smells of the city, the tones and shades of which he couldn't yet make out . . .

"The stores were closed; apparently he'd arrived in this place in the early morning. He looked above the display windows at the store signs, but he couldn't make out the text on them. He tried to place Czech words on some signs, and he saw immediately that they didn't belong; obviously, the city wasn't in Bohemia or Moravia. Besides, the smell of this place wasn't that of a Czech city. He tried putting various other languages on the store signs, none of which looked right against the walls of this city. Evidently, this city was in an imaginary country. But rather than giving the city space over to arbitrariness, this discovery gave Tomáš a feeling of a greater responsibility for the scene and the sharpness of its focus, as there existed no guidebook to correct mistakes in his description.

"He tried hard to figure out what kind of country he was in, and the position held by this city within it. He knew immediately that it wasn't the capital. He suspected it lay at the edge of the country, but obviously it wasn't a small town of little importance. Most likely, it was the administrative center of one of the provinces. Although most of the buildings that appeared to him were marked by the international style of the late nineteenth century, mixing historicism with elements of Art Nouveau, there was much—such as the metal railings of small balconies, high wooden shutters and front doors, some of which opened directly into the living space, where many various cloths and doilies lay across tables and couches—to suggest that the city was somewhere in the south. This assumption was supported by what was on display in the windows of the produce markets: Among the oranges, lemons, and eggplants, he saw figs, okra, and prickly pears. He hadn't yet reached the edge of the city, but from the layout and rhythm of the streets he read that to the west and east it opened out into fields and grassy plains, while to the north it appeared to be bordered by foothills; he looked over the rooftops at ridges of gray rock that headed into the clouds. As yet, he was unable to make out what was on the south side. Tomáš was in no hurry to map out the city: To do this, he had two weeks, and besides, he knew that a dearth of patience might cause the city to disappear."

2. First Pedestrian

"By now, Tomáš had covered eight pages with small handwriting. He was glad that it had occurred to him to write about the imaginary city; in this way, he could keep himself amused for the duration of his illness, he told himself. He was sticking to his initial decision not to concern himself with style, although he saw that the city was settling into its own style, by transmitting its rhythm into the dark space of a nascent language. This transmission caused the mesh of sentences and clauses to submit to an urge to imitate the network of the streets, and to mark the rhythm of a pedestrian's progress. Having so far headed north, he happened upon a broad, busy street that ran from west to east; this, it seemed, was the city's main boulevard. He didn't wish to walk this, so he turned and headed back in a southernly direction. He sensed a growing restlessness: On the city's south side was a restlessness that made itself known in the shape and course of the streets, the smell of the stucco, and the breath that came from open first-floor windows. For a long time, he didn't know what this was. Then, at the end of a narrow, sloping street, he saw a flash of sea. Up to this point, it hadn't occurred to him that he was describing a city that was by the sea. He walked down the narrow street to the old port, where he paced back and forth along the pier. Further east, he saw what looked like a modern port: Above the roofs of the flaking apartment buildings, their balconies hung with laundry, he saw the tops of big white ships."

I'd been wriggling in my chair for a while now, and at this point I felt the need to interrupt. "Hang on a minute. I don't want to offend you, but it's easier to believe that Petr Quas was visited by a fur-coated figure from the darkness than Tomáš Kantor writing about a strange city as if describing a film he was watching."

Martin was obviously irked by the interruption. "I'll describe that winter morning to you as Tomáš described it to Kristýna, and as she described it to me," he said. "I can't be sure it was exactly as I say. It's possible that everything he told Kristýna about his writing was an illustration. But that illustration may be truer than an official statement on what happened that day. It's more than likely that the origins of the city were somewhat different; it could be that Tomáš considered various options, compared various visions, and made his choice from among them. But maybe the story he told that December morning was intended to show that the city that had emerged from his writing was oddly complete before he began to write, and that it wasn't a product of his desires or preferences; besides, who can say whether Tomáš had any desires and preferences at the time? The city imposed itself on him, allowing him no latitude in his description. This was the main thing Tomáš was trying to convey—whether he described the city in his very first attempt with no crossings-out or if it emerged in its final form after the tenth or twentieth rewrite is of no importance.

"When he saw his first human figure, disappearing around a corner, it was noon in Prague and seven-thirty A.M. in the imaginary, nameless city. At first, Tomáš saw only the tail of a gray coat. As Tomáš's double paused on the street, so, too, did the pen over the paper. Tomáš didn't know what to do; he'd started writing with the thought of creating a quiet, peopleless world, and now he knew that more pedestrians would soon appear on the city streets. At this point, he considered abandoning his writing, to save the city from a human invasion. But his indecision was brief. He realized he had no cause to fear the people who were about to exit the buildings: They wouldn't be intruders, but beings born of the breath of the streets—figures the city craved and summoned to fill its space.

"No sooner had Tomáš decided to admit people to the streets than the population began to build. Most of those he encountered had dark, wavy hair, although they weren't especially dark-skinned. The appearance of the people and many other features scattered about the streets allowed Tomáš to place the city on the map: It lay to the very north of southern Europe, more or less where the South begins in the mind of a Central European. It was a port and trading city on the south-eastern border of the country. Tomáš was glad to have established the coordinates of the place he was writing about. He was indifferent to the fact that Europe has no space for such a country."

3. Stranger in the City

"As Tomáš roamed the city, he realized that along with the streets and the people, he was witnessing the birth of a new perspective, and it was by this perspective that he was looking at the streets, squares, and quays. What's more, this perspective was rooted in a new body. Although Tomáš was happy to produce a description of a non-participant, it was obvious that the eye trained on the city wasn't the indifferent eye of a camera—and he knew that it wasn't his own eye. He was looking at the city through the eyes of a character who, like everyone else in the city, was born out of the white mist present at the beginning of his writing. He set about finding out what he could about this character. Judging by his attentive, somewhat puzzled gaze, it was clear that the city wasn't his home; plainly the unknown pedestrian whose body Tomáš had entered, had come to the city only recently. And the perspective grew out of a body whose gait betrayed hesitancy, detachment, and an undefined movement toward distant places.

"Tomáš began to elaborate the past of the pedestrian into whom he had transformed himself, drawing on the perspective and the gait. The man and he were about the same age, a little over thirty. The man had recently been through something that continued to cause him pain and related to his stay here, a city that wasn't his home. Apparently, he had spent his whole life in the country's capital, where, it seemed, he had taught at the university—yes, Tomáš figured out that he was a lecturer in the history department; he had been married for several years, but had no children; a few months earlier, he had learned that his wife had been unfaithful to him; the anguish at the discovery had gradually given way to indifference and apathy; he and his wife had agreed to live apart for a while; he had applied for a transfer to a city in the far south-east of the country, whose streets he was now walking. And the name of the city? Only one emerged from the murmur, but it was so indistinct that Tomáš struggled to catch it. Was it Parma? No, Stendhal had written about Parma. Was it Pearl? No, that had been described by Alfred Kubin. Then Tomáš had it: The name of the city was Parca. Some of the country's historians claimed that it had been named by the Romans after a personification of destiny. Others among them declared the name to be derived from the language of the country's aborigines, and that the Romans had merely adapted it.

"The transfer had been easily achieved—Parca's university didn't have a great reputation, and it struggled to attract new staff. Often it was the last resort of a teacher who had failed elsewhere, or a first port of call for a recent graduate intent on a move to a more highly esteemed college. But Marius Sten—for that was the name of the pedestrian whose body Tomáš had occupied—could hardly wait to get started in Parca. He was glad to be free of the stifling atmosphere of his marriage. He was looking forward to a calm life in a city where no one knew him, and especially to the sea, which he had seen only a few times in his life, as the capital was in the country's interior, and he had taken most of his vacations in the Alps. He arrived in Parca on the first day of August. There was practically nothing to do in the department, as the start of the semester was still a long way off, giving him plenty of time to explore this new city."

4. History of Parca

"Although the city could look back to Roman times, in the late nineteenth century its councilors pushed through a comprehensive program of redevelopment. Consequently, there were few monuments worth seeing. The walking man was heading along the main boulevard, which ran parallel with the coast, toward the ports—new and old—on the city's south side. Above his head on the Renaissance Revival and Neo-baroque facades were dusty festoons, mascarons, and Fortuna's horns. He reached a point where the main boulevard opened into a square; in the middle of this was a monument to one of many battles in which the city had defended itself from enemies attacking from the sea. To the north of the main boulevard most of the buildings in view were from the twenties and thirties; on the outskirts of the city from east to west was a development of dilapidated high-rise concrete housing that on the map looked like teeth in a gaping maw about to gobble the city up. Just beyond the city's northern edge a range of mountains began its rise; gentle slopes across which villas of the rich were scattered gave way suddenly to a steep wall of rock. The peaks of the mountains, which in some years remained capped with snow into July, were dotted with transmission towers whose red lights shone out at night above the rooftops. The villa quarter was divided from the first tenements by a long strip of buildings set far apart; this was the university campus and the pavilions of the university hospital.

"Until the early twentieth century only the western side of the bay served as a port, protected by a long stone quay with a lighthouse at the end that flickered at night. Now this served mainly for the amusement of tourists, who dined in the restaurants on the pier. Nothing was berthed in the old port but plastic galleys, their shapes inspired more by Disney movies than the history of the country. Signs mounted on the sides of these boats encouraged tourists to take sightseeing trips along the coast in the company of local folk groups. The port proper had shifted to the eastern side of the bay, where cargo ships, fishing boats, and large ferries were docked.

"The only part of the city practically untouched by the grand demolition of the late nineteenth century comprised the narrow streets diverging from the central point of the old port. But a tourist wanting historical sights was disappointed here, too. In the alleys of the port quarter, one frequently happened upon a stranger standing on the sidewalk, guidebook in hand, his confused gaze roaming the fronts of buildings; more than likely he was looking for the Romanesque monastery, or the fortress of the Knights Templar that were said to be here. The guidebook wasn't lying as such: The monastery and the fortress were indeed still present, but over the centuries they had been covered by outbuildings, courtyard galleries, balconies, workshops, and garages; new interior walls had grown up, breaking large, somber spaces into many rooms, closets, and chambers. The corridors of the monastery had been partitioned up. Tall palace halls had had new floors built into them. Thus a Roman bath or a Norman church remained almost intact, but to reach its original spaces among all that had grown through and over them, one would have to perform the kind of exercise known to children from drawings in puzzle magazines where the outline of an animal or fairy-tale character emerges from a jumble of lines.

"Marius was renting a room on the second floor of a building in the old port, where he would open his shutters to a view of the beige awning that kept the sun and the rain from the tables of the fish restaurant on the first floor, the lighthouse, and a thin strip of sea. Most days, he left the office assigned to him at the university shortly after lunch and spent the afternoon and evening wandering the city's narrow streets. He had always been a keen walker. Several times he found himself on a high-rise housing estate, looking through the gaps between blocks at fields and the greenhouses of a large market garden. It was here, among various graffiti scribblings, that he saw, on the side wall of a high-rise, an inscription composed of four letters of the Lygdian alphabet.

"The Lygd nation was said to have lived on the site of today's city at the time that the region became a Roman province. Some claimed that the letters Marius was looking at were all of its alphabet that had been preserved, although most modern historians doubted that these were a true remnant of an ancient script. Having been taken aback at first by his encounter on a modern housing estate with what might be the script of the autochthonous people of the region, Marius told himself that the characters were probably the work of a gang that painted illegible inscriptions on walls as it searched for a new form of esoteric expression, and he stopped thinking about them. Over the next few days, however, he saw the Lygdian lettering several more times, on the walls of buildings in different parts of the city, and in various groupings. He had no idea what these inscriptions might mean: The clusters of letters made no sense to him. Besides, it was surely very difficult to make a meaningful inscription out of an alphabet with only four letters, especially when no one knew how to read them.

"Marius would dine each day in one of the restaurants in the port. One evening, he went to a trattoria whose tables were arranged on the site of the erstwhile monastery, in a courtyard enclosed by ivy-covered walls. As he was finishing his soup, he became aware of a droning noise that was beginning to override the sounds of diners' conversation and the clinking of silverware and glass. As the drone became a roar, he realized it was made by human voices. Soon he could distinguish individual words, such a 'freedom,' 'struggle,' and 'justice.' Figures appeared and disappeared from the empty portal in the middle of the monastery wall, like Apostles in the doorway of an astronomical clock. Marius saw frowning men and women of all ages, many of whom were waving placards in the air. From where he was sitting, Marius couldn't properly see what was written on them, but on some he thought he spotted Lygdian letters. Only a few of the diners at the neighboring tables looked up to watch the procession, which wasn't particularly long. By the time the last figure had gone, and the view through the opening in the wall again comprised only the closed gate of the house opposite, with its knocker in the shape of a lion's head, all diners were again bent over their plates of spaghetti. The calls for somebody's freedom and a struggle against someone again dissolved in the drone; the drone faded and was soon lost in diners' conversation and the tinkling of forks and spoons. Marius decided that tomorrow at the university he would ask about what was going on with the Lygds in Parca."

5. Conversation with an Assistant Lecturer

"The next day, he asked the assistant lecturer with whom he shared his office about the Lygdian script. At the mention of the Lygds, the young man pulled a long face. He started to pace the room while explaining to Marius that the New Lygdian movement had appeared in the city the previous year. So far, no one seemed to know who its leader was and what its intentions were. It was his own belief that even supporters of the movement were unclear on these two points. Marius tried to elicit more information. At first, the assistant lecturer spoke with reluctance; it was obvious that he was uncomfortable talking about local peculiarities to someone from the capital. Like most of his colleagues, he was convinced that scientists and university teachers from the metropolis looked down on the intellectual life of the provinces; perhaps the Lygdian ravings that had recently enthused some of the locals vindicated this attitude of disdain.

"At the same time, however, as a historian he found the origination and development of the New Lygdian movement enormously interesting; over the past few months the monitoring of this unexpected, hard-to-comprehend phenomenon had become his biggest hobby. His desire to explore Lygdomania had soon come to prevail over his reluctance to reveal this embarrassing side of local life. Before long, the young lecturer was talking at length about his observations. He had a wealth of these, as he was one of few local citizens to have been aware of the New Lygdian movement since its barely noticeable beginnings—when the first signs appeared on walls, and the first utterances charged with vague hopes and nostalgia for a distant past were heard in the hum of café conversation.

"At present, he told Marius, the Lygdian movement was broadly divided into two groups. The first was made up of researchers in the field of Lygdian language and history, a pointless activity because—'We're both historians, so we may as well be honest with each other,' he said—nothing at all was known about the history and language of the Lygdians; still, in itself this activity was pretty innocent, he supposed. This couldn't be said of the actions of the second group, the Lygdomaniacs. It included some who claimed that local people were Lygdian by nationality, and so demanded for themselves and their representation the kind of privileges accorded to minorities. Bearing in mind that it was highly doubtful the Lygdians had ever existed (even if they had, their genes would have been wiped out long ago), such demands were outrageous. For a long time the city authorities refused to comment, taking the line that if something couldn't be discussed reasonably, it was better not to discuss it at all. This tactic turned out to be unwise: In the several months that supporters of the Lygdian movement carried on a monologue, the people of Parca grew accustomed to the slogans spouted by the Lygdomaniacs. (Over time, a cluster of words heard every day becomes a taken-for-granted part of our world, even if it makes no sense at all.) Anyway, people ceased to perceive strangeness in the phrases.

"It was unclear which of the two groups was first on the scene. Had the Lygdian movement grown out of a professional interest in a topic shunned by official historians (doubtless with good reason)—an interest whose research had then become politicized? Or had it been born out of some dark intention to cultivate Lygdology as a tool for its realization? According to the assistant lecturer, although no one in academic circles had a current interest in Lygdology, fertile soil for the seeds of the new discipline were soon discovered. This soil was provided by amateur historians and linguists, most of them retired high-school teachers who sat about in the municipal library and regularly submitted articles to professional journals. The editors of these journals, having read the return address on the envelope, would usually drop the submissions straight into the trash. Occasionally, however, someone would open one of the envelopes; after a while, the editors reached the surprise conclusion that most of these submissions were papers on Lygdian mythology, Lygdian verbs, or Lygdian ceramic art. It could be supposed that Lygdology was an ideal science for retirees with a taste for academic research: As practically nothing was known about the

Lygds, the bold hypotheses produced in the retirees' minds were confronted with no facts that could unpick their loose-bound, wide-ranging connections."

6. The Movement

"Although amateur Lygdologists could hardly be suspected of dishonest intentions, it seems that by their inquiries they unwittingly served the aims of the political wing of the Lygdian movement. The wealth of publication opportunities that suddenly came the way of authors who till then hadn't accounted for a single line in a scientific journal was truly remarkable. It was unclear who was paying for all the pamphlets, festschrifts, and journals with titles such as *Studia Lygdologica* and *Lygdian Gazette* that had appeared in the past year, although it was assumed that the money was coming from the political wing of the Lygdian movement. This didn't have to mean that these dubious circles were comprised of fools who couldn't tell sound research from naïve, if sincere, gibberish. The decision to support amateur Lygdologists probably came from (i) the belief that articles bursting with enthusiasm and sensational discoveries were more likely to arouse the public's interest than strictly academic papers, and (ii) the supposition that the obsession with Lygdian themes that straddled naïve Lygdomania and serious history would eventually spread to genuine scholars, and that many esteemed scientists held an unacknowledged desire for involvement with a happy discipline whose form would submit to their own thoughts. Lygdian studies had so far received no academic recognition, but the assistant lecturer feared that such recognition was on the horizon; several times, he had spotted a colleague taking a sneak peek at printed matter produced by a Lygdologist.

"Whatever their motives, the political leaders of the Lygdian movement were giving generous support to Lygdology as practiced by retired high-school teachers; evidently, they felt that for now the scientific output of the retirees sufficed for promotion of the movement's aims. Marius asked what these aims were, and again the assistant lecturer sighed. This was a subject of much discussion in Parca, although so far debates were carried on largely in coffeehouses and bars rather than in the pages of magazines. Coffeehouse debaters held all kinds of suspicions about the leaders of the movement. And no wonder, as Lygdian themes had no ties, and they were so vague that they could relate to anything, from Marxism through Catholicism to the extreme right. Although the pamphlets that appeared were full of dramatic phrases, apart from generalizing about self-determination and cultural identity, they had very little to say.

"The fact that no one knew the identity of the movement's leader contributed to the uncertainty that surrounded its true nature. Although a Lygd Revival Party was established, all indicators suggested that the person who acted as its chair was just a front man. As to who the head of the movement might be, the oddest opinions were expressed, including one that the current chair was the true boss cunningly masquerading as a front man; this over-complicated theory, remarked the assistant lecturer, was presented in a coffeehouse at one A.M., at the end of a long evening devoted to discussion on the hidden objectives of the Lygdian movement, and it was little more than a testament to the fact that Lygdology-inspired whimsicality was infecting the discourse even of those sceptics who were trying to uncover its hidden meaning.

"Although most participants in the coffeehouse debates readily came round to the view that the aims of the Lygdian movement were unlikely to be of pure intent, there was less agreement as to what those aims actually were. Some believed that the whole New Lygdian Movement was nothing but a cunning ploy to force the central government to grant greater autonomy to the Parca region, which would have huge implications for the awarding of public contracts, for instance. The fact that the right to autonomy was reliant on the idea of a nation that had died out long ago—if it had ever even existed—was maybe not as absurd as it first appeared: The rights of a community are often based on a notion of unity that is more fabulous than a commonwealth of mythical beings, and besides, the imaginary community of the Lygd nation was already forming a community of Lygdomaniacs that was real and potent. (Lygds may not have existed, but Lygdomaniacs existed for sure.) Early pressure applied on the central government was apparently using the tactic of flooding authorities in the capital with appeals for Lygdian self-determination (in the form of folklore ensembles, museums, the teaching of Lygdian history in schools, etc.). Only after some time would claims be submitted that addressed what the applicants were really after. By this time, ministry officials would be so relieved to be spared the irritation of further requests too bizarre to satisfy, or even to furnish with a meaningful response, that they would be more willing to oblige.

"Others disagreed with this theory, instead tending toward the view that the Lygdian game had darker motives. From time immemorial, this port city had had encounters—some wary, some eager—with a great variety of communities from all over the world. Beneath the quiet, dull surface of the Parcan everyday was continuous, pulsing chaos; it was a jumble of battles, negotiations, short-term alliances, trade in every imaginable commodity, deception, and crime. It was presumed that the Lygdian movement had deep roots by which it reached out to this thriving, slippery life and drew nutrition from it, although the retired high-school teachers turned Lygdologists would surely have been outraged to be told that the world they inhabited included the mysterious gangs they read about at breakfast in the *Parca Herald*—and that not only their fees but also the aims of their articles were determined at meetings held at night at the docks, in the bowels of rusting tankers. There was talk that the true movers of the Lygdian movement were mafiosi from Russia or the Balkans, or terrorists from the Middle East; the involvement of large shipping companies and various espionage networks was debated. And indeed it was quite probable that some of these organizations were or had been somehow involved in the origination or development of the Lygdian movement. Maybe the movement had emerged by self-fertilization, as an expression of a vague channeling that had arisen within the swarming, invisible life of the bowels of the city; as it was there already, the individual groupings of the Parca underground had invested it with their own aims. Had the Lygdian movement originated as an instrument for the aims of a single group, whatever this group was, its members would have struggled to contain its activities and operations within the original program. No sooner had the movement been established than everything that flourished in the sticky climate of Parca's underground began to grow through and into it. Before long, it was impossible to tell what was the original body of the movement and what was a parasitic—or symbiotic—organism; all that was in it gave life to the rest but also sucked blood from it.

"On reaching this point in his narrative, the assistant lecturer made a dismissive gesture with his hand, expressing that this was where his private investigation had brought him. He looked at his watch, heaved another sigh at the thought of what his home had come to, and left the room."

7. History of Lygdology I: From Ancient Times to the Seventeenth Century

"Marius was left alone in the office. He sat down at his desk and looked at the sides of the mountains, whose peaks were lost in gray clouds. The assistant lecturer's explanation had done little to help him understand why the specter of the Lygd nation had appeared in this tranquil city at this moment, nor why its mood was so belligerent. Being a historian, naturally he knew something about the Lygds: Purportedly they were an ancient people who inhabited an area that comprised the site of today's Parca and its environs; their army was defeated in battle by the Romans in Marcus Aurelius's time (the army was probably nothing more than several groups of peasants armed with axes, the battle a few skirmishes in the woods), after which Lygdia became a Roman province commonly referred to in Latin writings as 'Parcia.' If indeed there had ever been any Lygds, there was nothing to suggest that they had felt the urge to revolt against the occupiers; over two or three generations, they had merged with the Roman troops and the colonists to such a degree that their language had disappeared, leaving very few traces in the local Latin, which became one of the sources of the language that was still spoken throughout the country.

"There had long been linguists who dug about in words in search of remnants of ancient Lygdian; such efforts at the partial reconstruction of Lygdian were especially animated in the mid twentieth century. But even at that time, other linguists raised doubts about attempts to revive Lygdian, claiming that the Lygdian roots of words were illusory. Skeptics pointed out the strange way in which Lygdian had been brought back to life: A vision of the Lygdian language had grown out of confused roots whose unraveling was better suited to psychoanalysis than linguistics; the researchers' vision had then been projected onto the country's current language, and phenomena in that language that in some way corresponded with this vision were declared relics of Lygdian. As there were several such visions, attempts at reconstruction of the Lygdian language resulted in emergence of three or four varieties that in no way resembled each other, which explained why in recent decades scientists had refrained from reviving the Lygdian language. Still, even the most light-minded output of linguists of the fifties and sixties was considered science; academics with an interest in it would protest in outrage whenever someone wished to draw comparisons with the new, savage Lygdian the assistant lecturer had spoken of.

"In historical records there was so little documentary evidence of a Lygd nation that serious scholars had always doubted its existence. The earliest surviving reference to Lygds was made by an anonymous Roman annalist; the next mentions were made by two chroniclers of early medieval times, one a Visigoth, the other Irish. The Roman author writes of a Lygd nation engaged in battle by Marcus Aurelius's legions; after Roman troops defeated their army, these Lygds founded an armed settlement on the site of modern-day Parca. Apparently, the Visigoth monk and his Irish counterpart were informed by this Roman source; all they did was expand the observation and develop some general themes, which then wandered from one book to another. The work of the Roman historian survived only in a late, somewhat messy copy, meaning that the reference to Lygds might have been inserted inadvertently by one of many scribes; if so, naturally it would have been retained in later copies. So, in fact the words about Lygds and their struggle might refer to a different territory and an altogether different people.

"The fact that nothing at all was known about the Lygds did not prevent them from playing a role in the history of the spiritual life of the country. Although Lygdology was an implausible science, the 'representation of the Lygds' provided some interesting topics of research for disciplines as far apart as history and literary theory, sociology, and psychoanalysis. Several times the Lygd nation underwent a rebirth, followed with regularity by a period when it lapsed practically into oblivion. Curiously, however, the awakening of interest in the Lygds was never connected in any way with the possible discovery of new evidence of the existence of the Lygd nation or relics from its history. The true reasons for all these waves of interest remain mysterious; although ultimately the representation of the Lygd nation was always exploited by some passing movement or fashionable folly, apparently this occurred only after some spell or other had summoned the specter of the Lygds from oblivion.

"The heyday of the first Lygd revival was the thirteenth century. Around 1230, a novel in verse described an idealized land in which the hero, a knight errant, embarks boldly on a journey and has a magical adventure. Then came a period of over two hundred years in which Lygdia appeared in various books as a land of magic; the literature of this time abounded with Lygdian sorcerers and Lygdian wood nymphs. Changes in literary taste cast the Lygds back into a long oblivion, although motifs from novels of Lygdian knights survived in folk puppet theater. The next rebirth of the Lygd nation occurred in the seventeenth century, a time when the nobles rose up in opposition to the growing power of the monarchy; it occurred to some author or other who supported the cause of the squires to present their struggle for preservation of their long-standing privileges as a repeat of the struggle between the Lygds and the Romans . . .

"When Tomáš got to the representation of the Lygds in the seventeenth century, it was one o'clock in the morning. As he lay in bed, the paper and the duvet were again illuminated by the lamp, whose white shade was bright in the dark window. Having completed his first day of writing, he knew that the story that had begun to evolve that morning—out of nothing, with no purpose, no idea, no thought, no need to communicate anything to anyone—wouldn't be over quickly. By now he knew his way around Parca pretty well, although some of its quarters he had explored only a little. And every place, every alley, every street corner breathed new stories; drama streamed out of the gloom beyond half-open balcony doors, forcing itself into words. The breath of certain places shivered imperceptibly with hundreds of gestures and words, with the occasional flash of a more distinct image; in this image, every object and every figure breathed another story . . .

"What was actually happening? Where was this wild stream of images coming from? Tomáš was feeling too tired to think about this. He turned off the lamp and fell asleep immediately. When he awoke the next morning, he put on his pants and coat over his pajamas and went out to buy food at the store in the next building. Having breakfasted, he got back into bed and went on with his writing."

8. History of Lygdology II: From Romanticism to the Present Day

"The fact that at a certain point in history the specter of the Lygds was invoked by campaigners for the rights of regional lords was no impediment for the Romantics, who a hundred years later equated the Lygds with the native poetic and democratic soul of the nation. Although over the centuries this had been violated, and thus gradually corrupted, by manners brought into the country by foreigners, the malign influence of the foreign could not spoil it completely. Its true nature did not expire; it was pushed deep down, beneath many layers of sediment, where it slept and occasionally spoke from its dreams. Romantic poetry and philosophy were intended as an enchantment that would rouse the Lygd soul from its long slumbers and transform its obscure mutterings into articulate speech. Although the old documents gave no support to such an idea, apparently no one was concerned by this absence, and dozens of authors composed poems in the Lygdian national style. Mere echoes of the German poetry of the time, by the next year these poems were generally regarded as originals of great historical value. Remarkably, it seemed that their authors came to believe in their ancient provenance; at the very least, they felt that in the act of writing, the hand had been guided by the Lygdian spirit of revival.

"Thus images of an idealized Lygdian life were formed. From the mid nineteenth century till the eighties, these images provided academic painters with favorite motifs—even today, the capital's museums abound in large canvases depicting scenes from the heroic engagement of the Lygds with Roman legions and the Lygdian family idyll (from a wooden hut, a woman is watching her husband returning from the tribal council; by the family altar, their daughter is strumming a very strange stringed instrument; their two small sons are fighting with wooden swords, building their strength for the struggle against the Roman usurper). It was interesting that none of the earlier Lygdian renaissances had begun in Parca, the alleged home of the Lygd nation; all had been produced in intellectual circles in the capital and reached Parca only as a faint echo. In this way, the current movement was different from all its forerunners.

"The Positivism of the second half of the nineteenth century was largely successful in the fight against the legends propagated by Lygdophiles and Lygdomaniacs, and by the end of the century it seemed that scientists had banished the specter of a Lygd nation once and for all. Now academic painting, too, turned from the distant Lygdian past to scenes from the present day. Although Symbolist poets continued to draw on a sentimental Lygdia, the image they chose was of an unreal country to which the artist resorted in dreams, as a refuge from a boring or hostile reality.

"After that, the Lygd nation fell into a long period of oblivion, although it underwent one more resurrection before the current one. In the nineteen-seventies, bookstores devoted ever longer shelves to works on yoga, Buddhism, Taoism, Sufism, Kabbalah, alchemy, and shamanism; having written all they could about druids, yogis, and shamans, New Age authors cast around for something new. It might have been expected that sooner or later they would come across the Lygds, and so it happened that the poor Lygd was roused once again and forced to play the role of a kind of local Celt. In the late seventies and early eighties, books appeared on Lygdian mythology and magic, and the natural healing of the Lygds; there were even Lygdian vegetarian cookbooks. On benches in front of the university, skinny, long-haired girls would sit with books in their hands, the copper of their Lygdian talismans glinting against their baggy sweaters. This was the time of Marius's puberty; his association of these fantastical metal ornaments with the hitherto inaccessible bosoms of the students meant that everything to do with the Lygds would always have a hint of eroticism for him. But also this wave of interest in the Lygds would ebb away, although for a long time thereafter one would happen across dusty books on Lygdian themes in secluded corners of bookstores.

"No one actually knew whether the Lygds had their own script. As for the characters Marius saw on walls in Parca, in the first half of the nineteenth century, it was believed that that they were remnants of the original Lygdian alphabet. Two of them were discovered by one of the first Lygdologists of Romanticism, in a little country church not far from Parca, in a fresco from the early Middle Ages. At this time of widespread Lygdophilia, no one dared say that these two smudges were of extremely

suspicious origin; everyone saw them as letters, the remainder of
an inscription in Lygdian; such firm characters did the human
gaze form from these smudges that the few skeptics who failed
to see them were accused of malice or blindness. In the end, the
inscription was restored by the sharpening of its lines in com-
pliance with the lines of the imagination. Consequently, no one
was sure what the smudges had looked like in the first place.
The origin of the other two letters was more dubious still. Not
long after the discovery of the characters on the wall of the little
church, another researcher, who happened to be a well-known
Romantic poet, saw some grooves, nicks, or cracks in a rock
beyond the city; he, too, wasted no time in declaring these to
be the remnant of a Lygdian inscription. Some scientists found
this difficult to accept, shyly putting forward the view that it
was probably a natural phenomenon; for this, they were labeled
renegades and dropped by their friends and acquaintances.

9. The Lygdian Movement Spreads

"Marius marveled at how quickly Parca's Lydian movement
spread, despite its lack of homogeneity and the fact that everyone who joined it seemed to have differing expectations. Not
only this: many of the ideas with which individuals and groups
entered the movement contradicted one another to an almost
comical degree, nor did it seem that these divergences could be
brought into alignment by the effect of the common destiny the
various groupings took on when they joined the movement; it
was more the case that differences engendered new differences,
on several levels. One faction pursued socialist aims, another
ultra-liberal ones. In a misty past that presumably belonged
entirely in the realms of dreams, one Lygdophile identified the
prototype of the great power of trade unions, another a model

of an unchanging patriarchal order to which today's wayward society should return. There were groups that attempted to revive the nature worship they claimed the Lygds had practiced; it was said that these groups celebrated Lygdian days of fertility through group sex (on hearing of these wild holidays, Marius was reminded of the connection he'd made as an adolescent between the Lygds and eroticism). The talk of sacred orgies may have been nothing but rumor and urban gossip, but if it were indeed a fiction, as soon as it got around, men and women were found within the movement who were willing to make it real in Lygdia's name.

"Surprisingly, rather than destroying the movement, these irreconcilable differences served only to strengthen it. The assistant lecturer had said that the movement's ideology was so vague that everyone could project his own dream onto it, but it would be more accurate to say that the movement was a magical mirror that showed the beholder his own dreams. The Lygdian movement proffered a dreamlike language in which its fascinated adherents learned clumsily to speak; so far they spoke only of the past, politics, and freedom, but Marius had the impression that their utterances were just the simple exercises of the beginner. He was amazed by the power of this nascent language: Even sensible, educated people were so enchanted by it that they were blind to the obvious contradictions from which their Lygdian faith was woven.

"When the assistant lecturer first told Marius about Lygdomania, he was right to say that serious academics had no interest in Lygdian themes, but in this regard, what was true in August was no longer the case in October and November. In these months, the wild stream of Lygdology began to undermine the banks of academe. For the first time, theses presented by amateur Lygdologists were admitted to official history, linguistics, and religious studies courses as hypotheses that needed verification. Again, Marius was perplexed by the lack of clarity on the root causes of this strange flirtation between respectable science and its poor, crackpot relation. The indulgence of some scientists toward something that was a pseudoscience as recently as the vacation was probably born out of conservatism (they had realized a sympathy with a distant time of supposedly strong and clear moral values); the willingness of others to be seen to take an interest in Lygdology could be justified by a belief in historical truth as a matter of interpretation, hence there was no fundamental difference in this regard between university disciplines and the products of Lygdology."

10. Lygdian Gods

"As Marius watched the Lygdian renaissance from a distance, he found all kinds of things in it that fascinated him. A new world opened up to him, albeit one disguised as ancient history. Although he thought it likely that the movement was, at its root, a dangerous one that might yet bear harmful fruit, he took pleasure in the unique performance by which it grew. Just as in his first days in Parca Marius had passed the time studying its buildings and streets, now he studied the birth and behavior of the Lygdian monster. And there was plenty to see. In the early nineteenth century, efforts to revive the Lygdian language and script hadn't gotten very far: Adherents of individual, contradictory schools of thought had been unable to agree on even the most basic facts. Attempts at the reconstruction of the Lygdian language in the mid twentieth century hadn't gone much better. Now Marius was present at the sudden opening-up of Lygdian language and script; although growing out of scanty seeds, dubious scratches on rock, clusters of sounds in local names, and opaque etymologies, they expanded with remarkable speed.

"The proliferation of Lygdian language and script was at its height in the late fall. Questions of the Lygdian language were debated by many groups of Lygdologists, producing preliminary answers that circulated in various social settings, where they were honed and enhanced, so that their origins as fantastical hypotheses were forgotten. By the time a new letter of the alphabet, word, case ending, or rule of grammar completed its journey in the urban labyrinth and returned to its inventor, it had been converted into a universally-accepted historical fact; the inventor acknowledged this new status as confirmation of his earlier uncertain assumption, without realizing that he was encountering his own idea cast as scientific truth.

"As they did the rounds of the city, not only did nascent fragments of the Lygdian language become more real; in every setting they reached, they encountered other fragments and grew together to form a tight fabric. Having been born out of the collective mumbling of the city, Lygdian no longer suffered from a lack of unity, as was the case when scientists had tried to reconstruct it; indeed, streams spurting from a great variety of sources somehow always met and reinforced one another. By the time the Lygdian language was almost complete, a consensus stated that there was nothing unscientific about placing fillers in gaps in its lexicon and morphology, just as when restoring an antique temple one would connect surviving fragments with concrete pillars. But even these declared additions grew into the fabric of Lygdian to such a degree that before long no one remembered their modern origin.

"Of course, as the Lygdian language grew, it needed to feed. It drew its material from the language of the country, turning in particular to its unofficial, unstable, and variable margins; there appeared in it groups of sounds and roots of words whose origins could be traced to vulgarisms, the argot of the underworld, the language of passion and despair whose words remained half-interjection, various slang, the mangled speech of foreign workers in the port, and the pidgins that originated and expired there, the babble of children, and the mumblings produced in fevers and dreams. Some of those who introduced the dense, bloody, sticky language matter of the margins into Lygdian claimed that they were merely restoring and replenishing fragments that had survived since time immemorial in the language's borderland swamps, beyond the leveling influence and supervision of the language center. Yet most creators of Lygdian words had no idea of the region of the subconscious that was funding their language-building, believing they were following a precise logic of reconstruction while all the time their thoughts were being invaded by amorphous, malleable material from the margins whose fascination resided in its apparent retention of the beginnings of speech in the chaos of pre-language.

"Thus the vocabulary and grammar of Lygdian were born as a cipher for desire and its flipside, anxiety; desire and anxiety pulsated in the body of the emerging language, flowing into its nascent case endings and manner of pronunciation. Not even the fact that none of the Lygdologists whose minds had spawned the putative ancient language understood the hieroglyphics of desire could detract from the magical appeal of Lygdian. (It seems that we touch on our desires only in signs that are incomprehensible to us, Marius said to himself.) Lygdian had some similarities with the present-day language of the country; it was rather like its counterpart in dreams. Although it coalesced out of an immeasurable number of sources, it took shape with such certainty, and in such strong and flexible form, that even skeptics came to believe that there was nothing arbitrary about it; from what was known so far, Lygdology might look suspicious, but apparently there was something in it after all. In December, Marius heard his colleague the assistant lecturer, his very first informant on the development of the Lygdian movement, say that their department should pay greater attention to Lygdian studies.

"Alongside the language, a history and religion of the Lygdians were gradually constituted; these came from the same sources, and as such it wasn't easy to find links between them and the emerging language. The development of the confused pantheon of Lygdian gods—which brought India to Marius's mind—was reminiscent of the growth of the declensions of the language coming into being at the same time. It occurred to Marius that the great number of grammatical cases and cohorts of deities were an expression of the same mix of blissful fertility and anxious striving to break through to the amorphous thing that always retreated from the shapes that were born out of it. He had a similar feeling that the convoluted syntax of Lygdian sentences, which were practically untouched by cohesion and collocation, was reminiscent of Lygdian myths—stories in which heroes and gods walked through never-ending labyrinths inhabited by dragons and winged wolves, mazes whose end points were just one more turning in a network of turnings. The Lygdian imagination worked—from behind the mask of scientific research, which it never removed—with such feverish activity that by October Marius had no doubt that it would succeed in constituting comprehensive systems of language, religion, and history. At that time, however, he had no idea that the inception of Lygdia would be complete by the next February."

11. The Lygdian Movement at the University

"Although Marius understood the attraction of Lygdomania and wasn't entirely immune to its charms, he was unable at first to imagine that it could take root at the university. It was much discussed in his seminars. In October, skepticism and mockery still prevailed; the students made fun of the Lygdian superstitions of their parents. In subsequent weeks, however, Marius observed a gradual change in the students' attitude toward Lygdian matters: The skepticism vanished, and there were fewer jokes about Lygdomania in seminars. Marius realized that from the very beginning the students had taken skepticism as part and parcel of youth—as a role that they were obliged to play because of their age, informed by the ages-old image of the student revolutionary. But in fact they longed for and loved the Lygdians like everyone else in Parca; they, too, needed material from which to render their dreams, and as theirs was the age at which people dream most, maybe they needed more of this material than others did.

"Odd as it seemed, many of those who had scoffed at Lygdomania in October were Lygdomaniacs by December. It wasn't difficult for former skeptics to justify their new opinions. The regeneration of student skepticism as the universal form of Lygdomania was performed in two steps. The first consisted in the student's announcement that the resistance of official science to non-institutionalized amateur knowledge and attempts to subordinate it to academic processes were a manifestation of what became known that fall as 'scientific imperialism.' The second step saw the supplementing of formal acknowledgement of Lygdology with something more substantial: The long-ago Lygdian struggle for freedom from the Romans became a model for the liberation struggles of every possible minority. Students could breathe a sigh of relief, as now it was possible for them to indulge in Lygdomania while assuming an obligation to be radical and 'young.'

"At the end of the year very little teaching went on at the university because the classrooms and corridors were practically given over to debates on the Lygdian question. While in the city the association of Lygdomania with conservatism on the one hand and the left on the other were fairly evenly distributed, at the university, it became a part of the union of emancipation movements, eventually placing itself at the union's center and becoming its heart and soul. This period was dominated by discussion among various groupings of the mainstream, which comprised leftist Lygdology partly associated with Marxism and partly a challenge to it. At the university, on the other hand, the relatively strong Young Conservatives' Club preached a return to values of family, patriotism, and religion on the model of Lygdian society, in whose organization they found support for the idea of a weak state. It was as though Lygdology were a magic box in which everyone found whatever he was longing for. An extreme right-wing student organization called Lygdian Action made some headway; it was composed of Lygdian skinheads who tattooed letters of the Lygdian alphabet on their shoulders (this was an abbreviation whose meaning Marius didn't know). Although these Lygdian groups hated one another, they were always able to unite for the purpose of bullying the university's few remaining skeptics—those who refused to believe in the newborn Lygdian world. Eventually most of the skeptics submitted to intimidation and preferred to keep their views to themselves.

"Marius watched developments at the university with amusement, amazement, and sadness. In his seminars, too, there was soon more discussion of the Lygds than actual teaching. Usually the Lygds became the topic of class within fifteen minutes, remaining so until the end of the session. Marius wouldn't try to put a stop to such debate and return the syllabus, like some of his bolder or more naïve colleagues, but nor would he participate in the students' debates, as teachers who courted the student movement did. He would sit comfortably at his desk with his legs stretched before him, watching the students, realizing that he was studying the nodding, turning heads and waving arms as in summer he had studied the stucco ornaments on the facades of Parca's streets and the bounteous leaves on the trees of its parks. He would listen to debates on the Lygdian question as he would the sound of the sea in the port; sometimes he followed the thoughts the students were expressing, sometimes, he allowed their words to dissolve in the vagueness of noise. Sometimes, he was anxious at the thought of how the all-consuming monster of Lygdomania, born of an idea that capitulated to desire, had succeeded in swallowing up the university within two months. What could now stand in its way? For a while, the students let Marius be, taking him for a conservative, basically harmless dope who couldn't be expected to take an interest in the exciting new ideas that were thriving at the university. Before long, however, this attitude of benevolence changed, thanks to a girl—one of the students. For the first time, an erotic motif appeared in Kantor's novel."

12. Rita

"Most discussions of Lygdian matters in Marius's classes took place in the presence of a student called Rita. Rita had a constant frown and black, bobbed hair; she wore a black miniskirt and a tight black top with a neckline so broad that her shoulders were left practically bare. In heated debate, other students would wriggle in their seats and turn in all directions, fluttering their arms like startled birds. Rita sat stiff among them, her hands resting motionless on the top of the desk. Marius didn't understand her at all, and he had no idea which group of Lygdomaniacs she belonged to. She tended to be at the center of the debate; the boys turned mostly to her as they were speaking, unaware, it seemed, that they were doing so. On his way home, Marius would try to recall the opinion she had advocated in the debate, always reaching the conclusion that she had given no indication of what she thought; she made vague remarks on the pronouncements of others, asked questions, and left her utterances unfinished, speaking so softly that her few words were difficult to understand. Maybe Rita's magical appeal for the other students was like the magic of the Lygdian world; she said so little that the others could take from her words what they wished to hear.

"It seemed that Marius was the only one who noticed that words spoken by Rita the sorceress had no content. In animated debate, the other students would project their own thoughts onto her incomplete utterances and understand her questions as prompts for thoughts already in their heads. Rita's silence, albeit one occasionally broken by a shaky utterance that soon disintegrated and dissolved, was the center point of the seminar, around which all spoken words hovered. It wasn't difficult to imagine why the other students were obsessed with Rita. As I said, from the very beginning Lygdomania was bound up with desire, so it was never just for old men sitting in the university library writing touchingly naïve studies. Indeed, it was a setting charged with sexual tension, and this tension wooed the young. As Marius observed, Lygdomania was immensely fertile ground for the growth of erotic relations of all kinds, from the unspoken, agonized love that originates in closed sects that define themselves in opposition to the rest of the world, to the orgies of Lygdian Neopaganism. The cumulus of intimated or unspoken words that settled around Rita encouraged the other students to see her as an initiate of some secret Lygdian knowledge, perhaps a member of some Lygdian kabbalah, and the secret of forbidden words that escaped in solitary whispers at dusk coincided with the secret of her body, as yet unknown to any of her classmates and, so it seemed to Marius, closed in on itself like a flower at night. This double secret created an aura around Rita that was cold but stimulating; in the boys at the university, it produced burning desire and dreams of sex.

"As I said, Rita was a mystery to Marius. He saw in her none of the sinister naivety that had lately come to dominate at the university and caused students to act like cruel children. He had no doubt that Rita had the courage of her convictions, would express them in opposition to all and even ridicule the others, if need be, yet she never raised an objection, not even to the most absurd Lygdomania-inspired stories served up in the seminar. At times, Marius had the impression she was an adherent of one of Lygdomania's most militant arms; at others, he was almost sure that Rita viewed the whole Lygdian movement as she would a poor comedy.

"In the university cafeteria, he once listened in on a conversation between two students sitting at an adjacent table. One of them was saying that he had managed to get behind the scenes at a session of the Lygdian Revival Party, where he had spotted Rita in intimate conversation with one of the leaders of the Lygdian movement. The two students had gone on to consider whether Rita was the man's lover; Marius had heard anxiety and jealousy in their voices. What they were saying might have been just make-believe—Lygdomania merged reality with fantasy in many minds—but Marius knew it could just as well have been true. He recalled the speculation about dark motives behind the Lygdian movement—thoughts that since the summer Parcans had somehow forgotten. Marius remembered them well, however, and told himself that Rita may be a figure in just such a game. Could she be working for a mafia-like organization, or even belong to one of the criminal networks? If it were true that a mysterious boss had entrusted Rita with the task of propagating the Lygdian movement at the university, she was making a wonderful job of it; all the students who took her silence and soft-spoken, vague words and wove them into wild thoughts took her for an avid Lygdomaniac, and they were keen to outdo one another in demonstration of their Lygdian zeal.

"Marius was attracted by Rita's secret, although he didn't believe in any secret initiation in Lygdian mysteries, and he suspected Rita of taking part in things that might be worse than Lygdomania. At the same time, he was aware that a grown-up, mature man should see no mystery in a taciturn, frowning girl student dressed all in black. The problem was, Marius knew that he had never been a proper grown-up, and he certainly wasn't mature. He had stayed on at university after his studies not because he was keen to disseminate knowledge and so follow in the footsteps of his teachers, but because he hadn't succeeded in becoming an adult, and he found the school environment attractive and comforting. Rita was probably only mysterious in the world of adolescents; but in this world, Marius was no stranger, his greater age notwithstanding. And he told himself that the mystery of the adolescent wasn't necessarily any worse than the mystery of the adult or the sage.

"So long did Marius ponder Rita's role in the Lygdian production, and so hard did he picture her face in search of its expression that he found himself unable to think of anything else. Rita's face would come to him as an apparition on the fronts of buildings he passed each evening, on the long detours he took on his way home from the university. Once, having paused in a quiet backstreet to look at the gray wall of the sea at its end, he realized to his amazement that he hadn't thought of his wife in the capital for several days; Rita's face had come to obscure hers entirely. This made him so sad that he preferred not to think of what lay ahead of him in Parca.

"Yet his strange love was without agonized longing, unlike that of the students. The kids he taught associated Rita with Lygdian esotericism, but Marius's love had different roots. For him, this girl student was part and parcel of the city he had been living in since early August—a city in which he was an unknown foreigner, and which made clear its indifference to him. For the very reason that no relationship had been established between him and the city, it could speak to him and provoke him with the shapes of its things, its ochers, grays, and greens, its murmurs and rumbles, its sweet scents of partial decay, and its disorderly, volatile, and mechanically repetitive movements. For this very reason, at every turn he could enter into a fanciful relation with a city space—a relation for which there is no name; as he was passing the closed doors of buildings, he could imagine himself a merchant in an Arabian tale; he could bind himself to the city by a thousand fine fibers, and then tear these asunder. For this very reason, everything in Parca could have an importance for him, and all its happenings could transform into a continuous, amazing pantomime. Marius's love for Rita grew out of this delirious, beguiled, indifferent, fantastical, nervous, hedonistic, cynical relationship with the city as a hotbed of fermentation, and it resembled it; for Marius, Rita became the demon of Parca.

"Soon the students were aware of the way he looked at Rita, and they began to joke among themselves about his having fallen for her. They didn't desist from their insinuations and ridicule in his presence; indeed, they competed for who could make the boldest comment. Although Rita must have known what they were talking about, her expression was the same as always. Marius knew he should feel embarrassed, but in a city that had succumbed to utter foolishness, what would be the point of embarrassment?"

13. Waterfront Encounter

"When his teaching was over, Marius would walk the city streets. Although the summer happiness exhaled by an unfamiliar place was ever weaker, still it could gush out at him, geyser-like—on a little cobblestoned square, in the gloom of a dank passageway, or by a tilting wall with an overspill of wild garden. But such encounters were rare. Since the summer, the city had changed; whispers rising from stains and furrows on surfaces had fallen silent—not so much because Marius now found this stirring script commonplace, but because the quiet discourse of walls was drowned out by the aggressive din of the large Lygdian letters sprayed everywhere in bright colors, so obscuring the long, mysterious sentence of scratches and cracks. On one of his evening wanders, Marius found himself in the streets of the neighborhood of the new port. He was glad of the strong wind that was pestering him like a big, playful dog standing on its hind legs. For the first time in a while, he wasn't thinking of Lygdomania, students, or Rita; he was fully occupied with the friendly wind. He took a steep, straight street down to the seafront. The gray plain of the water opened before him as several screeching gulls glided over his head. He walked past a row of Neo-baroque houses, their flaking stucco ornaments reminding him of the district in the capital where he had spent his childhood. The opposite side of the street comprised just a strip of gray asphalt lined with a low concrete barrier that the waves were breaking against; some of the waves were so high that their spray reached the walls of the buildings, and Marius felt it on his face. There were rails in the middle of the roadway, and before long Marius was overtaken by a streetcar, its windows already lit and damp with sea spray. As the streetcar pulled up at a nearby stop (no one got out), Marius saw it as a lantern atop drapery woven in various shades of gray. The vehicle moved off, around a bend in the road that made it appear as though a row of houses had decided to walk into the sea before having second thoughts. Marius was reminded of how much he had looked forward to the sea before his arrival in Parca. He regretted seeing it so rarely in daylight during his months here. He had seen the sea mostly as a dark plane filled with cold lights and known its presence by the sweet smell of decay wafting from the dark port through the open window of his room.

"Walking toward him was the bowed figure of a woman wrapped in a damp coat. As she passed him, she lifted her head. Marius recognized Rita. He uttered a confused greeting and prepared to move on, but Rita stopped and asked something about the subject matter of his seminar. Marius listened to her in amazement: Who at this university still cared about the histories of the real nations of this planet? Again there rose in him a suspicion that Rita was mixed up in something shady underpinning the New Lygdian renaissance. What did Rita truly want of him? Was it really just a coincidence that had brought them together in this deserted street? As they stood facing each other, tiny droplets of seawater landed on their faces. Marius started on his explanation, although he barely knew what he was explaining, and in any case, through the roar of the sea his words were difficult to make out.

"Beyond the concrete barrier on the other side of the street, a wave reared up like a gray phantom bird flapping cold wings. Rita interrupted Marius by laying a gentle hand on his arm. Then she pointed at the palely illuminated glass front of a café in the nearest building. There were no customers inside. They sat down next to the cold glass, against which drops of water were shivering in the wind. Again, Rita said practically nothing. Marius knew already the power of the round face with its pursed lips. He knew how Rita's magical silence could summon torrents of words from others, so he wasn't very surprised to find himself speaking continuously. He moved from Roman history to conditions at the university where he had taught until the summer, and from there to his life in the capital. He couldn't resist telling Rita about his childhood, the scholarly plans he kept putting off until they turned into dreams, the marriage that seemed to him like an abstruse book he did his inadequate best to understand, his wife's infidelity, the evenings of agony in their apartment, and his escape to Parca. He cared little whether Rita would repeat his confession to other students the very next day, and so render him ridiculous in their eyes forevermore. The only thing Marius didn't want to talk about was the Lygdian movement, although it raised its head in connection with practically everything, and he had a hard time keeping it out of his monologue.

"Whenever his talk generated an opportunity to ask something about Rita, he took advantage of it. She drew on her ability to speak while saying nothing, turning her every answer into another question that was an invitation to him to continue with his story. And so it went on, with Marius as the only speaker. Not that this bothered him: Rita could keep her secret, he told himself—in any case it was probably just a phantasm born out of the erotic dreams of her schoolmates, all of whom moaned with lust for her when alone. Now, it was enough for him to look at her face against a backdrop of waves whose ghostly dance was slowly lost in the advancing darkness. The suspicion that Rita was questioning him with the purpose of determining how he could be used in some dark game simply dissolved. Although Rita's expression didn't open—apparently, she lacked that ability; her face was closed to the world for good and all—it became a little more accessible and a little less grim than the one she wore in seminars. The sense that Rita was looking at others from the depths of a darkened room with long, unmoving drapes—sometimes Marius even imagined he smelled the room's antique furniture—remained unchanged, but now Marius had the impression that shyness rather than scorn had driven her into that gloomy, inaccessible space, and that here in the protective shadows her face was asking for forgiveness for the fact she couldn't draw closer to him. Earlier, Marius had reproached himself for being attracted to Rita for her very coldness; but it hadn't been so: He felt that the new, almost amiable face before him now, as though hatched from the cocoon of the earlier one, intensified the agony of his desire.

"And again he was assailed by doubt. He told himself that Rita's amiability was some kind of trick connected with the shady doings in Parca. He was realizing that his desire for Rita was so desperate that for her sake he would be capable of writing an essay on Lygdian deities or entering the service of one of her underworld bosses. But there was no suggestion that Rita wanted either of these things from him. Indeed, Marius was increasingly confident that she wanted nothing at all from him, and that she felt good just listening to what he was telling her. He couldn't help but feel proud to see, beneath the frowning face, an unexpected, bright face that none of the students would have recognized. So on he talked. The sky and the sea darkened until they merged and disappeared. No other customers came into the café. Now Marius was looking at Rita's face against a background reflected in the window—of empty chairs and tables, and the lamplight from across the street, scattered into droplets, floating above her head like a swarm of shining bees. The blurred lights of a streetcar passed through the scene. Suddenly, Marius couldn't go on; he couldn't even finish his sentence. Helpless, he raised his hands above the tabletop. The silence was disturbed only by the muffled sound of the rough sea and the patter of its spray against the glass. Out of these barely audible sounds, another originated in Marius's throat—a slurred whisper containing a confession that Marius, instantaneously cut off from everything to which he had been connected a moment earlier, uttered over and over. Then he leaned forward and kissed Rita's face. Soon he felt her hand stroking his hair, shyly and awkwardly.

"Without speaking Rita stood up, took Marius by the hand, and led him out. Having left some money on the table for the waiter, Marius allowed himself to be led. His mind empty, he watched the rising of the waves by the light of the lamps across the street. They had passed five or six buildings when Rita stopped at a heavy, coffered double door, which was wet with seawater. Rita unlocked the door, they stepped into an unlit hallway, and Rita closed the door, enveloping Marius in darkness and silence. He heard the groping of Rita's hand along the wall, as it searched for the light switch. The light this produced was so weak that he could barely make out the steps they were climbing. Rita lived in a studio apartment on the third floor. As soon as they were inside, she clung to him, as if afraid that he would dissolve in the darkness. Not a word was spoken."

14. Marius in Love

"A strip of white light made by a streetlamp lay across one wall. Rita's faint sighs were lost in the sound of the waves, itself muffled by double glazing that acted like soft velvet. Marius's lover said not a single tender word to him, but there were times when she clung to him so tightly as to cause him pain; Marius had the feeling that she was telling him something to the effect of: 'I need your help and protection.' Again he wondered if Rita was involved in foul play of some kind, something she was no longer able to get out of. They barely spoke. It was late at night when Marius broke the silence that lay between them with a question: 'Do you believe it?' Although this was his first mention that day of the Lygdian madness that held the city in its grip, he knew Rita would understand what he was asking her about. She gave no answer; although in the darkness he couldn't see her face, by a slight change in the rhythm of her breathing he knew that she was considering whether to tell him everything, and that something was preventing her from doing so. It was as though the hum of the sea beyond the window were a voice of warning, reminding her of a promise, or a threat, made to keep her silent. Maybe Rita needed Marius to convince her; maybe she wanted his words to drown out the menacing murmur of the sea; maybe just one more utterance, or even a repetition of the same question, would suffice for Rita to offload on Marius everything she had been agonizing over day after day for many weeks. But at that moment Marius was overcome by reluctance to talk about the Lygdian movement, put off by the thought of a crowd of noisy, arrogant students, and fanatical, half-mad Parcans barging into their quiet room. So he embraced Rita again and immersed himself in the sound of the sea, gladdened by the realization that it had been unfair of him to hear threats in it and link it with the madness of the Parcans; he assured himself that the sea could never be his enemy. Soon after, he fell asleep, content.

"This was the start of Marius and Rita's strange love affair. They took long seafront walks together, spending their nights alternately at Rita's studio and Marius's apartment in the old port. At seminars, Rita's behavior remained the same, although she made no attempt to hide the fact that she and Marius were lovers. Students constantly saw them together, and soon their relationship was the second hottest topic of conversation at the university, after the Lygdian question. For the students, the relationship was another of the incomprehensible ciphers by which Rita's mystery made itself known. In class, she was still at the center of the debate; all that changed was that the students' torturous desire for her was imbued with yet more jealousy and humiliation. The suffering of some was so plainly unbearable that it caused them to dispense with all self-esteem and follow Rita and Marius around. As Marius walked with Rita along the seafront street toward her building, he would sometimes spot a student in hiding, peeking from a recess or around a corner.

"While the students' love for Rita was now even stronger than before, the benevolent disdain they had felt for Marius transformed into a hatred whose extent was commensurate with the depth of their suffering and sense of humiliation. For some, Marius was a seducer and a corrupter, who had surely beguiled Rita by dishonest means; others inclined to the view that Rita had seduced Marius as part of a secret plan, linked, of course, with the Lygdian movement. Although these two groups often argued with each other, they hated Marius with equal intensity.

"In the capital city, there had always been a few students for whom Marius was a favorite. At his seminars in Parca, the eyes turned on him—with the exception of Rita's—were brimming with hatred. The students did everything in their power to humiliate Marius in front of Rita, speaking in clear allusions about people too dim to understand new thoughts and too cowardly to voice their own opinions. As he was at his place of work, it was impossible for Marius to dodge all the evil stares that came his way. The sight of one face rapt with hatred after another gave him a strange delight; he learned to wallow in fumes of derangement and malice. Thanks to his experiences in Parca, Marius was surprised to discover in himself a feeling akin to sadism. Over time, his face assumed an expression of mockery that had never crossed it earlier. This expression drove the students to silent fury, as obviously it was saying: 'Yes, I'm sleeping with the Rita all of you are in love with, and we spend every night together. I don't believe in your Lygds, and I think your struggle is ridiculous.' Rita never spoke of her schoolmates with Marius, although once, as they stood in some archway or other, she said to him: 'Watch out for yourself. I'm afraid that they'll kill you.'

"As Marius and Rita walked along the shoreline from one apartment to the other, their progress was often monitored from afar by a desperate student. On the few evenings when they didn't see each other, perhaps Rita was at a session of the covert leadership of the Lygdian movement, a meeting of Russian mafia bosses, talks with intelligence agents, a New Lygdian paganist sacral orgy . . . Marius never asked where she had been, nor did he wonder about it. Sometimes, it seemed to him that her sighs in his embrace were on the point of a whispered utterance, and he waited for them to produce a declaration or confession, but the transformation of breath into words always stopped on the threshold of speech. By then, Marius had abandoned all curiosity, anyway; he made no attempt to fit the rudiments of words in Rita's whispers into sentences, allowing them to drift away, their only common factor being the incessant murmur of the sea."

15. Dragon of the Void

"Tomáš got to the description of Marius's love affair as his two weeks of illness were coming to an end and he was preparing to return to his glass tower at the streetcar terminus," said Martin, to my momentary confusion as I struggled to return from Parca to Tomáš's Prague apartment. "By now his nightstand bore several dozen streetcar schedules covered with dense handwriting."

"By that time, he was aware of what had happened to him and his father. They had exhausted themselves fighting the monster of the void, which had settled within them like an alien fiend in a science-fiction movie—a monster which sometimes induced an all-consuming fever, while at others gave rise to apathy. His father had fallen in the struggle, and for a long time Tomáš spared himself the same fate by surrendering to the void and living as its prisoner. After that, the void was mostly benevolent toward him, granting him peace, and sometimes even an insipid sense of happiness. But Tomáš continued to perceive the void as his archenemy, and to blame it for ruining his life—it never occurred to him that it might be his ally and greatest benefactor; he never guessed that behind the mask of the demon, which had terrified him all his life, was the radiant face that his desire had always sought, without knowing its name.

"Every now and then, Tomáš would lay down his pen, look out at the snow-covered yard, and consider the strange event that had come to pass a few days ago, an event he could never have expected: He realized that the terrible desert of the void was in fact his lost home, the garden of Eden he had dreamed about and never been able to remember. But these moments of wonder didn't last long: The void straightaway commanded him to go on with his work, and he obeyed without delay. In the past, Tomáš had painted, composed music, and written to destroy the void; he had thrown words, images, and tones at it, although he knew that the battle was lost before it began. He had tried to block out the void's icy silence, more terrible than any scream, with a thought, an aim, a message, a theme, or an opinion, just as his father had done years earlier. But with the years spent in the glass tower and taking endless walks through the city, all the thoughts, aims, opinions, messages, and themes had been put to sleep. If he had begun then to write a poem, short story, or novel, maybe his instincts would have woken them as a defense against the monster of the void. Now, however, Tomáš wasn't writing to silence the void; this was no literature—he simply wanted to enjoy and calm himself by playing a game of words and images that consisted in a description of the streets of an imaginary city.

"So it happened for the first time in his life that he wrote without struggling against the void, and without trying to drown out its silence—and to his astonishment he realized that the silence of the void was not complete. He listened to the very faint buzzing it contained—he had time to do this, for there was nowhere he needed to be, nor was he trying to make sense of it. And as he concentrated on his listening, in the buzzing he caught the whispering of a language, and he realized that the silence of the void was filled with words, sentences, and stories. The stories were strange to him—he neither understood them nor imagined any kind of message in them, and he suspected that they made no sense, yet they were so remarkably close to him that they might have been long-forgotten tales from his childhood. Tomáš was so fascinated by the voice he was hearing that he knew he would listen to it forevermore. He acknowledged that fate had cracked an excellent joke: Emptiness and what filled it most were one and the same thing. Wrapped up inside it were thousands of stories; in each image and sentence of these stories, other stories were wrapped, in the others yet others, and so on. And the stories didn't just lie there unconcerned—they pushed their way out, demanding to be developed, and that every image, tone, melody, and thought contained within them should be opened out.

"Until then, Tomáš had believed that for many years the void had swallowed up, with no advantage to himself, everything that fell into his memory—buildings, windows, and streetlamps he saw on his walks in the city, designs in which the cobblestones of sidewalks were arranged, gardens behind wire fences, books, articles about foreign countries in illustrated magazines, adventure movies he saw on TV . . . Now he saw that none of this had been lost; everything had remained in a great reservoir, which was now flowing forth and crystallizing in images.

"Tomáš told Kristýna that there was one thing that didn't

change even after he started writing: The emptiness never disappeared behind the content that gushed from it, and it never ceased to rule. Kristýna believed that this was still the case in the last months of his life, when she no longer saw him. She said that Tomáš envied people who inhabited a solid construction of ideas and thoughts, but at the same time, he couldn't help despising them a little. He realized how little he was interested in the thoughts of those who didn't drink from the same well of emptiness as he. He saw now that his father had failed because he had battled the void for many years by trying in vain to fill it, to find ground on which images and thoughts could grow, and exhausted himself in the process; he could have accepted the void, tended it with love, and waited to see what matured from it. Maybe in moments of despair, when the paper before him was covered with remote, detached words in his own hand, it seemed to him that the collapsing text, the very heart of the void, was putting out a ripple that would allow him to recognize words and outlines of stories; maybe there were moments when it flashed through his mind that there might be a point in listening to these strange sounds—but then he always dispelled this idea. Wasn't the void his archenemy? Wasn't it the void that caused him to fail? Surely it would be foolish to expect anything good from it. Tomáš came to think of young people whose life force was being drained by a vain struggle with the void, as his had been; and it was this thought that first suggested to him that his novel could be published. Although the idea that he would be somebody's teacher was ridiculous to him, he told himself that the experience that he knew to emanate from each sentence of his work could be of help to those who were thrashing about in the void like flies in a bowl of soup."

16. Demonstration

"Students in the Lygdian movement held demonstrations with ever greater frequency, mostly in the evenings on the main square, where a student leader would climb onto the pedestal of a monument and make a speech that was sometimes somber, sometimes fiery, always containing a call to the government for the immediate meeting of all student demands, many of which were far more radical than anything in the program of the Lygdian Revival Party. They campaigned for support for Lygdian culture, and the teaching of the Lygdian language and Lygdian history in schools. They demanded that the building currently housing the income-tax office, which, it was alleged, sat on the foundations of the Lygds' greatest shrine, be surrendered to the Lygdian Revival Party, for it was the most notable site from Lygdian history. They demanded that the region be granted greater autonomy, and they called for all manner of social and cultural rights accruing to the Parcans as descendants of the Lygds. But sometimes all they did was shout, so that not a single utterance, not a single word, could be made out in the coalescing voices. It wasn't clear whether the unintelligible noise was produced by the volume of communications in the mix, or it was just an unarticulated roar, but that was of no matter. The chorus of voices in which Parca spoke to Marius occupied a space between two formless sounds—the murmur of the sea and the roar of the crowd. Marius realized that the students saw themselves in the same light as the ancient Lygds fighting for their rights against the Roman oppressors, although he was forced to concede that their commitment to the fight probably went far beyond that of the ancient inhabitants they took as their model—so much so that it began to appear that the leaders of the Lygdian Revival Party, who had initially welcomed the university's take-up of the Lygdian cause, were getting nervous about the students' radicalism. For a long time, the police left the demonstrators alone: Worried that a crackdown could lead to an escalation in the violence, the police prefect waited for the wave of demonstrations to subside of its own accord. In the meantime, it was enough, he decided, to send mounted patrols to the square. He was well aware that many police officers, some of them in senior positions, sympathized with the Lygdian cause.

"By March, there was a demonstration every evening. Parca's rainy season reached its peak at this time of year. Although it was rare for the city to be hit by an intense downpour, the practically continuous drizzle soaked through everything and left tiny drops on every surface. Rita attended every demonstration, and from the beginning Marius took it for granted that he would go with her. They would meet in a small café near the university, drink coffee together, and then head out for the square. Once there, Marius would stand silent among the shouting students. Rita, too, was silent, although the noise was at its greatest around her; while in class her silence provoked arguments, here it fed the roar. It was dark when the demonstrations began. Marius watched the anger-contorted, rain-drenched faces of the students, their teeth bared and gleaming in the lamplight as they chanted their slogans. Some of these slogans were in Lygdian, which by this time had developed and spread. Marius stood there unembarrassed, although occasionally he wondered what his wife and friends in the capital would think to see him there, and he felt a sting of shame.

"The students' hatred was turned on an imaginary foe they would have struggled to describe if prompted to do so. This foe comprised a vague army of all those who checked their right to return their land to Lygdian purity. This army was still the force of the Roman occupation that had humiliated the country so long ago, which had never left and simply transformed over the centuries, becoming a sinister network of officials, egoists, skeptics, and heartless scientists. In class, the students had to subdue their hatred for enemies and renegades; here, they could luxuriate in it. On the square, no one stood in their way. The few local police officers shuffling awkwardly from foot to foot or trying to calm their frightened horses didn't bother the students, who turned their wet faces toward the darkness and shouted at the blank facades, fancying they saw the enemy army projected there. The students' gazes sometimes wandered and landed on Marius, and Marius saw that their expressions retained the hatred: For the students, he was one of the army of foes; by the cynical mockery of Lygdian ideals the students read in his face in class, he was a participant in the spreading evil, all the more by his violation and corruption of their beloved Rita, the star of the Lygdian movement at the university. Although he feared the hostility of the crowd, Marius was confident that Rita's presence protected him; he suffered nothing worse than a few crude shoves."

17. Fighting

"For as long as the demonstrations broke nothing but a few storefront windows, the situation in Parca provoked little interest in the capital, either at the police presidium or the Ministry of the Interior. Then, at the end of April, the violence escalated, and after demonstrators torched several parked cars on the main square, as local police stood idly by, the Ministry decided to intervene. Police units from the metropolis and other regions were deployed to Parca. No one took the trouble to give these officers details of what was going on in the city; when one evening they jumped from their armored personnel carriers onto the wet pavement of the main square, they had little idea what the crowd they had come to oppose was calling for. The young demonstrators were yelling and waving banners bearing strange characters. The police officers stared at each other in amazement; it was as though they had landed in a weird dream.

"Skirmishes broke out, causing injuries to demonstrators and officers, as both sides became ever more enraged. One officer was struck on the head by a rock and taken to the hospital, where he lay unconscious in intensive care; the following night, a student hit on the head by a police baton was laid on the bed next to his. The police crackdown sparked a new hatred; now, the square was illuminated every evening by tall arcs of light drawn in the darkness by Molotov cocktails, as bellowed police commands and Lygdian cries of demonstrators were joined by the whoosh of rubber bullets, the use of which had been authorized by a special order of the Minister of the Interior.

"In this atmosphere of combat, the image of Lygdia was shaped and cemented: followers of the Lygdian movement submitted to its most absurd fantasies, the doubters among them now believing that to doubt on the battlefield was weakness, if not betrayal. Lygdian language, Lygdian history, and the Lygd religion were consolidated. A definitive Lygdian grammar, a Lygdian dictionary, and a great work of Lygdian mythology were published. Marius bought these and read them in his room in the old port. He was enchanted by many of the legends and myths and confused by the great variety of the fruit the Lygdian movement had borne: outrageous loss of reason, fanatism, and hate, but then these wonderful writings, and—perhaps the most beautiful product of all—the magnificent palace of the Lygdian language, born out of the dreams of Parcans and the refuse of his own native language, with its glittering halls and dark chambers. He was particularly taken by a drawing in one of the books—a reconstruction of the Lygd shrine that was said to have stood on the site of the income-tax office. It showed an austere space reminiscent of an early Christian basilica, with an impressive altar, the stone of which was embellished with a carved symbol of the Lygd religion. This symbol was a shell with an inset of a large, wide-open eye (maybe meant to symbolize a union of inwardness and cognition, or mystical meditation and mindful awareness). Before long, miniature replicas of the altar, made of various materials, were appearing in the apartments of Lygdomaniacs; in the student dorms, rooms without any such altar became a rarity, while jeweler's storefront windows displayed shells of gold and silver with inset eyes of all possible sizes.

"It was obvious that this had become a fight to the death. Some of the regular demonstrators took fright, and before long those gathered each evening on the square comprised only the most hard core of the university-based Lygdomaniacs. Marius and Rita continued to meet at the café; Rita never suggested it might be better not to meet like this, nor did Marius consider the possibility. Several students and leaders of the Lygdian movement were placed under arrest. A major protest was planned for the twenty-seventh of April, a Lygdian pagan holiday that it seemed appropriate to celebrate by fighting for freedom.

"Marius and Rita stood toward the front. As usual, it was drizzling. For the moment, the demonstrators were divided from the police by a wet strip of pavement that gleamed in the streetlight. The square was enveloped in a tense silence. Marius watched with curiosity the tight, motionless lines of police, their black-uniformed bodies concealed by shields of transparent plastic, their helmets and large protective eyewear making them look like enormous bugs. The students around him also stood rigid—Marius had the feeling that the whole square had been turned into a great sculpture. Looking from one wet face to the next, he saw the same expression of rapt concentration; everyone's hair was lank, and a smell of damp clothing hung in the air. Suddenly, Marius thought of his wife; he imagined himself returning to the capital and their reconciliation; he imagined them living together in their old apartment, maybe having a child . . .

"Pandemonium suddenly broke loose, so quickly that Marius failed to notice what sparked it. An insult shouted by a demonstrator? A rock hitting a plastic shield? Or did a policeman simply lose his nerve in the dreadful quiet made still more monstrous by the monotonous drizzle? The roar was everywhere at once. Through the air Molotov cocktails rose high and with a weird slowness, illuminating the facades. There were shouts in Lygdian, barked orders from police commanders, the stamping of heavy boots, rocks striking pavement and plastic shield, cries of the injured, hysterical female screams. The convulsed faces that emerged in the pale light around Marius, and were then lost in the crowd, reminded him of the mascarons on the fronts of Parcan buildings he had looked at in the summer. He watched the clusters of bodies come together and then spread out again, as though buffeted by waves of an invisible sea. He was about to grab Rita's hand, something he had never done at a demonstration, when a surge of bodies forced them apart. As figures rushed everywhere about him, Marius wandered as though in a dream, calling Rita's name, although he knew that in the commotion of battle she wouldn't be able to hear him. Suddenly, the wall of bodies around him flew off in all directions, confronting him with an apparition from the hell of Hieronymus Bosch, in which objects come to life; this object was a glass receptacle for garbage swaying on dark legs shod in high boots. This specter raised a baton-wielding arm before Marius could recognize it as a policeman behind a plastic shield. This was the last thing he remembered."

18. Green Room

"He lay with his eyes closed. He first conscious sensation was a mix of pleasant smells. The first he was able to distinguish belonged to old, heavy furniture, the next of a library that had grown up in a room for the whole long life of the room's occupier. Obviously, this wasn't his room in the old port, nor Rita's place, nor his apartment in the capital. The room was lit only by a weak bulb, which was surely somewhere nearby at the level of his eyes: Through his eyelids, Marius saw it as an orange blotch in a warm, velvet universe filled with blurry, blinking stars. He heard the ticking of two clocks—one somewhere near his head, the second a little farther away—and a faint rattling. At first, he took this sound for the working of nimble teeth belonging to a small rodent; then, his mind produced the image of a minuscule machine with many cogged wheels, and the idea of their regular rotation was extremely pleasing to him. The pleasure dissolved the moment he realized what he was hearing: distant automobiles and streetcars through many walls.

"He went on with his investigation without opening his eyes. In the mix of smells, he succeeded in identifying a trace of something else: Apparently, the floor of the room was covered with a worn Persian rug. Marius didn't want to move; he was happy to wallow in the darkness and scents of this unknown space. On his body, he felt the weight of a thick duvet. When he moved a little, his eyes still closed, he was gratified that the subtle sounds were joined by another, the creaking of old, dry wood. He thought the room was filled with the vapors of a drug of some sort, which was soaking into his body through every pore, bringing a sense of bliss. But as his being recovered from its swoon and rid itself of the remnants of dreams, it occurred to him that the pleasing calmness within him may have been induced by a tranquilizer.

"When at last he opened his eyes, the first thing he saw in

the half-light was an unlit chandelier, the eight brass arms of which cast indistinct shadows on the ceiling. Then he turned his head, without lifting it from the pillow, and saw a table lamp with a green fabric shade fixed over a metal frame, with several green tassels along its bottom edge. This lamp stood on a desk, next to a white china vase with a blue picture of cows grazing in front of a windmill. At the other end of this desk was a clock, its face between two rounded alabaster columns. It was half-past eleven. On the table was a thick book whose dark marbled binding bore no title, and several minerals of irregular shapes whose names Marius didn't know, and which probably served as paperweights. The green shade was glowingly reflected in the gloom of a large mirror, which hung on the wall above the desk and showed the backsides of the vase and clock. The frame of the mirror was of gilded plaster cast in the shape of branches of laurel bound together by crossed ribbons; the lower leaves were separated from the desktop by a thin strip of wall only. Although the room wasn't large, at its edges the light of the lamp was weak, with brighter spots emerging here and there out of the gloom. After a moment's thought, Marius told himself that he was looking at the extensive library that had announced itself to his sense of smell.

"Wherever the lamplight reached the wall, it was covered with dark-green wallpaper of a fuzzy material reminiscent of velvet, with a delicate pattern in a lighter shade of green. Marius also saw a window with closed shutters; as no light penetrated the room between its wooden slats, he concluded that it was half-past eleven at night. On the nightstand next to the bed was a heavy, round alarm clock; pushed up to the desk was a chair with its seat and back covered with purple plush. In the lower part of the mirror, he saw a white area of irregular shape, which at first reminded him of a snowdrift; within seconds, it dawned on him that this was the duvet that covered him. After another moment's thought, he decided to raise his arm. To his surprise, this went well; his arm appeared as a pale image above the frame of the mirror.

"Only now did Marius recall the events of the past few months and his own role in them; he remembered the summer facades of Parca drifting above his head, the birth of the Lygdian language and Lygdian history, the nights spent with Rita in two apartments, the roar of the sea, the hatred in the eyes of the students, Molotov cocktails illuminating the nighttime square, a hand brandishing a baton. And he felt immense happiness at the knowledge that here in this room no one would shout, gesticulate, or spout nonsense. After a long time, he was again in a place that exhaled an atmosphere of satisfaction."

19. Painting

He sent his hand out into the world; he touched his forehead where he felt a thin fabric of a pleasingly ribbed structure—a gauze bandage, he thought. He placed his index finger into the gap between the gauze and his skin and felt a crumbling crust of dried blood; he didn't feel any pain. He decided to continue his exploration in the darkened face of the mirror. Above the duvet, he saw a section of wall covered with dark-green wallpaper, the same paper as above the desk. Above this was a lighter strip, with many lavish shapes in bas-relief, some of which, situated as they were in a part of the room dominated by gloom, caught the reflection of the feeble light of the lamp; no doubt this was a gilded frame like the one in which the mirror was set. The whole upper part of the mirror above this second frame was filled with a dark area and a light spot situated in its right half, in precise accordance with the golden ratio. Again, it took Marius a while to realize what it was—a painting that hung in the gloom right over the bed. His hand fumbled along the smooth wallpaper until it appeared in the mirror again. He moved it up the wall, studying its reflection; now his fingers were touching the points of leaves of gilded plaster, and now, a little higher still, small cracks on the surface of an oil painting. Having verified that the dark area reflected in the mirror was indeed a canvas, he concentrated on the indistinct dark shapes and the light spot, trying to figure out the subject of the painting. Judging by the position of the light within the darkness that spread across the whole picture, he concluded that it was a baroque painting from the seventeenth or eighteenth century. Although for some time he tried to place various figures and objects within the painting's vague outlines, he reached no further conclusions. He became caught up in his game: After a while, he felt it more important to know what was in the painting above his motionless body than how the massacre on the main square had played out.

"Having braced himself, he placed his hands on the wooden sidepieces of the bed and sat up. He was startled by the gaunt, unshaven face that popped up in the mirror; the wide bandage was marked with a large russet-red stain with an outline so regular that at first he thought his head had been dressed in a Japanese flag. After staring at the apparition in the mirror for a while, he returned his attention to the jumble of shapes in the painting. Now he believed himself to be looking at the figure of a saint being stretched on a rack by mercenaries. Needing to verify this conclusion, he placed both hands on the edge of the nightstand and succeeded in standing. He took three steps across the carpet before sitting down in a chair at the desk, with his back to the mirror. After this strenuous journey, he rested. Then he looked again at the picture above the bed. Even now it wasn't easy for him—in this room lit only by a desk lamp—to figure out what it showed. The saint on the rack disappeared, and soon after that the dark and light spots agreed on a completely different scene. What he saw in the painting now made Marius marvel.

The distribution of light and dark, the brushwork, the excited gestures of the figures, even the network of cracks all testified that the painting above the bed was a work of the Baroque; but the scene in the picture was neither biblical nor mythological, nor did it depict a legend, or portray a king or a commander. It showed a diver in a black wetsuit with long frog-like flippers, goggles, and a tube coming from his mouth that fed into an oxygen tank on his back. The diver's hand held an electric lamp; the cone of light this produced in the water was the place in the painting that Marius had mistaken for a taper-lit space in which the artist had placed a group of figures from the Bible or legend. The light of the diver's lamp fell on a coral reef, where brightly colored fishes, rippling anemones, and all kinds of crustaceans could be seen; in the darkest areas of the reef, the lamplight was reflected in scales and shells. Marius didn't know what to make of this Baroque painting of a diver with a flashlight. He was attracted by the idea that a painter of the Baroque could travel in a time machine to the present day, to paint scenes from modern life in a style he was accustomed to. But he had to concede the greater likelihood of the painting being the work of a contemporary artist, who for some reason had wished to imitate work of an earlier time.

"He noticed a black line twisted in various ways in many places. This line ran diagonally across the part of the reef that was lit by the diver's lamp. Was this supposed to be an especially thin sea serpent? It occurred to him that the shapes in which the serpent's body was twisted resembled letters of a cursive script. He stood up, returned gingerly to the bed, leaned against the headboard, and studied the painting up close. To his amazement, he saw that the dark line really was twisted so as to form a sentence written in a cursive script. The sentence the diver was reading was in Spanish. It meant: *As Richard's car plunged toward the green hillside of the Chapultepec, a dark figure holding a submachine gun leaned out of the back window. There were three flashes and the sound of three short bursts of gunfire.* Apparently, this sentence was made from an ordinary length of wire, not an especially thin sea creature; someone had taken the time and trouble to twist the wire into the shapes of cursive letters. Marius read the sentence several times as he pondered its meaning. He had once been interested in the history of the House of Habsburg-Lorraine, so he knew that Chapultepec was in Mexico City, and that it was here that the hapless Emperor Maximilian had established his seat. Now he wondered why someone would write a sentence in wire, and how this sentence came to be found on a coral reef, but he didn't come up with any answers. Before long, he was overcome by such fatigue that fell back down on the mattress, where he lay staring at the metal chandelier, waiting for someone to show up."

20. Hector and Hella

"A short while later, the door opened, revealing two silhouettes on the threshold with an illuminated hallway: a tall, slim male figure, and the short, rounded figure of a woman. As the man walked briskly toward Marius, the lamplight fell on an angular face with a carefully trimmed beard and wavy gray hair, and Marius saw that he was older than he had looked at first. Judging by the deep lines on his forehead and around his mouth, he might be sixty-five or even older; plainly he prided himself on his upright bearing and brisk stride. The woman was leaning on the door jamb, still disguised by the gloom. Marius looked at the man's arms, which rested casually but confidently alongside his body; it occurred to him that these were the arms of a doctor. The man pulled the chair up to the bed and sat down. Marius wanted to ask where he was, but the muscles in the face wouldn't obey; hardly had he uttered the first abortive words than the man frowned and placed a forefinger on his lips. Then the man took hold of the Marius's arm, checked his pulse, and carefully removed the bandage from the patient's forehead. He muttered to himself before calling to the woman with a request for his bag, from which he removed gauze, cotton wool, and an amber-glass bottle before setting about the gentle cleaning of the wound. The woman had fetched the lamp from the desk and was holding it in one hand; the other hand rested on the back of the chair the doctor was sitting in. She had a kindly face and fine hair swept up in a chignon, reminding Marius of his mother, who had died a few years earlier.

"Having redressed Marius's forehead, the doctor asked him how he was feeling. Marius managed to say that he was feeling very well indeed. He rested and then asked again where he was. The doctor unfastened Marius's pajamas and treated a wound on his shoulder that Marius hadn't realized he had, leaving the answer to his wife. Marius learned what he needed to know, and all sorts of things besides. The people caring for him were Rita's grandparents, Hector and Hella. Hector was the senior physician at the Department of Surgery of Parca's hospital, Hella a conservator-restorer. At yesterday's demonstration, Rita had found Marius on the pavement, unconscious and with a bloody head wound. Students had helped her to drag him from the square into a side street (Marius imagined the students' distaste and thought how there was no one among them who would refuse to do Rita's bidding). Rita had managed to get hold of a car to take him to her grandparents' apartment; she hadn't wanted to take him to the hospital, as after earlier battles the rumor had spread that the police searched the hospital for injured demonstrators.

"At this point, Rita's grandfather spoke up to confirm that he had experienced several fierce scenes with police commanders demanding access to his hospital department.

"'I didn't let them in, of course, but all the same, it's safer here,' he said.

"Rita's face again came into Marius's mind; in the presence of this kindly, calm couple who were plainly satisfied with their lives, he felt ashamed of the folly of his love, and of his life in Parca as a whole. Now it seemed to him that the Lygdian movement could justify neither its extraordinary stories of legend nor the ingenuity of the new language that these had spawned; they were beautiful flowers that had grown in a slew of stupidity and intolerance, and they still bore the stink of it. In the presence of this physician who treated the sick and injured while he, Marius, was taking part in demonstrations charged with anger and hate, and which made idiotic demands, Marius felt distinctly embarrassed. His expression was also contrite and apologetic in front of the doctor's wife, who smiled at him indulgently, as if he were a small child. Yet his belief that the Lygdian epidemic that held the city in its grip could never penetrate this room, where every object caught in the lamplight spoke of focused, serious work, was a source of delight to him. If at that moment he could have made one magic wish, it would have been to stay in the green room forever. Marius preferred not to imagine what the doctor and his wife must think of him, a man who within weeks of his arrival in the city had succumbed to its fashionable folly, and had his head bashed in as a consequence. He imagined them excusing Rita's actions by her youth, and in any case a granddaughter could be forgiven anything; but he didn't know how his own behavior could be condoned. He should have been teaching History to young people, instead, he had gone to the square with them to scream for the rights of a fabricated nation. He searched in the faces of Hector and Hella for signs of indignation, scorn, or reproach, but to his surprise, he found nothing of the sort. Then it occurred to him that Hella had realized his love for Rita, and found it sufficient explanation and, perhaps, excuse for any oddities of behavior. Hector, meanwhile, had surely encountered all types at the hospital and knew that men could commit still greater follies than participation in demonstrations for the rights of nonexistent peoples.

"Although the green room was like Heaven on Earth for Marius, he tried to sit up in the bed; whispering that he had to go, he began to hunt for his clothes. The physician silenced him: In this state he wouldn't get as far as the front door of the apartment; now he would sleep again, after which he would spend a week or two in bed, in Hector's care. Because of the unrest in the city, there was no teaching at the university, but if an excuse should be needed, he would write Marius a sick note explaining that he had fallen down some stairs. Parcan houses had steep flights, and such falls were common accidents among those who came from the capital, he added with a smile. Not waiting for Marius's reply, Hector turned and left the room, along the strip of pale light that lay across the carpet. Hella smiled at Marius before switching off the lamp, which Marius heard her place back on the desk. Then she, too, left the room, closing the door quietly behind her. Again Marius lay in silent, fragrant darkness. He pictured the faces of Hector and Hella, wishing that they would accompany him into sleep. For a moment, Hector's face merged with Rita's, and Marius was surprised to realize how alike they were. The double face dissolved in ornaments of the pale light that danced beneath his eyelids; then these ornaments turned into a jumble of grimacing faces of demonstrators, and Marius was momentarily anxious before a wave of sleep overwhelmed him."

21. Visit

"When he woke the next morning, Rita was sitting by his bed. Now the room was filled with light, which was pouring in through an open window, with long, white rippling drapes in front of it. At one moment, a gust of wind grappled with the hem of a drape, clipping its reflection in the smooth surface of the mirror. Rita took Marius's hand; again they were silent, as they had been for most of their time together. Yesterday, Marius had imagined the green room rejecting Rita as an unwelcome alien, owing to the extent of her involvement in the Lygdian folly. But the cool early-morning light of conciliation lay across her dress and arms just as it lay across the other things in the room; this light separated everything in the room from common relationships, while placing it in a single unbroken fabric of pure existence that needed no justification, reason, or sense, and to which no such terms could be applied. It was as though Rita had simply become one of the things in the room. Marius was surprised to see that the room's objects accepted the visitor in friendship; he saw that the sorrow that had left its mark on Rita's face, as a creek in winter leaves ice formations on the bank, wasn't entirely strange to the accumulated wisdom, knowledge, and tranquility that breathed from the room's surfaces; he saw that the light dance of the drapes communicated with the script of the folds of Rita's dress, and that the wallpaper didn't object to being a backdrop to her face.

"Marius realized that the things around him must have known Rita for a long time, and that Rita had surely spent a lot of time in the room. Furthermore, it seemed to him that her gestures were more expansive here, shaped by contact with the rounded spines of the books and the cool minerals on the desk, retaining something of the space from which they originated. At last, Marius knew the mysterious room that Rita always carried inside. What the students took for a Lygdian mystery, a view Marius had sometimes shared, was in fact a room in the tranquil apartment of Rita's grandparents, which had seeped into her body, and lodged in her features and gestures.

"This transformation caused Marius to feel a rising wave of tenderness. Last night, in the solemn calm of the green room, a large portion of a love that had drawn him into so many awkward, undignified situations had dissolved; now, in the pure light of early morning, he saw that his love contained something more than foolishness and a childish fascination with a mystery that was possibly fake—there was also a longing that roused in him the sadness of an existence lodged in the intimate space of his childhood, on the flipside of world events, and which was shyly offering him an accumulated treasure.

"They talked of unimportant things, each taking greater care than before to steer the conversation away from the demonstrations and the Lygdian question. In what Rita was saying, Marius heard a voice that contained an echo of guilt; he heard a plea for forgiveness for what had happened to him, and another that he remain in her work—a work he knew nothing about. Rita still lacked the courage to tell him the truth, maybe because her secret was so awful, maybe because it was so trivial.

"Rita's grandparents' apartment was in a quiet street in the north of the city. From the window of his room, Marius saw nothing but a part of the facade opposite, and only rarely was a car heard in the street. When he fell asleep at night, woozy with painkillers, in the distance he heard cries of demonstrators, calls of police commanders, and the swish of rubber bullets fired from rifles; he might have been listening to sounds accompanying a puppet play. Marius wasn't frightened by these sounds; indeed, he found himself enjoying their music as it escorted him to sleep. It was as though the ages-old language of silence had eventually vanquished the noise that had recently dominated the city.

"Early each morning Hector left for the hospital, returning late in the evening. Rita would come sometime in the morning; all her visits were like the first. For the rest of the day, Marius would bathe in the calm glow of the things in the apartment, watching the dance of the drapes, dipping into the odd book he pulled from the bookcase, or talking with Hella. He spoke of his life in the capital, and he listened to all kinds of stories from her life as a restorer of old paintings and frescoes, which took her to many castles and monasteries. They didn't speak of the Lygdian movement; to mention it in this peaceful home would be an obscenity, Marius thought. But one day, he couldn't stop himself from asking Hella's opinion on Lygdomania. She simply shook her head, as if unprepared to waste words on it. She knew that her granddaughter was somehow involved with the Lygdian movement, but she had never questioned her about it or reproached her for it, nor had Rita ever referred in her presence to her connection with Lygdomania. Hella had reached the conclusion that this was down to the craziness of youth; Rita would soon get over it, so there was no point in trying to talk her out of it. But Hella was afraid that something could happen to her during the demonstrations."

22. Mayan Fresco

"One morning, as the wound on his forehead was being redressed, Marius asked Hector about the painting above the bed. Hector smiled and looked at his wife. The picture was Hella's work, Hector revealed. He was hurrying off to the hospital, but Hella would surely be happy to talk about it. No sooner was Hector out of the room than Marius asked Hella to do exactly that. The old lady sat by his bed and began a story that had played out forty years earlier, when she had been a senior-year student of Restoration at the Academy of Fine Arts. These were the days when she got to know Hector, who was just finishing medical school, and fell in love with him, causing her to break up with the classmate at the Academy she had been dating since her freshman year.

"One day, the professor who taught History of Art at the Academy took his students to a museum, rather than giving his usual lecture. Hella lingered in the room dedicated to pre-Columbian civilizations in America, by the Aztec figures. When at last she caught up with her classmates, she found them gathered around a single exhibit, gesticulating with excitement. As she approached, they fell silent. Alarmed, she asked what was going on, but no one answered her. When she went to look at what had so impressed them, her classmates stood back in silence to let her through. In a display case she saw fragments of a wall from a Mayan temple; on these fragments were paintings. On one such piece, Hella saw a scene that was strange indeed, and it was obvious that this fresco was the cause of her classmates' alarm. It showed, on the left, the figure of a man in a close-fitting blue suit like Superman's. On the chest, the suit had a red triangle standing on its apex, but instead of the 'S,' it contained the letters 'PYA' and the head of a violet. The man wore a wicked, lustful expression, and he was holding a whip that was dripping blood. The second figure was a naked girl whose splayed hands and feet were chained to two metal rings in the wall; her belly, breasts, and thighs were covered with bloody welts apparently inflicted by the debauched Pseudo-Superman's whip. There wasn't the slightest doubt that the girl's face was Hella's: She was wearing a blue-and-white Alice band of the kind Hella often wore at the time, and which all her classmates recognized; furthermore, the artist had taken the trouble to show the birthmark on Hella's left breast that was known only to her parents and the two men who had seen her naked. For a minute or two, Hella stared in silence at the Maya painting that depicted her in circumstances of such terrible humiliation. Then her eyes closed, her legs buckled, she lost consciousness and fell. The classmates standing next to her were only just able to catch her before she hit the floor.

"For Hella, the most dreadful thing about the fresco wasn't that it portrayed her, nor the circumstances in which it showed her. Most awful of all was the man in the blue suit. Hella knew him well: He was the Protector she had invented for herself when she was eight years old, and since that time she had always turned to him for advice in times of personal trouble. Having spent her childhood in his company, she had never forgotten him entirely—even at the Academy, she thought of him occasionally. The letters 'PYA' meant '(I Will) Protect You Always.' Little Hella had added the violet to the letters simply because it was her favorite flower. Hella was certain she had never told anyone about her dream Protector; she had always kept him to herself, as a secret.

"When she came round, it was dark. Someone was holding her hand; anxious, she asked who it was. She was relieved to hear Hector's voice, and she asked him to turn on the light. He replied uneasily that it was daytime and the window was wide open. Owing to her experience in the museum, Hella had been struck blind, and she would remain so for three weeks. When the narrative reached this point, Marius knew the dark mystery would develop. And the good-hearted grandmother didn't keep him in suspense, telling him immediately how the shadowy case of the Mayan fresco had unraveled, even though she herself had had to wait twenty years for an explanation. Aged forty-three, she had met in the street the man she had left for Hector, and they had gone to a café together. There, her erstwhile lover had confessed to her that he was the painter of the Mayan fresco. He had suffered terribly after Hella left him, torturing himself night after night with visions of Hella and Hector embracing on the bed of her room, which he knew so well. In those days, he had been supplementing his income by working as a conservator-restorer in the museum of ancient cultures. On learning that Hella's class would be taking a trip to the museum, it occurred to him how he might hurt Hella—and he did something for which he would feel shame for the rest of his life. He remembered the party he and Hella had attended to celebrate the end of exams after their freshman year. Hella had been in high spirits and drunk more than she was used to. As he walked her home, she had talked without stopping, obviously feeling the need to get all kinds of things off her chest. She had talked, too, of the Protector, confessing that she had never mentioned him to anyone. The next day, she had woken with a dreadful hangover, vomited from morning till evening, and remembered nothing of the previous evening.

"For several days, he had walked about as though in a trance, working on his idea. As Hella and her class were entering the museum, he ran to the display case he had chosen for his purpose and exchanged one of its exhibits for his own work; then he followed the school group stealthily, flitting about among the Mayan and Aztec sculptures to ensure that he was unseen; he watched the unfolding of events from behind a large statue of the god of rain. His revenge had given him no satisfaction, of course: He had suffered his whole life from a guilty conscience, which his confession to Hella years later had relieved a little."

For some moments now, I'd had the feeling that insects of the night were flying around our table; but as the buzz got louder, it turned out to be coming from an engine. A boat drew up, and the son of the owner of a neighboring boarding house jumped out on to the beach, having probably spent the evening at a discotheque in Hóra Sfakion. The music coming from the bar by the landing stage had stopped, and all the tavernas were closed. Martin and I were the only two people in Loutro still seated at an outdoor table.

The Story of the Wire Book I

1. Paradise Sonata

"When Hella was blind, the doctors recommended absolute calm and a change of surroundings—so Hector took her away to his parents' woodland cottage and cared for her there. In the evenings, Hella wished to be read to, but the only two books Hector could find in the place were an out-of-date public transport schedule and a handbook for gardeners. So Hella asked him to make up a story of his own. Hector considered how he should do this: As he wanted to keep Hella calm and stimulate pleasant thoughts in her, he decided that the right genre would be the idyll. He began on a story of two lovers who escape a bustling city and live in a cottage in beautiful countryside—in a clearing in a fragrant jungle that is like a welcoming garden, where most of the time they run about naked. The scene is reminiscent of a painting or etching by Max Švabinský. In the distance, through gaps between the juicy leaves of tropical trees, they see the city they have left, which looks like a wall of gray rock by day and a swarm of glittering fireflies by night. Hector described their days of happiness, their early-morning bathing in the creek, their expeditions to the heart of the jungle, their exhilarating trips by canoe below overhanging branches that

form a scented baldachin over the creek, their evening conversations on the terrace to the sound of birdsong. As he still
didn't know what he was going to do with the naked lovers,
and their frolicking about the clearing was becoming slightly
monotonous, he considered introducing something more dramatic—perhaps a story of how on a trip deep into the jungle they discover, in the humid air amid the lianas and roots,
the entrance to a mysterious ancient temple, where they find
either gold or some mysterious text they go on to decipher. Or
they might encounter the priestess of an ancient cult—yes, that
would be even better.

"Then something strange happened: The sentences of his
story were disrupted by the mysterious transmitter of another
tale. At first, the new voice was just an indistinct hum, in which
Hector could make out just a word here and there, but these
words disturbed him, not least of which because their tone
was very different from that of his idyll. The dark hum grew
louder, so that the words spoken by the naturist lovers became
ever fainter; soon, Hector was struggling to hold his sentences
together. Meanwhile, the hum was producing words with ever
greater frequency and of ever greater distinctness. The new story
grew in the body of the old like a diabolical parasite that was
taking possession, feeding on and growing stronger by Hector's
words and phrases, using them for an aim yet undeclared.

"Later, Hector told Hella that the nagging, glutinous runners of the other tale's sentences, which suffocated the original
story, broke through a crack in the dark hotbed in which the
germs of all stories thrive, and which may even reside at the base
of every person's consciousness, forever covered by a heavy lid.
Hector felt the warm, damp breath it gave off, a combination
of wild growth and decay, and he breathed in the scent of the
attractive but also slightly repellent juices that create stories—all
stories, irrespective of whether they were merry or sad, comic

or tragic. And he had to ask himself how far these suspicious juices, this dark blood of fiction, was involved in the shaping of our lives; now, he had the feeling that life was an endless repetition of strange tales . . . So, even as he was telling of an idyllic clearing in the jungle, Hector sensed—in the dark-green depths between the trees and their leaves—hitherto barely perceptible germs of another story; he heard how the faraway babble of creeks was joined by sounds of gunfire, and curses and cries of the wounded. Apparently, this was no ordinary war: It was a wild struggle conducted without rules or mercy. Hector was bewitched by its sounds—they wooed him like the song of the Sirens. He became ever more eager to learn about these distant battles, although for Hella's sake he tried to keep to his love story and not stray too far from Švabinský's clearing.

"Soon, however, he was no longer able to complete so much as a sentence. When Hella asked him what the matter was, he admitted that another story had settled in his own like a parasite. Hella said that she would like to make the intruder's acquaintance. With a sigh, Hector explained that he knew very little about it, but judging what from he did know, it was nothing for a patient with a nervous illness. Hella understood what Hector was talking about: Before her blindness, she had painted a lot; she had often found herself working on a picture for which she had long prepared when the lines she had committed to canvas turned into a picture unfamiliar and incomprehensible, yet fascinating and strangely close. In such a situation, she knew that the best thing to do was to place oneself at the aggressor's mercy. She told Hector to leave the lovers in the clearing to their own devices and to track the new story, insisting that a story grown in unknown soil would be of greater interest to her than an idyll in the jungle and tales of mysterious temples; he needn't worry that a tale of brutality and monstrosity could cause her state to worsen—if it truly was the case that in some corner of Hector's mind a murky horror was taking shape, she imagined the tension it would bring could help her more than his peaceful narrative, which—she was forced to admit—she hadn't been enjoying much. Hector said he was glad of Hella's permission to explore the new story, to which he was becoming ever more drawn. He would need two hours alone to make out the first outlines of the plot in the fog, and to think everything through."

"Maybe in this part Tomáš Kantor was describing his own experience. It reminds me of how his innocent game produced an unknown city and its story."

"Let's not jump to conclusions on how alike Hector's and Tomáš's experiences were. We don't know yet how far we can trust Hector's assertion that a completely unknown world revealed itself to him from the gaps between trees in a jungle, or gaps between words in his first story," said Martin mysteriously. "Maybe he had a reason for not telling Hella the whole truth."

2. Flying Eye

"Leaving Hella inside, Hector went to sit on the terrace. He studied the dense foliage that surrounded the cottage, while letting a house in the jungle present itself to his inner eye. For a short time, an image of rippling foliage and one of two naturists cavorting among heavy orchids tried to dislodge each other; but then the two came to terms, so that the iridescent, silver-green tapestry of the leaves did nothing to interfere with the images projected onto them by Hector's mind; indeed, its shadows and the restlessness of its dull silver helped new images to life by waking change in them and offering them new forms. Hector's mind was able to create a new organ—a flying eye of the mind with which to explore the world clamoring for his attention.

Hector was reluctant to call this an 'inner world,' as he couldn't find a place within him from which it was developing.

"Now, however, Hector had matters to attend to other than the origin of images appearing against a backdrop of leaves stirring in a breeze. Transformed into a flying eye, he flew through the dense jungle like a missile—and, as a pair of mental ears was attached to the flying ear, he heard the swish of branches and large leaves as he shot by them. (Hector imagined his invention: ears protruding from each side of a round eyeball, like stunted wings.) He came to rest in a place by a group of bearded men dressed in a mix of town clothes and various military uniforms; some were cleaning rifles, others cooking broth in a large pot, others playing cards, others sleeping in the grass, their faces covered by their hats. For the moment, Hector decided not to investigate who these men-at-arms were. He allowed the eye to rise above the trees. It rose so high that the jungle took on the appearance of a soft carpet of moss; eventually, it became a green spot on a thin strip of land that wound between two blue oceans, where giant tankers could be made out as glittering dots. The mainland he was looking at was probably a chunk of Central America; way down below, the jungle with the lovers' clearing and the camp of the partisans or bandits were enclosed in a border area in the south of a tiny country composed only of a thin strip of Pacific coast.

"The flying eye sighted a few spots of gray—obviously towns. Like a predator after its prey, it swooped down headlong toward the biggest. As the eye got closer, amid the undifferentiated gray it began to make out the lines of streets; it headed for a large, gently sloping square lined with inaccessible, colonial-style palaces with closed shutters behind a latticework of balconies, before pulling up boldly a couple of feet above the square's surface, which was composed of trampled loam shining in a sun still high in the sky. The square was empty, apart from a few children and three or four dogs chasing a ball at the bottom end. The clock face on the church tower showed that it was one o'clock. After a while, a small truck drove across the deserted space, churning up the fine sand, before disappearing into one of the streets.

"Hector was finding this game with the flying eye increasingly entertaining. Having discovered that the eye could pass through walls without difficulty, he sent it to look at the insides of the palaces. The eye flew through the gloom of large rooms with hardly any furniture, and closed shutters casting light in strips across ceramic floors, tablecloths, and beds, some with sleeping figures stirring under covers. At the very center of the palaces were atria, where, on a wicker chair under a bush with large white and red flowers, was a romance novel in Spanish, open in the middle and lying spine upward.

"The entire upper side of the square was occupied by a palace with a row of high, narrow windows. The eye whizzed across the square to this palace, flying through a gap in its shutters and finding itself in a hall, the largest room it had yet visited. The floor of the hall was composed of small, square tiles; at its center was a table, around which three people were eating lunch in silence. One was a stocky man with a shiny bald head and small, shifty eyes; he was wearing an unfastened uniform jacket (like the garb of an Uhlan in an imaginary Hungary) over a sweat-soaked white undershirt. The others were a bored-looking youth with a thin mustache beneath a pointed nose, and a heavyset woman who bore a remarkable resemblance to the Queen Maria Luisa of Goya's portrait. Servants stood in a motionless line by the wall, the men in liveries, the women in the kind of black dresses and white aprons worn by French chambermaids as illustrated in nineteenth-century erotic novels. No one spoke; the only sound was the clink of silverware."

3. Magazine Office and Villa

"The eye returned to the square, rose high above the rooftops, and descended on a small square amid a jumble of narrow streets. Although this place wasn't far from the sleepy main square, life here was busy, and everything movable or flexible was in thrall to waves of restlessness. The eye slipped between stalls where men and women in wide-brimmed straw hats were offering their wares in loud voices; it swerved around buyers chattering in several Amerindian vernaculars, braying donkeys, and cars with horns blaring that were attempting to cross the square. Through an open door leading to a tiny balcony came a monotonous rattling—the tap-tap-tap of many typewriters. Flapping its ears, the eye rose above the canopies of the stalls before passing over the balcony and bursting into a room that was as busy as the square below. Young men and women were running to and fro between tables, sheets of paper in their hands, shouting across the room to one another. The typewriters clattered, the ceiling fan (which was adorned with green-and-blue maps of mold) buzzed, and the noise was intensified by an influx from the square. In the wall was an opening covered by a bead curtain which led to a second, much smaller room reminiscent of a monastic cell; apart from a bunk, this room contained only a desk, behind which sat a young man with curly black hair. The man was wearing an unbuttoned white shirt, had a cigarette in his mouth, and was bent over a pile of typewritten sheets. Although the eye flew all the way around him, it failed to catch a glimpse of his face.

"The eye flew out of the cramped little room through the beads before hovering for a while near the ceiling of the large room. Then it returned to the square and rose above flat roofs bedecked with barrels filled with rainwater and miscellaneous junk. After that, it flew to the edge of the town, where the rectangles and ovals of swimming pools shone bright blue. It swooped down toward the largest of these, finding itself on the patio of a low villa whose lines combined the temperance of European Modernism with the intimacy and melancholy of colonial architecture. It entered a room where seven elderly men sat in leather armchairs around an oblong table of polished wood. The men were silent, and they looked worried. Although their dark-skinned faces had certain Amerindian features, their suits, hairstyles, and even the way they sat tended to the European. The silence, broken only by the drone of water-filtration apparatuses and the regular calls of a bird walking along the edge of the pool, which were coming through the open door to the patio, had obviously held sway in the room for some time; the faces of those present were marked by concern about a decision they were about to take. The eye didn't wait around; it flew out of the room and high above the town again. The details of the streets dissolved into the wall of green leaves in front of Hector's cottage. The images in Hector mind's eye were slowly seeking each other out, sending out tangles of slender rhizomes that grew gradually together. Although Hector didn't yet know the whole story, he was poised to utter the first sentences. He went inside to Hella, who had fallen asleep. He sat down next to her and waited. The moment she awoke, he took her hand and began."

4. North Floriana

"The story was set in a country called North Floriana. The man in the colorful uniform was a dictator who had ruled the country for twenty years. He was taking lunch in the dining room of the presidential palace with his wife and son, whom he had earmarked as his successor. Over the years, his government had regularly alternated periods of heavy repression, in which only one daily newspaper was issued and anyone at all suspicious to the authorities was in prison or had disappeared, with periods of relative moderation. It was said, however, that the easing of repression occurred not because the mind of the president-for-life occasionally gave birth to more enlightened ideas, but due to the fact that the underground resistance had become too rampant and complex, meaning that the ministry of the interior had lost track of what was going on within it. The president and his ministers apparently reckoned that liberalization would cause many enemies of the regime to emerge from their hiding places, giving the authorities a chance to take a good look at them, and then strike against them when the moment was right.

"This was indeed how things had been up till now; enemies of the president and government had a pretty clear idea of what would happen in times of relaxation—newly permitted magazines would wrestle with censorship for a few months, before, from one day to the next, all organs of the independent press would be outlawed by presidential decree; in the coming months and years, the progress of their editors would be dependent on which list their names were on, blue, red, or black: They would be placed under house arrest, in a detention camp, or they would disappear forever without trace. But the allure of new freedoms was always so strong that few could resist them; at last, people would say, things had finally taken a turn for the better, and they would cite all kinds of reasons in defense of this claim—the president's influence was weakening, he was more sensitive to international opinion because of the weak economy, his supposedly free-thinking son was being given a say, etc. Oddly, the partisans had the most realistic view of the situation; their continuous, hopeless struggle against the president's rule, waged from their bases in the jungle, took no interest in the declaration and removal of freedoms.

"In times of repression, those remnants of opposition that had somehow avoided arrest, went underground (perhaps in a shack with a corrugated-iron roof among thousands of similar shacks in a great slum in the east of the capital, a pit with a concrete covering in the yard of a house in the country, a smelly little hotel on the edge of the wilderness, or one of many shady rooms in a patrician's palace with valuable furniture). Not only the state found the underground opposition difficult to track; so, too, did the underground opposition itself. It evolved into complex networks that lacked a center (or dozens of centers, both real and illusory, emerged and perished within them); members of one cell knew no one in neighboring cells except for two or three messengers (and as these shadowy operators weren't greatly trusted, they were often given distorted messages); a single network might comprise a highly diverse set of groups, from moderate reformers to assassins. The authorities—and, indeed, the resistance movement—struggled to understand how in circumstances that made agreement and unified leadership impossible, the opposition was more effective and capable of action than in times of relaxation. A well-aimed blow was often produced by the buzz of the many confused, contradictory, suspicious, false, and barely comprehensible commands that passed from one underground place to another, while in better times most actions dissolved in endless quarreling among factions.

"When Hector's story began, one of these more liberal spells had been in progress for two years. As was usual at such a time, the tangled lines of the underground resistance had arranged themselves into three streams, so dividing the opposition into moderates, radicals, and militants based in the jungle. The radicals gathered around the *Emerald Falcon*, a literary magazine with its office in the room above the marketplace that was visited by the flying eye; the young man bent over the stack of manuscripts was Fernando Vieta, the magazine's editor-in-chief.

"The leader of the party of moderates was his father Ernesto Vieta, a university professor of economics. This was the man the flying eye had seen at the meeting, which he had convened at his villa. Fernando and his father were estranged. Fernando had left the family home when he was seventeen, shortly after his mother's death. For a few years, he had lived in a squat in a half-wrecked house, reading Bakunin and eating soy rissoles. Not much was known about his political opinions: He always refused to participate in the kind of talk about ideology that his fellows took such delight in. Nevertheless, everyone acknowledged his leading position in the movement; Fernando was the only one able to keep the squabbling factions of radicals together, apparently because he didn't embrace the opinions of any one of them.

"The liberalization never went so far as to allow independent political magazines. This explained the large number of 'literary reviews' with little real interest in literature that emerged in each period of relaxation. It had become customary to speak of opposition politicians as 'writers,' although most of them wrote little apart from essays characterized by copious political allegory and bad style. In this sense Fernando, too, was a writer, and no one expected that he would ever write a true work of literature. So, when he published a collection of sonnets with a long title—*The Iron Rail of a Winding Staircase in a House on the Waterfront*—he caused quite a surprise, confusing the opposition and the government in equal measure. Both sides scanned Fernando's poems for secret political messages, and, as tends to happen in such instances, in the end everyone found what he was looking for, even though it was a real chore to find political meaning in melancholy and bizarrely detailed descriptions of metal ornaments on the stair rail of an old house and marks on a wall. Fernando never said anything about any of the interpretations of his work, in public or in private."

5. Martial Law and War

"The older Vieta called a meeting of leaders of the moderate party at his villa because he had received disturbing reports from several associates or bribed persons who had access to the presidential palace. All indications suggested that the authorities were again about to strike against the opposition. At the meeting, various courses of action were proposed. At first, the leaders argued about which tactics were best, until suddenly they realized how ridiculous their dispute was: Not one of the ingenious plans they had proposed stood a chance against a military force answerable only to the president. Then came the moment of quiet in which the figures formed the silent picture Hector's mental eye had seen as its flitted about the city.

"A short while later, Professor Vieta excused himself and went into the next room, where he telephoned the office of the *Emerald Falcon*, to warn his son of the danger. As he waited to hear Fernando's voice, he felt his heart pounding: He had last spoken with his son seven or eight years before. But when at last the call was taken, the voice he heard at the other end of the line was a stranger's; Fernando had just gone out somewhere, he was told. That day, the older Vieta tried several more times to reach his son, in vain. At dawn, a booming sound cut into his dreams and woke him. Ernesto Vieta knew what was happening before he opened his eyes: The caterpillar tracks of tanks were thundering through distant streets.

"Martial law was declared. The office of the *Emerald Falcon* was occupied and its staff taken to an unknown location. The older Vieta was placed under house arrest. He wasted no time in trying to discover what had happened to his son, but he found that the telephone in his villa had been disconnected. After several weeks, he was given permission to leave the villa; wherever he went, he made inquiries about his son, but no one had heard anything. There were whispers in the coffeehouses that the army had set up a detention camp for subversive elements in the arid conditions of Cormorant Bay, on the country's northern coast; even quieter voices spoke of atrocities that were said to be happening there. Many people voiced the concern that Fernando might be interned in the camp, although no one knew anything for certain, and reports were contradictory. Sometimes, the older Vieta was told that his son had succeeded in fleeing the country; at others, he heard that Fernando had gone into hiding among the partisans in the jungle. With the help of his intermediaries at the presidential palace, he attempted to achieve an audience with the minister for war. Although everyone took his money, he was told repeatedly that he would have to wait for the right time.

"The most recent liberalization had gone farther than ever before; thus the consequent repression was more severe. As a result, many more people withdrew to the jungle than usual, and the raids on garrisons in the city were bloodier and more frequent. Arms were smuggled from neighboring South Floriana, on paths that wound through the jungle or, at night, on fishing boats by sea. South Floriana had good reason to support the resistance: The two states had been in a territorial dispute for longer than anyone could remember, and the generals of South Floriana were hoping that a government in North Floriana formed by today's rebels would be forthcoming in negotiations with its wartime allies, and demonstrate its gratitude to them. The dictator of North Floriana exploited every opportunity to refer to connections between the government of South Floriana and the rebels; every day his voice boomed in the streets from loudspeakers, accusing traitors of selling their country to the enemy. The front page of the newspaper published a text purporting to be a secret agreement between rebel leaders and the government of South Floriana, which addressed the ceding of large tracts of land to the southern neighbor. Although the text was a forgery produced in a special department of North Floriana's ministry for war established for just such a purpose, rebel leaders were unnerved by it, as the forgery was pretty close in content to an actual secret agreement they had signed with the government of South Floriana.

"In the end, the army of South Floriana became directly involved in the conflict. Troops crossed the border at one of the mountain passes, and at the same time marines landed at the country's southernmost port. Allied partisan and South Floriana units seized several towns in the south, quickly and without heavy losses, eradicating all hope of victory on the government side. From this point on, government forces waged their battles in retreat, as weary troops withdrew to the capital along hot, dusty roads; less than a month later, all government troops were entrenched in suburban streets of the metropolis. After three days of fighting, the capital fell. The dictator and his family were seized from their car as they attempted to flee to the port. As to what happened to them after that, very little was written, although some interesting xeroxed photographs were passed from hand to hand; these were best ignored by people of a sensitive nature."

6. Cormorant Bay

"There was still fighting going on in some quarters of the capital when old Vieta got into his car and headed out to Cormorant Bay. He wove his way through streets clogged with tanks, armored personnel carriers, and crowds of people. On the northernmost edge of the city, he was stopped by guards wearing the uniforms of South Floriana; luckily, it turned out their commander was a former student of his. The roads to the north of the city were still quite dangerous, so the commander offered Vieta a lift to the camp in his jeep.

"The camp was made up of low barracks standing in a long row on a sweltering plain of sand and rock above the sea. The government troops had by now abandoned the place. Confused and emaciated prisoners were wandering about the scorching sands; they bore witness to the departure of the troops the day before, in a ship that had been waiting below in the harbor. They had seen the troops loading some heavy crates aboard; presumably, these contained documents they hadn't succeeded in burning and intended to dispose of at sea.

"The professor asked all the prisoners about Fernando. Many of them had met him in the camp. Vieta discovered that his son had arrived there the very day martial law had been imposed. But none of the prisoners knew what had become of him. This was an ominous sign: Vieta was told that prisoners would be driven away in trucks that later returned to the camp empty. Eventually, he managed to find a man named Pablo, with whom his son had worked for several weeks in the depot. He had Pablo lead him there. From the outside, the depot building looked like all the other barracks, except that it had no windows. Professor Vieta walked about a long, dark room whose floor was covered with battered crates, iron bars, clamps, and large balls of wire. He walked right to the end, where there was a view of wide-open gates, forming a rectangular screen on which were projected the glowing yellow sand and the rock. The sunbeams that penetrated the room carried in a fine, whirling sand. The tin roof over Vieta's head was incandescent; it was incomprehensible to him that anyone could bear the heat in there for longer than five minutes. The prisoner waited in front of the depot. Vieta rejoined him and he explained that Fernando had struggled most with the fact that he was prevented from writing. He never complained about anything else; all those weeks Fernando spent in the sweltering depot he thought of nothing but literature, it was as if nothing else had any importance for him. He once confided in Pablo that in his last weeks of freedom he had planned a novel. Pablo knew that Fernando's only desire in the camp was to write his novel.

"But writing was strictly forbidden. The camp warders took pains to ensure that no prisoner ever came by the merest scrap of paper or anything that could be used as a writing implement. Once, Fernando managed to steal several blank record sheets, which had escaped the attentions of the warders because they were printed on both sides and as such not considered fit for use as writing paper. After this, Fernando would get up early, before reveille; guided by the first cold rays of the sun to appear over the barracks, he would use a nail in place of pencil or pen, inscribing his text into the forms. Then he would he bury the lacerated sheets in the sand behind the depot. Someone informed on him, however, and an officer forced Fernando at gunpoint to dig up all the papers and burn them. His punishment was a week in the darkness of the solitary-confinement cell.

"Fernando without pen and paper reminded Pablo of a narcomaniac whose drugs had been taken away. Often, Pablo would catch Fernando in front of the depot with a piece of metal piping in his hand, carving in the sand letters that were immediately smoothed away by the wind; or he would find him scribbling something invisible on a wall with his finger. After a while, Pablo was put to work elsewhere; he never saw Fernando again.

"Some days later, the Conservative Party held its first conference, at which Professor Vieta was elected party leader. Thanks to the work connected with his new position, he was sometimes distracted from thoughts of Fernando, but every time the telephone rang he felt sick with fear that the call might bear tidings of the discovery of his son's body. But the body of Fernando Vieta was never found.

"Although the leaders of the partisans and radicals were in the majority in the provisional parliament, their disagreements ran so deep that they failed to agree on a common candidate for president. Thus it happened that the race was won with relative ease by Ernesto Vieta, the candidate proposed by the Conservative Party, whom no one had taken too seriously to begin with. Vieta spent most of his time in the presidential palace, working long into the night, then pacing the empty corridors and meeting the ghost of his son, or standing on the palace balcony looking down at the sand of the empty square as it shone in the moonlight."

7. Wire in the Sea

"On a yacht at anchor by a belt of small islands off the coast of North Floriana, within view of the mainland, a group of students from the capital saw in the new year together. They had diving gear with them, and on the first day of the new year, after a night of champagne and fireworks, they swam down to inspect a coral reef whose many colors and shapes were illuminated by rays of sunlight that penetrated the warm, shallow sea. One of the students separated from the others and went deeper, into some kind of gorge that opened before him. In the beam of his flashlight, he saw tentacles wriggling about, then big, round, staring eyes and a flash of grooved fins. He was suddenly aware of a dark, twisted line, which continually vanished and reappeared amid the pink and white feelers of the anemones. The lone diver thrust his hand in among the pulsating anemones and felt the hardness of metal. What he was holding appeared to be wire; lifting it out of the bed of anemones, he

saw that the twists in the wire described carefully shaped letters of the alphabet. He bent to read, with astonishment, the
following: *As Richard's car plunged toward the green hillside of
the Chapultepec, a dark figure holding a submachine gun leaned
out of the back window. There were three flashes and the sound
of three short bursts of gunfire.* As the student began carefully
to extricate the wire from the stinging jungle of anemones, he
witnessed the flight on uncertain little legs of a school of small,
translucent shrimp that lived among them. There were places
where he had to tear the wire away from shells that had become
affixed to it. The wire seemed to have no end; in the flashlight
beam above the rippling anemones, more and more words and
sentences presented themselves. There in a rift in the coral reef,
the amazed diver read a story about a car chase through the
streets of Mexico City—a fragment of some kind of wire-book
thriller. Several meters in, he came to a place where the wire
was knotted and clogged with aquatic plant life. His touch provoked a soundless, dreamlike explosion—a school of fish of the
widest variety colors and shapes that had made a nest in the
tangle of wire, pursued in a dignified march by a hermit crab
in its shell. After this, the diver followed the wire in the other
direction and found another knot; here, too, was a confusion
of wire sentences in which fish, sea snails, and small crustaceans
had made their home. The wire was fractured in several places;
around the knot and in among the anemones there were several
smaller broken-off fragments.

"The student called his friends, and together they pulled
the wire out of the water and laid it on the deck next to empty
champagne bottles. Boys and girls in diving kits and swimwear
grouped together around the undersea wire text, the words of
which were plugged with seaweed, shells, and thrashing fish.
The wind had dropped, and the surface of the sea was still,
like a great floor of smooth blue stone. The students began to

tidy up the wire, pulling out aquatic plants whose long flexible stalks had woven themselves into its bends, tearing off mollusks that clung to it. As the debris of the sea was stripped away, the rusty curves that came into view in the radiant sunlight revealed themselves as fragments of wire sentences about the torments of love and hate, of ecstasy and humiliation, of demons and man-made men, of despair; then there were sentences describing gunfights and car chases, and others describing the torpid atmosphere of a roadside motel and then a stuffy hotel in some big city. The students succeeded in working one of the ends of the wire free; it comprised the sentence *Diamanta disappeared behind the low rocks that lined the coast,* and a little further along, the word *Finis.* To all appearances, this was the end of the text. The students turned immediately to the second great knot of wire and groped about in its damp and greasy innards; it wasn't long before one of the girls pulled out the other end. The students cleaned off the slime to reveal the words *The Captive,* which were written in letters somewhat larger than the rest of the text. After the last letter of the second word the wire ran straight for about ten centimeters before forming the next two words: These gave a name that all the students recognized, that of Fernando Vieta. Everyone was now aware that they were looking at a sort of title page, bearing the title of this work and the name of its author. What they had found in the sea was a book, a book such as had never been seen before, a book written in wire by the national martyr, the son of the President, during his time in the detention camp.

"The students decided to stop their work: The wire was so badly corroded they were afraid they might damage it. By evening of the same day, the tangle of wire sentences, still scented by the sea and covered with the corpses of tiny marine creatures, was on the carpet of the President's study. Ernesto Vieta sat next to it, running the ends of his fingers along words the hands of his son had fashioned in wire in the unbearable heat of the depot; the father, too, was afraid to straighten out the brittle wire. Fernando had succeeded in outwitting his warders after all: There in the camp he had found something that was at once pen and paper. Ernesto remembered seeing in the dim light of the depot coils of wire scattered about. Obviously, it had occurred to Fernando to use the wire as a solid ink, an ink that need not be applied to paper or any other base. The President imagined his son in a corner of the depot, patiently performing the endless task of bending the wire into a long string of words. Perhaps he didn't even bother to hide it, left it scattered about the depot for everyone to see; it would never cross a soldier's mind that this jumble harbored a work of literature. In all likelihood, the wire text had been noticed only at the end of the war, by one of the commanders, when all documents were being destroyed. It had been loaded on a ship along with everything else that needed to be disposed of and thrown into the sea. Professor Vieta imagined Fernando's joy at managing to complete his work despite the guards' attentions. He tried to fix in his imagination the expression of bliss on Fernando's face, but it was so many years since he had seen his son that he couldn't guess at what he must have looked like then. All that came to him was the face of a ten-year-old boy."

8. Conservation Institute

"The wire was entrusted to the restorers. For the next three months, they tended to it and treated it with oils; painstakingly, centimeter by centimeter they opened it out on the floor of the great hall of the State Conservation Institute. As Fernando's text was gradually revealed, the restorers were taken aback by what they read. But it was not their task to criticize the President's son's novel, so during their regular meetings with the elder Vieta they kept their feelings to themselves. They proposed to the President that his son's work should be cut up into lines, each about a meter in length, making it possible to set it on panels, each of which would form a page of a great book. But the President would not permit such a drastic modification. So the unfolded, restored segments of wire text were placed along the wall of the Institute's main hall, which was circular, and gradually arranged in a spiral which revolved inward and whose outer perimeter more or less matched the circumference of the circular hall, which was thirty meters in diameter. The scents of the sea gradually faded, to be replaced by the smells of conserving agents.

"Every day the President made time to have himself driven over to the Institute, where he would see how the work was progressing. On each visit, he would kneel and read over and over the passage that had been revealed since the previous day. On some days there would be a whole meter of newly restored text, on others just twenty centimeters. Images from Fernando's work would settle in his brain and then present themselves with painful insistence during governmental meetings; wire sentences would appear with the clarity of a hallucination between the lines of pages of dossiers prepared for his attention. This made it difficult for him to concentrate on his work; with increasing frequency he left the handling of affairs of state to his advisors. Complaints about his idleness proliferated. But at this time all the newspapers ran daily updates about the salvage of the wire manuscript of the President's son, a man tortured to death by the previous regime. This moving story aroused great sympathy and love for the President, not least among the lower classes, who, until recently, had regarded him with perfect indifference. For sale in the markets, in among pictures of the saints and figurines of Our Lady of Guadalupe, there were now statues and color-print portraits of the President and his son. Young people wore T-shirts bearing portraits of both Vietas. Such a ground-swell of sentiment was useful for the Conservative Party, and it served to strengthen the government, which in the chaos of the immediate post-war period had been quite unstable. Not even the opposition, composed of members of the radical parties and former partisans, dared challenge too openly a President so beloved by his people.

"The nation was impatient for the restorers to finish their work. All but the President and the team of seven restorers were expecting a great work that addressed the struggle for freedom from tyranny—a work that would yield passages for recital on festive and ceremonial occasions and sentences to be chiseled into the plinths of monuments. The President forbade all outsiders from entering the Institute until work had been completed. Although every evening the Institute was thronged with journalists who thrust microphones at anyone departing the building, the restorers were silent about what was slowly emerging from the submarine tangle, thus keeping their promise to the President.

"Restoration work was still in progress when Vieta announced he would build a mausoleum with an empty tomb as a symbol of his son's remains. The mausoleum would also contain a room that would be the final resting place of the original wire book. All the publishing houses battled for the right to publish *The Captive*; after long deliberation, the President granted permission to the Golden Age Press. The contract stipulated that the book would be published in three forms: The first would be the usual means for reading works of literature, the second a facsimile edition of the wire original, in which the lines of pages would be reproductions of segments of wire, the third a single page in the form of a long strip of paper that would bear a facsimile of the wire text in unbroken flow. The paper strip of the third of these editions would be rolled up and attached at each end to a roller; in the manner of ancient scrolls, reading would progress across the page from one roller to the other.

"By the beginning of August, the last section of wire was restored; on the floor of the hall of the Institute Fernando's book lay in an almost perfect spiral. Its last turn, into the sentence *Diamanta disappeared behind the low rocks that lined the coast*, took it to what was practically the dead center of the room. After the word Finis, there was a space in the shape of an irregular circle about twenty centimeters in diameter. Regrettably, the wire was broken in several places. The President had three expeditions of professional divers sent to the coral reef, and these succeeded in fishing out from among the anemones a few more sentence fragments. But some of the missing pieces were never recovered. Soon all three versions of the book were published in a print run of many thousands. On the day of publication, lines formed in front of the bookshops before first light. By evening, the book was sold out, and the publishers began planning the next edition."

9. A Nation Reads *The Captive*

"But the book was received with disappointment and consternation. Instead of the novel about the struggle for freedom so keenly anticipated by readers, what appeared was a tale so strange that no one could make much sense of it. Indeed, it was no easy matter to establish its genre; it was set in 2001—which was then still the future—like *A Space Odyssey* before it, so eventually the critics decided it was science fiction. Still, the incomprehensibility and oddity of Fernando's novel was in no way detrimental to the Vieta cult of the father and the son as it existed among the people: These qualities belonged in the world of the sacral, for the Vieta cult had taken on something of a religious character. In the villages and slums that skirted the cities, *The Captive* went unread (nor would anyone there have read a novel about the national struggle for freedom), but newspaper cuttings containing extracts from Fernando's novel were pinned to household altars, next to pictures of the President and his son. When people there read, syllable by syllable, the incomprehensible sentences, they found the text was not entirely without meaning: The readers invested them with veneration, love, and hope.

"The reaction of the educated classes was far less favorable. Intellectuals had imagined a great personal theme (probably love) woven through scenes from the revolutionary struggle. The motif of subjugation suggested by the work's title was indeed present, as was the motif of love, but the account of the hero's yearning for freedom and the story of his amours had little in common with what the impatient intellectuals had imagined. It was as though Fernando had known what his readers were expecting and was making fun of them. The educated classes would have been accepting of the work had it been composed of a formless, difficult stream of interior monologue that broke down the contours of things, connections between elements of plot, and the unity of character; it would then have been a simple matter to declare the book *a modernist work* and thus assign it to a familiar category. Nor would it have been difficult to ideologize such a work of modernism—by declaring it a protest against the classical forms of art promoted by the previous regime, a representation of the struggle for freedom of expression within the national struggle for greater freedoms. But Fernando's wire was bent into chains of words in classically constructed clauses, in which were set out long, detailed descriptions of characters and places, together forming a strange but completely coherent story. In bending the wire into thousands and thousands of words, Fernando had surely cut his fingers to shreds; the writing of the book must have caused him unspeakable pain. Many of his readers imagined the bloodied hands forming word after word in the sweltering heat of the depot, and they said to themselves, 'Why did he suffer so for *such a thing as this?*' Few of them read *The Captive* to the end."

10. Critical Opinion

"The literary critics were as bewildered by the book as everyone else. But their profession demanded that they be able to write something about anything; polite reviews began to appear in newspapers and literary magazines close to the Conservative party. Some of these praised the novel for the elegance of its form, others forced some underlying message on it; typically, the critic would use his closing paragraph to express regret that the tragic circumstances attending the book's creation had not permitted the author to address its deficiencies in the final version and make of it a truly exceptional work. In this way, the reviewers made clear they did not, in fact, think very highly of *The Captive*. And their hypocrisy was founded on a fallacy: To all appearances, the work was properly finished and its author had reworked it thoroughly to make it so. It was possible to straighten and re-bend the wire in the act of revision, and the state of the wire testified that Fernando had performed many such rewrites and deletions in the search for expressions that at first escaped him.

"Critics of magazines supportive of the previous regime thought it in slightly poor taste to write unfavorable reviews of a book whose author had been a victim of a dictatorship under which they themselves had prospered, so they expressed a hypocritical regret for the fact that the young writer had been unable to develop his talent to the fullest. Typically, such a reviewer would make this position clear in his very first paragraph; this allowed him to devote the remainder of the article to an enumeration of the work's perceived shortcomings. It must have been a pleasant task to describe in detail how the son of the current president, whom the reviewer detested and who in turn held him in open contempt, was a bad writer.

"So it was that the wire book from the bottom of the sea became first a subject of incomprehension and indifference, then of weary debate that excited no one, not even those taking part. Above all, this debate provided a forum for declarations of loyalty, spiteful taunts, the settling of old scores, toadying, exhibitionism, the repairing of reputations, ridicule, and several other, similar demonstrations of foolishness and immorality. Perhaps someone could be found who was able to read the book without prejudice—a young person with no interest in the conflicts of his father's generation and no desire to understand them, for example. But young people had no wish to read a work that had become—its incomprehensibility notwithstanding—the official book of the regime merely because its author was the son of the current president and a hero of the resistance. Perhaps the only person in the whole of North Floriana able to read Fernando's book for what it was, to understand it, to realize that the work was a crystalline growth of images born of the borderlands between the realms of nothingness and sense, was an old man who was indifferent to political discord. Such a person, however, if indeed he existed, did not step forward to bear witness to his reading.

"But the governing party was loath to give up on the work of a national hero who had died in the struggle for freedom. By the circumstances of its genesis the work was bound to become a tool of propaganda; its actual content was of no great importance. It was necessary only to find in it some sentences and phrases that could be used when honors of state were being conferred, that could be chiseled into the plinths of memorials. These sentences and phrases were easily found: Any phrase chiseled into marble will take on the meaning we require of it. Fernando's father was not resistant to such interpretations; although he knew them to be a violation of his son's work, he also knew that this violation was of no account; in the depot, Fernando must have foreseen the fate awaiting his book if ever the wire should be found, and without doubt he would have been utterly indifferent to it. But the elder Vieta, like everyone else, was mistaken in his view of the book. Although he knew the text of his son's novel by heart, he read it as a testimony that replaced his lost memories. In the cadences of its sentences he distinguished Fernando's movements, gestures, and facial expressions, all of which he had known and forgotten; out of the flow of language there emerged, albeit faintly, other gestures he had never known. Thus, the currents and forces of language begot a false image of the son that he had never known.

"Marius thought that Hector was describing the reactions of different people to a work whose content remained unknown, remarking that this was a technique favored by Henry James, whose work he enjoyed. But Hella smiled at this, saying Hector didn't resort to such intricate tricks; he had a simpler style of storytelling. After relating how *The Captive* was received by different groups of North Floriana's population, he had dutifully retold Hella Fernando Vieta's entire novel—except for those parts whose wire records hadn't been found. (Although Hector was a classic storyteller who saw into the mind of his characters, not even he could see beneath the sand of the Pacific Ocean, where the lost pieces of Fernando's wire lay.) Hella remarked how strange it was that Hector and Fernando's 1960s science fiction resembled the world of today; many of their predictions had come to pass, although some of the more fantastical motifs (such as the industrial production of artificial humans) were as yet unrealized. For some reason, Hector had never wanted to return to the story he had invented for Hella at the time of her illness, and he had refused to write it down. Hella had told the story to several of her friends, however. She confessed to Marius that in the part with the description of Fernando's novel, she had gradually introduced certain modern inventions that hadn't existed at the time she had heard the story from Hector, even if Hector's ideas had run them close. Marius was impatient for Hella to get on with the story, and he asked her to do so."

The Captive I

1. The Building

"Hella explained that the world described by Fernando Vieta in his novel was remarkably similar to our present, differing from it only in two fundamental ways: that it had achieved a far higher level of artificial intelligence, so that the production of artificial humans was spreading across the entire planet, and that the demons of ancient religions and fairy tales, previously considered beings of myth and fable, had recently been proved to exist. The literary critics of North Floriana were pretty irritated by these two motifs; it wouldn't have bothered them if Vieta had written a tale of classic science fiction, a story about demons, or even a mix of the two, but they had no idea how to approach a story in which both motifs were woven, entirely inappropriately, into an otherwise realistic narrative, which would, they believed, have managed perfectly well without them.

"The novel began in an unnamed metropolis somewhere in the northwest United States. Its main character, Leo, was thirty-two years old and for the past ten years had been happily married to Patricia, whom he had started dating at high school; they were still childless. Throughout his childhood and into his high-school years, Leo had wanted to be a painter; he had been admitted to the academy of art, but after a year decided to switch to design. At the time the action of the novel began, Leo was a successful, well-known interior designer. In the mail one day he received a letter whose envelope bore a simple depiction of a dolphin jumping out of the sea; the space between the curved body of the dolphin and the sea was filled by a semi-circular rising sun and five sunbeams. This image was known to Leo just as it was to millions of people worldwide. It was the logo of the Dolphin company, seen in many countries on multiple continents on the front of huge concrete halls, most of them near big cities. Each hall contained hundreds of workers seated at long tables, assembling computer parts. In recent years, Dolphin had invested huge sums in the development of artificial intelligence, becoming one of the first companies to reduce the production costs for robots (some of which were indistinguishable from humans) to such a degree that wealthier households could afford to buy them.

"Edward Willis, Dolphin's owner, was a local man. A few years earlier, he built in the city a large trade and administration complex, known simply as the Building. Leo remembered the opening ceremony, when amid all the speeches Willis had declared that the Building was his gift to the city that he had grown up in and launched his career. Since Willis moved Dolphin's head office into the Building, so few people had actually seen it (rumor had it that it comprised only three rooms appointed with antique furniture) that there was some doubt as to which part of the Building it was in. Perhaps Willis was capable of commissioning only colossal buildings, which was why he had bought and demolished a large area of housing and had the Building raised in its place. The Building was a maze of walkways with many terraces and suspended galleries whose spaces were laced together by horizontal and diagonal bridges, glass tunnels, and escalators. From down below, all these unmoored passages and the innumerable rows of lights with which they were set came together and crossed, forming star-shaped ornaments. Pressed against the walls were broad tubes of glass in which cylindrical elevators moved up and down constantly, like connecting rods in a piston engine. Anyone walking through the passages could watch the ongoing interplay of patches of pale color—reflected from the neon signs of stores on bars—on the smooth marble surfaces and the glass of the walls. The first-floor arcades and lower galleries contained restaurants and bars, cafés, cinemas, theaters, and luxury boutiques; the upper stories housed the offices of lawyers, realtors, and various other businesses. In several places, the passages opened out into vast halls that ended in vaulted metal grating fitted with a sheet of thick, greenish glass.

"The letter in the envelope comprised only two computer-printed lines, with a request for a meeting. The signature was a single word: *Willis*. Naturally, Leo hoped that the matter was a commission, and as it was inadvisable to stall over an offer of work from one of the richest people on the planet, he immediately called the telephone number given in the letter. Having introduced himself to a courteous male voice presumably belonging to one of Willis's secretaries, Leo was asked to present himself at five o'clock that afternoon in the main hall of the Building, by the door immediately adjacent to the window of a famous jewelry store. Leo was so impatient for the meeting that he couldn't do anything that day; by half-past four, he was standing at the appointed place, hopping from foot to foot. It took him a while to find the door; there was no sign or name-plate on it, nor even a lock or a handle. The only indication of a door there was given by four slits in the smooth marble wall. At five o'clock precisely, Leo watched as a rectangle of marble, bounded by the slits, moved backward slightly and then slid silently into the wall. To his great surprise, Leo found himself looking at a small room with purple wallpaper and a large mirror above a sofa with purple cushions. To the left of the sofa was a round marble table on a single slender leg, bearing a decanter and cognac glasses. To the right stood a dark-skinned young man in a tailcoat, his straight black hair slicked neatly back. It occurred to Leo that the symmetry of the scene made the young man look like a painted statue. Only after noticing long vertical rows of mother-of-pearl pushbuttons that stood out from the wallpaper did he realize that he was standing in front of an elevator. He stepped inside and the door closed behind him, again without a sound, drowning the noise of the passage. With a gesture in which only his head and his right hand stirred, the man in the tailcoat invited Leo to sit on the sofa; then he pushed the button at the very top; as soon as the elevator was in motion, the man froze, his hands on his belly.

"It occurred to Leo that the man in the tailcoat might be one of the artificial beings produced in Willis's factories. He sat on the soft, gently vibrating sofa as closed doors passed before his eyes; in the upper stories, the elevator was freed from its opaque shell into a glass tube; now Leo saw below him the green vaults of the halls looking like walls of great aquaria, and he remembered how prodigiously high the metal ribbing had appeared to him from the passage below. He was excited by the prospect of finding himself in Willis's mysterious office. Now that he was at last seeing the Building for the first time as a whole, he realized how it was arranged. Its inner part was enclosed within a ring of structures that were much taller. From the street, Leo had often looked at the Building's outer belt; its structures were of different heights, their relations banishing any thought of regularity—it seemed that the architect had wished to give the Building the appearance from a distance of the ruined walls of a giant castle in outline. One of the structures jutted high above all others, making it reminiscent of a watchtower built into a stronghold; Leo looked for this now, but he couldn't identify it. Then he realized that the elevator was rising along its wall."

2. Glass Nest

"The elevator came to a soft halt and its doors opened. Leo stepped out into a smallish, windowless hall. Dim light from its vintage chandelier glittered on the dark-green veined marble with which its walls and ceiling were lined. Leo turned and saw that there was nothing but marble wall behind him now; it took him a while to find the slits that marked the edges of the door he had just walked through. A simple low fountain, also of marble, was built into the facing wall; Leo heard nothing but the murmur of the fountain's gradually fraying and dwindling streams as they worked their way through a cascade of five bowls before landing in a shallow pool. On either side of the fountain were black leather sofas. Leo had just reached the tentative decision to sit down on one of these when a rectangle of dazzling white light appeared in the wall to his left. Out of this luminous deluge stepped a tall female figure. Smiling, she gave Leo her hand.

"Leo recognized her immediately as Vanessa, Willis's twenty-eight-year-old daughter—and it dawned on him that the signature on the letter wasn't necessarily that of Edward Willis. Two weeks earlier, in a dentist's waiting room, he had sifted through a pile of well-thumbed magazines that lay on the table, finding a photo of Vanessa in almost every one of them; Vanessa Willis at a garden party, Vanessa Willis at a ball, Vanessa Willis at the premiere of an opera . . . Vanessa told him that she admired his work and would be delighted if he would agree to design the interior of her apartment, which occupied the entire top floor of the Building's highest tower. She led him through the rooms around its edge. The nucleus of the apartment comprised a few artificially lit rooms; Vanessa explained that these contained the quarters of the domestic staff, various technical facilities, a kitchen, and pantries. The Building was set in a steel structure, to which the outside walls were hung—this frame made all-glass walls a possibility. Leo passed through a room whose only wall

was a cloudy sky that looked like some fantastical, ever-changing wallpaper. He was falling under the spell of this glass nest
high above the roofs of the city, and he was also increasingly
enchanted by the woman who inhabited these luminous spaces,
apparently alone. Judging by the photos he had seen of her in
magazines, he had always imagined Willis's only daughter to be a
superficial snob—but as she guided him through rooms flooded
with soft light, asked for his opinion, and listened attentively to
his answers, he told himself that he had been swayed by silly
prejudices about billionaires' daughters, and that Vanessa was
in fact a modest, amiable, educated woman.

"From top to bottom, the glass walls were filled with dreary
sky (in this city, the sky was almost always overcast), but when
Leo stepped right up to the glass, the rooftops way below
appeared to him like gray floes. In one of the rooms, Vanessa
asked Leo's opinion of a fashionable glass vase for which she
had obviously paid a large sum; unable to lie, Leo told her that
he found it ugly. Without saying anything, Vanessa picked the
vase up, dropped it, and looked with satisfaction at the shards
on the floor; then she went to the desk and pressed a green
button on its top. (Leo had noticed similar buttons in many
places in the apartment.) Almost immediately, a dark-skinned,
tailcoated athlete appeared. He so much resembled the man
in the elevator that for a moment Leo assumed they were one
and the same. Vanessa ordered the man to clear up the shards
before turning to Leo and informing him that she was willing
to destroy every object in the apartment that displeased him.

"With a smile Leo said that this wouldn't be necessary: He
would be happy for about a third of the objects to remain.
When their tour brought them to a desk of dark polished wood,
Vanessa stopped, opened one of the drawers, drew out a check-
book, and wrote out a check. She handed this to Leo, saying
that of course it was only a down payment; the sum she had

entered was appreciably higher than Leo considered a good fee for the whole job. Vanessa insisted on one condition only—that Leo work right there in her apartment; she was looking forward to watching him at work, and she would have one of her rooms made into a studio for him."

3. Leo in the Tower

"So Leo spent the coming days in Vanessa's glass tower. As the soft, cold light and changing patches of cloud had come to dominate the life of every object in the apartment, he decided that the furniture he brought to the room would submit to its rule; he placed tall, slim objects in simple shapes and bright colors (vases, plant pots, and lamps) against the windows and watched them soar into the changing sky; at the back of the room he placed rounded, segmented closets of polished wood, whose surfaces transmitted the dance of the light deep into the room. At first, he asked Vanessa's consent for his every suggestion, but as she refused him nothing, he gave up this practice. As Leo was also well known as a fashion designer, Vanessa asked him to design some homewear for her; he came up with a simple, loose-fitting dress in orange silk. It gave him pleasure to see a bright-orange figure moving against the gray surfaces, as if walking along the shore of a cold sea; when she came to rest, she looked like one of the tall vases he had placed in the apartment. At moments such as this, Leo told himself he would miss his work in the tower once it was over. As the silence in the tower was absolute—no city noise reached this far, the manservants didn't speak, and the sound of footsteps was absorbed by the carpets—when Vanessa came to see how his work was progressing, Leo heard the swish of silk from the next room already.

"The athletic manservants in their dark suits and white

shirtfronts moved about the living spaces like characters in a silent movie, before disappearing into the enclosed center of the apartment, where Leo never went. There might have been six, seven, nine, or even twelve of them: Leo was constantly mixing them up, and he never succeeded in counting them. Like the genies of Arabian fairy tales, one would appear at the door of any given room almost as soon as Vanessa pressed one of her numerous green buttons, which must have set a light flashing in one of the inner rooms. Leo looked on in amazement as they performed even the dirtiest servant's work in their black suits and white shirts. Once, he asked Vanessa if the manservants weren't by any chance automatons produced by her family's company; Vanessa laughed at this, saying there was no doubt that they were live humans. When Leo wondered aloud why they didn't find more dignified work, Vanessa replied: 'They receive a higher salary than the directors of Father's factories.'

"Every morning at nine, the elevator, operated by the silent, motionless manservant, would arrive for Leo. He was always waiting in the hall, eagerly looking forward to the rapid, soundless glide of the elevator and the moment it would shoot out of the darkness and he would see spread out below, like an enclosed city suspended in air, the roofs, glass vaults, towers, covered terraces, projections, and depressions of the Building; this enclosed city was completely hidden from the outside world by the belt of outer structures. He also looked forward to the opening of the elevator door, when an ever-smiling Vanessa would come to greet him, just as he looked forward to his work in spaces flooded with a calm light that fell across the papers on his desk and, so it seemed to him, whispered to him its dreams and guided his hand as he drew. Often, he would remain in the glass tower when his working day was over, and he and Vanessa would discuss the day's drawings over a glass of wine. Before long, their conversations were no longer confined to the appointing of the apartment. One evening, Vanessa confessed to him that she was writing a book; it would mean a lot to her if he would listen to a few pages and give her his opinion on them. Leo awkwardly agreed; it turned out that Vanessa's creation was a psychological novel set on a large ship sailing from Europe to America, its protagonists a thirty-eight-year-old divorcée, her seventeen-year-old daughter, and a ship's officer. Although Leo's understanding of literature wasn't great and he struggled to grasp the plot, he gave the novel vague praise, which seemed to satisfy his client."

4. Celebrating a Birthday

"His praise had an unfortunate consequence: From then on, Vanessa read to him from her work practically every day. Soon, Leo was bothered by having to feign interest in it; besides, Vanessa was keeping him from his work, an increasing nuisance. He realized he was becoming irritated by other things she did, too—the way she would constantly stop by his office, her permanent smile, her admiration for everything he said . . . At the same time, he told himself that this irritation was unjust, and in trying to treat her kindly, he praised the novel more and more, even though he barely listened to her readings and thought about his work instead. One day, Vanessa asked him to stay with her a little longer: It was her twenty-ninth birthday, and she was having a small party. This was inconvenient for Leo, who had arranged to go to the cinema with Patricia and in any case wasn't in the mood for company; the thought of having to converse with strangers put him out of humor. Yet he saw how important it was to Vanessa that he stayed, so he called his wife and explained that he was forced to stay longer at the Building.

"At seven o'clock, a manservant came to Leo's desk and led

him away to one of the rooms. Vanessa sat at the end of a table in a long, iridescent green dress and a necklace of large pearls. It was dark beyond the window, and the room was lit by a crystal chandelier whose reflection hovered like a strange spaceship in the night sky behind Vanessa's back. To Leo's surprise and dis-comfiture, the table was set for two people only. He asked where the others were; Vanessa told him she had invited no one else. The conversation stalled, and Leo's discomfiture increased. He found himself waiting for the moment when he could go home without his departure giving offense to his client. Vanessa had decided to hold a seafood banquet, and the manservant brought to the table platters of octopus, cuttlefish, shrimps, mussels, oysters, and lobster. Leo wasn't keen on deep-sea creatures, and as he looked down at the dead bodies on the platters, he thought of nature's irresponsibility and stupidity in experiment-ing with unstructured tentacles and external skeletons; nature could only be excused these experiments because it preferred to hide its results underwater. He impaled pieces of food with his fork and put them into his mouth; the incomprehensible tastes of these invertebrates were repellent to him, and he swallowed the food only with great effort.

"He had just placed the small, soft body of a shrimp peeled from its shell in his mouth when he saw that Vanessa had laid down her fork and risen from the table, and that now she was walking toward him. Moments later, she knelt and laid her head in his lap. Leo was so surprised and frightened that he forgot to chew and swallow the shrimp on his tongue. Lifting her face to look into his, Vanessa told him in her usual, calm voice that she loved him. In the bowl right next to her head, a brick-red crab lay staring at him, its eyes on stalks. With an uncomprehending, silly expression, Leo gazed back at the two faces. To his dismay, Vanessa took hold of his arms and pulled herself up in stages; when her face appeared next to Leo's, she attached herself by the lips to his mouth. Leo was frozen to the spot. On Vanessa's lips he tasted a salty, tart reminder of oyster drizzled with lemon; he had the fleeting thought that the creature pressed up against him was herself a life form from the sea, which had risen from the deep at the head of the company of the creatures on the table. And it crossed his mind that the shrimp in his mouth, which Vanessa's insistent tongue was now trying to reach by forcing itself through his pursed lips and clenched teeth, was a marine worm that had climbed from Vanessa's mouth to his; at that moment he was entirely incapable of swallowing it, but in such a situation it was obviously unthinkable that he should spit it out. In his panic, he imagined the creatures on the table joining their mistress in forcing themselves against him; they would get under his clothes and crawl about his bare body.

"Leo's growing horror and disgust were compounded by the fact the manservant stood in the room, in his usual attitude of respect, for the duration of the silent scene. It seemed to Leo that the scene lasted an inordinately long time. At last, Vanessa slid away from him and returned to her seat. Before starting on the lobster that lay in front of her, she apologized for her behavior, and using the tone she employed when discussing with him his furniture designs, she said that although she loved him as she had never loved before, and had felt compelled to let him know it, she would never bother him with her feelings again; she wouldn't wish for what had happened to be a cause of tension in their relationship, and she hoped that things between them would be just as they had been before. Leo stammered words to the effect that he wasn't angry with her. Although he felt like an idiot, he was reassured that the terrifying sea creature Vanessa had turned into had apparently gone away. In the elevator, Leo felt distinctly awkward in the presence of its manservant operator, although he saw in the mirror that the man's face bore the same expression as always. He relaxed only when the door of the elevator had closed behind him."

5. Game

"On waking the next morning and realizing he would have to go to Vanessa's, Leo felt queasy. He remembered how he had felt as a child on the morning of a school day when one of his transgressions would surely be investigated. But Vanessa treated him amiably once again, repeating her apology the moment he arrived, saying that she had drunk more than she was used to, and that she was sorry if she had spoiled the evening for him. Over the next few days, their relationship returned to how it had been, with the bonus that Vanessa didn't distract Leo from his work or read to him from her novel. Neither of them mentioned the scene at the birthday party. Within a week, Leo again looked forward to going to work at the Building.

"One day, Vanessa came running into Leo's office. She had something to tell him: Her novel had been accepted by a publisher. She explained that this turn of events meant a great deal to her, and she would like to celebrate it with Leo. Before he could respond, she laid a hand on his shoulder and said with a smile that there was nothing for him to worry about. Leo was in a good mood; he laughingly assured her that he wasn't worried in the least. Again the party comprised just two of them, with a manservant in attendance. They sat across from each other at a small table set right against a glass wall, beyond which the night sky was starless. This time, there were no mollusks and crustaceans on the table, nor did Vanessa transform into a phantom from the sea. The mood of the dinner was relaxed from the beginning; Vanessa even made a joke about her love, and Leo couldn't help but be flattered. Both had more than enough to drink, and so it happened that they found themselves leaning over the empty bottles on the table and kissing; it may even have been Leo's elbows that were the first to cross the dangerous divide in the middle of the table, toward which each had been working for two hours. It was as though their kisses were part of a game of dare, played by friends of opposite sexes at high school. The game was made more amusing by their having to stand up from their chairs for their faces to touch, their bodies forming a wobbly arch over the clinking bottles. The somewhat drunken undressing that followed was filled with laughter. Leo began to wonder how far their game would go.

"Vanessa ordered the manservant to turn out the lights; then she asked Leo if she should send the man away. Leo knew that she was doing this for his own sake only; for her, the presence of the servant was probably no more significant than the presence of furniture. But in his drunkenness Leo was delighted by the presence in the dark depths of the room of a white-shirtfronted figure who saw the silhouettes of their naked bodies in front of a glass wall, at whose lower edge the luminous haze of the city glowed; it heightened his joy in the game, which was like a return to his first erotic explorations and adventures. Now he was sorry that by marrying so young he had left the world of unforeseen encounters with unfamiliar girls' bodies; in his embrace with Vanessa, he felt that he was experiencing at least an echo of this almost forgotten world. He was grateful that Vanessa didn't speak of love; perhaps she sensed Leo's thoughts and fears and was keen to accommodate them, and indeed her effort to prove that this was all part of a jolly, frivolous adventure was a little suspicious.

"So instead of answering the question, Leo looked into the gloom and instructed the manservant to bring over their glasses, which were on the table. To the sound of Vanessa's laughter, the servant emerged into the dim light with a silver tray, then stepped back into the gloom. Glasses in hand and still locked in an embrace, Leo and Vanessa slid down the cold glass wall, until Vanessa was lying along its length and Leo was on his knees beside her. By continuing with this game, he would soon cross another—the last—frontier, and he was hesitant and anxious. But Vanessa's slender form was awash with purplish light from the city far below: It was as though the glow of a magical lost world were flooding through her.

"After they let go of each other, Leo remained sitting, Vanessa lying. Neither spoke. Leo's drunkenness had left him. The wonderful world of adventure was the one down there. Leo avoided Vanessa's gaze, looking instead into the darkness that lay over most of the room, broken only by dim patches of white: undergarments strewn across the carpet, the shirtfront of the motionless standing figure of the manservant. Leo realized that the servant was indeed looking at them, and again he felt queasy. At last, he said that he had to go home. Vanessa just nodded; as he stood, she sat up on the carpet, leaning her back against the glass wall with its dim lights. As Leo searched for his clothes in the darkness, he bumped against the table, sending the silverware jangling against the floor. As he placed his hand on the door handle, Leo was unsure whether Vanessa could see him from the other end of the room, so he decided against waving to her before he disappeared without a word. A moment later, the manservant followed—to call the elevator and travel with him to the first floor."

6. Anxiety

"When Leo got home, Patricia was already asleep. As he lay in the dark next to her, his mind was filled with several images of Vanessa that he couldn't bring together: the snob at a celebrity party, the gracious, generous client, the tiresome writer, the slimy undersea creature, the merry friend, the silent dark silhouette before the faint luminous breath of the city . . . What character would he discover in Vanessa next? On his way to the Building the next morning, he was a little fearful of their next encounter, although he told himself that she would probably greet him with a conspiratorial smile that would wipe from their lips the bliss of the previous day once and for all—the kind of smile exchanged by two children with a shared secret.

"When he entered Vanessa's office, she stood up from the desk, walked over to him, and kissed him on the mouth. She told him that she had always known that one day he would love her as she loved him, and she was so happy that this had indeed come to pass. Leo wasn't prepared for this. He began to stammer excuses for last night's behavior: He had been drunk; it wouldn't happen again. The gracious smile on Vanessa's face didn't even flicker. When Leo's explanation was over, she only said that, in the end, he was bound to understand how well suited they were. She knew how confusing all this was for him, and that he couldn't be expected to free himself from the preconceptions and habits that bound him to his wife just yet. To prove that she understood, it would be enough for them to be just lovers at first. There was no need for him to say anything at home for the time being; there would be plenty of time to prepare his wife gradually for divorce. Poor Leo explained to Vanessa that this couldn't be: What had happened yesterday was just a game; he loved his wife and would never be able to leave her. Patiently Vanessa heard him out. Then, in her usual amiable voice she informed him that if he refused to do what she was proposing, she would call Patricia immediately and tell her all about last night. Again she kissed him on the mouth. Then she went back to her work.

"That day, Vanessa didn't appear at his desk even once. As

evening approached, Leo began to hope that he would never see her again. But as he was preparing to leave, a manservant appeared and notified him that his mistress wished to speak with him. This time, Leo was led not to the library as usual, but to the bedroom, one of the rooms designed and arranged by Leo. At its center was a large bed with turquoise linen that merged with a carpet of the same color, giving the bed the appearance of a frozen wave in the sea. Vanessa was in the bed in her nightdress, half sitting, half lying, writing—making the final changes to her novel, perhaps—by the light of a bedside lamp. When Leo appeared, she closed her notebook, rose, walked over to him, and attempted to embrace him. This made Leo extremely angry; having shaken her off, without a word he turned and made for the door, in which the manservant was still standing. He was on the point of leaving the room when he heard something that made him freeze in horror: the little beeps of a number being tapped into a telephone. He was in no doubt that the number in question was his wife's. By the time he returned to her, the lady of the glass tower had switched off the phone and laid it down on the nightstand. Now she was ordering the manservant to bring wine.

"The section of wire describing the early period of Leo's stay in the tower was somewhat damaged. From the fragments that remained, it was clear that Vanessa blackmailed Leo, and that he didn't dare stand up to her. His life was transformed into a nightmare; even on the short trip to the Building each day, he had a sinking feeling in his stomach. He would sit bent over his desk in the tower, his hands shaking as he committed his design to paper, screwed it up, and threw it in the trash. Vanessa sat in the next room writing a new novel, the telephone poised next to her notebook. Leo despised himself for his failure to stand up to Vanessa, but he was afraid that if Patricia found out about his infidelity, she would leave him—and he thought that without her his life would have no meaning. On several occasions, he wrenched himself furiously out of Vanessa's embrace, threw her to the floor, and left the room. When this happened, Vanessa neither complained nor called for the manservants to act against him. She stood up calmly, picked up the telephone, and began to tap in Leo's wife's number; this would always bring Leo back.

"Leo could hardly wait for his work in the glass tower to be over. But when it was finally finished, Vanessa continued to blackmail him. Whenever she wished him to, Leo had to go to her. He had to think up ever more new excuses to give Patricia. His hatred for Vanessa grew by the day. He could no longer think of her as a woman—she was a vile creature, a great mollusk that pressed itself against him and clung on. He imagined with great delight, thousands of times, and in the minutest detail how he would pick up this loathsome thing and throw it from the glass wall of the tower; and he imagined the deep fall of the bloody body riddled with protruding shards of glass, before it hit the metal bars of the Building's main hall and broke up."

7. Caged

"After three weeks of this, Leo could bear it no longer; he decided he would confess all to Patricia and beg for her forgiveness. When he called Vanessa with the news, there was a long pause before she told him not to say anything at home just yet. Then she asked him to come to her one last time: She realized now that she had behaved badly, and she wished to apologize to him and for them to make their peace, after which they could part with no need to see each other ever again. Leo was delighted at the prospect of being rid of Vanessa without having to say anything to Patricia. He entered the glass tower to find Vanessa recumbent on the sofa in the orange dress he had designed for her. All she said to him was that she loved him too much to let him go. Furious, Leo left the room without a word. Once he was out in the empty marble hallway, he realized he didn't have the key card he needed to open the door of the elevator. Since no manservant appeared, Leo was forced to return to Vanessa. 'Please stop this silliness,' he said. 'You can't keep me here forever.' Now it was Vanessa's turn to say nothing; she just looked at him and smiled. Suddenly, Leo realized that with the help of her athletic manservants she could keep him here as long she wished, and that she was eccentric, stubborn, and self-centered enough to do it. He realized too—with horror—that he had told no one he was going to her apartment; once his disappearance was noted, no one would think to look for him here.

"So it happened that Leo became a prisoner in the glass tower. At first, he yelled and yelled for Vanessa to release him immediately, to which she responded with more smiles and silence. Several times, Leo was on the point of striking Vanessa when one of the manservants appeared as if from nowhere and placed himself between captor and captive—the lady of the glass tower didn't even need to press a button. Leo realized that in all likelihood every moment was monitored by invisible cameras. Whenever Leo threw himself at a manservant, he found himself on the floor without realizing how it had happened. On the fifth day of his captivity, before the manservants could stop him, he worked his way through the apartment, tearing, knocking to the floor, and smashing all the objects he had filled the place with over the recent weeks. Not even then did the manservants lose their manners, a reaction so comical that Leo almost laughed despite his despair. When the manservants came to restrain him, they would go into their karate moves straight out of a respectful bow, to which they returned at the end. Even during the fight, they retained something of the servant's attitude. What a weird, silly slapstick game this was, Leo would think, as he lay on the carpet at their feet and Vanessa's.

"After another week of furious shouts, curses, and toothless threats, Leo fell silent and ceased to speak altogether. At this point, Vanessa took to speaking to her prisoner almost constantly, all the while smiling and never raising her voice. Leo's presence was no impediment to her social life; during the day Leo was usually alone in the apartment with the manservants, although as soon as Vanessa returned in the evening, she would go to him. Leo would try to leave the room, but he was never able to open the door Vanessa had just closed behind her: One of the tasks of the manservant on screen duty in the out-of-bounds center of the apartment was the operation of remote-control equipment that locked and unlocked doors, which he performed in accordance with Vanessa's instructions. So Vanessa would come home, sprawl on the sofa, and speak incessantly to silent Leo until late; she spoke to him as though they were a husband and wife in the happiest of marriages. She would complain about how tired she was, telling Leo how she envied him that he didn't have to trudge from one boring social event to the next; she would tell him about her experiences that day, offering her observations on people she met; she would speak of the novel she was working on. She would ask Leo for his views on all kinds of things, and would ask what he wanted for dinner, after every question leaving a pause for his answer, something she never received in all the weeks of Leo's imprisonment.

"This game of Vanessa's didn't surprise Leo; naturally she was mad, and in the context of her life in the tower, to which all threads connecting her to the rational world below had been cut, it didn't strike him as especially bizarre. Owing to the ingenious game with the remote locking of rooms, it was impossible for Leo to flee from Vanessa and her talk, but before long he

developed an ability to deprive his captor's voice of any meaning, noticing only its noise, as he would notice the rustling of
the wind or the murmur of water in a creek, so that she could
talk for many hours without his knowing what she was talking
about. Always there came a point in the evening when the locks
of all rooms except the bedroom would softly snap shut, leaving Leo no choice but to sleep in a bed with Vanessa. He never
touched her or paid any attention to her, and she didn't pester
him; even in bed, she played the role of contented wife in an
exemplary marriage, telling him what she thought of a new film
she had seen that day, the character flaws of a girlfriend, or her
own stomach problems, before falling asleep in the middle of
a sentence.

"Her sleep brought Leo no relief; he hated her contented
heavy breathing as much as he hated her unctuous voice. He
would lie in the bed for hours with his eyes open, looking
through the window at the strip of lights strewn along the
lower edge of the glass wall—lights that sparkled like an unreal
last hope; he watched the colored lights of aircraft passing
slowly through the darkness. When at last he closed his eyes,
he imagined that he was at home with his wife, begging for her
forgiveness; and Patricia would say that she forgave him, and
everything would be as it had been. After this, Leo sometimes
managed to sleep for a while."

8. Butterfly Woman

"One day, in the midst of her incessant talk about everything
imaginable, Leo's captor happened to mention that a young,
avant-garde composer had based a ballet on Kant's *Critique of
Pure Reason*, and she asked Leo to design a dress she could wear
to the premiere, which would take place in a month's time, in

the large theater her father had commissioned as part of the Building. As ever, she left a pause for Leo's response, even though she was expecting none, before going on with her chatter. Leo didn't respond this time either—but in that moment of silence a thought came to him that he would develop and refine all that night. When Vanessa got home the next evening, she found on her desk a dress design that included detailed drawings of the cut. She ran straight to Leo, who was standing at the window, looking down at the city. Although she got no answer to any of the questions she bombarded him with, she was gladdened by the suggestion that Leo was missing his work; she told herself that what he had done should be taken as a sign of the kinder treatment he had in store for her. She was delighted with the design, and she sent it to her dressmaker straightaway.

"But Leo's thoughts weren't as she imagined them to be. Several years before, he and Patricia had taken a vacation in Jamaica, where it had become their early-morning habit to walk along the shore collecting pebbles with brownish-gray and white markings. They would place these stones on the table of their hotel room, admire the markings, and speak for hours about what their shapes reminded them of. The pebble they liked best had a light-brown marking in the shape of a woman with fine wings. They brought the winged woman home and named her Papillia; she became their talisman, and they took her everywhere with them. Leo remembered Papillia's every detail, including the slight tremors in her outline—and now he had produced her likeness on the front of Vanessa's dress. There was no doubt that Vanessa and her premiere dress would appear on the cover of at least one magazine. Leo was hoping that Patricia would see this photograph and figure out that the Papillia design was a message from him—a message that was at once a plea for help and an indication of where he was being held.

"Vanessa's dress did indeed cause a stir at the premiere of *The Critique of Pure Reason*. In front of the theater she stepped out of her car to a veritable explosion of camera flashes and paparazzi running about her like a troop of frightened monkeys. And so it happened that while waiting for a bus, Patricia saw on the cover of a magazine displayed at a newsdealer's kiosk a color photo of a smiling Vanessa Willis wearing a dress that bore a depiction of a creature known only to her and her husband. Patricia had long suspected Vanessa of having a hand in Leo's disappearance; now at last she had evidence for her suspicions. She went back to the police commissioner who was dealing with the case and placed *Dolce Vita* magazine on the desk in front of him. Next to the magazine, she placed the Papillia pebble.

"The commissioner was having lunch; he had a slice of pizza in his hand as he examined the magazine cover and the pebble. He acknowledged the striking resemblance between the figure on the dress and the marking on the stone. But, as he wasted no time in explaining to Patricia, the police couldn't open an investigation on someone because of a pattern on her dress, and certainly not when she was the daughter of one of the richest men in the country, who was also the city's greatest benefactor. Realizing that her efforts were in vain, Patricia left the commissioner's office without saying goodbye. As she walked the long corridor toward the exit, wondering who else she could show the magazine and the pebble to, she realized that any subsequent visit to the police would have the same outcome; she felt so terribly helpless that she began to sob. The next moment she heard a hurried step behind her and a woman's voice calling her name. She turned to see running toward her the young sergeant who for the duration of her interview with the commissioner had been sitting at the next desk, working at a computer, giving not the slightest impression that she was taking in what Patricia and the commissioner were talking about. The sergeant told

Patricia that her name was Kate, the commissioner was a fool and a coward, and that she believed her and wished to help her."

9. Rescue Expedition

"Kate got hold of a compact disc with a detailed plan of the Building. (Of course, Hector wasn't such a prophet that he had come up with the compact disc in the sixties; he had spoken vaguely of a tool for the storing of digital data; in this place, as in several others, Hella had slightly modified and improved his story.) The two women spent a whole night in Patricia's apartment, before a computer screen on which green lines representing walls shone against a black background, planning the rescue mission together. From the beginning, Patricia insisted that she would go with Kate; at the university, she had gone in for mountaineering and judo; she could handle whatever she was faced with, she assured the sergeant. As she and Kate searched for a way to the tower, Patricia was reminded of the computer games of her childhood, a Persian prince (Marius guessed that Hella had added this to the narrative), and many other characters that walked an intricate maze of corridors on many levels but were sent back to their starting point by a single wrong step with only one wall separating them from the door of the treasure chamber. It seemed that their path through the Building would be like the journey of the Persian prince; it transpired that the Building linked—by stairs or elevator—only the fifth, eighth, eighteenth, and nineteenth floors, and the fourth with the eleventh; if someone did manage to make it to the right floor, they would find that the room they were looking for was beyond a locked glass door in another part of the passage, and so approached from another floor. It could happen that to reach the next room, visitors would have to pass through practically the entire Building. On top of this, it would be necessary to dodge guards and cameras; unlike the Persian prince, the two women each had only one life.

"Whether the elaborateness of the Building was a result of chaotic planning or deliberation on the part of Edward Willis was unclear; perhaps he was hiding something inside it. Whatever the reason, it gave Vanessa a great advantage. The two women tried out dozens of routes; the flashing green lights on the screen representing themselves penetrated the most distant and weirdest parts of the Building, but they always came up against a wall, a locked door, or a floor that was off limits, forcing them to return to the last fork in their way, only for their next attempt to take them to another impassable wall. On several occasions, the green phantoms came near the lower floors of Vanessa's tower, but in searching for an entrance they would again find themselves at the far end of the Building. Both women fell asleep in the small hours, by which time they had concluded that the only way to the tower through the maze of the Building was the purple elevator, which was out of bounds to them. As the pale light of morning appeared at the window beyond the computer screen, Patricia told Kate she should get some sleep before she went on duty. Kate said nothing to this; she just pointed to a dotted line on the screen they hadn't noticed before. This represented a passage connecting the closed circuits they had been roaming in vain.

"Shortly before midnight, Patricia and Kate were walking the passages of the Building; the pistols Kate had gotten for them were carefully concealed in their coats. The Building was a creature of the night, sleeping briefly only in the early hours. The two women were passed by streams of people returning from the cinemas and theaters; through the glass walls, they saw into restaurants filled with customers; most of the stores, too, were still open. They took an escalator to the highest freely accessible gallery, where, the map they had loaded into their small electronic notepad informed them, they would need to turn toward an inconspicuous staircase that led to some lawyers' offices. Having taken this, they ascended and descended more staircases, walked long corridors, turned dozens of corners, took passenger and freight elevators up and down, crossed roofs belonging to lower parts of the Building, descended to the boiler station in a freight elevator, and then walked up a fire escape. Like Catwoman, they crept on all fours across the dome of a hall, the green-glass glow of which lit their faces from below. After three hours, they found themselves in front of an open hatch giving on to the shaft of a freight elevator, which reminded them of an empty stage at a puppet theater. They crawled inside this, and Kate turned her flashlight upward; its beam picked out a dusty structure attached to the walls, although the distant ceiling of the shaft remained in darkness. Then they climbed up the tangle of greasy, smelly cables and wires, as though these were lianas in a dark ravine in the jungle.

"At last their hands touched the ceiling; now they needed to crawl through a narrow horizontal ventilation shaft. Kate went in first, flashlight in hand. For a long time all Patricia saw in front of her was the soles of Kate's shoes. Then the soles stopped and Patricia heard a faint creaking; she guessed that Kate was carefully unscrewing the cover of the exit from the ventilation shaft. They had reached their destination at last; beyond the cover was one of Vanessa's rooms. Kate switched off the flashlight, lowered herself quietly to the floor, and helped Patricia out. They ran across the carpet on tiptoe. Kate cautiously opened the door to the next room; it was in complete darkness—obviously the drapes were drawn across the glass wall. For a long time the two women stood listening; there was total silence in the room, and in the apartment as a whole. At one point, Patricia thought she heard someone breathing;

if so, she supposed it was Kate . . . Then the room was flooded
with bright light; two yards away from Patricia and Kate stood
six men in black tailcoats, forming a regular semicircle. All
had guns trained on the women—four submachine guns, two
pistols. No one in the room spoke."

10. Captives

"As resistance was futile, Kate and Patricia allowed themselves
to be disarmed and taken to Vanessa. She was sitting at her
desk, looking at the screen of her computer, which showed a
plan of the Building with two blinking lights on it; Patricia and
Kate realized that Vanessa had monitored their whole climb.
She could have had them apprehended a thousand times, but
obviously she had been curious to learn if they would find a
way through the maze, and she had been entertained by their
efforts. Vanessa's expression made it plain to the intruders that
she was glad of their appearance in her apartment. She was getting bored by life with Leo, and the arrival of these two women
delivered hope of new amusements.

"And things got off to a splendid start: Patricia yelled at
Vanessa to tell them where she was holding her husband. Vanessa
waited until she had finished before saying that she would call
Leo immediately. This took Patricia and Kate so much by surprise
that for a moment they didn't know what to say. Meanwhile,
the yelling had woken Leo from his fitful sleep. On recognizing
the voice of his wife, he came rushing to Vanessa's office; he
embraced Patricia, and the two of them burst into tears. Once
Leo had grasped what had happened, he spoke to Vanessa for
the first time in many months, to plead with her not to harm
the women. Vanessa was thrilled realizing the benefits for her
of the changed state of affairs achieved by Patricia's loyalty and

Kate's bravery: She was rid of the danger Patricia had posed for her on the outside, she could tell that the relationship between the captive spouses would provide a fascinating spectacle as well as psychological experience she could use in her novel, and she had gained a means by which she could blackmail Leo. In different circumstances, she might not have bothered to make the effort—her love for Leo, now a pitiable, helpless figure, was cooling—but the prospect of Leo having to pay attention to her in the presence of his wife revived her desire. Extortion was a weapon Vanessa liked above all others, and the one she worked with best.

"Vanessa devised a simple yet effective strategy based on her refusal to give Patricia and Kate food and drink, and a brief announcement to Leo that it depended on him whether his wife and her friend would be left to die of hunger and thirst. That night, Leo came to Vanessa; so before she fell asleep, Vanessa ordered a manservant to serve a fine dinner and the best wine to the two women in their room. Now Vanessa had not one prisoner, but three. She made no attempt to stop them from associating with each other. At first, Patricia and Kate kept coming up with plans of escape, but all these came to grief in the first moment of realization. After months of imprisonment, the eyes of Patricia and Kate, too, took on an expression of listlessness. The captives clung to one another; often the three of them sat on the carpet, huddled together, holding hands like children, Patricia's head resting on Leo's shoulder. When they went into such a huddle, there was always a danger that Vanessa would appear, sit down in a nearby chair or sofa, and start talking; now she spoke to all three captives as she had earlier spoken to Leo, and all were as silent as Leo had been when alone. God only knows why Vanessa did this—maybe she liked the idea of placing all her prisoners in the game she had invented to show

Leo her kindly face. She was evidently delighted that her chatter infuriated Patricia and Kate.

"Whenever Vanessa was at home, her voice—by now the worst instrument of torture for the prisoners—hardly ever stopped. Every evening, she would read to them the pages of her book she had written that morning. As she did so, the prisoners would sit on the carpet, hold hands, and watch the changing gray clouds beyond the window. For Leo, Vanessa's voice had long been mere background noise to which he attached no meaning; after many evenings of readings, he still had no idea what the novel was about. After a while, however, he noticed that some of Vanessa's sentences woke Patricia from her torpor, and that at times she couldn't resist listening to the novel with interest. Once, she became so involved in what she was hearing that unwittingly she let go of Leo's hand; at that moment, Leo's despair was greater than at any time since he was first imprisoned. He had a gut feeling that Patricia's hand was pulling away from him for good, and when seconds later it slipped back into his, it felt like someone else's. He noticed that Patricia's gaze, which, like his and Kate's, had hitherto been fixed beyond Vanessa's head, allowing it to roam the gray sky, had found its way to the reader's face and was resting there. Although Patricia's hand remained in his, Leo could sense that his wife was scarcely aware of his presence. When he pressed her hand, Patricia's response was mechanical, and Leo felt worse still. Later, when he saw her listening to Vanessa's story with particularly close attention, Leo pressed Patricia's hand, and she snatched it away crossly.

"Soon after that, Patricia interrupted Vanessa in her reading to request an explanation of some point in the plot whose sense she hadn't entirely grasped. With her usual patience and perverse graciousness, Vanessa spelled everything out, before asking for Patricia's opinion. This first time Patricia held her tongue, thinking she had gone too far; at the next reading, however, she and Vanessa embarked on a long discussion about literature. After that, Vanessa often turned to Patricia for her opinion on the passage she had just read; to all appearances, she valued her opinions and gave them serious thought. It was now plain that Patricia looked forward to the readings. It seemed, too, that Vanessa looked forward to her conversations with Patricia."

11. Isolation

"At first, Leo reproached his wife for her behavior. Patricia defended herself by saying she was doing it for the sake of the three of them; if their behavior toward their captor became less hostile, she said, Vanessa would be less vigilant, which might enable them to escape, or she might even release them. Leo wasn't taken in by such talk; he could see that his wife's fascination with Vanessa was ever stronger. Although he had very little self-respect left, he was indignant at Patricia's suggestion that he should treat his captor more kindly. He thought, too, of how much more learned his wife was than he; although this had never bothered him before, now it was painful for him to realize that the two of them had never had a conversation as lively as the ones Patricia had with Vanessa.

"The time of Patricia trying to explain certain things to her husband or to lead him to believe them, didn't last long. Soon, she was avoiding him so she could spend whole days with Vanessa. As he trudged about the apartment, it seemed to Leo that he heard echoes of conversation between his wife and his captor from all sides. When Vanessa was out, Patricia stayed out of Leo and Kate's way. She sat in front of Vanessa's bookcase and read from its contents; as soon as she heard Vanessa's step in the hall, she would snap the book shut and rush to her new friend. Leo and Patricia stopped speaking to each other; if they met in one of the rooms, they passed on in silence.

"Patricia's betrayal brought Leo and Kate closer. Patricia stopped speaking even to Kate, the woman who had risked her life and lost her freedom for her. The daily reading now proceeded with Vanessa and Patricia sitting at opposite ends of the sofa, while Leo and Kate remained on the floor in the captives' corner, huddled together and holding hands. Patricia listened to Vanessa with close attention, interrupting now and then with a question; after the reading, the two of them would have lengthy debates, as though alone in the room. Then came an evening when, during the reading, Kate's hand released itself from Leo's, and he saw in her eyes the same expression of admiring attention as in the eyes of his wife. At that moment, he knew that he was again the only prisoner in the glass tower.

"Now Kate, too, was involved in the literary debates. Kate lacked Patricia and Vanessa's education; for her, Vanessa's readings and conversation with Patricia represented a voyage of discovery into a world that had little in common with the world she had known before her arrival at Vanessa's apartment—one of undercover agents, thieves, pimps, and drug dealers. Now Kate thanked fate for having delivered her and Patricia to the tower, and for the failure of their attempt to rescue Leo. She apologized repeatedly for her ignorance, and the women treated her kindly. She responded to their teaching by proving herself to be an exceptionally gifted pupil; Vanessa and Patricia were delighted.

"The three women gave ever less thought to Leo. Now he could sleep whenever he wished. As he was no longer obliged to listen to Vanessa's readings, when they were in progress he wandered about the room; or he stood motionless at the window, his forehead against the cold glass, looking down on the rooftops of the city; or he went to the other side of the apartment and looked at the sparkling green-glass vaults of the halls. Sometimes, he crossed the living room like a silent phantom as Patricia and Kate listened to Vanessa or the three of them were in passionate discussion about literature. One day, Kate suggested they dramatize the dialogues from Vanessa's novel; Patricia and Vanessa were delighted with this idea, and the three of them divided the roles between them. After that, Leo would pass through the living room to the sight of his wife, Kate, and Vanessa acting out an endless soap opera. He realized that the novel was about three women who had met somewhere on the Baltic coast, where they were trying to discover the truth about their lives; as they talked Patricia, Kate, and Vanessa would look to the distant horizon of an imaginary sea, their hunched-up bodies telling of a cold wind blowing from its surface."

12. Three Sisters

"Before long, it wasn't enough for Patricia and Kate merely to recite lines written by Vanessa; and so, with Vanessa's encouragement, they altered them and added words of their own. Soon the three of them were composing a joint work during the day and acting it out in the evening. They spent all their time together: Thanks to their joint writing/acting project, Vanessa hardly ever left the apartment anymore. Surprisingly, Kate turned out to have the most remarkable talent; it was she who came up with the brightest, most unusual images. Perhaps her day-to-day contact with the argot of the street had awakened in her a sense for creative language in all its physicality, while her role in police actions had given her a knowledge of expressions and rhythms of the body. Vanessa and Patricia praised her and were a little jealous of her talent. All three considered these to be the happiest days of her life. Often, they likened themselves to the Brontës, and they spoke of themselves as sisters.

"Patricia and Kate could now leave the apartment whenever they chose. Often, the three women went together to the theater or an exhibition; on their return, Leo would hear them arguing passionately about what they had just seen. So heedless had Vanessa and Kate become of Leo that by now he was little more to them than a large, inconspicuous pet dog moving noiselessly and wearily about the apartment. Whenever tiredness caught up with him, he would sit or lie down at the place he happened to be, remaining there for five minutes or five hours before getting up and resuming his wandering. At the occasional moments the women registered the disagreeable fact of Leo's presence, they discussed what was to be done with him. It was unfortunate that they couldn't set him free: The police would surely be interested in where he had spent the last year. Vanessa and Kate inclined toward the simplest solution—to keep things as they were for the time being, after which they would see. Leo's silent rambles bothered them little, although sometimes his presence got on their nerves.

"Patricia disagreed with her girlfriends on the subject of Leo, advocating more radical action. Once a mere irritant to her, the sight of him shuffling stolidly about the apartment as he transformed into a zombie now filled her with rage. Patricia's hatred for her husband was probably her way of coming to terms with the fact that he had become a dumb animal, a transformation for which she was principally to blame. She would never have believed herself capable of such powerful negative feeling toward someone. Her hatred of Leo was almost as delightful to her as her creative friendship with Vanessa and Kate. But her antipathy for Leo was more than the product of a bad conscience; its seeds had long been growing unheeded in her mind. Now her hatred was able to evolve and thrive, and it took in all kinds of nourishment: repressed guilt, memories of past misunder-standings and embarrassments, Leo's indiscretions in the course of their marriage, her own past devotion to and love for him, sorrow for the fact that they hadn't been able to have a child, feelings of reproach for his having slept with Vanessa while she, Patricia, was waiting for and worrying about him at home. Once-suppressed images came to her unbidden: She thought of the way he ate, and was disgusted by the memory of his chewing mouth at dinners they had shared . . . So when the women discussed what to do with Leo, Patricia always insisted that they kill him; indeed, she offered to do it herself, provided that the manservants disposed of the body. But Vanessa and Kate balked at murder. Whenever Patricia spoke of the necessity of doing away with Leo and described the best way of going about it, they felt afraid of her.

"Patricia humiliated Leo in front of her girlfriends system-atically. At first, she mocked him and spoke of embarrassments in their marriage. 'When I married Leo,' she would say, 'he didn't even know not to put his knife in his mouth.' She was disappointed to see that her words had little effect on Leo. Was he still able to perceive their meaning? She took to treating him like a servant, following him about and giving him all kinds of orders, none of which he carried out, enraging Patricia to such a degree that she would call a manservant to hold Leo's arms while she drove her fists into his face and belly, all the while yelling at him that he must do as she told him. Disturbed by these scenes, Vanessa and Kate would walk away from them. Patricia would then apologize to her friends for letting herself get carried away, but the next day, on encountering Leo in the hallway she would again lose control of herself, and the scene would be repeated. Leo several times overheard Vanessa and Kate discussing Patricia with concern in their voices."

13. Flight

"Early one morning, while the women were still asleep, Leo was making his cumbersome way through the marble hallway when a manservant arranging flowers in a vase turned to face him, pulled a magnetic card from his breast pocket, fixed Leo with a steady gaze, and swept the card through the electronic lock by the door of the elevator; then he walked away, leaving Leo alone in the room. It took Leo's devastated mind a moment or two to figure out what he had just seen. He brushed his fingertips across the marble panel on the door, which moved aside to reveal the elevator's dark-purple inside and his haggard face looking back at him in the mirror. No sooner had he stepped inside than the door closed behind him. He pushed the button at the bottom and the elevator began to vibrate. Leo still refused to believe that he was about to walk free; he was, he supposed, the victim of a cruel prank played by Patricia, and he was expecting the door to open to reveal his wife and her spiteful laughter. But when the elevator stopped and its door soundlessly slid sideways into the wall, he was confronted with a large space filled with people. In a daze, he paced the arcades of the Building as the voices of the crowd came together in a monotonous hum; he looked at faces awash with the pale light of neon signs; he passed glowing storefronts that put him in mind of underwater caves in a fairy tale. Still he believed that this journey through the arcades was part of Patricia's joke, and he waited for a manservant to grab him from behind and drag him toward an elevator, the doors of which would close behind him once and for all. He knew that in the busy arcades, whose lighting made people and objects look unreal, no one would attend to his abduction.

"But the arcades came to an end, and Leo found himself on the sidewalk, looking at the facades of tall buildings, their lines converged in a dizzying perspective. Above these buildings was the cloudy early-morning sky, pierced, at the far end of the

street, by a bundle of angled streams of sunlight. He thought of
the manservant—the only one in the glass tower to have shown
him any compassion. The noise of the cars and streetcars put
him in a trance. He couldn't recollect the layout of the streets
around the Building, but this mattered nothing to him. He
walked straight on, turning into each new street he reached,
irrespective of right or left. He believed his walk to be aimless
until he reached the street where his own building stood. He
stopped on the sidewalk opposite his apartment and looked
at its windows; then he walked on—how could he possibly
return to the rooms he had shared with Patricia? Little did he
know that he would owe his freedom to this distaste for his old
apartment: At that very moment, the living room was occupied
by three manservants with tranquilizer guns, and a van with
blacked-out windows parked by the entrance was poised to take
him back to the Building."

14. Uptown

"As evening approached, Leo reached an uptown district he
didn't know. He came out of his trance and looked around,
seeing houses with unplastered, dark-brick fronts with large,
illegible scribble on them, metal fire escapes, overflowing garbage containers, old, battered automobiles parked in the street.
On passing a niche containing an ATM, he remembered the
bank card in his pants pocket. (By now Marius knew better
than to ask Hella if the ATM was one of Hector's prophecies,
or if she had added it herself.) As he was hungry, he withdrew
some cash and went to a snack bar, where he wolfed down a
beefsteak and French fries and drank a beer before going on
his way. Before long, the sidewalk was lost in clumps of dry
grass; the city had come to an end. The blacktop fought free

of the buildings and turned into a shiny road that headed into darkening open country, taking two sharp turns before disappearing into the saddle of a hillock, beyond which a red, setting sun peeped from behind dark clouds. Leo looked away from the yellowing grass of the plain, which was littered with plastic bottles and supermarket bags, back the way he had come, at blind side walls with peeling paint on both sides of the street. These walls belonged to the city's last tenements. Rising over the roof of one of the buildings, he saw Vanessa's tower, looking like a ridiculously tiny extension built by an eccentric resident.

"As he didn't wish to return to the city, Leo walked on. The tenements at the end of the street were not the very last buildings after all; soon, he came to a long, single-story construction that looked like a worn-out couch tossed into the dry grass along with all the other trash—maybe at night and in secret, by a resourceful city-dweller. At the far end of this building was a mounted frame that cast a vertical row of four neon-lit letters into the turquoise dusk. A large 'M' sat on the highest crossbar of the sign, a fat 'O' was pressed against the feet of the 'M,' and an 'L' was attached to the lowest rung; above the 'L,' an 'E' hovered crookedly; between the 'E' and the 'O,' a 'T' glowed palely and intermittently, as though trying to come back to life but lacking the strength to do so.

"Before Leo reached the motel, darkness fell. Unless he intended to walk all night along the road to the nearest town, he would have to stop here. So he entered the pleasingly empty reception area, where he booked a room and bought a bottle of wine from an old man. He crossed a courtyard containing several beds of pansies and a shallow pool with an artificial-stone statue of a Red Indian at its center, reaching a row of doors, above each of which was a rounded lamp surrounded by swarming flies. The door to his room opened with a loud creak. On turning on the light, he saw that the room was small and its walls were covered with rococo-patterned wallpaper peeling in several places. The picture above the bed was a reproduction of a sunset over the Bay of Naples. On the nightstand were two glasses standing bottom-up and a lamp with burnt spots on its ivory-colored shade. There was a table in one corner and a TV on a shelf. The curtains were yellow from smoke.

"Leo stood on the threshold, inspecting his new room and inhaling its fusty scent. He was filled with happiness, and the happiness grew. Then he put the bottle on the nightstand, switched off the light, and lay down on the bed, the feathers of which jumped up to meet him. The window had a view of the road, which was only a few yards away. In at the upper right-hand corner of the window was the shiny bottom of the neon 'L'; a square turquoise glow lay across the floor. Leo bobbed about on the mattress, sipped his wine, and studied the lights of passing cars through the curtains. He fell asleep after the first glass. Although his dreams returned him to the glass tower, he cried out several times in horror and woke up in a sweat; on opening his eyes to a piece of turquoise letter shining against the curtains, he felt his happiness flood back, and he fell asleep again quickly. At one of his moments of wakefulness, he heard, through the thin wall at his head, a sound of soft weeping. The sound soon stopped."

15. Life at the Motel

"Leo stayed in the motel; meanwhile his mind slowly healed. Still lacking the concentration required to read books, he spent his days watching TV, flicking through the tattered pictorial magazines that lay around the reception area, or sitting in the yard on a plastic chair, sipping wine. One bottle would last him several hours of daydreaming, for most of which his thoughts were on the Caribbean coastline he knew from his vacations. Although Patricia had been at the seaside with him, he succeeded in blanking her out of these memories. In the tower, he had often imagined that if he managed to escape, he would travel a lot; now he marveled that the picture of the Bay of Naples and his memories gave him all the travel he desired . . . At this time, he enjoyed nothing more than to lie on his bed watching the cars drive by.

"Sometimes, he would walk in the direction of the city, albeit never far from the motel. Everywhere visible over the rooftops, Vanessa's tower radiated evil, or so it seemed to Leo; but the rays of evil seen against the gray sky by his mind's eye weakened as they got further from their source, eventually fading to nothing so that the streets of the city's outskirts were practically untouched by the tower's force. He tended to take lunch and dinner in the motel's restaurant. He liked to watch the faces of the people who checked in at the motel, mostly for one, never for more than two nights, and to catch snatches of their conversations, out of which he tried to figure out details of their lives. Sometimes it crossed his mind that he should go to the police and inform on the women in the tower, but the thought of forsaking his happiness at the motel somehow to deal with Vanessa, Patricia, and Kate was so repulsive to him that he banished it whenever it came. Nor did he wish to visit any of his friends in the city; the Leo that came out of the glass tower wasn't the same Leo that went in, and the new Leo had no friends.

"Apart from Leo, two young women were the only permanent residents at the motel. Their room was next to Leo's; it was from there that Leo had heard weeping on his first night; and this weeping was repeated on many subsequent nights. He saw the women practically every day, on sunloungers by the pool in the courtyard; they spent most of their time reading or talking together in hushed voices. He and the women always greeted each other, but they never talked; Leo had the impression that the women had no desire to start a conversation with him or anyone else, and he was grateful to them for their reserve. As Leo sat with his bottle of wine, from time to time his thoughts would drift from warm, faraway shores back to the yard, and then he would observe the women discreetly. In the face of the dark-haired, shorter one, who was apparently somewhat the younger of the two, he read the expression of a permanently frightened child. Sometimes her eyes were red; it was she, Leo supposed, who wept at night. He was slightly irritated by the fact that he was never able to read the face of the fair-haired woman; it was as though it drew on a different wardrobe of expressions than the impoverished one the rest of us use. This woman's expression made him think most of all of sorrow, but also of great strength lying fallow in an empty life, as well as compassion grown out of a sense of overwhelming futility.

"Leo noticed that whenever a new guest appeared in the yard, the women would go to their room. 'Maybe they've run away from their husbands together, or they've robbed a bank and gone into hiding,' he thought. In any case, having gradually gotten used to the women, Leo wasn't afraid of them. Before long, the three of them fell into conversation. Leo learned that the dark-haired one with the childlike expression was called Linda, while the other woman went by the unusual name of Diamanta. In their conversation, both women took care to avoid anything that might give rise to questions about their pasts; at the slightest sign of danger in this regard, they would swiftly change the subject. As Leo had no desire to talk of what he had been through, their conversation remained in the narrow confines of the present tense, which had little more to offer aside from the traffic, the weather, and the food in the motel's restaurant. Nevertheless, such conversation seemed to suit all three of them. Leo enjoyed the women's company, and he believed that each time they met in the yard, the women were glad.

"During one of his walks on the outskirts of the city, in the storefront window of a thrift store, Leo spotted some opera glasses with a mother-of-pearl inlay, which he bought. Sitting by the pool, he would train the glasses over the roof of the motel and study Vanessa's tower; when it was dark, he would see that the lights were on in Vanessa's apartment, although the lenses were too weak to allow him to make out any figures. The sight of the tower held no fear for him; in fact, Leo enjoyed looking at the tiny pavilion this playful prospect made of his prison. Now that they were aware of the Building's tower's attraction for Leo, the anxiety that prevented Linda and Diamanta from speaking about the past was challenged by their curiosity. Whenever Leo was looking through his opera glasses, which were obviously trained on a single point, the women would sit on their loungers in a state of agitation. Eventually, Diamanta succeeded in reassuring herself that a query about Leo's daily watch wouldn't bring down an avalanche of questions about their pasts. Why, she asked, was Leo so drawn to the city's tallest skyscraper? Startled, Leo mumbled an answer that was open to multiple interpretations. Half-expecting this kind of response, Diamanta and Linda asked no further questions. But in the silence that opened around the pool, Leo's thoughts were suddenly invaded by a long-held desire to tell someone about what he had been through in the past year. It was unlikely, he told himself, that he would find better listeners than these two gentle, attentive women, who, it seemed to him, were tainted with misfortune just as he was.

"So, just as the women's thoughts were returning to their magazines, he spoke up. He spoke for a long time, in a calm voice, telling his new friends of his experiences in the glass tower, of Vanessa, Patricia, and Kate and their drama serials, of the manservants, of Vanessa's smiles and endless prattle, of Patricia's frenzies, of Kate's gift that had shown itself so unexpectedly that perhaps she hadn't realized it would be steeped forever in the evil of its origins. Leo told Linda and Diamanta everything. As he went over details of the most humiliating episodes, he saw that the two women understood his approach; they knew that he was telling them all because he appreciated that they and he belonged to the same nation."

16. Diamanta's Story

"After Leo finished his story, no one spoke for some time. As it was around noon, drivers were arriving at the motel for lunch; in the silence, they heard trucks pulling up and driving away on the other side of the building. Leo watched the two women squinting into the distance at the sunlit glass tower; no doubt they were imagining the scenes of humiliation he had spoken of. Linda was the first to speak. 'Tell him about us,' she said softly to her friend, and Leo had the feeling that Diamanta had been waiting for just such an appeal. From the very first sentence Diamanta spoke, Leo learned that neither of the women was human: Diamanta was a daemon, Linda was an artificial being created three years earlier in laboratories of the Massachusetts Institute of Technology, on the east coast.

"Leo wasn't really surprised to discover that Diamanta's face, whose expression he had wondered about so often, was that of an immortal being; indeed, he considered this an immediate solution to the mystery. Suddenly the signifiers scattered about her features like letters of an unfamiliar alphabet refusing to come together formed a unity: Diamanta's face was of someone whose immensely long life had been filled mostly with boredom, whose loss of all hope meant the loss of all need to hurt others, and whose feelings and passions had been extinguished, although their ashes quietly continued to give out sympathy for the world and its creatures.

"Nor was Leo surprised to learn that Linda was an artificial being. Although there was nothing automatic about her behavior, Leo knew that to the untrained eye the state-of-the-art robots produced in Vanessa's father's factories were indistinguishable from humans. Linda's origin explained the anxious expression that never quite left her face and was surely a consequence of her living in a world that belonged to beings of a different birth where there were no rights to protect her; no statute book had a category for artificial beings. The need for new legal regulations regarding the treatment of robots was a common topic, and for many years a committee appointed by an international body had been working on some; however, as artificial people were part of a rapidly developing field of technology, and there was a lucrative business in them with a great many interests involved, the committee had so far yielded no results worthy of the name, to the surprise of absolutely nobody. Even when a minor modification to a law could be agreed upon, this law had to undergo a ratification process so complicated that in most instances it eventually crumbled and dissolved. So there was no legal protection for artificial beings—apart from that given by the fact that causing damage to robots that were the property of someone else was unlawful.

"Leo questioned Diamanta on the world of daemons, about which he knew little. Thirty years earlier, science had made the surprising finding that daemons—long considered by the modern era to be products of fiction and the imagination of the ancients—actually existed. At more or less the same time, there was an unexpected breakthrough in robot evolution, resulting in the sudden need for humans to come to terms with the fact that they weren't the only inhabitants of Earth capable of rational thought. That daemons and robots arrived on the scene at the same moment was surely a coincidence, and these two groups of beings lived side by side without paying much attention to each other; but later, three hundred years after the time of Leo's story, they would form an alliance directed against humankind, for which the consequences would be fatal. (The critics of North Floriana didn't know what to make of this last remark. What was the point of such a glimpse into the fictional future of the novel? There was no other reference to it in the entire length of Fernando's wire. Was it just whimsy on Fernando's part or perhaps an indication that he was intending to write a sequel? Had he mentioned wars between humans on one side and daemons and robots on the other on a piece of wire that had remained on the ocean floor?)

"It turned out that daemons were less scarce than was at first believed. The fact that until then no one had seen any was probably because their appearance bore little relation to the traditional idea of what a daemon looked like; indeed, daemons were very similar in appearance to humans (some humans, at least). It was pointed out many times that 'daemon' wasn't the right designation for these beings, and many other names were suggested; but as we know, once people get used to a name, no matter how unsuitable, they aren't keen to change it. Besides, the languages of the world had no word for an immortal, neurotic being distinguished by its insufferable character, very poor memory, and obsessive fondness for useless old junk. No one noticed a daemon for so many years in part because daemons spent a lot of time among humans; they were invisible because they occurred in places where no one was looking for them. Some of them even took jobs, doing so mainly out of boredom or the need to escape the company of other daemons. They didn't have to earn money, as they had hardly any human needs. They ate almost nothing, and their bodies radiated some kind impregnator that kept their clothes clean, meaning that they made do with one set of clothes without recourse to washing machines and dry cleaners. Nor did they need to rent an apartment: They didn't feel the cold and mostly slept for just an hour a day. When not passing the night in an abandoned factory, warehouse, or junkyard, they tended to walk empty streets. Given the choice, most daemons would rather spend the night in a dreary factory yard stinking of grease and diesel fuel than the Ritz hotel. Were it not for Linda, Diamanta told Leo, she would be happiest under a collapsing fence in a bed of nettles, in a scrapyard, or in a ditch, from where she would fall asleep to the sight of the city's glittering lights."

17. A Natural History of Daemons

"The revelation of the existence of daemons had caused a sensation. The scientific journals of the time were filled with articles on the newly discovered beings, foundations were laid for daemonology as a scientific discipline, and several books were published that remained standard works in the field. Since the revelation much had changed, however. It hadn't taken long to realize that differences between daemons and humans were so slight—aside from the immortality and the strange tastes—that it was barely worthwhile establishing a special scientific discipline for the former. As a result, the great wave of interest in daemonology soon subsided. Nor did research of daemons prove particularly interesting from a practical point of view; apparently daemons did nothing to influence the human world. No conclusions were reached on how they might be employed, although in the early days the possibilities fueled many daydreams. Either they had no supernatural abilities, or for some reason they were keeping these hidden from humans.

"By the time Leo met Diamanta, mentions of daemons appeared mostly in 'human-interest' magazines, which, when they didn't happen to have anything else to write about, invented various sensational nonsense about them. One might say that the journalists of these magazines created a new being—by crossing the 'daemon' discovered by science with the mythological figure of the same name. This fantasy figure occupied the pages of the sensationalist press alongside pop singers, actors, and all manner of celebrities. They often carried news that some movie or music star had a daemon lover, or that the star him- or herself was the daemon. This kind of news was mostly spread by the actors and singers hoping to get themselves talked about. The magazines in question also regularly published articles on mysterious murders with daemons as suspects. People liked to read this kind of thing, caring little that it was nonsense. Most daemons had no interest in other species, and there was not one recorded case of a daemon deliberately harming a human.

"As a rule, daemons didn't help humans either. They lived in their own world and attended to their own affairs, often grumpily, even among society. For most of their lives they were alone, spending much of their time in warehouses, factories, yards, and on roofs; it wasn't uncommon to find a daemon curled up in the grass behind a kiosk at a streetcar terminus, amid crumpled-up plastic cups and cookie wrappers. Hector told Hella that although Fernando had devoted almost twenty yards of wire to Diamanta's description of the nature and behavior of daemons, his own narrative referred only to a passage about two yards in length, which spoke of daemons' liking for broken, moldy, and rusty things. On coming across old junk, they could rarely resist taking it, discarding it only when they came across something else they wanted. In the golden period of daemonology, when daemons were still being picked up for purposes of scientific research, these propensities were exploited by their hunters.

"Leo had read that although daemons did no harm to humans, contact with them was unpleasant, as most of them were solitary, irritable, neurotic, mistrustful, and quick to take offense, while some were unbearably maudlin—all qualities perhaps associated with their great age. But he had read, too, in articles in the Sunday supplements, that on occasion there appeared among them an extraordinarily humble being who was kindly and good. These rarer qualities, too, might be due to great age, in this instance revealing to the daemon in question the futility of time-driven aims. Leo recognized immediately that Diamanta belonged to the smaller group. This didn't mean, however, that she was free of the strange likings of other daemons; later, Leo would see her face light up when they passed a dump or she saw junk lying in a ditch, although she was ashamed of this reaction and tried to conceal it. As Leo had taken no great interest in daemons up to this point, it was from Diamanta that he learned that the gift of immortality was counterbalanced by a very short memory. Most daemons remembered with clarity only events of the past ten years or so, although it might happen that a certain image or overheard word would wake a memory from the more distant past."

18. Fortress

"It was probable that daemons hadn't always shared such character traits. Dim flashes of memory indicated that daemon tribes had once been at war. Perhaps their cantankerousness and hostility toward all other daemons—which in Leo's time mostly took the form of whinging, malign gossip, and tittle-tattle—were an awkward hangover from heroic days of struggle, a pathetic remnant of the fighting spirit of their ancients that had stayed in the blood for centuries and spoiled there. No doubt the origin of the strange ritual of periodic returns to the world of the daemons to contest its throne was also to be found in the daemons' ancient history. As Leo knew little about the world of the daemons, he asked Diamanta what it was like. It was sometimes shown in magazines as a fantastical place, but the origin of these spectacular images was always traced back to some science-fiction movie or other. With a smile, Diamanta explained that there was no similarity between the daemon world as shown in the human-interest magazines and the real one. It occupied something like the reverse of the human world, and it was possible to reach it through several holes in space, much as we insert a finger in a hole in a suit in order to touch its lining. Diamanta would have gone on to give Leo details, but he demurred, fearing that this would entail a lecture on the fourth or fifth dimension or the space-time continuum, which he knew he wouldn't enjoy; at Leo's behest, therefore, Diamanta skipped the expert commentary. She had last visited the world of the daemons during the Great Return eight years earlier. Naturally, she had no memory of earlier visits.

"Diamanta was just embarking on the story of her visit to the world of the daemons when they became aware of voices coming from the rear entrance to Reception—those of the receptionist and a man unknown to them. Obviously agitated, Linda stood up and prepared to leave. But when the receptionist appeared in the company of a man, a woman, and two small boys, whom he proceeded to lead across the yard, Linda concluded that she had nothing to fear from this family, and she sat down again. Diamanta went on with the story. 'There is something insect-like in the behavior of daemons,' she said, 'and during the Great Return they resemble insects more than ever. The preparations are like the swarming of ants or bees. The daemons gather at holes that lead to their world and run to and fro there, humming and buzzing. Then at night they swarm through to the other side.'

"The urge to return to the fight, which stirred in the blood of daemons once every thirty-three years, was impossible to resist, she said. She remembered a day six years earlier when she had witnessed, without understanding what was going on, some confused, restless, aggressive daemons running about in front of her house, shoving and hissing at each other. On waking the next morning, she had been too restless to stay at home, and soon she was running with the others, bumping into them, and pushing them aside with her elbows. In the world on the other side it was always dusk; there were lines of red light amid the clouds of its dark sky, but the sun never showed itself. On arrival in their world, the daemons found themselves at the bottom of a cliff overlooking a lake. On the top of the cliff, looming against the dark sky, was something darker still—a fortress. The daemons referred to this as a castle, although it looked more like a large warehouse or an evacuated factory. This was where the daemon lord—something between a barbarian chieftain and a gang leader—lived with his retinue. Trembling with impatience, the daemons scaled the rock like ants, all the while shoving and crawling across one another. Thus they forced their way into the fortress, where battle was joined between the newcomers and the garrison; the weapon of choice was the dagger. Daemon battles were brutal in the extreme; not to the death, of course, as daemons couldn't die, but combatants suffered all degrees of physical pain known to humans, as well as other, more terrible ones that humans were spared by unconsciousness and death. These daemons were able to heal even the most severe, painful wounds relatively quickly by the laying on of leaves of an ivy-like climbing plant that grew on the walls of the inner courtyard of the fortress. No sooner had they scrambled to their feet than they plunged back into the fight.

"Only during the actual invasion, as the swarms fell on the gloomy fortress, did groups and cliques begin to form. Certain combatants were declared commanders, and temporary alliances were established. Each passing day brought new tricks and betrayals; everyone was perpetrator and victim of treachery, and it was common for assailants to secretly unite with defenders against their own allies, and for defenders to sell out their commander to assailants in return for the promise of a place close to the new ruler. She, too, had done all this, Diamanta said, although today she could scarcely understand how she could have done it. She was so ashamed that she had mentioned it to no one apart from Linda and Leo; yet she knew that in twenty-five years she would again be running through the halls of the fortress, dagger in hand, stabbing at every shadow, scheming with and betraying fellow combatants.

"The group that emerged as the winner and captured the ruler named its own commander the new king. The new ruler always treated his vanquished predecessor and his retinue mercilessly and cruelly; he demonstrated the same lack of pity with members of his own forces and allies who fell into disfavor. Unable to kill those he imprisoned, he had them chained to the walls of the dank, dirty hall in which he lived with his own retinue. Members of the defeated army who escaped imprisonment fled through the holes in space back to the human world, where immediately they made plans for a retaliatory expedition. But the amok on the other side soon died down, plans for retaliation were abandoned, and after ten or eleven years no daemon could remember the battle at the fortress. Thus the daemons led their restless, shallow lives until the urge to fight returned to stir their blood thirty-three years later.

"Diamanta had been gravely wounded in the last invasion, resulting in her failure to escape and her capture. Her oppressors had put her in an iron collar attached to the wall of the gloomy hall, where she had lived with several other prisoners similarly restrained. She had been lucky: One day the drunkard charged to guard her had fallen asleep within her reach, allowing her to pull the keys from his pocket and so unlock her collar. She had run from the fortress down to the lake, and from there through to the human world."

19. Skaters

"Diamanta found herself in a frosty white landscape. The sun was shining from a clear blue sky and the hard snow crackled underfoot. She had no idea where in the human world she was, although she was quite sure she wasn't in Africa. The country was interlaced with canals, each with a thick covering of ice. The bare black trees that stood in the snow were too widely spaced to be considered woods. She heard the cries of crows and every now and then the flapping of wings as one flew around her head. Amid the black trunks she saw a group of low buildings with snow-covered roofs, from which unmoving strips of pale smoke rose like marble columns. She headed across a sparkling white field toward yards and orchards at the back of a village, her approach monitored from afar by the barking of a dog. After a while she heard a man's call, in German. She passed the village and continued across the snowy plain before stepping onto a frozen canal and following this for a long time. The lighter lines on the surface of the ice had been left there by skaters, she supposed. Eventually, she spotted among the trees on the bank a snow-covered structure that she took for a deserted factory. And as all daemons are attracted by old, abandoned industrial buildings, she set off toward it to take a look. As the heavy metal gate creaked open, a large, screeching crow flew through a large hole in the roof, where the blue sky peeped through. The inside of the building was a single room filled with rusty machinery, the shafts and cogwheels of which were half-hidden under drifts of snow. Dried leaves blown in through broken windows were scattered about the decomposing floor. In such an environment, every daemon would feel as comfortable as a millionaire in the penthouse of a luxury hotel on the Riviera. So Diamanta made this place her home while she recovered from the wounds inflicted in the fighting at the fortress and torture in its throne room—without the properties of the ivy-like leaves, wounds took longer to heal. When she was feeling better, she went for long walks along the canal, meeting only a lone skater once or twice a week.

"One morning, she heard human voices. She clambered onto the metal casing of one of the machines and looked through the metal grating of a window that had lost nearly all its panes. A red sun was weaving its way through the black branches, casting shadows on the pink snow. Amid the tree trunks she saw skaters flashing past, only the top half of their bodies visible above the sloping bank. About an hour later, Diamanta heard footsteps in the snow near the factory, and muffled men's voices. Again she climbed on a machine and listened keenly. For the next two hours or so nothing happened; the men stood in one place and conversed in German. There were ever fewer skaters on the canal; individuals passed by at ever greater intervals. Suddenly a woman screamed, followed by sounds of a struggle. Diamanta ran outside to see three men trying to subdue a young woman. Two of the men, wearing green quilted jackets, were holding the woman down in the snow; the third, overcoated man was telling the others what to do, as he prepared to tie the woman up with strong cord.

"The operation wasn't going too well: Although the woman was small and apparently delicate, she was showing surprising strength in the struggle, and she was using the skates on her feet as an effective weapon. Several times, her kicks almost slashed the brutes' faces. So the men changed their tactics: They decided to unlace and remove her high skating boots before tying her up. The sudden appearance of Diamanta startled the men and momentarily broke their concentration. Seizing her opportunity, the young woman aimed an accurate kick at the man in the coat, slashing his face with her skate. He let out a yell and fell to his knees, both hands over his face. Diamanta saw the blood drip from his fingers and onto the snow. For a second or two the other men froze, their eyes on their commander as he crawled screaming through the snow. His screams frightened the crows over a wide area; the howling and wheezing was joined by the sound of flapping from dozens of pairs of wings.

"The young woman leapt to her feet. Diamanta grabbed her hand, and they fled together through the trees. Still in her skates, the young woman struggled to make progress, and the ruffians might have caught them easily. But Diamanta looked back to see their assailants departing, the men in jackets flanking the wounded commander, who was still moaning and leaving a trail of red spots in his wake. So this was how Diamanta and Linda had met.

"Diamanta took Linda inside the factory, realizing as soon as she began to examine her that Linda wasn't a human. At first, Diamanta thought that Linda was a daemon too, but it didn't take her long to figure out that she was a robot. It was from Linda that Diamanta learned where she had been living for the past two weeks: This place of crisscrossing canals was in the southern part of Brandenburg. Later, Linda would tell Diamanta the story of how she had ended up there."

20. Massachusetts Institute of Technology
"At this point in the narrative, Diamanta invited Linda to pick up the story. Up till then, Linda had listened in silence,

although she surely knew Diamanta's story very well. As Linda didn't wish to speak of herself, she asked her friend to do so on her behalf. Besides, she was feeling unwell, and she preferred to go and lie down in their room. Left alone with Leo in the yard of the roadhouse, Diamanta embarked on the sad tale she had heard from Linda in the freezing-cold abandoned factory.

"Linda had been created three years earlier at the Massachusetts Institute of Technology, as a prototype of a new generation of robots. Diamanta was about to explain to Leo what constituted the exceptionality of this type, but Leo—who, as we know, had no head for exact science—made it clear that he didn't wish to hear the technical details; so Diamanta had to settle for telling him that the production of Linda represented an entirely original merging of technological and biological processes developed by a team led by a Professor Burns. A robot's character was more or less a matter of chance, so the fact that Linda was born as an extraordinarily gentle, kindly being prone to melancholy, couldn't have been foreseen. For financial reasons, the series for which Linda was the prototype never went into production, meaning that now she was probably the most advanced product on the robot market. This explained why she bore a greater burden than most beings of her type.

"Linda's sufferings began in the institute of her birth, when one of the team of scientists—a certain Dr. Jones—fell in love with her. Unfortunately, Jones was engaged to be married to Dr. Williams of the same team. The more competent scientist of the two (more competent, indeed, in all kinds of ways), Williams had the more senior position—she was assistant to Professor Burns. Linda loved clumsy, high-strung Jones in return. A description of the tragi-comic relationship of the scientist and the artificial woman took up about fifty yards of wire. Fernando recounted at length how the lovers lived in a constant state of anxiety. They had to hide themselves in warehouses, deserted laboratories, broom closets, and storage rooms, where Linda listened to Jones's breathless confessions of love. Although there were hundreds of small rooms at the institute, all of them known to Jones and Linda, still they were constantly being disturbed, and Jones would have to pretend that he was conducting a scientific experiment on Linda. On the verge of a nervous breakdown, he was having trouble sleeping, and he lived on little more than tranquilizers and antidepressants. In spite of all this, they succeeded in keeping their love secret from institute staff, with a single exception: Dr. Williams soon noticed a change in Jones's behavior toward her, even though he did all he could to disguise it. And Williams was astute enough to figure out the identity of her rival.

"It came as a shock to her. Williams had always been repelled by artificial people, much as she was disgusted by insects. She was humiliated by Jones's love for Linda; she had always had a remarkably high opinion of herself, and now it seemed that Jones preferred a monster to her. She felt hatred as well as disgust for Linda. Williams put off her punishment of Jones to concentrate on his artificial lover. She was a powerful enough at the institute figure to make Linda's life hell. There were many things Williams could do to harm Linda, and gradually she tried them all. Fernando described the pain-inducing, extremely humiliating experiments Williams conducted on her. Williams concealed from Jones her knowledge of his love for Linda, so she could ask him to assist in her sickening abuse and abasement of his lover. By now, Jones was taking so many sedatives that he wandered about the laboratories in a stupor, his eyes barely open, test tubes falling from his hands. But he was terrified of Williams, and besides, he cherished the foolish belief that by standing up for Linda, he would betray the secret of their love. He was too much of a coward to confess his feelings and protect defenseless Linda from his feral fiancée. Though Jones didn't protect Linda, MIT internal regulations did, by preventing Williams from destroying or causing serious damage to the joint work of her team. Still, Linda knew that Williams would soon come up with a way of killing her with impunity. She was on her guard always, knowing that the final onslaught on her unhappy life could arrive at any moment, and that she had to be ready for it."

21. Chase

"Linda slept in a laboratory at the institute. A light sleeper like all robots, one night she was woken by the rattling of the elevator. She looked at her watch and saw that it was three A.M. She jumped out of bed and ran out into the empty corridor, which glowed a dim fluorescent purple, and succeeded in hiding in a dark alcove, from which she watched the ominous broadening of a line of light between the double doors, followed by the entry of a white-coated Dr. Williams holding a syringe. Williams stood still and looked about, the fluorescent light flitting about in the lenses of her spectacles. Although Linda pushed herself against the wall, she couldn't conceal her shadow. She made a run for it through the long corridors of the institute with Williams in hot pursuit. Whenever she looked back, there was Dr. Williams, her unfastened white coat flapping behind her. The clack of the heels of the two women overrode the quiet buzz of the strip lights and the ticking of instruments whose green and blue lights shone beyond doors of laboratories.

"Fortunately, Linda's design allowed her to run fast. Not only was Dr. Williams fueled by hatred, however, she knew her way around the maze of corridors and stairwells far better than Linda did. Many times, Linda came up against a locked door and had to retrace her steps. At last she found the emergency

stairs and raced down them. Meanwhile, though, Williams had
traveled to the first floor by elevator. Linda opened the doors
to the corridor that led to the exit to find herself confronted
by Williams, her hair disheveled from the chase, wielding the
syringe in a raised hand. Linda slammed one of the doors against
the doctor's face and heard her scream in pain, before sprinting
past her and down the unlit staircase that led to the boiler room.
A strip of dim light from the streetlamps penetrated the barred
window by the low ceiling and lay across the floor of the otherwise dark room. Linda ran alongside pipes from which white,
hissing steam escaped at several places. After a while, the pipes
forked off into different streams, which were lost to view. Linda
took advantage of the near-darkness by disappearing into it,
moving further into the labyrinth contained in the hot, twisting
pipes. Her course was guided only by light reflected weakly by
the aluminum foil insulation wrapped around the pipes. She
stopped and strained her ears for the sound of her antagonist's
breathing or the rustle of her coat; she knew that Dr. Williams
was close, perhaps right next to her separated only by a pipe,
standing and listening. For a long time, pursued and pursuer
stood in a silence broken only by the occasional rattle of some
machine or other, the hiss of steam, and the muffled sound of
a late-night car passing along the embankment of the Charles
River.

"Cautiously and on tiptoe, Linda moved on through spaces
where the darkness was absolute. So as not to lose her way,
as she moved forward she ran her hand along a pipe at head
height—until she touched something soft, then something
hard. The next second it dawned on her that the soft thing was
Williams's face, the hard thing her glasses. Then she felt a hand
seize her own and a sharp pain in her belly. Gathering all her
strength, Linda wrenched herself free of Williams's grip and
threw her aside, before speeding off into the darkness. As she

ran, she pulled out the syringe that Williams had stuck into her. She came to the main corridor of the boiler room. As she hurried back toward the stairs, from deep in the darkness she heard banging and a squawking voice that sounded more animal than human. Dr. Williams had lost her way: The noises were produced by her pain as her face struck hot pipes and metal stopcocks—and her terrible curses and threats. As she opened the door, Linda looked back to see Williams, her face bloodied and blood stains on her gleaming white coat, staggering toward the exit. Linda was struck by how this woman instrumental in her manufacture now herself looked like an artificial monster.

"Linda ran up the stairs to the first floor, out of the building past the night porter's lodge, and onto Memorial Drive. For a moment she stood still and looked to the opposite bank of the dark Charles River, where beyond a string of lights on the waterfront the Boston skyline rose black and jagged. Then she ran across the Harvard Bridge, which at that time of night was deserted of all pedestrians and vehicles. She was already on the far side of the bridge when she heard an engine behind her. She turned back and was dazzled by the headlights of a car turning onto the bridge. Again Linda ran as hard as she could, as the car gathered speed and careered toward her. Linda stayed close to the rail, but the car approached her with two wheels on the sidewalk, sometimes clipping the rail so that sparks flew from its hood. It was almost upon her when she reached the bank and darted down to the riverside, where she hid among the trees. The car stopped. Keeping to the shadows, Linda lay flat against the earth. She saw Dr. Williams step out of the car and look around. After that, the car drove around slowly, like a sniffer dog, along the embankment and neighboring streets, its lights coming and going, until at last it turned back to the bridge and returned to Cambridge."

22. Life on the Run

"Linda knew that she couldn't go back to MIT. She knew, too, that the life ahead of her—that of a fugitive robot—would be a desperate one. Having taken one last look at the sleeping institute on the other side of the river, she headed east along Massachusetts Avenue. On reaching Commonwealth Avenue, she rested under the trees, even managing to sleep a little. She spent all that day wandering the streets of Boston, with no idea of where she should go. She was shivering with fever: The few drops of lethal poison that had entered her body from Dr. Williams's syringe were eating away at her insides. As the buildings were turning pink in the dusk, a white van pulled up at a kiosk, and its driver dropped a bundle of evening newspapers at Linda's feet. On its front page, Linda saw a photograph of herself and one of Dr. Williams with her face covered in blood. Below the photographs was the following caption in large print: 'DANGEROUS ROBOT FLEES MIT AFTER ATTACKING SCIENTIST.'

"This was how Linda's life on the run began. The chase would go on for several years; indeed, there was still no end to it. It took her to many cities, towns, and villages, in America and in Europe. Diamanta told Leo that Linda never wanted to speak of this period of her life, not even to her, her good friend. As a fugitive being without rights, with a high reward offered for her capture, Linda must have known unimaginable pain and humiliation. Anyone could abuse, blackmail, or otherwise hurt her, and she was forced to do things most people never dreamed of, even in their worst nightmares. She found herself in terrible places whose existence the world wasn't prepared to admit; she was sold, bought, and exchanged . . . Diamanta inferred that Linda herself had several times been forced to commit acts of wickedness, even crimes, to ensure her survival. Although few people would recognize Linda as artificial, at that time there were many hunters who took advantage of loopholes in the law to make a lucrative living out of the apprehension of fugitive robots. Some of these hunters stole artificial beings to order; they could identify a person as artificial within seconds. So it happened more than once that Linda settled in an out-of-the-way village, made friends with her neighbors, and began to cherish the secret hope that she would live there for the rest of her days, only for someone who made his or her living stalking robots to turn up on the village square. Having seen in this person's eyes the avidity of the hunter who had just spotted a 'fine specimen,' she would be forced to flee again, she knew not where . . .

"All the time, Williams was waiting for Linda at MIT. Now that the robot was considered uncontrollable and dangerous, she would have the consent of her superiors to kill her. Linda was spared from delivery to the institute that had created her by the fact of her being the only robot of a new type—there was no shortage of rich snobs willing to pay a sum for her several times higher than the reward offered by the institute (Williams tried and failed to have this raised). Linda's exceptionality also saved her from excessive physical violence on the part of her owners. Although she was cruelly punished for disobedience and attempts to escape, each of her owners was very aware of her value and careful not to break or otherwise damage her. In any case, as Linda was such a fragile soul, there were many ways of torturing her that didn't involve significant damage to her body."

23. Linda in Vienna

"Linda remembered all her owners, although her memories of them blended together, returning in her nightmares as a monstrous tapestry, the scenes of which she crawled through as though they were woven from bloated faces, foul-smelling mouths, soft white bellies, fleshy lips, and chubby fingers with dirty nails; the tapestry rippled and whispered, yawned, snored, panted, sweated, drooled, stank, laughed brayingly . . . Linda no longer remembered the paths that took her to Vienna, where she lived with her last owner. Not one of the worst, he was a skinny young man called Oskar, who lived on an allowance provided by his father, one of Austria's wealthiest industrialists.

"Linda spent whole days alone, locked up in a large apartment cluttered with antique furniture. She would look beyond the drapes at the dusty ornamentation on the facade of the house opposite. She would pace the apartment amid the shiny varnished, inlaid surfaces of beautifully preserved Baroque commodes and Empire writing desks. The ticking of dozens of clocks of various kinds differed from room to room, creating a sad, never-ending mechanical piece of music; at regular intervals the clocks set up their multifarious chiming before returning to silence. (This part of the story reminded Leo of his own wanderings in Vanessa's apartment.) Oskar tended to get home late in the evening, in high-spirited male company. Linda had to serve everybody. Although in front of his friends Oskar treated her with condescension, once the friends had left he babbled drunkenly and sentimentally until morning, telling her some story of unrequited love (this story varied from one night to the next, although apparently he always spoke of the same woman). Typically he burst into tears around three-thirty and wanted Linda to comfort him. As at last he prepared to go to bed, he would blather something about God and the soul and how Linda was his only friend. When he awoke, at noon, he was surly and rude toward her, however; and when he went out he never forgot to lock every door in the apartment.

"One day, Oskar went off leaving Linda with the feeling there was something different about this particular day. She stood in the middle of the apartment wondering what it was. Then it came to her—she hadn't heard the clicking of the locks. She pushed down the handle and the door opened. Linda breathed in the damp smell of the stairwell, considering it the finest scent in all the world. She ran down the stairs, and, as so many times in the past few years, wandered the streets of a city she didn't know. After a while, she reached an avenue with streetcars moving along it; she skirted a fence made of metal poles, beyond which she saw a park with carefully trimmed bushes and trees shedding colorful leaves; she passed large, richly ornamented buildings and dark monuments. Her quiet happiness soon evaporated as the thought became more and more insistent that she was back on the desperate merry-go-round of wandering, captivity, and escape. She realized that she no longer had the strength to live such a life; she felt a terrible weariness and a longing to be at peace. Her aimless course took her farther and farther uptown. Now she was walking along a straight, seemingly endless street bordered on one side by a railing, beneath which were tracks for the trains that traveled out to the suburbs, which indeed passed from time to time. On seeing a concrete bridge that crossed the tracks, it occurred to her what she should do if she intended never to run again. She mounted the few steps to the bridge, placed her elbows on the barrier, and looked down at the shining rails running off into the distance. She stood like this for a long time—not because she was afraid of death, but because she still wished to revel in the peace and joy she hadn't felt for so long."

24. Professor

"Someone placed a hand on Linda's shoulder; she screamed and turned around. But she had nothing to fear: The kindly face she saw beneath the white hair certainly wasn't that of a robot hunter. The old man addressing her was a neuroscientist—a professor emeritus who had taught at many universities, all over the world. And the team that built Linda had made use of his work in the field of artificial intelligence. On seeing her in profile as she stood on the bridge, the professor had recognized her immediately: In professional circles, Linda's case was very well known. He had even met Dr. Williams several times, and could well imagine the background to the rumors spread by the MIT scientist about the danger that Linda posed.

"As he introduced himself to Linda, he told her immediately that he knew who she was, and he made it clear what he thought of Dr. Williams. Then he offered her a place to stay. Linda was unsure whether to accept: On the one hand, she didn't want to give up the peace she had found at last, but on the other it dawned on her—to her amazement—that this was the first kind-hearted, truly good human she had met. So she let the professor take her to his home, a villa on the outskirts of the city. There, at the fireside and into the small hours, Linda told the story of the night of her escape in Cambridge, and of what had happened to her since. The professor listened without interrupting; he simply smoked his pipe and nodded. A widower with an ailing heart, he lived alone. Linda began to take care of him and his household. As the professor seldom saw his children and grandchildren, he soon began to treat Linda like a daughter.

"The professor often spoke of his childhood. He had been born in a village in Brandenburg, in a landscape crisscrossed with canals. He liked to look back on this, particularly the ice-skating races that had been held on the frozen canals every Three Kings' Day. In the professor's younger years, this had been a great event in the area, not least as it gave the villages an opportunity to compete with one another. With a smile, the professor explained to Linda that his favorite daydream had cast him as the winner of the competition, although in reality he had never taken part, being too weak for it—he had suffered from all kinds of illnesses since early childhood. In his daydream, he saw in detail how he would move smoothly between the snowy banks, overtaking every other skater until the landscape was his and his alone, as the others were left far behind. Again and again, he saw himself arriving at the finish line, where the spectators would fall on him in congratulation. He confessed to Linda that the power of his daydream had no doubt been heightened and developed by the fact that for boys the race was laced with eroticism: The victors had been admired by all the girls, and the admiration often had a continuation.

"Linda could see that the professor still regretted that he hadn't been able to compete with the other boys. It crossed her mind that he may have become a celebrated scientist—he had once been regarded as a serious candidate for a Nobel Prize—in an attempt to come to terms with his failure in the skating race. Whether the attempt had been successful, Linda couldn't tell. She wanted to help the professor, and there was only one thing she could do for him that would express her gratitude to him. She realized that what she was about to propose was nonsensical, but also that its very absurdity was what made it worth doing. She would show the professor how much she cared for him by doing something for him, and as there was nothing meaningful she could do, she would at least do something meaningless. She told him: 'I will enter the Three Kings' Day race on your behalf. Then I'll come back and tell you about it.' She saw that the professor understood and was glad. He didn't spoil the moment by trying to talk her out of it."

25. Winter

"Linda moved into the villa in October. A week before Christmas, the professor had a seizure and was taken by ambulance to the hospital, leaving Linda alone in the house. In the early morning Linda was informed by telephone that the professor had died during the night. She took some money from the professor's wallet and left the villa. Out in the streets, large snowflakes rolled in on many sides from the main avenues, swirling in the cones of light produced by car headlights. She stood at the crosswalks waiting for the green light through the blizzard. In the pedestrian zones, she threaded her way through crowds of snow-covered figures under festoons of lights hanging from the facades. Christmas music was playing from loudspeakers, and the aroma of punch and roasted chestnuts wafted over from the market stalls. She slept at railroad stations or on the front steps of buildings. She liked to sit at a window table in a coffeehouse, just to watch the snow fall, but whenever she did, she felt the eyes of another customer resting on her, so she hurriedly paid up and left; she would spend the next hour making sure that nobody was following her. She saw that her life in the villa had been nothing more than a three-month postponement of her suicide—perhaps a gift from some deity to help her on her way into the darkness. Linda was unsure about her religious beliefs, but she was certain there was no afterlife for robots. The period of deferral over, she was again ready to do the thing she had been preparing on the bridge above the tracks; this time, however, she felt far weaker and less brave. In any case, before it came to that, there was a promise she had to keep.

"On New Year's Eve, Linda's last night on Vienna's streets, the snowfall was especially heavy. Just before midnight she found herself in a square filled with revelers. At the center of the square was a great cathedral with a slender tower, the tip of which was lost in the darkness. As the bell sounded, dozens of multicolored fireworks shot up into the eddying snow and exploded high in the dark sky, illuminating the steeply-pitched roof of the cathedral, casting the falling snow in all colors, making Linda feel that birds of paradise were flying above the city. After midnight, people drifted away from the square; as dawn approached and the snow stopped, she found herself walking alone in a sleeping city. As soon as it was light, she headed across the virgin snow to the railroad station and went straight to the ticket office. On the platform she passed a souvenir stand where a vendor was showing a little boy a small glass globe, shaking it to bring down snow inside the glass which settled on the roof of a great church; Linda recognized the church as the cathedral where she had seen in the new year. She bought the toy so that in the days that remained to her she would be reminded of her time in Vienna. Then she got on the fast train and traveled through snow-covered landscapes and cities to Berlin. There she bought some skates in a department store and spent several days on the streets, spending the nights on the surface of a frozen lake. In the early morning of Three Kings' Day, she stepped out of a train at the small station in the village the professor had told her about."

26. Race along the Canals

"Tables from the local tavern had been placed along the banks of a canal. Here wurst, punch, and mulled wine were on sale. There were a great many people around these tables—some of them competitors, others mere spectators. The competitors were required to complete twelve laps of the course, which was a complicated one, as the canals branched off in many places. The organizers explained to the competitors that they should pay close attention to the red flags tied to the trees, so as not to stray from the right path.

"Later, Linda and Diamanta learned what actually happened during the race. In the crowd was a robot hunter called Hellmut, a sturdy thirty-year-old with ruddy cheeks who was a native of a nearby village. At fifteen, Hellmut had gone to Berlin to become a beater for a robot hunter. Having worked his way up to the position of hunter, now he was the owner of a thriving agency with its office on the Kurfürstendamm that specialized in the finding, sale, and exchange of fugitive robots. Owing to the lack of laws in this area, more and more such businesses were being founded all over the world, and they operated entirely in the open; the police would challenge their activities only in obviously demonstrable cases of theft.

"Hellmut had attended every single ice-skating race since he was a child, albeit in recent years only as a spectator. He was standing with his two younger brothers, who had stayed in the village. The brothers admired Hellmuth immensely, considering him a very successful man. They were drinking grog that Hellmuth had graciously paid for, and they were laughing at his jokes. As an expert in his field, the moment Hellmuth saw Linda at the registration of competitors, he recognized her not only as an artificial being, but as the robot that had fled Cambridge in the United States; he knew, too, that there was a large reward for her apprehension, and that this reward was small compared with what certain of his clients would be prepared to pay for her. Although he had come here to have a good time, drink too much grog, and reminisce about his childhood, as soon as he saw the robot, his lust for wealth and passion for hunting were awakened, driving all thoughts from his mind but those relating to Linda's capture.

"He wasted no time in telling his brothers about the prey that had come into view; honored that Hellmuth wished to collaborate with them, if only on one day, they listened carefully to his plan for the hunt. Having skated the complicated course many times, Hellmuth knew it well. He decided that they would lie in wait for Linda near the old factory, a spot on the bank where there were rarely any spectators. They would seize Linda on the eighth or ninth lap, by which time the few remaining skaters would be passing by individually at great intervals. The brothers expressed the concern that Linda might quit this difficult race at an earlier stage, but Hellmuth assured them that her design was such that she would surely last all twelve laps, and that indeed she had a great chance of winning the race. Before setting off for the factory, they bought a bottle of rum, which they drank as they waited among the trees. Linda passed them several times, but she was always hemmed in by other skaters. There was a gradual thinning-out in the number of competitors until at last the brothers saw their prey come out of a bend all on her own—whereupon they jumped her, pushed her onto the ice, and dragged her to the snow-covered bank, where they attempted to tie her up. At this point, they were disturbed by Diamanta."

27. Daemon and Robot

"Although she could barely stand without support, Linda wanted to go on with the race for the professor's sake. She was terribly upset, and she was consumed by self-reproach that she had failed to keep the promise she had made in Vienna; this, she believed, was the greatest defeat of her life. The two women sat on the floor of the factory amid the snow-covered machines, looking beyond the open doors at the brilliant white and the black silhouettes of trees. At first engrossed in thoughts of her failure, only slowly did Linda become aware of what Diamanta was saying to her and begin to answer her. Diamanta told Linda that she had identified her as artificial, but that Linda had no cause to fear her. Linda could tell that Diamanta wasn't human either; she asked if Diamanta was also a robot. Identifying herself as a daemon, Diamanta explained patiently what kind of creatures daemons were.

"Then the two women began to talk of what they had been through; their stories were descriptions of isolated images and scenes from the short period that the memory of a forgetful daemon could contain and the three years the robot had been operational, and there were frequent pauses in the interaction. In the moments of silence, they listened to the cawing of the crows and the occasional swish of a passing competitor's skates. From the mere fragments she was told, each of the women learned everything she needed to know about the other; they saw that they were sisters, aliens roaming the human world. Both thought about the similarities between the tangled paths of their aimless, senseless journeys, which together formed a single intricate ornament of futility and sorrow. Although Diamanta tried to convince Linda to stay with her, Linda continued to insist that she had to get away. Linda was delighted to have made a friend just before her life's end, but the conversation didn't provide a reason for prolonging her stay on Earth; she was determined to accomplish what she had postponed on meeting the professor on the bridge over the tracks of the Vienna S-Bahn. Her delight was mixed with sorrow for her failure to keep the promise she had made to the professor, but to wait until next January was out of the question—she lacked the strength for another year of life. She was afraid that if she deferred her suicide for even a day she would lose the courage to go through with it. So shortly before nightfall, Linda opened the backpack she had worn during the race, which contained the glass globe and her shoes. She changed out of her skates and showed Diamanta how the snow fell on the roof of the cathedral; then Linda and Diamanta embraced before Linda walked away.

"Although Diamanta didn't know what Linda had in mind, she was worried about her. She had grown fonder of her factory than any other place on Earth she could remember, and before Linda appeared, she had imagined herself spending the next months or even years there. But left alone in the freezing hall, next to Linda's abandoned skates, she told herself that she shouldn't allow Linda to go off into the world alone. And she realized that until the memory of her dissolved, she would miss the unhappy artificial being with whom she had spoken for just a few hours, more than her factory. So she ran outside and through the snow, fearful that Linda was lost to her forever. Before long, however, she spotted a solitary figure that cast a long, pale shadow across the pink-tinged, snowy plain. Diamanta ran toward Linda, shouting her name. As she stopped in her tracks, Linda knew that she would no longer be able to kill herself. After that, the two women stayed together.

"The artificial being's anxiety compounded by the daemon's restlessness ensured that they never stayed long in one place. They traveled in many countries of Europe, Asia, North Africa, and America. The wire book described scenes from their lives in a Paris suburb, Manchester, a colony of dachas near Moscow (a whole winter), the rundown Greek quarter of Alexandria, a Beirut prefab baking in the sun, a tenement in Berlin's Kreuzberg, and Chelyabinsk. As the elder Vieta moved his finger along the arcs and loops of wire that made up this passage, he wondered from where in Fernando's mind the images of these cities and landscapes had emerged. Had he known them from guidebooks and travel films? Had he dreamed them up in the blistering heat of the depot, or had he traveled half the world in the years of their estrangement? When the war was over, in an attempt to find out more about his son's life he sought out Fernando's colleagues at the *Emerald Falcon* and a number of women with whom Fernando had been intimate, but it turned out that not even his lovers knew very much about him.

"For the first time in her short life, Linda had a friend. Diamanta, too, had spent the last few years alone, although she had dim memories of feeling agonized love for daemons and humans before the last battle at the fortress. There were robot hunters everywhere: Linda and Diamanta needed to be as wary of them in a Cairo marketplace as in the English Garden in Munich, or in the port of Marseille. Although as a couple it was easier for them to avoid the hunters' traps, Diamanta was powerless to protect Linda: In the human world daemons were as weak as children—the life force mentioned by the old myths had dwindled over many centuries. Linda and Diamanta preferred to live in cities, where they felt safer. As robot hunters seldom dared strike in a crowded street, it wasn't unusual for the women to notice the covetous eyes of a man who had stopped in his tracks to watch Linda. Having considered the risks, in most cases he turned away with regret and went on his way. But the hunters were becoming ever bolder, and on less frequented streets the women suffered several attacks like the one by the factory. Most recently, a group of hunters had ambushed them on New York's Fifth Avenue, just as a police car was passing. The hunters broke into a run as Diamanta and Linda made off in the opposite direction: Like criminals, they needed to steer clear of the police."

28. Motel

"They now lived in cheap hotels on the outskirts of cities, where robot hunters seldom appeared, occasionally earning money by taking work as waitresses, chambermaids, or in fast-food restaurants. They never stayed anywhere more than a few nights; and this had also been their plan for the motel where they met Leo—but both of them had fallen for the musty atmosphere of serenity and sorrow that had seeped into the wallpaper and breathed from the bed coverings, so typical of stops on long journeys. Daemons and artificial beings shared many tastes. In the beginning, Diamanta told Leo, so strong was the appeal of their room at this motel that it put them in mind of the snow-covered factory; by now, however, memories of the factory had dissolved to nothing in the room's welcoming breath. And as the women believed the motel to be relatively safe, they postponed the moment of moving on again and again, until at last they decided that nothing was forcing them to do so, at which point they stopped discussing the matter.

"They had been at the hotel for more than six months when Leo appeared on the scene. It never crossed either woman's mind that she might one day have a home, but after some time at the motel, both realized with amazement that their happiness in the room with yellowed curtains and nightstands with empty drawers wasn't unlike what humans meant when they spoke of home. At the motel, the three escaped prisoners—a human, a daemon, and a robot—developed a strange but intense happiness. Images of past wrongs and suggestions of desolate days to come reached the surface only at night, when a wakeful Linda sobbed quietly, her face buried in the pillow.

"As the days passed, however, a shadow crept over the happiness of the three friends. Linda felt worse and worse: It was clear that if she didn't get an overhaul in the next few months, she would die. Diamanta and Leo spent many hours at the computer in Reception, trawling the internet for information on where they could seek help for Linda. But it was obvious that apart from MIT, where since the retirement of Dr. Burns, Dr. Williams-Jones—Williams had married poor Jones after all—was heading the team, there was nowhere for them to turn. Diamanta sent Jones an e-mail, in which she described Linda's condition and asked for his help; she was prepared to take Linda anywhere in the world, she wrote. But her only reply was a sentimental letter in which Jones reminisced about wonderful moments with Linda, expressed regret that there was nothing he could do for her, and wished her a speedy recovery—cowardly drivel, as Jones surely knew that without his help, Linda was unlikely to live into the new year.

"Before long, Linda was spending most of the day in bed. The women were running out of money, and Leo was glad that he could at least help them out with this; there was still enough in his bank account to support several dozen daemons and robots. Diamanta insisted on earning—she agreed with the owner of the motel that she would help in the kitchen and wash dishes. Leo came to spend a lot of time alone with Linda in her room. He was touched by her fate, she by the fact that he was the only man who had ever treated her with kindness, apart from the professor. Leo knew that Linda was in love with him, although she didn't dare speak of it. He came to love her, too, out of the emotion stirred in him by her silent devotion and his compassion for her. They made love on two occasions, but though she tried not to show it, he recognized that in her weakened state, physical love was a torment for her. After that, they spent most of their time in the room in an embrace, some-times chatting, sometimes silent."

Linda's Lament

"One day, when Linda and Leo were lying together, Linda began to speak of all she had been through since her escape from MIT. She told him things she had never mentioned to anyone, including the professor and Diamanta. She spoke for several hours without a break, while Leo listened in a horror-induced trance. The story he heard formed a chain of unimaginable suffering, degradation, and revulsion. People who met Linda told themselves that as she wasn't a human being, no moral laws applied in their relations with her. This idea and the fact of her outside-the-law status woke the cruelest and most perverse desires in the men, women, and children into whose clutches she fell. Linda saw that her tormentors were themselves surprised, even horrified by what they discovered in their souls, but that at the same time the spurting forth of evil aroused in them feelings of intense pleasure the like of which they had never known.

"In a surprisingly firm voice, Linda described to Leo in detail all that had been done to her. As she had journeyed through the inferno, before long nothing at all had surprised her. For instance, there was the thirteen-year-old boy, a model student considered by all to be a kind, cheerful child, who invited his friends to his home, where they gave Linda an afternoon that still came back to her in her most horrible nightmares. Even animals hated her: Recognizing that she wasn't human, animal, or object, they had no idea what she was, and felt threatened by her. Some marks on her body had been made by dogs, horses' teeth, and cats' claws. On the run, Linda fell into the company of some other fugitive robots hiding in a tumbledown house in the country. But they, too, tormented her, considering her to be more human than robot. Once, she came across a camp of grotesque figures in the woods—robots whose manufacture hadn't been a success, and who had escaped from the laboratory. With them, she spent the most terrifying three days of her life, until she managed to flee. Right up until her decision to end it all in Vienna, Linda's main purpose had been survival, and she told Leo without inhibition about the degrading, shameful acts she had performed when it became clear that they offered her only chance of avoiding death. Amazingly, she had also known moments of strange ecstasy and dazzling beauty, which had arrived, like gifts from a compassionate angel escort, amid the greatest suffering. At times when she was able to rise above the horror that was her lot, her body might be racked with almost unbearable delight at the sight of a red sun over gray buildings, the shape of a cloud, the shadow cast by a branch on a wall, the chaotic arabesque of a bush. At moments like these, it seemed to her that the universe had been created for just such brief manifestations, and that nothing else was of any importance.

"This chapter, which Fernando had named 'Linda's Lament,' was the most badly damaged section of the wire book. A feverish Fernando had apparently made many rewrites here, straightening the wire before twisting it into new words; perhaps he had taken fright at the brutality and obscenity of the images, or else these words had seemed to him too innocent designations for the horrors that arose in his mind. Wire already weakened

by repeated twisting and straightening had been further damaged by seawater, so that in some places the book had come
apart. Although it had been possible to recover some of the
broken fragments from the seabed, many descriptions of fright-
fulness had disappeared into the anemones and coral and been
covered with sand.

"As he cautiously handled the surviving fragments of 'Linda's
Lament,' Fernando's father was reminded of Sade's *Justine*, and
he wondered how his son's mind could have begotten such
scenes. Imagining the reaction of the public, he decided that
the four most horrific passages in the chapter should be excised
from the restored text. He locked the four stretches of wire
in question in a safe in his bedroom. But he would awake at
night with a sense that scenes from his son's book were glowing
through the steel door. Often, he couldn't resist its dark enticement; he would switch on his bedside lamp, rise and put on his
dressing gown, open the safe, remove the wire text, and read it
over and over, as if it were a diabolical invocation.

"But the published remnants of 'Linda's Lament' aroused
more interest among the public than any other section of the
book (indeed, this was the only part of the book that aroused
public interest of any kind). The rumor leaked out from the
restorers' circles that certain passages in this chapter had been
censored on the President's order, on moral grounds. The earliest rumors put the censored passages at thirty yards of wire,
although a few months later this had gone up to a hundred
yards; after that, the missing wire was extended in the popular
imagination by an average of one yard per day. A wide range
of tales originated about the missing content, various obscure
publishing houses produced books they claimed to contain
the confiscated part of Fernando's work, a pornographic movie
was made with the title *Linda's Adventures*, to be followed by
Linda's Adventures II, and more than one sex club with the

name 'Linda' was established. The strange thing was, the pieces of wire locked in the President's safe contained scenes more terrible and obscene than the imagination of the masses could come up with, even though authors of the apocryphal works did their best."

The Captive II

1. Secret Clinic

"Linda's condition continued to deteriorate. In their desperation, Leo and Diamanta considered taking her to Boston. After all, Linda was now in such a bad way that there was no longer anything to lose, and perhaps Dr. Williams had cooled down since her wedding; and even if she hadn't, she was under the supervision of the scientific board and couldn't simply do as she pleased. But when they suggested this course of action to Linda, she said she would rather die at the motel than come face to face with Williams again. Leo and Diamanta were forced to accept that they could do no more than accompany Linda to the brink of the emptiness she was heading for. Then one day, Leo overheard a speaker on TV mention an illegal clinic or workshop for the repair of artificial people, somewhere in Mexico City. The clientele of this place comprised mostly robot hunters who were having their booty improved before selling it on to their own greatest advantage. The secondary activities of the clinic included the forging of certain highly valued brands of artificial people, as well as the production of copies of living or deceased individuals that were indistinguishable from the original. (These were actually the only activities that members of the international commission for artificial intelligence had agreed to ban and so pushed through to legislation in the long years of that body's existence; the copying of human specimens was obviously too socially dangerous to be permitted.)

"Yet interest in such copies remained great, and they fetched vast sums. When crimes were committed, they provided the perfect alibi, and they also came in handy for the compromising of enemies. It became fashionable in both Americas for wealthy widows to acquire a copy of the dead husband (often in the form of his younger years). There were cases of a copy being delivered before the husband had quite managed to die; a little later, the widow might return from the funeral to find her husband waiting by the hearth, reborn and rejuvenated, with a glass of sherry in his hand.

"No wonder, then, that the clinic's revenue was huge. It had proved impossible to track down the clinic's location in the enormous city, even though an international arrest warrant had been out on its director for several years. Leo and Diamanta sought out every mention of the clinic on the internet. All mentions were largely in agreement that the clinic's equipment surpassed that of every legal institution, as thanks to its huge income it was constantly upgrading, and it could afford the world's top specialists. Leo proposed that the three of them fly out to Mexico immediately. At first, Diamanta was against the idea: Surely it was beyond them to find a place for which the Mexican police, Interpol, and the CIA had been searching in vain for years. But at last she conceded that it was the last hope they had of saving Linda."

2. Ciudad de México

"Leo bought flight tickets to Mexico City, and the three of them said their goodbyes at the motel. Standing at the door of his room and taking a last look inside, Leo wondered if he would ever again experience so much happiness in one place as he had in his first months here, when Linda was still relatively well. As he quit the motel, it didn't even cross his mind that he owned a large, luxurious apartment in the city's downtown. (As Hector was telling of the southbound plane containing Leo, Linda and Diamanta flying through the night sky, Hella suddenly sat up straight in the bed. Seeing the expression of astonishment on her face, he asked in trepidation what had happened. 'I can see,' she said. Hector wanted to break off the story, as it had originated only on account of Hella's blindness, and for them to return to the city, but Hella asked if they could stay in the country until he had told it to the end. She was terribly curious to know whether Hector's heroes found the secret clinic in Mexico. Admitting that he was, too—he knew no more than Hella about what would happen next—Hector went on with the story.)

"At daybreak, Leo, Diamanta, and Linda were sitting in a taxi from Aeropuerto Benito Juárez, heading into the unknown metropolis. They had left the United States in such a hurry that they had had no time to buy a map. Although all three of them were intimidated by the great piles of concrete, steel, and brick that seemed to be pulling them in, they felt that the very inscrutability and vastness of the city admitted all possibilities and therefore offered hope for the impossible, a cure for Linda. At the airport, in answer to the driver's inquiry about their destination, Leo had muttered embarrassedly only that they were heading downtown.

Now, they just stared out of the taxi's windows in silence. There were columns of cars to either side of them, all going in the same direction. A murky orange light lay on the cars and across the large letters on the fronts of gray, crumbling concrete buildings; occasionally, a low tree growing on the edge of the sidewalk would emerge over the tops of the vehicles. The cars would disappear into dark underpasses before re-emerging into the early-morning light and rejoining the current toward the monotonous gray facades, trees, and big letters. The taxi drove ever slower, until it was making only fitful progress; the lines of downtown-bound cars took turns crawling a few yards before coming to a halt. Although Leo and the women didn't know where they were going—up to this point they hadn't discussed the details of their journey, or even seen a basic map of the Mexican metropolis, and they didn't know where they would stay or who to ask for help in this huge city, where they knew no one—they grew impatient. In the north, they hadn't had the time to think the trip through; not one of them, it seemed, had seen a point in planning, as they believed their situation to be so desperate that all that could help them was a miraculous accident.

"The cars were moving forward at the speed of a funeral procession. The taxi driver's curses became ever louder; on at last reaching a corner, he spun the wheel to the right and proceeded to navigate the side streets in an attempt to overtake the column of paralyzed vehicles. They moved further and further away from the highway until there were very few cars around, nor any pedestrians, apart from a few children apparently on their way to school. As the taxi passed through a quiet little square at whose center a twisted tree grew out of a traffic island, the passengers spotted a four-story concrete building with a sign bearing the word 'HOTEL.' Leo and Linda, who were in the back, looked at each other at the very moment Diamanta turned around to face them. Leo told the driver to pull over. There was no need for Leo to explain himself to the women: It was clear that the concrete building reminded them of the home they had shared, their beloved motel on the edge of town—although in fact it was nothing like it.

"As soon as they stepped onto the worn red carpet of the reception area, they saw that they weren't mistaken: Here was the rapture they associated with the smell of old hotels. Indeed, this Mexican hotel and its location in the north of the city was part of that happy, musty land of tattered plush and peeling wallpaper that spread over many continents. It crossed Leo's mind that if his death were to transport him to paradise, it would look like a room in a shabby hotel. The three of them checked in to one rather large room, on whose brick-red wallpaper were several color photographs of the city and its surroundings. Their small balcony offered a fine view of whatever was going on down in the square.

"Leo reasoned that to give themselves the best chance of discovering anything about the illegal clinic, they would need to get to know the locals. For the time being, they would spend their time in and around the hotel. For the first few days of their stay, they had no idea how far they were from the city center, and they knew its sights only from the photographs on the walls of their room."

3. Cantina

"They took to spending the afternoons in a cantina opposite the hotel. Their hotelier Miguel would sit here from morning till evening, and they came to enjoy the ceremony of his greeting. Miguel rarely showed up at the hotel, apparently leaving all the work to his wife and daughters, who all looked remarkably similar and whose exact number Leo was never able to establish. While Leo and Diamanta each drank several glasses of beer, Linda necessarily kept to water, and even that caused her pain.

Soon her condition was so bad that she was forced to remain in the room alone while Leo and Diamanta went to the cantina, where they fell into conversation with the locals, as Leo had hoped they would. Before long, everyone knew them; but still they lacked the courage to ask directly about the clinic.

"They focused their attention on the hotelier, who seemed to them the kind of person who might lead them to the clinic. All kinds of people came to Miguel to ask for help or to do business with him; apparently, he knew everyone and was able to arrange whatever was asked of him. Many people came to Miguel with respect, to thank him for his services, so he was obviously very successful in his dealings. Leo and Diamanta long wondered how Miguel could manage all this by spending day after day sitting over a cerveza, but eventually they realized that the heads inclined toward his had attentive ears as well as whispering mouths. Evidently, the table at the cantina was the center of an extensive network, which might reach over the entire area of this vast city—so allowing Miguel to perform his magic without moving a muscle. If no other seats at Miguel's table were taken, Leo and Diamanta would join him and chat to him about all kinds of things. Although for a long time they didn't dare ask him straight out about the clinic, they would hover over the topic of artificial people; they were waiting to be certain that the hotelier wouldn't denounce them to the police or tip off robot hunters about Linda's whereabouts. While he listened to their clumsily expressed musings, Miguel tended to squint into his cigar smoke, all the while smiling and saying little. Leo and Diamanta had no idea what was on his mind. Had he grasped what they were driving at, or did he have no inkling of what they were here for? Was the smile on his lips that of a crafty schemer or an uncomprehending fool?

"But their opportunities to speak with Miguel were few and far between: The hotelier spent most of his time at the cantina talking business with someone or other. As they sipped their Mexican beer, for the first time in ages Leo and Diamanta came to speak of matters other than Linda's sickness; they resumed their talk of daemons, which at the motel they had been forced to break off. Leo wanted to know about daemons' place in the world—he had read somewhere that Plato claimed they were the link between humans and gods—but Diamanta knew of no place for daemons in the world, nor did she hold with Plato's opinion. It turned out that she was a somewhat dogmatic atheist. There was no borderland between humans and gods, she said; Plato had settled daemons in a nonexistent place. Leo, who tended to agnosticism, disagreed with her, although he had no clear view on the matter. And so their time in the cantina passed in pleasant disputation, as they ordered and savored one cerveza after another and watched the moving shadow of the tree at the center of the hot concrete square, a shadow which reminded them of the style of a sundial. Sometimes, their eyes would flit to the dark, open balcony door beyond which Linda lay, and they would feel their guilt keenly.

"During these long conversations in the cantina, Leo and Diamanta came to the realization that they were in love. Now, Leo conceded that 'love' was the wrong word for what he felt for Linda; what he truly felt was compassion and a longing to be needed. He conceded too, as did Diamanta, that it was unthinkable for him to leave Linda in her helplessness.

"For a long time, their feelings remained unspoken. But one evening after they had left the cantina—and were walking in the neighboring streets, as they often did, having chosen not to go directly to the hotel and to sleep—they suddenly forgot all thoughts of bad conscience and the pain they might cause Linda, rendering resistance futile. Under a tree with the light of a streetlamp streaming through its branches, they pounced on each other like starving beasts. Having torn themselves apart almost painfully, without a word they ran down the street to the little hotel whose name shone out at its end, went to the front desk, took a room, and raced up the stairs. After a remorse-filled hour, they hurried back to Linda. After that, they tried desperately to conceal from her what was going on, but they couldn't be sure that Linda hadn't figured it out for herself, nor would they ever be."

4. Ricardo

"Although Leo and Diamanta went to the hotel in the neigh-boring street almost every day, these visits didn't cause them to neglect their conversations with the owner of their own hotel. But these talks didn't appear to be making any progress. Miguel just smiled all the time, drank his beer, was silent, or spoke about all kinds of things, and still Leo and Diamanta lacked the courage to ask him directly about the clinic. One afternoon, as an awkward Leo was again tiptoeing toward the subject that interested him most, and was still a long way from it, Miguel raised his glass, first to Diamanta, then to Leo, and said: 'Why not come straight out with it, my friend? That Señorita Linda is artificial I noticed when I first laid eyes on her. It doesn't look good with her, and you need to find the clinic. You have noth-ing to fear from Miguel. Miguel will denounce the señorita neither to the police nor to the cazadores, the hunters.' (At moments when he wished to emphasize his importance as an institution, Miguel spoke of himself in the third person.) 'Had he wished, he could have done so long ago. Señor Leo and Señoritas Diamanta and Linda are guests at my hotel and my friends, and I will help them. I do not know where the clinic is, as I do not need to know, but it is no problem for Miguel to find this out.'

"For two days after that, Miguel made no mention of the clinic. He sat as his table, as always, listening to many whispering mouths and giving orders and counsel to many ears. Whenever Leo and Diamanta joined him, he expounded his ideas on politics and football. On the third day, they sat silent at his table as he complained about the government. After about an hour of this, he ordered another beer before drawing from his pocket a folded slip of paper, which he handed to Leo, saying: 'This is the address of the cantina where tomorrow at noon someone will be waiting for you. This person will take Señorita Linda to the clinic.' He went on to name the sum they would need to pay. As Leo and Diamanta were thanking him, Miguel added only that the man they would meet was called Ricardo; he had no wish to speak more of the matter.

"Leo and Diamanta returned immediately to the hotel, to give the news to Linda. The rest of the day was given over to feverish preparation, even though there wasn't really anything to prepare. Leo and Diamanta scuttled about the room, moving things from one place to another and getting in each other's way, while Linda watched them pensively and wordlessly from the bed. Leo wondered what was going through her mind. Was she contemplating what awaited her at an illegal facility where her lack of rights would be blatantly obvious? As she watched him and Diamanta, did she have some inkling of their visits to the other hotel?

"The next day, their taxi driver spent a long time searching his street atlas for the address on Miguel's slip of paper, and when at last he found it, his expression led them to believe that the address wasn't a good one. He proceeded to drive them to a slum, where shanties of sheet metal spread sprawled across the side of a hill. The car climbed steep streets of hot asphalt lined with wondrous abodes composed of all kinds of materials. The cantina they were headed for turned out to be a block of white concrete without a front wall; judging by the gasoline and oil stains on its floor, until recently it had served as a garage. Five people sat around the tables inside. Several shelves containing bottles of bright-colored liquor were mounted on the back wall, behind the bar.

"They sat down at a table. In the reflected, dazzling sunlight the asphalt of the street looked like molten metal. Even in the shade it was unbearably hot. Linda began to feel sick almost immediately; in the hot air saturated with smells of asphalt, stale beer, and gasoline, Leo and Diamanta, too, were having difficulty breathing. After about ten minutes, Ricardo came over to their table. A small, bald man with a mustache, he had spent the time since their arrival sitting by the back wall, sipping his beer and watching them. All he told them was that unfortunately the clinic wasn't admitting today, and that in three days' time they should be waiting with the money at eight A.M. precisely on the corner of Tacuba and Bolívar Streets, where they would be met by the car that would take Señorita Linda where she needed to go. Leo asked if they would be able to accompany her, to which Ricardo's only answer was to wave an index finger vigorously from side to side in front of Leo's face; then he repeated that they mustn't be late, stood up, and walked off into the shining asphalt.

"At the cantina opposite their hotel that afternoon, Leo and Diamanta told Miguel in detail about their meeting with Ricardo. Miguel looked pensive; Leo noticed wrinkles on his forehead. Eventually, the hotelero said that he would take them to the rendezvous point in his own car.

"So it happened that three days later Linda, Leo, and Diamanta were driven by Miguel through streets totally unfamiliar to them, although by now they had been in the city for several weeks. In the early-morning mist, the reflected sun gleamed fitfully on the asphalt, streetlamps, and door handles of buildings, which were wet after a night of rainfall. Leo sat in silence in the back seat, holding Linda's hand, reminded of times when he had traveled a lot. He and Patricia had visited many American and European cities and breakfasted on the terraces of restaurants on splendid avenues. He wondered if he, Linda and Diamanta would ever walk around Mexico City, guidebook in hand, taking in sights, sitting in cafés and parks . . ."

5. Automobiles

"Miguel stopped the car on a long, straight street, where the portals of baroque churches and faded colonial palaces alternated with the fronts of cantinas and snack bars. He remained seated in the car, as did Linda and Diamanta, but Leo, too restive to stay inside, paced the sidewalk, on which at this early hour there were few other pedestrians. He heard the rattle of a roller shutter as a storekeeper opened a nearby produce market; then all was quiet again. At eight o'clock precisely a car drove out of a side street, swerved to avoid Miguel's vehicle, then braked sharply right in front of it. Leo saw Ricardo sitting behind the wheel, next to a woman in a hat and dark glasses, whose head was bowed so that Leo couldn't see her face—a member of the clinic's staff, he assumed. The man lounging on the back seat was similar in appearance to Ricardo. Under his jacket, Leo spotted a dark strap that might be attached to a leather holster. This man got out of the car. As Leo handed him the envelope with the money, Diamanta led Linda from Miguel's car to Ricardo's. Leo was suddenly overcome with anxiety. Who was he delivering Linda to? Linda embraced him and Diamanta, got into the car, and waved at them through the window. At the moment Ricardo started the engine, the woman in the front seat looked up, turned to face Linda, and took off her glasses. Linda let out a cry of desperation and reached for the door handle, but the door refused to open. Then the car darted forward and away. Now Leo and Diamanta were shouting, too: They had recognized the woman as Dr. Williams, having seen her photograph many times on the MIT website.

"They chased after the car, an entirely futile act. Miguel called to them; they sprinted back to him and tumbled into the back of his car, which then sped off down Tacuba Street. By now the mist had lifted, and they could see, at the end of the straight road, the car in which Linda was captive. Leo and Diamanta had never seen Miguel angry before; he was red in the face and muttering strings of curses. The hotelero was the victim of something he hadn't known for a long time, the kind of act that his world considered the greatest crime of all—he had been cheated by a business partner. Leo and Diamanta, too, had figured out what had happened: At their meeting at the cantina, Ricardo had immediately recognized Linda as an artificial being known by those engaged in illegal trade with robots to be immensely valuable, and he had made the snap decision to play the game by his own rules. He had claimed that the clinic was full to gain time. He had gotten a phone number for Dr. Williams—perhaps he had had one in his notebook for some months already—and called her up.

"The hatred Dr. Williams felt for Linda had in no way diminished since her wedding—indeed, maybe it was stronger now that she knew that Jones's love for an artificial woman had caused irreparable damage to his soul. Leo would discover that Williams had recently made a private offer to robot hunters for Linda's capture that was far in excess of the official MIT one. Nor was it out of the question that Ricardo had demanded an even higher sum, to which Williams had agreed on one condition—that she herself be involved in the abduction: After all these years, she was hardly likely to pass up the opportunity to witness Linda falling into her trap, and to this end she would have taken the first plane from Boston to Mexico City. Ricardo had probably violated Miguel's protocol with some reluctance, as it had long been in his own best interests to observe it. Maybe money wasn't even the decisive factor; maybe he was simply too much of a cazador to allow such a trophy to get away from him."

6. Pursuit

"As yet there was hardly any traffic on Tacuba Street, and Ricardo's car, although far away, remained in their sights. None of them spoke as the car sped along the straight road in pursuit of what appeared to be a mirror. Leo was in a strange state; it was as though his horror at what had just happened had erased his thoughts, ideas, and feelings, leaving in his head an empty space which was being filled with sharp, surreal images of things they were passing; as in a vivid dream, Leo saw down to the finest detail the figures and faces of passersby, the leaves on the trees, the walls of buildings marked with graffiti and peeling plaster; but all the shapes had slipped away from their names and contexts. The wet road glistened in the light of the low sun, as though the car were gliding along the surface of a canal. Above the glare were the dark, silent faces of houses, mansions, and churches all grown together, like a single, indifferent mass, which for reasons incomprehensible to the human mind had assumed a shape dreamed up in its innards that had nothing to do with human purposes. Leo wouldn't have been at all surprised if the portals, windows, and roofs had transformed into monstrous, giant figures.

"The rows of houses on each side suddenly fell away, and the gleaming surface of the road spilled over into a large square with a pole at its center whose flag stirred lazily. On its left, the car passed the dark mass of the cathedral, which Leo recognized from a photograph that hung in their hotel room; but now it was a cathedral for him no longer, as the curves and bulges of its facade produced hundreds of different shapes, none of which came together in a meaningful image. What Leo saw was a hill made of clay, the shapes made by jumbles of figures above the portals in the dark, trickling mud, some fixed, some on the move, but all on the point of dissolution. Meanwhile, the car in which Linda was captive had disappeared into a street that led away from the square, between the cathedral and a palace with monotonous rows of windows that stretched into the distance in dreamlike perspective.

"The two cars wove through stalls, odds and ends that had fallen into the roadway, cylindrical stoves on which wrinkled old women with chignoned black hair were baking tortillas, clusters of people, and chasing dogs. Ricardo and Miguel sounded their horns almost continuously and were followed with screams and curses. Miguel had the advantage here, as his car was following in the wake of Ricardo's, and he was gradually gaining on the kidnappers as a result. On their right, a side street opened up that was altogether deserted. There was a screech of tires as Ricardo swerved to the right to take a corner and then did the same again. The two cars were now back on the square, on its southern side. At the far end, Leo glimpsed the dark mountain of the cathedral, just before Ricardo's car disappeared into another side street.

"Now the sun was at their backs, so the glare on the road was gone. The two cars went down a busy street overshadowed by a ponderous skyscraper that Leo knew from a photograph in their hotel room, then a narrow street lined with low buildings with, at ground level, open stores, car repair shops, poultry markets, and taprooms. Leo read the signs painted on the white and gray walls: Ricos Caldos, Pollo Fresco, Tubas y Conectiones Plasticas. Again, Ricardo and Miguel sounded their horns furiously: The roadway was filled with cars, vans, cyclists, pedestrians. Then another broad avenue opened up, revealing a series of glass skyscrapers, one of which reflected the sun into Leo's eyes, momentarily blinding him. Then they wove their way through the deserted streets of what looked like an administrative district, bringing them out on a straight road where the cars hurtled by in several lanes, into the distance and out of sight. Leo figured that this was Paseo de la Reforma, the city's greatest thoroughfare, whose name he had often heard spoken by habitués of the cantina.

"Miguel wove through the cars, changing lanes as he overtook them, making sure that he never lost sight of the vehicle containing Linda. Leo and Diamanta were amazed by the masterly driving skills of this man who spent most of his life sitting about in a cantina. But Ricardo, too, was a good driver, so the distance between the cars remained more or less the same. At a certain point, the road opened out into a sort of piazza, at the center of which stood a tall column whose top was adorned with a gilded angel with wings outstretched, glistening in the sun. A moment later Leo saw—above the streams of traffic, through the smog backlit by the sun—the indistinct form of a tree-covered hill topped by a castle with splendid glassed-over arcades. This place, too, Leo knew from a photograph in the hotel room, and he remembered the caption that went with it—'Castillo de Chapultepec.' As Ricardo's car was zooming up Chapultepec Hill, a figure bearing a submachine gun leaned out of a back window and produced three short bursts of sound and bright light; fortunately, the shots missed Miguel's car. Again, Ricardo was gaining on Linda and her captors. But then came a sudden screech of tires as the leading car skidded, turned full circle, and went speeding back along Paseo de la Reforma toward the downtown. Ricardo's maneuver caught Miguel by surprise, and he lost time in turning his own car around; worse than that, for some moments his view of his antagonist was obscured by a bus. When at last he succeeded in overtaking the bus, there was no sign of Ricardo and his crew; clearly, he had turned off into a side street. Miguel, too, turned off the main drag. He spent a long time scouring the streets on either side of it, until Diamanta laid a hand on his shoulder and told him what she thought: that there was no sense in continuing the search. Miguel drove them back to the hotel; not a word was spoken on the way.

"Leo and Diamanta refused to give up hope. They had faith in Miguel, whom they expected to resume his post in the cantina, where he was at his most powerful, at the center of a network that infiltrated the whole city, even the slums and most distant outskirts. This network, they believed, was buzzing with messages and instructions, commissions, offers, questions and answers, dreams, longings, and hate. From his table, Leo and Diamanta told themselves, Miguel would be able to find Linda sooner than if he were driving blindly about this vast city. So no sooner had Miguel dropped them off at the hotel than they crossed to the cantina, to witness what would happen next. But Miguel didn't appear in the cantina that day. Late in the evening, as they were preparing to return to the hotel and to bed, the patrono came to their table with some news: On one of the city's steep suburban streets, the police had found four bullet-ridden bodies. One of them was Miguel's; obviously, the hotelero had set out in search of justice, to mete out punishment for the violation of the rules of business. No doubt he had considered the risks in advance and told himself that his own death was a price worth paying for the reestablishing of order."

7. Decision

"The next day, Leo and Diamanta sat in the cantina, drinking their coffee in silence and looking across the square at the hotel. They had long seen its facade as a tired, friendly face, and today, too, they were consoled by its presence. 'Let's fly to Boston,' said Leo. Diamanta agreed. Most likely this trip would be pointless, but what if they really did succeed in breaking into the laboratories at MIT? And what if Jones were prepared to help them?

"That morning, they considered various plans, all of which were dreamlike and fantastical. The TV above the cantina's bar was always on. Now it was tuned to a news channel. Neither Leo nor Diamanta followed what was going on on-screen, as they couldn't keep up with the rapidly changing images and the uninterrupted flow of speech at low volume. But when Leo heard the words 'Massachusetts Institute of Technology,' followed by 'Doctor Williams-Jones,' he looked up. The screen was filled with Dr. Williams's face. Leo and Diamanta heard her say that the dangerous, long-searched-for fugitive robot had at last been apprehended, and that it had been rendered inactive and placed in the museum of artificial intelligence. Then there was a shot of Linda lying motionless in a glass case; her skin bore obvious signs of having been subjected to an autopsy.

"That evening, they retired early to the wide bed in which Linda used to sleep with Diamanta. They lay in a silent embrace, staring into the darkness, listening to the babble of voices that reached them from the cantina and the square."

"Just as Marius and Rita would listen to the sea in the quiet of the night," I remarked. Although I had no watch, I knew it must be long after midnight. Loutro was sleeping; we saw no one about; the lamps lit empty tables and chairs that were waiting for their morning customers. All windows were dark at the Porto Loutro hotel: There was no need for a night porter, as no guests came to this place at night. Apart from paths in the rock, so narrow that walkers had to go in single file, no ways led here by land, and the boats weren't in service at night. All we heard was the splash of gentle waves in the bay, the most beautiful sound in the world.

"That's right," said Martin. "When, out of the blue, Diamanta said, 'I'm going to ours,' at first Leo didn't know what she was talking about. 'It's the only chance we have left for saving Linda,' Diamanta continued. Leo was alarmed. 'But Linda is dead,' he said, sitting up. He tried to make out the expression on Diamanta's face, but the shadows hid it from him. He was worried that Diamanta was taking leave of her senses.

""The only cure that will work on Linda now is ivy from the fortress,' Diamanta continued in a calm voice. 'I've been thinking of it for a long time, but I've lacked the resolve and the courage to go for it. In the car with Miguel, at a certain place I had the feeling we were close to a way through. It was somewhere near there . . .' She was pointing at the wall, where a patch of dim light from outside lay across one of the photographs. The light was too dim for Leo to look at it now, but he knew that it showed the skyscraper known as Torre Latinoamericana, and that they had seen it from Miguel's car. 'Don't go anywhere, I beg you,' he said. 'Stay here with me. Not even your people's magic can help Linda now, and at the fortress they would take you prisoner, chain you to the wall, and torture you. Because of your escape, no doubt they have some terrible punishment in store for you. You might be trapped there for centuries.'

"Diamanta paid little heed to what he was saying. 'I can't leave Linda in that glass coffin,' she said, several times. Then she turned to Leo and stroked him gently. 'Don't worry, I'll be careful. And maybe I'll be lucky.'

"Leo asked her to reconsider, but obviously Diamanta's mind was made up. For Leo, too, it was difficult to imagine life without Linda, although at that moment he couldn't imagine how he would manage his relations with the two women—what would be worse, to deceive Linda indefinitely or to tell her the truth? In any case, it seemed that fate had answered this for him. He no longer believed that Linda could be saved, and now he was worried that he was about to lose Diamanta, too. What would become of him if he did? Over the past hours, he had begun to believe that he and Diamanta would come to terms with Linda's death; he had imagined them living together in Miguel's little hotel, and that in time its quiet spaces and beloved square would help them find peace and maybe even something akin to happiness. Now he was worried that he would have to let go even of this dream."

8. Fountain

"When Leo awoke, Diamanta was standing by the window, brushing her hair; she was already dressed, and she had a canvas bag slung over her shoulder. She turned to tell him that she was going out to look around, with the intention of finding the exact point of passage to the fortress. Knowing there was no point in trying to talk her out of it, Leo jumped out of bed, pulled on his pants, and announced that he would go with her. After all, he told himself, Diamanta was only going to look around; maybe she wouldn't find the passage, and if she did, he might then succeed in persuading her not to use it. Once they were outside, the chill of early morning crept under his shirt; the square was in shade, the sun behind the surrounding low buildings, making itself known by the pinkish glow over the flat roofs with their thickets of antennas and satellite dishes. As they waited for a taxi, Diamanta gazed at the square, taking in the cantina opposite, the peeling walls scribbled over with spray paint, the twisted gray tree at its center, so disconcerting Leo and making him anxious.

"Nor did they speak in the taxi. They got out of the car by the skyscraper on Avenida Lázaro Cárdenas. Diamanta took up a position amid the throng of hurrying pedestrians, turning her head slowly. As he watched his girlfriend, Leo realized that she had slipped out of her human behavior as though it were a suit she was comfortable in and liked wearing, but which she now she didn't need, and which indeed would be a nuisance to her. For the first time, he was struck by the fact that Diamanta wasn't human; now she seemed to him more like an animal trying to catch a scent. Saying nothing, she pointed to the nearby park and set off toward it, paying no attention to Leo, who followed. They passed an ornate building, its honey-colored glass roof lit by the sun. Diamanta had obviously picked up the trail; her step was certain, and her pace quickened, so that Leo had to trot to keep up with her.

"The paths of the park were in the shape of a symmetrical star. At its center was a fountain adorned with two female figures whose smooth, dark-metal bodies spurted streams of water. Diamanta circled the fountain slowly. For a moment, she seemed at a loss as to what to do. Then she sat down on one of the benches set around the fountain. Leo, confused, sat down beside her. Not daring to speak, he looked into the spray, which was bright against the dark trees. "Wait here," said Diamanta. Leo watched her stand and approach the fountain. She didn't look back before her figure disappeared into the droplets of water and white light. Leo leaped up and raced around the fountain. Apart from a dirty, sleeping dog, there was no living soul far and wide. Leo understood that Diamanta had found the passage to the fortress, and that she had wanted to spare them the pain of parting.

"Leo paced the park's paths until evening. He fed himself with a tortilla bought from a street vendor. He kept returning to the fountain, telling himself that Diamanta would emerge out of thin air just as miraculously as she had disappeared into it. She might even succeed in creeping through the outer court-yards to the inner, picking a few ivy leaves, and returning to this side within a few hours; if so, she would reappear in the park any moment now. After darkness fell, he convinced himself he had missed her as he was pacing the park; perhaps she would be waiting for him at the hotel or their cantina. He hurried off in search of a cab.

"But Diamanta was neither at the cantina nor in their hotel room. It crossed Leo's mind that she might have reemerged through a passage that dropped her somewhere in South Africa, for instance, and that her journey back to him in Mexico would be a complicated one. Besides, once she had Linda's cure, she would probably first head for Massachusetts. Since Diamanta's exit, he had noticed that one thing was missing from their hotel room: Linda's glass globe from Vienna. Diamanta must have taken it with her on her perilous expedition, as a kind of talisman.

9. Waiting

"From then on, Leo's stay in Ciudad de México was nothing but a wait for Diamanta's return. At first, he returned to the park— he had learned that it was called the Alameda Central—every day, sitting for hours on a bench by the fountain, in whose hiss he heard Diamanta's words and Linda's wails; later, he also began to hear in it the voices of Patricia, Vanessa, and Kate, which were sometimes so clear that he wondered if he was going mad, but still he found it impossible to do without his daily dose of this melancholy radio. He knew the fountain in all its colors, and he knew all the kinds of light cast in its waters by the sun's wanderings above the Alameda. It became his habit to return to his empty hotel room late in the afternoon—on foot, even though the walk took him two hours. At first, he paid little heed to the streets he was walking, nor did he register faces, or develop a feel for the places he passed; but as his despair gave way to a dull pain, his senses slowly reawakened.

"This wasn't because he was beginning to forget Diamanta and Linda. In fact, his memories of the robot and his hope that the daemon would return to him were as strong as ever; but they were losing their shape and moorings, and dissolving into the passage of time, as though a haze of sorrow were seeping into all his thoughts, impressions, and sensations. Remarkably, he was coming together with the exhalations of the city—its smells of hot corn tortillas, concrete, gasoline, dust, early-morning rain, and thousands of others that dissolved into the thin air of the plateau. Every morning, though, he would wake at three, and long, red-hot knives of despair would thrust themselves into him. To drive away the harrowing images that then descended on him in a swarm, he would turn on the light and stagger out onto the balcony, there to study the sleeping square and the interplay in the nighttime breeze of the streetlighting and the leaves of the lone tree. Only after three or four hours would he be overwhelmed by the need to sleep and return to bed. By the time he awoke in the afternoon, his sorrow would have quietened.

"The sorrow no longer clouded his perception. The few goals he had clung to before Diamanta's departure had fallen away, at last delivering to him the calm of hopelessness and releasing a space into which sensations could flow, so allowing him to face whatever came his way, and to be a quiet, attentive observer. The city as he now perceived it had little in common with the city he had encountered in his trance in Miguel's car, a mountain range that by some strange chance assumed humanoid forms. Things and spaces took back their names, whispered them to Leo, and told him stories about their lives with humans, and of their secret dreams and affinities that humans knew nothing about. In this way, Leo became acquainted with the city. He approached and returned from the Alameda Central always by different streets, taking ever more roundabout ways, until one day he never reached the fountain in the park and continued his wanderings, looking at the city's buildings and other objects, entering spaces that opened up to him. He became an urban pedestrian, just as Marius—who was in the green room, listening to Hella's story—was an urban pedestrian; just as Tomáš Kantor, who had dreamed up Leo and Marius, had been one.

"A time came when Leo knew the huge city better than its own people did. There were dozens of backstreets, parks, plazas, cantinas, arcades, bars, and cafés he liked to return to. No longer a green phantom hovering menacingly over the car in which Linda was being abducted, the Chapultepec park was where Leo would go to breathe the atmosphere of calm Sunday afternoons, as he sat on a bench watching families taking their walks, children at play in the grass, and Native Mexicans performing Aztec-type dances for the tourists. The Alameda Central had ceased to be maze of paths among trees around the gateway to another world through which Diamanta had disappeared; now it was a shaded garden where Leo went to get out of the burning sun of the streets, and when he sat on a bench by the fountain, he no longer heard voices in its babble. One day, he was sitting in a café on Tacuba Street, drinking coffee and looking out of the window, when he exclaimed in amazement: 'Good God! This is the street where Miguel's car chased Ricardo's!'

"He had no thoughts of moving out of Miguel's hotel. Now it was his home as well as a holy place and a secret center of the city. It was also the place where the day's images matured into a sweet juice. Leo didn't yet know what to do with this juice, so for the time being he simply reveled in its flow through his body as it carried him to sleep. His nighttime despair returned occasionally, but by morning he tended to have forgotten it. The hotel was now run by Miguel's widow and daughters, exactly as before. Leo spent the evenings at the cantina table he had shared with Diamanta, drinking beer and Mexican wine from Baja California, allowing images of the city, some mixed with memories of Linda and Diamanta, to float to and from the surface of his mind. From time to time, the face of Patricia or Vanessa would rise to that surface from an immense depth."

10. Colors

"On waking one morning, Leo's eye fell on a greasy, sunlit stain on the wallpaper. He felt a joy that he barely understood; all he knew for sure was that this joy somehow arose out of the relation between two projections on the rounded top of the stain and seven small fringes on the bottom, and how this relation was connected with all he had been through—captivity in the glass tower, life in the motel in the north, the search for the clinic, the losses of Linda and Diamanta, even his recent wanderings in the city. As Leo stared at the stain, it dawned on him that he could use the sweet juice pressed every evening from images and memories. So far, he had only drunk it in; now he saw that he might allow it to crystalize into a new form.

"Leo thought back to when he was eighteen and would paint pictures in his room at home. Now, years later, the longing to create new shapes—shapes found nowhere in the world, and for this very reason able to reveal the world's hidden currents and to speak secrets that objects, bodies, spaces, and events kept to themselves—was reawakened. No sooner was he out of bed than he went to a stationer's store for pastels and a sketchpad. This was the first day in many weeks that he didn't embark on his wanderings about the city. Instead, he went straight to the cantina and set his sketchpad down on the table. He began to draw an orange vortex, out of whose center emerged an emerald-green mark. The force of the swirling tore several pieces from this mark, tossing them across the orange surface. Immediately after this, dark-purple oblong spots appeared at the edges of the vortex; although these gave the impression that they knew nothing of the green at the center, perhaps these were in league with it; indeed, the green and the purple may have had a common origin, and maybe they were working together to quench the orange flame; then again, their appearance may have been an expression of a hidden dream on the part of the orange fire, yes, perhaps they were its secret children . . . Leo was excited to see how the incipient drama on the paper in front of him would play itself out. He felt that he was drawing as he would write an adventure novel, yet at the same time he knew that the forces unleashing the shapes and initiating a complex strategy of struggle and symbiosis had somehow arisen from a dissolved past maturing in the darkness, and from images from his wanderings in the city and everything he had been through in the tower, the motel in the north, and Miguel's hotel; all this was now returning as a geyser of color.

"As soon as it seemed to him that the colors had reached a state where they held each other in check, he stopped drawing. Then he turned to a new page in his sketchpad and developed another story, this time about a creeping, protracted fight between a blue flame and some grayish mesh whose intentions were unclear. That day, he drew several more pictures, telling of the fights, alliances, loves and desires of colors. From time to time, other customers at the cantina would come to his table to look at what he was drawing. Evidently, they liked the pictures; oddly enough, none of them seemed to mind the absence of figures and objects. Before long, Leo would sit drawing in the cantina every day from early morning, drinking six or seven cups of coffee in the process. Then, after a light lunch, he would embark on his wanderings in the city. In the evening, he would return to the cantina, where he would drink cerveza or wine, listen to the murmur of conversation, and look at the facade of the hotel, all the while observing how the images he had saturated himself in all day reconstituted themselves into a fragrant juice, out of which new color shapes would emerge the next morning.

"After a month, he asked the stationer, also a regular at the cantina, if he might exhibit his pictures in his storefront window. There they were noticed by an art critic who happened to be in this part of the city. Not long afterward, the critic approached Leo in the cantina, and not long after that, an exhibition of his work was held at a gallery downtown. The exhibition was well received and followed by others, and consequently Leo's name became more and more well known. He began to paint in oils, which naturally he couldn't do at his table in the cantina, so he made his hotel room into a studio, painting by the open window to the balcony. Soon his paintings were being exhibited at famous galleries in Mexico City, San Francisco, and Paris, and they were selling for ever higher prices. Two years after he, Diamanta, and Linda had arrived at Mexico City's international airport, a large exhibition of Leo's work opened in the Palacio de Bellas Artes near the Alameda Central, which he had first seen on the way to the fountain with Diamanta.

"At the opening, Leo had a strange thought that he couldn't shake—that Diamanta would appear among the guests. The party lasted long into the night, and for all that time Leo was restless and watchful; at a certain point, he snuck away to a dark, empty terrace on the side of the palace that overlooked the busy Avenida Lázaro Cárdenas. It was drizzling as he leaned on the stone parapet with glass in hand, watching the rain-fragmented beams of car headlights pass below him. Turning the open door that gave onto the radiant hall, from which voices reached him as a continuous murmur, he readied himself for Diamanta's appearance in the doorway. The wine may have been to blame for the strange trance in which he found himself, and after a while he came out of it. Diamanta didn't come to the terrace. Leo returned to his guests."

11. Coyoacán, Malibu

"The fact that a rich and famous man should live in a cheap hotel, in a room with a hard bed and a wonky table, was taken as a brilliant artist's eccentricity; indeed, some suspected that Leo had chosen such a bizarre base because of the publicity it earned him. By now, however, Miguel's little hotel was more of a home to Leo than the motel in the north and the apartment he had lived in for many years with Patricia; indeed, he could no longer even picture the latter. Some evenings as he sat in the cantina, he had the feeling that Diamanta had gone out for a while; or he would look beyond the tree-top to the window of his room and imagine a sick Linda waiting for him there. Overall, however, he thought of Diamanta and Linda seldom. They came to him mostly as shapes in the pictures he painted, when he saw briefly, painfully a facial feature or a small gesture, which then disappeared in the deluge of color.

"Leo became one of the sights of the Mexican capital. Ever more people showed up at the cantina to get a glimpse of him; some even knocked on the door of his hotel room. As a result, Leo was deprived of the peace he needed for his work, and he felt guilty that his presence was destroying the calm the square and its neighborhood had known for many years. So in the end he moved out of the hotel. By that time, he had so much money that he could afford a villa in Coyoacán, a quiet part of the city. The house stood in a garden and was surrounded by a high wall. Leo lived in it alone, and he painted every day. Several years later, on one of his walks about the city he came across a bookstore selling a translation of the book Vanessa and Kate had written together. He read on the jacket flap that they had become a well-known writing duo. For the first time in ages, Leo thought of Patricia and wondered what had become of her. Perhaps she had felt shame for what she had done and left the tower; or perhaps her rage had given way to madness, and she was living off Vanessa's money in a sanitarium somewhere.

"When Leo was sixty-two, his business agent told him of a villa for sale in Malibu on the Pacific coast. With advancing age, Leo felt an ever-stronger longing to live by the sea. So he bought the villa and moved to California. One summer evening he was sitting on the terrace, watching the reddish light of the setting sun on the high waves rushing to the shore. Then he noticed, walking along the wet sand, a woman with a canvas bag over her shoulder. The low sun was tracing her footprints before the incoming waves washed them away. The woman was heading for his house. As she came closer, he recognized her as Diamanta. She looked exactly as she had almost thirty years earlier, when she had disappeared by the fountain in Mexico City's Alameda Central. She told him that she had seen a photo of him in a magazine someone had left on a seat in a café, and his face had reminded her of something from her past; perhaps they knew each other, although she couldn't recall where they had met or the nature of their relationship. She explained, somewhat apologetically, that she was a daemon, and daemons had short memories . . . If he had indeed known her, maybe he could tell her something about her lost past. The first thing she could remember was living chained to a wall in the daemons' fortress; she had no recollection of what she had been punished for, and her captors, too, had forgotten what it was. Two years earlier, she had heard fighting in the halls of the fortress. Thirty-three years since the last invasion, fortunes had again been reversed and the fortress re-conquered. The insurgents had taken the room in which Diamanta was being held and set all prisoners free, so that they could join their cause. At the end of the battle, Diamanta had returned to the world of humans.

"Leo told Diamanta briefly about Linda and the snow-covered factory in Germany, the motel in the north, Mexico City, and their love for each other. Diamanta said that the story was very sad, but she could remember none of it; to her mind, it could have been a stranger's story. As Diamanta said her goodbyes, Leo didn't try to hold her back. Just before she left, she opened her bag, took out the glass globe, and gave it to Leo. It had been with her for the duration of her captivity, she said, and if it had some connection with Leo's life, she would like him to have it. By then, Leo had forgotten all about Linda's globe. He lifted it and shook it, bringing down on the Stephansdom a shower of snow illuminated and colored by the orange sun reflected from the surface of the Pacific. As Leo watched Diamanta make her way along the shore, he considered calling her back and suggesting that they try to live together, as Diamanta had once called to Linda as she walked away across the snowfields of Brandenburg. He deliberated whether love, returning after many years like a painful, penetrative sting, was more important than peace in which to do concentrated, solitary work. Before he could make up his mind, Diamanta disappeared beyond the low rocks. This was the final scene of the wire book."

The Story of the Wire Book II

1. City in the Jungle

"After some time, an official interpretation of the President's son's work emerged from the camp that had the government at its center: Fernando Vieta's novel was allegorical. Leo's captivity in the glass tower symbolized the period of oppression under the previous regime; Patricia and Kate were symbols of the centrist parties whose leaders had at first supported the revolution but became increasingly critical of certain methods of the struggle; the bodyguard who unlocked the elevator door for Leo was said to represent the governor of one of the southern provinces, who had joined the uprising at the last moment. In this interpretation, Leo himself embodied the revolutionary spirit of the nation awakening from a long sleep; critics in the government's press tended to write articles that made it clear that this spirit should be identified with the ruling Conservative party. To find allegorical meaning for the characters of Diamanta and Linda was a more labor-intensive task, but in the end, it was decided that they represented all those who regrettably didn't get to see a liberated, happy homeland (as represented by Leo's life in California).

"It wasn't exactly smart, but then the circumstances attending the President's son's book made no special demands on the intellect. Critics in the anti-government camp didn't polemicize the government's interpretation in any way—indeed, they were happy to accept it, as they realized it could work in their favor that a book they, and many others besides, thought manifestly bad and nonsensical, was identified with the ideology of the government. The rest of the population had no interest in it. Although very few people read *The Captive* from start to finish, the wire book lived several lives in North Floriana: in schools, it was taught as a novel of revolution; quotes from the book were carved into the plinths of monuments; critics loyal to the government made ever more improvements to the canon of allegorical interpretations of the work; journalists writing for papers of the opposition insinuated that the author was mentally ill and as such provided an eloquent testimony to the identification of the government's vision of history and society with that of a lunatic; village-dwellers and people living in poorer urban neighborhoods pinned up on their home altars passages from the novel which each evening before bed they would mumblingly recite; meanwhile, the figure of the daemon Diamanta became real in their imaginations and transformed into a powerful new deity that was incorporated into the folk pantheon (images of Diamanta appeared on home altars alongside color prints representing the Virgin Mary); one pornographic fake after another appeared, each masquerading as the novel's lost middle. The late Fernando Vieta was no doubt indifferent to all this.

"The President of the Republic was only vaguely aware of matters surrounding his son's novel. He read *The Captive*, the original of which remained at the Conservation Institute, over and over, walking for hours along the spiral like a mouse in a labyrinth, bending to the floor to pick up and read the wire sentences whose tremors enabled him to form an image of his lost son. His pursuance of this sorrowful magic meant he had little time for affairs of state. Deputies representing the opposition complained in parliament about his lack of activity, while within the party of government the grumbling also became ever more frequent. Nevertheless, all politicians feared that unseating the President would provoke a popular uprising. Still, increasing dissatisfaction with the President's behavior was reflected in parliament's decision—by a large majority—to reject Vieta's proposal that a mausoleum should be built for his son. Oddly, when the proposal was debated, no one argued that it was pointless to build of a mausoleum when there was no dead body. Deputies from all parties expressed the opinion that a mausoleum would surely be a work pleasing to God, but that the money demanded by its construction was, in this difficult period of social transformation, needed for the other things.

"Although in recent months the elder Vieta had given the impression of somnambulance, in matters that were truly important to him he retained his ingenuity and ability to think keenly. Now, nothing unconnected with his son's book was important to him. Vieta was no longer urging his proposal on parliament, and for several weeks it seemed that he had given up all thoughts of it. But three months after parliament rejected his proposal, Vieta appeared on television, delivering a speech in which he called for the building from scratch of a new capital city in the jungle, based on the Brazilian model.

"The President's call took everyone by surprise. Vieta had played a masterstroke, as the deputies realized: The very next day, parliament would be awash with lobbyists for the large construction companies stuffing wads of cash into hands in return for promises to vote for the proposal. Before long, everyone would be happy—the deputies because the bribes would buy them new villas, cars, and yachts, the owners of the construction companies because they would be getting the best commissions of their careers, and most of all the President, because now it was in the cards that the construction companies would build him his longed-for mausoleum out of gratitude, in a new capital.

"Everything went ahead as expected. At the vote in parliament, the vast majority of deputies assented to the building of a new capital; in fact there was a suspicion that those who raged about a waste of state funds and voted against, were paid to do so by the construction companies, whose bosses reasoned that they would appear more trustworthy if plans for the development of a city in the jungle were approved after rigorous debate and unavoidable squabbling.

"The plans were swiftly drawn up; renowned architects from around the world descended on the country; on a chosen site in the jungle about seventy miles from the existing capital, roads were built, trees felled, and swamps drained. The lovers in the clearing from the beginning of Hector's story made a brief reappearance. One morning, they were woken by an unfamiliar sound that overrode the babbling of their creek—a sound that brought together the distant wail of power saws with the rumble of bulldozers and trucks. On rising from their bed, the lovers wandered a couple of miles through the jungle toward the new sound, reaching a precipice, from where they watched a large brown spot that had appeared in the green of the jungle down below, as people and machines swarmed about it; it was as though a stone had been lifted, leaving black bugs running about in exposed confusion in the bare space it left behind."

2. Mausoleum

"The first buildings to go up were those on the main square—the presidential palace and the parliament building. Owing to the gratitude of the construction lobby, getting the mausoleum built, on an avenue that would cross the main square, was a simple matter; and here Fernando's wire would be placed. Wishing to oversee the building of the mausoleum, the President moved into the palace before it was finished. The windows of its front side looked out onto the square, giving a view of cranes and the steel frames of embryonic buildings; the windows at the back of the palace showed only the dark-green leaves of the murky jungle. Whenever the President was doing his rounds of the palace and looking into the empty rooms on this side, he had the feeling that he was walking through a long gallery of monotonous abstract paintings; when he entered a room and leaned out of a window, however, he could make out, down below the trees, interlaced with the torn lianas and broken branches, muddy black cables, and steel and plastic pipes. As most civil servants were still in the old capital, Vieta's dealings with them were mostly by e-mail. He would manage his correspondence in a provisional office in the back part of the palace; the computer monitor stood on a desk in front of a high window, bright against the green gloom of the jungle. The fact that the President was living seventy-odd miles from the seat of parliament and government resulted in a number of difficulties, but before long it became clear that this arrangement actually suited all sides: The President could devote himself to the building of the mausoleum and his memories, while members of the government were glad that Vieta didn't interfere with their decision-making, and that little by little a precedent was being set that meant that from then on the president would be head of state in name only; nor did the deputies regret that the President, with his right of veto, took no part in sessions of parliament. As the government ruled and the deputies argued and cursed one another, the President lived alone in an enormous unfinished palace, with a few low-ranking civil servants, bodyguards, a cook, and a chambermaid. Occasionally, a surprised senior diplomat from a foreign country would be sent to the jungle on an official visit; seated in the presidential lounge, he would look on in amazement as a green lizard ran across the mantelpiece.

"Although Vieta was necessarily parted for some time from the spiral of wire at the Conservation Institute, by now he knew his son's work by heart and could recall every curve in the wire. The mausoleum's architect proposed that the wire be rolled out into a helix that would trail across the inner wall of the circular central hall. Believing that the work should be unbroken, the architect proposed filling the gaps in the text with straight gold wire. Construction work on the mausoleum was completed within six months. The empty tomb of Fernando Vieta stood symbolically at the center of the hall; light entered the building through a glass dome, the diameter of which was two yards less than the diameter of the hall's ground plan; the space between the top of the wall and the perimeter of the dome was filled by a circular metal strip containing a system of grooves in which were held twelve telescopic rods that could be let down to the floor; each of these rods ended in a seat, so that the whole apparatus looked like an overelaborate swing carousel. The armrests of the seats had buttons for the extension and retraction of the telescopic mechanism, so adjusting the height of the seat; a little wheel at the top of each rod regulated movement left or right along the wall. Should two seats moving in the groove happen to meet, the apparatus in the ceiling would automatically open a switch, moving one of the rods to the neighboring groove.

"Thanks to this apparatus, up to twelve people could read the manuscript of *The Captive* at one time, at a speed that suited each reader. Following the ceremonial opening of the building, however, it turned out that visitor interest in the mausoleum was less than even the greatest skeptic had anticipated; educated people had no interest in *The Captive*, while the villagers and slum-dwellers, who had passages from Fernando's novel tacked up on their home altars had no money for a trip to the new capital, which was far from everywhere. Therefore, it often happened that every seat was empty, or that a figure circled the wall alone—and this figure had been attracted to the mausoleum more by the apparatus that made the reading possible than the reading matter itself. Before long, the youth of North Floriana realized the entertainment value of the seats and began to hold races in them. Soon, groups of high-spirited youngsters would appear at the mausoleum most days, there to have themselves hoisted up so that they could chase each other around the wire sentences, like swarms of flies. The walls of the mausoleum were covered with notices listing what was forbidden on the premises, but nobody read them. Often, an attendant would stand over Fernando's tomb, shouting threats up toward the dome, but the laughing boys and screeching girls at the top of the hall didn't seem to notice him.

"The President would enter the mausoleum in the evening, when quiet had returned to the hall and the cleaners were getting busy with their buckets and mops. He would take a seat and rise and fall along Fernando's words until deep into the night. After the departure of the cleaners, he didn't wish for the lights to remain on purely on his account, so he used his own flashlight, sometimes lingering over a single place in the text, sometimes drifting about restively.

3. Raid

"At that time, relations between North Floriana and its southern neighbor were worsening. The rebels would never have been victorious without military assistance from South Floriana, and once the revolution was achieved, there was much fraternizing between the two states. But when representatives of South

Floriana began to insist on the opening of long-promised negotiations about changes to the border, the letters of reply from
the Ministry of Foreign Affairs of North Floriana were filled
with flowery sentences about the friendship of the two nations,
but as for a date for the negotiations, there were but a few words
in the final paragraph, postponing everything until an indefinite near future. It was obvious that the new regime was just as
unwilling as its predecessor to give up so much as a scrap of land.
The new government was taking it for granted that the army of
South Floriana, whose senior officers were still seen on public
holidays on North Florianan platforms in uniforms heavy with
gold, would be reluctant to invade the territory of its closest
ally. But the politicians of South Floriana had finally run out of
patience with warm-hearted letters from North Floriana, which
were coming increasingly to resemble mockery. The generals
persuaded the government that, all recent fraternizing notwithstanding, a military campaign should be mounted as soon as
possible, as the best time to strike would soon pass. And this was
a good time because the army of the old North Florianan regime
was crumbling and a new army was still forming, from ill-disci-
plined partisans and guerilla commanders, who were well-versed
only in the tactics of skirmishing and nighttime raids.

"Then something happened at the mausoleum that was
widely viewed as an inexplicable if not supernatural, occurrence. (Even so, intelligence chiefs immediately put it down to
worsening relations between North and South Floriana, and
they submitted a report to that effect to the government—
although no state institution officially declared itself to have
any interest in the occurrence.) One night, following the departure of the cleaners and then the President, the attendants had
fallen into a deep sleep, which, rumor had it, was produced
by magical means (the local form of voodoo included a ritual
even a beginner could manage, which resulted in putting the

victim to sleep). When counter-espionage experts arrived on
the scene, however, at the threshold of the mausoleum they
recognized traces of a sweet smell; obviously, nitrous oxide had
been released into the building, probably through the air-con-
ditioning system. On waking in the small hours, the attendants
had discovered that Fernando's novel was damaged. Although
the wire helix was still whole, twenty of its rings had been torn
from the wall, and the stretch of wire in question had been
formed into a strange new shape that hung like a great, irregular
spider's web. At first, the horrified attendants assumed that the
wire book had been destroyed, but they soon discovered that
not so much as a single piece of wire was missing, and not a
single word had been violated. All that had happened was that
the stretch of wire detached from the wall had been bent into
new words without the loss of any of the original text. From the
sequence of words in Fernando's novel, the mysterious nighttime visitor had created, in upper-case letters, a new text, which
now hung in the middle of the hall:

*It seems that those who come over roofs wearing black masks
adorned with figures of constellations are at last approaching your
apartment; the time of waiting is coming to an end. Hopefully,
they will show you mercy and not the meaning of what terrified
you most—the loathsome words repeated incessantly by the mal-
functioning mechanical dummy in the abandoned bus shelter in
the middle of that field. Remember how surprised you were to find,
after twenty years of marriage, those words written in your wife's
diary, which was hidden carefully at the bottom of a drawer, under
the cookbooks—it is not advisable to search the bottom of drawers.
When your wife then left in a shiny black automobile driven by a
handsome man with a suntan, you were sad, but also relieved that
the period of anxiety was over. For some time after that, she continued to send you postcards, which you hid from your children. In*

these cards, she wrote of the sadness of living in an apartment with a large bookcase filled with squirming, squelching books, which produced, in a permanent trickle, a thick, black, sweet-stinking juice; she wrote how she didn't understand her new children, who lived with her and did nothing at all except lick the sticky library. Perhaps these were not actually books, although her new family referred to them as such, and there were marks supposed to be letters on their twitching, veined pages. You wrote to her that the situation in her old home was by now quite similar and there was nowhere to return to—that here, too, fraying and crumbling prevailed over all other processes, so that nothing remained that was not hemmed with fringing. Geometry had collapsed (it was necessary to wait for the birth of a new geometry for the world of fringing), and time was badly rumpled; so far only dodecahedrons composed of irregular pentagons more or less kept their shape. When one day your children announced that their school had added instruction in a new language, you knew immediately what was going on. By now you lacked the strength to take action; you preferred not to ask about the new teacher: You did not wish to know which coast he was from, and what the tattoo on his left arm depicted. You did not attempt to find out why it was that after written tests your children fell sick with illnesses borne by a dreamy bliss, producing rashes that attacked the furniture and the plaster of the house's hallways. Sometimes you told yourself that it might after all be for the best if you were to go to the school to investigate, and a few times you actually set out in that direction, but the school building was in a dark part of town, and to reach it you had to pass so many sad storefront windows and fierce dogs that hated you, that you never made it that far. So when your children told you that the meaning of your name in the language they were learning was Despair, you pretended not to hear; whenever they memorized words filled with crackling, gurgling, and frenetic grammar, you closed yourself up in your room. Worst of all were the conjunctions, all of which expressed disgusting, perverse relations you didn't want to think about, although deep in your soul you knew them well. You had no choice but to wait for the moment your children would come to you and pass judgement on you in the language they had learned at school. Having heard them pass an incomprehensible sentence on you, you fall back on the last things in the world that still mean something to you— large, cool diamonds; and perhaps you will accept an invitation to a city at the bottom of the ocean, which you declined years ago. The prospect of wandering down long underwater avenues, where the pale light of streetlamps and storefront windows shines through undulating seaweed and illuminates the sadness of underwater palaces, is still better than staying in an apartment whose walls will be covered with frescoes showing the life of your family in a revolting paradise—pictures your children are already painting, along with animals and monsters. Recently you have often been compelled to wonder about the extent to which the matter with the animal is to blame for your wife's departure. Fifteen years have passed since your discovery that your wife enjoyed secret caresses with an animal she had brought with her and kept hidden for many years behind the closet. You hated it so much that in the end you decided to kill it, and you will never forget the terror in its face as you raised the knife. At that moment, it occurred to you that this was the only creature that could ever be your friend. That evening at dinner, you watched your wife's face as she discovered, behind the dresser, the dead body, which had dried blood stuck to its fur; she betrayed no emotion apart from a slight shaking of the hands, and she went to bed early. What happened in the years after that? Nothing special: For sure the sauces she prepared sometimes tasted threatening, but more often their flavor was of inconsolable despair; and later her rissoles came to contain tones of comfort.

"The intelligence people suspected the involvement of their South Florianan colleagues, although they struggled to figure out the sense of the act. They advised the government to hush up the whole affair, so for two days the mausoleum was closed 'for technical reasons' while restorers removed all bends in the wire that didn't belong; meanwhile, the spies tried to find out what was going on. The lack of wisdom that informed the government's decision to keep secret the nighttime transformation soon became clear: Rumors current among the population about happenings in the mausoleum assumed ever more features of the fantastical and the supernatural. For people of the villages and slums, the mausoleum became akin to a shrine, and reports of a terrible supernatural event that had taken place in it were met with horror. One of the attendants repeated to his wife a sentence he recalled from the nighttime text, thus violating a prohibition; the sentence was spread by word of mouth, changing little by little until it became a prophecy of doom for the whole country. Obviously, the mausoleum had been entered by an unknown deity more powerful than Diamanta, to whom people had been praying. Panic spread throughout North Floriana; the future was viewed with dread, wedding plans were dissolved, deeds were nipped in the bud. People ceased to believe in their own strength, as they believed it to be stripped of divine protection.

"Of course, the educated classes didn't believe in the coming of an evil god, but they, too, were affected by the atmosphere of disquiet, anxiety, and defeatism from the slums and villages. Worst of all, this sickness infected the army still more than other segments of society: In the battles of the civil war, soldiers had become accustomed to worshiping Fortuna as the supreme deity, and they were more susceptible than others to the power of omens. Before long, therefore, all North Floriana was infected with helplessness and demoralization. An incomprehensible poem couldn't have had such fatal consequences on its own, of course. The strange incident in the mausoleum did no more than release the anxiety and uncertainty that had settled in the hearts of people used to waiting. Following the victorious revolution, they had lost the enemy they despised but that gave meaning to their lives, and now there was no longer anything to wait for.

"Just as the country was overwhelmed by this sickness no one could cure, South Florianan gunboats appeared in the half-light of early morning in the sea off the country's southernmost port; soon the fortress in the port was under fire. This was followed by a radio broadcast in which the President of South Floriana made a short statement; because of the conscious violation of an international treaty, he said, South Floriana was declaring war on its northern neighbor. Shortly thereafter, the army of South Floriana was again marching through the mountain passes to North Floriana."

4. Meeting on a Terrace

"The incident in the mausoleum had nothing to do with supernatural forces, of course. North Florianan intelligence was right to assume that the secret services of its southern neighbor were behind it. It all began with a meeting of the South Florianan intelligence service on a raised terrace at the private villa of General Varela, a hulking figure with a crew cut who was the only one present in uniform. The secret-service chiefs sat around a table placed in the middle of square floor with a chessboard design which was bounded by white balusters with large, dark palm leaves poking between them. By this time, the plan for the invasion had already been approved. The meeting had been called to discuss an action that would support military intervention by shaking the trust of the people of North Floriana in its government and weaken the morale of its army.

Most proposals made that day called for the forging of documents that would attest to corrupt behavior or sexual affairs on the part of senior representatives of North Floriana. One of the figures around the table was the agent Henriette Fox, known in intelligence circles as Vulpécula, whose French mother and American father, adventurers both, had met on their travels in South Floriana. Head of a unit composed only of women chosen by herself, Vulpécula was renowned for her ability to make intelligent, dispassionate decisions during dangerous actions. For a long time, she played no part in the discussion. When at last she got to her feet to speak up, she proposed that they break into the Fernando Vieta Mausoleum, where they would twist the wire of the President son's novel into new text.

"When she finished speaking and resumed her seat, silence fell. Everyone but Colonel Ramirez, Henriette's immediate superior, wondered if Vulpécula had been joking. When General Varela demanded to hear her plan, Henriette explained that for simple people in North Floriana, the wire book had become a sacred text and a magical object, even though no one read it. Were they to succeed in defacing and dishonoring this object of popular worship, it was likely that the superstitious classes—meaning practically the whole nation—would be thrown into confusion and terror, thus weakening the nation's ability to resist an enemy.

"The other participants conceded that there might be something to say for Henriette's plan after all. General Varela wondered aloud whether it might not be more effective to destroy the wire book altogether. Vulpécula's patient answer to this was that the people would consider the destruction of the wire book as its heroic death; if, however, its words and sentences were to remain undamaged but were forced to serve other words and sentences, the sacred book would be dealt the greatest humiliation imaginable. The general then came up with the idea of

bending the wire into propaganda directed against the government of North Floriana. Again, Vulpécula explained that such
an act would be pointless, as everyone would guess who was
behind it. If the identity of the perpetrator remained a secret,
the North Florianans would reflect all their anxieties on to it,
the upshot being that they would create their own enemy, and
this enemy would be invincible. Vulpécula proposed that they
leave the writing of the text to her.

"As always, what Vulpécula said was convincing; and as
always, her plan was perfectly thought through. Still, more
than this was needed if the elite of South Floriana's secret
services were to approve such an outlandish action. Only
Ramirez stood up for Vulpécula, his best agent, and an argument erupted between him and Varela that ended only when
the colonel proposed a bet, the stake a crate of twenty-year-old
whiskey. The general, a passionate gambler and a lover of alco-
hol, accepted this immediately; and so the action was authorized. Vulpécula climbed into her black convertible and headed
back to her women's unit. On the way, she thought about the
words into which Fernando's wire would be twisted. When on
a mission, she was in the habit of carrying a copy of Rimbaud's
Illuminations, which she would read when required to wait
around. She had written several prose poems herself, modeled
on the work of Rimbaud, her favorite poet. For her mission
in North Floriana, she would write an entirely new poem, she
now decided.

"The mission entitled 'Wire' went off without a hitch. That
night, Henriette and her unit flew out from a military airport and parachuted into the jungle in the vicinity of North
Floriana's new metropolis. Women in camouflage put the attendants to sleep by releasing nitrous oxide into the air-condition-
ing system. Then, wearing gas masks, they descended by rope
from the glass dome of the building to the hall, where they

carefully detached the wire from the wall. Each of the women bent her section of wire as instructed by Henriette, so creating the passage she had been assigned. The only thing that surprised Vulpécula was how working with the wire made her feel; she had the impression that rather than the women humbling the wire, the wire was toying with the women; that the women's hands were extolling the wire by creating new words in it that realized its secret dreams; that the wire was longing to be twisted into hundreds of texts, only one of which was Henriette's poem; that the wire had summoned Vulpécula and her women to the jungle to make its dream a reality. It seemed that her poem was no more than an outline asking to be formed into the letters of a larger text, the words of which were now palely luminous around the twice-twisted wire, like St. Elmo's Fire. At moments, she thought she saw certain words surface out of the faint glow, and she was tempted to re-twist the wire in larger letters, as the wire itself seemed to be suggesting. She sensed that the birth of new letters wouldn't end with this giant text; that ever-larger letters were present in the wire, conversing and feeding on each other's plots. Vulpécula wondered where it would end. Perhaps with a single enormous letter—a hieroglyph formed from all the letters and texts, radiating their meanings and whispering their contents."

5. Defeat

"There was no doubt that Henriette's mission contributed to the rapid defeat of North Floriana. Shaking his head in disbelief, Varela sent Ramirez a crate of whiskey, which the two of them polished off in a week. As it made headway in the North Florianan interior, the invading army laid siege to the new capital in the jungle. This city was protected by a considerable garrison, a luxury bearing in mind that, as yet, the new metropolis comprised only a mausoleum and a few unfinished buildings, and that apart from the crazy President, no one lived there. (On hearing the approaching artillery fire, the construction workers and staff of the presidential palace had fled.) Yet the muddy building site in the jungle was still the official capital city of North Floriana, and as such it had high symbolic value for both belligerents. The result was a bloody battle in which South Florianan tanks mounted a continuous attack on the city for five days, supported strongly by the air force. When at last the city's few surviving defenders raised the white flag, all that remained of the buildings were piles of rubble. Under one of these piles lay the body of Ernesto Vieta, President of North Floriana.

"Three days later, North Floriana capitulated, so agreeing to withdraw from all disputed territories, plus a few more hills and valleys. Immediately a new retaliation movement was formed; after several months of inconvenience, people were relieved that they had something to look forward to and were no longer forced to live in the present. Also, the government undertook to pay heavy war reparations. No one thought of rebuilding the city in the jungle, so it died before was properly born. The jungle soon grew over the ruins of the houses and palaces; within a year they were hard to distinguish from the shapes of nature. Also swallowed up by the jungle was the pile of broken concrete slabs that had once been the mausoleum of Fernando Vieta. Before long, the wire book was as overgrown as it had been when found by the diver on the coral reef, although now tropical vines, branches, and aerial roots entwined its sentences rather than seaweed. Living creatures again built their shelters in its words, although this time, rather than fish and shrimp, they were parrots, nimble rodents, ants of many colors, and large, shiny bugs. Thus letters, plants and animals again settled down together, and the work that had once been part of a coral reef was transformed as a text/jungle that was simultaneously decaying and proliferating. The letters became objects that grew into shrubs and nests; meanwhile, bugs and lizards became letters, merging with Fernando's letters to form weird and wonderful words—a wire sentence would end halfway, then recommence in the green script of a rhizome or vine. Although the text/jungle pulsated to thousands of different beats, it exhaled a heady breath of decay the style of which was remarkably unified; this went unappreciated, however, as apart from the ancient daemons of the jungle, there was no one there read it. As new tales for unknown eyes were born in the humid darkness out of Fernando's broken narrative, it was returned to a life of juices and blind urges that existed before the words that may have borne it.

"As the catastrophic defeat was blamed on the President's dilatoriness in the final weeks of his government, his son's book ceased to be considered a national monument. It was removed from the school curriculum and gradually lapsed into oblivion; in any case, only the author's father had ever read it properly. Quotations carved into the bases of memorials were erased; home altars shed their photographs of Fernando and color prints of Diamanta looking down on North Floriana from a cloud in the heavens. There remained a few S-M clubs called Linda, whose clients soon forgot about the origin of the name. And all that remained of Fernando's novel was a few false and fading images in the memories of the people and a great plant made of wire, roots, and leaves—i.e., the piece of jungle that the text in the bombed-out mausoleum had become."

Escape to Parca II

1. Conversation at Night

"The defeat of North Floriana marked the end of Hector's story, as told to the wounded Marius by Hella, who added the spice of modern inventions to replace Hector's vague ideas about technologies of the future. Hella told Marius that she and Hector had married immediately after her graduation, and before long their daughter Elisa, Rita's mother, was born. Hella remembered wondering what to give Hector as his thirtieth birthday present. She decided to surprise him with a picture representing a scene from his story. She thought long and hard about which scene this should be. In the end, she chose the moment when the diver discovers Fernando's wire book on the seabed. As a restorer, she knew a great deal about painting techniques of the Baroque. Her idea was to paint the picture just as an artist of the Baroque would have done, had he happened to find himself in the twentieth century and hear the story of the wire book; Hector was bound to be amused by this.

"Marius's wounds were slow to heal. Every day, he claimed to be feeling better, indeed, well enough to return to his apartment in the old port; every day, Hector forbade him from getting out of bed. Hella, too, wished to keep him there, and

Marius was easily persuaded to stay in the room where every surface breathed the kind of happiness he hadn't known for many years, where even the hate-filled nightly roar of the demonstrators and police was transformed into soft, sweet music.

"So the days went by in the light-filled room. Rita came to see him every morning, and Hella often came to his room to discuss the story of the wire book. He would have liked to talk about it with Hector, too, but Hector refused to speak of the only literary work he had ever produced. Marius believed that the smile that lit Hector's face whenever the story was mentioned was an indicator of shy apology for a young man's folly. Marius found it slightly confusing that such harrowing narrative images could emerge from the mind of a man who appeared so equable. Hella wasn't at all unsettled by it. In her opinion, there was a source of dark imagery at the bottom of every soul, which occasionally spilled out in bad dreams; in Hector's case, an opportunity had arisen for this source to burst to the surface in his waking life. Having once asked Hella whether she was afraid that such an outburst could erode the solid substratum of deed and thought, Marius heard pride in her answer: 'If we were talking of someone else, maybe I would be. But every day Hector's scalpel must be accurate to one tenth of a millimeter, and not once has his hand trembled. Can you imagine that such certainty would ever allow his world to crack?'

"One night, Marius awoke at one-thirty. On his way through the dark hallway to the kitchen for a glass of water, he saw that a light was burning beyond the rectangle of frosted glass in the top half of the door to Hector's study. A pale light lay across the tiled floor and in the folds of the coats on the stand. He heard the muted voices of Hector and Rita coming from the study; it seemed that Hella was asleep. What could Rita be doing there so late at night? Marius stood and listened. Although he managed to catch only a few words, he understood that Rita and her grandfather were talking about the Lygdian movement, the situation at the university and the hospital, and preparations for more demonstrations. Marius was amazed: Until then, he had been convinced that such matters were not spoken of in this apartment. And he was disturbed by the tone of the two voices, which gave him to believe that Rita was urging something on her grandfather that he was reluctant to undertake. Marius heard Rita say repeatedly and emphatically, 'We need to do' this and this, and this and this 'must be carried out,' followed by Hector's demurrals and refusals. Marius was upset; in recent days, he had ceased to seek a solution to the puzzle posed by Rita to such a degree that he had begun to wonder if there was any puzzle at all; he had stopped caring whether Rita was a fanatical adherent of the Lygdian religion, an agent of the mafia, or she found entertainment in manipulating people; all this applied only beyond the walls of the apartment where he was now living, if at all. He felt growing fury at the thought of Rita bringing the Lygdian poison into the happy, pure home of her kindly grandparents, who had nothing to do with the Lygdian madness. He needed all his self-control to keep from bursting into the study and ordering Rita out of the benevolent world she was apparently corrupting with such callousness; her grandfather was obviously too considerate to throw her out himself. In the end, Marius returned to his room, where he walked back and forth across the carpet for many minutes, shaking with rage. Then he took some sleeping pills and lay down on the bed. A little while later, he heard Rita's and Hector's voices in the hallway, followed by a soft click as the door of the apartment closed. He tossed and turned for a long while before he fell asleep.

"When Rita appeared in his room that morning, Marius sat up in bed before she could even cross the room to him. The reproaches spewed out of him—albeit quietly, so as not to alarm Hella, whom he could hear in the kitchen. Rita could manipulate whomsoever she chose, he said, if she left the best people he knew in peace. As she heard Marius out, Rita stood motionless in the middle of the room. When he had finished, she appeared to consider whether to answer him. Then, without having said a word, she walked out of the room and out of the apartment. Marius got out of bed and went to Hella. He told her that he would never forget what she and her husband had done for him; had it not been for them, he would have lost his mind, perhaps even died in Parca, but now he really had to return to his own apartment.

"It felt strange to be back in his own place, to look at the bare walls and the papers and books on his desk, and to hear the sea for the first time in weeks. The next day, he decided, he would telephone the university in the capital and ask to return; maybe he would be able to resume his classes in the fall semester. He imagined his departmental colleagues referring to him as the Lygdian bard or something similar, and he smiled at the thought. That evening, he left his bed to go to the little store in the building next door, for bread, cheese, and wine. He ate his supper sitting at the window, watching the lights of the boats on the water. He realized that there was probably a demonstration going on at this very moment, but as the port was some way from the square, the sound of voices that might have reached it in muted form was absorbed by the lapping of waves. At around nine o'clock, the doorbell rang. He opened the door to find Rita standing there."

2. Hector and Rita

"Rita sat down on the bed and began to tell Marius about herself and her grandfather. An only child, she had been born in Parca, but when she was a few months old, the family moved to the capital. She remembered little from that time except for afternoons spent alone in a large apartment: the intricate pattern of the carpet she played on, with its slowly shifting borders of sunlight and shadow, the bent legs of the furniture that ended in metal lion claws, the windows in which gray giants dressed in leopard skin held up on broad shoulders the balcony on the front of the house opposite. In those days, she saw her grandparents rarely. Then, when she was twelve, the family returned to Parca; every Sunday after that, Rita and her parents would lunch at Hector and Hella's, where Rita would be extremely bored at the table. As soon as they finished eating, she would slip quietly from her chair and embark on a journey about the living room. She would study the minerals on the shelves, and the human anatomy, male and female, in the medical textbooks that lay on her grandfather's desk. She would open bound volumes of old magazines and look at the copperplates depicting cities unknown to her and figures in strange folk costumes under skies with hatched-in clouds; she would try to decipher the twisting and turning Gothic letters of the captions under the pictures. Turning the pages of atlases, she would read the names of rivers, mountain ranges, and deserts. She would examine the painting on the wall with the mysterious, submarine theme, and she would think up stories that the scene with the diver and the coral reef might belong in. Meanwhile, the voices of her parents would reach her from the dining room, often complaining of the suffering their solitary child imposed on them.

"Then her grandfather would come to her. He would hand her a stone with a fascinating pattern on its smoothed surface, or a book with pictures of vast city squares under white domes and minarets, or a well-thumbed magazine, or a black, angular figurine of a woman with pointy breasts, or just an empty tin box, its sides adorned with pictures of mountain waterfalls, pagodas, and Chinese men with long braids. Without a word, her grandfather would then return to the others in the dining room. Rita would marvel to discover that each of these objects had its predetermined place in her world. It seemed that her grandfather knew her dreams, dreams that no one—her parents, schoolmates, or even Rita herself—had any idea about, and she began to think of him as a magician. For a time, she wondered how it was possible that he could speak at length with other adults about boring matters, but then she told herself that a true magician had to be able to dissemble in public so that no one but a few friends entrusted with the secret knew of his mastery. Strange to say, the ideas of Rita the child were closer to the truth than those of the three adults in the room with them, all of whom thought they knew Hector well.

"Although Rita's grandfather was indeed a magician, he wasn't a clairvoyant. Only several years later did he read in Rita's gaze that she lived in the land of his own childhood—a land he had in fact never left. After that, a long time passed before Rita and her grandfather began to speak to each other, and eventually become singular friends and loyal conspirators. Now, however, Rita was the only person to whom Hector could speak of his whole life—everyone else knew but fragments of it; Hector had never imagined he would find such a person. In childhood Hector, too, had roamed the secret landscapes of the family apartment; its rooms, too, had been filled with cold lusters and slow ripples, with a golden dust settling on its things. He listened to the incessant hum of stories resonating from the closed, smooth doors of closets, the glass fronts of display cases, the restless drapes; he heard whispers from dark spaces between the backs of closets and the wall, chinks in which dust balls shivered in the draft. As though it were the roar of surf, the hum drowned out the voices of his parents, teachers, and classmates; for Hector, everywhere was like the seashore. Occasionally, utterances and images would emerge from the hum. Some of these were magically beautiful, bright with the purest light, while others seemed to mock him by revealing anxieties and dark wishes he was afraid to think about. Nor did the hum of objects and spaces quieten as he reached adolescence; in fact, the utterances and images he made out in it became longer and more distinct respectively, producing ever more wonder and anxiety, delight and disgust, pure light and shameful filth of the soul.

"Hector didn't wish to listen to the voice that issued from the hum of spaces—a voice unlike any other in the world. He began to fear it and seek protection from it. He decided to study medicine in the belief that only a conversation with a sick person in need of his help could drown out the clear, dark voices he heard all around him. This idea was the right one: At the university, no one had the slightest inkling that Hector was such a good student because only study and work could dispel the mumbling, singing, and guffawing of objects, and the strange stories that every space he entered regaled him with."

3. The Sickness Returns

"So it happened that for the years of Hector's studies the chattering of objects and spaces subsided to such a degree that it practically stopped. Now he was rarely addressed by a piece of wall as he passed it, and seldom did some convoluted story emerge from the stench of the blackened inside of a vase, dissolving before its ripples could form characters and faces. Possibly, the voices would soon have fallen altogether silent. But then came Hella's blindness and her need for him to tell her a story. At the moment of her request, Hector felt like an abstaining addict offered his favorite drug for free. Deep down, he knew how this would end. He knew that the whisper of things hadn't ceased at all; it was just that he had learned to ignore it. The quiet hum was still there all right, whether or not Hector was listening to it. It had sunk into his memory, there to generate images like crystals in a supersaturated solution. And these crystals were waiting for the membrane covering the depths to rupture, and the black liquid of memory mixed with dreams and desires to spurt forth. Hector suspected that when this happened the impact of the crystal detritus born in his memory would be enough to demolish his existence. Nevertheless, with Hella's appeal he was unable to resist the gorgeous well that had been forming so long within him, and with it the longing to submit to childish indulgence and orchestrate the birth of unreal events. And his weakness was supported by a fine excuse: How could he refuse the request of a sick person?

"Hector knew that in starting to tell his story he would be plunging back into the opium smoke that emanated from things, a dubious delight of which he had almost succeeded in ridding himself—but he persuaded himself that he could handle it. As we know, he embarked on his story with caution. As it was necessary to give sick Hella a tale from which she could take heart, he undertook not to poke about under the crust of reality, and to steer clear of story streams that led into darkness. Little did he know—or maybe he refused to acknowledge—that there are no pure story streams; all stories are scary, all come from a single strange-smelling wellspring that seeps into the folds of things and collects in dirty corners of the spaces we inhabit, all trace patterns of desire and fear that aren't even ours but those of a monster whose dream is our life. And so it happened that after a few sentences whose content he foolishly considered to be innocent, he began to feel the tug of a current well known to him; he knew that his sentences were in the grip of this current and bending to its rhythm, and that words charged with menace were being deposited in their folds. The rest we know.

At first, Hector did try to swim against the current; but soon he received Hella's blessing to surrender himself to it, and he did so joyfully. Before long, his story had produced an internment camp in the wilderness, cruel women, a confused daemon, an unhappy robot . . .

"He was right in surmising that it wouldn't end with the story at the log cabin. On his return from the woodland cottage, he once again heard things and spaces. The city of Parca was humming with activity, every gesture of its every pedestrian developed some kind of plot, the facade of every building whispered the stories being played out inside, everything was at once a beginning and a lead. He was terrified that this deluge of fantastical past and present, which teemed with characters jostling for full formation, would render him incapable of a physician's work, but to his surprise the sentences that slithered, like squirming maggots in some disaster movie, from the world's folds recoiled from the sick bodies he treated, and the voices of his patients weren't drowned out by the hum of stories all somehow related to Leo's captivity and his confused wanderings in strange cities. Thus, Hector embarked on a double life. A respected surgeon and exemplary family man, at night he would lie in bed watching the weavings of dark stories with his inner eye."

For the first time in ages, I heard something other than Martin's voice and the lapping of the sea: the sound of an engine, which soon subsided. In the distance, a light bobbed on the dark surface; the father of the proprietor of the taverna next door, one of the last inhabitants of Loutro still in his original occupation, was going fishing.

4. Locked-away Book

"Hector soon realized that the story from the log cabin was but a part of a great tangle of stories, the outer and inner limits of which were inaccessible, as new shoots were forever sprouting from the outside edges, while the inside was in a constant state of fraying. The nighttime proliferation of stories exhausted him, but as luck would have it, this growth ceased the moment he passed through the hospital gates. For three years, Hector lived among the breakers in a sea of nighttime tales. His mind was unable to contain all the storylines and characters as they branched off into ever new episodes. Heroes transformed in his mind; two characters would merge into one, or a character would disintegrate; it even happened that storylines from different episodes became intertwined, or that a character who was writing a novel himself became a character in that novel. Life in this crumbling, forever-transforming palace of stories exhausted Hector, so that he came to the realization that he should give the volcanic storylines an unchanging, verifiable form and a fixed place, and so find relief. Thus, on his return from the hospital at night, he took to going into his room to record the stories in the corners untouched by the desk lamp. He locked the sheets of paper he had written on in the bottom drawer of his desk. Although he would have found time to write when working the night shift at the hospital, it was plain to him from the start that he would never break his rule: The world of the hospital and the world of his book must remain forever separate. Hella and Elisa believed that he went to his room to study his medical books.

"When Hector began to write, he knew that he could start anywhere, even from the most obscure episode—an utterance overheard in the hum of conversation on the Boulevard Saint-Germain by a minor character in a short story published in a magazine whose pages fluttered in a salty sea breeze as a hero in a novel by Vanessa Wills stood reading it on the deck of a transatlantic ship, for instance. Still, whenever the nib of Hector's pen struck blank paper, he longed to return to the place where his work had been born and begun to grow—the jungle of North Floriana. Thus, the first sentences he wrote were from the story of the wire book. But it was a different story now: When he had told it to Hella in the log cabin, he had suppressed darker and more brutal images from the civil and interventionist war, the captivities of Fernando and Leo, Linda's life on the run, and Diamanta's imprisonment in the fortress, driving them away as soon as they began to form in his mind, for fear of troubling both Hella and himself. But as he sat alone in the act of writing, he had neither the strength nor any cause to resist the frantic pressure they applied. As the harrowing scenes formed themselves into words, other, yet more dreadful images and stories were born out of them. Yet it happened regularly that an image of ecstatic beauty and pure light would flash through the violence, decay, and filth.

"No one had the faintest idea that this gifted, kindly physician, whose abilities had allowed him to scale the heights of his chosen career, who was loved by his patients, and who was an exemplary family man, was in fact a brother of the Marquis de Sade who spent hours of the night writing a novel whose brutality and obscenity would have shocked the world. Although Hector dreaded ever having to show his handwritten sheets to Hella, he was tormented by having to keep this secret from the person closest to him. The thought of walking about in a mask until his dying day was unbearable to him. Hella would at first be horrified by what she read, that was for sure, but later she would understand; she would accept what he was doing and continue to love him, his strange night sickness and monstrous book notwithstanding. So he braced himself in anticipation of his confession. Then something happened, and neither Hella nor Elisa ever found out about Hector's writing."

5. Sylva

"When Elisa was two years old, a young woman was admitted to Hector's department with appendicitis. Hector learned from her admission records that her name was Sylva Cerrano, and that she was an architect. Marius asked Rita if she was *the* Sylva Cerrano. The name was well known to him; Parca-born Cerrano had become one of the world's most celebrated architects—she may have been the most famous person living in Parca at the time. 'That's right,' said Rita. 'But at the time she was only twenty-six and quite unknown. Not a single building had yet been built to her design, and apparently there was little hope that anyone would choose to make her unusual vision a reality.' Anyway, one evening, on entering Sylva's sickroom, Hector saw that she was sitting up in bed, working with a pencil on a large sketchpad propped against her knees. He asked to see what she was drawing, and Sylva turned the pad around for his benefit. The light in the room was dim, and at first Hector took the gently sloping lines on the paper for a spider's web. Then he realized he was looking at a faint sketch of a vast hall. In somewhat exaggerated bottom-view perspective, lines marking elevator shafts and vertical strips of lights converged on a high vaulted roof made of sheets of glass set in metal grillwork; beneath this roof Hector saw galleries, bridges straight and slanting intersecting at many points, escalators, and the mouths of many corridors.

"It struck him immediately that what he had before him was a drawing of the Building from his book. When thinking up the story of Leo, he had perceived every detail of the Building very keenly, from the decorative curves in the walls to the smells of the rooms; new, phantom arms had grown out of his body, sprouting fingers that touched the glass of illuminated storefronts, ceramic, and metal surfaces. But as a whole, the space was shrouded in fog—all he felt of it was an undefined breath. Now he realized that the fog out of which his images had emerged was contained in the space drawn by Sylva. For a long time, he studied the drawing in silence. Then he recalled a detail he had described in his story. He laid the tip of an index finger on top of the cylindrical cage of an elevator and asked if its roof was in the form of a spiral-shaped shell. Astonished but saying nothing, Sylva flicked through the pages of her sketchpad and found one on which was drawn an elevator cage with a spiral-shaped roof.

"Hector made a quick getaway to the doctors' room, where his thoughts were dominated by the woman who had drawn his dreams. He knew that this was no case of telepathy; he had encountered a person to whom the world was revealed as it was revealed to him, whose hands and his, groping in the dark, had touched the same shapes—the space he had seen in Sylva's sketchpad and the Building in his own novel were two crystals whose similarity meant they originated in the same source. For a long time, he had observed how the wildly growing tangle of his nighttime stories was overcharged with a throbbing power to keep pace with the endless incestuous encounters of their own shoots and their new entanglements. He felt the tangle stretch the very ends of its runners into the darkness, in a fumbling search for a related thicket with which to intertwine. And now at last it had happened: His story was presented with an image that had emerged from elsewhere, although he was in no doubt that he himself was a part of its wild, rampant tangle. Immediately he recognized in Sylva's drawings signs of his own vice; should he turn the pages of the sketchpad, he knew he would find the same space growing and metamorphosing, producing halls, galleries, and corridors in a never-ending stream.

"Hector had the felt the touch and keen draw of this other, proximate universe on the universe of his own imagination. He knew that were he to stay in Sylva's company, the coalescence of the two universes would begin in earnest, and the thought of how this merging would proceed and what would come of it caused him great anxiety. The outcome would amount to more than intellectual friendship, he was sure of that. The growing-together of two unruly tangles would be monstrous yet blissful and bound to beget a relationship which—like the stories he wrote at night—was filled with torment and delight. Such a wild process would likely cause great injury to Hella and Elisa, the people he held dearest. Sylva Cerrano was due to leave the hospital in three days' time, and Hector decided to stay out of her way for the duration. Hopefully, she would be out of his life after that.

"No sooner had he made this decision than there was a knock at his door. It was Sylva, wanting to know how it was that he knew her vision so well. It was obvious to him that her visit was fueled by more than curiosity; her thoughts in her hospital bed had been like his in the doctors' room. He couldn't just brush this off as mere coincidence. Although he felt a powerful desire to tell her all about himself, he was still trying to protect himself and his family. So he invented a story, telling Sylva that he had once read a novel that featured a space like the one he had seen in her sketchpad; he had forgotten the author's name. Sylva wanted to know what this book was about. Instead of sending her back to bed, he did as she asked, talking long into the night about the political situation in North Floriana, the discovery of the wire book in the coral reef, the captives in the glass tower . . . He had reached the part where Patricia and Kate break into

Vanessa's apartment when he was called to a patient whose condition had worsened, and Sylva went back to her room. It was a Friday. When Hector appeared for work on the Monday, he was saddened and relieved to find another woman in Sylva's bed."

6. Meeting in a Café

"A few days later, Sylva telephoned Hector at the hospital and asked him to meet her. They met in a large café on the main boulevard. Today, Rita explained, this place was empty and boarded up (during the demonstrations, its windows had been broken so many times that the proprietor had thought it best to close down and wait for calmer times), but in those days it was always filled with customers. They met in the evening, with the room abuzz with conversation and a constant stream of white and red carlights beyond the window. Sylva began by speaking of her work. For her architect's drawings she used a special method she had discovered while at university: She created stages for the unfolding of undetermined plots, novels whose words mostly reached her as the mere melody of speech beyond a wall, although she sometimes caught a sentence fragment describing a gesture, a scene, a snatch of an argument . . . All she knew of her wordless novels was their mood, expressed in the tone of their encounters with the people, objects, and spaces that governed them, and the formless flow of forces and figures reminiscent of moving abstract paintings. Each of the novels from which her buildings originated was different, but all contained tones of anxiety and ecstasy. In Sylva's architectural vision, these two tonalities and their connection in a hidden common source were reflected in the contrast between the intricate labyrinth of corridors on the one hand and vast, undivided space, with sky, landscape, and sea displayed through walls of glass on the other.

"As she was making her first drawings of a complex of arcades for an international client, she had the feeling that she was carefully plotting a scene in some dark tale she didn't know. Now she knew that this was the story of Leo's captivity and escape. She had always wondered about the origin of the mysterious, wordless stories her spaces grew out of. She was extremely curious about this origin: By finishing the tale of the wire book and remembering the name of the novel's author, Hector might tell her what she needed to know.

"So that evening in the café—and the next three evenings, too—Hector went on with the story. He included all the shoots that had sprung from it in recent years. Whenever Sylva urged him to recall the name of its author, he prevaricated, blaming his bad memory. On the fourth evening, however, he confessed that the novel about the wire book was his own work. He told Sylva how the story had originated and later been overgrown by other stories. He told her how he wrote at night in secret, of his double life . . . Sylva appeared little surprised by these revelations; perhaps she had suspected all along that he was the author of the book about Fernando and Leo."

7. Space Born Out of Words

"So began the symbiosis of two monstrous organisms, each of which nourished itself on the dubious sludge of the deep while turned toward the burning white light. Hector's sentences and Sylva's visions of structure intertwined, and one was born out of the other. And the lives of Hector and Sylva came together just as their work did; they became lovers and remained so for over thirty years. Used to living in two worlds, Hector succeeded in keeping his love for Sylva secret from Hella just as he concealed from her the work he did at night. Hella would often speak with Hector about the buildings of the famous daughter of Parca, without having the faintest notion that they arose out sentences written by her husband in the room next to where she was sleeping, or that the face she saw in magazines was one of two centers of the world in which Hector was most at home—the other lay like a secret North Pole in the locked bottom drawer of his desk.

"Sylva never married, and she had no children. After several years of her love for Hector, her face reflected a silent sorrow; as if ashamed by this, Sylva covered it with a smile like a light, transparent veil, which she never removed. She lived on Olive Street in the old town. Her apartment overlooked a spacious yard in which tall plane trees grew; above the roofs were bare, pale hilltops, with cloud shadows chasing across them. Here, Hector would read to Sylva new chapters of his book, and Sylva would draw architectural designs that grew out of stories her lover described to her. Events from his books would be transformed into nameless, pulsating force fields, which would eventually form stable spaces she would clothe in brick, metal, and glass. Her work was always recognized by its conjunction of dark labyrinths on the one hand and practically non-material glass, non-material rooms and terraces bathed in sun- and moonlight on the other. Many were puzzled and disturbed by this conjunction, but few denied its strange humor.

"Spaces of Sylva's design grew outward in much the same wild, unpredictable way as Hector's book. On the one hand, they evoked visions of other buildings as their own dreams or phantom doppelgängers—these would seek a place in a different landscape, perhaps even a distant continent; on the other, Sylva's buildings penetrated their surroundings, sending out projections, distributaries, terraces that jutted boldly into emptiness, slim towers jetting into the sky. It was as though they couldn't stay in one place: Houses advanced, their glass corridors running for bushes, tree-tops, or the surface of an artificial lake, their airborne bridges at the level of a thirtieth or fiftieth floor heading for the void. The ends of corridors, colonnades, and bridges would sprout new buildings, and these would sprout yet more rootstocks before the building could close.

"Most of Sylva's buildings were restless and eccentric. They burrowed into the ground, bent over rivers and lakes and pulled them deep within, opened themselves up to the wind and let it wander their corridors, received tree branches, and ironically violated boundaries between dwellings and forests or jungles. They had no fear of spray and the monotonous music of waterfalls, and they rose in terraces reminiscent of cyclopean stairs to form steep slopes, there to look over clifftops to the ravines beyond. On the coast, their basements went below the surface, where, with the aid of floodlights, they opened large windows onto the undersea world. It was as though Sylva's buildings were trying to escape their center: They cracked and burst open, bringing their interiors to the surface, as though they had been turned inside out, or absorbed themselves—they included bedrooms with walls of glass transparent from one side only, spilling over the abyss of the boulevard, so that the facade ended up on the inside, with the glass laid open to the wind and rain like an exposed mucous membrane. Such centrifugal processes might mean the absence of an actual structural body—the building was nothing but projections over nothing. Sometimes, however, a sketch would appear among Sylva's designs of a building closed in on itself, as though it were cancelling all relations with its environment."

8. Words Born Out of Space

"Hector looked forward to seeing drawings of the new spaces that thus grew out of and detached themselves from his stories of his book, which would remain connected to them only by thin, imperceptible threads. Having seen the drawings and studied them for a long time, he would wait until the spaces matured in his mind into new stories filled with people, wild beasts and birds, metal robots, monsters, and ghosts. But before all Sylva's spaces could produce characters and storylines, out of them there arose, like murmuring, colored smoke, a lurking, a roaming, searching, dreamy, foolish self-concealment, a struggle which, deep within, longed for defeat, a snooping, slow, ecstatic floating through space, an unclean persuasion and a wicked humility, energy surging and subsiding, discreet extortion, the movement of thoughts perverse and tender, spreading through the space like foam, suspicious confession, lamentation permeated with threat, hesitation before decision, daydreams of sparkling gemstones, a blissful expectation of emptiness, action dominated by a slow, swaying motion, action dominated by wheezing, the oppressive control of victims, escape that now and then becomes pursuit of the pursuer, fatigue that allows the egress of luminous shapes, a ripening of aims which is actually rotting, decay which contains the inception of new, unwitting scheming, betrayals, reproaches, and many types and tones of waiting."

Martin spoke these words with a monotonous rhythm, his voice in harmony with the rhythm of the surf. The windows and doorways of all rooms in Loutro had long been in darkness. Provided there were no insomniacs beyond the rocks in Finix or way up in Anopolis, there was no one else awake within several hours' journey of where we were sitting.

"Out of this formless action, like a pattern created by iron filings on a magnetic board, new images, characters, and stories arose: a room with a glass wall through which a snow-covered

wood was visible would become the stage for the meeting of
dreamy conspirators who were planning the robbery of a large
sapphire; on a terrace, a girl leans on a metal rail, watching a
curve in a coldly gleaming river in silence, as she is persuaded
by a young man in a tuxedo to carry out a crime; a leopard lifts
its head from a carpet and turns it slowly toward an opening
door; a sixteen-year-old girl puts on a black facemask, while
in the next room her parents speak of neoliberal economics;
in an underground garage, an extremely beautiful woman in
a black miniskirt and an unbuttoned fur coat stands next to
a shiny Aston Martin car, explaining to two attentive scientists a metaphysical system of her own design based on a new
Neoplatonism and the spirit of glossy fashion magazines.

"Hector was particularly fond of the outermost places in
Sylva's rooms—places in which the energies that created them
seemed to be concentrated, and where they were transformed
into a kind of *scintillation*. These were the farthest places the
substance of the building succeeded in reaching, and where it
was forced to stop: Had it gone any farther, the terrace would
have crashed into the ravine, the sea would have poured into
the hall, and drops from the waterfall would have hit the bed-
covers. In Hector's book, such outlying places provided a stage
for scenes in which the lines of unrelated stories became entangled or at least crossed (in a glass-covered porch above an overgrown garden, the path of a robber fleeing with a precious stone
intersected with that of a philosopher seeking her master, who
years before had left the university for the drab suburbs, from
where and since when dreary theories on a muddy emanation of
some kind had seeped through to the academic world). Hector's
plots were commonly characterized by the same centrifugal
force as Sylva's buildings; stories ran off into the distance, frequently ending up on a foreign continent, at a hill station, or
deep in the sea—Hector's favorite means of transport was the

submarine. His characters undertook research expeditions, were fugitives from the law, and by series of improbable coincidences reached the inner gardens of strangers' homes. Wherever they went, unknown spaces—which had emerged in Sylva's mind before being committed to the white pages of her sketchpad, there maturing into precise architect's plans—opened to them.

"So it happened that Sylva and Hector's joint work, composed half of words, half of shapes, each born out of the other, a centaur and an ouroboros eating its own tail, came into being. It was now out of the question that Hector should tell Hella about his work. It became his and Sylva's secret; besides, his speaking up about the handwritten pages in his desk would expose many years of marriage as a sham. Was it out of consideration for Hella or because of ordinary cowardice that Hector kept his work a secret? It was difficult to say. But there were ever more reasons why only one person would learn, after many years, of Hector and Sylva's joint work. That person was Rita."

9. Fame

"Before Sylva met Hector, none of her designs had got beyond the paper stage. In the early days, to gain acceptance with the commission for architectural design competition, she had kept her vision reined in. Still it was considered too bizarre; she often met with thinly veiled ridicule, and she could tell that many of her colleagues wondered about her sanity. Over and over, she heard that her designs were technically unworkable. Such objections were nonsense. Sylva loved vertiginous equilibria that conquered seemingly intractable forces and rendered them compatible. Her devotion to dreams both dark and light and her capacity for rapture combined with a brilliant mathematical brain and an exceptional gift for solving problems of structural mechanics, so managing the forces that threatened to destroy her buildings. There was such balance and synergy in her work that the resulting form was stable, even though it gave the impression of being seconds from collapse.

"But once she began her joint work with Hector, and her designs were born out of Hector's writing, it seemed to her that scenes and stories from her lover's book dictated the nature of the architectural space so unequivocally and adamantly that there was no question of their requirements being subjected to checks and mitigated by compromises. Thus Sylva decided that she would no longer think in terms of what was acceptable, popular taste, and the sacred axioms of the architectural community. What, she asked herself, was the point of listening to mocking reproof and condescending advice if her designs never got beyond the paper stage? At the moment she gave up all hope of seeing her buildings made real, the sorrow that overwhelmed her was mixed with relief and a new sense of freedom and great peace. If need be, she would make her living as a cleaner, drawing her visions in her free time as she worked on her and Hector's project.

"What happened then was beyond her wildest dreams: Her untamed, inconsiderate, never-seen-before projects—which arose as scenes for the intricate plots of Hector's book, as designs that couldn't be held to mock the popular taste, for they had nothing in common with it—were so fascinating and masterful that once seen, they were never forgotten. At the sight of Sylva's drawings, people at city halls and ministries, as well as private individuals, felt a longing to witness the transformation of her dreams into objects of steel, brick, concrete, and glass which they could look at and walk deep inside. Suddenly, there were clients and investors aplenty; before long, buildings of Sylva's design were on all continents, springing up one after another. Perhaps her vision was so appealing because the forms of her buildings reminded people of the mother's labyrinth of bliss and the angst at the bottom of their minds, the ground plan of which had become the secret pattern of all events in their lives. Soon, Sylva could no longer reply to all the offers she was getting. She became one of the world's wealthiest and most sought-after architects. Still Hector and Sylva worked jointly, but while one part of the work was known by millions, the other was locked away in a desk drawer, known only to Sylva and Hector. Some who wandered the corridors of Sylva's buildings had a sense they were hearing the murmur of some kind of phantom plot, but they could have no idea that they were encountering the ghosts of Hector's characters, which had called Sylva's spaces into being.

"The money mounted up in Sylva's bank account, but she had no idea what to do with it. She continued to live in her old apartment in Olive Street, where she felt at home, designing spaces born out of Hector's dreams, waiting patiently for the time he would be able to come to her. In the beginning, Sylva had tried to persuade Hector to have his book published, but he had refused. In addition to the book's being bound up with their secret love, there arose a new reason for its concealment. It seemed to Hector now that the sense he and Sylva shared of a vertiginous equilibrium demanded that their work preserve certain symmetries: In contrast to the light airiness of Sylva's buildings, the other part of the work should be forever in darkness; in opposition to the world renown of one of the originators, the name of the other should remain completely unknown; while one part spread itself across the globe, the other should never leave the confines of the drawer; and finally, the immobility of the buildings should be balanced out by a flow of words that never froze into the final text of a published book."

10. Late Work

"Hector's heroes were travelers, inventors, spies, sages, mathematicians, criminals clambering about city rooftops in the moonlight, mystics, heads of corporations, chemists, and poets. In most cases, several such lives came together in one character, who either lived them concurrently or gradually transformed to live them one after another. Another cause of astonishment at Sylva's buildings was that each of them contained something of the never-ending office, factory, caliph's residence, criminal's lair, magical villa, oil refinery, monastery, lighthouse, dock, mountain hut of a Taoist sage, frivolous residence of a Hollywood film star, secret service headquarters, and suspicious laboratory. In later years, the once-extensive section of Hector's book with the undersea adventure disappeared, although the submarines, their heroes discussing metaphysics by round portholes, still roamed the deep somewhere, even if Hector was no longer following them. His life gave him ever greater cause for despair, and the underwater world was no longer a place in which he could escape his deepening depressions; its impenetrable darkness, panic-stricken hustle and bustle, listless rolling and rippling, the never-ending parade of strange shapes, and the struggle that never, ever stopped reminded him darkly of the world of the surface.

"His characters' adventures broke away from the land and the sea, whose associations with his despair were too strong; instead, they moved ever higher up futuristic skyscrapers. The stories that played out in these luminous heights little resembled their terrestrial counterparts, although they were composed of the same elements, being mixes of industrial espionage and metaphysics, love and ecstasy, and treasure-hunting, advanced mathematics and dreamlike debauchery. Although despair did penetrate to the higher floors, it was imbued with city lights in blinking constellations, and it changed its substance, as if by an alchemical process, to a *prima materia* of feelings, in which pain and pleasure were impossible to distinguish. Hector loved precious stones, although he had never owned any. They appeared with unusual frequency in his work from the very beginning; this late phase was characterized by the appearance of ever bigger and brighter diamonds and other gems in ever greater numbers.

"The rhythms of Sylva's and Hector's lives had long been synchronized. Sylva was now designing ever taller, ever less corporeal buildings connected by bridges that spanned cities, superhighways, and rivers at even more dizzying heights than the skybridge that joined the Petronas Twin Towers in Kuala Lumpur. In cities and open landscapes all over the world, structures of breathtaking slimness—hieroglyphs of concrete, glass, and steel characterizing the despair, dreams, and rapture of a respected hospital doctor and secret writer from Parca—spurted for the skies. The glow of a book locked in the bottom drawer of a desk spread across the planet.

"The skyscraper period was succeeded by the bridge period. At a distance, Sylva's suspension and cable-stayed bridges looked like finely drawn scratches in the sky. The great distances between pylons was a cause of wonder, and still they were able to withstand storms and tornadoes. Then the bridge period, too, came to an end. When Hector and Sylva at last returned to residential buildings, what they produced reminded people of stars, fire, and cloud, even though the buildings bore no resemblance to these shapes."

11. Sickness and Despair

"Sylva's apartment was one of a few buildings that had originated by the breaking up of former palaces into pieces, and which were then grouped together in new units. Sylva liked her apartment so much that she had never considered living in a house made to her own design. Three years earlier, after conducting a search for a home for its newly established revenue authority, Parca City Hall had settled on a block of houses in Olive Street; the former palace would be at least partially restored so as to house the new offices. Sylva was left with no choice but to move out of the rooms she loved so much. She was very unhappy about this, as she couldn't imagine living anywhere else. Eventually, she bought a modern white villa by the sea on the western edge of the city, in a wealthy neighborhood. But she failed to settle there. She missed her old apartment. She was surprised to realize that she had been happy there, her loneliness and constant waiting for Hector notwithstanding.

"Not long afterward, Sylva became seriously ill. She was over sixty, and she felt extremely tired. These days, when Hector read new chapters to her, to her surprise and sorrow she realized that they didn't inform her ideas of space. She accepted that the mental powers that summoned up the interiors of buildings, which hundreds of workers would then dress in reinforced concrete, had been extinguished. She told Hector that she was sorry, but her work in their shared project was over. She would never design another building.

"When Hector came to her now, usually he would find her sitting on a sofa in front of a glass wall, watching the white-crested waves. For a while, Hector's protagonists continued to develop under pressure from their unresolved subplots. But in his many years of cooperation with Sylva, Hector had become used to the support of her drawings and finished buildings; he could create only characters and stories that had been breathed on by her spaces. As his stories slowly died away, he waited for a conciliatory or tragic ending for his book to emerge, to bring his and Sylva's joint work to a close.

"Sylva's illness became progressively worse. There came a time when her life at the villa alternated with stays in the hospital. Now she looked much older than Hector: Her hair was completely white. Hector told her of his intention to leave Hella so that he could stay by her. She talked him out of it: She didn't want to cause anyone pain, and she didn't expect to live much longer. She was afraid. Only now did she confess to Hector that every day of their long relationship she had imagined the two of them living together in a happy marriage; she had dreamed up two children for them, given them names and lives, then children of their own, and now she feared that real life had become confused with the invention. Whenever despairing Hector told her that he would do whatever she asked, she gave the same reply: She didn't want him to move in with her, nor did she still have the desire to continue with their joint work; she was reconciled to the fact that the time had come for the work to end. The only thing she wished for was to move back to her old apartment—but this was a wish that only a wizard could grant. Sylva was convinced that a return to her old apartment would restore her health. Hector saw more in this belief than mere superstition: Surely the breath of furniture and walls steeped in memories of the time when they composed their joint work was a more effective medication than the pills Sylva's doctors were prescribing?"

12. Encounter at a Station

"Although the one thing Sylva wished for was out of reach, Hector found himself in the depths of despair at his failure to help her. He was no longer able to write; rather than reaching a conclusion, the action of his book had frozen mid-gesture and mid-sentence, like a snapped reel of film. He didn't know how to go on, so when one day at dawn he had the idea of taking his own life, he felt relief and something akin to joy. He made the firm decision to end his life—a course of action from which even thoughts of Sylva, Hella, Elisa, and Rita failed to dissuade him—one night while on duty at the hospital, sitting in his office, looking at its white door. As his ability to think in exact terms was undiminished, there and then he prepared everything he would need, including a pack of sleeping pills from the cabinet. Shortly after seven, having been relieved by a colleague, he headed straight for the train station closest to the hospital, which was on the edge of the city. His intention was to take a train to a nearby village, where he would approach a cliff overlooking the sea; in a grove of tall trees whose name he didn't know, he would lie down in the grass and swallow the pills.

"The station was little more than a halt, and few people used it. Hector saw just one person—a slight, white-haired man in a threadbare coat, who was sitting on a bench. As this was the only bench on the platform, Hector sat down next to him. Although the sun was shining, the cold of early morning was still in the air; melting frost glittered on the gleaming tracks. With astonishment, Hector realized that these would be the last images of his life. He was afraid that the old man would try to engage him in conversation; and sure enough, before long the man turned to him and asked if he had change for a banknote: He wanted to buy a coffee from the vending machine. Hector reached into his pocket and pulled out a handful of coins; he refused the old man's banknote, and the old man didn't insist that he take it. Hector hoped that the conversation would end there, but obviously the old man wanted someone to talk to. When he returned with his steaming cup and once again took up his seat next to Hector, he asked if Hector was traveling far. Hector answered with a mere shake of the head, but the old man was not so easily rebuffed. Looking and nodding at Hector, he said, 'Things on your mind, eh?' before adding wise words about how life wasn't as easy as people made it out to be. The old man's intrusion was the last thing Hector needed, and he was bothered by having to listen to such banalities an hour before his death. He decided to leave the bench and walk about the platform. But before he could stand, the old man embarked on a tale about his own life; he had once been in a hopeless situation, pining for a woman who was completely out of his reach. The old man's voice was high and thin; Hector waited impatiently for him to end or at least pause, so that he could say his goodbyes and flee.

"But the old man plowed right ahead. All those years ago, he had considered killing himself, and had even been looking forward to the act. But then a crazy idea had occurred to him: As there was no possible means of achieving what he wanted, how about trying an impossible one? At this point, Hector couldn't help but pay greater heed to what the old man was saying. 'I'm not sure I understand,' he said. 'Time after time I'd tried all the routes I could think of in pursuit of my aim,' the old man explained, 'and all had proved completely impassable, all contained an insuperable obstacle. The woman and I were separated by several universes. But then I said to myself: "Why not take a path that doesn't lead to my goal? Why not forge a connection whose direction is completely different?"' Hector still didn't get it, but now he was listening closely. 'In short, I told myself I'd take a path determined by chance—any path at all,' the old man continued. His voice was suddenly deeper and stronger. 'And this random path really did lead me to my goal. I won't bore you with the details, but why don't you give it a try? What do you have to lose? If it turns out not to work, you can always go back to your original plan.' 'Very well,' said Hector. 'I'm beginning to see what you mean. But tell me one thing: What guarantee will I have that my choice is truly a random one? I've gone over the matter so many times that if I asked chance to show me the way, how could I resist unwittingly choosing a way that ran close to ways I've already considered?'

"'But it's perfectly simple, my friend,' said the old man. 'Certain accidents are exactly that. What I did was close my eyes, open a book at a random page, point a finger at that page, and allow myself to be guided by the word it fell on.' 'And that word got you the woman you so yearned for?' asked Hector, incredulous. Sipping his coffee, the old man merely nodded in reply. 'But I don't have any book with me,' said Hector. 'I'd expect you to show a little more imagination,' sighed the old man. 'Let's say you decide that your path will be determined by a headline in the top left-hand corner of that page of newspaper being blown about the platform. Want to catch it? Or how about this? See the boy and the girl at the ticket window? Now they're heading for the platform, obviously in conversation. How about taking as the key to your future the first words you hear them speak as they pass? But there's one thing I should make clear. All this will work only if you accept without reservation whatever chance presents you with. It makes no difference if the gift appears altogether useless or even detrimental to the cause. And probably it *will* appear that way. Remember, the goddess of chance bestows her gift only at the first time of asking, and only *her* gift is miraculous.' 'But what if the gift chance bestows really is completely useless? Not every means suits every end. You can't use an electric shaver to solve a mathematical problem.' Still the old man kept patience with Hector. 'If the gift bestowed by chance seems useless to you, so much the better. Then it plainly has nothing in common with the means you have used hitherto—means that have led you down a blind alley. Besides, are you really so sure that an electric shaver can't be used to solve a mathematical problem?' Hector stared at the old man in surprise. In the course of their discussion, not only had his voice changed, his facial expression and whole bearing had changed, too; now Hector wondered if his neighbor on the bench was even as old as he, Hector, was. Although still undecided on whether to take the man's advice, as the boy and the girl—they appeared to be students—approached the glass doors that gave onto the platform, Hector strained his ears to catch what they were saying.

"As they stepped onto the platform, he heard the girl say something about 'Lygdian motifs.' He didn't properly catch the rest of her utterance; perhaps she was telling the boy that since she had a seminar paper to write about Lygdian motifs in Romantic poetry, or some such thing, she couldn't go to the cinema that evening. That was all that Hector heard: The girl and the boy headed straight for the other end of the platform. The old man looked at the tracks and sipped his coffee, saying nothing; Hector couldn't tell whether he'd caught anything of the students' conversation. 'What nonsense!' Hector thought. 'How could Lygdian motifs help me acquire the headquarters of the revenue authority? Maybe I *should* give it another try . . .' But apparently the old man had guessed what was on his mind. 'The very first words!' he said strictly. 'They must be the very first.' He even raised a finger of warning from his coffee cup.

"The whistle of a locomotive sounded in the distance. Having again thanked Hector for the change for the vending machine, the magical old man walked toward the track. Seen from the back, again he looked very much older than Hector. A gray locomotive emerged from the pale mist. Hector got to his feet; he knew that he had only a few seconds in which to make his decision. Although he was reluctant to defer a decision for which it had taken him so long to gather the courage, the old man's words resonated in his head; deep within, he understood what the man had said—he knew the magical power of chance from the writing of his book, so he knew that it could produce the most sought-after treasures. As the old man boarded the train, he didn't look back."

13. Imaginary Army

"The next train to the place Hector had chosen for his death wasn't due for two hours. In the end, he decided to stay at the station for those two hours, considering the feasibility of putting to use the words with which Chance, in the form of a student stranger, had presented him. If no new idea came to him—and Hector couldn't imagine that one would—he would board the train and, after just a slight delay, carry out his original plan. But no sooner had the first train left than he flew into a rage with himself. Now he would have to gather his courage all over again, making everything so much worse, and his end even more ignominious. Still, he forced himself to address the strange exercise Chance had set him. He walked back and forth across the empty platform, searching for an explanation for how a legendary nation could help him recover an apartment whose rooms were now given over to a large official institution. What was he supposed to do—dress up as a Lygd and attack the revenue authority building? He wished that the two hours had passed and it was all over. As the exercise he had been set evidently had no outcome, he allowed his mind to wander through a variety of absurd scenarios. He imagined Lygds dressed in bear skins laying siege to the revenue authority building, as the police tried to protect it . . .

"He told himself that if the Lygds were more than just a romantic fiction and still living in the city, they would indeed have a certain claim on the revenue authority building. At the very least, they would be able to argue that this claim pre-dated the claim of state bureaucracy. If only there were some kind of magic that could bring the Lygds to life! But this was beyond the powers of any deity—not least because the Lygds had probably never existed. And even if they had, today's Parcan soul would not retain the faintest whisper of them. The sun emerged from the early-morning haze; Hector had to squint to stop the glint from the tracks bothering his eyes. But was it really so important that there weren't any Lygds? Did it even matter that there never had been?

"Then he had a crazy idea: What if the Lygds' greatest strength was their non-existence? Hector began to see the possibilities this offered—far-reaching connections could be made with all kinds of things. The very fictiveness of the nation meant that it could be transformed into an army of mercenaries deployable in any war. In his mind's eye, Hector saw the Lygds in battle formation, ready to strike out at the revenue authority. Maybe there really was something in what the magical old man had told him! Hector looked on as nonsensical Chance created a new space very different from the depressing labyrinth he had roamed in recent weeks; hope dawned within him, then grew ever stronger. And in this space produced by two words over-heard, thousands of wonderful paths began to open.

"As the Lygds were without definite characteristics, they were malleable. Although he didn't yet know what needed to be done, he had an inkling that the Lygd nation was a vessel that everyone could fill with their own dreams, and so it would be attractive to everyone. As the people awoke from these dreams, they would want to assist in the birth; everyone would want a share in the Lygd revival and its aims—aims that Hector, the secret creator, would determine. And once the Parcans had helped him create the Lygd nation, it would be possible to demand all sorts of things in its name. Hector even imagined using such an army to conquer a fortress far less pregnable than the revenue authority building.

"He was startled by the blare of a train approaching the station. He looked at his watch: the two hours were up. It was time for him to decide. Would he board the train or not? The excitement brought on by his musings vanished; now he saw that his latest thoughts were fantastic and foolish, akin to the intricate dreamer's plans he had hatched in his childhood. Bizarre images of fierce Lygds battling police were banished from his mind, to be replaced by an enticing image of a magnificent, peaceful grove with a sea view. As he approached the train of death for the second time that morning, it struck him as comical that he must decide whether to kill himself in the space of ten steps.

"In the end, he remained on the platform; he remained alive, in the knowledge that he had just committed himself to the craziest enterprise of his life. He would have to put the fantastic ideas he had cooked up at the railroad halt into practice. He would have to create a new nation and cause it to capture the headquarters of the revenue authority. He sat back down on the bench and remained there until long past nightfall, apart from an occasional stroll about the platform; he bought eight cups of coffee from the vending machine, and, from the kiosk, a pad of paper he made notes in, and he telephoned Hella to say that he would be late getting home. When he did get home, after midnight, his Lygdian campaign plan was clear, albeit in broad outline. He put the notepad in the desk drawer next to his book, and he locked the drawer."

14. Conspirators

"Hector told himself that the Lygds might succeed in taking the revenue authority building if they could prove a meaningful connection between it and their history. Although it would be necessary to invent this connection, that shouldn't pose too great a problem; Hector didn't foresee much trouble in finding volunteers to assist him, even without their knowing anything about the goals of their work and the cause they were serving. Even if his present to the city was formless, confused, self-contradictory, and embryonic, he imagined the city grabbing it with alacrity, then tending it and working it until it became a monument to Lygdia—a monument to its dreams, both light and dark. All this would come to pass, of course. But what Hector didn't foresee that day at the station was the great speed at which the community of the new nation would evolve.

"Hector would need to take to care to prevent the process of the nation's birth taking a direction incompatible with his aims. The leadership of the movement he was about to found would need to direct its natural development without putting the brakes on it. As to his own position in the movement, it should be an important one, although for the sake of his plan it would be better if he remained in the background, unseen by the public and the outer circle of followers of the Lygdian idea; the best role for him would be secret advisor and schemer . . . If he succeeded in keeping all this secret, he wouldn't have to explain anything to Hella. He had been deceiving her for years, of course, but still he couldn't see how he would get her to believe that he took the struggle for Lygdian independence seriously.

"Nor did he wish to discuss his plan for the Lygds with Sylva. The only person he could take into his confidence was Rita, whom he had been avoiding recently for fear that she would intuit that he was preparing for death. He called her early in the morning after his day at the station. An hour later, they were sitting together in a café halfway between the hospital and the university, and Hector was telling his granddaughter about his despair of recent weeks, the grove with a sea view, how the magical old man had saved his life, and how on a railroad platform he had come up with the craziest plan any Parcan had ever devised. Hector knew that Rita was the only person who would hear him out without questioning his sanity. She took his hand and said: 'Don't worry. Together, I know we can do it.' Having discussed all details, they divided out the main tasks: Hector would get the movement started and create its ideology and direction, without ever appearing in public; Rita would work on expanding the reach of the Lygdian movement at the university.

"They set to work immediately. From the beginning, everything progressed more easily than they were anticipating. Under various pseudonyms, Hector wrote the first articles on Lygdian themes; these were immediately seized upon by retired high-school teachers, who wrote study after study in the same vein. On this front, Hector's work was soon done—amateur Lygdologists took the bait in droves. Before long, the Lygdian monster had taught itself to find nourishment everywhere, and it grew rapidly.

"Hector and Rita assumed that the creation of the movement's political wing would be more problematic, not least as in Parca, unlike other peripheral areas of the country, there was no tradition of separatism to use as a starting point. But their fears in this regard soon proved unfounded. Hector came up with several Parca personalities to form the core of the Lygdian Revival Party. All were men of the middle class who were active in local politics and characterized by ambition, nationalistic tendencies, and a certain talent for organization. Hector watched them for some time from a distance before opting for Albert Albert, the editor-in-chief—indeed the only editor—of a magazine that modeled itself on *Action française* and was bought by about thirty Parcans. Hector decided to cultivate Albert as leader of the movement and chairman of the party."

15. Albert

"Having found the address of the magazine's office in the rag itself, Hector paid Albert a visit. It was situated in one room of the shabby apartment in which Albert, a scrawny, nervous man with a goatee, lived with his aged, apparently mad mother. Hector had brought several recent articles by amateur Lygdologists for Albert to look at; the heyday of new Lygdian research was just getting started, he explained. The emergent new spirit would doubtless soon exceed the boundaries of the academic world, leading to the birth of a much broader movement that would return it to its roots; a consequence of this would doubtless be a political and moral renaissance. The main battle should be waged in pursuit of the restoration of the fixed norms of Lygdian society; central to such a struggle would be an endeavor to assert the rights of descendants of the ancient Lygds. It was of crucial importance that the indisputable claims their political representatives would make regarding Lygdian sacred sites should be fully respected. One such site was currently occupied by the revenue authority building; as the editor-in-chief was surely aware, this had once been the home of a major Lygdian shrine.

"In closing, Hector informed Albert that he had come to him because he knew his articles and saw in them the presence of a large, light spirit that should not be left out of the most important movement of its time. For the duration of Hector's long speech, Albert remained in his chair, tugging at his beard. Enormously excited by what he was hearing, it seemed to him that he had at last found his true mission, and that Hector's message had given his life a purpose. As soon as the guest's exposition ended, Albert jumped from his chair, pumped Hector's hand, and declared that Hector himself would make an outstanding leader of the new movement. Hector replied modestly that he lacked talent as an organizer, and besides, his work as a hospital doctor made it impossible for him to engage in politics. But he knew of one man in Parca who was far better qualified to stand at the head of the forthcoming struggle. In the short dramatic pause that followed, Albert's mother was heard to mutter as she shuffled through the dark hallway; then Hector announced that the only man worthy of such an exalted task was none other than Albert himself. As he descended the staircase, which smelled strongly of disinfectant, Hector experienced mixed feelings: satisfaction at having gotten closer to his aim vied with disgust at the sham that had just given Albert Albert the happiest moment of his life. At the corner of the street, he went into a bar, where he drank several shots of rum.

"After that, Hector frequently visited Albert Albert. Sitting at a table covered with books, notepads, unwashed coffee cups, and piles of greasy paper, they carried on long conversations. From time to time, Albert's mother, her white hair in disarray, would look in on them and squawk something. Hector and Albert examined the situation in the Lygdian movement, the former advising the latter on action he should take. Albert was impressed by Hector's lack of self-interest; he considered Hector the brightest figure in his life, and he loved him more than anyone else in the world.

"Before long, teething problems with the financing of the movement sorted themselves out. All adherents invested their dreams in it—hitherto unknown dreams that were revealed in the movement's magic mirror; this also applied for the financial dreams of the city's magnates. The movement soon had no need of wealthy sponsors, who saw in it a source of future profits. It transpired that the attraction of the movement for them was more than a mere illusion. Indeed, support of the movement paid off right from the start; even when it existed in semi-illegality, the movement's adherents established relationships like those of the lodges, and naturally they were relayed to the levels of business enterprise and financial speculation.

It became increasingly apparent that the time was approaching for the Lygd Revival Party to wield official power in the city, and that its leadership would have a say in the awarding of important contracts; no one doubted that the party would remember its benefactors from the time of its heroic dawn. Many shady figures from the world of crime were attracted to the movement by the opportunities it offered to conspire and prospects of lavish reward for investment—there was a lot of truth in the rumors that the Lygdian movement took money from murky sources. Those who spread the rumors were mistaken in one regard only: the shady bosses weren't the actual founders of the movement—they joined it only once they saw in it a potential for profitable business and an ideal playing field for their games.

"While all this was going on, Rita got to work at the university. By instinct, she understood right away that her best tactic was to do practically nothing; in such a case, the only propaganda concerning matters Lygdian would be silence and sentence fragments that rarely made sense . . . Hector and Rita tried to remain coolly in control of the nascent Lygdian monster, but within a few months it was clear to them what they had unleashed, and it was enough to make their heads spin. For Rita, the sight of the drunken city losing its last scraps of reason was a source of ever greater dread. She told her grandfather more than once that they should give it all up. Probably Hector, too, was dismayed by the Lygdian delirium, but apocalyptic images of decay in his native city were overwhelmed by a keen vision of a happy, recovering Sylva in her Olive Street apartment. If ever greater frenzy in the city, so paving the way for still greater disaster, would lead him to his aim, Hector was quite prepared to make it happen. In any case, he couldn't have stopped the Lygdian movement, even had he wanted to: It had long had a life of its own . . . 'If I hadn't met you,' Rita told Marius, 'this wild dream we've plunged the city into would have driven me mad.' This was the first time Marius saw her cry. Her love had

become her only island in a sea of madness she and her grandfather had summoned, and in which all Parca was drowning."

16. Olive Street

"'So what happens now?' asked Marius. 'I don't suppose you've
paid much attention to what's been happening in the city
recently,' said Rita, before going on to tell him Parca's news.
With no sign that the clashes between demonstrators and
police were coming to an end (indeed, they were becoming
ever bloodier), the government had agreed to negotiate with
representatives of the Lygd Revival Party. As the government's
main aim was to stop the demonstrations, it had indicated that
it was prepared to make concessions. The party leadership had
approved a list of ten requirements it would insist on being met.
The true author of this list was Hector. As he was dictating its
points to Albert, he had stressed the importance for the party of
point eight, the handover of the building in which the income-
tax office was based. The negotiations had begun three weeks
earlier, gone on for several days, in the course of which the government had agreed to the Lygd Revival Party's demands.

"As soon as the delegation got back to Parca from the capital,
Hector hurried to Albert's place to ask about the income-tax
office. Albert answered proudly that naturally he had insisted
on the Lygdian shrine, before going on to enumerate his other
successes. But Hector was no longer listening: He cared only
about the building on Olive Street. Albert embraced Hector
and told him in a voice trembling with emotion that he didn't
know how to repay him for his immense contribution to the
great Lygdian victory. Hector replied that he wanted nothing
but two small rooms in the palace that housed the soon-to-be
former income-tax office; again, Albert was impressed by his

colleague and mentor's modesty. The removal of the income-tax office from the palace was achieved within ten days and followed by the renovation work that would convert it into the Lydgian Center.

"When Sylva moved into the villa, her first act had been to arrange in it the furniture from Olive Street. Ever the architect, she understood the language of objects and saw that her closets and tables were as unhappy in the villa as she was; they yearned for the windows overlooking the courtyard with its plane trees, and they reflected the seaside light with distaste. Sylva's furniture evoked sorrowful memories, so she placed it for hibernation in an empty garage. On the day that the Lygdian Revival Party took over the building that housed the income-tax office, Sylva was in hospital. Hector had the furniture taken from the garage to her old apartment; with assistants assigned to him by Albert, he installed all tables, closets, cabinets, and chairs in the places they had occupied for years. After Sylva discharged herself from hospital, Hector drove her straight to Olive Street. Awestruck, Sylva climbed the familiar stairs with Hector's support, to discover that her lover had performed a miracle on her behalf: She was back in her beloved apartment. Still leaning on Hector, she inspected the two rooms and vestibule; everything was exactly as before, when she and Hector had worked on their joint creation.

"Marius asked Rita about the dispute with Hector he had overheard that night. Rita explained that the Lygdian Revival Party had recently begun to split, and that its anti-Albert wing was gaining power to an alarming degree. She had been trying to persuade her grandfather to do something to consolidate the position of the party's chair. If members of the new faction were to seize the leadership, there was a danger they would eventually drive Sylva out of Olive Street. Although Hector saw that his granddaughter was right, the achievement of his sole aim had apparently so exhausted him that he lacked the strength to do anything more.

"Rita stood, took Marius by the hand, and led him to the door. Marius didn't need to ask where they were going. The building of the former income-tax office wasn't far from his apartment. Although it was almost midnight, the streets in the distance were a hive of activity; the lights of cars slid across the facades, creating many shadows; cries and blows dealt by metal rang out. They arrived at the palace's illuminated courtyard entryway to find a patrol comprising two students Marius knew by sight; sporting armbands adorned with Lygdian characters, they were checking the passes of all comers. Having greeted Rita with respect, they stepped aside to let her and Marius pass. Rita led Marius up some steps to a corridor, where they met men and women hurrying from one end to the other, carrying books, papers, files, revolving chairs, and computers.

"At last they came to the right door, which Rita unlocked. Having passed through a dark vestibule, they reached a room dimly illuminated by a nightstand lamp. The nightstand was next to a bed in which an old woman was lying, her white hair spread across the pillow. Sitting on a chair and leaning down to her was Hector; he, too, looked old. Rita went toward them but stopped in the middle of the room. Marius was a few steps behind her. Hector looked round, smiled at them, then turned back to Sylva. Marius studied Sylva's gaunt, wrinkled, sweat-drenched face; her eyes were closed and lips whispering, or perhaps trembling with fever. Six or even two months ago, the room in Olive Street might have been able to cure Sylva, but now it was too late. Yet she was smiling, happy to be back there. Perhaps by the time she was presented with the miracle, the question of how it had come about had been too difficult for her to grasp, so Hector had explained nothing . . . The silence of the courtyard and hallways was broken by the voices of workmen, and the sounds of hammers and drills. Again Rita took Marius's hand, before leading him from the room and closing the door. Just a few streets away, the city was wide awake. They walked on in silence to the sea, which was remarkably calm that day. Then they headed for Rita's apartment. There wasn't a star in the sky. At one point, they stopped, leaned against the concrete rail, and gazed at the dark place where sea and sky converged."

Tomáš and Petr II

1. Song of Emptiness

"It was with this nighttime image of Rita and Marius at the seafront that the novel ended. As he was writing, Tomáš Kantor had realized that he liked his words and imagery to emerge within a kind of ring; when he was writing about the wire book, he developed its life between two points of chaos in which objects, beings and words emerged, were born, and grew—between the undersea mass of a coral reef at one point and the snarl of a jungle at the other. He closed the novel with the image of a starless night that erased all shapes—an image that was intended to correspond with the opening image of a white mist from which shapes were yet to emerge. For four years, Tomáš worked on his novel in his tower apartment with its view of a yard, writing at first on backs of pages on which streetcar schedules were printed; after a few weeks of this, he bought a computer and printer. When he completed his novel in the fall before last, Kristýna delivered the manuscript to a publishing house, where it was read with favor and included on the list.

"But things didn't turn out as planned. Kristýna blames what happened on a single question she asked Tomáš. Because of that question, she believes, the book still hasn't been published;

because of that question, Tomáš left her for another woman, and later died in Turkey . . ."

"What did she say that was so terrible?" I asked.

"Kristýna told me about a December day when she and Tomáš took a walk along the Vltava embankment. There was a cold wind, and a crust of ice was building by the stony shores. They were under a railroad bridge when Kristýna asked out of the blue about Marius's wife's infidelity before he left for Parca. That's all it was. Kristýna isn't the naïve type of reader who believes that everything can be discovered about the lives of a novel's characters before the novel opens and after it closes. Her question about Marius's wife was a kind of game with no real significance, and Tomáš accepted it as such. But as he was working it through, he fell silent. Although Kristýna then changed the subject, she could see that Tomáš wasn't really listening to her. When they reached his apartment, she waited for him to invite her in, but he said that he had something to do, and they went their separate ways.

"Over the next two weeks, each time she called him he said that he couldn't see her because he had too much work. Then one day he called at seven in the morning and asked her to come over. That night's snowfall was already turning to mud in the streets, but in the yard next to Tomáš's apartment it still lay in a pure-white drift. It crossed Kristýna's mind that the yard may have looked exactly the same on the day five years before when Tomáš had started to describe the streets of the strange city on a first piece of paper, before he knew that the sentences he was writing would grow into a long novel. As she stepped into his room, she saw that the desk by the frost-patterned window was covered with printed paper, with crossings-out and insertions scattered all over the text. On top of the paper was an odd wire construction with white spaghetti tubing wrapped around it. The whole still life was illuminated by the calm brightness of fresh snow, making Kristýna think that she was looking at a photograph by Josef Sudek. The sight of all this writing disturbed her. Had Tomáš started rewriting his finished novel? As for the wire construction, she had no idea what to make of it. Could it be some kind of brainteaser that helped Tomáš relax from his work?

"As Tomáš made tea for her, he talked of what he had been doing over the past two weeks. First, he spoke of his novel. He reminded Kristýna of how it had originated: A city had appeared to him in the midst of a white void; a figure had arrived in the city's streets; a storyline had been drawn from the figure's gaze, and the rhythm of his steps; this storyline had developed several branches, which themselves developed some of their own, which moved together and apart while always remaining connected, each reacting to the appeals of the other lines by emitting images. The branching abated before crossing over to the recoupling stage; now, whatever sprouted bent over to touch the original branch, and what had split apart grew back together. When this process ceased of its own accord, once all the small limbs and outgrowths had grown back into the stem, the book was finished. Now, Tomáš confided in Kristýna for the first time that when *Damp Walls* had been at the publisher's for some weeks, he had begun to feel dissatisfied with a book he so little understood himself. He tried to put to it out of his mind, as the thought of it made him nauseous.

"Kristýna's question had made it possible for him to understand his feelings. The problem was, while the storylines were separating and coming together, Tomáš forgot about their origins and early evolution in the slowly solidifying discharge of the void. Because of the large number of stories that appeared in his book, he lost sight of what it was about. *Damp Walls* was a book about emptiness—a book about nothing. Emptiness was the content and meaning of the work; its author. Marius and Rita,

Hector, his wife, and his lover, the elder and the younger Vieta, Leo, Patricia, Vanessa, Diamanta, and Linda—all these characters were words that spoke emptiness, a mumble of nothingness, which Tomáš recorded without asking what emptiness wished to express through them. Tomáš's book was a discharge of the void, a song of nothingness. In this, it was different from every other book he knew. No other book was about emptiness and nothingness only, even those in which the words *emptiness* and *nothingness* appeared on every page. All those other books had something to say, and Tomáš admired many of them, envied their authors their talent and many opinions and ideas, but he felt that they belonged in a world different from his, and he wasn't particularly interested in any of them. With a certain pride, he told Kristýna that of all the writers he knew, he was the only one with absolutely nothing to say.

"Tomáš's dissatisfaction was rooted in the book's failure to correspond with what he meant. It falsified the emptiness it wished to express, although it owed its existence to this emptiness and drew its strength from it. Books that were about something could have one or several stories, and that was fine. But for a book about nothing, it wasn't fine at all; any number of stories couldn't satisfy a book about nothing. There was nothing so rich that it could be expressed merely by an endless proliferation of stories, a never-ending cascade of events in which other events spurted forth from every object, space, and gesture, then yet more events from the spaces, objects, and gestures of these. Tomáš felt that even the entire cosmos would be too little for the expression of nothing; a cosmos that expressed emptiness would have to be endless.

"Tomáš's book had its origins in what spurted forth from nothingness, but as time passed it somehow forgot this; it broke away from the welling-up of emptiness from which it had been born and closed in on itself. It wasn't of the void, although it owed its existence to it. Kristýna's question reminded Tomáš of the space that surrounded his stories, a space of buzzing emptiness from which the novel dropped, and so was its true meaning disguised. Now Tomáš was again hearing the hum of all the stories and words concealed in the void. The book slipped back seamlessly into its native space in emptiness, the never-ending proliferation of stories whose words drowned each other out, so producing a quiet hum. When this happened, Tomáš picked up a page of his novel and recognized immediately that the book had come back to life; the flow of nothingness again streamed through its letters and were absorbed into its dried-out words, giving them back their life."

2. The Diagram

"Now that the novel was again imbued with emptiness, new stories began to sprout from it. Tomáš suppressed the immediate temptation to record them all. He knew now that it wasn't possible to replenish words' longing for the mother's milk of emptiness; he knew that he was about to exhaust himself by the writing of an endless book, and that he would latch onto anything within the orbit of his story. He remained convinced that the only way to be faithful to the meaning of the book, make pure its relationship with nothingness, and let the emptiness shine through its story, so illuminating its images, was to show its plot as part of an endless proliferation of images and events; but he realized too that the presence in the book of a rainforest of growing images could be achieved only by means of the quiet hum that surrounded the letters; this hum would serve as a reminder without transforming into words or maturing into images.

"It was necessary to show that the book didn't exist in

isolation, that like each of its parts—stories, images, words, char-acters—it was part of an endless network, a galaxy of images in which some were close by, others extremely far away, and still others inside, in the worlds of its interior. These images were connected by thousands of golden threads running through every word, syllable, and character. Grown out of the exploded void, these threads ran through the entire world, making remark-able connections, weaving the world's fabric. He saw that each image, word, and character of the book shone with a light that reflected the radiance of all emerging, newborn, decaying and extinct words and images that swirl about in the transforming universe. It was impossible to depict the gallery of images, and the work could be incorporated in it by one means only: The nebula around the work, the parent substance of all images, gave rise to a small number of works that formed a constellation with the original book. This connection prevented the book from closing in on itself. Also, it ensured that its seeds weren't released into the fertile void, maintained its inner ferment, and kept it alive by steeping all its sentences in the mother nothing-ness. The works surrounding the book would continue to point beyond themselves and one another to the universe of possibil-ities, drawing lines of connection with unformed images and uncreated works whose light matter was nevertheless already playing an active role in the birth of words.

"It was immediately apparent to Tomáš that the works he allowed to grow out of his novel should represent a variety of genres: Rich nothingness could not be satisfied by a single form. He carefully examined everything that began to grow from the newly begotten nothingness. His hopes were highest for the story of a man and a woman who meet on a couch high in the reading room of Fernando Vieta's mausoleum (it would make a novella in itself, according to Kristýna), a collection of poetry in prose written by Henriette Fox-Vulpécula, and the catalogue of an exhibition of Leo's paintings in the Palacio de Bellas Artes. He was considering whether to make a novel by Vanessa and Kate, discovered by Leo in a Mexico City bookstore, a part of the constellation, too. In the end, he decided to let the images and plot outlines mature for a time; when they were ready, he would sift through them and harvest the ripest.

"In this way, the Work-Network was born. Although Tomáš was largely successful in subduing the proliferation of images and plots, the book's new growth continued to paint a pretty confused picture; it wasn't uncommon for Tomáš to lose his way in the new storylines as the paths crossed or didn't. He had tried to solve this problem, he told Kristýna, by making a chart on a sheet of paper and pinning it to his bookcase; but it soon transpired that a two-dimensional model did little to help him negotiate the complex network of relationships. Then he remembered Fernando Vieta and thought that he, too, might use wire; having been to a hardware store for spaghetti-insulated brass wire and a small pair of pliers, he created a three-dimensional chart of his book. Tomáš lifted the wire construction from the table and handed it to Kristýna. "I call it the Diagram," he announced. Bewildered, Kristýna turned the object this way and that; it put her in mind of a strange tree, its branches forking and crossing, growing together or back into the central trunk.

"As Kristýna inspected the wire creation, Tomáš explained how a few days earlier the Work-Network had undergone another important transformation. He had just started on the writing of Leo's catalogue when it occurred to him that rather than writing about imaginary paintings, he could paint them. This was, he felt, more than just a quaint idea resulting in an act of willfulness: To express the rich nothingness, an abundance of literary genres wasn't enough—the Network would need to contain works from different art forms. So Tomáš bought pastels of different colors and set about painting the work Leo produces in the cantina opposite his hotel, as described in Tomáš's book. When the picture was finished, he signed it with Leo's name."

3. The Work-Network

"Tomáš picked up a sheet of paper and read to the surprised Kristýna the list of works that comprised the Work-Network:

1. *The Cloudy Boat*, a novel by Vanessa and Kate

2. *Abandoned City Square*, a collection of poetry by Henriette Fox

3. A comic book about the adventures of Vulpécula

4. Leo's paintings, exhibited at the Palacio de Bellas Artes

5. A collection of Lygdian myths

6. A chapter on the grammar of Lygdian, discussing noun declension

7. A ballet of *The Critique of Pure Reason*, for whose premiere Leo designs the dress that betrays Vanessa's secret

8. Sylva's sketchpad, which she shows to Hector in the hospital

9. Torn-up sonnets; a novella about a meeting on a couch in a mausoleum. (He could rework the latter as a stage play or an opera, Tomáš remarked.)

"Tomáš even began to hum a tune—perhaps an aria from the opera he was working on. For the whole time he was speaking, Kristýna just stared at him. She was little convinced by his words about nothingness, golden threads, and networks, and she was worried that his complicated explanations pointed to a single truth: that his childhood malady had returned, making him incapable of renouncing any possibility, for he longed to possess them all. She was concerned that his Diagram notwithstanding Tomáš would again lose his way in the jungle of

possibilities that opened before him, and that the untamed
vegetation of this treacherous primeval forest and the unknown
beasts living in it would destroy what he had done already.
Kristýna was angry; for the very first time, Tomáš had made
her mad. Exercising self-restraint, she suggested he reconsider.
It was her view, she said, that *Damp Walls* needed no additions,
and besides, it would take a very long time for Tomáš to write,
draw, and compose everything he had in mind. Tomáš told her
that he had already reconsidered and was counting on finishing
the Work-Network within five years. Obviously, he added, the
work must appear all at once. He had called the publishers and
asked them to delay the publication of *Damp Walls* until the
whole thing was ready. On seeing the impact of his words on
Kristýna, Tomáš tried to soothe her with the information that
Marcel Proust had waited to publish *À la recherche du temps
perdu* until the last line of the last volume was written.

"At this, Kristýna could contain herself no longer, and she
did something I struggle to imagine her doing, because Kristýna
is the most mild mannered girl I know. At the end of Tomáš's
speech, she stood up without a word, walked from the sofa to
the window, and opened it. The drapes rose like white wings,
snow flew into her eyes, and the papers on the desk were blown
to all corners of the room. Then she drew back her arm and
tossed the Diagram as far as she could into the yard. Then she
closed the window and yelled at Tomáš that he was like a junkie
who had kicked his habit after years of rehab but was again
experimenting with drugs, claiming they could no longer harm
him. Tomáš had no answer to this; he stammered for a moment,
then fell silent. Having calmed down a little, Kristýna went out
to look for Tomáš's toy. Between two fluffy drifts in the middle
of the yard, she spotted a cluster of white wires sticking out of
the snow. She picked up the Diagram and inspected it. Then
she looked up toward a square of gray sky between gray walls,

the windows narrow black holes with snow-covered ledges. The snow was coming down in large flakes. The snow-coated wire was cold in her hands. She was learning to accept that Tomáš was embarking on a high-risk journey that would take him God-knows-where. But maybe the risk was worth it; maybe he would find his way in the jungle and succeed in creating something new. She went back inside. Tomáš was still standing frozen in the same place, like a character in a bad comedy expressing amazement. Kristýna put the Diagram back on the desk—rapidly melting snow dripped from it onto a page of Tomáš's work. She began to talk to him about his new plans, as if nothing had happened . . .

"Tomáš set to work simultaneously on all nine parts born out of the violet glow of *Damp Walls*—and three months later, he left Kristýna. He didn't even call to tell her he had done so; she received a letter, in which he wrote that he was in love with another woman. He didn't tell Kristýna the woman's name, just that she was a sculptor. He asked Kristýna not to come to see him anymore, and he asked her to forgive him. As Kristýna was telling me this, she burst into tears. I didn't ask her any questions; there was no need for her to tell me more, as I could figure out for myself what had happened. Once he began to listen to the murmurings of other possibilities, Tomáš also heard the murmurings of women that are everywhere around us, and a buzzing, luminous women's nebula gave rise to characters of the work . . .

"Apart from this, I had the feeling that the scene with the Diagram had played a part in Tomáš's separating from Kristýna. She told me very little about him. I've never seen a photo of him, and I don't know how he talked and moved, or even the color of his hair. The idea I had of him was composed from characters he created—his face emerged from the intermingled faces of Marius, Leo, Hector, and Fernando, even of Rita, Diamanta, Linda, Vanessa, Patricia, and Sylva. Yet it sometimes occurred to me that my knowledge of Tomáš was fuller than Kristýna's, who saw him only as a person living in a world of pure images. Women often know little about the filthy breeding ground from which even the purest images grow. I believe that Tomáš, like all writers, was an egoist. More than love, he needed peace and quiet to work in and someone he could talk with about this work. Had he had the time, he would probably have been a libertine—but women weren't so important to him that he would devote to love affairs time he could spend writing. When he realized that Kristýna could make problems for him, so disturbing him in his work, he found a woman who could give him the peace and quiet he needed. But I'm just guessing how Tomáš felt, we'll never know for sure . . .

"Kristýna's world was in ruins. She never saw Tomáš again. She went out of her way to avoid the streetcar terminus, and as soon after she and her parents moved to the Letná part of the city, since the split she hadn't even seen the glass tower. That fall, Kristýna learned that Tomáš's body, pierced by thirteen deep dagger wounds, had been found off the coast of Turkey. The next spring, Kristýna saw a poster announcing that the Flamingo theater company was preparing a production of the ballet of *The Critique of Pure Reason*, one of the works of Tomáš's lost constellation. Tomáš had been working on the ballet in the days before he left Kristýna. Unsure of his ability as a composer, he had told Kristýna that he intended to show it to a distant relative who was a professional composer of music; perhaps this relative had furnished the Flamingo company with the libretto and score. Kristýna attended several performances of the ballet. At the last of these, she witnessed the murder of Tomáš's stepbrother."

Murder at the Theater II

Martin was quiet for a moment. We looked eastward, to Hóra Sfakion, where the sky was turning pale. Below it, the outline of the mountain range descended to the sea.

"For two weeks, Kristýna and I met in small restaurant gardens on the Letná plain, close to where she lived. I listened to her soft, calm voice telling me about Tomáš, his childhood, his brother Petr (whom, like me, she saw just once, in the Tortoise Theater with a bullet hole in his forehead), Tomáš's book, his abandonment of her, and his death. Hour after hour, I watched her face against a backdrop of dark facades; it seemed to me that the features were drawn, like lines in the sand, by a never-ceasing current from the past.

"Kristýna must be very different from the person she was three years ago, I realized. Her new being must have been born in response to the strange world she had experienced after getting to know Tomáš—a world that attracted her even though she was little prepared for it. This world contained all the stories she had come to know: that of Tomáš's life, beginning in a Prague tower-block apartment filled with sorrow and ending with his unexplained murder in Asia Minor, interwoven with stories of captivity and pursuit, struggle and betrayal, distant, sometimes nonexistent cities from the books Tomáš wrote in his tiny apartment and in the tower above the streetcar tracks. I believe these stories became ever more mixed in Kristýna's mind, until at last they dissolved into a single humming, ever-changing ocean, in whose waves memories and images from Tomáš's narration and novel were but dimly outlined.

"And I saw that in response to her encounter with a strange world, Kristýna's being had become composed of sorrow, softness, fragility, and quiet astonishment. Tomáš's life and death had opened an unbridgeable gap between Kristýna and things that were present; in the zone that extended around her person, I noticed, things lost their intimate warmth while acquiring a glow like magic stones. Kristýna had slipped free of many human bonds; the sorrowful, amazed expression with which she viewed the strange landscapes she passed through perhaps resembled the expression of Linda, the artificial woman from Tomáš's novel. Although Kristýna was turned to the past, her being was stuck in the time of her new birth and the purity of a future just beginning. Shivering around her like a cool aura was an array of yet unpolluted possible new relationships, deeds, and occurrences.

"I desired this newborn creature as I'd never desired any woman. Her ghost appeared to me on the pages of my thesis-in-progress. Work is an obsession with me, as it was with Tomáš Kantor, but since Kristýna and I had been meeting in gardens, I was incapable of writing a single word, or even reading a sentence to its end; it was terrible. I was under no illusion that Kristýna met me for any reason other than to talk about what had happened to her. When Tomáš left her, she had come to a standstill, and since then she hadn't moved; all she did was gaze with fascination at past events that stood before her like landmarks of a fantastical, incomprehensible city below a setting sun in the middle of a wasteland. Sometimes, I saw these clearly;

the shadows cast by the city's towers reached across the plain to Kristýna's feet, and she couldn't turn her gaze from them. At these moments, she didn't see me—it was as though she was talking to me over her shoulder, and only then because she was hoping her words might help her come to terms with the past.

"After she lent me the manuscript of *Damp Walls*, I no longer made any attempt to concentrate on my thesis. I spent each morning bathing in the algae-filled sea of the novel's cadences, and each afternoon listening to Kristýna. Maybe I was reading a book that no longer existed, she told me. She didn't know how many of the new works Tomáš had intended to write around the first book he had managed to complete, and she was worried that vapors from all the poems, drawings, ballets, and comics might have done damage to Damp Walls, or even seriously undermined it. Maybe, she said, the subverting proximity of so many new images had caused an entirely new book to emerge from the ruins of the old; or maybe the ruined novel had given rise to a musical composition, a sculpture, or a fresco.

"I had planned to finish work on my thesis over the summer, after which I would relax by the sea in France or Italy for two or three weeks. Instead, I spent July and August in the gardens of Letná and at home reading Tomáš's novel. It didn't cross Kristýna's mind that she could take a vacation. Travel was pointless for her: She perceived every place as a cairn over her lover's broken body. One day at the end of August, I awoke with a new determination to pull myself together before Kristýna the mermaid dragged me deep into the ocean of her past, where I would join her other spectral curiosities. I realized that the characters of Kristýna's memories and Tomáš's novel had become more real to me than living people. For the first time, I didn't call Kristýna. To my surprise, she called me in the afternoon; although the sound of her voice was a great temptation for me, I told her that I was too busy with my work to see her.

She didn't call a second time. Slowly, I got back into my work, although the ghost of Kristýna was difficult to dispel. I made a great effort to put the events of the summer, beginning with my visit to the Tortoise theater, out of my mind (I knew they still had power over me), and I achieved my first successes. Then, in mid-September, I went to a café on Řetěz Street and picked up a Slovak visual arts magazine . . ."

Libyan Sea II

Again Martin fell silent. I didn't ask him what he had seen in the Slovak magazine. Was it a clue that had set him on the journey that had ended here, in the south of Crete? Could it be that the murderer of Tomáš Kantor and Petr Quas was hiding in a Loutro boarding house? If so, was Martin hunting him? I knew that Martin had decided to tell me everything, and I also knew that we would have plenty of time for this. In Loutro, it was easy to break the habit of impatience. We looked toward the east in silence. The color of the sky over Hóra Sfakion was now turquoise, shading into dark blue higher up. After a while, a bright orange glow appeared and grew rapidly above the mountains. Between this and the gray-green light of the sea was the solid black of the cliffs; a few pale stars continued to glint in the sky. A red sun appeared over the distant mountains, flooding the west of the bay with light, beginning with a low rock and the tower of a Venetian ruin. We watched in silence as the light descended to white wall, first pouring a pink light over the upper floors of the Sifis boarding house, which was the last in a row of white houses. It occurred to me that such a glow only ever appeared on walls in Greece. The flash of sunlight in the windows of the boarding house made us narrow our eyes.

A ferry lying at anchor at a concrete landing pier moved out of the blue shadow into the pink light. Moments later, the waters of the bay were a blaze of gold, the waves black corrugations. I heard the whirr of an engine; as though in a fairy tale, a black fishing boat returning from the night's catch was seen bobbing on the golden surface, pulling into the bay in a wide arc.

"Let's call it a night," said Martin. "Somehow I haven't gotten around to telling you about my journey south. If you like, I'll tell you about it some other time."

He stood up and waved a hand in parting. I sat on a while, watching his progress past the empty tavernas, toward his boarding house across the bay. We hadn't arranged a time for our next meeting; in Loutro, appointments are unnecessary— on its only street, people meet several times a day. My own boarding house was nearby. Once there, I went out onto the balcony. For a little while longer, I looked at the golden sea and the houses across the bay and listened to the splashing of the waves and the buzzing of the bees as they flew around the large flowers of the shrubs on the balcony. Then I went to bed and fell asleep immediately.

PART TWO
CITIES AND TRAINS

The Story of the Demons of the Night Train and the Corso Café

1. Lassitude

I awoke at one-thirty. I lay in bed for a while, watching the sparkling sea through the open door. Then I made my way down the narrow staircase. Outside in the sun, hot air saturated with fragrances of flowers, heated plaster, and damp pebbles washed over me like clear honey. I knew that in the north of Crete the autumn rains had begun, but the high mountains over Sfakia would hold the clouds back for a few more days, so protecting the coastline of the Libyan Sea. At the Pavlos taverna, the Dutch couple were having lunch in the flimsy shade of a taut canopy; Tanya was sitting close to the door to the kitchen, chatting with a friend from Kiev who had arrived on a visit the day before. The leaves on the trees and the blue-and-white canopy were still, and the movement of the sea was languid. Most of the tourists were enjoying the last of the sun on the beaches under the cliffs. Loutro was dozing; it was as though one could hear the heavy breathing produced by its dreams.

I sat down at my usual table. When Tanya came to me, I ordered a croissant and some Greek coffee. The day before, I

had decided I would take a trip—I wanted to climb the winding path up the cliff to the village of Anopolis; but in the last
days of the season Loutro was even lazier than usual, so I gave
in to its mood. I remained seated, drinking one cup of coffee
after another, looking toward the horizon, where Gavdos shim-
mered in the fierce sunlight. Children's voices from the coastline
opposite carried to my ears on the still air, then faded away;
from Tanya's table, I heard conversation in Russian.

It was about three o'clock when I stood up and went for a
walk past the tavernas, which at this time of day were practically empty. I passed a tiny store in front of which batik fabrics
were hanging limply from a rack, and a convenience store in
semi-darkness, from which the smell of bread and black olives
drifted toward me. On passing the Blue House, I exchanged
greetings with Vangelis, who was standing in the doorway to
the kitchen, arms folded. I reached the end of the village in
five minutes. As I wasn't yet ready to walk back the way I had
come, I climbed the low rocks to the ruins of the Venetian
and Turkish fortress. From there, Loutro was hidden behind a
low stone wall, with twisted breadfruit trees growing in front.
I stopped and looked up at the parched, ocher hillside, where
sheep were grazing on gray thyme bushes; every now and then,
I heard the soft tinkling of a bell. For a few moments, I stood
looking at the sunbaked rocky amphitheater. No human anywhere; the only signs of human presence were the ruins of the
fortress, which were overgrown with dry grass and low bushes,
and a few houses some way farther up that looked like slightly
lighter stones in the rock, part of the village of Livaniana. After
my wakeful night, I felt too weak to go any farther, so I went
back down to Loutro.

As I was returning to my boarding house, I saw Martin
in the open internet café, sitting at a computer. He waved to
me and called. Would I be having dinner at Vangelis's place?

I understood this as an invitation to listen to the next part of his story. I nodded. Maybe we would get to his journey south at last.

2. Magazine

Martin and I were sitting facing each other in the Blue House taverna on the western side of the bay. I was eating moussaka and Martin stuffed cuttlefish. We spoke little while we ate, but no sooner had Martin cleared his plate and dabbed his mouth with a napkin than he picked up the story where he had left it the previous day.

"I went back to work on my thesis. But in my room at home, I struggled to concentrate—thoughts of Kristýna and dozens of sentences from her lover's book went round and round in my head like a swarm of persistent flies. To escape these irritating insects, I trained myself to work in cafés, where the murmur of background noise is as good as the splashing of the sea at washing away sorrowful and tiresome thoughts. At eight-thirty on the morning of the thirteenth of September, I went into the Literary Café on Řetěz Street, in my bag a manuscript of a chapter of my thesis I needed to correct. I was looking forward to my work. The café was almost empty, its only other customers a young man and woman sitting at the back in quiet conversation. I sat down by the large window next to the entrance and worked on my thesis until midday. I was pleased: The work was going well—I had rewritten the whole of one chapter, while thinking of Kristýna only about twenty times. I ordered a sandwich, intending to pass the time while I waited for it leafing through a thick magazine with dog-eared pages I had found on a shelf.

"It was a Slovak visual arts review. There wasn't much in it for me: Its glossy pages were filled with unimaginative modernist works based around the vaguest semblance of an idea. I was about to return the magazine to the shelf when something caught my eye—a print of a painting in oils of a classroom scene. It showed a picture hung from a nail protruding from the top of a blackboard. Next to the picture, facing the class, stood the straight-backed teacher, a beautiful young woman in glasses, her expression strict, her wavy hair loose. She reminded me of Kristýna. The teacher was explaining something to the pupils, who were sitting at their desks listening attentively. In her right hand she held a pointer, its tip placed against the picture on the board. The depiction was realistic except for one thing: The teacher was stark naked.

"The picture hanging over the board had the word *Kedd* written across the top of it. Below this, painted in the style of old-fashioned encyclopedias of anatomy and other natural sciences, were three objects labeled by Roman numerals. 'I' was a depiction of a chain bridge. 'II' was a picture of a scrap of paper with irregular edges that had been screwed up then straightened out, on which two groups of capital letters—'OM' and 'ANT'—could be read. 'III' showed a symmetrical, gray-green scallop stood upright, like the logo of the Shell company. Set in the center of the shell's grooves was a large, wide-open, undoubtedly female eye, the upper edge of which traced the arc of the shell; the white of the eye was gold, the iris emerald green, the pupil and the long, thick lashes a dark violet. The dreamlike presence of unconcealed female nudity, which was unstirring, unsurprising, perhaps even uninteresting to the clothed persons in the picture, reminded me of the work of Paul Delvaux.

"The title of the painting was *Tuesday*, its artist a Hungarian painter called József Zoltán. The photograph was accompanied by an article, which I read but didn't learn much from.

It was about a collective exhibition of central European art in Kraków, and it mentioned at least a dozen names, with Zoltán's appearing just once. The shell with the eye was familiar to me, although it took me a while to realize where from: Tomáš Kantor mentions it in *Damp Walls*, as a sacred symbol of the Lygdian cult. How could an emblem of the Lygdian religion have come to be in a painting by a Hungarian artist? Tomáš's novel had never been published, which made me wonder if the painter was one of very few people who knew about *Damp Walls*; maybe someone had told him about it. Then I remembered that Tomáš had published two extracts from his novel in magazines, so maybe Zoltán had read about the shell in one of those. It was also possible, of course, that the shell with the eye wasn't Tomáš's idea—the shell motif may have been an unacknowledged borrowing from a source known also to Zoltán. Or it may have been a total coincidence that Tomáš and Zoltán had each come up with the same motif. I put the magazine back on the shelf before tucking into the sandwich the waiter had brought me. Then I went back to Kant. But my concentration was gone—the violet eye was staring at me, keeping me from my work."

3. The Mystery of the Lygdian Shell

"None of the possible explanations for how the shell might have ended up in the painting served to convince me. Even if the Lygdian shell had been mentioned in the published extracts from Tomáš's novel, it's highly improbable that a Hungarian painter would be a follower of Czech literary magazines. But nor could I believe that the similarity between Tomáš's and Zoltán's scallops was a matter of coincidence. It occurred to me that although I hadn't been surprised to discover that a painter had used the same motif as Tomáš Kantor, I was surprised to find that I had imagined the sacred shell in *Damp Walls* exactly as Zoltán had painted it. From the beginning, I was in no doubt that the picture in the magazine was truly a Lygdian evil eye, born out of the dreams and fears of the Parcans. For the same reason, I thought it unlikely that both writer and painter had plagiarized the same source.

"It was clear to me that I would do no more work on my thesis that day, so I closed its folder and went back to the magazine. I took a long, hard look at the strange classroom scene. The shell with the eye wasn't the only mystery the picture presented. What, for instance, did the words 'om,' 'ant,' and 'kedd' mean? What was the meaning of the scene as a whole? And why was the picture called *Tuesday*? I wondered whether to call Kristýna to tell her of my discovery. Maybe Zoltán's picture really did contain some kind of clue that could help us solve the mystery of Tomáš's death, with which Kristýna was still obsessed. I had recently come to suspect that Kristýna returned to the shifting sands of the past with ever greater frequency because of this agonizing unsolved puzzle rather than for the sake of her lost love. Perhaps clarification of the circumstances of her lover's murder would at last allow her to accept what had happened. I reached into my pocket for my cellphone. I was about to tap in Kristýna's number when it crossed my mind that things might turn out very different. What if the Hungarian trail, be it genuine or false, marked the beginning of a long, hopeless quest, with the result that Kristýna lost her way in the labyrinth of the past for good? So I sat there over the open magazine for almost an hour, cellphone in hand, unable to decide what to do."

The white *Daskalogiannis* was slowly approaching the bay; there were fringes of light in the dark water underneath it. Martin was silent for a moment, as the two of us watched a scene that played out at the Blue House every evening. The square bow of the ferry came menacingly closer until the entire view was obscured. Just as it seemed that it would sweep into the tables, crushing them and their occupants against the wall of the taverna, the boat turned and pulled up softly at the concrete landing stage. We looked on, just as we had the day before, as the iron front of the boat tilted forward and a few last passengers walked across it to the shore.

"In the end, I did tap in the number," said Martin. "Did I do it because I had convinced myself it was the best thing for Kristýna, or because I was missing her and longed to see and speak with her? I didn't know then, and I don't know now . . . And there's no point in thinking about it. In any case, at that moment I embarked on the journey that has brought me here.

"In my phone call to Kristýna, I described Zoltán's picture in detail; she was particularly interested in the coloring of the shell and its eye. Then she said: 'I'll be with you as soon as I can get there. Keep hold of that magazine.' So as I watched out of the window for Kristýna, I clutched the magazine, even though it was unlikely in that empty café that someone would try to take it from me. Within twenty minutes, Kristýna appeared at the corner of the street, in such a hurry that she was practically running, as though worried that the picture in the magazine had appeared for a short while only and would soon disappear. She studied the print for a long time, in silence. I feared that by getting her hopes up, she was leaving herself open to disappointment and even greater suffering, so I voiced all the objections to her I had earlier made to myself—maybe József Zoltán knew the shell with the eye from the magazine-published extracts; maybe the painter and Tomáš had drawn on the same source; maybe it was a simple coincidence.

"'I'm sure it's no coincidence,' Kristýna said. 'One of the chapters Tomáš published in a magazine really does include the Lygdian shell with the eye, but there's no mention in it of its coloring. But the colors in the painting are in exact correspondence with how Tomáš described it in the original manuscript. At a later stage, Tomáš came to consider this passage too descriptive, so he changed it. Let each reader decide on the colors for him- or herself, he told me at the time. Neither in the magazine nor in the manuscript Tomáš submitted to the publisher's is there any mention of the coloring of the shell or the sacred eye.'

"'Maybe one of his friends knew something about it,' I countered.

"'Tomáš didn't have any friends,' said Kristýna.

"Kristýna said that the letters 'OM' and 'ANT' might be fragments of the name 'Tomáš Kantor.' This seemed improbable to me, but apparently Kristýna took it as irrefutable proof that this work by a Hungarian painter had something to do with her dead lover. She reached for her cell and tapped in the Bratislava number given in the magazine's imprint. In reply, she got the tone announcing a canceled connection. Then she called Directory Assistance, to be told that apparently there was no longer any such magazine. After that, she just sat there beside me, despondent, the phone still in her hand. I felt very sorry for her. I mentioned that I needed to go the university in Bratislava for a consultation with an associate professor called Hudec; I would do this as soon as I could, I said, and while I was in the city, I would try to find out something about the lost magazine, and about Zoltán. At this news, Kristýna brightened. She wanted to know how soon I could go. Such was her impatience that there and then I called Associate Professor Hudec to make an appointment. I could come whenever I liked, he said, so I announced I would do so the very next day. To begin with, Kristýna insisted on going with me. But then she remembered that the next day was her father's birthday, and that she had promised to spend the evening at home. I promised to call her from Bratislava the moment I found out anything about Zoltán's shell.

"The express train to Bratislava departed from the Main Station at midnight. On my way from the café, I succeeded in solving one of the mysteries presented by the painting. I stopped at a bookstore on Kaprova Street to look up the word 'kedd' in a Hungarian dictionary; it means 'Tuesday.' Back home, I put my thesis, *The Critique of Pure Reason*, and a few other books into my backpack. I didn't take all these books because I suspected I was embarking on a long journey, but because I couldn't make up my mind which of them to take. It's always like that when I take a trip—my friends make fun of my backpack full of books, calling me the Book Sherpa. As I was standing in a long line on the station concourse, waiting to buy a ticket, Kristýna came hurrying across the shiny tiles toward me, a backpack over her shoulder. The enticement of a Hungarian shell had proved stronger than the promise she had made to her father."

4. Night Train

"As midnight approached, we stood on a platform flooded with pale fluorescent lighting. The express to Bratislava was already in. Alongside its cars, people paced and smoked in silence, their faces sorrowful masks in the cold light. A clean-shaven man in a suit jacket stuck his head out of the upper part of a compartment window, his soft, white-shirted belly pressing against the glass. His conversation with a woman with a gray perm sliced into the silence. From high up in the invisible vault came the sound of a bird flapping its wings. I was suddenly anxious—fearful even—at the thought of being alone with Kristýna in a train compartment at night. Not only was I worried that this shared experience would be agonizing and embarrassing, I was apprehensive about the journey I was embarking on; for the first time, I was overwhelmed by a sense that this pilgrimage would not end any time soon, and of having no idea where it would take me. The landscape of a journey's end is always magically shaped by anxieties and dreams, so I had plenty of reasons to fear what awaited me in Bratislava. To what strange Slovakia would the train deliver us in the early hours? I longed to flee— back to my cafés and my Kant. It seemed to me that Kristýna, too, was made fearful by the train that was about to carry us off into the night, although her disquiet and anxiety were probably different in kind to mine. I believe that she was convinced that the reproduction of the painting in the magazine was a message from her dead lover, telling her to make a journey, calling her to him; although fearful, Kristýna was impatient to learn what his ghost had prepared for her in Bratislava.

"We boarded the train and found our compartment. Kristýna climbed onto the top bunk, no questions asked. I leaned out of the window and watched the conductor slamming the car doors. Then the whistle sounded and the train slowly gathered speed, passing riveted steel pylons. I remained standing at the window for a long time, looking at the backs of houses, their illuminated windows like sad aquariums featuring light fittings and dark fragments of furniture, and the backyard shrubbery. Before long, however, everything beyond the train was in darkness, but for the occasional swarm of lights and distant constellations of streetlamps and village windows.

"I turned back to see that Kristýna had removed her pants and jacket. She was lying on the top bunk, on her back with her eyes closed, a blanket pulled right up to her chin. I opened the cabinet in the wall; it contained a shallow washbasin and a mirror, lit by a blinking fluorescent strip. I went to Kristýna

and watched her face, which was slightly agitated by the movements of the train. The pale-yellow light from below revealed
roundnesses and depressions in it I hadn't noticed before. I
had the feeling that Kristýna's face had been molded by her
odd fate with Tomáš Kantor, and I wondered if the original
face was somewhere beneath this new one. The shadows scattered across the face were like letters in Tomáš's hand. How
long would Kristýna have to wear this inscription on her face?
How many months or years would be needed to wear it away?
Some of the inscription was legible to me: I saw signs of the
insult of Tomáš's abandonment of her, the pain of his absence
and death, her long contemplation of this death's cause. I also
saw signs of characters from Tomáš's book. I thought back on
a certain moment of the summer—waiting for Kristýna in a
garden restaurant, and realizing as she approached along the
long, straight street that not only was her face Tomáš's creation,
her whole body was, as well; her movements were invested with
the movements of all characters in her lover's novel, so that she
herself had become one such character; in her walk, I saw Leo's
weary perambulations in Vanessa's apartment, the nimble elegance of Henriette Fox, Marius's light-footed wanderings about
Parca, Linda's anxiety, Diamanta's resignation . . . Had these
characters come to her from the outside, or had they long lain
dormant in her, to be roused by her reading of *Damp Walls* . . ."

Vangelis was hurrying by; Martin gestured to him that our
brass jug was empty. Then he went on: "I know I may be making things up, to explain the fear I felt from Kristýna, and to
justify the personal embarrassment this feeling caused me. But
at that moment in the train, I really did have the impression
that a whole bunch of ghosts had gotten into her body, and that
all these ghosts were wary of and hostile toward me. And yes, I
was afraid that I would have to do battle with them."

"You're speaking like an exorcist," I said.

"You misunderstand me. It wasn't that I wanted to drive the demons out of Kristýna. As a legacy from her dead lover, of whom I was jealous, I didn't like them, of course—but I couldn't deny that they were the cause of Kristýna's attraction for me. In the dim, fluorescent light, the sight of ghostly, ever-transforming faces in hers, which I knew intimately, roused in me a painful, almost unbearable longing. My God, who had I fallen in love with? Was I, like Kristýna, in thrall to a dead dark magician?"

Plainly agitated, Martin shook his head almost imperceptibly. Then he tried to shake a last few drops from the brass jug into his glass.

"After a while, she opened her eyes, perhaps because she felt my breath on her face. She looked back at me in astonishment. And I was foolish enough to start babbling something about ghosts, hoping that at last I would get around to telling her what she meant to me, and perhaps to observing that, unlike Tomáš Kantor—who no doubt had been amazing—I had the advantage of being alive. A lousy argument for getting the girl, I admit, but what was I supposed to do with so many ghosts up against me? In any case, I needn't have worried: it soon became clear that Kristýna was paying no attention to me. Ever since she'd seen József Zoltán's picture in the café, all she could think about was the message of the Lygdian scallop. Realizing the futility of my attempt at a confession, I broke it off in the middle of a sentence . . . Kristýna had made me angry. What was she expecting from the Hungarian shell? It seemed to me that she was clinging to it as to a magic vehicle that could bring Tomáš back from Hades. I wanted to yell at her that they had found his body in the Mediterranean; that she had told me herself that the Turkish police had reported thirteen deep stab wounds in it, so no Lygdian sorcery would be bringing it back to life."

5. Lights and Voices

"I said nothing, of course. I closed the door of the cabinet with the fluorescent light, and in so doing took care not to glimpse my own face in the mirror. Then I lay down on the lower bunk. The compartment was bathed in a dim light—as the train passed through a town whose station and its street were illuminated from tall lamp-posts—before being plunged back into darkness. I waited for sleep to come and stared into the darkness with its fleeting lights, all kinds of thoughts flashing through my mind. Did Kristýna truly long to discover the truth about her lover's murder? Wasn't her real wish to engage in an intoxicating jaunt around places that glowed with Tomáš's absence? Wasn't this detective work first and foremost a titillating, erotic dance with a dead man? And if so, her excitement and impatience would no doubt be heightened by the delightful awareness that the unknown woman for whom Tomáš had left her was out of the lovers' competition. Dead Tomáš, too, was now defenseless against Kristýna; there was nowhere he could run from her love. I realized that my being alive placed me at no great advantage over Tomáš.

"The train passed a factory building with many lights and intricately interwoven pipes on its outside wall. I saw that the factory exhaled clouds of white steam at different places as it slept, and I said to myself: If the detective work in this game was just a cover-up for an erotic orgy with a dead man, hadn't Kristýna's love for Tomáš long been a cover-up, too—for her longing for self-discovery? This longing may have originated on Kristýna's first contact with Tomáš's world, when she made the amazed realization that she understood the ghosts deep in his soul, and that the strange legend they told of was about her. Kristýna's lover's book may have been a mirror for her. If this were so, who was this person I had gone on a journey with? It occurred to me that this quiet, dependent, timid girl, who was

afraid to travel on her own, might be stronger than me—and
Tomáš, too. Maybe she was a queen in disguise, and we were all
in her service: Tomáš wrote a book for her, although he had no
idea he was doing so, and now I was her escort on a pilgrimage.
Once again, I wondered what was ahead of us. What kind of
Transylvania were we heading for? What kind of monsters' ball
were we involving ourselves in?

"The quiet, regular rattle of the train covered the sound of
Kristýna's breathing, so I didn't know whether she was asleep, or
staring into the dark as I was. After a while, the rocking of the
train lulled me into a light sleep, out of which I was half-woken
by the lights of the stations we passed through and announcements from station PA systems. At daybreak, I heard voices in
the corridor—customs officers and border guards. I handed
my passport to a woman in a green uniform without the need
to get out of bed: I had the document ready under the pillow.
Above me, I saw Kristýna's hand thrust out, then pulled back
in, like that of an inquisitive but shy animal. After the customs
officers had left, I continued to listen to their voices as they
moved down the corridor, and it dawned on me with a certain
regret that after this year, I would never again experience this
nighttime manifestation, part of the magic and mythology of
train travel—as no doubt you know, borders within Europe
are set to disappear at the end of the year, marking the end of
these ghostly apparitions that break the sleep of night travelers.
Anyway, after that, I didn't go back to sleep. Instead, I looked
out on brown fields, factories, industrial towns, and long, gray
pipelines apparently adrift in the dim light."

6. Sun on a Square

"We alighted in Bratislava to a cold, cheerless morning. Right there in the station, we drank vending-machine coffee and ate two limp sandwiches. Then we took a half-empty street-car through unknown, uniform, slightly mist-blurred streets. Throughout this time, we spoke barely a dozen words to each other. I studied Kristýna's face furtively. In daylight, I saw no ghosts in it; maybe I'd been a victim of night-train sorcery. I no longer took too seriously my small-hour thoughts on the hidden true purpose of Kristýna's journey, and I told myself that she simply wished to find out the truth about the death of a person she still loved.

"The rooms of the erstwhile magazine office were now occupied by a real estate agency. We were told by a gray-suited secretary that the magazine still existed but had been renamed and moved to new offices downtown. Out on the street again, I explained to Kristýna that I had to go the Faculty of Arts for my meeting. She looked unhappy about this—because I was leaving her alone and afraid in a strange city, or because she wished to express her disapproval with the fact that I was prioritizing something over the investigation of the mysterious death of her lover, I didn't know. In the end, though, she accepted that she would have to look for the magazine office on her own. We agreed to meet at noon in the Corso café on the corner of Hviezdoslav Square and Rybné Square, a place we both knew.

"I spent about an hour speaking with Associate Professor Hudec. At the end of the conversation, he asked me to check an article he had written for a collection on Kant, to be published in November, before my departure from Bratislava. As I left the school building on Šafárik Square, the sun was beginning to break through the mist of the early morning. Rybné Square wasn't too far away, so I decided to walk. I reached Hviezdoslav Square via the Fajnor Embankment and Mostecká

Street. Although most of the square was still in shade, at its end, at the round tables in front of the Corso café, students and Bratislava's idlers were enjoying the last sun of the year, paying no heed to the cars speeding past them a few yards away along the high slip road to the bridge across the Danube.

"I sat down at a table and began to read the article. The sun got higher in the sky, bathing everything in a golden light. For the first time since we left Prague, I felt happy. To my surprise, the concrete ramp and the traffic on it gave the impression that the café was at the bottom of a kindly ravine forgotten by the careworn, trouble-burdened world. I unfastened my jacket and sprawled in the comfortable chair, preparing to take a walk through *The Critique of Pure Reason*, a beloved palace whose every nook was familiar to me. Now the halls, rooms and chambers of the Transcendental Aesthetic and the Transcendental Analytic seemed to me a refuge from girls who wanted to pull me down into the well of their past, the suite of ghosts that travel in their train, and their dead bridegrooms.

"When the waiter brought my espresso, I raised my head from my papers and looked around, taking in trees whose sunlit leaves looked like small flames, the warm, glowing pavement, and a column topped by a saint from whose head a silver disc apparently rose to the top of a pillar of the suspension bridge, as if in some Dadaistic collage. Now I was glad to be traveling. After a night of worry and unpleasant thoughts, I had the feeling that the silent, light-filled festival I found myself in now was a sign of hope. Gems lay all around; the gentle September light smoothed the edges of things and relations among them, endowing their chromatic existence with a sense of magnificence that overwhelmed all other considerations. Whether Kristýna was a defenseless girl in need of protection or an adventuress on a monster hunt was no longer of interest to me; in the soft light of this late morning, such distinctions had lost their importance. I hoped that this

Bratislava light would continue to shine on my gloomy Prague fall, for a few days at least."

7. Day and Night in Bratislava

"I returned to my work in a contented mood. Another hour or so elapsed before a soft-contoured shadow fell across my page. I looked up at wavy hair lined by an aura of September sun. Without sitting down, Kristýna announced that she had found and visited the magazine office and managed to get Zoltán's address—he lived in Budapest. She wished to go there straight away; leaning on the edge of the table, she told me that our train left in an hour, so I should pay up. My sense of well-being was gone in an instant. Kristýna was obviously assuming that I would continue to help with her task, which, after all, was so important that the impertinence implicit in the assumption could be excused. Again, I felt my anger rise. I explained that I had work that would keep me in Bratislava until evening at least, and after that I would be returning to Prague; she might travel alone to Budapest, which she would reach by train in three hours. I turned back to my work.

"Kristýna sat down next to me. She knew no Hungarian, she said miserably, and her English wasn't up to much . . . She was plainly unused to traveling alone. Her lament fell short of a direct appeal to me to go with her, however. When it was over, she just sat there in silence. I pretended to read the article, which my mind was no longer on. When I looked up, I saw tears running down her cheeks. This was too much for me, of course: I promised to go with her to Budapest as soon as my work was done.

"As I stayed on at the café table, proofreading the article to the end, Kristýna walked about the city, examined the train schedule, and bought needless items for the journey; period-ically, she would return to see how I was getting on with my work. Although the fall sunlight improved my temper, the joy I had felt that morning didn't return. Evening came, and my work still wasn't done, so we agreed to spend the night in Bratislava before taking the eight o'clock train to Budapest the next morning. While Kristýna was finding a cheap hotel, I finally finished the proofreading.

"We slept at a small hotel on the riverfront, in a double bed, to the drawn-out hooting of freighters on the Danube, with dead, smiling Tomáš Kantor lying between us. In vain, I tried to recall the joy I had felt that morning, and to revive that luminous world against whose amiability all ghosts were powerless; the colored lights of the boats on the river had no place in this world—they were in league with the writer/vam-pire traveling with us. Again, I was angry with myself for hav-ing left my work to take a journey in the company of Kristýna and her dead lover; I felt miserable in the same way as the hero of the Stevenson story who is forced to travel with a suitcase containing a body. I consoled myself with the knowledge that Budapest wasn't far away; we would question József Zoltán, to whom Kantor had likely described the colors of the Lygdian shell at a séance, and then return to Prague immediately.

"I awoke to darkness and couldn't get back to sleep. Then I noticed that Kristýna, too, was awake. The phosphorescent hands of my watch showed four o'clock. I turned to Kristýna and said: 'The first train leaves in an hour. We could be in Budapest by eight . . .'

"So we left Bratislava at five in the morning, seated alone in the dining car, in silence, drinking weak black coffee and watching colorless images in the glass. After a while, a horizon-tal orange line appeared in the windows of the dining car, like a crack in a black wall."

The Story of Meditating Ants, Gunfire on Gogolevsky Boulevard, and the Sociologist Who Tries to Hang Herself

1. Balcony

"The train arrived at Budapest's Keleti station at eight-fifteen. When we reached the street, I waved down a taxi. Kristýna showed the driver a slip of paper with Zoltán's address on it, and it turned out that the painter lived on the opposite, west bank of the Danube. We drove along the early-morning streets. At one point, the houses that lined both sides parted, then disappeared altogether. In the sun-filled haze, like a huge tuft of multicolored cotton wool, the Gellért Hill appeared to us, as did light-drenched bridges floating over the river. My joy of the previous morning returned; I realized that the happiest times of my life were mornings in strange cities. The early-morning joy exhaled by the walls of buildings, the surface of the river, the asphalt of the road, the leaves of trees, and the flashing of the light on the hoods of cars dispelled the last of the moroseness I had felt in the night. No longer did I see this trip as an unreasonable diversion undertaken with an unattainable girl and her dead bridegroom. Again, I was glad to be traveling. At that time of day, thoughts of the senselessness of our undertaking couldn't prevail over the amiability of the autumn sun and the slow flow of the Danube, which spread peace as far as a horizon dissolving in a warm mist. Having reached the other side of the river, the taxi turned into a broad, unpopulated boulevard with glinting streetcar tracks down the middle. As we climbed a gentle slope, I read on a plaque on one of the buildings that this street was called *Bartók Béla utca*. At the end of its second block, the street turned back toward the river. We passed through a neighborhood of quiet streets.

"Zoltán lived on the sixth, top floor of an unremarkable residential building. The door to the apartment was opened by a tall, muscular man in shorts and a striped sailor shirt; he was about forty. I began to speak in English about the painting called *Tuesday*, right there on the threshold. Before I had uttered anything substantial, the painter made a gesture that invited us into the apartment. It crossed my mind that he took me for a critic who had come to look at his new works, girlfriend in tow. He led us through a well-lit, spacious room, which surely served as his studio, to a small balcony, where he had obviously been having breakfast; on a child's table stood a coffeepot, one cup, and some toast on a plate. Before stepping out onto the balcony, I studied two unframed canvases on the facing wall. Of the same size—about one square yard—they were hung next to each other at the same height, with seven or eight inches between them. Projected onto them by the velvety sunlight were the shadowed, breeze-stirred leaves of a hibiscus that grew in a pot on the balcony.

"Both of these works were in the style of *Tuesday*. The first was strictly symmetrical. It showed a yellow ant sitting in the lotus position—if indeed a six-legged animal can be said to sit in such an attitude. The painter had solved this problem of anatomy by having the central pair of legs rest in the curve of the back pair, which were crossed. The front pair of legs were raised slightly, their toes and index fingers—the animal in the painting had human digits—touching, so producing a posture well known to us from depictions of the Buddha.

"The second painting was a view of the intersection of two deserted streets. Judging from the metal fire escapes and the cylindrical water tanks on the roofs, I assumed that this was a scene from the United States, most likely from the outskirts of a large city. One of the streets headed for the horizon in a regular perspective, ending after a few blocks in a dockyard with many tall cranes; whether this gave on to the sea or a river was unclear. All that was visible of the second, foregrounded street was a stretch of asphalt roadway and a sidewalk whose curb ran in parallel with the painting's lower edge. Beyond the sidewalk was a windowless wall, the area of which occupied most of the painting. On the sidewalk in front of the wall was a fire hydrant, which in this deserted, strangely paralyzed city had the appearance of a grotesque being. The wall was featureless but for a small expanse of bare brick where the plaster had flaked away; this spot was shaped like a dog's head. Attached to the top edge of the wall was a billboard showing a girl in a dirty, torn dress with a rope around her neck and an expression of horror on her scratched, bruised face. At the end of the rope was a white hand clutching a white baton; this looked like a broken-off part of a statue. In the background was the Grand Canyon, illuminated by the setting sun. Across the whole billboard, a slogan in white lettering set against the red sky declared: *Find the right health plan for you.*

"The small balcony was lined on all sides with boxes containing dense plant life, so there was barely enough space for the low table and three wicker armchairs. Once Kristýna and I had taken off our backpacks and left them on the floor of the studio, Zoltán seated us in the armchairs, pushed the plate of toast toward us, then went away before reappearing with two cups; all this took place without a word being spoken. I looked down—the balcony was floating in the sunlight like the basket of a hot-air balloon, over a quiet street whose depths were still swathed in shadow. An early-morning chill came up to me. The sun was shining low in the cloudless sky over Pest, stinging my eyes, which I shaded with my hand. Now I could see, beyond the roof antennas, the green strip of the Danube, looking like it was made of frosted glass, and beyond it in the distance, buildings on the far riverbank, their facades, still untouched by sunlight, forming an undifferentiated gray belt. On turning my head, I saw, rising from the haze beyond the sun-flooded rooftops, the Gellért Hill, looking like a mass of multicolored leaves.

"Once the painter was reseated at the table, although I had a piece of toast in my hand, I began to tell him about *Damp Walls*, the Lygdian symbol, Tomáš's death in Turkey, and the murder of his brother at the ballet. My words were accompanied by sounds of the early morning, the hooting of steamers on the Danube, and the muted rumbling of streetcars along Bartók Street. I did so afraid that Zoltán would interrupt me, tell us he didn't have time to listen to such nonsense, and throw us out. As he sipped his coffee, his gaze flitted about over the Danube; I had no idea whether he was even listening to me. He hadn't actually spoken yet, and it struck me that he might not understand English."

2. Lost Week

"As soon as I finished, he disappeared back into the apartment. He returned a little while later with more coffee, which he poured into our cups. Then he broke his silence. 'The sacred symbol of a nonexistent nation, a body found in the sea, the *Ding an sich* with a gun in its hand . . ." he said contemplatively, in rather good English. "Yet I'm not surprised by it. I was expecting something of the sort as soon as you mentioned *Tuesday.* The thing is, a year ago something happened that wasn't particularly interesting of itself, but which set in motion a long, strange chain of incidents and events I lost control over. For a long time, it seemed that the chain would never end, but in the spring the incidents stopped, and I was starting to think that the series had run its course. Now you two turn up with the cult of Lygdianism, a murdered writer, and dancing Kantian categories . . . Anyway, I'll tell you where I saw the shell with the eye, and about everything that has spilled out of it since—or at least all I've heard or read about it. But what I tell you may not help you—maybe it'll even confuse you further. But that's up to you.'

"Zoltán began by speaking about a Sunday evening a year earlier. He had done some painting during the day, but his work hadn't gone very well. As evening fell, he quit what he was doing and went to sit on the balcony, where he drank wine and watched the bank opposite, as the strings of lights were coming on. He was restless, dissatisfied with the whole of the past week. Then he had an idea that promised to rescue that wasted week: He would identify at least one important moment in each day and paint a series of seven works that would express those moments. He explained that he came up with moments related to important aims in life; in his opinion, truly important moments were apparently unremarkable ones, when the transparent, hermetic case that overlays things and bodies is briefly torn, so that suddenly one smells the past that flows through them and the strange essences of their and our past and future. When we encounter a strangely twisted flue attached to the side wall of a building, see the slow gesture made by a woman at the table next to ours in a café, smell the breath of an open book that holds a wonderful world inside, this is such a moment; others include spotting the rusty, twisted skeleton of an instrument of some sort as we walk past a dump, and having our gaze drawn to a stain on an expanse of plaster, which is trying to tell us something fundamental about our life; such moments may be carried to us on the boredom of an afternoon idled away, or they may come to us on a sleepless night, as we gaze into the dark.

"He sat on his balcony above the sparkling city long into the night, meticulously examining the past week hour by hour, a patient prospector sifting through the sands of memory—and he was surprised to find many precious seconds on the territory of a week that had seemed boring and pointless. He couldn't help but think of the weeks and months he had allowed to pass without joy, and it occurred to him that the missed seconds might be hidden in time, and he began to hope that they weren't lost without a trace but were somewhere at the back of the mind, from where their glow could still reach out to the present, illuminating his life and work.

"In the following weeks, he painted the pictures *Monday*, *Tuesday*, *Wednesday*, *Thursday*, *Friday*, *Saturday*, and *Sunday*. *Tuesday* grew out of an episode that had begun in a bar on *Fő utca*, on the riverfront below the Buda Castle, where he had gone for a glass or two after work, and where he had gotten into conversation with a student sitting at the table next to his. Obviously bored by the company she was keeping, the student talked with him until two in the morning, when the bar closed. When at last they were out on the street, the student said that they were close to her home, where she had a few bottles of good wine. Zoltán explained that *Fő utca* is in the lower part of the old quarter of Víziváros, on a steep slope leading from the Danube to Buda Castle. They climbed some steps, followed some winding streets, then climbed more steps; at a bend in one of the streets, the student unlocked a gate with a high grille, beyond which was a garden lit by a lantern. They entered the house, which was at the far end of the garden, and climbed the stairs to the attic, where the girl stopped at a door, which she unlocked."

3. Apartment in Víziváros

"Zoltán didn't give many details of the night he spent in the little room, where there were mattresses on the carpet in place of a bed, and the surfaces were covered with books, course materials, professional journals, and handwritten notes. When the night was over, the girl went with him to the garden gate. Rather than make an embarrassing promise to call her, the painter kissed the girl on the cheek and hurried down to the riverfront; he never saw her again. As he sat on his balcony wondering if he could find a moment in the Víziváros episode, about which he still felt bad, one that would provide a theme for *Tuesday*, his first thought was of when the girl went to the bathroom, leaving him in the room alone. Finding an English-language science magazine on the carpet, he flicked through it before starting to read an article about an expedition mounted by an international team of scientists, who earlier that year had traveled by yacht to the Mediterranean to study invertebrates. His attention was drawn to one of the photos that accompanied the article. It showed a shallow bay lit by the rays of a red sun that was nearing the horizon at sea; lying in the sand just inches from the water was an unframed painting that depicted a shell with a wide-open eye. But there was something more interesting still in the picture: shiny blue lettering like a strange marine neon sign, which went right across the shell. The lettering was composed of several words on three lines. Its message made no sense in any language known to Zoltán.

"He had time to read that the scientists had spotted the luminous lettering from the yacht, in the Dodecanese archipelago, not far from the Turkish coast, as they were passing a remote bay on an uninhabited island, and that the lettering was formed from the luminous bodies of a species of small marine worm. When Zoltán mentioned the Turkish coast, I saw Kristýna shudder. Zoltán would have liked to read more about worms that write unintelligible messages under the sea, but then the student came back into the room and switched off the desk lamp. After that, the only illumination in the room was from beyond its long white curtains: the arced lights of the chain bridge and their reflection in the Danube.

"Awake during the night, Zoltán looked at the lights in the curtains and then at the unknown body lying next to his. He saw the dull reflections on his skin—he didn't know where they came from—as a mysterious marine creature that had swum out of a nest of clothes below the surface of the night. The feeling this gave him reminded him of the photo in the magazine, and he thought about it for a while; he imagined the marine worms undergoing a kind of training that taught them how to write; they had been writing their message for hundreds of years, and it had become part of their genetic make-up. As to the content of the message and the language it was written in, he was none the wiser. Although he had stayed awake for only a short time, when he came to look for a theme for his painting *Tuesday*, it occurred to him that the substance of that Víziváros night—a mixture of adventure, suspense, evocations of stories from the *One Thousand and One Nights*, mystery, curiosity, sorrow, disappointment, shame, closeness that resists expression, embarrassment, delight, tenderness, guilt, and a sense of pointlessness—was concentrated in its purest form in this very period of wakefulness. He tried to recall the worm lettering in the photograph, but he remembered nothing but the groups of letters 'OM' and 'ANT' that made up the bottom line. It was out of this melancholic mixture that the painting *Tuesday* came into being.

"Zoltán had never thought about what his paintings should mean before he painted them; only after he finished one would he sit in front of it and try to make sense of it. One afternoon last September he sat in front of *Tuesday* and thought about it. It occurred to him that more than anything else, the painting expressed the anxiety that lay at the bottom of all his erotic adventures; it also addressed how the pleasure he sought through them was pleasure in the victory over an anxiety that had been with him his whole life. This anxiety had its source in his childhood, when, it had seemed to him at the time, he was constantly aware of spending whole days and nights in a lake of anxiety, whose surface he could never reach. The strange thing was, but for this anxiety, he would never have become a painter. He had started to paint when the ubiquitous threat emitted by all shapes in the strange world, from the hostile look of things, began to transform into something else unknown—a magical glow that urged him to allow it to mature into new shapes, fans, nest, and thickets of color on his white paper or canvas. Yet this alchemical transformation was incomplete: beneath the fascination for shape and color, the anxiety of childhood still sounded; the magnificence of the visible world still contained a threat. And so the motif of the mysterious undersea lettering and the strange shell with the eye blended with motifs of eroticism, anxiety, and pleasure, memories of childhood and nighttime lights in curtains, and out of all this originated the picture of a teacher standing naked before a class of obediently seated pupils.

"I asked myself why Zoltán was speaking of personal matters with people he had just met; he didn't seem the type to confide easily in others. Maybe it was because he realized from what I had told him that the life of Tomáš Kantor, too, had been an ongoing battle with ghosts from childhood . . ."

4. Meditating Ant

"Looking at his picture, Zoltán was certain that the teacher knew the meaning of the glowing lettering and was at that moment telling her pupils about it. And he couldn't shake the feeling that the letters were asking him to read them too. It occurred to him that the two groups of letters he remembered were seawater-damaged remnants of words or indeed fragments of a single word. He tried and failed to complete them: In the time that the letters had lived in two groups in his picture, they had gotten used to one another and teamed up, and now they refused to be supplemented. But since the letters demanded to be read, Zoltán did his best to read them. He told himself that the first group was perhaps a sacred syllable in Sanskrit, the second the English word for a small social insect. He acknowledged that his achievement was less than amazing and the solution less than satisfactory, yet it seemed to him that the letters accepted the meanings he had accorded them; the meanings settled and grew into them immediately, so that it was no longer possible to tear them out. So it was that the luminous letters formed by the worms in the Mediterranean Sea told of a Sanskrit mantra and ants.

"The painter didn't know what to do with this two-word combination. By throwing a dice or opening a book at a random page, sometimes a remarkable affinity can be revealed, opening a door long searched for in vain. But often such a gamble produces only banality or nonsense giving rise to nothing. This was a case of the latter, Zoltán thought. (It crossed my mind that the old man at the station in Parca thought differently.) Having come to accept that the words in the picture would remain indifferent to each other, Zoltán saw to his surprise that their meanings were coming together by a strange chemical reaction; this process was an interplay of appeals, provocations, enticements, and exchanges of meaning in which both words were involved, culminating in the idea of a meditating ant. Also strange was the fact that he immediately saw this remarkable creature in the form in which he would go on to paint it.

"In which realm of reality or the imagination could a meditating ant be found, he wondered. The first idea that came to him was based in science fiction: On a faraway planet, astronauts have discovered a theocratic civilization of giant ants; by his profound wisdom and knowledge of mysteries of the universe, the superior of one of many monasteries impresses a beautiful woman astronaut to such a degree that she falls in love with him despite his strange appearance, so inspiring jealousy and anger in the captain of the spaceship, who determines to kill the monk-ant. The result is a fight in which the ant uses a magic weapon . . . Zoltán had no intention of writing a work of science fiction; he was simply considering painting a scene from the story.

"He wasn't completely happy with the extraterrestrial ant, however. By sending the meditating ant to another planet, he had made his task a little too easy, he thought; he needed to find it somewhere on Earth. Above all, he realized that he had no clear idea of how such meditation was practiced. He remembered reading somewhere that it was necessary to stop the flow of ideas in the mind, which was what he tried hard to do, to no avail; he felt like Charlie Chaplin trying to push a stream of water back into a hosepipe. But then he looked carefully at the streams of constantly transforming, confused, restless, intrusive thoughts and feelings, and the eddies of unnamable substances of his mind, which hadn't yet managed to render them as thought and feelings, and at once he saw this action as magical, moving ornamentation, a tangle of many, ever-changing patterns woven into a carpet that stretched out forever without a single hole or unfilled space. Although the tension didn't lessen, it changed into a stream of strength that formed the patterns on the carpet. He gazed in wonder at the magical ornamentation of colored fibers that twisted and stretched, creating in the process many various patterns that intertwined, traced, or rejected each other. He wondered how it was that he had never before seen the ornamentation when it had been in front of him his whole life long; now he realized that everything he had seen was part of the ever-changing pattern, so forming archetypes of everything he had ever painted.

"The never-ending carpet glowed slightly, as though lit by a soft afternoon sun; and the painter knew that he had to embrace it, heed its calls, and proceed along it slowly, without hurry or anxiety. He realized too that what he had taken for isolated seconds of brightness in his past were points of radiance in a continuous pattern linking past, present, and future. He felt as though he had entered, along with the whole room and the whole city, a strange, slow dream. He went out onto the balcony, leaned against the railing, and gazed out on the afternoon city. What he saw was woven into the magic carpet. Then he closed his eyes, and, to his surprise, there was no blank space in the carpet even then; he watched marvelous, luminous shapes swirl about behind his eyelids, and between the inside and outside shapes there was no interruption, both were parts of a single fabric, these shapes grew out of those and were in no way obviously different; well-known human faces, trees, and objects were an arabesque flickering behind his lids, like cloud shapes; eddies on the surface of a river and stains on walls were pictures of objects and beings so far unnamed, but which seemed to him just as important as those for which humans had found names.

"As the painter looked at the river, it seemed to him that the flow of time had merged with its slow rhythm. He remembered that the poet Hölderlin had written that the Danube was too patient; and suddenly he grasped the sense of these words, because for the first time in his life—while filled with confusion, fear, and dissatisfaction with himself—he realized what patience was. Also, for the first time in his life, the anxiety disappeared, or at least transformed in a remarkable way: It had become one of the threads twisted into the carpet, and the same glow lay on its patterns as on all other figures. There was no longer any need to worry or any place to hurry off to. It was enough to walk slowly and patiently about the carpet and watch the patterns of magical ornamentation; its every turn contained the rest of the carpet—a whole universe, as nearby patterns referred to distant, hitherto invisible, or forgotten ones, summoning their hallucinatory images and blending with them, plaiting together a magical network that extended on all sides.

"Nor was that everything he experienced that afternoon. Without any disruption in the unity of the carpet, Zoltán began to distinguish in it layers dating back to different times; beneath the most recent patterns, which were concerned with human knowledge, he made out images of animals, insects, and plants, and beneath those, a long way down, vague figures from the dreams of rock and water, in which neither consciousness nor life had yet awoken. And he had the feeling that together all these layers composed the consciousness of a great cosmic monster, which was also his consciousness, and all of them participated in its perceptions, ideas, thoughts, and actions; its gaze always contained the eyes of animals, while in its thoughts there was forever a distant echo of the ancient sorrow of rocks and restlessness of comets. Every place in the carpet contained its whole, infinite area, and referred to patterns near and far with which it was joined in the great weave, so that also the whole of its past, which had remained in place and alive, was everywhere present.

"In this way, Zoltán found, in the company of many beings of his own consciousness, the meditating ant written about by luminous worms under the sea. He told us that this experience of perfect peace and a completely joined-up world lasted one evening. Then, although the old restlessness and anxiety returned, nothing was as it had been before . . . Shortly afterward, he began to paint his portrait of the meditating ant, which was also something of a self-portrait."

5. Ant under Arrest

"We were the first people he had told about the origin of the Meditating Ant, Zoltán said. In its time, the painting attracted a lot of attention. Many people pestered Zoltán with questions about what his canvas meant, but he refused to give any kind of explanation. As a result, the Meditating Ant was widely understood as an expression of Neo-Dada, which indeed came into existence shortly afterward. Because of its bizarre subject matter, the picture garnered popularity even in strata of society not renowned for their interest in the visual arts. With a smile, Zoltán explained that for a while the phrase 'meditating ant' reveled in a fame among the fools of Budapest like that enjoyed by Raymond Roussel's 'rails of calf's lung' among fools in 1920s Paris.

"The Manhattan bar on Andrássy Avenue was frequented by singers and actors. Its owner had been considering changing its name to something showier. The constant talk of Zoltán's painting gave him an idea he thought ingenious: He would re-name the bar the Meditating Ant. He called Zoltán to ask his permission; as far as Zoltán was concerned, the bar owner could call his business whatever he liked. Before long, a sign-board appeared above the entrance to the bar that drew heavily on Zoltán's painting. The bar owner embellished the meditating ant by putting it in the orange robe of a Buddhist monk adorned with the words 'OM MANI PADME HUM,' in lettering that gave the appearance of Tibetan script. Thanks to the bar on Andrássy Avenue, the phrase 'meditating ant' soon became known to almost everyone in the city.

"That was last November. In mid-December every year, there is a fancy-dress party in Budapest attended by all kinds of celebrities from the world of show business. On this occasion, a famous pop singer came in a meditating-ant costume. The singer wore an ant-head face mask with two antennae, made from small springs, swinging this way and that; sewn onto the sides of his orange habit, which was adorned with the mantra 'Om mani padme hum,' was a third, central set of limbs, made from padded plush. When the party was in full swing, two uniformed policemen appeared on the threshold of the hall, before heading all the way across it to the ant, who happened to be standing with his back to them, at the buffet, loading his plate with slices of roast beef and a lobster cream sauce. On reaching the ant, one of the cops placed a hand on his shoulder from behind and announced that he was under arrest. It turned out that the singer was suspected of involvement in drug trafficking.

"At the moment of his arrest, he had had rather a lot to drink. We don't know if he knew that he was being addressed by real policemen; maybe he really did think that this was a costume party joke, as he later claimed in his defense (one of the cops was tall and thin, the other small and stout—as a pair, they might have been taken for characters in a slapstick movie). As the case may be, the singer turned to see the larger cop right in front of him, and, without a second thought, made to push the plate of food into the man's face. The smaller cop showed remarkable presence of mind: Reading the singer's intention, he brought his baton down between antennae on his head a split-second after the plate hit the larger cop's face. The singer fell to the floor, holding his head and groaning. While the smaller cop clapped on the cuffs, the larger one picked up a napkin and wiped the lobster cream sauce and roast beef from his face. Both then lifted the detainee to his feet and led him to the exit along an aisle created as the revelers stepped back to allow the strange trio to pass; they left a trail of lobster cream sauce behind. The despondent singer's padded limbs hung limp, making a pitiful impression. But he would spend less than twelve hours at the police station: First his manager bailed him out, then his lawyers got the charges dropped."

6. Snow-covered Ant

"There are always plenty of photographers from the tabloid press hanging around the guests at the fancy-dress party, and this year was no exception. One of them succeeded in getting a shot just as the plate hit the first policeman's face and the other's baton was three or four inches from the singer's head. This photograph appeared on the front page of the newspaper the paparazzo worked for the very next day, after which it was reprinted in many Hungarian magazines. So it happened that, by chance, it was seen by a young Moscow sculptress called Larissa Kuznetsova, just as she was gaining world renown for her hyperrealistic sculptures on provocative themes. (For a Paris exhibition of new Russian art, for instance, she sent a sculpture representing the French President in his pajamas, standing over a washbasin cleaning his teeth.) Although Larissa knew no Hungarian, and so had no idea what the photo was showing, she was so impressed by this action scene with a giant ant and two policemen that she created a sculpture in colored plastic out of it, showing the whole group in her usual veristic fashion. This work put the three figures in the exact poses the photo had caught them in, and it even included the buffet with the bowl of lobster cream sauce and the slices of roast beef.

"A certain Moscow art theoretician came up with the idea of mounting an exhibition of the work of young sculptors in the park that runs through the center of Gogolevsky Boulevard. This took place last February. Larissa's sculptural group stood alongside other works on the snow-covered grass, under white trees; broad caps of snow appeared and grew on the heads and shoulders of the singer/ant and the policemen, and the roast beef, lobster cream sauce, and their table were entirely submerged. The organizers wanted to remove the snow from the sculptures, but Larissa forbade this, saying that the weather was her collaborator and the snow part of the work.

"About a week after the exhibition opened, a bank was held up on New Arbat Avenue. The two robbers escaped in a car along Gogolevsky Boulevard to the river, with three police vehicles in hot pursuit. That day, the snow fell heavily; the Moscow police officers felt as though they were fighting their way between thick white drapes hung across the street, and they kept losing sight of the robbers' car. In the end, however, the cops managed to shoot out one of their tires. Having lost control of the car, the robbers jumped out with two sacks filled with money, a shotgun, and a Kalashnikov before fleeing across the white park. They soon saw that their flight had a guard of honor, comprising statues of stone, metal, and plastic. When the cops appeared under the snow-covered trees, the robbers saw there was no escape, so they decided to hide and return fire.

"Taking a quick look around, they saw that the best shelter was the ant sculpture. They tossed the sacks with the banknotes into the snow and hid behind it. One of the robbers rested his submachine gun on the arm of the Hungarian cop with the baton, the other the barrel of his shotgun on the arm of the singer that held the plate. Then they opened fire. During the gunfight, which lasted about a quarter of an hour, the sculpture was struck by several dozen bullets. One of the robbers was hit; his blood soaked into the snow, forming a circle of red into which he eventually fell. His associate tossed his submachine gun into a snowdrift before stepping out from behind the statue with his hands up. (Whether Larissa enlisted Fate as another of her collaborators and declared the bullet holes part of the work, Zoltán didn't know.)"

7. The Ant and the Grand Canyon

"An article on the exhibition on Gogolevsky Boulevard, with a mention of the shootout, appeared in a San Francisco magazine; it included a photograph of the bullet-ridden sculpture. The curators of a certain American gallery had just come up with a plan to mount a sculpture exhibition on the tops of rocks in the Grand Canyon, and it was for this very exhibition that an artist from New Orleans had sculpted in white stone a representation of a scene from the Moscow shootout: a shot-up sculptural group capped with snow, providing shelter for two robbers, their guns resting on the arms of a plastic ant and a plastic cop. And the work really did come to be placed on top of a rock in the Grand Canyon. Zoltán went back into the apartment for a newspaper clipping showing a white sculptural group sitting on the edge of the flat top of a red rock.

"Zoltán took it for granted that the white statue in Arizona would mark the end of the chain of images that had grown out of his canvas, but a short while later another was added. A young woman student at the university in Berkeley had

happened to fall in love with a professor of ancient philosophy. As the professor was married, they met in secret in motel
rooms. Things went on like this for several months, and maybe
they would have continued thus for another couple of years, but
for a scandal: it transpired that the professor had published a
falsified edition of the fragmented writings of Heraclitus, adding some of his own ideas and passing them off as the thoughts
of the Ephesian philosopher. As she had considered her lover an
embodiment of perfection, the young woman was so disturbed
by his deception that she determined to commit suicide. And as
she longed for a truly spectacular death—no doubt to punish her
lover to the maximum for his dishonesty—it occurred to her to
hang herself from the white statue at the Grand Canyon, which
she had seen in a photo in a magazine. The baton-wielding white
arm outstretched over the abyss was an obvious invitation to
the desperate, she thought. So she bought a strong rope, got
into her car, and drove from California to Arizona. In the late
afternoon, she reached the Grand Canyon, where she tied the
rope to a Hungarian cop's arm, closed her eyes, and jumped
into the abyss."

Vangelis happened to be passing our table. Although it
wasn't yet late, Martin waved his billfold at him.

"But the arm of the statue failed to bear the student's weight
and broke off, and she went rolling all the way down the rocky
slope. Then she wandered about the Grand Canyon in shock,
bruised and bloodied, the white arm of the Budapest cop swinging against her belly, until she reached a camp site, where the
campers stared at her in amazement. As it happened, there
was a photographer among them, and this photographer was
working on a large picture book about the United States. The
bizarre apparition sent him scrabbling for his camera. The resul-
tant shot won him a Pulitzer Prize in the Feature Photography
category, and an American health insurance company thought

it so eloquent that it used it in its advertising campaign. The scene from the Grand Canyon appeared in magazines and on billboards all over the States, and the photographer and his model made a lot of money. On hearing of this, Zoltán painted a picture showing a wall with the insurance company's billboard on it; he called the picture *America at Noon*. And as he believed that this really was the last in the line of images that had begun with *Meditating Ant*, he hung it next to that first picture, so closing the circle. But now he was wondering if a new round was starting up . . ."

8. City

"We said our goodbyes and left him thinking about this. No sooner were we out on the street than Kristýna began asking me about parts of the painter's story she hadn't fully understood. I asked her to bear with me as I pulled out my cellphone and searched for the number of a friend who was an assistant professor at the Faculty of Science in Prague. He picked up, and I asked him if he knew anything about an international scientific expedition that had studied invertebrates in the Mediterranean last summer and been the subject of an article published in English-language science journal. He didn't, but he promised to investigate and call me back.

"Walking slowly along the river, Kristýna and I went over what Zoltán had told us. It didn't seem to me that all these stories, sculptures, photographs, and mystical occurrences described to us while we gazed at the Danube would bring us further in our investigation into the mysterious deaths of two brothers—and as for the writing worms, well, they were a mystery in themselves. But Kristýna tended to see important clues in everything, so she waited impatiently for my cellphone to ring. Although she couldn't explain why marine worms had used their bodies to write strange words on a picture of a Lygdian shell, she was convinced that once we were able to read their text in its entirety, it would somehow show us the way; she may even have hoped that the worms had included the name of Tomáš's murderer in code. The idea that the marine worms had witnessed the murder and written about it in the Roman alphabet appealed to me despite its improbability.

"At a kiosk, we bought a map of Budapest, which we occasionally consulted. After half an hour, we realized that we had arrived at the lower end of Víziváros. Kristýna proposed that we explore the quarter; maybe she was attracted by the place where the painter had seen the photo which, she felt sure, contained an important message about Tomáš's death. We climbed the steps and wandered the winding lanes Zoltán may have wandered. We passed several fences with grilles in them before we reached the top of the hill and found ourselves in front of the cathedral."

Vangelis hurried back with the check and three glasses of raki. We clinked glasses with him, knocked back the spirit, and paid up.

"I looked at the map again," Martin continued, "and told Kristýna that we were at a place known as Halászbástya—fisherman's bastion. We leaned on the stone rail and looked down on the roofs and yards of Víziváros, the slow barges with their cargoes of sand, the chain bridge, and the houses scattered about the bank opposite as far as the eye could see. I remembered how we used to sit on the pedestal where the Stalin Monument had once stood in the Letná park, where Kristýna had first told me about her and Tomáš. After two practically sleepless nights, I felt tiredness overwhelm me; the gentle hooting of the boats and distant sounds coming from the bridge and the opposite bank were working on me like a lullaby. Then there was a ringing in my pocket—my cellphone. Last summer's scientific expedition had most likely set out from the University of Ljubljana, my friend told me. As I explained this to Kristýna, she gave me a pleading look which left no need for words.

"'I know,' I sighed. 'Ljubljana isn't so far from Budapest.'

"At the first internet café we came to, we ascertained the address of the university in Ljubljana and checked the schedules; there was a train that left Keleti station for Ljubljana at midnight. For the rest of the day, we walked about the city, several times crossing the river on different bridges. We stopped by six or seven cafés, where I doused my weariness with coffee, in vain. We went over and over what the painter had told us, reaching no conclusions. But Kristýna was pretty satisfied with the results of our stay in Budapest; for her, the fact that a scientific expedition had found a picture of a Lygdian shell near the place where fishermen had recovered Tomáš's body was proof that we were on the right track, and she was convinced that in Ljubljana we would learn more still, perhaps even the identity of Tomáš's killer.

"It's true that I, too, was struck by the fact that the Lygdian shell wasn't the only thing in Zoltán's story somehow connected with Tomáš's life and work. I couldn't help thinking about the great similarities between Tomáš's all-engulfing emptiness and the infinite fullness without spaces to which the lettering in the sea had guided Zoltán. And how strange it was that Zoltán had discovered something reminiscent of Tomáš's fate in a text apparently so badly damaged by seawater that it made no sense! Stranger still, in interpreting the two fragments he remembered from the worm inscription, the painter hadn't thought too hard, simply accepting the first meaning to occur to him. And this meaning was the result of the interplay of a few coincidences. How could it be that it concurred so remarkably with something that was in the soul of Tomáš's world? How could it be that chance had produced such strange connections?

"We got to the station at around ten. Sitting on a bench, I drank several more cups of coffee. When the train got in and we reached our compartment at last, Kristýna again lay down on the top bunk, where she talked and talked about Zoltán's message. Fortunately, the combination of her voice and the rattle of the train soon turned into a fantastical composition reminiscent of Tomáš's music for *The Critique of Pure Reason*; all the strong Budapest coffees notwithstanding, I was soon fast asleep. On the border between Hungary and Slovakia, a customs officer had to shake me awake. After he left the compartment, I couldn't get back to sleep, so I just lay there with my eyes open, wondering what to expect in Ljubljana, listening to the voices from the loudspeakers at the stations, and watching the cold light of the new day as it poured itself slowly into the compartment."

It was clear that Martin had no wish to repeat the vigil of the night before, and that we had reached a point in the story where we might break off. He drank the last of his raki, set the glass down on the table, wished me goodnight, and walked away. As there were still plenty of customers at the taverna and I wasn't yet ready to go to bed, I ordered a jug of wine. As I drank the wine, I watched the lights on the dark water and listened to the hum of conversation and the splashing of waves.

The Story of the Underwater Lettering, the Keter Sapphire and the Beautiful CIA Agent

1. Room with a River View

The next day, I travelled from the eastern end of the bay on the ten-thirty motorboat to Sweetwater Beach, bathed in the sea, which was still as hot as in summer, and lay about on the bright, sunbaked pebbles. In the afternoon, I returned by the narrow, winding path along the coastal cliffs, where thanks to all the years I had been coming to Loutro, I knew every stone and thyme plant. I wandered about the village for a while, ending up with a *frappé* in a café on the western side of the bay, in a comfortable armchair with floral-décor upholstery, looking out for Martin. I was keen to know if he had succeeded in Ljubljana in figuring out the meaning of the underwater lettering. He appeared before I had finished my coffee.

As soon as he sat down at my table, I offered him a reminder. "When we finished yesterday, you were on the night train from Budapest to Ljubljana."

"When we got to Ljubljana, we dropped off our backpacks at the station's left-luggage office," he began. "Then we set out for *Kongresni trg*, where the main building of the university is. At the gatehouse, they told us that the Biotechnical Faculty was on Jamnikarjeva Street. At the Faculty, we discovered the name of the marine biologist who led last year's research expedition to the eastern Mediterranean, and we found out that he was the author of the article in which Zoltán had read about the glowing letters. He wasn't at the Faculty that day, but we managed to get his address. He lived on the fourth floor of a building on a quiet stretch of the Hribarjev Embankment, in an apartment beyond a heavy paneled door. Next to the door was a little plate on which were engraved the occupant's name and titles.

We rang the bell and heard a little girl's voice call out in Slovenian. The door opened to reveal a broad, suntanned face framed by curly, graying hair and beard. Again it was necessary for me to reel off the story of the two murders and the origin of *Damp Walls*, this time with the addition of the new installment from Budapest, complete with a telling of Zoltán's nighttime adventure in Víziváros and the creation of the surrealistic *Tuesday*. Although I left out several things, notably the ant, the shootout on Gogolevsky Boulevard, and the Berkeley' student's unhappy love affair, there was more than enough to tell. The marine biologist heard me out patiently; it was my good fortune that he appeared entertained by my story. As I was trying to explain the connection between the shell with the eye and Kant's murderous *Ding an sich*, he opened the door wide and led us through a dark, spacious hall at whose end we saw our reflections in a large mirror, into a long, high-ceilinged, impeccably neat room with a window view of the waterfront.

"That Ljubljana morning was not at all like the morning of the day before in Budapest. Sunlight was yet to penetrate the narrow ravine comprising a line of houses on either side of the Ljubljanica River; all that lay across the objects in the room was a scattered white light, which caught the glass of a round-cornered bookcase taking up the whole of one wall, a large, oval, dark-wood table, at whose exact center stood an earthenware bowl filled with apples and pears, and a densely stuffed sofa covered with smooth black leather. The light also extended softly across white walls and a faded Persian rug. On the latter, a girl of about seven was playing with two dolls, a solemn expression on her face. When we appeared, she raised her head and inspected us before turning back to her toys.

"The marine biologist bid us sit on the sofa. Before I could speak again, a telephone rang somewhere in the apartment. Our host excused himself and left the room; the little girl, whom he had addressed as Miljana, picked up her dolls and ran out after him, leaving Kristýna and me alone in the room. We didn't speak; the only sounds were the loud ticking of a square-faced Art Deco clock from the bookcase and our host's muffled voice coming from another room. I looked at the bent photographs stuck behind the glass doors of the bookcase, seeing palm trees, high mountains with snow-covered peaks, and unknown faces; I didn't get up to study them more closely. Beyond the window, I saw colorful treetops and gray facades of buildings on the other side of the river. I thought of the buildings on the far bank of the Danube as seen the day before from Zoltán's balcony, and how they had looked to me like a mirage that might dissolve at any moment. Here, the windows and cornices were so close that it was difficult to believe I was separated from them by a river. Kristýna looked at the carpet; maybe she was thinking of Zoltán's metaphor of the day before."

2. Photograph

"When the marine biologist and Miljana came back, I was made to tell the whole story again, in detail, from the beginning.

This time, I included the meditating ant and the Muscovite hyperrealist. Having described the shell with the eye, I gave a more in-depth account of the Lygds. At first, the marine biologist struggled to understand what was real and what was from Kantor's novel, and he kept stopping me to check. Clumsily, I also wove into the story the wire book, Leo, Diamanta, Dr. Williams, and Linda's abduction in Mexico City. There came a point when the marine biologist stopped asking questions: either because he understood everything or he had given up hope of making heads or tails of my narrative. Perhaps it was enough for him to understand what was most important: that the glowing letters he had discovered in the Mediterranean were part of a complicated puzzle Kristýna and I were trying and failing to put together, and that we were asking for his help.

"He was amused by Zoltán's idea that someone had taught the luminous worms to write. It would be a fine thing, he said laughing, although his explanation of the luminous undersea lettering was a simpler one: The worms had gone over something that was already written. The luminous letters were no great mystery: The worms lived on the picture because they fed on its canvas. As the oils used to paint the shell were inedible for them, they had settled only places where the paint had been removed. Most likely, someone had scratched the canvas with a sharp object, and the luminous text had formed as the worms settled in the scratches. The canvas had obviously been in the water for a long time, so the worms illuminated only the letters that were left on it.

"I asked if the expedition had brought the picture home. There had been no reason for them to do so, the biologist replied. From a scientific point of view, the luminous worms weren't a particularly interesting phenomenon—their life was well known and described in detail in scientific literature. He had photographed the glowing letters merely out of curiosity;

initially, he hadn't even intended to mention them in his article. He had added the photograph and written a passage about the letters only at the insistence of the magazine's editor-in-chief, who had considered the article too specialized while admiring the photograph of the evening-time bay, with its glowing blue letters beneath the darkening surface, as art. The editor-in-chief reminded the marine biologist that the magazine had a lay readership, too; it was always good to include something to impress the non-expert.

"Of course, what we wanted to know above all was which letters appeared on the painting. The biologist put on his glasses and went to a drawer for an envelope stuffed with photographs. As he started to flick through them, I noticed that Kristýna was sitting on the very edge of the sofa, holding her breath. As the biologist finally plucked one of the photos from the pile and laid it on the table, I, too, was excited; Kristýna and I jumped up in unison, like a couple of jack-in-the-boxes.

"The photo showed an unframed canvas lying in the sand, in the shallow water of a bay, as József Zoltán had described. Painted on the canvas was a shell with an eye (the painter had remembered its shape and colors very accurately); over the eye were three lines of letters, which came together in an incomprehensible message:

ET AS ILLE
E MAG IYT
OM ANT

"What strange invocation is this? I wondered. As the three of us stared in silence at the photo, Miljana's serious face appeared over the edge of the table. By now I knew Kristýna well enough to realize she was convinced that the luminous lettering concealed the truth about the death of her lover, and I could tell that she was trying to figure out the undersea puzzle. The biologist, too, was deep in thought; it had struck him, perhaps for the first time, that things could whisper of secrets wholly different from those he was trying to coax out of them. Maybe it occurred to him that in revealing themselves below the dark surface of the sea, the glowing letters might have an important message for him, just as they had for József Zoltán. The silence was broken by Miljana reading aloud the mysterious words on the photo; obviously, she, too, was wondering what they meant. The biologist may have been contemplating the great volume of such tracks, characters, puzzles, clozes, signs, and messages on land and in the sea; perhaps it was possible to read the natural world in a way other than the one he was used to; maybe the text he read was charged with many other texts.

"As we were leaving, the biologist gave us his calling card, along with the photo. He asked us to call him if we found out anything that cast light on the meaning of the undersea characters. It was clear that over the next few days he, too, would be spending a lot of time thinking about those eight groups of letters. He made a note of my cellphone number and promised to call me if he should discover anything that might prove important for us in connection with the luminous worms."

3. Ljubljanica

"On the opposite bank of the Ljubljanica, scattered about the tall trees, were several garden cafés. It was clear to both Kristýna and me that we would sit down in one of them and go straight to the deciphering of the text. We walked along the embankment. I looked at the dense clutter of skittle-shaped lights above the river, and at a viridescent monument that stood nearby at the center of a small square, looking like a creature from a fairy tale. As we approached, the outline of the monster split into two figures; the upper jaw of the open mouth became a Muse with an outstretched arm, the lower the head of a man in a suit of clothes from the nineteenth century. Having reached the square, we discovered that the clutter of skittle shapes above the river was in fact six balustrades belonging to three short bridges that crossed the Ljubljanica close to one another; 'It's as if the builder was worried the facing bank could tear itself free and float away, so he wanted to attach it to the square as firmly as possible,' remarked Kristýna. I was delighted by this playful bounty of three bridges springing across the river at the same point, as I was by the grove of lanterns topped with white balls that floated above them; this was a good sign, I told myself.

"After we crossed the first of the bridges, Kristýna stopped to lean over the balustrade and look at the dark-green water, even though her urgency was still greater than my own. Maybe before we set about solving the puzzle, she wished to greet the spirits that dwelled in the river's depths and plead for the help of their ages-old magic. This seemed to me neither strange nor inappropriate; under the fantastic whirl of skittles and lamps, I felt that the dark, narrow river was so immensely deep that a dragon might be sleeping on its bed. Kristýna and I stood side by side looking at the turbid surface of the Ljubljanica. Then I raised my eyes and let them wander, coming to a bend in the river where the facades of the houses on one bank appeared to come together with those on the other, so transforming the space above the river into a bright ceremonial hall. This river had looked so slight in comparison with the Danube in Budapest, but now I saw that it had a similar degree of control over its surroundings—in a different, hidden, but perhaps even more effective way.

"It seemed to me that the ivy on the walls of the embankment and the trees up on the bank had been born from the breath of the river; that the tangle of rootstalks, branches, and foliage was a continuation of the life of its algae. I even had a sense that the buildings themselves had arisen without human agency, like crystals of a dark breath, and that the streets traced the magical paths this breath blew. It seemed to me now that the even the calm light of the biologist's apartment was complicit in something that came from the depths of the river. I had the impression that the waters of the Ljubljanica rose from incredible depths, from cracks in the Earth's surface. What did they bring to light from those depths? How strange it was that this river, like the Danube, exhaled peace. Yet it was a peace imbued with a secret of the swampy deep and a vague threat. I asked myself if the tranquility, charm, and coziness of urban spaces that opened like hospitable halls, protecting us from the sorrow of the distant horizon, were nothing but protection from the dark, swampy breath of the river.

"On the far bank, in a square called *Rybji trg*, we sat down at an outdoor café and each ordered an espresso. I reached into my pocket for the photo, blew twisted dry leaves from the wooden tabletop, and put the photo down on it. For a moment, we studied it in silence. Then Kristýna pointed to the last letter in the second row of luminous letters. I had had the same letter in mind; like Kristýna, I was struck by the fact that only one of them wasn't in Roman script: It was either from the Greek alphabet or the Cyrillic. Given where the picture with the lettering had been found, it was probably a Greek gamma. The Greek alphabet hypothesis was supported by the fact that the group 'IYΓ' might form part of a Greek word; in Serbian and Russian post-revolution Cyrillic, there is no iota. The possibility remained, however, that the iota could be a disfigured 'j'. If so, and the Cyrillic was Serbian, this group of letters would read 'jug', meaning 'south': Such an explanation wasn't complete nonsense. One more thing occurred to me: The letters of the last two groups were the same in the Roman and Greek alphabets, so it was possible that the first part of the wording—to the word 'MAG'—was in Roman and the rest was in Greek. So was the inscription in two languages? If so, it would be easier to decipher. (I thought of the Rosetta Stone.) But my attempts to find commonalities between the two parts came to nothing. As for the rest of the letters, the group 'ILLE' was suggestive of French.

"The words captured in the picture were evidently fragments. I can't say that we came close to solving the puzzle. Dozens of possible solutions—dozens of words that would fit—occurred to us; indeed, they whirled around in the photo like a swarm of bees. After about two hours of deliberations, we realized that we might keep this game up until snow fell on the tabletop and still we wouldn't know the solution to our marine rebus. For a while longer we looked cluelessly at the photo, blowing away the dry leaves that fell on it. New words continued to swarm about the letters, but now we let them fly away without taking them in.

I realized that Kristýna was holding back tears. I was sorry that our attempts to solve a puzzle we had crossed three borders to find had ended with such a whimper. What a pitiful end to our three days of detective work! I tried to find pleasure in the prospect of returning to my work, but I failed. I saw a tear run down Kristýna's cheek. By the time I felt brave enough to stroke it away, I saw that she was looking at and speaking with a dead man. She may have been apologizing for our incompetence, she may have been reproaching him for setting us riddles that were too hard to solve. I drew my hand away."

4. Feast

"Anyway, I told Kristýna that the least we could do was have a good lunch. She appeared to say goodbye to her ghost and return to me, and had nothing against a memorial feast for our failed expedition. As we hadn't had a decent meal since we left Prague, I ordered *kisla juha, ribji brodet, pršut, zelena solata, ocvrta skuša, rakci, meso na žaru, gibanica,* and *melona*—half the items on the menu. We had a good idea what some of these meant, but others we chose simply because we liked their names. As plates were set down on the table, the photo remained between us. As it disappeared under fallen leaves, my feeling of disappointment turned gradually to pleasure at the thought that my absurd journey was ending. I was hoping that after our return my foolish love, too, would come to an end. I began to wonder what would remain in my life from this strange summer and early fall. As we were finishing our feast, my gaze returned to the photo, and I saw among the dry leaves the mysterious trio IYΓ. I felt the stirrings of a buried memory—yes, I had the overwhelming sense that I had come across these letters once before. I stopped eating. From the depths of my mind there emerged an image of pages of a book. But before I could read a single word, it had slipped back beneath the surface. Several times I almost had a fragment of text in my grasp, but always the book eluded me. Telling myself it was probably a false memory, I gave it up and went on with my dessert.

"Then an image sprang to my mind: a double-page spread from a book I had read five years ago, when I was preparing for an examination in Renaissance philosophy. Kristýna saw straight away that something had occurred to me. At first, she just watched me intently, not wanting to interrupt my train of thought, but soon she couldn't help but ask what I was going on. But before I had checked out the image, I didn't want to tell her. I remembered seeing a large bookstore on our way from the station, on the main street *Slovenska cesta*. That was where we must go, I told Kristýna. So we rose from the table with its plates of fish bones, melon rind and unfinished desserts, grabbed the photograph, returned to the trio of bridges, and dashed across the small square with the monument and along a short street before coming to the busy main street. In the bookstore, I raced from one shelf to the next, Kristýna following me in confusion, until I found the Philosophy section. I was in luck: The book I was thinking of was there, a slim volume among many thick ones. The following was written on the front page:

"'Giovanni Pico della Mirandola
De dignitate humanae naturae
Oration on the Dignity of Man'

"I opened the book, which was a bilingual edition—the Latin text on the even-numbered pages, a Slovenian translation on the odd. I flicked through the pages frantically, worried now that back in the café my memory had fooled me. At last I came to what I was looking for. Since that day, I've read that passage so many times, I know it by heart."

Martin leaned back in his chair a little and fixed his gaze on the water of the bay. Then he recited rapidly: *"Haec, inter sparsas Dei beneficio et inter seminatas mundo virtutes, quasi de latebris evocans in lucem, non tam facit miranda quam facienti naturae sedula famulatur. Haec universi consensum, quem significantius Graeci συμπάθειαν dicunt, introrsum perscrutatius rimata et mutuam naturarum cognitionem habens perspectam, nativas adibens unicuique rei et suas illecebras, quae magorum nominantur, in mundi recessibus, in naturae gremio, in promptuariis arcanisque Dei latitantia miracula, quasi ipsa sit artifex, promit in publicum, et sicut agricola ulmos vitibus, ita magus terram caelo, idest inferiora superiorum dotibus virtutibusqe maritat."*

A German family of four was sitting at the table next to ours. The middle-aged parents and their two sons looked up from their ice-cream sundaes to stare at Martin in amazement.

"I took the photo from my pocket and laid it on the facing page. And it was as I had thought: All the letters of the under-water inscription appeared in Pico's text, in the same order; the only difference being, the worm letters were in capitals. I showed Kristýna, whose gaze had been flicking impatiently from the book to me and back again, how the letters in the photo matched with those in the book."

Martin leaned over the table to write something in ballpoint on a paper napkin, over the blue map of Sfakian coast printed thereon. He handed the napkin to me. It was a quotation in capitals, and he had underlined the letters that appeared in the underwater inscription.

. . . NATIVAS ADIBENS UNICUIQUE REI ET SUAS ILLECEBRAS, QUAE MAGORUM IΥΓΓΕΣ NOMINANTUR . . .

I was about to ask Martin what it meant when he proceeded to explain the Latin to me. "The text is in praise of magic," he said. "The passage comes from a discourse composed by Pica della Mirandola in 1486, which is usually published under the title *Oration on the Dignity of Man*. Literally, it means: This benefi-cent magic, in calling forth, as it were, from their hiding places into the light the powers which the largess of God has sown and planted in the world, does not itself work miracles, so much as sedulously serve nature as she works her wonders. Scrutinizing, with greater penetration, that harmony of the universe which the Greeks with greater aptness of terms called *sympatheia* and grasping the mutual affinity of things, she applies to each thing those inducements (called the *iugges* of the musicians), most suited to its nature. Thus it draws forth into public notice the miracles which lie hidden in the recesses of the world, in the womb of nature, in the storehouses and secret vaults of God, as though she herself were their artificer. As the farmer weds his elms to the vines, so the 'magus' unites earth to heaven, that is, the lower orders to the endowments and powers of the higher.'"

5. Wryneck

"I read the text several times, then and there in the bookstore. Kristýna, who knew neither Latin nor Slovenian, stood next to me, shifting her weight from one foot to the other. When her patience ran out, she asked me what the text was about, and what it had to do with our search. I explained to her that the passage in Pico's discourse dealt with magic, and that so far, I wasn't able to find any connection between it and our search. But I would need to go through the text carefully. And before I did, I needed to know the meaning of the word *iugges* (or *jynges*) Pico had introduced me to.

"When I read Pico's discourse in preparation for an exam, I hadn't had time for such details. Now, however, I would learn all I could about the unknown Greek word which appeared in part on the underwater canvas. On the other side of the river we had passed an internet café. For a third time, we crossed one of the trio of bridges (we would learn later that they are known as *Tromostovje*). Having sat down at a computer, I went to the search engine and typed in the word *jynges*. To my surprise, it pulled up several dozen links to pages on ornithology. It turned out that *jynges* is the plural form of *jynx*, and that *Jynx torquilla* is the Latin, or rather the Graeco-Latin name for the Eurasian wryneck."

"The Eurasian wryneck?"

"The Eurasian wryneck." Martin wrote the words 'wryneck' and 'JYNX TORQUILLA' on the paper napkin.

"But why does the letter *n* appear in the Latin prescription? It's gamma in the Greek."

"The Greeks have always designated the velar nasal with a gamma. Try saying the word 'England' and you'll hear that the sound really is more of a g than an *n*," Martin explained, with some impatience. Perhaps he was disinclined to supplement all his digressions and interpolations with an excursion into linguistics. "Do you get it?"

I assured him that his explanation was more than adequate. And I promised not to ask about any more minor points.

"We discovered that the wryneck is an unremarkable-looking bird in the woodpecker family, that it's not much bigger than a sparrow, that it lives in holes in tree trunks, and that unlike other woodpeckers, it doesn't carve out its own nest—if it finds a nest it likes, it simply drives out the current occupant and takes the nest over. Anyway, as we went on with our search, we did indeed discover a connection between *jynges* and magic. In ancient Greece, the wryneck was considered a magic charm that could find a way to a beloved, man or woman. The dead bird, its wings outstretched, was affixed to a wheel of some kind. As the wheel spun, incantations were chanted, the purpose being to establish a connection with the gods, who would then arrange for everything else. The internet also showed us a poem by Theocritus, in which a girl appeals to a wryneck to bring her beloved home . . .

"The word *jynx* came to mean magic in general. Eventually, it was given a special meaning in the Chaldean Oracles—a text that probably originated in the second century AD, in which Neoplatonist philosophy takes on elements of magic in the folk tradition; here, the word *jynges* denotes spiritual beings that operate as intermediaries between the gods and human souls, the magical names of things, and also the degrees by which the absolute spills over itself in a cascade, rather like the sefirot in Kabbalah. These three meanings of the word *jynges* relate to three aspects of what connects them vertically and horizontally due to their common source—remote existence and sympathy—i.e., that which weaves the network of kinship and affection that exists between them, which Pico also mentions in his discourse. Otherwise, all the internet had to offer on the Chaldean Oracles was a lot of occult-related nonsense; the only thing that distracted me for a moment was the information that W. B. Yeats took an interest in them, and that they may have influenced his work.

"Kristýna remained convinced that the shells were painted by Tomáš. I asked her if she believed, too, that he had carved the quote from Pico's book into the canvas. She considered this for a moment: With capital letters, it was difficult to recognize a person's handwriting. Then she said that as she couldn't think why Tomáš would wreck his own work, she assumed that someone else had made the inscription. I tried to visualize what may have happened in the eastern Mediterranean. I could imagine about twenty different stories featuring a character using a knife or a nail to carve the words of a passage from a Renaissance discourse on magic into Tomáš's canvas, but none of them would be worth much. To tell them the truth, I was annoyed that of all the words we had made in the outdoor café with the letters 'MAG,' the one we had ended up with was magic. As you know, *The Da Vinci Code* still has many readers, and the bookstores are awash with translations of all kinds of imitations. I've always detested works of this kind, which promise magic and mystery before raising the curtain on banality blatantly disguised as mystique. Right then, I feared that I was a character in just such a story. But then I told myself that the god who had devised the journey Kristýna and I were on, so bringing us together, had better taste than to have Tomáš Kantor murdered for cracking a closely guarded secret. But this surmise wasn't enough to put my mind at ease. So far, the enigmatic director of my story had divulged so little about what he was up to that I still had cause to fear the worst."

6. Tree of Life

"When it was plain that we wouldn't find any more important stuff online, I suggested we sit down at a table and have a glass of cognac. But Kristýna grabbed the mouse, refusing to give up on the only lead we had. After that, I just sat and watched the cursor as it fluttered in jerky motions about the screen, like a seismograph reflecting the tension and impatience she was feeling. I looked on as Kristýna plunged along long corridors of link after link, only to pull up helpless at some distant junction and then search for a way back. Gradually, I ceased to take in all the words and magical shapes that appeared before me. Pleasantly tired, I felt myself drifting off to sleep; my head dropped toward the keyboard, my eyelids began to close, the white keys grew so large that they turned into the trio of bridges, one of which I tried to cross to reach the far bank, but it got farther and farther away, growing into a network of bridges with an endless number of branches, and I lost my way under a clear blue sky . . .

"Kristýna shook me, and I awoke to see on the screen something that at first sight reminded me of the Expo 58 Atomium building in Brussels—a system of eleven spheres arranged in three columns and connected by double lines. Within the balls were inscriptions in Hebrew. It occurred to me that I was looking at the Kabbalistic Tree of Life. Having once read something about this, I knew that the ten spheres represented the ten sefirot—stages which form a cascade to create an overflow of the Absolute, and which make individual levels of reality; the cascade is also a staircase that can be ascended, i.e., in the other direction. So the spheres on the screen, and the tubes that connected them, represented an emanatory waterfall and a geyser of ecstasy or meditation. (The eleventh sphere was the connector of the second and third spheres—most kabbalists don't regard it as a sphere in its own right.)

"Kristýna waited for me to recover my wits. Then she told me that the picture of the sefirotic tree the links had led her to while I slept reminded her of something. If an aspect of what the Chaldean Oracles and Pico della Mirandola called *jynges* was identical with the sefirot, there must be a connection between Tomáš's work and the marine inscription. Again I was assailed by the worry that we were about to follow an occult-related clue, so I was relieved when Kristýna explained that the Kabbalistic diagram put her in mind of an episode from the comics series on the adventures of the agent Henriette Fox-Vulpécula. 'That was the part Tomáš finished reading just before he left me,' she said. I learned that the story was set in the present, but because Vulpécula, like James Bond and Ellery Queen, had the miraculous ability not to age, she remained as beautiful as she was in the Sixties, when the young Hector had created her for his tale about the wire book, as told to the blinded Hella.

"At the time in which the comics were set, Vulpécula was living in Washington, an elite agent of the US Central Intelligence Agency. Sometime earlier, there had been a putsch in South Floriana. The new government had had General Varela arrested; the arrest of Colonel Ramirez had turned into a fierce shootout, in which Henriette's boss was killed. Vulpécula was already collaborating with the North American secret services, without the knowledge of her superiors. One night, the CIA sent a military helicopter to South Floriana from an aircraft carrier. It was on this helicopter that Henriette and her entire girls' troop left the country."

7. The Nefarious John Wind

"For this part of his comic, Tomáš Kantor wished to create a bad guy who would be a worthy adversary for his favorite heroine. He came up with John Wind. Wind's crimes were characterized by a unique style in which uncommon cruelty was powered by an eccentric, often self-serving imagination. In addition to the committing of perfect crimes, Wind had two other great interests: precious stones and Kabbalah studies. Although born in Chicago, he now lived on the French Riviera—in a villa he had had built that overlooked the sea. Here, he often closed himself up in his favorite room, to spend hours on end studying his collection of sapphires, rubies, and diamonds, or to read the Zohar, the foundational work of the Kabbalah, in Middle Aramaic, all the while sipping on the very best French wines. The room also contained a computer attached to twelve screens, which Wind used to manage his activities when they didn't require his presence in the field. Above the screens, three portraits hung. One was of Thomas De Quincey, author of the book *On Murder Considered as One of the Fine Arts*, which Wind had decided to take seriously. The second was of Moses de León, publisher and perhaps author of the Zohar, the third of Vincente Peruzzi, a seventeenth-century Venetian diamond cutter who had gone down in the history of diamond cutting for increasing the number of facets from seventeen (as there were in the so-called Mazarin Cut, in use at that time) to thirty-three.

"Wind's ingenuity enabled him to conceal the life he truly led behind a veneer of respectability; he passed himself off as a speculator on the stock market and a notable philanthropist. So original were his crimes that even the lowliest of detectives could recognize his handiwork at first glance. Yet it was their very uniqueness of style that made the guilt of their perpetrator impossible to prove. From start to finish, Wind performed each of his crimes with the precision of a poet in search of the only right word, or the painter who selects a shape from among the thousands whose nebulae float around the tip of his brush. He planned his crimes as though they were ballets whose choreography had to be flawless. For all its unpredictability, the logic that informed his heists, kidnappings, and murders was unshakeable; it was the logic of a work of art that made the next move impossible to guess, yet constituted a fully coherent whole. Wind was never where he was looked for, and he was forever doing the unexpected. Not once did anyone succeed in catching him in the act, or in building even the flimsiest of cases against him.

"One day, as he was reading the Zohar, Wind came up with the idea of building a tower on his land that would represent the Tree of Life of the Kabbalah, with its rooms corresponding to the sefirot and its staircases and corridors to the relations that obtain between the individual sefirot in accordance with the Kabbalah's teachings. He drew a diagram of the sefirot and emailed it to the architect who had designed his house, adding a brief note stipulating the structure's location and dimensions, the date for completion, and the fee he was offering.

"The architect completed the Kabbalistic tower on time and in exact accordance with Wind's drawings. It comprised eleven rooms connected by corridors and staircases. Seen from outside, the rooms were perfectly spherical; inside, each perfect hollow sphere was breached by a horizontal floor. On the left from top to bottom were the sefirot Hod, Gevurah and Binah. (Using a pencil as a pointer, Kristýna showed me the circles and their names on the screen.) The sefirot Netzach, Chesed, and Chokhmah were on the right, while the sefirot Yesod and Tiferet were in the middle. At the top, between the sefirot Binah and Chokhmah, was the Da'at room to mediate between them. As I have said, Da'at is not itself a sefirah in the truest meaning. Each of the well-appointed, luxurious rooms contained a comfortable sofa, a table, a library, and a bar containing the finest wines and distilled liquors. Many of them boasted pictures by Wind's favorite artists. The furniture was shaped to sit in perfect alignment with the convex walls. Wind began to spend most of his time in the room at the top, which was situated centrally above the Da'at and represented the sephirah Keter. He had the central computer brought here from the villa, plus the portraits of his three masters."

8. Maharajah's Ball

"Having realized that Wind shared many qualities with his best woman agent, Henriette's boss at the CIA sent Vulpécula to Europe with instructions to catch him in the act and arrest him. As Henriette and her girls' troop were landing at the airport in Nice, Wind was at work on his latest opus—the robbery of a large sapphire belonging to an Indian maharajah. He planned to take the jewel during a masquerade ball at the maharajah's palace in Monte Carlo. As Wind was hoping to make this work into one of his best, he made several improvements to its style and composition as he honed every detail. Never he had suffered such creative torment.

"He showed up at the ball with three assistants, each of whom, like Wind himself, was dressed in a long, dark cloak and a white Venetian *volto*. Wind's mask was that worn by Il Capitano in the Commedia dell'arte, with a long beak-like nose. Within moments of their arrival, Wind was making good use of the mask, issuing discreet, virtuoso directions to his men in a play of signals and voices, feigned love interest, behind-fan whispers lost in ballroom noise, attendants bribed or seduced, tiptoes along dark corridors where long white drapes billowed, ropes lowered from windows, soft clinking from an anchor whose line clung to a chimney, nighttime garden rendezvous with shadows dancing in large illuminated windows, fake gems gleaming in the moonlight and the glare of chandeliers, and figures concealed behind heavy curtains. Henriette appeared at the ball in the company of Elena, one of her commandos who had also been her best friend since childhood, when they had attended the same Roman Catholic girls' school in South Floriana. Slim Henriette was wearing a figure-hugging Harlequin costume adorned with colorful rhombuses, a black eye mask, and a tricorn, with her hair in a chignon. Elena was dressed as Colombina, her face concealed by a *moretta* of black velvet.

Quick on the uptake, Henriette attuned herself to the style of Wind's campaign like a violinist finding her way around a piece of music. Her fight with Wind wasn't about destroying his art; instead, she stepped inside it, became a part of it, conformed to its aesthetics and the tone which established itself as drunkenness set in, fireworks played beyond the windows, and the processions of masked revelers roaming the darkened corridors became ever more *féerie*-like and fantastical. Wind's most powerful weapons had long been the singularity and coherence of his style; now, Henriette turned these against him, as the instrument by which she would defeat him. To the brilliantly planned game of exchanging true gems for fake, Henriette added an element of her own, so making the odd number of substitutions even. As a result of her intervention, the true gem—which, unbeknown to the maharajah and his guards, had been doing the rounds of the palace while the ball was in progress—was inconspicuously returned to its place on the maharajah's turban.

During the ball, Wind and Henriette were three times so close to each other that the white nose of Wind's *volto* made contact with Henriette's black eye mask. (Kristýna offered the observation that Tomáš's black-and-white comics nicely brought out the contrast between the two masks.) So Wind didn't get the sapphire, but the evening wasn't a great success for Vulpécula and Elena either: They failed in their attempt to arrest Wind. Although the house was surrounded by police, Wind withdrew from the campaign by performing his famous disappearing act. An hour later, he was sitting in his villa in his silk dressing gown, with ten police cars just beyond his windows, blue lights flashing. Wind explained to the commissioners from Monte Carlo and Nice that he had spent the whole evening in bed, reading the tenth chapter of the Zohar.

"Though disappointed to have missed out on the stone he so much desired, Wind was enchanted by the tasteful style of Henriette's intervention, which had in no way spoiled his art; indeed, it had added new, unexpected tones to a beautiful, harmonious effect. And the touches of his mask against Henriette's, those three light taps amid the whirling dancers, were for him an unforgettable erotic experience. He knew already about the activities of Henriette's paratroops in the mausoleum of Fernando Vieta in North Floriana, and he was very impressed by what he had heard. Nevertheless, he believed that for reasons of the ethics of his criminal state and aesthetics alike he must get his revenge; without such culmination, it seemed to him that the work he and Henriette shared would remain a fragment. The Revenge he intended would be the second part of the work entitled *Crime at the Ball*. After long deliberation, performed in his revolving chair in the Keter sephirah at the top of his tower, he inclined to the view that his sequel should be very different in tone from the fantastical lyricism of the first part; it would be darker and more dramatic. And in this second part, he and

Henriette would meet, a meeting he was very much looking forward to."

9. In the Kabbalistic Tower

"Not long afterward, Wind's men broke into the hotel where Elena was sleeping, where they etherized, then abducted her. Wind ordered her to be flown in his private plane to Tuscany, where he had bought a crumbling rococo mansion (which sat atop a hill in an overgrown olive grove) and prepared it for Elena's imprisonment. The moment Henriette learned of the kidnapping, she was in no doubt as to the identity of the perpetrator. But Wind had disappeared, and no one had any news of him. One week after the abduction, Vulpécula was driving her red convertible at noon under the palms of the Promenade des Anglais when she spotted Wind in front of the Hotel Négresco, getting into his car. There followed a wild chase along the Promenade, in the narrow streets of the Old Town, and around the switchbacks of the Moyenne Corniche, which are carved into the cliffs above the sea. The car chase takes up two whole pages of the comics. Tomáš evidently enjoyed furnishing the pictures with large balloons to contain a great variety of cries and exclamations, expressing noises made by the engines, tires, and brakes. On reaching Èze-sur-Mer, Wind headed up toward Èze le Col, before returning to his estate along a side road. As Henriette's automobile flung back the closing gate, Wind drove past the villa and headed for the Kabbalistic tower.

"Henriette saw him go through the entrance, which was situated in Malkuth (Kingdom), the tenth sephirah, which represented the immanent force, or life. (Kristýna pointed to the screen, and the lowest sphere in the middle row.) Henriette jumped out of the car and ran after him. By the time she entered the room, it was empty. She was surprised to find that the room was like the lobby of a luxury hotel. She was standing next to a soft beige leather armchair. Stock-still, her cocked Beretta 92 in hand, she listened; but apart from the cawing of the crows from outside, she heard nothing. Holding the pistol in both hands, slowly and noiselessly she ascended the marble staircase to Yesod (Foundation), the ninth sephirah. (Kristýna pointed to the screen, and the sphere above the Malkuth sphere.) The moment she stepped into the room, she saw, at the top of the staircase leading to Hod (Glory), the eighth sephirah, Wind's silhouette, dissolving in the sunlight that flooded through Hod's large window onto the dark staircase. She saw Wind raise his pistol-toting hand. A shot rang out. But Vulpécula had managed to take cover behind a bookcase. As the shelves had no side panels, she heard the bullet tear into the second volume of the Larousse encyclopedia, stopping somewhere in the middle. (Kristýna explained that the upper floors had provided Tomáš with the opportunity he sought to try out unusual angles and exaggerated comic perspectives, while using the contrast given by the dark staircases and light flooding through the windows to experiment with expanses of black and white.)

"The silence resumed. Pistol in hand, Henriette ran up the stairs, but the room Hod was already empty. Along a horizontal corridor, Vulpécula slowly approached Netzach (Victory), the room of the seventh sephirah, which together with Hod and Yesod forms the realm of nature. No sooner has she stepped into Netzach than she was again forced to take cover. This time, the gunfire came from above and the room of the sephirah Tiferet, which together with the rooms of the sefirot Gevurah and Chesed comprises the higher triad of the spiritual realm. As Henriette crouched behind an armchair, bullets thudded into a shelf bearing bottles of brilliant liquor, producing the sound of shattering glass. Looking around carefully, Henriette saw liquids of many sunlit colors cascading across the carpet. (Tomáš conveyed the impression of colored light in a black-and-white drawing, Kristýna confirmed.)

"On the screen, Kristýna showed me Henriette's route of ascent through the rooms of Wind's tower. Still feeling the lack of sleep, I struggled to follow. I interrupted the explanation to suggest I fetch two cognacs; Kristýna had no objection. As I was waiting at the bar, I looked outside to see a fine but keen rain falling, and people hurrying along the sidewalk bent forward; the wind picked up a plastic bag and with it wrote a sentence in an unknown language as it flew by the windows."

10. The Five Highest Sefirot

"We finished our cognacs and put the glasses down on either side of the keyboard. Then Kristýna went on with the story. She doesn't have a particularly good memory, so I was struck several times by the precision of her recollection where her dead lover was concerned; even then, she could reconstruct Tomáš's comics about Henriette and Wind, panel by panel . . . Vulpécula made it uninjured to the fifth sephirah, Gevurah (Strength), also known as Din (Justice); and from there to the fourth sephirah, Chesed, where Edward Hopper's *Early Sunday Morning* hung on the wall. Bullets from Wind's pistol made six holes in the canvas, in the place with the row of windows with half-pulled blinds.

"Wind's bullets tore into the wallpaper and the upholstery of the sofas and armchairs; they smashed vases and bottles of wine. Tomáš's pictures made freeze frames of all this—showing, for instance, the moment at which a bullet bored into the pages of a thick book, or its tip pierced the back of a Chinese vase as the front burst into dozens of pieces. Vulpécula stepped quietly around the shards, which gleamed in the sunshine. She, too, left a trail of spent cartridges on the floors of the sefirot, corridors, and staircases. Except for Malkuth, each of the rooms had several doors, beyond which were corridors expressing the complicated relations among the sefirot. All these doors were locked, however, but for those which led directly to a higher sephirah in the shape of a sefirotic lightning flash, a path of emanation and ecstasy winding through a thicket of connecting lines among the sefirot; along this path, Vulpécula, trigger finger at the ready, made her cautious way toward Keter, the highest of the sefirot.

"There followed the ascent of a long staircase to the sephirah Binah (Reason), which together with Chokhmah (Wisdom) formed the realm of understanding. All was silent again. Henriette followed the stairs to the Da'at room, which was on a slightly lower level. (At first, Wind had been unsure whether to include this eleventh room in the building, as this link in the sefirotic tree was introduced only in the sixteenth century, in the scheme of Isaac Luria—meaning that his beloved Moses de León hadn't known it. Then Wind had realized that the placement of Da'at between the second and third sefirot appealed to his sense of symmetry.) On the computer screen, I read that Da'at was but an aspect of Keter, the highest sephirah, which Henriette was now approaching. She had no doubt that it was here that she and Wind would come face to face. Having stepped into the room of Chokhmah, the second sephirah, she froze. Again, I looked at the commentary on the screen: Chokhmah represents the primary force in the creative process.

"Vulpécula listened long and hard. Absolute silence reigned in the tower. She considered her options. She knew that Wind was waiting for her in Keter (Crown), the topmost room, and that here the showdown would take place—there was no escape from Keter; only Ein Soph, the Endless One, was above it. (In the on-screen commentary, I read that Ein Soph is a side of the Absolute that stands beyond a descent through the sefirot, which explains why it isn't shown on emanatory schemes; for this reason, it seems, Wind didn't build a room to it at the top of his tower.) Henriette had a different worry, however: For some time, she had been aware of the position of advantage held by Wind in this Kabbalistic ascent; it was clear to her that if he truly wished to, he could kill or wound her easily. What game was Wind playing with her?

"Pistol in hand, she climbed slowly from Chokhmah to the final—or perhaps the first—sephirah, Keter. From above, she heard the music of Mozart. Again, I looked at the commentary. The sephirah Keter, I read, means a flow from Nothing that rushes over shapes . . . Although the stairs were in darkness, when Vulpécula got closer to the room, she saw that it was flooded with light from a sun that still sat high above the Mediterranean. When she entered the room, John Wind didn't turn. He was sitting in front of a computer at a broad desk, sipping champagne from a glass with two large strawberries in it, listening to the music. Above the computer keyboard, Henriette counted twelve dark screens, each reflecting the window and the horizon on the sea; above these, she saw the three famous portraits she had heard about at CIA headquarters in Washington; higher still was the white Il Capitano mask, whose long nose had touched her three times at the ball. Wind's pistol lay on the desk, next to the keyboard. From the wide window, she could see far below, beyond all sefirot, beyond the rock, beyond the pantile roofs of the village of Èze, the elongated peninsula of Cap Ferrat, dotted with white villas and reaching far into the warm sea, as if wishing to tear itself from the land. As Henriette cautiously approached Wind with pistol in hand, she wondered at his strange behavior. Even when she pressed the muzzle of the gun against his temple, still Wind didn't move."

11. The Sephirah Keter

"My tired eyes were closing, demanding a rest from the glare from the computer screen. Now that Henriette had at last reached the crown of the Tree of Life, i.e., the topmost room of Wind's tower, I suggested to Kristýna that we leave the computer. We took a seat by the window, where we ordered more cognac and coffee. It was still raining, and the gardens in front of the cafés had emptied. I was saddened by the thought that this strange summer would soon give way to fall . . . Slowly, Wind turned to face Henriette. She may kill him if she wished, he said, but if she did so, she would be condemning Elena to a terrible death. Vulpécula had been expecting something like this; she lowered the gun. Wind invited her to sit in the other armchair. He poured her a glass of champagne, adding several strawberries to it from a bowl. She should hear him out, he said. He wished to show her an invention of which he was very proud. Although several IT specialists had worked with him to bring the instrument into existence, still he considered it his child, as the idea behind it was his.

"Henriette should imagine a room with white walls, containing nothing but a few pieces of old furniture, he said. Its barred windows overlooked an untended garden, and branches of its dense vegetation scratched against the glass. The room was always in semi-darkness; only just before sunset did a few rays penetrate the leaves and force their way inside. On opening the window, a smell of damp, rotting leaves would waft into the room . . . Henriette sat down and listened.

"'All the walls look the same—smooth and white,' Wind continued. 'But in fact, one of them contains a cutout ten feet by ten, and this hollow square is filled with a part of my instrument I call the screen. The border between the screen and the rest of the wall can't be made out. The screen comprises several thousand very small rods stacked tightly together and of the same white as the surrounding wall. A precision mechanism concealed behind the screen and operated by a computer program slides the rods in and out. Different programs can be inserted in the computer to determine exactly when each rod should be slid out, and how far.'

"It occurred to Vulpécula what the purpose of this invention might be. She began to suspect that Wind intended to use her for something monstrous. But she couldn't prevent herself from listening to his description with interest. She even picked up the glass of champagne—with her left hand; the right was holding the pistol—and drank from it. 'Perhaps, dear Henriette, you have guessed already what the instrument is used for,' said Wind.

"'I imagine it being used to create reliefs of different kinds,' Vulpécula said slowly.

"'And so it is!' said Wind. 'And surely you've also realized that not only can the reliefs on the wall be alternated, they can move, too. Can you imagine the impression a moving relief would make on the living-room wall of a millionaire snob? Plus, there's a simple program that converts your holiday videos, let's say, into a moving relief—naturally, I'm not interested in working on such nonsense. I believe that my invention will one day give rise to a new art form, combining sculpture, film, and ballet. How I look forward to having more time, so I can devote myself to the creation of works of art the likes of which the world has never known! I can tell you that first I would like to make a *féerie*-play moving relief on themes of your wonderful poem from the mausoleum of Fernando Vieta, which I know by heart.' To prove he wasn't making this up, Wind began to recite from the text, which Henriette had forgotten long ago. She asked him to desist and return to the point. 'Unfortunately, this pet plan of mine will have to wait,' Wind sighed. 'The moving reliefs are about to become part of the work I'm currently engaged with.

I'm hoping you will join me in creation of this work. Together, I believe we will make something unparalleled.'

"Henriette didn't ask why Wind was telling her this. She said nothing. 'In the room I described to you,' said Wind, 'your girlfriend awoke a week ago. She has been closed in there ever since. The room has a bathroom and toilet facilities. There are people in the house to provide Elena with sufficient fine food and drink every day. But the prisoner has no contact with any of them: the food and drink are conveyed to the room in a special elevator, arriving at a recess in the wall. By the way, the house with the room in it is in a place you will never, ever find; not you, not your friends at the CIA. There are twelve hidden cameras in various places, following Elena's every movement.' Wind tapped on the keyboard and all twelve screens above the desk lit up. Some showed just a blank stretch of wall, but others showed, from various angles, Elena sitting on a couch in a room with white walls and barred windows overlooking dense vegetation."

12. Moving Reliefs

"Wind finished his glass of champagne and poured himself another. Then he leaned toward Henriette and said quietly, 'I'm putting on a show for your friend. I started by having a relief move out from the wall for just a short time every day. On the first occasion, the rods appeared in such a way that for a fraction of a second Elena saw her own face on the wall; that was all that happened on the wall that day. The next afternoon, Elena's face emerged from the wall again. But this time, it transformed into a giant insect with terrible moving mandibles. The show follows a meticulously thought-out plan, in which reliefs of innocent content alternate with disgust-provoking reliefs of violence and incest. At present, reliefs appear at different times of day, albeit only once per day, and always for a few seconds only. If I wanted to, however, I could put on a relief film of ten hours' duration. Do you happen to know, dear Henriette, why I use the instrument so sparingly?'

"As Vulpécula said nothing, Wind answered his own question. 'I've spent a lot of time and trouble making the reliefs as agonizing as possible. My agents in South Floriana found out all they could about the country, and about Elena's life. Their report was evaluated by a psychologist, who determined which visions were the most nightmarish for Elena, and what lies at the very bottom of her fear—a bottom she herself does not know, as she has always been afraid to look there. Now she is getting to know these visions, in moving reliefs I present to her on the wall. But there is one thing far worse than the most terrible of these images: the waiting for what will appear, and the not knowing when it will do so . . . Today's show is yet to take place, so I can demonstrate my invention to you . . .'

"Again, Wind tapped something into the keyboard. Henriette considered trying to stop what he was doing, but her desire to see how Wind's crazy invention worked got the better of her. On the screen, Henriette saw the wall in front of her friend start to ripple. Before long, it had formed itself into a relief that depicted Elena herself. Elena stood up from the sofa with a terror-stricken expression (on some of the screens, her face was seen in detail), went up to the relief, and touched her own face. Next to the face, a second relief face emerged from the wall; Vulpécula recognized this face as her own. Relief Elena threw herself at Relief Henriette and proceeded to strangle her, laughing as she did so. Eventually, Relief Vulpécula fell to the ground, where she lay twitching as Relief Elena kicked her in the face several times. After that, Relief Henriette lay motionless as the vilely laughing face of Relief Elena grew across the wall before exploding into hundreds of small pieces. The pieces transformed into cockroaches and caterpillars; insects scurried about this way and that, grouping themselves in letters spelling out obscene utterances, before sinking back into the white wall, the surface of which was soon as even as it had been at the beginning. The whole story had been told in just a few seconds.

"'That was horrible,' said Vulpécula in a soft voice.

"'Yes, it was, wasn't it?' Wind agreed. 'I worked hard to come up with such a powerful script. I saw that you watched with interest.'

"'You want to drive Elena mad,' said Vulpécula.

"'That Elena should go mad isn't my intention, believe me,' Wind replied. 'I won't deny that I was counting on madness as I made the first sketches for my work. But then I came up with something better. At first, I wanted to get my revenge on the two of you, if only because the work we embarked on together at the maharajah's ball was unfinished. I bear you no ill will. But as Aristotle says, a work of art must have a beginning, a middle, and an end. According to Aristotle, the end must follow naturally, either by necessity or as a rule, from what has gone before, and conclude the action. But I realized that in the Aristotelian sense, revenge wasn't the right end. In its essence, every act of vengeance is a banal, bourgeois affair, and as such it doesn't befit a work of art. It is a manifestation of the mercantile thinking of debit and credit. So, I decided to end the work in another way: There would be no revenge, but I would get the maharajah's sapphire.'

"Wind smiled at Vulpécula as he sipped his wine. She said nothing, and the Beretta remained in her lap.

"'Having thought the matter through,' Wind continued, 'I came to the conclusion that for many reasons—one of the most important being that the two parts of the work should be in symmetry—it would be best if you were to steal the sapphire.

The maharajah is a fat fool who isn't worthy of such a stone. Should you refuse to do as I ask, I will continue with the relief performances for Elena. And if I do, you know that your friend really will go mad. That wouldn't be the perfect end to my work, but in the end, irrespective of Aristotle, it wouldn't be so bad. Should you accept my offer, as soon as you hand the sapphire to me, I will give the order for Elena's release. And as compensation for her suffering, she will be given one of the most precious and beautiful of my rubies.

"'I have the feeling that once I have the sapphire, I shall give up for good the part of my work people refer to as "crime." From then on, I will concern myself only with my collection of precious stones, my Zohar, and the making of works of art using the instrument of my own invention. I've long been governed by the high principles instilled in me by study of the Kabbalah, and I'm sure you, Henriette, will appreciate that I have lived my life as an ascetic. But my achievements are worth all the sacrifices: To the sphere of crime I have introduced concord, symmetry, and aesthetic harmony; I've succeeded in bringing the pure waters of Ein Soph to a realm as far as possible from the source; I've returned to its governance the farthermost sphere that still eluded it, so removing the last hindrance to emanation; I've opened the floodgates to the magnificent Niagara Absolute . . . But I've become tired. I think I truly shall become the philanthropist that until now, in the interests of my work, I have only pretended to be. And I'm really looking forward to it.'

"As she listened to Wind, Vulpécula realized that he was mad, and that this madness grew from his fondness for precision. But should she refuse his offer, he would carry out his threat, and Elena would end up in a lunatic asylum . . . So she told Wind she would get the sapphire for him.

"In the meantime, the maharajah had moved to his palace

in London. The panel on the last page of the comic showed Henriette in a black top and a black mask on a London rooftop glistening in the light of a full moon.

"Kristýna never did find out how the story of Henriette, Wind, and Elena ended: Several days after completing the comic book about the Kabbalistic tower, Tomáš left her. Tomáš liked to end each of the exercise books in which he composed his comics with what is known as a cliffhanger, typified by an ending where the hero or heroine hangs from a cliff by his or her fingertips, with no help for miles around. Tomáš completed the book on the fight between Vulpécula and Wind in this spirit: The third picture from the end showed Henriette making her way along a narrow ledge on the highest story of a London building; the penultimate picture showed dilapidated masonry crumbling under Vulpécula's feet, and her losing her balance; the final panel gave a bird's eye view of Henriette falling into the London abyss, toward converging lines of buildings. Although the situation looked hopeless, Vulpécula had become Tomáš's favorite character, so Kristýna was convinced that he wouldn't let her die, and that the first page of the next book would present her salvation. Maybe Superman would come flying over to catch her just before she hit the sidewalk . . ."

The Story of the Colored Threads, the Harmony of the Universe, and the Fruit-gum Candies

1. Colored Threads

"So Kristýna retold me a story from one of Tomáš's comic books. But how could the story of Vulpécula, Elena, and Wind help us in our search? Did it tell us anything more than Tomáš's fondness for adventure literature—which I had noticed in any case when reading *Damp Walls*. I doubted it. I would have said that Tomáš used the motif of the Tree of Life only because he found the combination of Kabbalistic mysticism and an all-action plot amusing. I had the feeling that Kristýna, too, didn't really believe that this story of Henriette had an important clue for us. When she began her telling of the comics story, she spoke too rapidly, her voice trembling with excitement at the thought of having spotted a connection between the mysterious marine-worm inscription and Tomáš's work. But as the story continued, with Vulpécula climbing the stairs of the Kabbalistic building, Kristýna's voice became ever more downcast. Plainly, she was beginning to believe that this was a false trail.

"After she finished, the two of us sat in silence for a long time, looking out of the window. Briefly, the sun reappeared, its rays causing the wet leaves of the trees to glint, the raindrops on the café's tables to sparkle, and the golden edges of Kristýna's hair to gleam, but it soon disappeared again. Dusk arrived; I was surprised by the speed at which the day had passed, as I had assumed it was early afternoon. I had the feeling that some silent magic was causing the gloom to rise from the Ljubljanica, invisible far below us, so flooding the streets of the city, the windows of the houses on the bank opposite, the stone balustrades, the monument on the square, the trio of bridges—all this melted peacefully into the bluish gloom. The milky-white balls above the three bridges lit up all together, as though we were in a magical luna park. It occurred to me that all foreign cities are beautiful.

"Kristýna asked me to tell her about Pico della Mirandola. I told her what I could remember about his life. She listened with concentration. When I finished, she said she thought Tomáš had a lot in common with the Renaissance philosopher, a comment which took me by surprise. 'But isn't it obvious?' said Kristýna. 'Pico della Mirandola lived a public life. He traveled around Italy and France. He was forever organizing things, and he corresponded with princes. He had discussion after discussion. He abducted women—well, one woman that we know of. Tomáš lived away from others, in a one-room apartment in his glass tower by the streetcar terminus. Apart from me, he saw no one. But Pico's reluctance to choose between options, his desire to take everything on, be everything—academic and adventurer, philosopher and kidnapper, Christian and pagan, Platonist and Aristotelian, scholasticist and humanist, kabbalist and man of science, explorer and lover, hedonist and ascetic follower of Savonarola . . . When you were telling me about him, I couldn't help thinking of Tomáš, who couldn't choose between his options either, even as a child, because he wanted to keep hold of everything, even things others had no use for.

That's why he fell in love with the void, which contains all possibilities . . .'

"Again I read to Kristýna the passage from Pico's discourse about magic, translating it word for word. I saw that she was starting to liven up. When I finished, she described something that happened in the final period of her relationship with Tomáš, after he reopened the book that was already concluded and had it grow into a thicket of texts, pictures, and musical compositions. Once, she arrived at his apartment to find him sitting on the sofa holding the Diagram, looking at it as though he were Hamlet and it was Yorick's skull. She noticed that the Diagram wasn't as she remembered. Various places along its wires were connected by colored threads which were woven into the frame, crossing inside the Diagram and on its surface. The white wire network was overgrown with a second, multicolored network, so that it resembled an ingrowing tree no longer, but a network of seaweed or rhizomes, or an entanglement of parasitic plants climbing the branches of a tree and wrapping themselves around them. Kristýna remembered the quivering of the ends of colored threads hanging from the wire frame in many places. 'There was always a draft in Tomáš's place,' she said. 'Lots of things in it were forever moving and rippling.'

"Tomáš explained to her his strange realization: The more the Work-Network grew, the more branches sprouted from it in all directions, detached themselves from the stem and lived their own life, the greater the number of characters, cities and stories became part of the Work, and the more distinct the entire universe appeared as the last horizon of the growing Work, the more obvious it was that in all the unstoppable growth, only a small number of figures appeared, over and over again. He had counted six of them, but to get the root of the problem, he had been to the notions store on the corner of the street for spools of red, yellow, green, orange, purple and blue thread, then used each color to connect places on the Diagram denoting parts in the Work expressing one of the patterns. (A single motif in the Work might be an expression of two or more figures, however; in places on the Diagram where this applied, threads of different colors crossed.)

"At the moment of Kristýna's arrival in the apartment, Tomáš was turning the Diagram this way and that. He couldn't make up his mind whether to be delighted by the fact that it hadn't vanished amid the thousands of images sprouting from his work or desperate at the poverty of his work, and the impossibility of the appearance in it of something entirely new, something which that escaped the monotony of repetition. But a few days later, this worry had evaporated. By then, the six colored patterns, too, had begun to disintegrate and multiply. In the appearance of things and the schemes and rhythms of events, Tomáš kept finding new patterns, relations, and affinities— requiring him to buy thread in more and more colors, which he wove into the Diagram. The thread became so tangled and knotted that before long the Diagram was so chaotically overgrown that the wire frame was inferred but not seen. Having first woven the thread into the Diagram to bring order to it, so helping him understand his work, he saw now that he was trying to explain one labyrinth with another, more intricate labyrinth . . . In those days, Kristýna would often find him with the Diagram—now an irregular tangle of thread in all colors imaginable—on the desk in front of him, staring at it with a pensive expression.

"At first, I didn't understand why Kristýna was telling me about colored thread. Then she explained it to me. 'When you were translating the words of Pico for me,' she said, 'I had the feeling you were speaking of something I knew. Then I remembered Tomáš's threads. According to Tomáš, they represented affinities that were unexpected, at first glance imperceptible, or trivial, but in fact essential, as they connected things distant from each other—high and low, commonplace and exotic, real and dreamed—so creating strange yet cohesive families. It dawned on me that the affinities Tomáš spoke of were jynges, which set things in a network of sympathy establishing universal consensus, universal harmony, which would see the tangle of colored thread as an entirety.'

"Resisting my desire to comment that the tangled ball of thread of Tomáš's creation surely didn't make a very harmonious impression, I said that Kristýna was probably right; who was to say whether universal harmony was like harmony as we understand it? Tomáš told Kristýna that when he looked at the tangles of colored thread, he realized that things we encounter emerge not in isolation but woven into magic nets. As each thing emerges, by some mysterious rule, so, too, do all the things and beings associated with it, and we may see these on the face of things; each thing is spun only from its strange affinities and images, in which other images and affinities are contained. And these affinities may be linked to things and beings from distant continents, strange planets, the undersea realm, dreams, or the world of good and wicked fairy tales.

"Sometime later, Tomáš told Kristýna that when looking at the entangled Diagram, he had also realized that the figures that appear in the life of things are secondary to something else; they are like meanders, drawing a river's course in the landscape; they are traces of currents of the life-giving, indifferent void, creating things, spaces, bodies, and thoughts. These currents share with actual rivers an ability to change their bed; the lake of emptiness, from which they flow, contains millions of possible rivers of all kinds and millions of possible beds carved by a river's course.

"Pointing at a place in Pico's discourse, I said, 'These invisible rivers Tomáš spoke about could quite easily be *sparsae et seminatae mundo virtutes*—forces scattered throughout the world.' I imagined an arm of a river from the void flowing across the room; its sound was a murmur in my ears, merging with the buzz of café conversation. Although this river of emptiness was with me for a moment only, I said to myself that it would remain one of the rivers I had encountered on my journey, and that once I returned to Prague, I would remember it as I remembered the Danube and the Ljubljanica. I thought of my Kant, too. Until then, I had considered the subject work of my thesis to be a description of a solid ground plan, in which all human experience was played out. Now, however, I was seized by the staggering notion that the forms of our life and our world were a labyrinth of shapes that carved their own path as a river from the void carves its bed; that as such they were random, and may have turned out quite different. I imagined worlds in which *The Critique of Pure Reason* was appreciated not as a work of philosophy but as fantasy fiction. It had never occurred to me that our world might have emerged from the other end of the kaleidoscope . . . Oddly enough, my first reaction of lightheadedness and dismay was superseded by a weird sense of bliss; now it seemed to me that randomness and unanchoredness charged all things with a solemnity and urgent beauty . . .

"This was all very well, but what did it have to do with the aim of our journey? That's right—at that time, I still believed that our journey had a goal. We ordered another round of cognac and sipped our drinks slowly, in silence. By now it was properly dark; I looked at the glowing, hovering white balls of the lamps beyond the window. In the artificial light of the café, Kristýna's face, bent over her book, looked extremely pale and tired; it was as though we had been on our journey for many months. As she read the long, unintelligible Latin sentences, her lips moved ever so slightly. Perhaps she was hoping to light on a word containing a clue as to where we should turn next.

I reflected on what we had truly found out: that Pico della Mirandola's discourse may or may not be related to what was truly essential in Tomáš's work. Even if there really was some connection here, we had no idea how it could help us; we had been looking not for signatures of things and magical sympathies that control the universe but for the truth about the deaths of two brothers. On top of this, there was the risk that the death of either or both was part of some stupid occult story, even though Kristýna had assured me that Tomáš Kantor wasn't in any secret society. I thought of Stanislas de Guita, who is said to have used magic to murder the Abbé Boullan. Once again, we had come to a dead end. I was going to propose to Kristýna that we go back to the computer to find out the time of the next train to Prague. Then the cellphone in my pocket rang."

2. The Lygdian Shell Makes Another Appearance

Martin looked around for the waiter, to order an ouzo. I suspected he wanted it because his story demanded a dramatic pause at this point. The waiter placed the glass in front of him. He drank before continuing.

"The caller was the marine biologist. Diffidently, he embarked on a narrative that at first I could make neither heads nor tails of. He began by asking me if I knew the gummy candy they make in the shape of bears, monkeys, and other animals. Taken aback, I told him that of course I knew it—I had eaten thousands of the things. The biologist said that he had remembered an incident from last fall. On his return from his scientific expedition, he had gone away again, on a late vacation with his wife and Miljana to Pula, a port city in Croatia. One day, when he and the girl were walking about the city, he bought her a pack of gummy candy in a store. Miljana ate all but the last piece, which she decided to give to her father. Before the biologist put the candy in his mouth, he noticed that it was shaped exactly like the shell with the eye from the painting he had seen in the Mediterranean. And that was all: The biologist ate the candy, soon forgot about it, only to remember it again that day, after our visit. He apologized for bothering us with his gummy candy tale. He was quite sure that the incident in Pula meant nothing at all and was of no help to us, and he had thought long and hard before calling us about it. In the end, he had decided there was nothing to lose, and so on.

"He asked if we had made any new discoveries. Clearly, our early-morning visit was still on his mind. He wasn't done thinking about his strange finding by the Greek island, I was sure. His sudden recollection of the strange candy had obviously disturbed and confused him. Lacking the strength to tell him about everything Kristýna and I had been through that day, I told him there were no new discoveries yet . . . Actually, I was angry with him. Why was he telling me about the gummy shell now that I had accepted that our detective work had led only to grief and was looking forward to finally going home? The Pula candy would rouse new hope in Kristýna, soon to be followed by new disappointment: There was no chance at all of a gummy candy having something to do with the death of her lover . . .

"No sooner was the cell back in my pocket than Kristýna was pumping me for information about the biologist's call. As I was expecting, she perked right up on hearing of something that might be considered a new lead. The thought of the biologist's message was making me more and more annoyed—not least of which because I knew the candy to be stuck in my brain, too, and that there was no hope of shaking it out. What a point we had reached! To the question of what connected the deaths of Tomáš Kantor and Petr Quas with Renaissance magic was added a question of their connection with gummy candy. I told Kristýna that what we had come across since yesterday—an ant mystic, statues of statues, a shootout in snowy Moscow, a student committing suicide at the Grand Canyon, a Florentine Neo-Platonist, a wryneck, a Chaldean incantation, the Kabbalah, the CIA, a comic-book bad guy, universal harmony, and now this gummy candy—was all a bit much for me.

"The inundation of pictures and words since our departure from Prague had made me enormously weary. There was nothing I wanted more than sleep. But Kristýna was restless again, sitting on the edge of her chair, prepared to head into evening-time Ljubljana, to embark on a new trail. Her enthusiasm was getting on my nerves, and I told her so. 'What in God's name do you want to do in the city?' I complained. 'Go around candy stores buying up gummy bears?' By the expression on her face, I realized that was exactly what she had in mind. I reminded her that the marine biologist had bought the candy in another country. She pointed out that the same products are sold all over the world, which is more or less true. Besides, a walk around Ljubljana buying up gummy candy was a better prospect than sitting in that café next to Kristýna in tears. So we paid up and went out into the streets . . . '

With a smile, Martin went on to say, as if to himself: "How could I have known that a small piece of gummy candy would be the most important lead in this whole case? And that it would bring us all the way to Crete?"

I asked no questions; I was in no hurry. As I sipped my third frappé, I waited for Martin to explain the connection between the candy and his presence in Crete in his own time, be it tomorrow or a few days from now. In Loutro, one quickly learns not to hurry . . .

"'So, we walked along streets and across squares, past lighted storefronts. Whenever we saw a confectioner's or a supermarket, we went in and inspected the bags of gummy candy on sale. In most cases, the pack was transparent, so we could tell what was inside. We saw hundreds of bears, monkeys, parrots, spiders, bananas, pineapples, dinosaurs, strawberries, raspberries, Coca-Cola bottles, ghosts, and Martians, but we didn't see a single shell, with or without an eye. If the pack wasn't see-through, we bought it and opened it up, but in every case it contained only more animals, apples, strawberries, pears, etcetera. We dropped by an optician's and bought a magnifying glass to better examine the candies. Still we found nothing suspicious or interesting. Having opened a bag, we struggled to resist a taste of the contents. Before long, we both had stomachaches."

3. Sound of the Sea

"The streets we reached were ever darker and more deserted. At eight thirty, we found ourselves in a housing complex, far from downtown. At the end of a row of houses we saw the red neon sign of a convenience store. We went through the candy rack from end to end, but we didn't find anything we hadn't seen already. We went out into the empty, dimly lit street. From an open window above our heads came the sound of a television showing some film or other. Now even Kristýna had to accept that there was no point in our continuing to roam the city. When Kristýna asked how far it was to Pula, I was again about to propose that we check the time of departure of the next train to Prague. My first reaction to her suggestion—that our foolish journey should have an even crazier continuation in yet another country for the sake of one piece of gummy candy—was anger. I was tempted to tell Kristýna that she could go on wherever she chose, but I would be going home.

"But before I put this thought into words, I realized that anger wasn't all I was feeling: A quiet, enchanting music had

entered my head—and after a moment I understood that it had
come to me from the name 'Pula.' Pula is on the Mediterranean.
Suddenly, the prospect of my standing on the seashore seemed
more important than any other; more important than the
folly of my traveling detective work, than my childish love for
Kristýna, than the images that bothered me by whirling around
in my head. Why I was attracted by the Mediterranean, I didn't
know. I had no idea whether it would deliver the solution to my
mysteries and boldness in love; or ultimate failure, acceptance
of loss, and forgetting; or indifference, peace, disquiet, greater
wisdom; or confusion; or something entirely unknown. What
I knew for sure was that its scent had drifted all the way to the
suburbs of Ljubljana, and that I found it difficult to resist . . .

"Now the question arose of what the true destination of my
journey was. I had believed I had left Prague to find the murderers of Tomáš Kantor and his brother, and because I was in
love with Kristýna. Now I saw there was a chance none of this
was true. Maybe I had simply been heading south, toward the
Mediterranean, from the very beginning. If the office of the
magazine I had found in the café had been in Berlin or Warsaw,
would I have taken this journey? Probably yes; but if the trail
from Berlin or Warsaw had pointed north, it's unlikely I would
have followed it. The North Sea didn't call to me. It didn't
seem to me to speak of intoxication, nothingness, the birth
and perishing of shapes; all its shores were good for was endless
contemplation of profound problems of psychology, something
I had had more than enough of. Right now, psychology concerned me still less than finding a solution to the rebus of the
lettering in luminous worms, something many wise folks would
consider an undertaking to be pitied.

"At last I understood the reason for the strange tremors
I had felt throughout our stay in Ljubljana. The realization
put a spring in my step as we wandered about the city, and

again I was impressed by the facades of the buildings. This was a sign that I felt the breath of the south—the world of the Mediterranean—on the banks of the Ljubljanica. I realized that it had drifted my way in the sun-drenched air of the streets of Budapest; the colorful trees of the Gellért Hill had been soaked in it, as had the calm air over the flat land of Pest stretching into the distance. I began to believe I had first caught a whiff of this intoxicating drug in the heat of Bratislava, at my sun-drenched outdoor table at the Corso café, the scene touched by light foam from an invisible Mediterranean wave spreading deep into the continent from the Mediterranean, as a gentle, bliss-soaked continuation of its surf. Who was to say that this secret bay didn't reach all the way to Prague? I remembered moments on Prague streets when I had the sudden sensation that I was standing on the seashore.

"But then I told myself I was being histrionic in thinking that our investigations into Tomáš's death concealed the true aim of my journey, the sea. Surely there was no connection between the two. But I couldn't shake the thought that the sea I was heading toward and the mysterious murder of Tomáš Kantor shared a close bond. If this were so, might the sea bring about the mystery's resolution? As I contemplated the sea and the south, Kristýna stood next to me, showing no impatience. She realized I was figuring out whether to go on, and she was eager to learn my decision. We might still catch a night train to Croatia, I said. We retraced our steps through dark streets; in one of these, we were by a bus stop when we spotted, coming our way, an empty bus with its interior lights on. Above the driver's head we read the name of the terminus: *Železniška postaja*—train station. On reaching the station, we collected our backpacks. The train was due to leave at nine thirty, to arrive in Pula at two in the morning."

4. Journey to Croatia

"An hour later, Kristýna and I sat facing each other in a compartment flooded with bluish light from a fluorescent bulb, as Slovenia glided past beyond the window, shrouded in darkness. There had been no time for dinner in Ljubljana. We were so hungry that again we raided the packs of gummy bears and monkeys, making our stomachaches even worse. I was almost certain that in Croatia we would find nothing to help our search. Even if we did find candy in the shape of a shell with an eye, how would we know what to do with it? In front of that convenience store in Ljubljana, I had imagined the roar of the sea including a voice that spoke of a connection between all the clues we had gathered on our journey. At night in the train compartment, that thought struck me as delusional. Because of my keenness to see the sea, I had fallen in with Kristýna's crazy plan to travel on to Croatia, and I cursed myself for it. Now, it was up to me to prepare her for the disappointment she was bound to experience in Pula.

"'God knows what the biologist saw,' I said. 'There's not much to see on a gummy candy. What looks like an eye might be random scratches or streaks. And even if what he saw on that candy was an eye, that doesn't mean it has anything to do with Tomáš.'

"'That's where you're wrong,' said Kristýna. 'Making gummy candy to illustrate his work, that was just Tomáš's style. And it's the sort of idea no one else would have.'

"I couldn't argue with that. I could easily picture Tomáš's work expanding into areas a long way from literature, painting, and music; it wasn't too much of a stretch to imagine it swelling to take in mathematical equations, cookbooks, even machines. Kristýna having curled up in a corner of the compartment and fallen asleep, I turned off the light and allowed sleep to claim me in pleasant thoughts of the sea, which I hadn't yet seen this year and had been missing. Each time the train pulled into a station and I was woken by the public address system, the feeling of blissful expectation returned."

Martin was sticking to his principle of speaking of no more than one country in one day. The narrative ended on a night train, as it had done the day before. We said our goodbyes with the sun low over the sea. I went to the store for cheese, olives, and a bottle of wine, before dining alone on the balcony of my room. I sat there watching the sea change color and lights come on all around the bay.

The Story of the Dockside Cranes and the Weiner Café

1. Pula

The next morning at breakfast it occurred to me that I hadn't visited the Marmara Beach this year. The Marmara is on the opposite side to Sweetwater Beach. I headed off toward it, avoiding the promenade by a hidden, winding path unknown to most guests in Loutro, house backs on one side and rocks on the other. I passed henhouses, garbage cans, and small, disorderly gardens, where cucumbers, squashes, melons, and tomatoes grow among all kinds of weeds, and the large leaves of banana plants hang over ramshackle fences. As I descended from the Venetian fort to the sea, Finix emerged from behind the rocks. According to the travel guides and the Bible, in ancient times Finix was a busy port. Today, all that remains under the high, ocher rocks on the shore of the small bay are two inconspicuous little whitewashed houses serving as pensions. Here, I stopped for a coffee on the terrace. Before long, I realized I wished to walk no further. I sat reading, drinking several glasses of ouzo. Then I went back to Loutro. In the evening, I met Martin at Vangelis's place.

"When the train reached Pula, I was fast asleep," Martin began, as soon as the waiter had taken away our empty plates. "Fortunately, Kristýna was awake, and she woke me. I grabbed my backpack and staggered from the train, across the station concourse and out onto the street. The pavement was wet: It must have been raining till shortly before we arrived. Several people passed us who had gotten off the same train. I heard the slamming of car doors and the starting of engines. Before long, we were alone in the street. The portal of the station building projected three squares of light onto the sidewalk. There were a few streetlamps farther along, but none of the windows in the dark house fronts were lit. I was saddened by the unfriendly welcome this city was giving me, and I could scarcely believe that the sea was somewhere nearby. We might have been on the outskirts of Prague. Could some spiteful genie have moved the train off course?

"As we stood on the glistening wet asphalt, a taxi appeared at a bend in the road. We waved it down and asked the driver if he knew of a cheap hotel. He drove us to a small guesthouse in the middle of a steep street. As we stepped out of the car, at last my face was brushed by a breeze, in which I smelled decay, seaweed, dead fish, diesel, and engine oil. Suddenly, my tiredness and sadness were gone. The receptionist was dozing; to collect our room keys, we had to wake her. Leaving Kristýna alone, I went out into the night. The clouds had parted to reveal a round moon. The pavement beneath my feet gleamed silver, like a silent waterfall. I hurried down the hill. I found myself looking at a huge wall with empty windows resplendent with light. Pula's Roman amphitheater, I remembered. I passed the dark trees of a little park before reaching a stone pier, from where I watched the gleam of moonlight on water and the giant metal structures of the shipyards, listened to the splashing of waves, and inhaled the smell of the sea. I didn't stay there long—I needed only a few moments to greet the sea. I knew that the sea was offering me but one of thousands of scents; now I believed that Pula wasn't the end point of our journey, and that in the near future my path would bring me to the Mediterranean several times. When I got back to the guesthouse, Kristýna was asleep. The room was filled with the fragrance from the large white-flowered bushes that grew in a neighboring garden, underlaid by the smell of the sea.

"When Kristýna woke me in the morning, she was dressed and eager to set out for the candy stores of Pula. Perhaps she had been driven from her bed by the prospect of the last bag of gummy candy being sold—the very bag that contained a coded message about the death of her lover. We climbed the steep lanes between the port and the citadel, all the way up and down again, past low buildings and garden walls. The sea appeared above the roofs, then disappeared, though the tops of the shipyard cranes were visible practically everywhere. The streets were windy; scraps of cloud chased across the sky; branches cast fleeting, lacy shadows on light-colored garden walls; gusts of wind set traffic signs rattling.

"The look and breath of these streets suggested their recent desertion by the last guests of summer. Pula had the magical atmosphere of a city whose season had just ended—a city suddenly and touchingly empty and clean. We came across lots of small stores, and we made a stop at every one. We discovered several brands of gummy candy that were new to us. Kristýna ripped open the bags there and then, in front of the store, even though the wind tried to tear them from her hands. As she rummaged through them impatiently, pieces of candy fell to the sidewalk. To her great disappointment, she turned up nothing but more bears, parrots, and monkeys. On a square in the lower town I saw a metal statue of James Joyce. Why he was sitting in an outdoor café, I couldn't say. Could he have lived in Pula at one time and been a patron of the café? When I stopped to inspect him, Kristýna, like a headstrong child, tugged at my sleeve to get me to move along, toward more candy stores and minimarkets. At this point, I rebelled: I sat down next to Joyce and insisted on our having breakfast. Kristýna bolted down a croissant more in sorrow than with appetite. Then she sat hunched against the wind, impatient for me to finish my ham and eggs and coffee, directing reproachful looks at Joyce and me.

"We walked on and on, buying more and more candy. As we wandered about the city, I saw very little of the sea, but I wasn't disappointed, as its breath was everywhere—floating on the wind, climbing the streets, quivering on walls, drifting in my direction from garden gates and open windows of first-floor apartments; I caught its raw smell off the stores we went into. I had a sense that the sea had written its code on the faces of the old women who were these stores' regular customers. Whether Kristýna sensed the sea and read its signs, I really couldn't say. For all I know, she may have been entirely ignorant of its nearness. I wondered if she noticed even the huge amphitheater, although we walked past it several times. On our pilgrimage through Pula, I don't believe her gaze ever rose higher than the signs above the storefronts, and nor did it stray into the gardens or passages. Kristýna was moving along a narrow corridor, on the confined trail of an old crime.

"When we entered a small store at the top of a side street, we had almost reached the citadel. Having greeted the old, black-dressed lady who was reading a magazine as she watched the store, we made straight for the candy rack. With barely contained impatience, Kristýna inspected one familiar package after another. I reached out for the last bag, which was resting against the wall at the very end of the rack. When I drew it into the light, we saw that it bore a color picture of the sandy shoreline of a tropical island. Between two sagging palms with bright-colored parrots on top was a see-through circle. And looking out at us from the middle of the circle was a wide-open eye within a purple shell."

2. Weiner Café

"Kristýna was desperate to open the bag, but I tucked it into my pocket, saying we should find someplace to sit down, so that we could examine the contents in peace. As we were approaching the harbor, a warm rain began to fall. We roamed the streets of the old town until we came to a small, empty square that reminded me of Italy; it had a Roman temple with Corinthian columns on its far side. Several wet tables and chairs stood on the pavement in front of a restaurant with two large windows, above which were the words 'Café Weiner.'

"Only a few students sat in the room, which was quite large, with spectacularly shabby furniture of various provenance. After the rigors of the tourist season, the café had apparently drifted off into pleasing sleep. We seated ourselves in low armchairs with threadbare corduroy covers. Kristýna tipped the candy onto a table and began to sort it with shaking hands. When she was done, there were ten piles, as follows:

1. three purple shells with an eye
2. five orange boats with a stemless flower growing out of the deck
3. five green daggers, their hilts shaped like a crocodile with open jaws
4. three white, irregular-loaf shapes
5. four brown monkeys
6. three light-blue seahorses
7. seven red parrots

8. two gray turtles
9. six dark-blue butterflies
10. four emerald-green lizards

"We took out the magnifying glass and examined the candies minutely. But apart from the shell with the eye, none of them appeared to have anything in common with Tomáš's life or work. Nevertheless, I was no more prepared to consign the presence of the shell with the eye to coincidence than Kristýna was. Besides, I couldn't shake the feeling that at least some of the gummy candies from the bag were letters, intended to be put together and read as a message. If so, who had sent us this message? Was it from Tomáš, from beyond the grave? Was it a message from his murderer, of the ironic kind found in detective stories? Was there some connection between the putative candy text and the luminous undersea lettering photographed by the biologist from the University of Ljubljana? Maybe what we were dealing with here was a single text written in two different alphabets. Or a transcription of the undersea words in candy text. What kind of letters would the next message be written in? Traffic signs? Scores in the rock? Stucco decoration on house fronts? Clouds in the sky?

"I might have been dreaming this situation requiring me to decode an important message contained in a bag of candy. While some of the candy shapes were unusual, most differed in no way from the ones we had seen in other bags, in Ljubljana and in Pula, a fact that confused me further. In fact, only four of the shapes were strange: the shell with the eye, the boat with the flower, the dagger/crocodile, and the unclassifiable white loaf. The prevalence of parrots, monkeys, and other animals did nothing to lessen my feeling that the candy in the bags represented letters in a rebus that demanded to be figured out. Maybe the animals were there to disguise a message that was written using four letters only. But it was also possible that the animals were the letters of the message—in which case the candy alphabet would comprise ten characters. Nor could it be ruled out that the animals were the true alphabet, the four unusual shapes an addition to mislead the puzzler. Of course, I had no idea what could have inspired someone to use such a bizarre alphabet and choose such an unusual way of sending their message into the world. But we decided to set such questions aside for the time being. First, we would try to crack the code by forming the candy pictograms into some kind of text."

3. The Rebus

"Kristýna and I again found ourselves at a table in a café, doing our best to puzzle out a mysterious text. The two rebuses we had so far encountered on our journey were of different kinds, however. The Ljubljana rebus had given us fragments of words, their letters arranged in a recognizable sequence; our job had been to fill in the missing characters. The Pula rebus appeared to be giving us all the letters, and it was our job to put them in the right order. Without knowing the grammar of the language the message was written in, it was extremely difficult to make the candy characters into a sentence. We didn't even know if the gummy figures were ideograms or graphemes. In my view, the best approach was to put the candies in a random sequence, consider the resulting formations, and wait for inspiration to strike. We set the candies out on the table in every kind of grouping we could think of. We came up with lots of ideas for solutions, just as we had in Ljubljana the previous day; these may have been plausible, they may have been absolute nonsense . . .

"I soon saw that our table-top games were leading nowhere. I gave up trying to compose in gummy candy and drank my coffee. But Kristýna remained bent over the table-top, pushing the candies this way and that. The sun emerged from behind clouds, its rays lighting up the dust in the café and waking sparks of color in the translucent candies on the table. Kristýna's mood of impatience had passed; now she was ordering the candies as ideas occurred to her, always paying careful attention to the symmetry of the figure she was creating. There were straight lines and crooked ones, circles, equilateral triangles, squares, stars. I couldn't tell if she was still trying to form the candies into a readable text; maybe she was simply indulging in a kind of melancholy game. I looked up and out of the window, to the square, which a cat was crossing, and to the slim columns of the Roman temple, with the shipyard cranes looming behind. Still lost in her thoughts, Kristýna swept the candies into a formless mass. Then she just sat there in silence. Again, the time had come for us to speak of returning to Prague. After my brief encounter with the sea, however, I would be sorry to move on. What's more, the city streets had started to tempt me southward; if we were to move on now, I would never know what the south had in store for me.

"Just then, it occurred to Kristýna that the candy rebus differed from its worm counterpart in one other respect: It bore the name and address of the entity that had sent it into the world. She began to search her pockets for the torn plastic bag. I saw the chaotic eagerness return to her hands. Having at last turned up the bag, she proceeded to examine it. After a moment, she handed it to me. There was no need for her to say anything: I could read for myself that the gummy candy was produced by an Italian company called *L'Elefante gaudioso*— Merry Elephant. The business had its headquarters in a town called San Benedetto, in the Veneto region. This time, there was no need for Kristýna to talk me into going on with our journey. Maybe she understood that I was drawn to Italy by more than a desire to crack the candy code; maybe she had some idea of what attracted me in the name of an unknown town and the dreamy expression of the little square in front of that Pula café.

"On a table by the bar was a computer connected to the web. We learned that San Benedetto was a small town situated on the vast plain south of Venice. Unfortunately, it appeared to be a dull, industrial place. Still, I wasn't too disappointed: I felt quite strongly that San Benedetto would be a stop on a journey that would soon send us farther south, to sun-lit squares and shores lining warm sea. Kristýna was again hopeful, and obviously convinced not only that the candies were a message from Tomáš but also that we would find someone at the factory to show us how to read the message.

"A train would get us to San Benedetto via Trieste and Venice. The train to Trieste would leave in two hours. I was sorry to be leaving windswept Pula, even though I knew little of it but its minimarkets. I would have liked to stay in that town magically emptied of its summertime guests for several weeks; in its cafés, I would have worked on my thesis and thought about Kant; I would have climbed its steep streets and strolled along the pier in the harbor. But it was necessary to follow the gelatin-candy trail to Italy, in the search for the murderer of Kristýna's lover. In Pula, I had experienced my much-yearned-for sea as little more than a strip of shiny ribbon, espied at the far end of a street, vanishing behind a wall. Still, I understood that this brief, glittering apparition was one of the languages in which the sea sought to tell me something important about my life, and I was sorry that I hadn't had time to figure it out. After drinking another coffee, Kristýna and I returned to the hotel for our backpacks."

The Story of the Irascible Sculptor

1. Merry Elephant

"The train moved toward the coast and away again. All I got to
see of the sea was a broken, narrow strip. In Trieste, we did no
more than cross the platform to an adjacent track, where our
connecting train was waiting. The train would reach Venice along
a northern route that took it through Udine. Before long, the
tracks moved away from the sea; a little later they were touching
the foothills of the Dolomites. We spent the whole way in an
overcrowded compartment. I looked through the window at
the signs of the stations we passed through. Gorizia Centrale,
Udine, Treviso Centrale. As far as I could tell, Kristýna didn't
look out of the window once. Her only thoughts were for the
message in gelatin. From time to time, to the amazement of our
fellow passengers, she reached into a little plastic package for a
little gummy figure, which she would inspect from all sides before
returning it to the bag. We got off the train at Mestre, where I
took the opportunity to look toward Venice, in the sea at the end
of a long bridge. But when I saw that Kristýna was unhappy at
the prospect of a pause in her quest for the mysterious gummy
candy, I thought it best to go and find the number of the platform from which our connecting train would be leaving.

"It took us less than an hour to reach the little station at San Benedetto. After our train pulled away, we were alone on the platform. We learned from a kiosk vendor that the candy factory was just beyond the town; he left his booth to point past the darkened cornfield beyond the other track to a place that stood out in the rays of the setting sun as a narrow strip. What looked like an alien spaceship in the process of landing, was in fact the factory's metal roof. Although Kristýna wasted no time in asking in broken English for the whereabouts of a taxi, I insisted we go there on foot. So we turned our backs on the unknown town and followed our long shadows toward the factory, cornfields to either side of us, the road like a never-ending wall pierced by many dark holes. The fields extended under the purplish sky to the distant horizon. All that loomed over their dark-gold surface was the roof of the factory hall and, radiant in the evening sun, two ugly campaniles, which no doubt indicated the locations of towns. At last we arrived at a light-colored block of metal—the factory. It was set between fields at a right angle to the road, its side walls brushed by large corn-plant leaves. There was no one around, and apart from the rustle of leaves in the evening breeze, there was no sound. A pink light lay across a parking lot stretching from the factory to the road, with the shadows of three cars at a slant. Evidently, it was long after working hours. The evening sun also lit up a huge plastic figure above the factory entrance—a baby elephant in a red-and-white-striped bobble hat and a short skirt doing a clumsy dance.

"As there was no one on reception, we mounted the staircase to a long, windowless corridor, which we worked our way along, knocking on a few doors and waiting for an answer. No sound came from behind any of them. Finally, we decided to open a door. We stepped through it to a kind of gallery, which sat above the empty factory hall. The hall itself was lit only by the fading, pinkish light, which entered through strip windows above our heads. In these windows, we saw a cloudless evening sky. The pink light lay across white walls and the curves of silent, motionless machines down below. We saw boilers of polished brass, small tubs and large vats, metal casings reminiscent of abstract sculptures, metal boxes equipped with claws, with tubes, belts and narrow gutters variously intertwined above them.

"Then we heard a man's voice calling to us in Italian, the words echoing as they would in church. A young man in a gray uniform was standing on the other side of the gallery. Moments later, he was standing next to us. After we made it clear we didn't understand Italian, he asked us in English, brusquely but politely, what we were doing in the factory. Having apologized for entering the place uninvited, I explained that we were looking for information about one of the factory's products. Kristýna joined in by showing him the open bag and pulling candies from it. The guard continued to behave in a forbidding manner. Indeed, he confiscated our passports and the bag of candies and asked us to follow him to a small office. Here, he placed the passports and candies on the desk before making a telephone call. Things weren't looking good for us. Although I didn't understand what he was saying, judging by the tone, I assumed that he was speaking with the police.

"When the guard picked up the bag of candies, I realized he was speaking about them. Then he picked up the passports and pronounced our names syllable by syllable. I understood the meaning of the words *Repubblica Cecca*. He hung up and again asked us to follow him, his tone still unfriendly. He walked past the many doors of the long corridor quickly and without speaking, occasionally turning around to make sure we were keeping up. I caught up with him as we were turning the fourth corner. I asked him where he was taking us. To the director, he said, and nothing more.

"Beyond the final corner we found ourselves in a corridor glazed along one side. In every window we saw a setting red sun over cornfields—leaves like gilded letters on a dark-green page—that reached all the way to the horizon. Our three shadows moved in the red glow that lay along the facing wall. It seemed to me that the sun was approaching the horizon extremely quickly; by the time we reached the end of the wall of glass, it had plunged behind the dark fields. Having opened the first door beyond the glass wall, the guard bade us enter a windowless space, apparently an antechamber. The room was illuminated harshly, by a fluorescent tube. Without speaking, the guard nodded toward a door on the far side; the door was ajar.

"'Could the director of Merry Elephant be Count Dracula?' I whispered to Kristýna.

"'Maybe his Italian cousin,' she whispered back.

"We were joking, but neither of us saw anything to be amused about. As the guard was standing right behind us, escape wasn't much of an option. Even if by some small chance we did manage to give him the slip, we were sure to get lost in the corridors of the factory. So, as there was nothing else for it, I pushed open the door."

2. In the Director's Office

"We stood on the threshold of a simply furnished room. The wide window in front of us looked like the flag of some state in the Caribbean, with three horizontal stripes—the bottom one black, the middle one orange, the top one dark blue. Before the window was a desk with a glass top and a bent metal frame. A small lighted aluminum lamp stood on the desk. At the desk, in a leather swivel chair, sat a woman of about thirty-five. She was slim, short-haired, in T-shirt and jeans. And she was smiling at us. She told us that her name was Giovanna Sulzer and she was the director of the Merry Elephant company. We sat down in armchairs in front of the desk. We mustn't be cross with the guard for his unfriendly treatment of us, said the director. She had been compelled to increase security at the factory because of several recent cases of industrial espionage, resulting in a loss to the company of a lot of money. The receptionist would be punished for leaving his post. Only after she explained all this did she ask what we wanted of her. Kristýna handed her the bag of candies from Pula. If she could explain the meanings of the four strange shapes of candy, we would be very grateful to her, I said. Naturally, the director wanted to know the reason for our interest. As I was tired of telling the story of the double murder, luminous worms, meditating ants, the Kabbalah, and Pico della Mirandola, I said only that it was possible the shapes of the candies had something to do with a certain mystery Kristýna and I were trying to solve; we had no wish to trouble her and keep her from her work. But she liked mysteries, she said, and she would be glad to hear our story.

"So I ran through the history of our search. But this wasn't enough for the director. For one thing, she wanted to know about Kristýna's and my relationship with Tomáš and Petr. Then she asked for all kinds of details about the deaths of the two brothers and our journey so far. I felt obliged to tell her about our findings in Hungary, Slovenia, and Croatia. As I spoke, I heard cars leaving the lot; otherwise, there was silence all around. I was confused by the level of interest the director was showing in us. Did she take such time and trouble with every guest at the factory outside her working hours? Or were we espionage suspects being subjected to interrogation? Was the director's amiability a mask to fool us by? And besides, industrial espionage at a candy factory—what kind of nonsense was that? Was she afraid that we would steal a recipe for chewing gum, or copy the shape of a chocolate figure?

"Then another possible reason for the director's interest in us occurred to me: that the bag of candies from the store in Pula really did contain something connected to the deaths of two people. Suddenly, there was something suspicious in the director's apparently pacific smile. Now the vertical wrinkle between her eyebrows seemed to cast a restless shadow across her forehead; that dark line gave the upper part of her face, shrouded by the gloom and so unreached by the smile, the expression of a watchful woodland creature. What was Giovanna Sulzer wary of? Why was she asking so many questions? What if she was involved in the murders of the stepbrothers and wished to know how far our investigations had taken us? It was quite possible we had reached a point that represented a danger to the killers of Tomáš and Petr, even though we remained in ignorance of the fact and believed we were still wandering around in the dark. At the realization that we were alone in the factory with a director who could be an accessory to two murders and a guard who apparently obeyed her every word, my nervousness returned. Built into the desk was a panel with many buttons, and I found myself unable to take my eyes off it. At any moment, the director might press one of the buttons, and moments after that, the guard might appear in the doorway with a gun in his hand, or even an ax . . .

"But then Giovanna moved so that the light of the lamp fell across her face at a different angle. Suddenly, the suspicious wrinkle was gone, and with it the features of a wild animal of the woods. In my mind, I chuckled at my foolish imagination. It must have been inspired by the tensions of the journey; besides, an abandoned factory hall was a likely setting for a horror movie. The simplest and most probable explanation for the time the director was taking with us, was her own state of boredom. Making and selling candy probably isn't very exciting work; no doubt our story was more interesting to her than the reports she had to deal with every day. After all, hadn't she told us that she liked mysteries?"

3. Party on the Square

"I felt calm again. As we answered the rest of the director's questions, I waited to hear what she had to say about the strange gummy candy shapes. When at last she got around to it, what we heard was a major disappointment to us. Having quizzed us about our journey and Kristýna's dead lover for almost two hours, Giovanna dealt with the story of the factory's locality in barely fifteen minutes. The only interesting thing to be said about it was that its setting and extras would make a good fit for a Fellini movie.

"The bag of candies we had bought in Pula belonged to series 8112, Giovanna explained. In telling us the story of the series, she started at the very beginning. The first thing we learned was that Merry Elephant was founded in the early twentieth century. At first, it was just a small confectioner's store on the square, with a room in back where the confectioner's wife made chocolate. Fifty years later, it had grown to be the largest factory in the area. For the past twenty-plus years, it had been a multinational concern with its headquarters in Switzerland. It remained the case, however, that all members of the board of the San Benedetto factory were related; board meetings were characterized by quarreling and cohesion, as is often the case with families. Last year, to mark the hundredth anniversary of the company's founding, a gala meeting of the board was held in a *trattoria* on the town square. As it was a hot, humid day, the owner set up a long table on the pavement in front of the restaurant. The members of the board, all in dark suits, and their wives, all in wide-brimmed hats, took their places around this table. I couldn't help but comment to Giovanna that I could scarcely imagine her in such company. She laughed at this. As a Swiss from Locarno who had arrived in the town just three years ago, by appointment of the CEO in Bern, there was much about San Benedetto that was strange to her, she said.

"'A countryman of mine was at the party, too,' Giovanna continued. 'A deputy of the company's Swiss owner. Because he was sitting opposite me, I saw that he kept looking at the clock on the tower of the town hall, obviously counting the minutes until he could go back to this hotel . . . The members of the board included a certain Rizzo, a fifty-year-old gentleman with a bit of a belly. A widower, he had recently married again. His new wife was twenty years his junior, from Rome, and her manner of dress caused quite a stir on the San Benedetto promenade. She claimed to be an artist, although no one was quite sure what she did. Having discovered some Bohemian tendencies of his own, Rizzo had taken to wearing orange socks and neckties which reproduced Andy Warhol's portrait of Marilyn Monroe. That afternoon, Rizzo said very little. Toward evening, the wind got up. Newspapers were blown across the square; above our heads, wooden shutters banged; the white tablecloths lifted at the edges, and more than one woman at the table had her hat blown from her head, sending her husband on a chase across the pavement. It seemed that a storm was on the way and the party would have to end early. In a moment of boldness, Rizzo stood up to make a surprising announcement. How about refreshing the production of little gelatin figures with some new designs? he suggested. When his cousins and uncles asked how this should be done, he said it would be easiest to commission a young, avant-garde designer to come up with at least one series.'

"'For a moment, we all stared at Rizzo in amazement. Then the knowledge sunk in that Rizzo's wife was behind his little speech. The other members of the board tried to rebuff Rizzo's proposal by stating that none of them knew any young, avant-garde artists. All no doubt feared that the artist in question was Rizzo's wife. Fortunately, Rizzo went on to explain that his wife knew a certain excellent sculptor from Rome. Mrs. Rizzo, who was sitting next to her husband, hadn't said a word till then. Now she explained that were she to ask him, the sculptor may consent to do the job. At that point, everyone assumed that Mrs. Rizzo was promoting a lover of hers who was struggling to find work.'

"'It's unlikely the deputy from the head office in Bern had much truck with the idea at first. But the sight of the unhappy Rizzo dabbing at his bald head with a handkerchief, having done all in his power to perform the task set by his wife, and the thought of what awaited Rizzo at home if the proposal failed, roused the deputy's pity. So he said, "Very well, let's give it a try." It seemed that after many years he had gotten the urge to do a good deed; besides, if it came to it, the international concern could easily absorb the failure of one series of candies. Rizzo's relief was touching to see, his delight infectious. The party proper started only after the exchange I've just described. Rizzo was happy with his success, his wife was happy to have promoted her sculptor, the envoy from Bern was glad to have done a good deed at no cost to himself, the others were happy to see how happy Rizzo was. So even though the wind got ever stronger, the tablecloths fluttered ever more wildly, and the newspapers reached the height of the church belfry as they cir-cled the square, more and more bottles of wine were ordered. Then at last the rain came down in a tide, and we fled for our homes.'"

4. Sufferings of a Young Artist

"'The young, avant-garde sculptor arrived from Rome a few days later. His name was Rossi, or Rossini. Maybe Rossellini. From the very beginning, a frown never left his face. He wanted everyone to know that the indignity of candy design was making him suffer, and what an honor it was for our company that he condescended to work for us. After he had been here ten days, the head of the art department and I went to the studio in the factory Rossi had been given the use of. He only had four models ready . . .' Giovanna picked up our bag of candies, tipped the contents onto the desk, rummaged through them, and picked out the ones made from Rossi's designs. 'I remember them well: this boat with the big flower, the shell with the eye, the dagger with the crocodile hilt . . . and this odd shape.' The director chuckled. 'I can still see the sour look on the face of the head of the art department as he picked up Rossi's models and inspected them from all sides, clueless as to what they were supposed to represent. When I asked Rossi to explain, he instructed us that the essence of art lay in the creator's combination of two things in and of themselves banal—like a shell and an eye, or a boat and a flower—which in coming together kindled a magical aura. I didn't tell him that there wasn't much art in candy production, nor that I saw no aura of magic around his designs. But I did ask him about the magical coming-together represented by the loaf-type thing. This question Rossi rewarded with his second lesson. At rare moments, he explained, the artist yields to automatic whispers urging him to create shapes unknown in the natural world. At this point, I realized that Rossi was crazy. I left him alone to complete his series for the sake of poor Rizzo, and because he was doing so with Bern's blessing.'

"'The head of our art department has excellent manners. He told Rossi that although his designs were interesting, he himself believed that animal designs were more suitable. At this, Rossi pulled a horrible face. Art could be made anywhere, he declared, even at a candy factory. Then he added, in a tone more forceful still, that he would never stoop so low as to make teddies and bunnies. At this, the patience of the head of the art department finally snapped. He made a few heavily ironic comments about Rossi's creations. Rossi made a move toward him. At first, I was worried that the sculptor intended to strangle his antagonist. In the end, however, he did no more than yell that he was done with whoring himself in this bourgeois backwater in the service of people who knew nothing about art. Then he stormed out of the studio, leaving his series unfinished. There followed a scene with the Rizzos that was heard right across the square. Then the sculptor made his way to the train station and returned to Rome.'

"'Everyone at the factory breathed a sigh of relief. I asked one of our artists to create new models for series 8112. But Rossi had made us all so tense and confused that when the series went into production, the designs he left behind were included. By the time we realized this had happened, over a thousand packages had been sent to stores. That's how the most bizarre candy series ever produced in Italy came into being . . . But it was no big problem: Adults don't tend to look at the shapes of candies they buy, and children look but don't think too deeply about them. You may be the only ones who noticed anything strange about those candies . . .' What happened next? I asked. The director shrugged. 'Nothing happened after that,' she said. 'Well, Rizzo got divorced, and before long he was again wearing black socks and neckties. We never heard another word about Rossi, or Rossini, or whatever his name was.'

"It seemed that we were on the wrong track again. It was highly improbable that Rossi's shell/eye had anything in common with *Damp Walls*. And what could the candies from Pula have to do with the deaths of Tomáš and Petr, the undersea lettering, or Pico della Mirandola? Even so, I asked the director if she knew Rossi's address in Rome. She didn't, but she remembered that when they were first introduced, he had given her a card of invitation to the opening of an exhibition of his, held at a gallery in the district of Rome called Trastevere. She had thrown away the invitation card long ago, of course, and she couldn't remember the name of the gallery. I insisted that she take down my cellphone number. Should she find out something about Rossi, she would call me, she promised.

"As we returned along the road between dark fields and under a starry sky, neither of us spoke. As no car passed us, we could only assume that the director had stayed on at the factory. The trail to Rome was so faint that not even Kristýna dared propose we go search for Rossi or Rossini in the capital. Once again, it seemed that our investigations were over, and we were left with no option but a return to Prague. Neither of us could get used to the idea of our pilgrimage ending here, on this road between fields. All the way back to the San Benedetto train station, we were expecting a phone to ring, as it had in Ljubljana—with words from Zoltán, the marine biologist, or the director of Merry Elephant that would send us farther on our journey. Kristýna even turned on her display to check the strength of the signal. But the only sounds we heard were the rustling of corn leaves and the buzzing of insects of the night. The funny thing was, we both really wanted to go to Rome but were embarrassed to admit as much to the other. Kristýna wanted to go on with her journey because she couldn't entirely discount the possibility that the similarity between Rossi's shell/eye and the Lygdian symbol was no coincidence, and she refused to give up on this last, probably insignificant, maybe even ridiculous hope. As for me, I wished to go to Rome because the moment I heard the director of Merry Elephant pronounce the English word 'Rome,' I had an image of sunlit squares, and I could smell hot walls . . ."

5. Night in San Benedetto

"When we made the decision to spend the night in the small hotel opposite the train station, we still hadn't discussed what we would do the next day. The room was on the second floor. Part of the neon lettering above the station entrance was visible from the window; its green light fell across the wide double bed. We didn't even turn on the lights. Kristýna darted into the bathroom to change for bed. Moments later she was under the duvet with her eyes closed, having bade me good night. I lay on the bed with my back against the headboard, looking down at her, watching the play of green and white station lights on her face, thinking about our strange journey. For me, its aim had been changing since Budapest. Meanwhile, Kristýna had been moving away from me; by Pula, she was little more than a shadow companion on my pilgrimage, which was leading forever southward. Now, when it seemed that our journey was ending, Kristýna's body had reemerged; like a drawing hitherto concealed, its relief standing out beneath the duvet in a tangle of white folds. It seemed as if the light on the duvet was a faint remnant of a glow from the sleeping body. I reached for the glowing body, but I was afraid to touch it: To do so, I would have to push through all the torn drapery of the past it was caught up in, and even then I would find it cold and indifferent.

"I had pangs of conscience for my betrayal of Kristýna. I had stayed at her side, and I wouldn't have left her, but my journey wasn't hers. Although I hadn't stepped away from her for a moment, and apparently she was the one who determined where we went, I was traveling elsewhere. It was clear to me now that to find a solution to the mystery of Tomáš Kantor's death was never the main purpose of my journey. So why did I leave Prague for Bratislava? Perhaps because I believed I would find something there that would free Kristýna from the spell of her dead lover, the vampire; I had gone on with the journey because I had wanted to be near her. Perhaps because of the night and day trains, which I have loved and dreamed of since I was small. Whatever the case may be, I had listened more and more to the soft whisperings of cities, first heard on Bratislava's Hviezdoslav Square. After a while, I knew that all city voices whisper of the same things—the south and the sea. In cities, the south called to me and promised me something—I knew not what; I could read the whisperings of the cities as little as I could read the worm and candy rebuses Kristýna and I had encountered on our journey. As to what was luring me ever farther south, I had no explanation: The ideas that came to me were contradictory and opposing. At times, I had the feeling I was attracted by a bright light that sharpened and fixed the contours of things, at others that I yearned for a heat in which all shapes melded in a single, formless mush. Sometimes, the image I held of the south was a silhouette of rock in sharp outline against the sky; sometimes, it was of a waste dump on the edge of a seaside village, stinking with decay and ridden with flies. Apparently, I was attracted by recognition and forgetting and sleep, victory, and defeat. The strange thing was, all these images and notions gave me pleasure.

"It seemed to me, too, that at many moments in my life I had turned my face southward, not knowing that I did so. My journey hadn't begun four days earlier at Prague's Main Train Station, for I had been on it since way back when. My ways to school and the university library, my walks about Prague, and my nighttime wanderings from bar to bar were all part of it. The south had always been the vanishing point for my restlessness. The thread of my desire was beginning to untangle. I regretted how long it had taken me to reach this point, yet I wondered if the south I was headed for had been born out of the delays.

"But I had continued to flounder like a sleepwalker, even on my journey with Kristýna. Where had the stories I had heard in strangers' apartments, the magazine photographs, the gummy candies from the out-of-the-way store brought me? To San Benedetto. I didn't know where I was going; nor did I know what was feeding my desire for Kristýna. In Prague, I had thought her attraction was in the sad music made by the brush of her gestures against things. On the train to Bratislava, I had thought myself attracted by the masks that appeared in her face. Now, in San Benedetto, I wondered if what attracted me most was Tomáš's void. If so, this void had penetrated her being, and it was out of this void that the gestures and ghostly figures that dwelt in her body were born. The emptiness had seeped all the way to her fingertips, from which it trickled like a delightful, exciting balm . . .

"San Benedetto was *en route* from Venice to Rome. There were many trains, all of which set the glasses on the nightstand tinkling, hardly any of which stopped at San Benedetto Station. Again I asked myself if solving the mystery of Tomáš's death was the true aim of Kristýna's journey. Perhaps her destination was as unknown to her as mine was to me; perhaps we were both sleepwalkers, and as such unknowing conspirators. Maybe we were so obsessed with the idea of decrypting the messages we found on our journey that we had overlooked the greatest cipher of them all—the unfinished hieroglyph inscribed on the map of Europe. For now, I had no sense of the final shape of this enormous character, nor of its meaning. But that night in San Benedetto, I realized the great calligrapher wasn't done yet, that he was still wielding his brush. So I decided we should go on—if need be, to that crazy Rossi in Trastevere . . .

"When they learned who their daughter had fallen in love with, Kristýna's parents were horrified. They hated Tomáš from the first moment. Kristýna had told me several times that her parents were convinced Tomáš had turned her into a mess. She thought this was funny. They liked me very much, however. In their view, a young man who worked at a university was worthy of respect, and so the right type for their daughter. They made this plain to Kristýna—the worst thing they could have done, of course. Now, I thought their idea of a good girl brought to ruin by an irresponsible artist was even more wrong than I had thought at first: I couldn't believe that on meeting Tomáš, Kristýna had become a completely different person; I couldn't believe that Tomáš had led her astray by teaching her to use the drug of emptiness, and to delight in the chimeras it summoned up. Now, I was almost certain that the voices she heard in Tomáš's book had simply woken figures that had long been asleep in her.

"What's more, it seemed to me now that Kristýna's being was darker still than Tomáš's—a conclusion that would have appalled her parents. Kristýna had told me that before she got to know Tomáš, her life had been like most other girls'. I believed this—although such a truth meant nothing at all. Kristýna admired Tomáš because she saw him as a gladiator who looked phantoms in the face and had the courage to fight them. But these fights took place within the confines of literature; the monsters that emerged from the void were confined to a small enclosure, which they couldn't escape. Kristýna's phantoms—known to her thanks to Tomáš—weren't caged: They occupied the entire territory of her life, and they transformed it. Kristýna had no place to hide from them; women don't build such refuges . . .

"A train passing through the station sounded its horn. Kristýna opened her eyes and looked at me. 'We're going to Rome,' I said. She smiled and took my hand. Moments later, she was asleep again, her fingers free of mine."

The Story of Entoptic Images, Monsters of the Cosmos, and Hot Walls

1. Sorrow in Trastevere

"We left San Benedetto just before daybreak, in a compartment to ourselves. We watched the Po Valley, in the dirty colors of dawn, slowly pass the window. Over the Tuscan hills, the sun began to warm up; before long, it was flooding the compartment and doing its magic with Kristýna's red hair. As we entered Lazio, it was high above the horizon. The glowing landscape showed very little trace of the coming fall. Shortly before noon, the train pulled in at Rome's Termini Station. Kristýna and I had agreed to find accommodation in Trastevere itself, to make our search for the gallery with Rossi's exhibition easier.

"We traveled to Trastevere by taxi. The driver recommended a pension on a small square filled with tables and chairs in front of *trattorie* and cafés, with a little space in the middle occupied by a stone fountain. Nearly all tables were taken by lunching customers. We were given a corner room under the roof, with a view from the balcony of the square and from the window of a narrow street. Having discarded our backpacks, we began our search for Rossi. We walked along side streets bathed in shadow, emerging suddenly into sunlit squares. Several times we walked up and down the broad, busy *Via Trastevere*, only to reimmerse ourselves in the quiet of the empty streets. Several times a side street brought us to the Tiber embankment, forcing us to retrace our steps.

"We came across quite a few small galleries, but no one knew of a sculptor called Rossi, Rossini, or Rossellini. Kristýna's pace slowed as she became ever more dejected. It was as though all the sludge acquired on our journey—a journey born of her inability to accept Tomáš's death—had flowed into these streets, and she was having to push her way through it. I assumed she now realized the meaninglessness of our search for a man whose name we didn't know, and who probably had nothing at all to do with the mysteries we were chasing. Several times when she looked at me, I thought she was about to say, 'Let's pack it in, it's pointless.' But perhaps she didn't wish our journey to end in a state of helplessness in the middle of street in a city we had come to because of a gummy candy . . .

"I, too, was feeling pretty low. I had the feeling the dead Tomáš Kantor was walking alongside, sneering at us. In vain, I tried to recall the joy in the journey I had felt in Pula. I looked up and allowed my gaze to wander over the facades. Here was everything I had been looking forward to, and more: stone portals with house numbers chiseled in, sun-faded plasterwork in many colors, tall wooden shutters, small balconies with metal grilles, sharp-edged shadows produced by cornices, laundry on lines stretching between neighboring buildings (a common sight in Naples, but not so much here). But it was no good: It felt as though I was looking at characters of a script unknown to me; at a text unfolding mechanically before me, on an endless scroll that lacked any apparent meaning. And I thought of worse things that might have happened but hadn't: I realized that every time I was told by a gallery assistant that they didn't know of a Rossi, I felt relief. The prospect of our journey reaching its climax in conversation with an arrogant sculptor was a torment to me. What could he tell us, anyway? That the shell with the eye was a vision produced by his genius? There was little doubt he would tell us that he had never heard of Tomáš Kantor, his novel, or the Lygds.

"Yes, it was our good luck that no one knew Rossi: In the evening, we made a discovery we hadn't reckoned with. Walking along *Via Trastevere*, we came to a movie theater. Kristýna stopped and pointed at a poster in the display case. It showed some Buddhist monks with shaven heads in front of a snow-covered stone building, presumably a temple, against a backdrop of mountains. In dark letters across the lower half of the poster ran the movie's title: *The Larva*. At first, I saw nothing to interest me in the poster. Then it dawned on me that this was the film co-created by Petr Quas. The box-office attendant informed us that *The Larva* wasn't showing at this theater until the day after next, but there was a screening of it that very evening at a cinema on the outskirts of the city. Of course, it was highly unlikely that the film would turn up any explanation of the deaths of Tomáš and Petr. Still, I told myself, even this was better than the mysterious Rossi; and I think Kristýna had the same thought. Besides, I was truly curious about the movie, as I couldn't imagine an American SF thriller featuring the character of Czech anatomist and physiologist Jan Evangelista Purkyně."

2. Images under Eyelids

"We rode a bus for a long time, alighting at a housing project that looked like a 1950s build. The sun was setting; the angular black shapes of the high-rise apartment buildings, with many dozen windows lit, were set against a darkening sky. Some of the windows had women leaning from them, calling to children playing on the sidewalk, and the children were shouting back. Kitchen fragrances mingled with the smell of hot asphalt. The cinema we were looking for turned out to be an open-air theater between rows of buildings. Empty chairs were strewn across the asphalt in front of a large screen. We were the first members of the audience to arrive. We sat down in the middle; eventually, we were joined by about ten others.

"The movie was in the original English with Italian subtitles. The opening scene was in a university lecture hall filled with keen young men in frock coats; all wore long sideburns and a high collar over a carefully tied cravat. The camera moved slowly over the heads of the students to settle on the lecturer, a middle-aged man dressed in the same manner as the students. He was standing on a platform, at a stand to which a thin sheet of paper was attached. On the sheet was a drawing of some kind; from a distance, it was impossible to tell what of. Plainly, the lecturer was Jan Evangelista Purkyně: Although the actor playing him wasn't a good likeness, his hairdo was an exact copy of the one I knew from Purkyně's portrait. Music started up (I recognized motifs from Chopin and Schubert), and the words 'BRESLAU 1842' appeared on the screen in large letters. The closer the camera came to the lecturer, the quieter the music became; meanwhile, Purkyně's voice became stronger and more distinct. The camera stopped at the point where the screen was filled with the upper half of the scientist's body and the sheet of paper. Now it was clear that the drawing was just a jumble of lines; had the movie been set at a different time, I would have taken it for modern art.

"The topic of the lecture turned out to be a strange one: Purkyně was talking about the classification of images we see on the insides of our eyelids when our eyes are closed. He had found a certain regularity among them allowing their classification in different groups, as one would classify minerals. Kristýna looked at me questioningly. I leaned close to her and told her in a whisper what the movie was about, explaining that I had read somewhere that during his stay in Breslau, Purkyně really had studied visual percepts known as entoptic images, and that in so doing he had obviously been influenced by the Romantic search for original forms as found by Ernst Chladni in magnetized iron filings, Goethe in a single form from which different parts of plants evolved, and Novalis in the chance designs made by grooves in rock and shapes of clouds.

"Unfortunately, I missed much of Purkyně's lecture, as his words were frequently drowned out by the comings and goings of cars and buses, and the calls of women and cries of children from the apartment blocks. Indeed, the noise would persist throughout the show. The next scene is set in a small, light-filled room simply furnished in Biedermeier style. Purkyně is sitting at a desk with thin, curved legs. On the desk are portraits of Purkyně's wife and a small daughter, both of whom died in Breslau several years earlier during a cholera epidemic, and two books, their titles written in *Schwabacher* script. One book is a copy of Goethe's *Farbenlehre*. On the front cover of the other are the words: *Johann Purkinje, Beiträge zur Kenntnis des Sehens in subjektiver Hinsicht, Prag 1819.* The scientist is looking at thin sheets of paper with drawings of entoptic images on them. On the floor, his two young sons are playing, supervised by a governess. Suddenly, Purkyně pauses in his perusal; apparently, something has caught his attention and disturbed him. Eerie music starts up—like in Jaws when the shark is approaching. Purkyně stands up and carries the drawings over to the window; then he lifts one sheet after another and studies it against the light. As an expression of horror breaks across his face, his lips move in an inaudible utterance. The drawings fall from his hand. The light sheets of paper are borne upward, then

downward on a draft, in a slow, sweeping movement. One of
the sheets reaches one of the boys on the floor, coming to rest
on top of the painting he is working on (presumably, he is
future artist Karel Purkyně). The quiet, expectant music takes
on grim notes of horror. The drawing that now fills the screen
is composed of smudges and haphazard lines. Over this, the
title 'THE LARVA' appears.

3. Judith Greenfield

"The camera returns to the scientist's face, on which the expression of horror has been replaced by one of deep contemplation.
Purkyně is standing motionless, his gaze wandering above the
steep roofs of the houses of Breslau. The camera eye looks up
slowly, along gray strips of smoke rising from the chimneys. For
a few moments, the screen is filled with nothing but clouds, the
shapes of which remind us of the under-eyelid images Purkyně
was showing to his students. The somber music gives way to a
tone of sorrow and resignation. A new, initially indeterminate
murmur mingles with the melody. Then a car horn sounds, and
the murmur gradually resolves itself into individual sounds in a
large, modern-day city. We hear the roar of engines, the screeching of brakes, the blaring of horns, the calls of news vendors.
The camera eye looks down. Along the bottom edge of the
screen, the tops of skyscrapers come slowly into view. The camera slides along vertical rows of windows that go on for a long
time. The words 'MANHATTAN 2006' appear on the screen.
The camera stops just above the roadway of a busy street. The
sidewalks are crowded with people in a hurry. At the crosswalks,
the lights turn from red to green, and back again; cars pull up
and away in a stop-start stream. The movie's opening credits
begin to roll. I wait for the names of the creators of the original

idea—there are three of them, including Petr Quas. After the last credit, the name of the director, the camera again moves upward, along a facade, before picking out a large window and going through it into the building.

"Again, we find ourselves in a lecture hall. The lecturer is a young woman scientist in a gray skirt suit and large horn-rimmed glasses, her hair combed smooth into a chignon. Her appearance is obviously intended to express her devotion to her research and her indifference to life's more commonplace plea-sures (although the visagiste hasn't forgotten to apply perfect make-up to the actress's face and eyes, I notice). The scientist inserts a portrait of Purkyně into an epidiascope, and the image is projected onto a large screen. She talks of Purkyně's research in the field of entoptic images, before informing her students that she has repeated this research. She returns to the epidiascope to place in it a transparent film bearing images that look like those we know from Breslau. The lecture ends, and the students leave the lecture hall. As the scientist is folding away the film, she is approached by a young man, obviously a faculty colleague, who makes a good-natured joke: She is the last person at the univer-sity who projects images by means of an epidiascope instead of a computer, he says. As the scientist and the young man converse, an older man with long, gray hair stands a short distance from them, his head down. After the young man leaves, the older man approaches the scientist. When he looks up, we see that his character is played by David Carradine. In a soft, monotonous, sorrowful voice, he asks the scientist to abandon her research of entoptic images; were she to continue, he warns, she might do harm to many people. Obviously thinking he's not right in the head, the scientist refuses to speak with him. She notices a tattoo on the stranger's wrist: an oval-shaped depiction of a fibrous form that looks like a silkworm cocoon.

"In the next scene, the scientist is in her apartment, sitting by an open window that overlooks Central Park. She is going through the transparent films with the images. Like Purkyně, she is struck by something she sees in them. The mysterious music heard in the Breslau apartment is reprised. In a state of agitation, the scientist orders the films in a neat pile. Then she walks to the window and holds the folder containing the films against it. The sun, which is high above the wall of skyscrapers lining the south side of Central Park, shines through it. As we expect, her face registers dismay. 'Impossible!' she whispers. The camera moves closer to the films, but the shot ends before the audience can catch sight of what is on them.

"The next shot shows the same room, at night. The scene is illuminated only by a computer screen, in front of which the scientist is sitting in a fetching nightshirt. The screen is reflected in her glasses. Her fingers are racing about the keyboard without pause. At the window, long purple drapes flutter in the breeze, a stronger gust occasionally blowing them open to show a dark sky above skyscrapers and, much farther down, lamps lighting the paths and trees of Central Park. A silence disturbed only by the tapping of the keys (and, of course, the sounds of a Rome housing estate) is shattered by the ring of a telephone. The scientist jumps, looks at her watch in surprise, then lifts the handset. She hears a gloom-laden voice; the audience recognizes David Carradine. Again, the mystery man asks the scientist to abandon her interest in visual percepts, and above all not to publish anything about her findings; he alludes to an unimaginable threat to humankind. The scientist hangs up as he is still speaking and goes on with her writing: science is the most important thing in her life, and no indeterminate threat is going to deter her from her research.

"In the next scene, the scientist, in a white-red skirt suit, is standing before her superior. He is the dean of the faculty, and this is his office. The dean is pacing the room in a state of agitation, huffing and puffing, waving a magazine about, shouting that the scientist has besmirched the good name of the university. We learn that the scientist is Dr. Judith Greenfield, and that she teaches Physiology at the Faculty of Natural Sciences. The dean opens the magazine and reads aloud with ironic emphasis one of the passages that irks him most. 'The investigation into spots on the retina projected onto the undersides of the eyelids when the eyes are closed, one of the so-called entoptic phenomena, meaning a visual percept originating in the body, produced surprising results. When we lay a longer series of drawings of entoptic images, or visual percepts, made on transparent films one on top of another, we see that spots on one image complement spots on other images in the pile, as if the patterns were composed of fragments of a single image. Curiously, the image that emerges in this way is figurative; it depicts a creature unknown to us. Although I am aware that emotion has no place in science, I cannot but admit that this creature is the most frightening thing I have ever seen . . .'

"The scientist wishes to make an objection, but the dean won't let her speak. It is of no interest to him whether Dr. Greenfield was confused by a chance occurrence (people can see all kinds of things in nature's marks), the whole thing is a silly prank on her part, or she has fallen victim to an act of mystification, he says. He is about to back up his words with another outrageous quotation from the article when his gaze falls on an accompanying picture. It shows a monster whose image is said to be diffused across all human retinas. Obviously, the picture has attracted the dean's undivided attention for the first time. We see the anger in his face turn to a mix of horror and disgust. He drops the magazine on the desk and growls at Greenfield that in view of her previous work he will keep her on at the university, provided nothing of the sort ever happens again. Then he waves her out of his office. As soon as he is alone, he returns to the magazine, picks it up gingerly, and looks again at the spot picture of the monster . . ."

4. Monastery in the Himalayas

"The scientist is at home, again sitting at her computer. It is evening: The trees of Central Park cast long shadows on the grass. Having scanned the drawings of the visual percepts, Greenfield is now stacking them up on her computer screen. As a monstrous face emerges from the spots, we see excitement and fear in Greenfield's expression. This emergence begins with the eyes, which are fixed on Greenfield. Before the features can take on more definite form, however, the telephone rings. (At no point in the movie does the audience get a clear view of the monster; its face and body are always just glimpsed, making them all the more terrifying.)

"Again, the caller is David Carradine. In a voice even more sorrowful than before, he says, 'You should have done as I said. This is just the beginning.' The scientist doesn't wish to speak with the stranger this time, either; she tells him in no uncertain terms to quit bothering her. Then she hangs up and goes back to her computer. A few seconds later, the phone rings again. In common with every other movie character in this situation, Greenfield assumes that the previous caller is calling back. She picks up and speaks angrily into the handset: 'I asked you to quit calling me . . .' It is a different caller, of course. In a voice that betrays his confusion, a young man explains that he has read her article and requests a meeting with her as a matter of urgency. When Greenfield asks why, the young man hesitates before telling her that he, too, has seen the terrible creature in the spots . . .

"Greenfield meets the young man on a bench in Washington

Square. His name is Terence Grady, and he is a traveler-adventurer with a taste for mountain-climbing. Three years ago, he explains to Greenfield, on a solo expedition to Nepal he was caught out by a snowstorm in the Himalayas. Having fought his way through it, he was at the point of exhaustion when the gates of a Buddhist monastery appeared before him. As he is telling the story, the sounds of automobiles give way to the howling of wind. The pigeons on the pavement of the square fade out, and the picture resolves itself into the scene of a severe blizzard, in which a gray portal can just be made out. A snow-laden figure stumbles up to the building, pounds on the gate with his fists, then collapses into the snow. The gate opens to reveal monks in orange robes. The monks pull the exhausted traveler over the threshold.

"Before the storm ends, Grady spends several nights at the monastery. Each of the silent monks has a picture of a cocoon tattooed on his wrist. Things happen at the monastery that Grady fails to understand, and which frighten him greatly. At night, he is sometimes woken by a cry of terror that echoes through the building. Several times, he witnesses one of the monks in the throes of what appears to be an epileptic fit; while this is going on, the others hold the monk down and pour some kind of drink into his mouth, after which he calms down and eventually falls into a long sleep. One morning, another of the monks is found hanged in his cell. All walls of the prayer hall are covered with a sacred fresco filled with images of gods and bodhisattvas. One part of the fresco is always concealed behind a heavy curtain fringed along its lower end with gold thread. The monks do not allow Grady to draw aside this curtain. The figures on the fresco look toward the place hidden by the curtain with a mixture of horror and disgust; their expression fills Grady with anxiety and confusion. What kind of horror can this be that even Enlightenment and the gods cannot resist it?

One night, Grady creeps from his cell to the prayer hall, the walls of which are aglow with the light of dozens of candles placed along the floor. He lifts the curtain. In the flickering candlelight, he sees a picture of a monster (the movie's audience see only a dim outline of a very strange creature). No sooner has Grady set eyes on the painting than he knows he will never forget it. Before his meeting with Greenfield, he has never spoken of the monster on the fresco with anyone. Although the entoptical-image picture that accompanies Greenfield's article is far blurrier in outline than the fresco at the monastery in Nepal, Grady is in no doubt that it depicts the same monster.

"The scene returns to the bench and pigeons on Washington Square. 'No words can express my feeling when looking at that fresco,' Grady tells the scientist. 'It was unlike any other feeling I know. It was barely human . . . Notions of horror and disgust don't get close to explaining all that it contained. I sensed in it some kind of consciousness of the awakening of some terrible evil . . . But the most horrifying thing about it was . . .' Grady falls silent. Maybe he can't find the right word; maybe some strange sense of shame is preventing him from using it.

"'It was joy in all the horror—an echo of an immense, long-forgotten, evil delight.' Judith Greenfield has finished his sentence for him.

"'And also impatience—a yearning for the nascent horror, for it to arrive as soon as possible . . .' As he spoke these words, Grady's voice was little more than a whisper. Don't worry, I'll try to keep it brief," said Martin, having seen me sneak a look at my watch. "As we might expect, Grady and Greenfield go out together to the snowy landscapes of Nepal, where they search for the mysterious monastery. The scientist has exchanged her skirt suit for a down jacket and baggy pants with lots of pockets. Grady and Greenfield fall in love, of course. On their journey, mysterious masked men make several unsuccessful attempts on their lives. In the end, high in the mountains, they reach the monastery unharmed. But the monks refuse to tell them anything about the fresco. All they will say is that it relates to a secret that must never be told, because if it were to be divulged, it would bring great suffering to humankind. Even now, the audience doesn't get a clear sight of the monster. During the movie, the curtain before the fresco is lifted several times, but on each occasion the fresco appears fleetingly, in the weak, flickering candlelight. Determined to get to the bottom of the mystery, the scientist and the adventurer remain at the monastery for several months. At the end of this period, they are summoned by the superior, who tells them that they have earned the right to know the great secret of the Nepalese brotherhood. He is prepared to tell it to them—provided they promise to tell it to no one else, as long as they live."

5. What the Monastery Superior Said

"The superior tells them a story about the origin of life on Earth. Great, bloodthirsty monsters roam the universe, fighting with and eating one another. When they reproduce, the fertilized female seeks out a suitable planet on which to lay her single egg. So it happened that millions of years ago such an egg was laid on Earth. Out of this egg, terrestrial life was born: All living organisms on Earth are in fact the scattered cells of a single, ever-growing, ever-evolving life form that feeds itself by the eating of one cell by another. The life form is still at the larval stage, but this stage is due to end within the next few thousand years—at which point the larva will pupate. When it does, all animal and plant organisms will develop white, fibrous runners; before long, everything living will be overgrown with these runners, forming one huge chrysalis; this white tissue will come to cover the whole planet. Over several hundred years, the continuing connection and transformation of all organisms inside the white chrysalis will bring about the birth of an adult life form. On that day, the monster will claw its way out of its hard cocoon, leaving behind a dead planet comprising remains of rock, desert, and products of humanity its juices have failed to erode, plus the torn white cocoon. Then it will set off into space, on the hunt. Stored on the retinas of all living beings are traces of the animal we are. We see these traces when we close our eyes. By putting all the small fragments together, we can compose a full image of the animal. The sight of the monster provokes such horror and disgust in us because we see ourselves in it; it is as though we are looking at a self-portrait—and we know this to be so, hence our delight.

"Judith and Terence are stock-still as they listen to the monastery superior's story. The top of a snow-covered mountain is visible through the window. Not for a moment do they doubt the truth of the story they are hearing. Indeed, they realize that they already know it—that part of their mind is a dark memory, containing recollections of the mother and a long childhood in prehistoric seas, primeval forest, and glaciers; they realize, too, that this childhood is not yet over. The moment they first saw the cosmic monster—Judith in the under-eyelid images, Terence on the monastery wall—each knew that they were looking at their own self; that they were seeing their true face for the very first time, although they weren't yet able to admit it. They ask the superior where he knows the story of the monster from. They aren't in the least surprised when he tells them that awareness of the cosmic monster is contained whole and intact in each of his temporarily scattered cells; indeed, it lies at the bottom of every consciousness. Hence it is possible to reach understanding of the true essence of humanity and all life on Earth through deep meditation, by descending into one's own mind. Humanity must be spared the terrible knowledge of what it is and what is the meaning of its existence, he says. If people were to discover that the entire history of humanity has but a single aim—to deliver it to a point where it will be able to pupate, grow as one under a great white blanket, and transform into a vile, bloodthirsty monster—they would be plunged into despair and insanity. Ditto if they were to discover that the true significance of the origin of all the greatest works of art, science, and philosophy is to refine the senses, intuition, and intellect for the brain of a killer monster, and that the love and care of a parent, lover, or other loved one are mere manifestations of the cohesiveness of that monster's scattered cells.

"Terence and Judith ask if there is any way of preventing the coming of the monster. 'But the monster is not coming,' replies the superior, in a soft voice. 'It is already here.' So they ask if it is possible to prevent its final transformation, and the coming of its truest form. The superior says there is only one way by which this could be achieved: the suicide of all humanity combined with the destruction of all that is living on the planet. If one living organism were to survive, the birth of the monster would be delayed by a few billion years, but it would still happen. And even if Earth's monster was denied, the universe would not be rid of the terrible inhabitants that turn it into a place of shame. For this to happen, before its voluntary death, humanity would need to send a message deep into space for all other civilizations of the universe, and this message would need to convince all these civilizations to self-destruct. Only after full destruction would the universe be a place of purity, with innocent stars roaming its skies undisturbed, until its dying day. The superior explains that a faction at the monastery favors the full-destruction solution, but that he himself thinks it is impossible to realize; in his view, it is best to keep people in ignorance so as to minimize their suffering. 'But maybe this attitude is a manifestation of the monster's desire for survival, at work at the bottom of my mind,' he adds quietly.

"'What is one who knows the secret supposed to do?' asks Judith.

"'Suicide is a great temptation,' answers the superior. 'But the voluntary death of one person—one cell of the great larva—is meaningless. There is one path that can protect us from madness and diminish our suffering, although it is a long way from victory and liberation. It tells us to learn to live at odds with our life and its meaning. The very point of the Buddha's teachings, known to but a few initiates, is that we should break free from the life of the monster we are; that the least we can do is identify with the life of stones, water, clouds, and silent stars, even though we can no longer join it. But this path is no guarantee of anything, either. As you have seen yourselves, there are cases of insanity and suicide here at the monastery, too. It may even be that the teaching of detachment is nothing more than a trick issuing from the genes of the monster, the point of which is to cultivate a resistance in humankind to knowledge of its true nature . . .'

"Greenfield and Grady promise the superior that they will reveal to no one the secret they have learned in the monastery. Both have the sign of the cocoon tattooed on a wrist by the monks. Although they return to New York as lovers, they soon go their separate ways: Their love has failed to survive the realization that their feelings are merely calls from the cells of a vile monster that wishes to join them together."

6. Cocoon

"The next scene is in the common room of a luxury rest home for the elderly. Old people sit watching TV, or playing checkers;

some are dozing, or just sitting, their gaze blank. A nurse goes from one resident to the next with a medicine trolley. The words 'VERMONT 2057' appear on the screen. As one of the old women reaches for her medicine, the sleeve of her gown slips back to reveal a tattoo on the wrinkled skin of her wrist; it is a picture of a cocoon. Although the meticulous visagiste has covered the woman's face in wrinkles, we see that Judith Greenfield is played by the same actor as before. Judith puts a tablet in her mouth and swallows. Then she struggles to her feet and walks out onto a sunlit terrace, which looks down on a forest, specifically the snow-covered tops of conifers. She pushes snow off the railing, so that she can lean against it. She stares at the branches of spruce and fir. The sun is high in the blue sky, and the branches are heavy with glittery new snow. No sound reaches the terrace from the building. Indeed, there is silence all around. From time to time, a sprinkling of snow like diamond dust falls soundlessly from a branch.

"The camera lingers on the old woman's face. What does the face express? It is difficult to describe. It isn't horror, though a horror remembered is in there somewhere. Nor is there acceptance in the face. There is almost certainly wonder in it, and, I think, questioning. Maybe Judith is asking if this view of white beauty and perfection is an illusion. Can it truly be that the point of this sight—indeed, of all views, feelings, and thoughts—is to bring to fruition the consciousness of a vile monster?

"In the next scene, we see weird futuristic buildings—tall, slender, helical, pearlescent skyscrapers. 'MANHATTAN 11,874' appears on the screen. Flying vehicles hover among the buildings, making no sound. One of the vehicles is transporting a tall, bald man in a white toga. The man is about to press a button on the control panel when he notices a small white rootlet growing from the ball of his thumb. With dismay, he watches the rootlet grow until it is slapping about among the colored knobs of the control panel, like the runner of a climbing plant . . . Again, the camera eye looks to the sky; the words 'EIGHT YEARS LATER' appear against the clouds. The camera comes back down to a terrible spectacle. The streets are filled with people. These people are staggering about, with white shoots growing from their bodies. Some of these shoots are thirty yards long; their wretched hosts struggle to drag them in their wake. Some are trying to pull the shoots from their bodies, although naturally these attempts cause them acute pain. And the white shoots aren't growing out of humans only: they are sprouting from every living organism—dogs, pigeons, trees, you name it. The shoots catch one another and interweave, making it harder still for the people to walk. Humans and animals alike have madness in their eyes. They fight and kill one another— feral dogs and savage birds throw themselves at humans, their teeth and beaks tearing into the bodies. During these deadly struggles, assailants and victims grow together. Amid all this, a woman with a dazed expression walks with a child in her arms; she and the child are growing together. There are screams and vain calls for help from all sides.

"The words 'TWO YEARS LATER' appear on the screen. The place is the same as in the previous scene, but the apocalyptic frenzy has left no sign. The city is quiet, apparently deserted. At first sight, the sidewalks and roadways appear to be covered in snow. But when the camera moves in, we see the white as a dense tangle of shoots, which have grown into an unbroken blanket. In several places, human bodies are visible beneath the blanket. Arms and legs move languidly, before transforming and growing into others. The words 'FOUR MONTHS LATER' appear on the screen. All we see now is a continuous white cobweb that is quite motionless, with pearlescent skyscrapers poking out. The last designation of time and place reads 'EARTH

14,481.' We see the white case of the cocoon swell and then tear, and we see something dark appear in the tear, something like a huge claw . . ."

7. At the Hotel

"Although the movie was riddled with cliché, I quite enjoyed it. But Kristýna, who is into arthouse movies, obviously suffered through it. During the movie, I looked at her several times, and I had the impression it lost her attention at around the midway point; after that, she was lost in her own thoughts. We got back to Trastevere just before midnight. Having bought pizza and wine, we sat on the balcony of our room over the illuminated square, which was buzzing with dozens of voices, and spoke about *The Larva*. We at least agreed that the film had no obvious significance for our search: There was little likelihood that Petr or Tomáš had been killed by a member of the brotherhood with the cocoon wrist tattoo for having revealed the secret of the history of humankind. It was strange, however, that the movie wasn't entirely out of sync with what we had encountered on our journey so far. Could not Pico's text, a fragment of which was found in the sea on the painting of the Lygdian shell, be understood as a description of the world as one huge organism? (The mysterious affinity between distant things discussed in the passage of Pico's work could be explained by one great, unifying body.) Didn't the movie chime with Zoltán's reading of the undersea text, which claimed that a consciousness of all other beings could be found at the bottom of the human mind? This double coincidence was interesting insofar as the Budapest and Ljubljana interpretations of the worm rebus were incompatible; the groups of letters OM and ANT on its last line couldn't be both words for a sacred syllable in Sanskrit and an ant, as in Zoltán's reading, and two fragments of the Latin word *nominantur*, as I read them in Ljubljana. Or could they? Perhaps it was possible to read the luminous lettering in several ways, all of which were correct. One more question occurred to me: How come Petr Quas's screenplay was caught up in the network of connections growing out of Tomáš's shell, when according to Kristýna, the brothers had had nothing to do with each other at that time?

"Even Kristýna was unconvinced by these connections, and up till then she had seen a lead for the mystery of Tomáš's death practically everywhere we looked. Furthermore, she had stopped believing that the similarity between Tomáš's and Rossi's shells was more than a coincidence. She barely spoke; the sadness she had felt that afternoon certainly hadn't been lightened by having to sit through a two-hour-long American thriller that made no attempt to pass itself off as art. Now she had the feeling that our entire journey had been fanciful and foolish, a trip to the movies on the outskirts of Rome being the last but not the least of the follies. I, too, was silent, preferring to listen to the soporific hum of many voices that rose from the tables on the square. At last, Kristýna spoke the words she had been putting off all day: 'Let's go home.'

"For a little while longer, I tried to hang on to the hope. Maybe the director of Merry Elephant had it wrong, I said; maybe the gallery wasn't in Trastevere. If we searched other districts of Rome, maybe we'd track Rossi down . . . But I knew there was no point in going on. Kristýna didn't want crumbs of comfort from me. From what I could tell, her feelings had dissolved into one. That feeling was shame—at the childishness behind all our wanderings, born out of a single picture in a magazine and her impatience; at the effortlessness and lack of responsibility we had brought to the making of connections between objects, images, and fragments of words, so sending us ever farther south, all the way to a buzzing square in night-time Trastevere, where we now sat and asked ourselves and each other what we were actually doing. Kristýna's shame was accompanied by self-reproach for having kept me from my work to bring me on a wild goose chase simply because she lacked the strength to break free of a man who had abandoned her—and furthermore, that man had been dead for over a year.

"I wasn't doing much better. In Rome, I no longer heard the whisper tempting me farther south, intimating that it would take me to my unknown destination. The walls of Rome were mute. It seemed to me now that the enticing voices I had heard in the streets and squares of Ljubljana and Pula were just hallucinations summoned by my desire. What I heard in the square below me now was noise, like the buzzing of a bothersome insect. Still, I would be sorry to leave a city whose spaces and light I had so looked forward to, having experienced so little of it. It occurred to me that I might accompany Kristýna to the station, then spend a few days on my own in Rome. In those few days, with any luck I would make sense of the city's language. Or I might travel on, farther south, to the sea. To Naples, or to the coast at Sorrento, which I knew from photographs . . . But the thought of parting from Kristýna on the platform made me so sad that I replied: 'You're right. We'll go back to Prague tomorrow.'

"Kristýna took a shower; then she went to bed. When I joined her in the dark room, she was lying on the edge of her side of the double bed, her eyes closed, curled up like a child. As I lay down beside her, it occurred to me that for the first time her dead lover probably wasn't between us; that if I reached out to her, I wouldn't have to go through his ghost. But instead of making me bolder, the thought of our being alone in bed together scared me. I justified this reaction by telling myself that it wasn't honorable to seduce a woman bound by feelings of guilt and indebtedness—although I knew this was just an excuse thought up by my anxiety. Kristýna may have renounced her dead lover that evening, but in her mind and her body Tomáš's ghost was still having a field day. If I were at last to cross the threshold I had stood shuffling before since spring, what kind of enchanted castle would I find myself in? I returned to the balcony, where I slowly finished the bottle of wine I had left there. When I went back into the room, Kristýna was asleep."

8. Hot Walls

"I awoke the next morning at seven. Kristýna was sleeping under a light duvet, with a strip of bright sunlight across it. In the open window above her I saw the purple wall of the building opposite, embellished by a slanting shadow. When I caught sight of the colorful rectangle on the wall of the room, I felt that nameless bliss rise within me; it was as though I had picked up a book of magic and found in it the very page I had been looking for for years. I got out of bed as if in a daze, went downstairs, and made my way through the streets and squares. It was the same place as yesterday, yet everything in it was changed. My gaze glided slowly over the vermilion, sienna, and purple walls, which were dotted with pale stains with blurred edges, some reminding me of the patterns inside the eyelids I had seen in the movie the evening before. The walls seemed to exhale the warmth that had built up in them all summer, just for me, along with a delightful lassitude, acceptance, and wisdom of forgetting, as promised by the breath of the waterfront in Ljubljana, and the wind in Pula, and as whispered softly by spaces in Budapest and Bratislava. Stains scorched by the sun and washed by the rain, and vast surfaces of many shades of vermilion and purple seemed to me more beautiful than the paintings of Kandinsky, Klee, Pollock, and all other much-loved artists; I had the feeling I was looking at the most amazing gallery in the world, and I was happy to be walking around in it.

"On all walls lay slanting morning shadows cast by window ledges, wooden shutters, streetlamps, and laundry on lines; today, these letters came together in a message that couldn't be misunderstood, bringing unexpected comfort, together with the hope that they might teach me to understand all the scripts and codes in the world. The splendid fabric of the future rippled in the mouths of side streets, its nascent seconds shimmering. Set against the purity of the coming moment and the mysterious promise of the corners and shadows on walls, how pitiable the investigative aim of our journey seemed! Glowing images floated calmly in the fragrance of walls, which transformed slowly, like a melody; into this early-morning fragrance wafted dozens more, such as those of the bakeries, and of the vegetable and fish markets, which were just opening. The heavy breath of the Tiber plowed a course through the backstreets; the scent of the stone pines—whose crowns rose above the rooftops, like the hanging gardens in Oriental fairy tales—drifted down from the Janiculum hill. I no longer cared if my journey had a mistaken aim. I told myself that all destinations were false, for the true destination emerged only on the road. We met it in some suspicious backstreet we had wandered into in error. It seemed that my destination was these few moments in early-morning Trastevere. And that was fine: What more could I ask? The thought of returning to Prague today no longer saddened me.

"I was slightly worried that the silent ecstasy in my gaze would disturb the repose of a monument around the next corner—a famous work of art, perhaps, which would proudly refuse me entry to the space where all objects had the same value, because everything is modeled from the prime material of the pure light of early morning. My worry soon turned out to be unfounded: beyond a bend in the road was a church. Facade, columns, cornices, sculptures, corbels, scrolls, shells—none of them denied affinity with the walls and their stains; indeed, they humbly and joyfully conceded it.

"I considered calling Kristýna. If she didn't wake soon, she would miss this wonderful morning. But I doubted that her eyes, wearied by the search for clues and bleary with sorrow and self-reproach, were ready to receive it. I feared that the magic of early-morning Trastevere would pall under her gaze. As I walked down a narrow backstreet, I came to a café. A waiter was out front, arranging chairs around three small, round tables. He smiled at me. I sat down, ordered a coffee and a croissant, and settled down to study the uncommonly beautiful stains on the wall of the building opposite . . . Soon, however, I realized the time had come for me to return to Kristýna. When I stepped into the room to pay, the waiter was in back somewhere. As I stood waiting for him, my sun-blinded eyes adjusting to the gloom, I noticed something interesting on the wall behind the bar. This thing was white and triangular. When my vision was clear, I saw that it was shaped like the piece of gummy candy whose likeness I hadn't been able to identify—the piece of candy the director of Merry Elephant said Rossi had claimed to be a product of its creator's imagination."

9. Church on an Island

"I was looking at a calendar issued by a travel agency for pro- motion purposes. There would be no need for me search for the location the image was taken from, as it was given under the picture. It was a color photo of the highly unusual Church of Panagia Paraportiani on the island of Mykonos, set against a backdrop of the Aegean Sea and a deep blue sky. Although the candy was short on detail, there could be no doubt that it was a tiny copy of this church. I had found the solution to one of the puzzles of the Pula rebus! It occurred to me immediately that this was the second connection between the Lygdian shell and a Greek island. The first had been the small island in the Dodecanese on whose coast the biologist from Ljubljana had seen and photographed a canvas with a painting of the shell. I reached into my pocket for my cellphone, to call Kristýna. But then it struck me that my discovery was worthless. Although I had found what we were looking for, the discovery answered the wrong question. What did it matter if Rossi had thought up the shape of the candy, or if for some reason he had decided to create a miniature in gelatin of an Orthodox church in the Cyclades?

"But maybe it did matter. When the waiter appeared, I ordered another espresso and went back outside to my table, to think it through. If Rossi had lied about the island church, he might have lied about the shell with the eye. If a building on a Greek island was the model for a piece of candy, who was to say that the inspiration behind another piece of candy wasn't the passage in *Damp Walls* about the Lygds. That the director of Merry Elephant had said nothing about this was neither here nor there. Or . . . could it be that no sculptor called Rossi, Rossini, or Rossellini existed? That Giovanna Sulzer had made him up? But why would she do that? To send us off on a false trail, that's why. Which could mean that there truly was some mystery behind the candies in the bag bought in Pula, and that that mystery may have a connection with Tomáš's death.

"Of course, anyone who learned that we were looking for a connection between a dead body found in the Mediterranean Sea and a strange-shaped gummy candy would have thought us ridiculous. Still, I had to ask myself, as I had done at the factory two days before, why the director of a large company would give two strangers almost three hours of her time for the sake of an ordinary bag of gummy candies. And again, I thought it unlikely that she had questioned us for so long just because she liked a good mystery and happened to be bored; her questions seemed too insistent for that to be so. I thought back on those questions, and how eager yet fearful they had seemed, how they had circled and sneaked around something that remained unspoken throughout the conversation. It occurred to me that the frequent pauses in her story about Rossi may not have been the result of a poor memory, but a sign that she was making it up as she went along. I remembered the shadow on her forehead, my uneasiness in the empty factory, and my hunch that the director's smile was hiding something.

"I closed my eyes and tried to recall the director's face, until at last it appeared to me quite distinctly among the entoptic images. I studied the face in detail. That smile was no mask, I told myself; I would say it had grown on a face ravaged by some great misfortune, and that out of this obscured foundation shone a long sadness, and that occasionally it showed a flash of something else . . . What could that be? Might Giovanna Sulzer's flimsy smile be an echo of a horror from the distant past? We could forget about Rossi; now our suspect was the director of Merry Elephant."

10. Message in Candy

"Still I couldn't imagine how Giovanna Sulzer could be involved in Tomáš's murder. Nor did I have any ideas about who could have reported on the crime in candy, and why they had chosen gelatin hieroglyphs for the purpose. I decided to set these questions aside for the time being. Now that I had identified the white shape, I would make another attempt to read the text the candy characters comprised. I had the bag from Pula in my pocket, so I poured its contents onto the table, between my espresso cup and my water glass. I was hoping that the messages whispered by objects that morning, which had led me believe I could understand all the secret languages of the world, would help me find the key to the Pula rebus. But as I tried to order the candies into a coherent message, again I felt like an archaeologist who had happened upon these strange letters in a desert, with no means of deciphering them.

"As I also had the magnifying glass with me, I inspected each of the candies in minute detail. The first one I looked at was the shell with the eye. Could it be emblematic of Tomáš Kantor? And if so, might it tell me who the candy message was for? As I considered such ideas, I doubted the good sense of what I was doing. Whether or not Rossi was a fiction, I told myself, it was still more than likely that the candies had nothing to tell—and that in trying to read them as hieroglyphs, I was making a fool of myself. But then I made myself forget my doubts and treated the whole thing as a game; I would simply assign meanings to the candies and see if any possible message came out. I held the glass over the next candy, the dagger with the crocodile hilt. The dagger might indicate the way in which Tomáš died, of course; but I could make nothing of the crocodile hilt.

"If the text in candy told of Tomáš's death, then Tomáš couldn't be its author; in that case, Kristýna was mistaken in recognizing her lover's style in it. There was, of course, a possibility that the message had been written by an epigone of Tomáš's—someone who had mastered Tomáš's style and shared his compulsive desire to work images into ever new genres, and had taken these beyond the confines of art, into the food industry. Yet how could someone be so familiar with Tomáš's work when only two short fragments of his oeuvre had been published, and, according to Kristýna, Tomáš had had no friends?

Then I remembered the mysterious woman for whom Tomáš had left Kristýna. Hadn't Kristýna said that she was a sculptor? If she made large statues from stone or metal, surely she could manage small ones in gelatin. Could she have killed Tomáš before creating an encrypted message about her crime?

"I studied the white candy through the magnifying glass. There could be no doubt that it was the church on Mykonos, rendered in precise miniature. What on earth could the church on Mykonos have to do with the murder of Tomáš Kantor? But maybe the church wasn't the point; maybe the candy was a synecdoche (a part representing a whole) and the miniature church signified Mykonos, or even the Cyclades . . . And if the candy truly did carry a message about Tomáš's death, maybe its role was to mark the place where he died. But this was very unlikely: The Cyclades and Anatolia are some distance apart, so the chance of Tomáš's body being carried by the sea from Mykonos all the way to the coast of Turkey was slim indeed. And I couldn't see why a murderer would carry a body such a distance by boat when it could be gotten rid of anywhere in the Aegean.

"These thoughts brought me to the last of the four strange candies. Under the glass, I studied the little boat from all sides, paying careful attention to the large flower growing out of its deck. There was little doubt that it was a magnolia flower. What could it mean? Was the unknown author of the text in candy telling us that the owner of the yacht was partial to the magnolia plant? Or that the owner grew magnolia plants? Or that the owner's name was a word like 'magnolia'? Could *The Magnolia* be the name of the boat? It occurred to me that the 'MAG' of the luminous worm text might also be a reference to magnolia, not a fragment of the word *magia*, as we had thought in Ljubljana. Or could the groups of letters of the undersea text belong to various words and various sentences, going their various ways before meeting again on paper and leading the way to far-off places?"

11. The Magnolia

"What I did at the café in Trastevere may have been just a game, but as I looked at the pieces of colorful gummy candy scattered across the little round table, I couldn't shake the feeling that they contained a message about a shadowy happening of some kind; there was something horrible about these candies. Having put the gelatin hieroglyphs back in the bag, I paid for my coffee and set out for the hotel, back to Kristýna. Although the early-morning tide of bliss had subsided, the walls were still bright. As I was passing an internet café, it occurred to me to check out the idea that 'Magnolia' was the name of a boat. Having passed over lists of ocean-going steamers, ferries, and cargo ships, I came to the European register of private yachts. And there I found a boat called *The Magnolia*. A relatively large luxury motor yacht, her owner was a certain Alexis Spiridaki. I checked to see where she was registered: Her home port was given as Mykonos.

"It may have been mere coincidence, of course. But at that moment, that didn't seem to matter, just as it didn't matter whether I was attracted to a Greek island by a bit of detective work or the idea of white walls in the sun set against the sea. My encounters with hot facades and the script of shadows had taught me that in any case I couldn't just leave the game of signs behind, as chance hieroglyphs could be a truer guide to the answers I was seeking than an obvious trail, and a false trail could be more important than a true one. Thinking of Hector at the station in Parca, I wondered if we should have allowed ourselves to be guided by a game of chance from the very beginning. Why not decide things by a dice thrown at a crossroads by a malicious or kindly god of the road? As I was already at a computer, I typed 'Ferries Italy – Greece' into the search engine. I learned that a ferry left Bari for Patras at four in the afternoon. In the early morning, a boat left Piraeus for Santorini, calling at Mykonos. If we hurried, we could catch the train for Bari that left from Termini in less than an hour.

"I emerged from the gloom of the café onto the street, where I called Kristýna. I told her briefly about the church on Mykonos and the yacht called *The Magnolia*. We should go to Greece straight away, I said. At first, Kristýna refused; she had accepted the idea of a return to Prague, and she thought the Mykonos trail too fantastical. She had had enough of being tempted onward by photographs, surrealistic paintings, texts written by luminous worms, candy hieroglyphs, and miraculous coincidences that probably originated in our heads—all fed by our obsession to join everything together and find similarities wherever we looked. 'You're right,' I told her. 'Maybe we've been on the wrong track since Pula, maybe since Ljubljana or Budapest. It's more than likely we've been on the wrong track since Prague. But what does it matter, after all? What if some random resemblance were to show us what we're looking for, as a poet's thought is revealed to him in a word summoned by a rhyme, a random resemblance in sound? The only clue we have is two pieces of candy that may or not tell us something about Mykonos. So let's follow their trail and see what shows up. Do you not think it remarkable that we keep following the most dubious clues, yet they bring us ever closer to where Tomáš's body was found?'"

"'No, I know how this will turn out,' said Kristýna, and I heard fatigue in her voice. 'We'll get to Mykonos, find another dubious sign, which we'll read as an order to travel to another place, where we'll wait for a new hieroglyph and a new journey to show up, and on and on it will go . . .'

"'Don't worry.' I said. 'Our journey will end in Greece. Our European Union passports won't take us farther.'

"I got back to the hotel a quarter of an hour later. Kristýna was waiting for me down at Reception, with the backpacks. The receptionist called a taxi for us. We made the train to Bari with seconds to spare."

The Story of the Sparkling Labyrinth, the Secret Name, and the Cold-shy Swede

1. Stations and Harbors

"On the train, my early-morning state of happiness persisted for a while, but soon faded. So, too, did my determination to continue with the journey. By the time the train reached the outskirts of Rome and their scattered homes and factories, nothing of the happiness or the determination remained, and where they had been I felt an emptiness. This time, the emptiness wasn't an embarrassing sense of the absurdity of our journey, nor one overflowing with images like milk froth boiling over from a pot—the emptiness felt by Tomáš Kantor on the winter day he began to write his novel. My emptiness felt more like sitting alone in a movie theater after the film has ended, my gaze fixed on the now-white screen on which snippets of memories and visions, pleasant and unpleasant ones, appeared in flashes, but which mostly remained blank. Kristýna's mood was similar, I think: There were moments when her old confidence in the success of our search returned, followed by torment at the likely pointlessness of what we were doing; most of the time, it seemed she felt as numb as I did.

"The state I had worked myself into had something in common with dreaming. The moments of the journey from Italy to Greece were linked neither by expectation nor impatience; I remember them as a cluster of unconnected images, with many gaps between. I recall the crowded train compartment, huddled in a corner with Kristýna for four hours, our fellow passengers chattering away in a language we didn't understand; set against our fellows' profiles, the Campagna, with mythological figures from the paintings of Poussin in my mind's eye; the railroad station in Bari, and waiting at the port with its great white ships; the wailing of sirens; the eighteen-hour passage, the cool of the night on deck, the inside of the ship with its bright, fluorescent lights; students sleeping on the floor, heads on backpacks; sunrise casting sparks of red on the dewy metal railing; again a packed compartment, on the train to Piraeus; the bench in the nighttime harbor, where Kristýna and I nestle against each other for warmth; long hours waiting for the ferry, with brief interludes of sleep; a ship as tall as a house opening itself to the gloom of the early hours; cars crawling into the ship's bowels; the harbors on Kea and Tinos, where the ferry stops . . .

"As the ferry approached the harbor, Kristýna and I stood at the railing, inspecting the town from a distance. It appeared not as a human accomplishment but as a block of white chalk. Then the block broke up into the grooves of streets: A fantastical settlement was revealed. The iron panel was lowered, and we walked across it in a crowd of tourists. Once on the pier, we and all the others made our way along an aisle thronged on either side with men and women calling, 'Rooms! Rooms!' and waving color photos showing hotels, pensions, and apartments. Having asked one of the men about the price of his rooms, we soon found we couldn't get rid of him. So we allowed him to grab our backpacks and load them into his car. Then he drove us to his house on Chora's hill."

2. Mykonos

"Before doing anything else, we wanted to see the church at Panagia Paraportiani. Although we bought a map, we were soon lost in the white streets, which are said to have been built in such an intricate pattern so that the pirates who regularly attacked the town from the sea would get lost in them; so as to protect themselves from horrors coming from the endless labyrinth of the sea, the town's inhabitants built the sea's mirror image in stone. We folded away the map and beat a random path through the glowing, baking-hot streets. When at last the white church appeared before us, I had the weird feeling that it was a huge model of the piece of gummy candy. We walked around the building several times. Then we peeked inside, where the light of dozens of candles illuminated the gold icons but couldn't chase away the dark. Having left the church and turned the next corner, we realized we were lost again.

"I thought back to the night in San Benedetto, when I had the idea that our journey was drawn on the map of Europe in one large hieroglyph. Now I had the feeling that it was more likely a text composed of many symbols, that each city that had opened up to me on our travels was a large pictogram, and that the pictograms came together in a statement for me to read. Maybe they wrote my secret name—a name I didn't know, but whose sounds I sometimes heard in the whispers of cities. Was knowledge of my secret name what awaited me in the southern place all the cities had sent me on to? And wasn't the solving of all the rebuses, jigsaws, and picture puzzles of our journey, and of the characters in worms and candy, just a part of a ciphered message that stretched across half of Europe? There are, I know, people whose secret name is written across a wall of their living room; those people are happy to sit at home and look at a blank wall. It was suddenly clear to me that if I wanted to read mine, I would have to travel to the very end of the continent . . .

"I realized, too, that each of the large characters on my path was different. The Mykonos labyrinth wasn't the same as its Roman counterpart. In Rome, I had walked between walls soaked in the happy intimacy of interiors, their vermilion plaster mixed with sunlight. Here, it was as if the walls hadn't been raised for the delimitation of interior space, and as if the human dwellings had originated by the sudden *en masse* creation of hollows in the white rock; I wondered if one day they would close again, or if an eruption of some kind would raise the reef from the sea, so exposing its grooves, protrusions, and caves to the baking sun.

"Both of the cities revealed and concealed its message, and the way in which the Mykonos town of Chora enshrouded the lines of its script was particularly sophisticated. They were hidden behind hundreds of color photos on calendars and the thick coating on the white walls to which the eyes of tourists were drawn. Briefly, I reproached myself for attending to the crossword puzzle whose solution would reveal my true name while Kristýna believed me to be her selfless helper in the investigation of her life. I drove this thought away by telling myself that the patient resolution of my personal rebus was perhaps the only way to make sense of things, especially as our chaotic journey seemed to be leading Kristýna ever closer to ghosts of the past.

"But maybe I really was being unfaithful to Kristýna. There was no doubt that as we traveled from city to city, my love for her had given way to a love affair with the cities we passed through. How difficult it was for me to resist their temptations! The strange towns and cities we visited were the most erotic and seductive beings in the world, not least very early in the morning, when they rose from bed. Sometimes, I would forget that I wasn't on this journey alone. But then Kristýna would reappear, and my desire for her would return. The new desire came about precisely because the face and body of Kristýna appeared to me against a backdrop of wonderful cities and were steeped in their breath. Like a mirror that collects and stores images, Kristýna's face reflected and conserved streets, squares, and facades. She had no idea about this, of course—she took nothing from the cities but particles that might evolve into clues in the search she believed set for her by her dead lover. If I had come to see Kristýna as a mirror in which cities were magically reflected, and so lost my desire for her, had I wanted her before because her body was the venue of a spooky ball where all the ghosts of Tomáš Kantor would dance forever?"

3. Four Letters

"At last we found ourselves back at the harbor. We walked along the narrow pier that ran far out to sea, looking at the yachts and small sailboats bobbing on the water. None of these boats was *The Magnolia*. In one of the boats we saw a thin, bronzed man in a T-shirt and baggy pants working on an engine. I asked him if he had ever heard of a yacht called *The Magnolia*. 'She's a nice big motorboat,' he said, in Greek-accented English, without soft consonants. 'But she isn't berthed here anymore.' I asked if he knew the yacht's owner. She had recently been bought by a Cretan, he said. Indeed, not long ago, he had seen *The Magnolia* in Crete, in the harbor at Chania. He didn't know anything about *The Magnolia*'s new owner, but he had known the previous one very well. 'His name was Gustaf, and he was a Swede,' he told me. 'At home (he waved an arm in the general direction of north), he was a university teacher. He had spent his every summer vacation here, on his yacht, sailing from island to island. Everyone here knew him. Maybe it was too cold for him in Sweden. Maybe his students got him down. Maybe his marriage was bad. I don't know, he never talked about what brought him here. But I know he quit the university, sold his house and everything in it, moved to Mykonos, and spent the next ten years here as a sailing instructor. Over time, he bought and sold several boats. *The Magnolia* was the last and largest of them. She had a different name in those days—it was the Cretan who gave her that name. Three years ago, Gustaf sold his boat and his house in Chora, and went back to the north. He didn't say why, but I think that in the end he had begun to tire of being on vacation all the time.'   .

"I asked what Gustaf taught in Sweden. He was a *zoologos*, the man said; he had first come to Greece on a scientific expedition. On learning this, the first thing I wanted to know was whether Gustaf was interested in marine life—luminous worms, for instance—but the man said he was a student of birds. Gustaf could recognize any bird by its call, he remembered. Probably, this ability impressed the man more than Gustaf's abilities as a sailor, which he shared with many others. Did he happen to remember what the yacht was called in Gustaf's day? I asked. He remembered that Gustaf had given each of his boats the name of a bird, in Modern or Ancient Greek, but he wasn't sure what the boat in question had been called. Could it have been *Aidoni*, meaning nightingale? I thanked the man and wished him a good day, and we turned to continue our walk along the pier. I was wondering what we would do next when the man called us back. '*Aidoni* wasn't Gustaf's last boat but his boat before last,' he explained apologetically. 'The last one was called *Jynx*.' For a moment, Kristýna and I stared at the Greek without speaking. Maybe he thought we hadn't understood him. He repeated the name, and with his finger he wrote four invisible letters on the side of his boat: I, Y, Γ, Ξ."

With a finger, Martin wrote the same invisible letters on the paper tablecloth, over a red-wine stain. Then he stood, wished me a good night, and walked quickly away. I saw him exchange a few words with Vangelis over the glass cooler, as he settled his bill. Then he disappeared.

The Story of Three Lazy Days in Chania

1. On Deck

The next morning, I set off along the steep, meandering path to Anopoli, a village perched high on the rock, invisible from Loutro. As I walked, Loutro fleetingly disappeared behind protrusions in the rock; each time I saw it again, it appeared smaller. As I approached the top of the rock, the houses of Loutro looked like a strip of white foam clinging to the stones of the bay. Then I emerged into a world I had almost forgotten, Anopoli before me on a broad plain, among gardens and fields, in the distance dark mountains, topped with motionless cloud. On the asphalt road, I was passed by a few cars; a green bus whistled by. I drank a coffee in a *kafenio* on a square with a white monument at its center. Then I walked down to the village, a calm, dreamlike world below the baking cliff, whose one street comprises the floors of terraces, one running into the next.

I headed straight for the Pavlos taverna, for a beer to quench my thirst. The only other customer in the place was Martin, sitting over a chapter of his thesis, making entries between the lines in pencil. I called over a greeting before seating myself at the table farthest from him, so as not to disturb. I noticed him cross out everything he had written, and I also noticed that he kept looking toward me. Probably he was thinking that if I were to join him, he would have a good excuse to stop with his work, which didn't appear to be going very well. In the end, he gathered his papers and wandered over to join me.

This meant, of course, that he was about to continue with his story. "When you finished yesterday evening, you were on the pier on Mykonos," I reminded him.

Having ordered himself a beer from Tanya, Martin picked up the story. "Because of those four invisible letters the Greek wrote with his finger on the side of his boat, Kristýna and I came to Crete . . . How odd to encounter the wryneck on our journey a second time! (We met it first in Ljubljana, if you remember.) We were filled with hope for what we might discover in Chania—maybe even from the mysterious Cretan owner of *The Magnolia* himself. Either the coincidence had sent us off on another wild goose chase, or the name of the Swede's yacht was connected with the worm lettering, the Lygdian shell, and the gelatin candy from San Benedetto, making it a link in a chain of signs—meaning we were on the right track, and a solution to the mysterious deaths of two brothers might be in sight. At the harbor, we learned that the next ferry to Heraklion left at six that evening, the one after that in three days' time. We returned to our lodgings for our backpacks and passports, paying our landlord for one night's accommodation so as not to leave him disappointed. Although we got lost in Chora's web of streets again, we managed to get to the harbor in time.

"After we put sea, it was soon dark. Kristýna fell asleep in a chair. I spent most of the night up on deck, leaning on the rail, watching the illuminated harbors of the Cyclades approach and recede, listening to the boat's hoarse-voiced PA announcements in English and Greek: Paros, Naxos, Ios, Santorini. Between the ports, all was darkness, monotonous engine noise, and wild wind. I thought of the labyrinth of Chora, and how it was beginning to merge with the other places we had visited in a single fantastical city. This city would take on a life of its own in my memory; I was curious about the many things I would encounter in its streets. It was born of memories of the square in Bratislava, trembling with a delightful fatigue at summer's end, of the steps in Víziváros, which in Zoltán's telling became a Baghdad of garden gates and miraculously opening strangers' houses, of the trio of bridges in Ljubljana, with its carnival-like parade of lamps, of the steep streets of Pula, chased by a crazy wind, of Trastevere, waking up to the early-morning sun. And the ground plan of this city of the memory opened new yet deeply familiar ways. I sensed what would originate in its spaces: new thoughts, feelings, gestures, ways of entering the world, and approaching people; ways of taking an object in one's hands, inspecting its contours and marks on its surface, and penetrating its structure. I knew that in these spaces my thesis would be transformed, and that it would copy them. I told myself that in the spaces of this city I must be reborn, as Tomáš's Marius was reborn from the breath of the streets of Parca.

"As I was thinking these thoughts, in the corner of my eye I saw the head and shoulders of a woman emerging from the lit stairwell. Turning toward her, I recognized Kristýna. At the point where only the top half of her body was above deck, she stopped to look around—slowly, as if she were an outsized marionette. With her frowning, pale face lit from below and her hair ruffled from sleep, she was a frightful sight, like the heroine of a story by Edgar Allan Poe. Still taking her time, she walked up to me, placed her elbows on the rail, and stared into the darkness. She was having a bad moment, I realized; maybe in her first moments after waking, her defenses down, she had been overwhelmed by fatigue and tension accumulated over the past few days, just as she was being assailed by the set of old ghosts traveling with her. To offer a little encouragement, I spoke of how we had almost reached our destination, and of my confidence that we would find answers to all our questions in Crete.

"As she said nothing to this, I kept on talking, until I was interrupted by a voice I didn't know. A voice that trembled with hatred and contempt. The voice was Kristýna's. 'I've had as much of you patronizing me as I can take,' she said. 'The way you try to protect me makes me sick. If you really think me incapable and crazy, why not just say so? Are you afraid of me? You run after me across half of Europe, clinging to me like a small child, yet you treat me as if you're my guardian. I'm not your child, and I'm not your mother. Why don't you tell me what you want from me? You're a coward.' Now she was shaking, and I was speechless. Once she recovered, she carried on. 'But I'm not crazy. I'm fully aware of how desperate and ridiculous it is to stagger from country to country, following weird clues found in Kabbalah teachings and gummy candy. This traveling from place to place is deadly serious for me. It's about what tore my life to shreds and what I must at least try to understand. If I make myself ridiculous in the process, so be it. For you, it's all just a game. Do you actually have any idea why you're on this boat? Could it be because you can't make up your mind whether to go home, just as you couldn't . . .' She paused briefly before saying: 'Know what? When we get to Crete, you go home. I'll carry on alone. I'll make myself understood here somehow . . .'

"She was about to go on, but then she thought better of it. She turned on her heel and went back to the illuminated stairwell, and from there below deck. For a long time, I stood rooted to the spot. Then I, too, went below deck. After a short search, I found Kristýna curled up in a chair, asleep. I returned to the deck, where I spent the rest of the night."

2. Arrival in Crete

"At first light, a town of light concrete came into view, stretching far along on the coast. Kristýna appeared next to me just as I was preparing to go and wake her. She smiled at me and asked how we would get from Heraklion to Chania. Neither of us mentioned the scene during the night, nor would we speak about it later, and it never happened again. She must have been sleepwalking, I told myself . . . As you know, there is no train service in Crete, so for the first time we rode a bus. It took us along the winding coastal road, stopping in every village. Those who got on and off were Greeks, most likely staff at the hotels along the coast; it was too early in the morning for tourists.

"We had no trouble finding *The Magnolia* in Chania's harbor: it was one of the largest boats at berth there. After a moment's hesitation, we jumped from the concrete jetty to the deck. We tapped on the glass of the cabin, but there was obviously no one on board. We looked through large windows, at leather upholstery, gold-plated fittings, mirrors, a well-polished floor. We tried all the handles; the door was locked. Not knowing what to do next, we walked on slowly to the old Venetian port, whose bay ended on the far side in an old fortress. 'What now?' Kristýna asked. 'How about breakfast?' I suggested. We were standing next to the outdoor seating of one of many cafés. We sat down in cushioned wickerwork chairs and ordered toast, yogurt with honey, and coffee.

"As we sat there thinking what to do next, it got hotter, and I smelled the stagnant water of the harbor. I breathed in this drug, stronger still than the agent of my intoxication in Rome. I allowed my gaze to wander in an arc over the cracked facades of the low, narrow houses that lined the harbor; I read signs that included 'Hotel Venezia' and 'Nostos.' I paused over lettering that was falling away, stains on walls, tall wooden shutters, crumbling balconies. Every inch of the facades and contours of these buildings came together in a time of happy deterioration—a dense time, in which it wasn't yet possible to distinguish passing seconds from changes in weather and the rhythm of the sea's breathing, and which crystallized every detail and worked on every bit of wall. On reaching the fortress, my gaze slipped to the sea and the horizon, before making its way back along the soulful landscape of dilapidated facades, the dilapidation making the buildings fitting companions of the sea they looked out on. Here, the border between sea and land wasn't a sharp one. The salty vapors seeped into and ate away at the buildings, turning them into things of the sea; the sea of the harbor received the smells of things of the town, mixing them with the non-human scents of its depths and distances. In this form, the sea, in invisible waves, poured itself out on the shore, so becoming part of the urban space, the streets, the houses and apartments, embracing all things and faces, sharing in every gesture and act; in conversations, it was heard in the gaps between words.

"The drug had entered my bloodstream. And this drug made me reluctant to concern myself with some guy called Tomáš Kantor, rebuses and other puzzles, Italian gelatin candy, a suspicious Swiss company director, Renaissance magic, or the yacht of a Cretan rich man I didn't know from Adam. All I wanted now was to spend a few lazy days in this place where the boundary between land and sea was blurred. To my surprise, I saw that Kristýna, too, had tasted the lotus; she, too, was avoiding talking about the mysterious yacht and what we should do next. Perhaps she had had enough of the endless string of clues pointing to other clues, a string she had sighted first in a Prague café and that had led her on a meandering course through six countries. Perhaps she just needed a rest to recover her strength, and this port, which sailed like a great dilapidated ship in the slow stream of seaside time, seemed to her a good place in which to take it."

3. Chania

"The three days we spent in Chania were the loveliest of our entire journey. We stayed in a small pension in the old harbor. When weren't walking along the seafront, we were wandering the narrow streets immersed in shade, snatching glimpses of the dazzling surface of the water, breathing in the scent of the South mixed with the breath of the Orient. The buildings there have been through marvelous transformations, having been Venetian structures and Turkish palaces before growing into their present form. Everything grows and decays in the heat. There are shrubs and trees in gaps in the crumbling walls, reeds in the corners of yards.

"Yet how different my happiness in Chania from the happiness I had known briefly in Trastevere! There, the streets opened onto a brilliant future; the intimacy of interiors flooded into the streets through windows and open doors, giving me the confidence to carry on with my journey. The streets of Trastevere urged me to venture into the unknown, whispering that a happy encounter was just around the corner, if only with gold dust dancing in the slanting sunlight. In Chania, it was as if the mysterious smells came ashore with everything drowned in the depths of memory—the accumulated past pouring into the present. But this was a reconciled, ghost-free past—a past of deep water that digested all beings and things, and transformed into a calming, slightly sorrowful symphony of scents of decay. In Rome, I had had the feeling I could read the large text written on the city's walls in a script of stains and shadows. Here, there was nothing to read or decipher, as everything had returned to the old world of mold and seaweed—a world from whose patterns script is yet to be born. In Chania, the South showed me its most pleasing face. Maybe it was Levantine repose, in which dreams and intricate, slow-evolving stories are born in the setting sun; maybe it was nothing but an illusion on my part—a buried dream that seeped through the walls and returned to me steeped in their breath.

"As we walked the streets of the old town, I couldn't shake the feeling that I knew them. At last it dawned on me why: The part of town around the port, whose only dwellings grew out of the disintegration of others, reminded me of Tomáš Kantor's Parca. It was more fantastical than the town of Tomáš's imagination, however—and warmer, too. I suggested to Kristýna that we go to the marina several times a day, to see if anyone had appeared on *The Magnolia*. Kristýna agreed to this plan. We both saw this as the comedy of hypocrisy it was, and we were a little embarrassed by it. We knew we were playing it out to relieve the pangs of conscience we felt for lazing around in Chania, doing nothing about the task in hand. It cost us nothing to stop by the marina or eat dinner in a taverna with a view of *The Magnolia*: We were walking by anyway, and the taverna seemed to have one of the best kitchens in town. But our patrol was in vain. All the indications were that no one had been on the yacht for a long time and the likelihood of anyone turning up there soon was slim.

"At this point, our investigations into the mysterious death of Tomáš Kantor involved nothing more than wandering over to the marina when we were in the neighborhood and lifting our eyes from our dinners of grilled octopus or red mullet to gaze on the still-dark windows of *The Magnolia*. Tomáš's name rarely came up in conversation. For the first time since Kristýna and I got chatting in the corridor of the Faculty of Arts building, our talk turned to painting and other things she had lived for before meeting Tomáš—things she may now be prepared to go back to. One evening at dinner, she said to me, quite out of the blue: 'You probably think I've been following this track blindly, like a dog with its nose to the ground, never lifting my head . . . And if you do, you're right. But I have seen the

gardens, beautiful walls, windows, and squares we've passed, out
of the corner of my eye. Those images aren't entirely lost on me,
you know. They surprise me by coming back, mostly in the evening, just before I fall asleep. And I try to concentrate on them,
to take them in, in every detail . . . It's as if the wasted journey
wishes to redeem itself by these images . . .' Then she said: 'I'm
glad we've taken this journey together. I'm very grateful to you.'

"I had the feeling that Kristýna had changed a lot in Chania.
As we walked, the streets lured new gestures out of her; it was as
if the warm Venetian stone woke and opened something within
her. I can't say that the ghosts in her body that had so frightened
me on the nighttime express to Bratislava were dispelled—they
had probably entered her bloodstream, so would be with her
forever. But I did feel that that through the thicket of cold, mistrustful gestures, a figure unknown to me was pushing toward
me, and maybe expecting my help. It occurred to me that this
pleasant stranger was perhaps the earlier Kristýna—Kristýna as
she had been before she met Tomáš Kantor.

"Each night before we went to sleep, we carried on our conversations in the large double bed in our room, to an accompa-
niment of noise from the tavernas in the harbor. Was the dead
Tomáš Kantor still lying between us? If so, this bugbear was losing its power, and it was ever less distinct. Had I reached out to
Kristýna in Chania—and maybe she was expecting me to—my
touch may have been enough to dissolve the ghost forever. But
I didn't reach out, and I don't know why. Maybe it was my old
cowardice. More likely, it was because I had come to depend on
the drug of lazy happiness, and so was unwilling to violate the
delightful film that lay evenly over all things; which I suspected
would happen if I allowed the serenity of those days in Chania
to be invaded by solemn emotion and the hard work demanded
by requited love . . . Among my superficial excuses for ignoring
the opportunity that was opening before me, I told myself I

had had enough in the North of profundity, inwardness, and suffering. I would later regret my laziness; this opportunity was a gift that didn't return.

"In Chania, I was reminded of the case of the two murders in rather curious fashion. As the new semester was getting close, it was necessary for me to contact my department. To do this, I went several times to an internet café. And on the server with my email, I spotted, among the digest of Czech news, the headline 'Was Petr Quas killed by a secret sect?' The article it ran above was from a magazine known for its sensationalist content. The writer had been to the movies to see *The Larva*, which premiered in Prague after our departure. Having been reminded of the bizarre death of one of the film's creators, it had occurred to him to make a sensation by drawing a line connecting the movie's theme of a strictly guarded secret about evolution of life on Earth and the unsolved murder. He hypothesized that Quas had been in on this great secret, and that by betraying his knowledge in the film, he had brought down on himself a punishment, meted out by members of the sect that guarded the secret . . . I don't know if the article attracted much attention in our homeland. But even if the writer had believed his own story, which I doubt, the very next day his amazing revelation would have been washed away by some new sensation."

The Story of the White Yacht

1. Evening at the Harbor

"On our third evening in Chania, as we sat in the taverna by the marina and Kristýna was telling me about her childhood, I happened to raise my eyes from the pile of batter-fried shrimp to see a light burning in the cabin of *The Magnolia*. I must confess that it crossed my mind not to draw Kristýna's attention to it; if she failed to notice, maybe our pleasant days in Chania would continue as they were . . . But I banished the thought: The last thing I wanted was to turn our journey into a farce that would shame me for years afterward. In any case, with what I was seeing now, the Levantine peace of the past few days was gone forever. I pointed over the heads of our fellow customers toward the yacht. Without a word, Kristýna laid down her knife and fork and stood up. In this one movement, it was as though she was shedding the new, light body she had acquired in the streets of Chania. She made her way past the tables, toward the yacht. In her wake, I saw that her legs were unsteady; she was back in her desert.

"In the light of the cabin, I saw a woman with dark hair. Her back was to us as she looked for something in a drawer of a secretaire of polished wood. We climbed over the boat's rail. Kristýna reached for the handle and opened the door. The woman screamed and turned around. At the sight of us, she seemed to regain her composure. Who was she afraid of? I wondered. The two women stared at each other, apparently oblivious of my presence. 'You're Kristýna,' said the stranger, in Czech. Could this be the woman for whom Tomáš had left Kristýna?

"She was about thirty, and very tan. At the sight of her strong, work-worn hands, I remembered that she was a sculptor. Then it occurred to me that those hands would be capable of delivering thirteen blows with a dagger. Maybe Kristýna had the same thought, since she asked: 'Did you kill Tomáš?' The woman didn't move. 'I saw Tomáš die,' she said. 'It was over there.' She pointed to the yacht's bow. 'You've been looking for me to ask if I killed Tomáš?'

"'I wasn't looking for you,' Kristýna replied. 'But I do have to know how Tomáš died. To put an end to it. To start again.'

"The sculptor gave a barely perceptible shake of the head. 'I, too, used to think this thing had to end somewhere,' she said. 'But that's nonsense. Nothing ever comes to an end. An end is just an idea, in most cases a silly one . . .'

"'I know that,' said Kristýna. 'And I did gradually get used to the unfinished story about Tomáš twisting itself into all other unfinished stories and finding a place among them. I had begun to believe that this would be just about okay, in the end . . . Then one day, in a magazine, I saw a picture of a shell with an eye, and five letters that made no sense. And I was certain they were an encrypted message from the dead Tomáš. And I knew that I had no choice but to try to read this message, because not to try would be a terrible betrayal.'

"'And those letters sent you here?'

"'We were on our journey already by then. In different cities, we looked for more scraps or letters of the message that we might be able to put together. Until now, we didn't know if they truly were letters. Maybe the words we made of them were just figments of our imagination. Maybe we were behaving like those crazy Parcans, who read scratches in stone as writing, which they then invested with meaning. But now I believe we have gathered all the letters. All that remains is for us to read them.'

Kristýna's use of the plural reminded the sculptor that I was there, too. When she turned to me, I said: 'I was at the ballet when the *Ding an sich* shot Tomáš's stepbrother.'

"'Martin is better at solving puzzles than I am,' Kristýna added. 'Without him, I would never have gotten this far.'

"So Tomáš's two widows met aboard *The Magnolia*. I was glad to see no resentment in either face. Sharing a dead lover made them allies."

2. Tomáš and Irena

"Kristýna told the sculptor about our journey. At first, the three of us stood in the middle of the cabin like a group of statues. Kristýna spoke in a soft, monotonous voice, fluently, with little show of emotion, as people sometimes speak in a dream. But the dreamlike torpor, which was affecting us all, gradually fell away. Kristýna's voice came to life, and I heard the pain in it. There came a point when we all sat down in armchairs. Not until she came to the taverna by the marina and the point where we spotted the light in the cabin did Kristýna pause in her story. Then the sculptor began on her story. Kristýna and I knew what it would be about: the death of Tomáš Kantor.

"A few sentences in, I interrupted to ask her name. 'Irena,' she said, after a slight hesitation. Then she went on with the story. At first, she spoke of things I knew a little about thanks to Kristýna. At the time Tomáš and Irena got to know each other, he liked to write in cafés. He enjoyed plucking words out of the hum of conversation and inserting them in new stories. When a new storyline was born this way, he would reach into a plastic bag for the Diagram. In it, he would seek out a place for the new storyline, which he would then weave in, among all the others. Sometimes, he would pull spools of thread from his pockets, there and then in the café, using different colors of thread to show on the Diagram relations between different lines of the Work. Someone engaged in such a strange activity in public is bound to attract the attention of others. Tomáš achieved a certain renown; he was referred to as 'the guy with the brainteaser.'

"Having heard about 'the guy with the brainteaser' from friends, Irena imagined him to be a kind of weirdo. One afternoon, she came across Tomáš in a café, searching his Diagram with a rapt expression on his face. The strange construction on the table before him was strikingly like a sculpture she was then working on. In fact, she happened to be going through a phase she called her 'maze period.' Such was her interest in the convoluted wire-thing that she went straight up to Tomáš and asked what it was for. Usually, Tomáš would talk about the Diagram only with reluctance and in general terms. But when he saw how well Irena understood his explanation, and how much she knew about mazes, tangles, and other types of convolutions, he became more expansive. By the time darkness fell, Irena knew almost all there was to know about the Work-Network. She knew about the origination out of the void of *Damp Walls*, the first part of the Work, its growth, its completion, and its new explosion.

"That same evening, Irena invited Tomáš to her studio. What happened to him there was comparable with what happened to Hector on encountering Sylva Cerran's drawings—he saw images from his own world in someone else's work. As Irena didn't want to say much about the beginnings of her relationship with Tomáš, out of consideration for Kristýna, she quickly changed the subject. Not long after she and Tomáš got together, she said, he and his stepbrother got back in touch. Petr had no idea that Tomáš was writing again. Last spring, for the first time in several years, Petr visited Tomáš at home. At the sight of sheets of paper covered with handwriting, drawings, and musical scores scattered across every surface, including the floor, he thought of his brother's childhood bedroom and his secret visits there. And he surmised the return of the convulsive sickness his brother had suffered in his mid-teens, which had resulted in many years of exhaustion and apathy. Petr wasn't particularly surprised: He had always sensed that the sickness was part of Tomáš's character, and that it would forever lie dormant in his blood, like malaria brought back from the Tropics.

"Petr picked up one of the handwritten sheets and read a few sentences. This was enough to show him that he was mistaken in his first assumption—what was going on in Tomáš's apartment was far stranger than the late return of a childhood illness. Petr was confronted with something entirely unexpected: clear, focused, calm text, whose words came from far away before settling slowly in their appointed places. He sensed that the author had waited patiently for them in a void that held no fear for him—indeed, he and the void were on friendly terms. It was as if Petr's body was filled with a strange lightness from the flow of language cascading from dependent clauses and soaking into the white sand of the page. Although Petr and Tomáš weren't close enough for Tomáš to tell his stepbrother about his struggle with the monster of the void and their subsequent conciliation, it occurred to Petr that this lightness could originate only in an empty space in which all structures, completed or uncompleted, had collapsed, and where neither fear nor hope could disturb the gradual, aimless birth of images and words."

3. A Balcony in Dobřichovice

"At first, I was taken aback by Irena's description of Petr's feel-ings and thoughts, which she couldn't have known. I even began to wonder if she was treating her story as fiction. But then I told myself that for everyone who came into Tomáš's orbit, before and after his death, visible objects and bodies became charac-ters, in which it was possible to read the hidden and invisible; naturally, Irena was no exception. Anyway, Irena explained how Petr asked about the manuscripts that lay about the room, and Tomáš described the winter afternoon on which the streets of Parca emerged from the void, the rapid growth of images, and the transformation of the book into the Work-Network. Petr asked Tomáš to send *Damp Walls* to him by email. Tomáš was reluctant: He didn't want to show a text he still thought of a mere fragment of the Work. In the end, however, Petr talked him into it. So eager was Petr to read it that he drove straight back to his villa in Dobřichovice. Once there, he took his laptop to the balcony and, above the blossoming treetops, got started on Marius's adventures in Parca. As he was reading the passages on political relations in North Floriana, darkness was falling, but he couldn't be distracted. From time to time, he would wave a hand at the flies that fluttered about in front of the lit screen, and sometimes he would gaze off into the garden, whose only light was between the trees, from the streetlamps; moments later, however, his eyes would again be fixed on the screen.

"Feelings swirled about inside him, like the swirling of paints of different colors in water. The first feeling was hope: If Tomáš, after years of apathy, had succeeded in returning to the agoniz-ing convulsions of his childhood and youth and transforming the energy they generated into patient work, perhaps he could manage something similar, Petr told himself. But this quiet hope soon gave way to anxiety. Petr realized that everything had changed that day. Before, he had never seen any reason to be ashamed of his weakness in front of his brother. He knew that Tomáš looked down on him for having spent much of his life making money off of bad writing. But Petr had written a volume of good poetry, too, and Tomáš acknowledged this. Unlike his father, Tomáš believed that Petr's poetry had brought something meaningful to the agonizing family drama of the Kantors, so freeing himself and his father from the enchanted castle of their folly, and he remained grateful to Petr for this. He had no intention of judging him for succumbing to one of the thousands of devils that tempt the writer. The stepbrothers' relationship was like that of two soldiers in a defeated army; the experience of defeat had brought them closer, and neither had any desire to discuss mistakes, fear, and cowardice, or the unfortunate and painful events of their lost campaign.

"Now, however, everything was different. Suddenly, the folly and convulsions of Tomáš's childhood had become a single act in a new story, resulting in the transformation of Petr's past, like in a movie about a time machine. After years, his weakness had become betrayal. Petr grew ever more anxious. He had the feeling that long-dormant ghosts from the haunted apartment of the Kantors were waking from their dreams, and that they were quietly, lethargically preparing to rise. On the balcony above the garden, he had something like a hallucination; he smelled the distinct, musty odor of the Kantors' tower-block apartment, which he hadn't thought about in years; he heard the creaking of the door when Tomáš emerged from his room, mixed with clinking of silverware at silent family dinners, the sound of a train on the track, and the bellows of drunks returning from the bars. He felt sick. Every childhood is a haunted house whose ghosts cannot be beaten, as they all fight as if in a dream, no one knowing the object of the fight; the battle usually ends when everyone gets tired and the dark house and its ghosts get left behind. Which is probably a good thing, said Irena on board

The Magnolia. This is one of those battles it's best not to fight to the end, leaving the outcome undecided. It is wiser to leave some wars neither won nor lost, but quietly smoldering, your whole life long. Petr was now faced with the dreadful prospect of re-engaging with the ghosts of the haunted house of his childhood, even though he was about to turn thirty-six and rightly considered an important figure in the world of business.

"Petr had always known that all that had happened to him had its origins in the moment he had moved into the Kantors' apartment, so assuming his role in a Kantor family drama that was no concern of his. The toxins and antitoxins of this apartment chock-full of unit furniture entered his bloodstream forever, although it was often difficult to tell what was poison and what was medicine. With the Kantorian drug of emptiness in his blood, Petr was a no-one, just like Tomáš. The two of them would remain no-ones for the rest of their lives. In their lifetimes, the fact that one of them spent many years in a glass booth watching the arching tracks of the streetcar terminus followed by a couple of years pulling stories by the dozen from the distillery of the void, while the other got rich and became a regular in the society mags, made little difference between them. 'I was surprised to learn how similar the flowers of nothingness were,' said Irena. 'And I wondered that the brothers had lived so long in ignorance of the similarity.'

"The Kantor poison had long been present in all Petr did. It had caused him to know the happiness brought by the forming of images from words and the comings-together of words in the void. But the same poison was the cause of his weakness, which was mysteriously related to the fear of the impenetrable darkness of the void suffered by both Kantors—the fear that had killed Tomáš's father, and which, so it now seemed, Tomáš had miraculously overcome by finding the strength concealed at its bottom. Petr's wealth had grown from this poison, too, of course; not only because the immeasurable hole of the void asked to be filled with something very large, but seemingly also because in the financial sphere, as in literature, emptiness manifested itself as a tendency to multiply to infinity whatever it generated.

"Another thing that originated in the haunted tower-block apartment, and one source of Petr's snobbery, was his need to be admired. The Kantor asceticism, idealism, and the cult of pure imagery came together in a tangle of all kinds of things, in which a longing for recognition and fame was relatively easy to identify. It isn't good to examine the purity of the figures into which the powers are bundled too closely, nor is it right to attempt to purify these bundles. The clearest crystal often results from the action of less than pure forces, working together in dreamlike fashion, their aim unknown. Perhaps strangest of all, Petr's love of luxury and money was born out of the breath of the tower-block apartment, as was his hedonism. In the poems Petr took from the drawers of his stepbrother's room, he found, alongside images of ruin and decay, images filled with light, glittering gemstones, white terraces with sea views, tan strangers on beaches, and dewy cups filled with colorful alcoholic beverages sparkling in the sun. Clearly, Petr felt that as well as being literature, these poems were expressions of a burning desire for life's delights. Even in Tomáš's early poems, it wasn't easy to tell what was humble worship of the pure image and what was self-indulgence and self-concern."

4. Mother

"Petr's mother went to the villa in Dobřichovice every Sunday. Once, over lunch, Petr mentioned that Tomáš had started writing again. Although she didn't let it show, his mother was greatly unsettled by this news. She could tell by the indifference in her son's voice that he was hiding his anxiety. What's more, she read into the situation something Petr probably didn't realize himself: that his mention of Tomáš's return to writing was a cry for help. She imagined Petr as a sleepwalker returning to each of the rooms of his life, until he came to the room of his childhood—and found himself in a dramatic game he could never win. Her reaction to this image was one of horror. She was touched that Petr had turned to her, as the only person who could enter the dream arena with him, to help him there with his dream struggle. For the rest of the lunch, as they spoke of inconsequential matters, the mother watched the son and assured him in her mind: 'Don't worry, I'll save you.'

"At this point in the narrative, Kristýna interrupted Irena to ask about Petr's mother's motivation. Wasn't her main worry that Petr might go back to writing poetry, and stop earning money? Irena was sure that this wasn't the case; Petr had so much money, if he so chose, he could spend the rest of his life writing poetry while continuing to live in luxury from his annuities. Besides, the mother could care less whether Petr was a wealthy businessman, an impoverished poet, or a popular lyricist. All her fears were concentrated on one thing: that the Kantor infection that had entered his bloodstream in childhood should rise again. For if it did, he would put on the ritual mask of old and sink into its dark drama. At that time, Petr was drawn to Tomáš irresistibly; to the mother's distress, they saw each other most days. She wanted to yell at Tomáš to leave her son alone. She would wake in the middle of the night from restless dreams, and mutter: 'For God's sake, don't let it all come back!' At the bottom of all this fear, however, she felt happiness, even delight at the prospect of Petr being her child again . . .

"She asked Petr to print out *Damp Walls* for her, thinking that it would help her gauge the enemy's strength. She found the book distasteful: Its sentences were filled with Kantor patterns and myths of the kind she had tried hard to forget. The calm ease of Tomáš's style irritated her; she knew Petr well enough to see that he would be enchanted by it, and she read in it a devilish subterfuge employed with the intention of seducing her son. She came up with various ways of discouraging Petr from seeing Tomáš. But the talks her son and her stepson were having about *Damp Walls* and the Work-Network in general (during which Petr returned again and again to the long-ago conversation with the man in the fur coat, and the question it posed about what he was doing with his life) became an indulgence Petr could no longer live without. He became like a child with a wound he couldn't stop picking and scratching, so as to watch the blood seep from it.

"Petr's mother wasn't the only one unsettled by the new closeness between the stepbrothers; Irena was concerned and saddened by the impure tones she read in Tomáš's new prose and saw in his new canvases. Tomáš's writing had always made use of trashy adventure fiction. Now, Irena had the impression that the transformative power that took storylines of the American thriller-type into the mythical void was weakening. In the new work, unlike the old, the vast space occupied by car chases and travels through exotic landscapes and over far-flung seas barely merged with the glowing expanse of emptiness. Tomáš was no longer capable of distilling the marvelous essence of adventure. And this was just one sign of the great change: Irena saw that Tomáš's images had no space in which to mature; the patience that had fed his long waiting for words and forms in the darkness of the void had disappeared. Whether this great change was because Tomáš's work had aged and the spring that first burst forth on that winter morning four years earlier had dried up, Irena didn't know. Perhaps the most recent changes were a consequence of his conversations with his stepbrother: The forms no longer matured in darkness and calm but before the eyes of another. Maybe the great change came for both these reasons: The work had aged and become so weakened by sickness that it could not resist the eyes of another, or ignore what these eyes saw."

5. Yacht

"In August of last year, Petr went on vacation to Greece, allowing Tomáš to devote himself to the Work without disturbance. He was working on a series of paintings on Lygdian themes. The imaginary artist was a Parcan character Tomáš had written into the new version of *Damp Walls*. (Marius got to know first the work, then the artist in a small gallery in Parca. Later, the artist fell in love with Rita.) On a visit to Irena's studio, Tomáš found on the desk a book of M. C. Escher's art. As he flicked through it, Irena saw that he spent a lot of time over the lithographs of conjoined houses in Valletta. 'How about we take a trip to Malta?' she said. To her delight, after a moment's hesitation, Tomáš agreed to this suggestion. Without saying anything to anyone, she bought the tickets. On meeting Tomáš in the departure hall, she saw that he was carrying a fold-up easel: He had no intention of sacrificing even a few days' labor on the Work; indeed, within moments he was telling Irena how much he was looking forward to painting in the bright light of the south.

"On their second day in Valletta, they were walking in the backstreets when the cellphone in Tomáš's pocket rang. Petr was calling from Mykonos. He was about to take his motor yacht out into the Aegean. For each of the past three years, Petr had spent the first three weeks of August on the yacht, which belonged to Alexis, a forty-year-old Greek whom Petr had met in a bar somewhere in the Cyclades. As a young man, Alexis had served in the Foreign Legion. Indeed, before he settled on Mykonos, Alexis had led a very colorful life—so colorful that Petr preferred not to know about it. Petr had paid for much of the yacht himself; at first, he had intended to be the sole purchaser, but then he had come up with a simpler, more convenient solution. The agreement between Petr and Alexis was as follows: (i) The yacht would be given the name *The Magnolia* (after the tree under the balcony of Petr's villa); (ii) Alexis would pay off his debt to Petr by captaining the boat for Petr and his friends for three weeks every summer. Although the boat was an expensive purchase, Petr may even have saved money on it, as the Greek was a fine captain and navigator, and he also served as interpreter, diving instructor, meteorologist, cook, and bodyguard. The luxury yacht attracted robbers, and there had been several attempted break-ins. Once, near the island of Patmos, there had been something resembling a pirates' raid. Alexis did everything himself, sticking to a principle instilled in his youth: Never involve the police.

"The trip Petr was planning this year was different from the trips of previous years. On returning from his last vacation, over a summer-time lunch at the villa, he had promised his mother that next time he would take her along. In the fall, he had started seeing a new girlfriend—a Swiss woman he had met on business abroad—and he had invited her, too. By the spring, having visited him in his home country several times, the girlfriend had learned to speak Czech fairly well . . . As soon as Irena mentioned Petr's Swiss girlfriend, a thought occurred to me. 'I don't suppose her name was Giovanna Sulzer?' I asked, though I knew the answer already. The cipher inscribed in the face of the director of Merry Elephant, an ongoing enigma to me, now had a reading. At that moment, I was in no doubt that the woman we had spoken with in San Benedetto was Petr Quas's girlfriend. It dawned on me, too, that the faces of Giovanna and Irena had been shaped by a wind from the same world. Irena answered my question with a nod. One look at Kristýna told me that she, too, was unsurprised to learn that the woman from San Benedetto was Petr Quas's girlfriend, and that the woman could speak Czech.

"When Petr, his mother, and his girlfriend were on Mykonos, where the yacht was berthed, making the final preparations for their trip, Petr realized how much he would miss his time with Tomáš. Over recent months, he had become so used to the ritual reopening of old wounds that he was struggling to manage without it. Under the striped awning of a café in the Mykonos harbor, where his mother and his girlfriend were exchanging false smiles, he pulled out his cellphone and called Tomáš. On learning that Tomáš and Irena were in Valletta, he perked up straight away. Valletta and Mykonos weren't so far apart, he said. He invited Tomáš and Irena to join him, his mother, and his girlfriend on the trip about the Aegean. Giovanna was glad for conversation partners other than her future mother-in-law. But the mother was so horrified by the new development that she pleaded with her son to think up an excuse to withdraw the invitation. Petr refused to hear of it.

"Tomáš didn't reply to the invitation immediately. Irena tried to convince him not to accept, as she disliked the idea. But she knew from the start that Tomáš wanted to go, and that she wouldn't be able to change his mind. Tomáš's keenness to accept wasn't fed by eagerness to talk with Petr, and he rather dreaded the stepmother he had last seen at his father's funeral. By this time, Irena knew Tomáš well enough to guess what attracted him to a cruise on the Aegean. You mentioned the strange origins of Petr's love of luxury, saying that it grew out of metaphors of light and sea in his brother's poems; indeed, this love was itself a metaphor for the pure poetic image, the lost light of inspiration. Later, Petr himself would say that he had acquired the boat because of the glow of the word 'yacht' in a surrealistic image in one of his brother's poems (found in a drawer of the young Tomáš's desk), although he couldn't remember another word of it. The odd metamorphosis from poetry to yachts and radiant swimming pools may even have occurred because images of light, scintillation, sea, shore, island, and sun had always been present in Tomáš's writing. These images had roots not only in the realm of language and pure form; they expressed a dream of southern happiness, glittering sea, and white boats. Indeed, the dream may have been the essence of Tomáš's every desire and wish—ones he had never identified (although they lived, echoed, and worked inside him) as well as ones he knew about. The lives of Petr and Tomáš were very different, but their love of the sea, boats, and the South had the same source."

6. The Boat Leaves Port

"The next morning, Tomáš and Irena arrived at the airport on Mykonos, where Petr was waiting for them. Within an hour, they were standing on the stern of the yacht, under a blue-and-white flag that was fluttering in the wind, watching Mykonos disappear in the glowing midday haze. *The Magnolia* sailed from island to island. Sometimes, they called in at a harbor, so that everyone but Alexis, who stayed on the boat, could go to a taverna for dinner. At others, they dropped anchor in a secluded rocky bay, where they would bathe in the warm sea. At first, the cruise went better than Irena was expecting. Tomáš either stood at his easel, working on his Lygdian paintings, or he and Petr sat in deckchairs, drinking ouzo or Metaxa, and discussing literature. A shared dread of Petr's mother brought Giovanna and Irena closer, and although neither could overcome her shyness in the company of the other, they formed an unspoken alliance. Alexis spent most of his time at the controls, where Irena often sought him out. He would tell her about the rocks they passed and point out changes in the sea's surface, each of which carried a different message.

"Although Petr's mother smiled at everyone, her eyes were watchful; it was obvious to everyone that she was forever on the alert. She would hang around Petr and Tomáš like a restless dog, although she never intervened directly in their conversation. The presence of a woman who for some years had been his mother, made Tomáš uncomfortable; he didn't know how to behave in her company, so he avoided being alone with her. Although the mother treated Irena and Giovanna with a treacly affability, both younger women were disturbed by her prying eyes, and they sensed her distrust and readiness to attack. The mother disliked both Irena and Giovanna, each for different reasons. She was wary of Irena as she thought of her as an ally of Tomáš, who had intruded on her vacation and was putting the soul of her son in danger. The searching eyes beneath the sweet smile bothered Irena to such a degree that several times she was on the point of telling the mother: 'Leave me alone. I'm not a pawn in some childish game of yours, you know.' But she kept quiet for Tomáš's sake. As far as Petr's mother was concerned, Giovanna, too, was an intruder. Unable to reconcile Giovanna's level-head-edness with Petr's neuroticism, she decided that Giovanna could only be interested in her son for his money.

"Petr's mother was doing her son's fiancée an injustice. Giovanna and Petr had gotten to know each other in San Benedetto, when the Phoenix Group was considering making the Swiss concern an offer for Happy Elephant. Petr was sent to Bern and San Benedetto to investigate the situation and conduct negotiations. Colleagues in Bern told Giovanna that Petr was an obnoxious snob, and as she guided him around San Benedetto, she found herself agreeing with this assessment; it seemed he couldn't decide whether to boast, albeit cautiously, about his fame in the world of celebrities, or to express his contempt for this world while dropping mentions of his splendid literary plans—as it was, he tried, clumsily, to combine the two. Giovanna was taken aback by Petr's choice of conversation, not least when she realized this was his way of wooing her.

"Yet she found Petr's awkward boastfulness and snobbery oddly touching. She read in them unhealed wounds, twisted signs of desire, the naivety of a child who for some reason hasn't been able to grow up, and so has become a rich man. She was intrigued by the mystery, and it was only on the cruise that she began to unravel it. Giovanna liked snobs. She appreciated the lengths to which snobs will go as they pay tribute to values unknown to her family and people they knew (office workers, all), indeed most people. In the antics of the snob, she saw the despair of excommunication, and awareness of the impossibility of salvation. All this distinguished Petr from the people she had grown up with, and among whom she lived still—people with no crack in their soul. Giovanna fell in love with Petr for the anguish that never left him. On the yacht, she saw his humiliation in Tomáš's company, and how the pain of this humiliation attracted him, and her love for him grew. Petr bragged that he had once had a volume of poetry published. When Tomáš described Petr's book as excellent, Giovanna was delighted. So Petr's snobbery had grown like a weeping willow over the tomb of a poet! Giovanna had never known anyone whose snobbery was fed by tears for a lost past of poetry-writing. On the boat, she had the feeling that in conversation with Tomáš, Petr's snobbery was cleansed, as the pure desire and reverence for art surviving in its depths were gradually distilled from it. She hoped that he would be able to come back from this."

7. Hate

"Petr asked Tomáš many questions about his work. To Irena's surprise and delight, she heard a new tone in his voice. Although it was hesitant and extremely quiet, she knew it to be a tone of budding friendship. Petr and Tomáš may have been connected by various bonds since their teenage years, but they had never been close. Irena hoped that Tomáš would pick up on the tone and respond to it before it faded out. Even now, she couldn't understand how this opportunity had been wasted. Maybe it was because in those days Tomáš was blind and deaf to anything but the work he was finishing; as he was incapable of paying attention to the sea and the islands, which he had dreamed of his whole life, perhaps it's hardly surprising that quiet tones in his brother's language passed him by. Most blame for what happened probably rests with the mother, who showed great ingenuity in devising ways to turn Petr against Tomáš. The cause of what happened, however, may have been the weather: The hot, windless days of their cruise on the Aegean blurred the senses, blunted vigilance, and suppressed any desire to start something new.

"The early atmosphere of calm didn't last. The voice of nascent friendship weakened until it fell silent. For a time, Irena had the impression that the stepbrothers' talks were played out in the void, and that some of the old ghosts appeared. Before long, Irena and Giovanna had the alarming sense that the drama of the Prague apartment block was playing out on a new stage; they looked on as the old roles awoke in the bodies of the protagonists, probably without their knowledge. Battle was rejoined—but this time under a clear blue sky, over a shimmering sea, between islands ablaze with light, not amid unit furniture, heavy, unshapely armchairs, and frowzy sofas. The older Kantor, too, was on stage: The behavior of Tomáš, Petr, and the mother made it clear that the father's ghost was around, listening in on conversations and studying the faces of his family, and that their words were also meant for him. Something bad was about to happen. In one of their few longer conversations, Giovanna told Irena—apparently out of the blue—that she would stand by Petr no matter what; plainly, Giovanna had a sense of foreboding. Petr's character combined a weak will with a fierce recklessness—it was better not to think about what it could be driven to.

"The change was gradual. The brothers continued to spend a lot of time together. Tomáš did more and more of the talking, Petr kept ever longer silences. Tomáš was devoting a lot of thought to the final arrangement of his *Gesamtkunstwerk*; this time spent with his stepbrother was a chance to give voice to his interior monologue. He paid little attention to what Petr said to him; when Petr spoke, Tomáš would wait patiently for him to finish, so that he could continue with the exposition of his own ideas. The arrogance with which the monologue was imbued began to annoy Petr; having at first been an expression of his interest and admiration, Petr's silence was more and more an expression of suppressed rage. He began to react to Tomáš's utterances with a range of grimaces and dubious shakes of the head. But Tomáš was so wrapped up in his own thoughts (maybe he was blinded by the brilliance of the sea, too) that he failed to notice Petr's dumb show. Irena tried to talk to Tomáš about his treatment of his stepbrother, but Tomáš paid her little more attention than he did Petr. His best reply was to accuse her absent-mindedly of exaggeration.

"Petr came to believe that Tomáš was speaking of his own work to mock and humiliate him, and Petr's mother supported him in his suspicions. The latest developments in the stepbrothers' relationship had been entirely to her satisfaction. She was hoping that the atmosphere on the boat would become too oppressive for Tomáš and Irena to bear, resulting in their departure at some port and their return to Prague. But Petr had nothing of the kind in mind: His anger and his burgeoning hatred for Tomáš bound him to his stepbrother more tightly than interest in his work and the need to wallow in loss had done. Realizing that his grimacing succeeded only in frightening Irena and Giovanna, he came up with a new tactic. Since it now seemed to him that Tomáš's only purpose in speaking as he did was to lord it over someone who had achieved nothing but authorship of a few pathetic song lyrics, he planned his defense, which would take the form of attack.

"He would wait for Tomáš to pause for breath in the middle of his monologue, then interrupt him to expound on a new claim that literature should make sense in its higher forms only, thus rendering every other form worthless. Whoever placed the right demands on literature would see that the honest course was to devote oneself humbly to one's craft, rather than to publish writing that merely masqueraded as real literature. The true craftsman deceived neither himself nor others, nor did he bow down before false gods. The point of this exposition was to show Tomáš that not only did Petr understand literature better than he did, he was also the more critical, honest, and humble thinker. Naturally, this thesis was far-fetched and lacking in logic. But the atmosphere of cunningly waged war that had descended on the boat had little need of logic and common sense; what's more, the heat and windlessness distorted reasoned thought to such a degree that the cause-effect relation became twisted. In this context, maybe Petr's idea wasn't so strange after all."

8. Fight

"It wasn't long before Petr's offensive defense of kitsch was irritating Tomáš as much as Tomáš's endless monologues irritated Petr. At first, Tomáš tried to raise objections, but he soon went back to waiting stony-faced for Petr to finish before picking up his monologue where he had left it, as if all he heard was just the splashing of the sea and the hum of the engine. Conceding the effectiveness of this approach, Petr adopted it himself. As a result, Irena and Giovanna became the audience of a weird performance in which the actors took turns reciting lines that had no connection with the lines spoken by the other. After a few days of this, Petr introduced a new tactic: He began to supplement his odd theory of literary honesty with allusions to shortcomings in Tomáš's books, adding to these apparently friendly, well-meant advice. Usually, Irena and Giovanna sat together in silence, saddened and afraid by the brothers' performance. The mother was never far away, looking on with wonderment as Petr and Tomáš returned to the evil swamp of the Kantor apartment, as if in a bad horror movie, vacillating between fear that the ghost-filled landscape was about to swallow her son for good and delight that Petr's burgeoning hate for Tomáš would finally rid him of his stepbrother's influence.

"Petr's assaults roused in Tomáš the kind of spite and vindictiveness the mother had never seen in him before. Eventually, Tomáš's conversation became what she had always taken it for: malicious mockery. And that wasn't all: on reading the last pages Tomáš had written during the cruise, Irena saw that the infection that had attacked the work in Prague was back; the splendid emptiness that abounded with imagery in the first sentences of *Damp Walls* was transforming into an emptiness that was dead and barren. Even worse, she realized that Tomáš was rewriting sentences and passages that had been finished, including parts of the original *Damp Walls*. So great was Tomáš's loss of trust in the void that had given him everything, he was ceasing to understand its language; he was able no longer to swim free in the ocean of emptiness; images born from the void that expressed nothing but its glow now seemed to him inadequate and ineffective, and he tried to improve them, furnish them with additional meaning, or rid them of detail he considered unnecessary, even though this detail was the most wonderful inflorescence of nothingness. So it happened that the void fell silent, then closed to him, the text of *Damp Walls* was gradually extinguished, and the Work as a whole quietly began to collapse in on itself. It occurred to Irena that Tomáš's work would have an even sadder end than Fernando Vieta's book. Although no one had read *The Captive*, and the wire original had been swallowed by the jungle, it had been published in thousands of copies, some of which remained in North Floriana—so there was still hope that years later someone would read and make sense of it. The way things were going with Tomáš, he would leave nothing behind.

"The mother, too, felt the impending doom, as she had a highly developed sense for anything that might threaten her son, as well as for what might work in his favor. She saw that Tomáš's fall had begun, and her pleasure at the realization outweighed all her other feelings. She was jubilant at the final humbling of the Kantor family. She felt the presence of the beast that had crawled the floors of the Prague apartment, baring its teeth at her son. She hadn't known its name then, and she didn't know it now. She didn't know that the dreaded monster was Emptiness, but she did know that it was about to devour Tomáš.

"Now she was glad of Petr's idea to invite his stepbrother on the cruise. A malevolent smile of triumph appeared on her face and never left. Although Tomáš and Petr were too caught up in their games to notice the smile and the threat it contained, the two other women could study it at their leisure. To the smile was added the ghost of Kantor the father. The mother couldn't shake the feeling that he was there with them; and how glad she was that he, too, was about to witness his son's fall! Seeing the seriousness of the situation, Irena tried to convince Tomáš that they should leave the cursed yacht at a nearby island and go home. But Tomáš was bound to the deck of *The Magnolia* by a thread of hate stronger still than his love of the sea, and he was incapable of quitting the wicked, nonsensical fight that could have no winner."

9. Last Breakfast

"After a time, Petr and Tomáš ceased talking to each other altogether. Silence settled over the boat. Each day felt hotter than the last, with a light breeze appearing only briefly, at sunrise. Tomáš hardly spoke to Irena either. He stood on the deck, at his easel, practically all day, working on paintings of his Lygdian series, although he took no pleasure in them. Only around noon, when the sun was at its hottest, did he retire to the cabin, to lie reading by the impotent, buzzing fan. Alexis minded his own business; as no one gave him any instructions, he sailed from one island to the next, as he saw fit. A series of sun-drenched towns and glowing shorelines appeared and disappeared before the bow, but no stops were made. The fearful gazes of Irena and Giovanna were mostly directed at the deck of despair. Tomáš, Petr, and the mother saw nothing of this fear, as their eyes were blinded by hate and turned inward, into labyrinths of evil. Sometimes, Irena would lift her eyes to a dreamlike view beyond the boat's rail, seeing white walls with blue shutters, terraces with parasols, the green tops of palms, or a rocky coastline shining in the distance; at such moments, she told herself: 'If we reject this gift, if we sully this purity, we deserve to be cursed.'

"One night, Irena awoke to find Tomáš sitting up in bed beside her. He was staring at the bright reflection of the moon in the water. 'What have we come to? What's happened to me?' he said. Again, Irena pleaded with him to go home with her. 'You're right,' Tomáš replied. 'We must leave, before I destroy everything. Maybe we'll manage to save something, if only we can get away from this dreadful boat.' Alexis was guiding the boat toward the Dodecanese Islands. Tomáš and Irena decided they would ask him to stop at one of these islands to set them down; then they would go home.

"The next day, Tomáš was out on deck at his easel from the early morning, working on the last in his series of Lygdian paintings. It was the one of the sacred shells with the eye. The table was set with the breakfast Alexis had prepared: bread, yogurt, thyme honey, feta cheese, taramasalata, Greek salad, olive oil, oranges, slices of red melon. Visible on the horizon was the oblong island of Kos, with smaller islands around it. One by one, everyone but Alexis appeared and sat down at the table. The heat of the day was yet to arrive. Pink rays fell across the still life on the table; it looked to Irena like the setting for a TV commercial. At last, Petr broke his silence with Tomáš. He did so to make fun of his stepbrother's Lygdian paintings. How clever Tomáš had been, he said, in choosing to release them as the work of a painter from Parca; in that way, he could blame all their failings on an imaginary artist and claim them to be intentional. In the night, Tomáš had determined not to be drawn into an argument with his brother, so he said nothing and went on with his work. Petr was so riled by Tomáš's silence, however, that he began to develop a new idea. Such excuses were nothing new for Tomáš, he said. Weren't they also a feature of the insertions in *Damp Walls*? The critics wouldn't know if the naïve story in which humans, demons, and robots work together should be charged to the account of Tomáš or that of Fernando, its author in the book—or even to Hector, whose invention Fernando was. Still Tomáš said nothing. But as he went on with his soft brushwork on the shading of the shell, Irena saw that his hand was shaking.

"Petr and his mother read Tomáš's silence as an expression of contempt. The mother's anger grew into rage. Until then, her participation in the fight between Petr and Tomáš had been limited to taunts in support of her own son. Now, for the first time, she was impelled to involve herself directly—and she did so on her feet and with her voice raised. She asked what Tomáš had done in his life, apart from writing the book he never stopped talking about, and which it was obvious he was never going to finish. Petr had at least published a volume of poetry, and hadn't the critics declared him a newcomer of the year? Tomáš could mock Petr's song lyrics all he liked, but he would never be able to write anything like them . . .

"Now her anger and hatred knew no bounds. As she wished to see Tomáš humiliated by any means, she decided to go at him with evidence of her son's abilities of which Petr, perhaps exaggerating his modesty, had forbidden her to speak. Petr, she declared in triumph, was the co-creator of a screenplay that was being made into a movie by a big American film corporation. She saw that Tomáš was taken aback by this news; his brother had mentioned nothing of the sort to him. His brush stopped moving at last. He looked from Petr to the mother and back again. The mother sensed that the moment of her greatest triumph was near. She ignored Petr's repeated admonitions for her to be quiet: Nothing could stop her now. A certain famous Hollywood director was very keen on Petr's proposal, she went on. She herself had seen the letter he had written to Petr: The man was greatly impressed by the originality of Petr's ideas.

"Tomáš spoke at last, to ask what the screenplay was about. Proudly, the mother embarked on the story that begins at the university in Breslau, with Jan Evangelista Purkyně studying images we see on the insides of our eyelids, and discovering them to be fragments of an image of a strange, cosmic monster, which will be born from all living organisms on Earth, as if from huge larvae, which are everywhere . . . Irena realized that she knew this story: With slight adjustments, it described the plot of an episode from Tomáš's comics adventure series about the agent Henriette Fox. The story of the entoptical figures and the cosmic monster followed on from an episode featuring the nefarious John Wind, which ended with a picture of Vulpécula falling from the sixth story of a building toward a London street. In the first panel of the new episode, Henriette had managed to grab a bizarre caryatid on a balcony. The next panel showed Henriette on the balcony, looking through an open glass door at a meeting of a strange society, its participants each marked with a tattoo of a cocoon on the wrist; Henriette listened to what they were saying, and learned that this society guarded the secret written in the entoptic images. Later in the episode, having dealt with the matter of the sapphire and Elena's imprisonment, Henriette seized some documents belonging to the secret society, including pictures of the monster. The rest of the episode differed very little from the story told by Petr's mother (no one believes what Henriette is telling them; her superiors ridicule her; a colleague from the CIA gets in touch, having encountered a picture of the monster in Nepal; he and Vulpécula travel to the Himalayas; and so on).

"Still holding his brush, Tomáš listened to all this in astonishment. Petr simply sat there, deathly pale. Seeing the expression on her son's face, Petr's mother suspected that something was wrong. It occurred to her that perhaps she should have kept quiet after all. She stopped talking. There was no sound but the purr of the engine. Irena saw the corners of Tomáš's mouth twitch. Then—notwithstanding his resolution of the past night not to provoke his brother—he burst out laughing. The laughter went on and on, and while it did, the four people seated at the table stared at him in silence."

10. End

"Later, Irena created a scenario around the affair of which Petr's mother had spoken. It went like this. Petr's busy social life was in some ways like Tomáš's solitude: Both were a long series of random encounters, whose traces soon disappeared. By the time Petr re-established contact with his stepbrother, many years after their last meeting, his attendance at celebrity parties was occasional rather than frequent. He did attend a reception at a certain movie festival, however. And it was there, as he was circulating among the groups with glass in hand, that he stopped at a small gathering around a well-known American director. The director happened to be talking about a science-fiction film he was preparing to shoot. It was the story of a cosmic monster that had planted seeds of life on Earth, where it cultivated life-forms, notably garden vegetables and livestock. Petr remembered coming across a similar idea in his stepbrother's work—and, unable to resist, he presented the idea to the director as his own."

"He might have said something like this: 'What if this humanity wasn't vegetable or livestock, but the monster itself?'"

"The director turned to Petr and asked, 'How do you mean?'"

"'Humanity could be its larvae,' said Petr. He spoke of an egg laid by the monster on Earth, and its development; he spoke of a secret brotherhood, and the secret it guarded to save humanity from a dreadful realization.

"The director attended closely to what he was saying. 'And the initiates are apparently of extraterrestrial origin, come to Earth to monitor the evolution of the monster?' he asked.

"'I think it would be more interesting if they, too, were part of the nascent monster,' said Petr.

"'But how could they live with such knowledge?' asked the director.

"'The conflict between clinging to life and realization of its dreadful essence would be the most disturbing thing about the film,' Petr replied.

"'I see. But how do they discover the truth about what they are?'

"'Maybe somewhere in the depths of the human mind or body is some evidence of humanity's origin . . . On the retina, let's say. I'm reminded of a certain nineteenth-century Czech scientist, who studied the patterns we see when we close our eyes. What if the monster's form was somehow present in these patterns?'

"'But isn't that . . . Although . . . I need to think about it . . .' Having stood there deep in thought for a moment, the director handed Petr his card. 'Could you write down everything you've just told me and email it to me?' he asked. 'And could you do it at your earliest convenience?'

"The director wasn't satisfied with his screenplay. He felt the movie lacked a new idea to set it apart from others of its type. He had the feeling that Petr's story was just what it needed. When Petr got in touch, the director told him that he wished to use his idea, and he promised him a large fee for it. As the movie was about to go into production, there was only just enough time for a rewrite of the screenplay. Petr found the director's offer irresistible. The thought of what would happen after the movie was released, and if Tomáš discovered that he had stolen his idea and been paid for it, was an unsettling one for

Petr. He dealt with it in his usual fashion: He simply stopped thinking about it. This didn't prevent him from boasting to his mother about his meeting with the director who would shoot a Hollywood movie based on his idea. His mother then improved the story by describing him as co-screenwriter of the movie.

"When the mother got to her feet, Tomáš was still at his easel, and still laughing. As she walked over to him, the laughter stopped abruptly. The others remained at the table, Petr white as a sheet. Irena and Giovanna stared in terror at these three people who had once tried to be a family. The sun was higher now, and it was getting hot. This motionless scene lasted but a few seconds. Then the mother struck the easel, sending it crashing to the floor, releasing the canvas with the shell from its confines. After that, she threw herself at Tomáš and pounded him with her fists. He and his father were the worst thing ever to happen to her, she yelled. She didn't care that they had ruined her life, but she would never forgive them for ruining Petr's. Had Tomáš no shame in bringing the awfulness of the Kantors to Petr's yacht? Tomáš put up with her blows for a while, but when she showed no sign of quitting, he pushed her away roughly, sending her sprawling. The back of her neck slammed against the metal rail, which she slid down for support before coming to rest in a half-sitting, half-lying position, eyes wide and mouth open, looking like a large rag doll that had been thrown against a wall. Blood trickled down her face from her hairline.

"Petr made a strange sound—something between a rattle and a howl. Then he ran to his mother and knelt to her. As she came to, the mother grabbed his sleeve with one hand and felt her head and face with the other. Then she stared at her red palm while appearing to babble softly—although the babble may have been air produced by her chin, which was waggling uncontrollably. Petr turned to Tomáš. Now that the long-accumulated hatred was released within him, his features were so changed that his face reminded Irena of an Oriental mask. He broke free of his mother's grip, leapt back to the table, and pulled a long knife from the breakfast melon. Then, with all his strength, he pummeled the knife into Tomáš's chest and abdomen. Tomáš stood there in astonishment, his torn white T-shirt soaking up blood until it was entirely red. Irena jumped between the brothers. Petr was standing so close to Tomáš that he, too, was covered in blood. And still he kept stabbing, dealing Irena several blows in the process. It was Giovanna who finally dragged Petr away. Realizing what he had done, Petr dropped the knife. Four bloodied figures stood motionless and silent on the deck. The mother continued to lie by the rail, groaning, spattered with her own and others' blood. The boat's engine purred softly. On the horizon, the island of Kos was coming into view. Just before Tomáš slid quietly to the floor, Alexis appeared in the doorway. Then Irena lost consciousness."

11. Tomáš's Letter

"Irena came around in a sticky pool of blood, to the realization that she couldn't move. When she opened her eyes, the sunlight was so excruciatingly bright, she had to close them again. Because the boat's engine was switched off, she could hear the splashing of the waves and voices in the cabin, the door of which was open. Petr, his mother, Giovanna, and Alexis had probably gone inside so as not to have to look at the bloodied bodies on deck. Now they were discussing what to do next. Obviously, they believed that Tomáš and Irena were dead. Irena heard Petr's sobs and soothing words from his mother. Alexis said that they would have to get rid of the bodies. Giovanna agreed with him, adding that it was unlikely anyone was aware that Tomáš and Irena were on the yacht, which was a stroke of luck. Irena was unsurprised by Alexis's realistic outlook; loyalty to his client was a given with him, she knew. She also believed that had he been able, he would have done all in his power to keep Petr from his dreadful deed, but now that it was done, he would do all he could to protect him. Nor was she surprised to learn that Giovanna was keeping a remarkably clear head, even though her teeth were chattering. Irena remembered Giovanna once saying that she would stand by Petr no matter what.

"The most important thing for Irena now was to find out what state Tomáš in. She was lying facing the rail, and it seemed to take her forever to turn onto her other side. She tried opening her eyes again. This time, the first thing she saw was an irregular red-and-white stain, formed by the mixing of spilled yogurt with drying blood. Lifting her gaze, she caught sight of Tomáš on the far side of the deck. He had managed to pull himself up on his elbows, and he was doing something Irena couldn't figure out. Irena tried to call to him over the few yards that separated them, but no sound emerged. Tomáš was using his left hand for support as his right worked with the bloodied knife to carve something into his painting. Irena began to crawl toward him through the pools of blood. She watched as Tomáš put down the knife and pushed the painting to the edge of the deck, extremely slowly and with monumental effort, as if the object were a marble statue, not a light canvas. Before the painting could fall overboard, Tomáš let go of it. Then he laid his head on the deck and moved no more. It took Irena what felt like an age to crawl to him. When at last she touched him, she found that he was no longer breathing. She wanted to cry out, but the only sound that came was a rattling sigh quieter than the splashing of the sea. Turning her gaze to the canvas, she saw the English words etched into it. In the moments before his death, Tomáš had written a last letter. For a pen, he had used the knife with which Petr had stabbed him thirteen times; instead of paper, he had used the canvas with the Lygdian shell. Tomáš had known that he was dying, and he had believed Irena to be dead already. He had written a message about his own death and the presumed death of his girlfriend, stating who had committed the murders, and where they had happened. To the new name of the boat, he had added the original one, by which it was probably still better known on the Aegean.

"'What did the message say?' I asked impatiently. Irena's story was so vivid to me, it was as though I was an eyewitness to its events. I looked through the window at the deck and the lights of the taverna on the shore beyond, picturing the scene of Irena's description in all its details. And I was so excited to think that all our puzzles were about to solved!

"'Tomáš carved into the canvas in large letters: PETR QUAS KILLED US ON BOARD OF THE MAGNOLIA (ΙΥΓΞ). Then he signed his name: TOMÁŠ KANTOR.'"

"Her face pale, Kristýna was listening with rapt attention to Irena's story. She, too, was looking at the deck, and the scene in her mind's eye was the same as in mine. But now the deck was spick-and-span, reflecting the lights on the shore. So this was the end of the tale that had begun in the apartment of the Kantor family in a Prague tower block; a tale that above all was one of emptiness. Or was there more to come? Although Irena's description of the murder on the boat upset me, I must admit that moments after I heard it, my thoughts returned to the prospect of Irena presenting us with the definitive solution to the rebus set before us in Víziváros and Ljubljana. There could be no doubt that she was telling us about the origination of the message carried by the current to the bay of a nearby island, a surviving fragment of which— ET . . . AS . . . ILLE . . . E . . . MAG . . . ΙΥΓ . . . OM . . . ANT—would be illuminated by marine worms."

12. Scenes on Deck

"Having gathered every ounce of her strength, Irena pushed the painting into the sea. Then she tuned in to the conversation in the cabin. It seemed that Giovanna and Alexis had agreed to hide the bodies below deck, wash away the blood, wait for darkness to fall, and then weigh the bodies down and drop them into the sea. The plan complete, the door of the cabin opened, and Alexis and the two women stepped out. Petr stayed in the cabin, his moans still audible; it was as if he were the injured party in all this. Unlike Tomáš, who thought of nothing but his work and saw as little in his brother as he saw in the islands and the changing sea, Irena had a good understanding of Petr. During the cruise, she had seen many different characters in Petr; the emptiness that had settled in his mind and body in his childhood years with the Kantors left plenty of space for them all. Not only was she fond of some of the characters, she had sensed that a stay on board *The Magnolia* would change Petr for the better. At first, like Giovanna, she had hoped he would find his way back to the purity of earlier days, or least come to accept his current place in the world. Now she saw that of all his characters, the one that had won out was the frightened, hysterical child.

"Giovanna and his mother left Petr alone with his wailing; there would be time enough to console him after the bodies had been dealt with. There were several boats within range, hence a danger that someone might notice goings-on on *The Magnolia*. Alexis grabbed Irena under the arms, Giovanna took hold of her ankles. Having lifted her, they were about to take her below deck when Giovanna realized that she was still alive; indeed, Irena was watching Giovanna. With a scream, Giovanna dropped Irena's legs. Alexis laid Irena down before going to check on Tomáš. Having assured himself that there would be no more trouble from him, he went back to Irena.

"As Irena lay there on the deck, the three figures bending over her were obviously wondering what to do with her. The mother was the first to speak, not caring in the least that Irena could hear what she was saying: 'This changes nothing. She won't survive in any case. Let's take her below deck. This evening, we'll throw her in the sea with Tomáš.' She took hold of Irena's legs and looked to Alexis for help. But he didn't move; he disagreed that Irena's survival changed nothing. Still the mother didn't drop Irena's legs. When it was clear that neither Giovanna nor Alexis were prepared to help with the removal of the injured, probably dying woman, grunting and groaning she dragged Irena toward the stairwell, as if she were a sack of potatoes. Although Irena seized the metal rail with both hands, she lacked the strength to hold on. And so she was dragged through a pool of sticky blood that now extended across the whole of the front deck, her eyes on the bloodied mother, who looked back at her with indifference.

"Giovanna placed herself in the mother's path. With a nod of the head, Alexis commanded the mother to let go of Irena's legs. As the mother tried to push her away, Giovanna explained that they should consider their next move very carefully. Still the mother pushed her, with one elbow, then the other; never letting go of Irena's legs. But Giovanna held her ground. The mother turned her head and shouted over her shoulder at Giovanna: 'What is there to think about? I've nothing against Irena, but she's half-dead already. And if she did recover, we could hardly let her go, could we? She'd go straight to the police. Or were you thinking of keeping her prisoner on the yacht forever?'

"Then she tried again to force her way past Giovanna with her bloody load. 'Tomáš ruined Petr's life!' she cried. 'He may not have deserved to die for it, but that's not important now. What's done is done. No way will I stand by while Petr goes to jail! What is there to discuss? Irena can't leave this boat alive, and that's that. If you're too afraid to finish things off, I'll do it myself.'

"Looking up from the floor, Irena saw the face of Petr's mother, on which the streaks of blood were now dry, the gleaming sea beyond her, and the blue-and-white flag drooping on its pole; although she heard what the mother was saying, she couldn't form the words into meanings, so she wasn't as afraid as she might have been. Giovanna, however, was horrified by the indifference with which Petr's mother was speaking of murdering Irena right in front of her. She made a grab for the terrible woman, and Alexis followed suit.

"'Calm down,' Giovanna said to the mother. 'I wouldn't let anything happen to Petr either. But that doesn't mean we should commit another murder. One is quite enough.'

"But the mother refused to listen. She clung to Irena's legs as if they were her most precious possession. In the end, Giovanna and Alexis had to pry her fingers from them one by one. Irena looked on impassively at the three of them fighting over her ankles, without speaking a word. Having finally gotten Irena free, Giovanna and Alexis carried her into the large cabin, where the sobbing Petr was crouched in a corner, and laid her on the sofa.

"They examined Irena's wounds and discovered that they weren't very deep. 'Don't be angry with me,' Giovanna said to Irena. 'I'm so sorry I didn't stop it from happening. But as Petr's mother says, what's done is done. I promise to protect you from her.' Irena didn't reply; she would never say another word to Giovanna. After he stopped sobbing, Petr just stared at Giovanna and Alexis blankly. As Giovanna and Alexis dressed Irena's wounds, the mother stood next to them, keenly inspecting the victim for injuries that could prove fatal. Petr yelled at Alexis to make for the nearest island, so that he could give himself up to the police, but no one paid him any heed. Alexis and Giovanna carried Irena into the cabin she had shared with Tomáš, surrounded by Tomáš's pictures and manuscripts. After nightfall, she heard bangs, shuffling sounds, and muffled voices on deck; she assumed that Giovanna and Alexis were tying weights to Tomáš's body prior to tossing it overboard. But she lacked the strength to get out of bed."

13. Kidnapped

"For the next few days, the yacht sailed aimlessly among islands that appeared fleetingly in the porthole of Irena's cabin. Giovanna came to her with food, and to change her dressings. No words passed between them. Judging from the sounds that reached Irena's ears, Giovanna spent the rest of the day comforting Petr and discussing with Alexis what they were going to do. Both knew, of course, that there was no satisfactory solution for what had happened on the boat. Sometimes, Petr's mother would open the door to Irena's cabin and look at her; the mother's anger increased in parallel to Irena's recovery. Occasionally, the mother took part in Giovanna and Alexis's discussions, but she rarely said anything. Irena imagined the mother sitting at a distance from the other two, with an ironic smile on her face, as if wishing to say, 'Since you refused to listen to me, the problem is of your own making.' For several days, Petr stayed away from Irena's cabin. When at last he came to her, he paced around the bed, pleading in his own defense; his main argument was that Tomáš had provoked him to the point of temporary insanity. He no longer spoke of giving himself up. Irena just stared at the white ceiling; she would never speak to Petr again, either.

"There could be little doubt that the mother continued to believe their problem would be solved by Irena's death, nor that she was thinking about how it could be achieved, for she had nothing to lose. The only obstacles in her path were Giovanna and Alexis. Several times during their discussions she broke her silence to remind the others that the solution she had proposed on the day of Tomáš's death was still available, and to state that she would happily do what needed to be done. Giovanna and Alexis would hear none of it. The peculiar notion of honor instilled in Alexis by his life of adventure didn't stop him from covering up a murder committed by his client and patron—a murder which he had been unable to prevent. And he took it for granted that once the deed was done, he would dispose of the body. Maybe it wasn't the first time he had been called upon for such a thing. But he made it perfectly clear to Petr's mother that he wouldn't allow a second murder on his boat. As Petr's life was in Alexis's hands, the mother couldn't insist. But she didn't stop thinking about how Irena might be gotten rid of without a fuss. There were so many wounds on Irena's body, and her psyche was so damaged, that no one on board would be surprised if she suddenly expired.

"The time came when all Irena's captors, except for Alexis, appeared to come to terms with the deadlocked situation. With the realization that there was no need for immediate action, a certain calm fell over the boat. Of course, Irena's kidnapping couldn't be dragged out indefinitely, but there was nothing to say that it couldn't continue for a while yet. None of the kidnapers needed to be anywhere else or had people awaiting their return: The mother was a retiree; Giovanna had handed over her responsibilities to her deputy for the indefinite duration of her absence, and so far no one had inquired about her; Petr was basically living off his annuities, and what little business he had, he could manage on his cellphone in internet cafés in the ports of the Aegean.

"The feeling of hopelessness worked like an opiate on

Giovanna, Petr, and the mother, granting them a numb satisfaction. Eventually, though, all three began to yearn for dry land—not because the situation on the boat had become insufferable, but because they could no longer stand the indifferent, ironic radiance and tranquil rippling of the sea. They felt as though they were in a bad dream, fleeing from something while standing still. No matter where they went, they remained at the scene of the crime. Every morning, they would wake to the sight of sparkling water, and they would feel queasy. How odd it seemed to Petr now that in his poems, the sea had been a symbol of hope! Giovanna began to fear that the sound of splashing waves would drive her mad.

"One day, Giovanna said to Alexis that she simply had to leave the boat. Alexis promised to make this possible. When they came to the island of Paros, he stopped at the harbor of a little town called Naoussa, went ashore, and spent the whole day on the island.

He returned to the boat with news of a furnished house for sale on Mykonos. The house's most recent occupant was a Sicilian who had lived there in retirement. Having done business with the Sicilian, Alexis knew the house, which stood behind walls high enough to repel any intruder. It was said that the owner had had good reason to live in such a fortress. Sadly for him, however, he had recently given in to homesickness and visited Palermo, where he fell victim to a fatal accident. So the yacht headed north, back to its point of departure.

"With Petr's money, Alexis bought the house of the careless Sicilian. When the house was ready for occupation, Giovanna dissolved some pulverized sleeping tablets in Irena's drink. Early the next morning, after the bars closed but before the fishermen returned with their catch, Alexis placed the sleeping Irena in a car and drove her to the fortified house on the cliff."

14. Mykonos Fortress

"Although some rooms in the house had been cleared, others were still furnished in the style of mafioso decorativism. Irena's room contained two pieces of furniture, a single bed, and a desk. The white walls bore hooks where paintings had hung; from the window, Irena saw the top of the high wall and blue sky. Petr and his mother stayed out of her way. Giovanna would bring her food and sometimes tidy the room, behaving almost like a maid. Even now, the two women never spoke to each other. Alexis's face was so expressionless that Irena had no way of knowing what he was thinking and feeling. He had taken on two guards, giants who spoke together in a Slavonic language Irena didn't recognize; it may have been Serbian, Macedonian, Bulgarian, or a mix of all these languages. She missed her work more and more, and so she learned to create sculptures in her mind. As she was lying in bed looking at the blank, sunlight-washed white wall, with the shadows of the hooks moving across it, she worked with imaginary stone, picturing all its bulges and depressions. When the sculpture was finished, she placed it in an imaginary exhibition hall, where she went to look at it.

"She couldn't help but think of Leo's captivity in the glass tower. It was as if her imprisonment in the fortress on Mykonos was a continuation of Tomáš's work, and that she was a component in the intricate network of images whose proliferation not even Tomáš's death could halt. She told herself that her experience on the yacht and now on Mykonos was one of the shoots of the work which, having grown through all possible genres, had broken through to reality. Would the Work-Network come to form the core of a far more extensive work that was growing around it, as the Work-Network itself had grown around *Damp Walls*? And wasn't her life an imitation of events in Tomáš's book? Would she have behaved as she had if she hadn't read the story of Leo, and all the other stories in the book? Wasn't her silence a repeat of Leo's silence in Vanessa's apartment?

"Once they left the sea behind, Petr and his mother were surprised to find that they were actually quite happy. Petr could delay his decision, life on a faraway island suited him well, and he taught himself to ignore the presence of Irena, who spent most of the time in her room anyway. He did all his important business on the internet, at a desk in a room that was always locked. The mother was delighted that fate had given her this unexpected time in the same home as her son. She no longer thought that its price was his becoming a child again, with all the fearfulness, sentimentality, and deceit that entailed. Petr tried to strengthen Alexis's loyalty by paying him a high wage. Even so, he didn't trust the Cretan. Petr knew that Alexis's moral code ruled out betrayal, but not mutiny. He insured himself against this by secretly paying the two Balkan giants more than he paid Alexis and making it clear to them that they were responsible to their employer directly. In return, he received from them an understanding that they would inform Petr of any indication that Alexis's loyalty to him was cooling.

"Every day was much like the last. Irena lay in bed, her mind projecting images of sculptures in progress onto the wall. She would hear snatches and fragments of conversation from various places in the house, and the laughter of the guards; sometimes, the wind would carry to her ears the voices of bathers on the beach. One day, she heard Tomáš's name—which was strange, as it was the first mention of the murdered man in this house. She tiptoed to the door and listened. At the far end of the hall, Petr was giving Giovanna some news. Irena heard fear in his voice. She understood that a report had appeared on the internet about the discovery of Tomáš's body by fishermen. It seemed that Alexis hadn't weighted the body down properly: Having floated to the surface, it had been carried to the nearby coast of Turkey."

15. Package from Italy

"Although Giovanna managed most Merry Elephant matters by email, from time to time the Balkan guards would drive to Chora to collect a consignment for her, and occasionally she herself would need to mail a letter. Irena waited for an opportunity to slip a message about her imprisonment into a letter that was leaving the island, or at least to scribble a cry for help on the back of an envelope. But Giovanna was careful to ensure that Irena never got anywhere near her correspondence.

"From time to time, Irena's wounds became inflamed and would open. This would put the mother in an especially good mood, and she would pace about in front of Irena's room and occasionally peek inside. The wounds always closed up again after some hours or days. One morning, Irena's body was in the grip of a particularly bad fever, and she was lying helpless on her bed. Giovanna's room was opposite hers. The jailer/caretaker/maid checked on the prisoner/mistress regularly, and she also brought her medicine. Between the silent visits, she left the doors of both rooms open. As she lay with her head on the pillow, Irena saw Giovanna pacing about her room, appearing and disappearing from the double frame of the two doors. Then she saw her step over to the desk, where she opened a package. At that moment, Giovanna's cellphone rang, and she picked up. The phone conversation appeared to be an argument; because Giovanna spoke softly, Irena couldn't tell who she was arguing with. She supposed it was Petr, who was in town with his mother and Alexis, presumably running an errand. Again, Giovanna disappeared. Moments later, Irena heard a car drive away. Now she was alone in the house, but for the two guards, who were probably in their room at the end of the hall, playing a favorite game of theirs, something like checkers. The doors of Irena's and Giovanna's rooms remained open. Either Giovanna had forgotten to lock them in her haste, or she had told herself that Irena was incapable of getting out of bed.

"Irena decided to take full advantage of this first opportunity to enter Giovanna's room and explore it. Slowly, she sat up in bed; then, leaning against the headboard, she got carefully to her feet. Much like Leo, it occurred to her. Or was she thinking of Marius in the green room? The characters from Tomáš's novel twisted and merged into one, with Tomáš's face. Irena shuffled to the door, using the wall for support. The hardest part was crossing the narrow hall to Giovanna's room without a prop. She almost fell, remaining upright only by grabbing the door frame. Having rested for a few moments, she at last reached the desk, which stood in the middle of the room. Like her own, the room had bare white walls and was scantly furnished. She collapsed into the chair. On the desk, sitting on crumpled wrapping paper, was a shallow box with its lid off. The box contained a folded piece of a paper with words of Italian on it. Under this, she found a sheet of plastic film with ten indentations; each of these indentations held the figure of an animal, bird, fish, or sea creature. The figures were made of white plastic and about a centimeter high.

"It took Irena a moment to realize what she was looking at. One of the duties of the director of Merry Elephant was to approve designs from which molds would be made for new candy shapes. From when she and Giovanna had still talked, Irena knew that Giovanna gave her designers free rein, and that her signature was a mere formality. It was likely that Giovanna would do no more with this than sign the cover document and return the designs to her deputy in Italy, who would then authorize their production. Irena's first idea was to write a message about her imprisonment and hide it inside the box, but she couldn't be sure that Giovanna wouldn't inspect the contents before sending the box back. When she saw the miniature shell, she was reminded of the Lygdian symbol in Tomáš's novel, which Tomáš had been painting on the day of his death. What occurred to her then was something so bizarre, she thinks today that it must have been a product of her fever: She would turn the figures into symbols and use them to write a letter; Merry Elephant would be the printer for her hieroglyphic call for help, producing thousands of copies; and these copies would be sent to towns and cities in many countries."

16. Irena's Letter

"Having examined all the designs, Irena decided on the hiero-glyphs she would turn them into. She planned a series of ten molds telling the story of Tomáš's murder and her own imprisonment. To convince herself that this idea wasn't as crazy as it might seem, Irena whispered to herself: 'Why shouldn't I give it a try? Maybe Giovanna didn't pay attention to the original designs. And even if she did, maybe she won't notice the changes. In granting her approval, maybe she'll be as undemanding and lax as I know she can be. Maybe the altered designs will go into production, and maybe someone who buys candy will realize that they are hieroglyphs comprising a hidden message. Maybe that person will succeed in reading this message. And maybe then someone will come to my rescue . . .'

"Obviously, there were so many contingencies in this plan that only someone with a 104°F fever would give it any chance of success. Nevertheless, the likelihood of the message being read was raised slightly beyond minimal by the possibility of Irena's letter being sent to many countries of Europe, including the Czech Republic—although this would happen only if the designs resulted in the production of shapes of candy, of course.

'Leo sent his wife a message embroidered on Vanessa's evening gown, which was even crazier than what I'm doing,' Irena told herself. 'And his letter reached its addressee. And its addressee read it right.' She had lived so long in the world of Tomáš's book that there were moments she couldn't tell Tomáš's images from the real world. It was the same with Kristýna. Even I find myself asking this summer if images in my mind are produced by memories of my own, or something Kristýna has told me about her life or Tomáš's novel . . .

"Irena had used the white plastic of the figures before, so knew it was easy to cut and rub down. She looked around for something to work it with, lighting on a safety pin on the floor by the window. Her journey to the window, made on all fours, was long and tiring. Having captured the pin, she dragged herself back to the desk, and then onto the chair. Her exertions so exhausted her that for a long time she sat on the chair with her head on the desk, recovering what little strength she had. At last she opened the pin and carefully removed the white shell from the sheet of film. She began work on the open eye, in the fervent hope that the candies would be bought by a reader of the published fragment of *Damp Walls*, and that this person would understand this character in the hieroglyphic letter to represent the murdered Tomáš Kantor. Fortunately, Irena has excellent eyesight, so she had no need of a magnifying glass. The problem was, her hands were so shaky with fever that she couldn't hold the point of the pin steady against the tiny shell. She dropped the pin and the shell on the desk. Because of her body's helplessness, she felt more desperate than at any point since her witnessing of Tomáš's death. She would have to return to bed . . . But then she made herself persist. She stared hard at the white figure and the point of the pin, to the exclusion of everything else. And then she felt the fever flow from her fingers, up her arms, to her shoulders, out of her body, and into a vacuum that surrounded her, where it stayed. The handshaking ceased. Having taken the shell between thumb and forefinger, Irena began, calmly and with concentration, to carve in the Lygdian eye.

"When the work was done, she blew the powdery residue from the figure and returned it to its indentation on the sheet. Then she picked up the jellyfish figure, turned it bell-down, and proceeded to scratch away at it until it looked like a boat; it was easy to make the standing tentacles into something resembling the flower of the magnolia. The second pictogram in the series meant 'a yacht called *The Magnolia*;' in combination with the other pictograms, it was to indicate the scene of the murder. As the outline of the octopus had something of the church on Mykonos about it, Irena used the pin to make the resemblance more apparent, so marking the place of her captivity. The fourth hieroglyph would tell of the act of murder. For this, Irena chose the crocodile with the good-natured smile. She transformed the half of its body with the long tail into the blade of a dagger. But before she could get around to turning the other half into the dagger's hilt, the silence was broken by the sound of an approaching car. Quickly, she returned the uncompleted figure to its indentation on the sheet, swept the white powdery residue from the desk into a handkerchief, and returned to her room, feeling the fever return to her body as she did so. She fell onto her bed exhausted, as if from a long day chiseling away at a large stone sculpture. Through the open door, she saw Giovanna inspecting the box, presumably to make sure that it contained no message from Irena. Giovanna gave no sign of noticing the changes to four of the designs.

"Once the fever subsided, Irena considered her attempt at smuggling a message from her prison with skepticism verging on ridicule. Even if she had managed to change all ten figures into hieroglyphs, the likelihood of someone deciphering them was slight, she told herself. Our story had astonished her. Her hopes in the madness of her fever hadn't been in vain: Not only had someone recognized the four gummy candies as a fragment of a message, they had read that message with a high degree of accuracy. By the time of our success, however, the message was no longer of use to her: She no longer lived in the house on Mykonos."

17. Flight

"Petr's mother worked hard to get her son to accept that Tomáš had provoked him. She maintained that Petr had acted in a state of temporary insanity, and she insisted that Tomáš had brought his end on himself. What her argument lacked in logic and morality, it made up for in repetition, and so the mother's few utterances became the basis of the son's conviction. Petr knew that the newly found gift of his innocence was too fragile to share with others, but he couldn't resist remarking to Giovanna, on several occasions, that he was the injured party in all this, and as such he deserved her pity.

"The mother was delighted by her son's improved mood. She resumed her plotting to get rid of Irena, in the firm belief that Petr would turn a blind eye to the act, and that he would protect her from Giovanna and Alexis once it was done. Before, she would never have believed herself capable of killing; now, however, what she was preparing seemed to her the most natural thing in the world. She would smile at the two Balkan giants, seeing them as willing allies, reading in their eyes proof that she lived in the same world as them, and that she was the boss they truly wished for. Thus, the balance of power at the house turned the mother's way. The guards regarded the prisoner as wolves regard a deer, tremulous in their eagerness to sink their teeth into their prey; but for fear of Alexis, they may even have acted on their own initiative. With the mother, they formed a terrible trinity. Irena's fear of them grew, as she knew that Alexis and Giovanna wouldn't be able to protect her forever.

"Although Giovanna viewed the growing bond between the mother and the guards with alarm, she was more concerned still by the change in Petr. When he was at his most desperate, she had stood by him and thought little about his guilt. But now that he was telling her he wasn't responsible for what had happened, spending more time with his mother than with her, and taking regular swims at Super Paradise Beach, she found it ever harder to support him.

"Giovanna listened to Petr's words of self-pity at first with annoyance, then with quiet range. She watched with sickened horror as the mother became the lady of the house, her court composed of sentimental Petr and two guards baying for blood. Alexis went about deep in thought, seemingly oblivious of his surroundings. Nothing remained of Giovanna's love for Petr. She longed to leave the house on Mykonos and return to her life of contentment in San Benedetto. But she knew that she couldn't leave Irena at the mercy of Petr's mother and the guards. The house on the cliff had become a prison for Giovanna, too. Although she knew she needed to do something, the weeks of strain had left her feeling exhausted and apathetic. Her life in the house became more and more like Irena's (and Leo's in the glass tower, of which she knew nothing). Like Irena, Giovanna spent most of her time in her room, looking from the window at the high wall and the blue sky, listening to an underlying hum of conversation elsewhere in the house that boded ill.

"But in thinking that Alexis had stopped taking an interest in goings-on at the house, Giovanna and Irena were mistaken. He had retreated into himself to observe the situation without attracting attention, and to consider what to do—a tactic he had learned with his unit during his time with the Foreign Legion in Somalia and Ivory Coast. When his client and patron was in danger of arrest, he had taken it for granted that he would stand behind him against the police and the law, and that he would somehow help Petr out of his dreadful situation. But now Petr was behaving as if on vacation, and his terrible mother was quietly taking control of the house, banding together with his subordinates as she resumed her plotting. And this plotting probably now targeted him as well as Irena. So at last he chose to take the situation into his own hands.

"One night, Irena was woken by a hand on her shoulder. She was about to cry out when the hand clapped over her mouth. Her first thought was that the guards had come for her, and that her end was near. But the figure by her bed was Alexis, and he was telling her to go with him. Irena pulled a coat over her pajamas and grabbed the bag that contained her papers. Then she paused for two seconds to consider whether to add Tomáš's last manuscripts to the contents of the bag. She decided that it would be better for his legacy if his writings from the time of his last sickness remained on the island. As she and Alexis were tiptoeing along the dark hall, they heard a creaking from behind them. They stopped, and Alexis reached into his belt for a knife. Giovanna was standing on the threshold of her room in a white nightgown, looking like a ghost. For a moment, the three of them just looked at each other. Then Giovanna went to Irena and touched her arm, as if about to embrace her; but the gesture went no farther, and she returned to her room in silence.

"Beyond a bend in the corridor, they saw a strip of light across the floor, coming from the part-open door of the guards' room. They snuck past the room, again on tiptoe, Alexis's hand again on his weapon. The guards were in the middle of an argument in their own language. Alexis was still the keeper of the keys; as quietly as he could, he released each of the locks on the front door of the house. After each click, he stopped and listened, but the silence of the house was broken only by the muffled voices of the guards and the snores of Petr or his mother. Outside, there was still the lock of the gate beyond the driveway to contend with. As Alexis worked on it, Irena watched the front door, her heart pounding. The door remained closed.

"They descended the cliff along a winding path, their progress aided by the bright light of a high moon. Irena's ankles and calves were scratched by dry thyme plants. *The Magnolia* was in the bay, bobbing about between pointed rocks, in a changeable patch of white light. By the time the boat growled and surged forward, Irena was standing at the stern, watching the long veil of light the boat was pulling in its wake, looking up at the house on the cliff. Then she went down to her old cabin, lay down, and fell asleep."

18. Lefka Ori

"As soon as she awoke, Irena returned to the deck. To her left, the red sun was rising—so they were heading south. Alexis was at the controls. Irena assumed that they had been traveling all night, without a break. She went to stand beside him, as she had done in the early days of the cruise. She didn't ask about their destination. Having reached its highest point, the sun began to descend. In the distance, islands appeared and disappeared, as if they, too, were gliding on the water. In the late afternoon, a long strip of land came hazily into view. Irena supposed that it was Crete, and that Alexis was going home. It was dark by the time they dropped anchor at the harbor in Chania. Having switched off the engine, Alexis spoke to Irena for the first time since their flight from the fortress on Mykonos. He was going to take her to a village in the Lefka Ori mountains on the south of the island, he said. There, his father, two brothers and their families would take care of her in her recovery. As soon as she wished to go home—be it the day after tomorrow, a month from now, or even a year from now—one of the brothers would book her a flight and drive her to the airport. If she chose to go to the police, she shouldn't try to protect him; he knew how to look after himself. Irena was happy with this arrangement; she wasn't ready to go back to Prague, as the thought of what awaited her there—her studio, Tomáš's empty apartment, a police investigation—was anything but appealing.

"They got into a car that was parked in one of the streets near the harbor. At first, they drove east along the coast, past large hotels with floodlit bunting, through towns catering first and foremost for tourists, passing store after store bright in the night like a string of Chinese lanterns. The car turned into a backstreet, after which it left the radiant world behind, climbing, via a long series of switchbacks, toward a plateau. The car's headlamps picked out dwellings made of stone and of concrete, crumbling stone walls, rusting wires reaching for the dark sky out of half-built houses, wrinkled, twisted olive-tree trunks, tangles of black cord for the watering system stretching along the roadside. Still the car climbed, until it came at last to a single-story house of unplastered stone. Before the house stood a tall, white-haired old man in high, black-leather boots, and two other men whose resemblance to Alexis was striking. Alexis got out of the car, walked to the passenger side, opened the door for Irena to step out, and introduced her to his father and brothers. He embraced his brothers and exchanged a few quiet words with his father. Then he got into the car and drove away.

"Irena stayed in the house with Alexis's father, two brothers, their wives and five children. Although she and they had no common language, they treated her with great respect, as though she were a queen who had condescended to share their home for a while. Before long, not only Alexis's family but the whole village was looking out for her. Every day she was invited to dine at a different house. The villagers taught her Greek, and she learned fast. Her wounds were treated regularly by a physician from a neighboring village, who, although he spoke English, asked her no questions. The window of Irena's room had a view of a rocky slope, adorned by the racing shadows of clouds. She went for long walks in the mountains, where often she encountered a shepherd and his sheep. As she climbed, the mountain range opened to her view in the cold light. Only atop the area's highest peak did she glimpse the sea, far off to the south.

"Sometimes as she walked, she imagined what Petr, his mother, and Giovanna were doing. Were Petr and his mother still on Mykonos, or had they returned to the villa in Dobřichovice? Were they perhaps hiding out on the Bahamas or the Seychelles, for fear of the punishment awaiting them for murder and kidnap? Were Petr and Giovanna still together? Was Giovanna still managing the factory in San Benedetto, or had she gone home to Locarno? Wherever they were, all three were no doubt living in fear of a police officer's knock on their door. But Irena still couldn't face the thought of delivering her testimony at a police station and in court. She wasn't yet prepared to entertain the idea of exchanging her life among the great people of these majestic, brilliant mountains for one of police interrogation and bearing witness in court, where she would have to look again on the faces of Petr and his mother. Nor did she wish to do anything to the detriment of Alexis, who had saved her from the mother and her helpers.

"Here in the mountains as at the house on Mykonos, Irena was struck by similarities between her fate and Leo's, in a story Tomáš had written before she knew him. The house in the mountains may not have become her home in the way that the motel beyond the city limits or the hotel in Mexico City became Leo's, but her village life brought her many moments of quiet joy. Unlike Leo, Irena couldn't forgive her erstwhile captors, although she told us she had no desire for revenge. What she felt was that the story growing out of Tomáš's work, and so becoming a part of it (her own life included), should be governed by the laws of that work; and that in common with other episodes in Tomáš's narrative, it should reach some kind of conclusion. It was plain that she herself should appear in the final scene . . . At that time, Irena took this idea no farther, preferring to think of other things."

19. Gallery in the Mountains

"There was another way in which Irena's fate was like Leo's: What they had lived through served to take them back to their work. The mountain paths Irena walked were lined with light-colored rocks. She often stopped to inspect them, run her hands over them, lean down to them, and breathe in their scent. One day, not far from the village, she happened upon an abandoned quarry filled with beautiful blocks of stone; it was as if they had been standing there waiting for her. She borrowed a hammer and a chisel from Alexis's brothers and began to turn the stone into sculptures. In this way, she filled the days of the fall, winter, and spring. She would go to the quarry first thing in the morning, day after day—even in winter, when she would have to sweep snow from her unfinished work that had fallen overnight. She would chisel away at the stone even in blizzard conditions, when she could see no more than a few yards ahead. The villagers brought her food and hot coffee; they liked to watch her work, always maintaining a discreet distance.

"Although Irena's new sculptures weren't figurative, they told of the summer cruise aboard *The Magnolia*, her love for Tomáš, and her memories of the Work-Network. She came to realize that her work drew her ever closer to the germ from which Tomáš's work, and her own fate, had grown—to *Damp Walls*; and from there to the moment on that winter morning when the novel was born from the fertile void in a sudden burst of images and sentences. Irena had the impression that the currents of emptiness that flowed through Tomáš's novel sentence by sentence were seeping into the stone, and even guiding her chisel. And so as the gallery slowly took shape in the quarry, it became one of the late shoots of Tomáš's work, which continued to grow even after the death of the author. 'I asked myself when this growing would stop,' Irena told us.

"It was then that Kristýna spoke up. Tomáš had once quoted to her the words of Paracelsus: 'As man cultivates the earth by his will, so he cultivates the heavens in their stars by his imagination.'

"'That's right,' Irena replied. 'I had the feeling that the tide would one day exceed the borders of Earth and rearrange the constellations of the heavens.'

"'But that's precisely what happened,' said Kristýna. 'Since Tomáš's death, the constellations of the heavens have changed.'

"'Yet I knew that the remarkable proliferation of Tomáš's work, which drew in everything that came into its path, had little bearing on whether the work was good or bad literature,' Irena continued. 'I myself am no judge of its quality.'

"Kristýna picked up the thread. 'Tomáš often said to me that he didn't think of himself as a writer. I think of him as an emptiness addict. He immersed himself in a stream in which the void endlessly changed shape, without ever being anything but a void, and without ever exhausting itself—provided Tomáš remained true to it. Bathing in the void was a drug he couldn't give up. That this indulgence first played itself out in literature was probably just a coincidence.'

"At that moment, the conversation between Tomáš's two widows was interrupted by a tap on the window. All three of us jumped, and Irena cried out; she may have been expecting to see the faces of the two Balkan guards, sent by Petr's mother to eliminate this witness to her son's crime. But it was only the waiter from the taverna where Kristýna and I had had dinner—a dinner for which we still hadn't paid. Having noticed us on the yacht, he had come for his money before cashing out. Apologizing profusely, we settled our bill. Then Irena went on with her story.

"The rocks in the quarry were roughly arranged in a circle, with three large blocks at its center. For a long time, Irena didn't touch these blocks—only at the very end did she make them into sculptures. And these were the only sculptures she gave names to. The first was *Emptiness*, and it represented the initial void that appeared to Tomáš Kantor on that winter day when he began to write *Damp Walls*—a void which still enveloped thousands of worlds, just a few of which would open in Tomáš's book and his subsequent work. The second sculpture, called *The Network*, depicted the developing void as a tangle of infinite growth. The third sculpture was called *Linda's Lament*. It represented the dark center of Tomáš's book and the whole of his Work-Network; the continuous transition of the void into shapes, and the blending of these shapes; the agonizing yet delightful surf of twisting, merging, and disintegrating lines; the sounds and scents from which words, images, and objects are born, and into which they crumble back; a whirl of unfinished monster images, heading for the light and searching for their finite form, with no guarantee that they will reach it, that they will not remain forever in the larval stage; the hum of words that are but convolutions of unknown sounds; and rippling tangles of lines, in which future characters can only be guessed at. When Irena spoke of the place where Tomáš's images were born, I pictured a dark, cold rift, from which something was forever rising, streaming, spurting, or slithering, much of it slipping back again. It seemed to me I could see the ghostly inhabitants of Kristýna's body crawl from the dark rift; I imagined the emergence of the swarm of lights on the trio of bridges in Ljubljana, and the many other lights of my journey south; I imagined the scents of early-morning Trastevere drifting all the way here; I imagined the smell of the sea, as it gave rise to a white matter that formed itself into the labyrinth of Chora. The three sculptures within the circle depicted the beginnings of the Work, its infinite growth, and its chaotic center moving in time with the Work.

"In spring, when the series of sculptures was finished, and the quarry beyond the village had become a Tomáš-inspired Stonehenge, Irena embarked on new work, in wood and in stone. Although this work grew out of shapes she had encountered in the mountains of Crete, it contained echoes of the old images, and Irena considered it a continuation of Tomáš's work. Her work attracted a growing number of buyers, and word of it spread far and wide. From her earnings, Irena bought a small abandoned house on the edge of the village, where she soon settled. Apparently, she was unmissed in Prague. As no one knew of her relationship with Tomáš Kantor, there was nothing to connect her with his death. She managed her affairs and kept in touch with her acquaintances in Prague by phone and online. Her memories of Tomáš still caused her pain, but this faded over time. Her life in the village was a peaceful one. Occasionally, she took a bus to Chania or Heraklion, where she bought tools for her work. Before her most recent trip, one of Alexis's brothers had asked her to go *The Magnolia* to fetch a family album Alexis had left on board. We had tapped on the window just as she was taking the album from a drawer."

20. Dream of a Trip to Prague

"Irena changed the subject abruptly. 'On that last night, if Tomáš hadn't woken me to tell me what was on his mind,' she said, 'I may have let the matter rest . . .' I knew what she meant by this, and I'm sure Kristýna did, too. In the silence that followed, the three of us thought of the same thing: the shooting at the Tortoise theater. The identity of the impostor Thing in Itself was the last unsolved puzzle of our journey. Neither Kristýna nor I had mentioned the theater, although both of us had guessed the answer to the riddle it posed. Here in Loutro, I've thought a lot about what happened there, and I've put the story together for myself—from what I remember of that evening at the Tortoise, from reading between the lines of Irena's story, and from what I read in newspapers reports of Petr's death about his solitary life in the villa in Dobřichovice. Maybe I've captured the truth; maybe I've made a few things up."

Martin called the waiter and ordered another ouzo. Then he told me what he thought had happened. "The way I imagine it, on one of her trips to the northern coast, Irena learned on the internet that the Flamingo theater company was preparing a production of Tomáš's ballet. Then she discovered that Petr had returned from Mykonos to his villa in Dobřichovice, where he was living with his mother. So he hadn't gone into hiding: Probably he had told himself that his fear of arrest would never leave him, no matter where in the world he was, and that he would feel better at home than anywhere else. In all likelihood, Giovanna had left him. He had become a prisoner in his own villa. How did he spend his days? Lying on the couch listening to the trains on the Plzeň line, as Irena had listened in the Mykonos house to the sirens of the boats? Did he complain to his mother about his fate? And, if so, did she comfort him, or did the two of them rarely speak and try to avoid each other? I imagine Petr thinking about his childhood—the early years, when he and his mother lived alone, rather than the years in the Kantors' apartment. In a strange way, the years had fallen away. Did he feel that his life in the villa was a continuation of his stepbrother's work, that he couldn't free himself from the web Tomáš had spun? I imagine his mother encouraging him to see friends, go out into the world, go on with his work, but giving up on this after a while. In her mind, love for the frightened, returned child merged with compassion for the castaway, and undying hatred of two dead men.

"Irena longed to see a performance of Tomáš's ballet, not least because, apart from the two published extracts from *Damp Walls*, it was the only part of his work to have reached the public. As she contemplated a return to Prague, she couldn't shake the idea that the story of the white yacht must have an end, and that it was her task to give it one. She was as committed to this idea as John Wind was committed to the poetics of Aristotle. At this early stage, I doubt Irena knew what the end should be, but I'm sure she knew that it would concern Petr and his mother, and that it would reflect the horror of Tomáš's murder and the depth of her own pain. Maybe her idea began as a dream, and the death at its center emerged as the idea took shape. Having spoken to Alexis about it, maybe she was surprised by how the idea acquired a logic of its own, and how the dream became a plan. I can't see Alexis trying to talk her out of it. He probably offered advice and promised to get her a gun, or least put her in touch with someone in Prague who could provide her with one.

"So Irena flew to Prague, where she attended the premiere of *The Critique of Pure Reason*, and all its subsequent performances. In the lobby and auditorium, she and Kristýna would have crossed paths, strangers to each other. Irena saw how easy it was to get backstage. As she considered how to put her plan into action, she went for long walks around the city. By now, she was firm in her intention to kill Petr—although sometimes she wondered if what she had in mind was truly the beginnings of a deed, or still a dream. I can easily imagine her waking each morning and wondering where she was: in Prague, at her house in Lefka Ori, on *The Magnolia*, or in the fortress on Mykonos? Maybe it happened like this. One night, Irena had a dream, in which Petr Quas was seated in the front row of the audience at a performance of Tomáš's ballet. One of the swirling dancers on the stage separated from the others. A gun appeared in this dancer's hand. There was a shot. A red dot appeared in the middle of Petr's forehead. This night-dream grew into her daydreams of revenge, and soon Irena couldn't get it out of her head. It was only a matter of time before she asked herself why she shouldn't do as the dream suggested. Recalling the success of Hector's Lygdian program, she told herself that the strangest, most fantastical plans could transform into the most effective, easiest-to-implement acts. There was nothing surprising about this: What she had in mind was so far removed from the life she had lived till then, it could only be added as a phantasmagoria; that it should have the character of unreality was all of a piece. Irena could only have killed in a dream . . .

"She had no difficulty coming up with a dream libretto. As she did so, Irena was aware of the great debt her style owed to Tomáš. Then she sent a letter to Petr, enclosing a ticket for the ballet. She composed the letter in characters cut from a newspaper—to disguise her identity not from Petr (he would know she was the author the moment he opened the envelope) but from whomever should find the letter after his death. Surely Petr had been expecting to hear from Irena, by some means or other, since her escape from Mykonos. No doubt his first reaction to Irena's communication was horror. But he may also have felt relief that the thing of dread that woke him several times each night was finally coming to a head. What's more, a letter from Irena was surely better than a police raid at the villa.

Her decision not to go to the police must mean that she wished to negotiate. So Petr went to the theater, with the intention of giving Irena anything asked for in exchange for her silence. Whether he recognized the shrouded figure pointing a gun at him from the stage, it is impossible to say.

"After Irena killed Petr and vanished from the labyrinth of storehouses behind the Tortoise, I suppose she went straight back to her house in Crete, having booked her return flight already . . . As I've thought about all this here in Loutro, I've reached the conclusion that Petr's death wasn't the main thing for Irena. More important still was the blow she dealt Petr's mother. It's my impression that the anger Irena felt toward Petr gradually dissipated in the Cretan mountains, to be replaced by sorrow, even compassion; but the hatred she had come to feel for the mother on board *The Magnolia* has never weakened. On learning of her son's death, the mother was in no doubt about identity of the perpetrator. But there was no way she could expose the killer. The possibility of her own exposure as a participant in Irena's kidnapping and as the main plotter in a scheme to murder her, with the prospect of many years in prison, was not, I believe, of much concern to the mother. I imagine her keeping silent because her confession would have revealed Petr's crime. The mother took it as her duty to protect the son's reputation, just as she had protected Petr while he was alive.

"Following Petr's death, each of these two women felt herself bound to the other by chains of hatred that never slackened, notwithstanding the fact that they lived hundreds of miles apart. Now, the mother's hatred for Irena was even stronger than her hatred for Tomáš and his father; her former husband, her stepson, and her stepson's fiancée were three devils who had entered her life with the intention of ruining and then killing her son. She remained alone with her hatred in the Dobřichovice villa, spending her days wandering the empty rooms, with their large windows overlooking the garden. First thing every morning, she would lie half-awake prepared to rise and go to Petr, before reliving the terrible moment of discovery that her son was no longer living.

"I've put all this together only since I've been in Loutro. I don't know if that's how things really were, and nor will I ever know . . . When Irena finished her story, she invited us to her little house in the country. Kristýna accepted the invitation without hesitation: The two women had a lot to talk about. I declined, not wishing to interfere in something that concerned only the two of them. Besides, I wished to be at the seaside; looking at the sea from a mountaintop wouldn't have been enough for me. I told Kristýna that I would wait for her in a peaceful spot on the coast. Irena recommended Loutro. She had come to Chania in a car borrowed from one of Alexis's brothers. I went with them to the parking lot, and there Kristýna and I parted. I spent a last night at the hotel and left Chania the next morning, by bus to Hóra Sfakion. I got to Loutro on the boat."

The Story of the Journey to Gavdos

1. The Point of the Journey

For all I knew, that was the end of Martin's story. After all, I now knew the identities of both murderers. But perhaps there was more to the story of the journey south than the detective part. In the early morning the following day, I was once again intoxicated by the superb laziness of Loutro, which is even more delightful, and even more like an opium dream than the laziness of Chania to which Martin had succumbed a few days earlier. The Loutro laziness rises like hot breath from the glittering water, the white walls, the glowing ocher rock, the mountains running to the sea, and many other layers, the last of which dissolve in the brilliant air of the distance. I walked several times from one end of the bay to the other, breathing in smells of breakfast, and listening to snippets of conversation. I took the back way that passes the gardens hidden under the rocks, after which I sat on the balcony until lunch, reading and watching the comings and goings of the white ferries Daskalogiannis and Samaria, which stop in Loutro on their way between Palaiochora and Hóra Sfakion. By one o'clock, I fancied some of Vangelis's sour fish soup. When I got to the taverna, it was full of people having lunch. Before long, Martin came by and joined me at my table; he ordered coffee and ouzo. As I enjoyed my soup, I waited for the story to resume, although I wasn't sure that it would. Martin took his time in getting started, but I soon discovered that he had plenty left to say. Again, he began without preamble.

"On my last night at the pension in Chania, in the room I had shared with Kristýna, I struggled to get to sleep. Images from Irena's story kept coming back to me. I saw the bloodied bodies on the deck of the yacht, and Irena's white room in the house on Mykonos. That night, I felt that the point of the journey south had been to solve the mystery of the death of Tomáš Kantor's and that of his stepbrother. My journey had ended in the marina in Chania, so it seemed. But the next day, as I rode the bus to Hóra Sfakion, I realized that the evening on the yacht was just one station among many, an episode in its own story, and that the story of Tomáš and Petr was but one thread in the twine of which the journey south was composed. The conversation with Irena was one of many encounters on a continuing journey, and the point of the journey was as mysterious as before. There in the almost empty bus, as we traveled from one mountain village to the next, I imagined that one day, maybe three years from now, I would discover that the point of this journey was the three days in Chania, or the early-morning shadow-play in Trastevere, or the encounter with the nighttime sea in the shipyards of Pula, or those few happy moments I spent at a café table on Bratislava's Hviezdoslav Square. I would discover that everything that came before those moments was preparation for them, and that everything that came after was their reverberation and extinction. Here in Loutro, I do nothing but consider the point of the journey south. In fact, the hardest detective work has come since Kristýna and I tracked down the killers of Tomáš Kantor and Petr Quas. Perhaps I've been so keen to tell you about my journey in such detail because

I hoped that by doing so, I would get all its events, feelings, intentions, delights, and anxieties straight in my head, and so understand them better. If that's so, I hope you don't mind."

"And have you got anything straight?

"Not really," Martin sighed. "The unrevealed center of the journey, around which all its moments are grouped, may reside in one of the cities Kristýna and I passed through, but it may just as well be in a few words from the conversation with Zoltán, the view of the lights of the San Benedetto railroad station from the hotel window, or the seconds we spent on the platform of Prague's Main Station on the night of our departure. As we traveled, I sometimes had the feeling that the whole journey was contained in the marionette-like movements of the figures in the cold bluish light, or words echoing through the station, thereby acquiring a strange, even eerie meaning, or the fluttering of a bird's wings up by the glass vault, and other things besides; and that all I experienced in the days to come was variations on the notes of that nighttime music of the platform—notes of expectation, restlessness, anxiety, and a strange happiness."

As I gazed over the heads of fellow customers to the glittering sea, my mind's eye saw the concourse of Prague's Main Station at night, and I felt cold.

"But the unrevealed center of the journey may be a brief view of a backstreet in one or other of the cities," Martin went on. "A view I've completely forgotten, even though for a moment it showed me a hieroglyph of my whole life. Even if it remains forgotten forever, its rays will covertly work on, and influence all moments to come, like those miraculous seconds József Zoltán found buried in his memory."

Having paused for a moment, Martin added: "But maybe the journey has no point, no center. Sometimes, I can't help but think that my journey has been just a random pile-up of images, which are beginning to fall away. And that one day these will dissolve in the memory, leaving nothing behind, nothing to grow from. I think of all the encounters with warm, fragrant walls, rivers and seas, dreamlike station concourses, sunlight lying across café tables, and the hypnotic gleam of train corridors, and it occurs to me that perhaps they were just isolated, incomprehensible spurts of light and color, which have left no trace. Then, I think that nothing will remain but a banal solution to one investigation . . .

"It's also possible that the journey has had many destinations, and many centers; that the light that served to illuminate things came from more than one point; that rays from many sources were reflected in objects, and crossed, merged, and strengthened . . . Or that the journey had a single center, but that this center was a void, and that the light that lay across objects was the silent light of emptiness, the glow of nothingness. But emptiness, too, can take many different forms; its light transforms, as if the void knows different times of day. And I don't know if my journey was ruled by the emptiness of overflowing images that appeared to Tomáš Kantor on the winter day he began to write *Damp Walls*, the tormented, anxiety-ridden, dreamy emptiness of his childhood, or a swirling chaos like 'Linda's Lament,' the empty center of *Damp Walls*."

2. Signs

"Here in Loutro, I keep asking myself what I've actually been doing on this journey. I'm too easily distracted by whatever comes my way to be a good detective. But I'm not much of a traveler either: I missed a great many images, passed up a great many gifts the journey offered me, walked by every half-open door, failed to open a single garden gate. And as to my role as

lady's companion and suitor, the less said, the better . . . What
I will say is, since the moment I caught sight of the print of
Zoltán's painting in the Slovak magazine in the café on Řetěz
Street, I've done nothing but try to figure out the meaning of
signs. I left for Bratislava in the hope of tracking down the
meaning of the five characters on the painting *Tuesday*—characters which, as it turned out, were a fragment of a text damaged
first by seawater, then by Zoltán's bad memory. At the time, I
thought I was trying to decipher the characters to get closer to
Kristýna. Now I wonder if it was the other way around: that
I desired Kristýna precisely because she lived in a landscape of
absence, and so was caught up in a seductive network of characters from the beginning. And what kind of strange delight
do the signs deliver when they open and close?

"The characters from Zoltán's painting weren't even the start
of the great inscription across half of Europe that I was trying
to read. Before them, like three great initials, came the three
hieroglyphs from bodies no one understood: the hieroglyph of
a dancer aiming a gun at an audience; the symmetrical hieroglyph of the corpse of Petr Quas with its arms outstretched; and
the hieroglyph of the corpse of Tomáš Kantor with its thirteen
wounds. In Ljubljana, more characters, Roman and Greek, were
added to the five from Budapest—but instead of filling the
gaps, all they delivered was a new emptiness that surrounded
them, and which quivered with many new texts. It soon turned
out that the strange rebus our journey had given us had more
to tell us, and that it was written in a great many alphabets."

"Its next part was in the gummy-candy alphabet," I said.

"But even that wasn't the end of it. More scripts appeared,
and I learned to recognize and understand their characters, too.
The rebus became ever longer and more complex. I realized that
the inscription I was trying to read was composed of more than
just luminous letters under the sea and pictograms in gummy

candy; it also comprised large signs from the ground plans of cities we passed through, and the fluent, somewhat monotonous script of rivers . . . Other characters were stains on walls, shadows on house fronts and pavement, constellations of lights at night; plus strangely dissolving ones—lights in the day, scents and stinks, shapes of waves in the sea . . ."

"And you tried to read all these characters . . ."

"Indeed I did. Perhaps I even succeeded with some of them. The task wasn't as hopeless as it may appear. At first glance, it seemed I had become an architect in a bad dream—a kind of confused Champollion, digging in the sand for a monstrous inscription composed of characters from dozens of diverse and dissimilar alphabets. In truth, however, those scripts weren't as different from each other as it first appeared. There were moments when they seemed to be telling me that they all had the same origin, and that the quiet music of their common birth lingered on in all, still audible . . . I heard the hum of the current from which characters of all alphabets emerge like crystals, and which throws them into clusters, so making words and sentences out of them; their constellations then refer back to the current that formed them, a current whose life endures in them. Also, over distances of space and time, they refer to and call to one another. So each emerging constellation brings in its wake whole networks of images—highly diverse networks that penetrate all real and dream worlds, in which we may occasionally glimpse a common, dreamlike pattern."

3. Noise of the Void

"I believe that the current whose noise I heard was the current of the void that gave birth to the work of Tomáš Kantor. The inscriptions in worms and gelatin proved to be parts of one large text. And as I learned to read this text, I realized that it told only of itself—of its birth, past, and future; of its interconnectedness with all other texts, and the entanglement of many other, hitherto indistinct texts within itself; of explosions of emptiness forming characters; of the scent of the void, as exhaled by characters of all alphabets; of their repeated gradual dissolution in the void, and of newborn characters."

As the waiter approached our table, Martin took the opportunity to order another ouzo. "But there are moments when the hum falls silent. When this happens, I find myself confronted with an inscription composed of unintelligible words; the silence spreads like a dreadful infection, and before long, all objects in the world become signs belonging to an incomprehensible script. The thing is, I don't really know what I'm dealing with, even when the signs speak to me. What am I to do with their messages? What's the use of an inscription that writes itself and speaks only of itself? What is the quiet, urgent noise telling me? I still don't know if the knowledge gained on my journey can change my life. Maybe all it has shown me is the futility of everything I've done, on this journey south and in my life in general. Has this journey brought me to treasure or shipwreck?"

Again, Martin paused, before saying with a sigh: "On top of it all, victory and shipwreck are indistinguishable . . .

"For a while, Irena's reading of the worm and gummy-candy inscriptions on *The Magnolia* overshadowed all other readings of the rebus we had made on our journey. But here in Loutro, those earlier readings have started to return. I've been thinking about Pica della Mirandola's sparkling rivers flowing through reality, spinning magical affinities between objects; and of the mysterious, remarkable chance patterns and original forms reflected on in Breslau by Jan Evangelista Purkyně, who tells us that what we think of as empty isn't empty at all, and that we can't escape metamorphosis, even by closing our eyes. József

Zoltán's great Dadaist ant took a trip around the confused palimpsest of all permeable texts, bringing in its wake that artist's whole creation: paintings, sculptures, stories, and mystical states Zoltán experienced on the balcony of his Budapest apartment. I've been reminded of the neurotic Rossi, and the wretched Rizzo and his affected wife, although these people were invented by Giovanna Sulzer to lead us astray. All these readings could exist side by side, passing one through another without intrusion, perhaps even supporting one another.

"I'm not saying it doesn't matter whether we read the luminous undersea inscription as a quotation from a Kabbalist of Renaissance times or as a message about a crime. Before he died, Tomáš Kantor wrote about his killing, not magic. Irena's reading of the undersea inscription is obviously correct. But here in Loutro, I've realized that its true meaning is also informed by all earlier interpretations, as these were born out of an interplay of chance and dream, and these are still present in it. Irena's reading was part of the great rebus of the journey, and it can't be extracted from it.

"The scene in which Tomáš Kantor uses a knife soaked in his own blood to carve his message in his painting of the shell shouldn't overshadow the other scenes in which the undersea inscription appeared—an island bay by evening; a magazine in a stranger's apartment in Víziváros, with unexpected encounters and mysterious gates; a photograph in a biologist's apartment flooded with gentle light; a table under dry leaves in a Ljubljana garden restaurant. These scenes have intertwined with scenes from *Damp Walls* and the Network. The story of the two stepbrothers has been woven into all the other stories, losing something of itself as a result. But the loss is charged with meaning, and the truth is in the weave . . ."

4. Current and Chance

"I also wondered how it was that Tomáš's book couldn't end, and how people touched by his work felt that their own lives became an extension of it. These weren't the observations of someone with no involvement in the matter: I, too, had the sense that I was becoming one of Tomáš's characters, all I experienced on the stops of our journey new chapters in his book. Kristýna and Irena were probably right to say that the strange, infectious proliferation of Tomáš's images had little to do with art and literature. The attractiveness of emptiness to the child Tomáš was the result of a sickness passed down to him by his father; having developed a sense for it, at a certain point in his life he simply fell into the current of the void. This current branches out and unites while spreading its sediment to all the constellations of objects, ideas, and thoughts, to which we give names like 'reality,' 'dream,' 'thought,' and 'image;' and the current continues to transform these constellations, which are also the current's loudspeakers, and the musical instruments on which the void plays its long compositions; still the current transforms and spills, creating yet more branches, and these branches, too, split and unite. The current of this infinite convoluted delta, which is also an endless source, took hold of Tomáš and carried him away; those who approached its banks by getting close to Tomáš were swept along. That's all there is to it; it had little to do with literature, at least not at first.

"That said, I feel that Kristýna and Irena overdid the fear that all that happens on Earth will become a continuation and constituent of Tomáš's work. Maybe it wasn't all fear; maybe it included desire that this should happen. I would say that the branch of the delta into which Tomáš fell was just a short stretch in a convoluted network of channels with no beginning and no end, many dead ends, and many beds, both nascent and drying. To claim Tomáš's stretch as a beginning would be a foolish mistake. After all, has anyone discovered a source of water that flows through all the Dutch canals?

"I believe that Tomáš understood that the rhythms of the current and the wonderful patterns of the constellations the current spreads, appear to us by chance. Here in Loutro, I've thought a lot about how a few words overheard by chance gave rise to the world of the Lygds, a magic mirroring of the people who dreamed it up. I've also thought about Zoltán in a stranger's apartment when chance set before him the seeds of characters, five of which would take hold and grow something remarkable, like the scene on the Gogolevsky Boulevard in winter and at the Grand Canyon, and Zoltán's mystical experiences when looking at the Danube. Maybe the five letters Zoltán remembered from the magazine photo told him an unknown truth about himself, as well as something important about the world—and all this happened because chance had picked them out from Tomáš's message. On our journey, Kristýna and I dreamed some things up and came to others by detective-like deduction. I realized that the dreamy game of the imagination and the kaleidoscope of chance on the one hand and strict logical cognition on the other are similar and related. They are simply two ways of revealing connections spread by the current of the void, and as such, two ways of understanding its nature and rhythms. I believe there is a word that contains the idea of both dreams about stains and constellations of chance, and the methodical exploration of objects. There is just one adventure, but this adventure takes many forms. Which explains why so many passages in *Damp Walls* and the Work-Network are like scenes from adventure novels."

"Isn't the movie *The Larva* about how figures created by the play of chance can mean something important?"

"It needn't take the form of a cosmic monster. But I agree—this may have been the idea behind the film, even if the director, screenwriter, and actors were unaware of it. Maybe even Petr was unaware of it; and Tomáš, too, when he composed the comics about bold, beautiful Vulpécula. Maybe the message of *The Larva* will find a way to someone who understands it, as Kristýna and I understood the message Irena sent from Mykonos in thousands of bags of gummy candy, with so little hope of success . . . It has occurred to me that if Tomáš and Petr had gotten past the awful moment on board *The Magnolia* that resulted in their deaths, the movie may have brought them back together. Petr's theft could be viewed as a show of respect and appreciation. Tomáš may have found within himself enough generosity, and Petr enough humility for *The Larva* to be declared a collaborative effort. A new friendship may have grown between them. And this friendship may have led to the reignition of Tomáš's burned-out imagination, and to Petr making a new beginning, or finding his way back to his lost purity."

5. Kristýna

At this point, Martin took a long pause. "But whatever I think about," he said at last, his voice soft, "I always come back to Kristýna."

"At last!" I thought. I had been thinking how strange it was that he was saying nothing about the girl for whose sake he had embarked on the journey.

"It was for her sake that I embarked on this journey," he said, as if reading my mind. "But as you know, there were moments when I lost my way in all the signs and characters, and so forgot all about her. Instead, I thought of sunlight on walls, and the sea, which I scented in Ljubljana, maybe even earlier . . . But there were also moments when Kristýna shone like a light, making everything else into her mirror image or a featureless background.

"Last night, I awoke in the early hours in a state of despair that was physical, as if with a monster weight on top of me. I got up and went to the balcony, where I looked down at the tables of the tavernas and the water in the bay. It dawned on me that the magical compass that had drawn me southward, to the sea, had missed its mark; that all the signs and meanings I had been tracking were parts of one big game; and that this game was insubstantial, because as I played it, my thoughts weren't with Tomáš Kantor, nor with Kristýna's pain. It was a frivolous game that disregarded the only serious, important thing on the journey—closeness to Kristýna. Now I know that the only meaningful part of the journey was the striving to get closer to Kristýna, across all the deserts that lay between us. I departed from the path—not because I was afraid of the swarm of ghosts born and grown in Tomáš's work, but because of my games with signs and other dubious raptures; because of stains on walls, and the noises, scents, and stinks of strange cities; because of my delight at the sharp contours of objects in bright light; because of my delight at a formless world; because of the promise of southern happiness I couldn't even imagine; because of dreams city spaces are made of; because of the laziness of the Levant, in which I luxuriated in Chania. Instead of guiding Kristýna out of her crypt, so breaking her hopeless marriage to a dead man, I allowed myself to lose her in a labyrinth of stains on walls; the opium of strange cities made me forget about her . . .

"As I was standing on the balcony last night, something happened I would never have expected: I felt myself begin to hate the sea, in the way that Petr and his mother hated it. It occurred to me that the sea was the worst of all the drugs by which I had been intoxicated on the journey, and that it was the essence from which all the other drugs were made. I was irritated by the monotonous splashing of the waves, the cheap magnificence created by tedium and formlessness . . . I took a couple of sleeping pills, returning to bed only when I felt them beginning to work. When the sunlight woke me this morning, my view on things had changed again. Perhaps my games with stains, lights, city spaces, and the sea weren't so superficial and reprehensible after all, I said to myself. They had taught me some kind of language, albeit one that told only of itself; but because everything that is, was created by its play (the regrouping of its letters), it told of everything, so assuring me that I would understand everything and be helpful with everything— that I would understand and be helpful to Kristýna. Maybe the point of my journey was to succumb to all the temptations of light, stains on walls, and scents and stinks of the sea; maybe the world of light and shapeless stains was no less important than the world of love, family, and work, even though no one writes novels about it."

At this point, Martin sighed. "That feeling lasted about an hour," he said. "Then came the doubt, and the echo of the night's despair. 'You've invented a very feeble excuse for your failure,' I told myself."

"You've been lured halfway across Europe by a vision of southern happiness. Apparently, all you've found is confusion and disquiet. Are you very disappointed?"

"But that's not how it is," said Martin. "I was lured southward by a convolution of many ideas I had little understanding of. An idea of happiness was just one of them. I thought of the South as a place where bright light shows objects in sharp outline, and where everything flows and dissolves in the heat and the proximity of the formless sea. Both these things, the hardness of shapes and their dissolution, is somehow connected with happiness and despair, as they are with confusion and calm, knowledge and rapture, dreams, concentration, sleep, apathy, and extinction . . . It was all this together that lured me southward—as a tangle of a nascent world with as yet no psychology, no aesthetics, and no other such useless things . . . I'm not disappointed; I have encountered here everything I expected to encounter, even if I couldn't give it a name; and many other things besides, exceeding all my expectations: sparkling sea, little white houses, boats large and small, beautiful olive trees and thyme plants, chiming bells, hot rocks and the goats that caper on them, good food and drink . . ."

6. Gavdos

"I hope you'll excuse me for saying so," I said, "but I might sum up what you have told me today as follows: You have found a treasure unlike any other, and you have been shipwrecked; you have pursued the most important things in life, and you have lost time playing superficial games; you have gained important knowledge, and you know nothing about anything; you have betrayed Kristýna, and you are on the right path to being with and helping her; you are enjoying your vacation in the seaside warmth, and you are in the midst of a breakdown."

Martin thought about this. "Yes, that's pretty accurate," he said. "But my journey isn't over yet, and all kinds of things can change."

I stared at him in amazement. Was he intending to go on somewhere?

"Having begun as a quest for answers about the mysterious deaths of two brothers, this journey became a quest for the south. We've already spoken of the necessity of finishing what has been started; on that, I even quoted Aristotle at you. On the journey's next leg, there will be time for further reflection and transformation. Kristýna called me. She's arriving tomorrow. Again, we will go south."

He gestured toward the horizon. At first, I thought he meant beyond the sea, to Africa. "But Libya isn't in the European Union," I remarked. "Have you got visas?"

"I don't want to go that far. Maybe I will go to Africa one day, but this is a European journey, on which each European city has sent us to the next; a journey southward through Europe, with the South as the point at which we should reflect on what the cities on our journey have told us."

I realized that Martin meant the island just visible on the horizon, dissolving in the haze. "You mean Gavdos?" I asked.

He nodded. "The cape of Tripiti on Gavdos is Europe's southernmost point. I checked it online this morning: 34 degrees, 48 minutes, 2 seconds north latitude. Where else could this journey south end? Gavdos will be the tenth and last stop—after Bratislava, Budapest, Ljubljana, Pula, San Benedetto, Rome, Mykonos, Chania, and Loutro."

"And you expect to discover the point of your journey on Gavdos?"

"We'll see. Maybe. Maybe the cauldron of feelings and thoughts will cook something up. It's possible that everything will finally fall to pieces there. Or that what I find there is indifference; that wouldn't be bad either. Or that I discover that the question itself is the answer, and that a state of disintegration is the best of all harmonies. Maybe all that awaits me on Gavdos is a few days' pleasant vacationing; there are still too many people here for my liking . . . Maybe on Gavdos I'll finally understand what Kristýna has meant to me, or maybe I'll stop thinking about her . . . Actually, though, I think I know what I'll encounter at journey's end. Whatever form it takes, it will probably be the emptiness that appeared to Tomáš Kantor on that winter morning when he started writing *Damp Walls*; the emptiness his work grew out of, as did his death."

"So you've been on such a long journey in order to end up with nothing?"

"Exactly. That's a pretty good destination, don't you think?"

Again, silence fell between us. I could tell that Martin had something more to say. Probably he intended to cast doubt on his last assertion, and then on all assertions he had made about his journey, as he had done yesterday. But then he seemed to think better of it, perhaps because he found it pointless and embarrassing to keep going over his ignorance and confusion. He waved a dismissive hand and kept the silence. I didn't speak again either. We each had a few more glasses of ouzo. Then Martin nodded to me in parting, as was his way, and disappeared.

I slept poorly that night. Fortunately, sleepless nights here aren't as hard to take as they are in Prague, as they carry the noise of the sea. I fell asleep toward daybreak, waking at ten. Sunlight lay across the white wall and the wooden floor. Through the open door to the balcony, I saw the shiny surface of the water. I heard the horn of an arriving ferry. I could see it would be another hot day. I dressed and went to the Pavlos taverna for breakfast, in the hope of meeting Martin there. I still had a few questions about things in his story I hadn't understood. When I was seated, Tanya came up and said in Russian: "Greetings from your friend. He and his girl were just here. They're on the boat to Gavdos."

She pointed to the pier on the opposite side of the bay, where a small boat was just pulling out, waved off by a group of people. The shine of the sea was so strong, I had to narrow my eyes. Soon, Martin and Kristýna would be standing on the southernmost beach before the very last sea. I would be leaving soon myself, I told Tanya: Two days from now, I would fly from Heraklion to Prague. My breakfast over, I went to the store for cheese, olives, and water. Then I took the path along the cliff to Sweetwater Beach.

CPSIA information can be obtained
at www.ICGtesting.com
Printed in the USA
JSHW022227220323
39357JS00002B/2